THE
KING'S CURSE

By the same author

History
The Women of the Cousins' War:
The Real White Queen and
her Rivals

The Cousins' War
The Lady of the Rivers
The White Queen
The Red Queen
The Kingmaker's Daughter
The White Princess

The Tudor Court Novels
The Constant Princess
The Other Boleyn Girl
The Boleyn Inheritance
The Queen's Fool
The Virgin's Lover
The Other Queen

Historical Novels
The Wise Woman
Fallen Skies
A Respectable Trade

The Wideacre Trilogy
Wideacre
The Favoured Child
Meridon

Civil War Novels
Earthly Joys
Virgin Earth

Modern Novels
Mrs Hartley and the
Growth Centre
Perfectly Correct
The Little House
Zelda's Cut

Short Stories
Bread and Chocolate

Order of Darkness Series
Changeling
Stormbringers
Fools' Gold

The Cousins' War

THE KING'S CURSE

PHILIPPA GREGORY

**SIMON &
SCHUSTER**

London · New York · Sydney · Toronto · New Delhi

A CBS COMPANY

First published in Great Britain by Simon & Schuster UK Ltd, 2014
A CBS COMPANY

1 3 5 7 9 10 8 6 4 2

Simon & Schuster UK Ltd
1st Floor
222 Gray's Inn Road
London WC1X 8HB

www.simonandschuster.co.uk

Simon & Schuster Australia, Sydney
Simon & Schuster India, New Delhi

A CIP catalogue record for this book
is available from the British Library

Hardback ISBN 978-0-85720-756-2
Trade Paperback ISBN 978-0-85720-757-9
eBook ISBN 978-0-85720-760-9

Typeset by M Rules
Printed and bound by CPI Group (UK) Ltd, Croydon, CR0 4YY

For Anthony

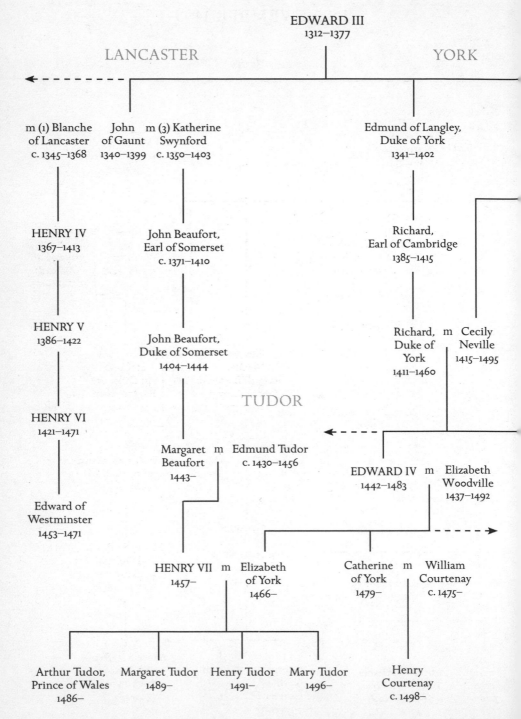

HOUSE OF PLANTAGENET

EDWARD III
1312–1377

LANCASTER

YORK

m (1) Blanche
of Lancaster
c. 1345–1368

John
of Gaunt
1340–1399

m (3) Katherine
Swynford
c. 1350–1403

Edmund of Langley,
Duke of York
1341–1402

HENRY IV
1367–1413

John Beaufort,
Earl of Somerset
c. 1371–1410

Richard,
Earl of Cambridge
1385–1415

HENRY V
1386–1422

John Beaufort,
Duke of Somerset
1404–1444

Richard,   m   Cecily
Duke of   Neville
York   1415–1495
1411–1460

TUDOR

HENRY VI
1421–1471

Margaret   m   Edmund Tudor
Beaufort   c. 1430–1456
1443–

EDWARD IV   m   Elizabeth
1442–1483   Woodville
                          1437–1492

Edward of
Westminster
1453–1471

HENRY VII   m   Elizabeth
1457–   of York
                          1466–

Catherine   m   William
of York   Courtenay
1479–   c. 1475–

Arthur Tudor,
Prince of Wales
1486–

Margaret Tudor
1489–

Henry Tudor
1491–

Mary Tudor
1496–

Henry
Courtenay
c. 1498–

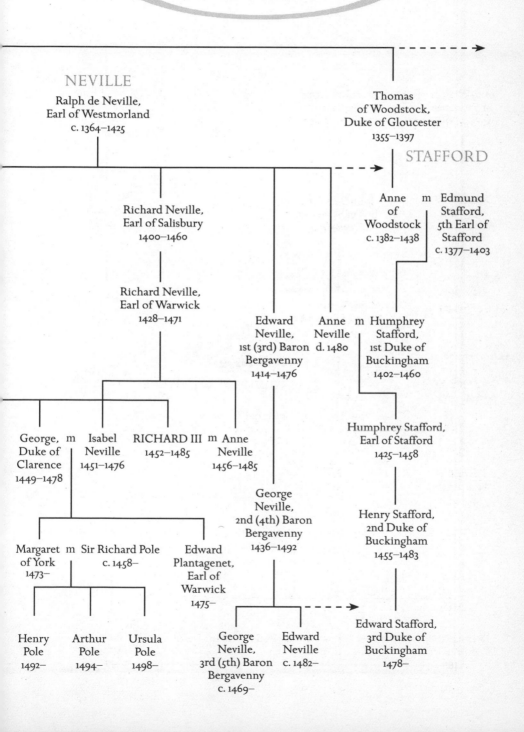

THE TUDOR AND PLANTAGENET HOUSES IN NOVEMBER 1499

NEVILLE

Ralph de Neville,
Earl of Westmorland
c. 1364–1425

Thomas
of Woodstock,
Duke of Gloucester
1355–1397

STAFFORD

Richard Neville,
Earl of Salisbury
1400–1460

Anne m Edmund
of Stafford,
Woodstock 5th Earl of
c. 1382–1438 Stafford
c. 1377–1403

Richard Neville,
Earl of Warwick
1428–1471

Edward Anne m Humphrey
Neville, Neville Stafford,
1st (3rd) Baron d. 1480 1st Duke of
Bergavenny Buckingham
1414–1476 1402–1460

George, m Isabel RICHARD III m Anne
Duke of Neville 1452–1485 Neville
Clarence 1451–1476 1456–1485
1449–1478

Humphrey Stafford,
Earl of Stafford
1425–1458

Margaret m Sir Richard Pole Edward
of York c. 1458– Plantagenet,
1473– Earl of
Warwick
1475–

George
Neville,
2nd (4th) Baron
Bergavenny
1436–1492

Henry Stafford,
2nd Duke of
Buckingham
1455–1483

Henry Arthur Ursula
Pole Pole Pole
1492– 1494– 1498–

George Edward
Neville, Neville
3rd (5th) Baron c. 1482–
Bergavenny
c. 1469–

Edward Stafford,
3rd Duke of
Buckingham
1478–

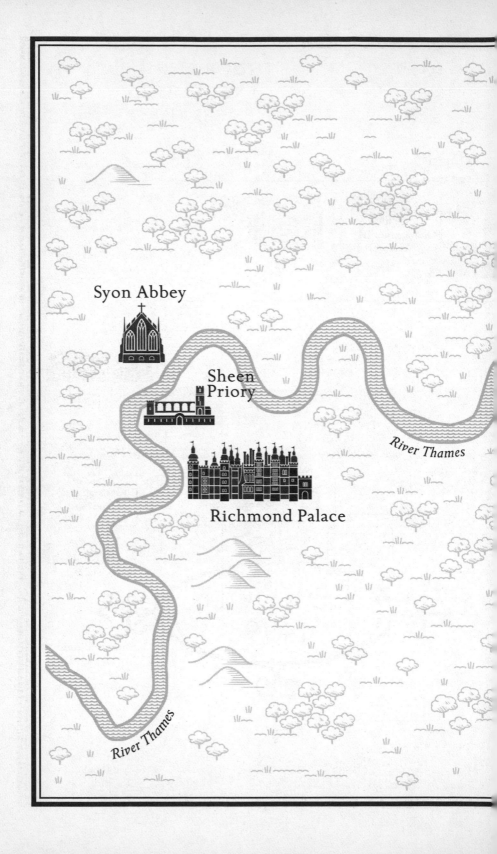

Syon Abbey

Sheen
Priory

Richmond Palace

River Thames

River Thames

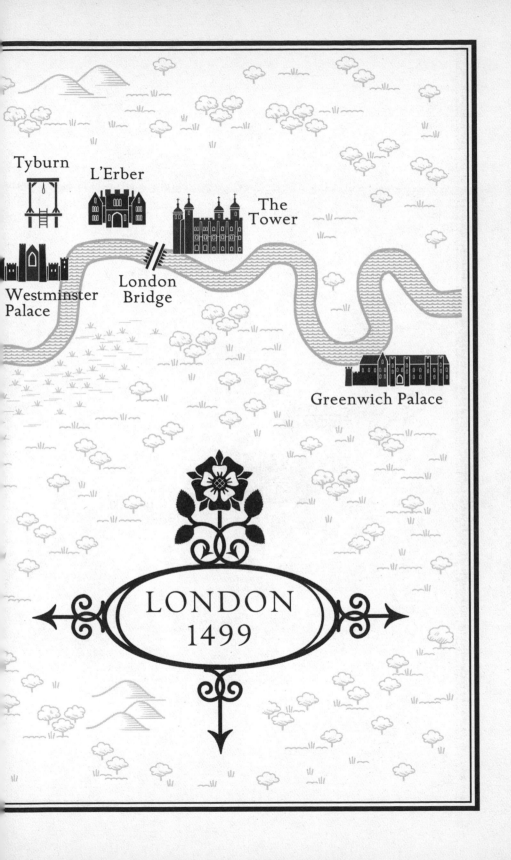

Tyburn

L'Erber

The Tower

Westminster Palace

London Bridge

Greenwich Palace

LONDON 1499

SCOTLAND

TUDOR
ENGLAND

York

Pontefract

Doncaster

Lincoln   Horncastle

ENGLAND

WALES

Ludlow
Castle

Stourton
Castle

Bockmer   Bisham

London

Cowdray House

Broadhurst

Dover

Southampton   Lordington

Warblington
Castle

In the moment of waking I am innocent, my conscience clear of any wrongdoing. In that first dazed moment, as my eyes open, I have no thoughts; I am only a smooth-skinned, tightly muscled young body, a woman of twenty-six, slowly waking with joy to life. I have no sense of my immortal soul, I have no sense of sin or guilt. I am so deliciously, lazily sleepy, that I hardly know who I am.

Slowly, I open my eyes and realise that the light coming through the shutters means that it is late in the morning. As I stretch out, luxuriously, like a waking cat, I remember that I was exhausted when I fell asleep and now I feel rested and well. And then, all in a moment, as if reality had suddenly tumbled down on my head like glossy-sealed denouncements from a high shelf, I remember that I am not well, that nothing is well, that this is the morning I hoped would never come; for this morning I cannot deny my deadly name, I am the heir of royal blood, and my brother – guilty as I am guilty – is dead.

My husband, sitting on the side of my bed, is fully dressed in his red velvet waistcoat, his jacket making him bulky and wide, his gold chain of office as chamberlain to the Prince of Wales splayed over his broad chest. Slowly, I realise he has been waiting for me to wake, his face crumpled with worry. 'Margaret?'

'Don't say anything,' I snap like a child, as if stopping the words will delay the facts, and I turn away from him into the pillow.

'You must be brave,' he says hopelessly. He pats my shoulder as if I were a sick hound puppy. 'You must be brave.'

I don't dare to shrug him off. He is my husband, I dare not offend him. He is my only refuge. I am buried in him, my name hidden in his. I am cut off from my title as sharply as if my name had been beheaded and rolled away into a basket.

Mine is the most dangerous name in England: Plantagenet, and once I carried it proudly, like a crown. Once I was Margaret Plantagenet of York, niece of two kings, the brothers Edward IV and Richard III, and the third brother was my father, George Duke of Clarence. My mother was the wealthiest woman in England and the daughter of a man so great that they called him 'Kingmaker'. My brother Teddy was named by our uncle King Richard as heir to the throne of England, and between us – Teddy and me – we commanded the love and the loyalty of half the kingdom. We were the noble Warwick orphans, saved from fate, snatched from the witchy grip of the white queen, raised in the royal nursery at Middleham Castle by Queen Anne herself, and nothing, nothing in the world was too good or too rich or too rare for us.

But when King Richard was killed we went overnight from being the heirs to the throne to becoming pretenders, survivors of the old royal family, while a usurper took the throne. What should be done with the York princesses? What should be done with the Warwick heirs? The Tudors, mother and son, had the answer prepared. We would all be married into obscurity, wedded to shadows, hidden in wedlock. So now I am safe, cut down by degrees, until I am small enough to conceal under a poor knight's name in a little manor in the middle of England where land is cheap and there is nobody who would ride into battle for the promise of my smile at the cry of 'À Warwick!'.

I am Lady Pole. Not a princess, not a duchess, not even a countess, just the wife of a humble knight, stuffed into obscurity like an embroidered emblem into a forgotten clothes chest. Margaret Pole, young pregnant wife to Sir Richard Pole, and I have already given him three children, two of them boys. One is Henry, named sycophantically for the new king, Henry VII, and one is Arthur, named ingratiatingly for his son Prince Arthur, and

I have a daughter, Ursula. I was allowed to call a mere girl whatever I wanted, so I named her for a saint who chose death rather than be married to a stranger and forced to take his name. I doubt that anyone has observed this small rebellion of mine; I certainly hope not.

But my brother could not be re-christened by marriage. Whoever he married, however lowly she was, she could not change his name as my husband has changed mine. He would still hold the title Earl of Warwick, he would still answer to Edward Plantagenet, he would still be the true heir to the throne of England. When they raised his standard (and someone, sooner or later, was bound to raise his standard) half of England would turn out just for that haunting flicker of white embroidery, the white rose. That is what they call him: 'the White Rose'.

So since they could not take his name from him, they took his fortune and his lands. Then they took his liberty, packing him away like a forgotten banner, among other worthless things, into the Tower of London, among traitors and debtors and fools. But though he had no servants, no lands, no castle, no education, still my brother had his name, my name. Still Teddy had his title, my grandfather's title. Still he was Earl of Warwick, the White Rose, heir to the Plantagenet throne, a living constant reproach to the Tudors who captured that throne and now call it their own. They took him into the darkness when he was a little boy of eleven and they did not bring him out until he was a man of twenty-four. He had not felt meadow grass under his feet for thirteen years. Then he walked out of the Tower, perhaps enjoying the smell of the rain on the wet earth, perhaps listening to the seagulls crying over the river, perhaps hearing beyond the high walls of the Tower the shouts and laughter of free men, free Englishmen, his subjects. With a guard on either side of him, he walked across the drawbridge and up to Tower Hill, knelt before the block, and put his head down as if he deserved to die, as if he were willing to die; and they beheaded him.

That happened yesterday. Just yesterday. It rained all day. There was a tremendous storm, as if the sky was raging against cruelty, rain pouring down like grief, so that when they told me, as I stood beside my cousin the queen in her beautifully appointed rooms, we closed the shutters against the darkness as if we did not want to see the rain that on Tower Hill was washing blood into the gutter, my brother's blood, my blood, royal blood.

'Try to be brave,' my husband murmurs again. 'Think of the baby. Try not to be afraid.'

'I'm not afraid.' I twist my head to speak over my shoulder. 'I don't have to try to be brave. I have nothing to fear. I know that I am safe with you.'

He hesitates. He does not want to remind me that perhaps I do still have something to fear. Perhaps even his lowly estate is not humble enough to keep me safe. 'I meant, try not to show your grief . . .'

'Why not?' It comes out as a childish wail. 'Why shouldn't I? Why shouldn't I grieve? My brother, my only brother, is dead! Beheaded like a traitor when he was innocent as a child. Why should I not grieve?'

'Because they won't like it,' he says simply.

THE HOUSE OF PLANTAGENET ON 29 NOVEMBER 1499

Plantagenet heirs

Executed Plantagenet heirs

EDWARD III
1312–1377

George, Duke of Clarence
1449–1478

m

Isabel Neville
1451–1476

George Neville, 2nd (4th) Baron Bergavenny
1436–1492

Henry Stafford, 2nd Duke of Buckingham
1455–1483

Edward Stafford, 3rd Duke of Buckingham
1478–

George Neville, 3rd (5th) Baron Bergavenny
c. 1469–

Edward Neville
c. 1482–

Jane Neville
c. 1495–

Margaret of York
1473–

m

Sir Richard Pole
c. 1458–

Edward Plantagenet, Earl of Warwick
1475–1499

Henry Pole
1492–

Arthur Pole
1494–

Ursula Pole
1498–

Catherine of York
1479–

Henry Courtenay
c. 1498–

WESTMINSTER PALACE, LONDON, WINTER–SPRING 1500

The queen herself comes down the great stair from her rooms in the palace to say goodbye as we leave Westminster after the Christmas feast, though the king still keeps to his chamber. His mother tells everyone that he is well, he just has a touch of fever, he is strong and healthy and resting out the cold winter days beside a warm fire; but no-one believes her. Everyone knows that he is sick with guilt at the murder of my brother and the death of the pretender who was named as a traitor, accused of joining in the same imaginary plot. I note, with wry amusement, that the queen and I, who have both lost a brother, go white-faced and tight-lipped about our business, while the man who ordered their deaths takes to his bed, dizzy with guilt. But Elizabeth and I are accustomed to loss, we are Plantagenets – we dine on a diet of betrayal and heartbreak. Henry Tudor is newly royal and has always had his battles fought for him.

'Good luck,' Elizabeth says shortly. She makes a little gesture towards the swell of my belly. 'Are you sure you won't stay? You could go into confinement here. You would be well served and I would visit you. Do change your mind and stay, Margaret.'

I shake my head. I cannot tell her that I am sick of London, and sick of the court, and sick of the rule of her husband and his over-bearing mother.

'Very well,' she says, understanding all of this. 'And will you go to Ludlow as soon as you are up and about again? And join them there?'

6

She prefers me to be at Ludlow with her boy Arthur. My husband is his guardian in that distant castle and it comforts her to know that I am there too.

'I'll go as soon as I can,' I promise her. 'But you know Sir Richard will keep your boy safe and well whether I am there or not. He cares for him as if he were a prince of pure gold.'

My husband is a good man, I never deny it. My Lady the King's Mother chose well for me when she made my marriage. She only wanted a man who would keep me from public view, but she happened upon one who cherishes me at home. And she got a bargain. She paid my husband the smallest possible fee on our wedding day; I could almost laugh even now, to think what they gave him to marry me: two manors, two paltry manors, and a little tumbling-down castle! He could have demanded far more; but he has always served the Tudors for nothing more than their thanks, trotted behind them only to remind them that he was on their side, followed their standard wherever it might lead without counting the cost or asking questions.

Early in his life he put his trust in Lady Margaret Beaufort, his kinswoman. She convinced him, as she convinced so many, that she would be a victorious ally but a dangerous enemy. As a young man he called on her intense family feeling and put himself into her keeping. She swore him to the cause of her son and he, and all her allies, risked their lives to bring her son to the throne and call her by the title she invented for herself: My Lady the King's Mother. Still, even now, even in unassailable triumph she clutches at cousins, terrified of unreliable friends and fearsome strangers.

I look at my cousin the queen. We are so unlike the Tudors. They married her to My Lady's son, the king, Henry, and only after they had tested her fertility and her loyalty for nearly two years, as if she were a breeding bitch that they had on approval, did they crown her as his queen – though she was a princess at birth and he was born very far from the throne. They married me to My Lady's half-cousin Sir Richard. They required us both to deny our breeding, our childhoods, our pasts, to take their name and swear fealty and we have done so. But even so, I doubt they will ever trust us.

Elizabeth, my cousin, looks over to where the young Prince Arthur, her son, is waiting for his horse to be led from the stables. 'I wish all three of you would stay.'

'He has to be in his principality,' I remind her. 'He is Prince of Wales, he has to be near Wales.'

'I just . . .'

'The country is at peace. The King and Queen of Spain will send their daughter to us now. We will come back in no time, ready for Arthur's wedding.' I do not add that they will only send the young Infanta now that my brother is dead. He died so that there was no rival heir; the Infanta's carpet to the altar will be as red as his blood. And I shall have to walk on it, in the Tudor procession, and smile.

'There was a curse,' she says suddenly, drawing close to me and putting her mouth to my ear so that I can feel the warmth of her breath against my cheek. 'Margaret, I have to tell you. There was a curse.' She puts her hand in mine and I can feel her tremble.

'What curse?'

'It was that whoever took my brothers from the Tower, whoever put my brothers to death should die for it.'

Horrified, I pull back so that I can see her white face. 'Whose curse? Who said such a thing?'

The shadow of guilt that crosses her face tells me at once. It will have been her mother, the witch Elizabeth. There is no doubt in my mind that it is a murderous curse from that murderous woman. 'What did she say exactly?'

She slips her hand through my arm and draws me to the stable gardens, through the arched doorway, so that we are alone in the enclosed space, the leafless tree spreading its boughs over our heads.

'I said it too,' she admits. 'It was my curse as much as hers. I said it with my mother. I was only a girl, but I should have known better . . . but I said it with her. We spoke to the river, to the goddess . . . you know! . . . the goddess who founded our family. We said: "Our boy was taken when he was not yet a man, not yet king – though he was born to be both. So take his murderer's son while he is yet a boy, before he is a man, before he comes to his estate. And then take his grandson too and when you take him, we will know by his death that this is the working of our curse and this is payment for the loss of our son."'

I shiver and gather my riding cape around me as if the sunlit garden were suddenly damp and cold with an assenting sigh from the river. 'You said that?'

She nods, her eyes dark and fearful.

'Well, King Richard died, and his son died before him,' I assert boldly. 'A man and his son. Your brothers disappeared while in his keeping. If he was guilty and the curse did its work, then perhaps it is all done, and his line is finished.'

She shrugs. No-one who knew Richard would ever think for a moment that he had killed his nephews. It is a ridiculous suggestion. He devoted his life to his brother, he would have laid down his life for his nephews. He hated their mother and he took the throne, but he would never have hurt the boys. Not even the Tudors dare say more than to suggest such a crime; not even they are bare-faced enough to accuse a dead man of a crime he would never have committed.

'If it was this king . . .' My voice is no more than a whisper, and I hold her so close that we could be embracing, my cloak around her shoulders, her hand in mine. I hardly dare to speak in this court of spies. 'If it was his order that killed your brothers . . .'

'Or his mother,' she adds very low. 'Her husband had the keys of the Tower, my brothers stood between her son and the throne ...'

We shudder, hands clasped as tight as if My Lady might be stealing up behind us to listen. We are both terrified of the power of Margaret Beaufort, mother to Henry Tudor.

'All right, it's all right,' I say, trying to hold back my fear, trying to deny the tremble of our hands. 'But Elizabeth, if it was they who killed your brother then your curse will fall on her son, your own husband, and on his son also.'

'I know, I know,' she moans softly. 'It's what I have been afraid of since I first thought it. What if the murderer's grandson is *my* son: Prince Arthur? My boy? What if I have cursed my own boy?'

'What if the curse ends the line?' I whisper. 'What if there are no Tudor boys, and in the end nothing but barren girls?'

We stand very still as if we have been frozen in the wintry garden. In the tree above our heads a robin sings a trill of song, his warning call, and then he flies away.

'Keep him safe!' she says with sudden passion. 'Keep Arthur safe in Ludlow, Margaret!'

STOURTON CASTLE, STAFFORDSHIRE, SPRING 1500

I enter my month-long confinement at Stourton and my husband leaves me to escort the prince to Wales, to his castle at Ludlow. I stand at the great door of our ramshackle old house to wave them goodbye. Prince Arthur kneels for my blessing, and I put my hand on his head and then kiss him on both cheeks when he stands up. He is thirteen years old, taller than me already, a boy with all the York good looks and the York charm. There's almost no Tudor about him at all, except in the copper of his hair and his occasional unpredictable swoop into anxiety; all the Tudors are a fearful family. I put my arms around his slim boy's shoulders and hug him closely. 'Be good,' I command him. 'And take care jousting and riding. I promised your mother that no harm will come to you. Make sure it does not.'

He rolls his eyes as any boy will do when a woman fusses over him, but he ducks his head in obedience and then turns and vaults onto his horse, gathering the reins and making it curvet and dance.

'And don't show off,' I order. 'And if it rains, get into shelter.'

'We will, we will,' my husband says. He smiles down at me

kindly. 'I'll guard him, you know that. You take care of yourself, it's you that has work to do this month. And send me the news the moment that the child is born.'

I put one hand over my big belly, feeling the baby stir, and I wave to them. I watch them as they go south down the red clay road to Kidderminster. The ground is frozen hard; they will make good time on the narrow tracks that wind between the patchwork of frosty rust-coloured fields. The prince's standards go before him, his men at arms in their bright livery. He rides beside my husband, the men of his household around them in tight protective formation. Behind them come the pack animals carrying the prince's personal treasures, his silver plate, his gold ware, his precious saddles, his enamelled and engraved armour, even his carpets and linen. He carries a fortune in treasure wherever he goes, he is the Tudor prince of England and served like an emperor. The Tudors shore up their royalty with the trappings of wealth as if they hope that playing the part will make it real.

Around the boy, around the mules carrying his treasure, ride the Tudor guard, the new guard that his father has mustered, the yeomen in their green and white livery. When we Plantagenets were the royal family we rode through the highways and byways of England with friends and companions, unarmed, bare-headed; we never needed a guard, we never feared the people. The Tudors are always on alert for a hidden attack. They came in with an invading army, followed by disease, and even now, nearly fifteen years after their victory, they are still like invaders, uncertain of their safety, doubtful of their welcome.

I stand with one hand raised in farewell until a bend in the road hides them from me and then I go inside, gathering my fine woollen shawl around me. I will go to the nursery and see my children, before dinner is served to the whole household, and after dinner I will raise a glass to the stewards of my house and lands, command them to keep everything in good order during my absence, and retire to my chamber with my ladies in waiting, my midwives and the nurses. There I have to wait, for the four long weeks of my confinement, for our new baby.

I am not afraid of pain, so I don't dread the birth. This is my fourth childbed and at least I know what to expect. But I don't look forward to it either. None of my children brings me the joy that I see in other mothers. My boys do not fill me with fierce ambition, I cannot pray for them to rise in the world – I would be mad to want them to catch the eye of the king, for what would he see but another Plantagenet boy? A rival heir to the throne? A threat? My daughter does not give me the satisfaction of seeing a little woman in the making: another me, another Plantagenet princess. How can I think of her as anything but doomed if she shines at court? I have got myself safely through these years by being almost invisible, how can I dress a girl, and put her forward, and hope that people admire her? All I want for her is a comfortable obscurity. To be a loving mother, a woman has to be optimistic, filled with hope for the babies, planning their future in safety, dreaming of grand plans. But I am of the House of York, I know better than anyone that it is an uncertain, dangerous world and the best plan I can make for my children is that they survive in the shadows – by birth they will be the greatest of all the actors, but I must hope they are always either off-stage, or anonymous in the crowd.

The baby comes early, a week before I had thought, and he is handsome and strong, with a funny little tuft of brown hair in the middle of his head like the crest on a cock. He takes to the wet nurse's milk and she suckles him constantly. I send the good news to his father and receive his congratulations and a bracelet of Welsh gold in reply. He says he will come home for the christening and that we must call the boy Reginald – Reginald the counsellor – as a gentle hint to the king and his mother that this boy will be raised to be an advisor and humble servant to their line. It is no surprise to me that my husband wants the baby's very name to indicate our servitude to them. When they won the country, they won us too. Our future depends on their favour. The Tudors own everything in England now; perhaps they always will.

Sometimes the wet nurse gives him to me and I rock him and admire the curve of his closed eyelids and the sweep of the eyelashes against his cheek. He reminds me of my brother when he was a baby. I can remember his plump toddler face very well, and his anxious dark eyes when he was a boy. I hardly saw him as a young man. I cannot picture the prisoner walking through the rain to the scaffold on Tower Hill. I hold my new baby close to my heart and think that life is fragile; perhaps it is safer not to love anyone at all.

My husband comes home as he promised – he always does what he promises – in time for the christening, and as soon as I am out of confinement and churched, we return to Ludlow. It is a long hard journey for me and I go partly by litter and partly by horseback, riding in the morning and resting in the afternoon, but even so it takes us two days on the road and I am glad to see the high walls of the town, the striped black and cream of the lathes and plaster of the houses under their thick thatch roofs, and behind them, tall and dark, the greater walls of the castle.

LUDLOW CASTLE, WELSH MARCHES, SPRING 1500

They throw the gates wide open in compliment to me, the wife of the Lord Chamberlain of the Prince of Wales, and Arthur himself comes bounding like a colt out of the main gate, all long legs and excitement, to help me down from my horse and ask me how I am doing, and why have I not brought the new baby?

'It's too cold for him, he's better off with his wet nurse at home.' I hug him and he drops to kneel for my blessing as the wife of his guardian, and royal cousin to his mother, and as he rises up I bob a curtsey to him as the heir to the throne. We go easily through these steps of protocol without thinking of them. He has been raised to be a king, and I was brought up as one of the most important people in a ceremonial court, where almost everyone curtseyed to me, walked behind me, rose when I entered a room or departed bowing from my presence. Until the Tudors came, until I was married, until I became unimportant Lady Pole.

Arthur steps back to scrutinise my face, the funny boy, fourteen this year, but sweet-natured and thoughtful as the tender-hearted woman, his mother. 'Are you all right?' he asks carefully. 'Was it all, all right?'

'Quite all right,' I say to him firmly. 'I'm quite unchanged.'

He beams at that. This boy has his mother's loving heart; he is going to be a king with compassion and God knows this is what England needs to heal the wounds of thirty long years of battles.

My husband comes bustling from the stables and he and Arthur sweep me into the great hall where the court bows to me and I walk through the hundreds of men of our household to my place of honour between my husband and the Prince of Wales, at the high table.

Later that night I go to Arthur's bedchamber to hear him say his prayers. His chaplain is there, kneeling at the prie-dieu beside him, listening to the careful recitation in Latin of the collect for the day and the prayer for the night. He reads a passage from one of the psalms and Arthur bows his head to pray for the safety of his father and mother, the King and Queen of England. 'And for My Lady the King's Mother, the Countess of Richmond,' he adds, reciting her title so that God will not forget how high she has risen, and how worthy her claim to His attention. I bow my head when he says 'Amen' and then the chaplain gathers up his things and Arthur takes a leap into his big bed.

'Lady Margaret, d'you know if I am to be married this year?'

'Nobody has told me a date,' I say. I sit on the side of his bed and look at his bright face, the soft down on his upper lip that he loves to stroke as if it will encourage it to grow. 'But there can be no objection to the wedding now.'

At once, he puts his hand out to touch mine. He knows that the monarchs of Spain swore they would only send their daughter to be his bride when they were assured that there were no rival heirs to the throne of England. They meant not only my brother Edward, but also the pretender who went by the name of the queen's brother, Richard of York. Determined that the betrothal should go ahead, the king entrapped both young men together, as if they were equally heirs, as if they were equally guilty, and ordered them both killed. The pretender claimed a most dangerous name, took arms against Henry and died for it. My brother denied his own name, never raised his voice, let alone an army, and still died. I have to try not to sour my own life with bitterness. I have to put away resentment as if it were a forgotten badge. I have to forget I am a sister, I have to forget the only boy that I have ever truly loved: my brother, the White Rose.

'You know I would never have asked for it,' Arthur says, his voice very low. 'His death. I didn't ask for it.'

'I know you didn't,' I say. 'It's nothing to do with you or me. It was out of our hands. There was nothing that either of us could have done.'

'But I did do one thing,' he says, with a shy sideways glance at me. 'It wasn't any good; but I did ask my father for mercy.'

'That was good of you,' I say. I don't tell him that I was on my knees before the king, my headdress off, my hair let down, my tears falling on the floor, my cupped hands under the heel of his boot, until they lifted me up and carried me away, and my husband begged me not to speak again for fear of reminding the king that I once had the name Plantagenet and that now I have sons with dangerous royal blood. 'Nothing could be done. I am sure His Grace your father did only what he thought was right.'

'Can you . . .' He hesitates. 'Can you forgive him?'

He cannot even look at me with this question, and his gaze is on our clasped hands. Gently, he turns the new ring I am wearing on my finger, a mourning ring with a 'W' for Warwick, my brother.

I cover his hand with my own. 'I have nothing to forgive,' I say firmly. 'It was not an angry act or a vengeful act by your father against my brother. It was something that he felt he had to do in order to secure his throne. He did not do it with passion. He could not be swayed by an appeal. He calculated that the monarchs of Spain would not send the Infanta if my brother were alive. He calculated that the commons of England would always rise for someone who was a Plantagenet. Your father is a thoughtful man, a careful man, he will have looked at the chances almost like a clerk drawing up an account in one of those new ledgers with the gains on one side and the losses on the other. That's how your father thinks. That's how kings have to think these days. It's not about honour and loyalty any more. It's about calculation. It's my loss that my brother counted as a danger, and your father had him crossed out of the book.'

'But he was no danger!' Arthur exclaims. 'And in all honour . . .'

'He was never a danger; it was his name. His name was the danger.'

'But it's your name?'

'Oh no. My name is Margaret Pole,' I say drily. 'You know that. And I try to forget I was born with any other.'

WESTMINSTER PALACE, LONDON, AUTUMN 1501

Arthur's bride does not come to England till she is fifteen. At the end of summer we travel to London and Arthur, his mother and I have two months of ordering clothes, commanding tailors, jewellers, glove-makers, hat-makers and sempstresses to put together a wardrobe of clothes for the young prince and a handsome suit for his wedding day.

He is nervous. He has written to her regularly, stilted letters in Latin, the only language they share. My cousin the queen has urged that she be taught English and French. 'It's barbaric to marry a stranger, and not even be able to speak together,' she mutters to me, as we embroider Arthur's new shirts in her chamber. 'Are they to sit down to breakfast with an ambassador to translate between them?'

I smile in reply. It is a rare woman who can speak freely with a loving husband, and we both know this. 'She'll learn,' I say. 'She'll have to learn our ways.'

'The king is going to ride down to the south coast to meet her,' Elizabeth says. 'I have asked him to wait and greet her here in London, but he says he will take Arthur with him and ride like a knight errant to surprise her.'

'You know, I don't think that the Spanish like surprises,' I remark. Everyone knows they are a most formal people; the Infanta has been living almost in seclusion, in the former harem of the Alhambra Palace.

'She is promised, she has been promised for twelve years, and now she is delivered,' Elizabeth says drily. 'What she likes or does not like is of little matter. Not to the king, and perhaps not even to her mother and father now.'

'Poor child,' I say. 'But she could have no more handsome or good-natured bridegroom than Arthur.'

'He is a good young man, isn't he?' His mother's face warms at his praise. 'And he has grown again. What are you feeding him? He is taller than me now, I think he will be as tall as my father.' She nips off her words as if it is treason to name her father, King Edward.

'He will be as tall as King Henry,' I amend. 'And God willing she will make as good a queen as you have been.'

Elizabeth gives me one of her fleeting smiles. 'Perhaps she will. Perhaps we will become friends. I think she may be a little like me. She has been raised to be a queen, just as I was. And she has a mother of determination and courage just like mine was.'

We wait in the nursery for the bridegroom and his father to ride home from their mission of knight errantry. Little Prince Harry, ten years old, is excited by the adventure. 'Will he ride up and capture her?'

'Oh, no.' His mother draws her youngest child, five-year-old Mary, onto her lap. 'That wouldn't do at all. They will go to wherever she is staying, and ask to be admitted. Then they will pay their compliments, and perhaps dine with her, and then leave the following morning.'

'I would ride up and capture her!' Harry boasts, raising his hand as if holding a pair of reins, and cantering around the room on an imaginary horse. 'I would ride up and marry her on the spot. She's taken long enough to come to England. I would brook no delay.'

'Brook?' I ask. 'What sort of word is brook? What on earth have you been reading?'

'He reads all the time,' his mother says fondly. 'He is such a scholar. He reads romances and theology and prayers and the lives of the saints. In French and Latin and English. He's starting Greek.'

'And I'm musical,' Harry reminds us.

'Very talented,' I commend him with a smile.

'And I ride, on big horses, not just little ponies, and I can handle a hawk too. I have my own hawk, a goshawk called Ruby.'

His mother and I exchange a rueful smile over the bobbing copper head.

'You are undoubtedly a true prince,' I say to him.

'I should come to Ludlow,' he tells me. 'I should come to Ludlow with you and your husband and learn the business of running a country.'

'You would be most welcome.'

He pauses in his prancing around the room and comes to kneel up on the stool before me, and takes my face in both of his hands. 'I mean to be a good prince,' he says earnestly. 'I do, indeed. Whatever work my father gives me. Whether it is to rule

Ireland or command the Navy. Wherever he wants to send me. You wouldn't know, Lady Margaret, because you're not a Tudor, but it is a calling, a divine calling to be born into the royal family. It is a destiny to be born royal. And when my bride comes to England I will ride to greet her and I will be in disguise and when she sees me she will say – Oh! Who is that handsome boy on that very big horse? And I will say – It's me! And everyone will say – Hurrah!'

'It didn't go very well at all,' Arthur tells his mother glumly. He comes into the queen's bedroom where she is dressing for dinner. I am holding her coronal, watching the maid in waiting brush her hair.

'We got there, and she was already in bed, and she sent out word that she could not see us. Father would not take a refusal and consulted with the lords who were with us. They agreed with him . . .' He glances down, and both of us can see his resentment. 'Of course they did, who would disagree? So we rode in the pouring rain to Dogmersfield Palace and insisted that she admit us. Father went into her privy chamber, I think there was a row, and then she came out looking furious, and we all had dinner.'

'What was she like?' I ask into the silence, when nobody else says anything.

'How would I know?' he demands miserably. 'She hardly spoke to me. I just dripped all over the floor. Father commanded her to dance and she did a Spanish dance with three of her ladies. She wore a heavy veil over her headdress so I could hardly see her face. I expect she hates us, making her come out to dinner after she had refused. She spoke Latin, we said something about the weather and her voyage. She had been terribly seasick.'

I nearly laugh aloud at his glum face. 'Ah, little prince, be of good heart!' I say, and I put my arm around his shoulders to give him a hug. 'It's early days. She will come to love and value you. She will recover from seasickness, and learn to speak English.'

I feel him lean towards me for comfort. 'She will? Do you really think so? She truly did look very angry.'

'She has to. And you will be kind to her.'

'My lord father is very taken with her,' he says to his mother as if he is warning her.

She smiles wryly. 'Your father loves a princess,' she says. 'There's nothing he likes more than a woman born royal in his power.'

I am in the royal nursery playing with Princess Mary when Harry comes in from his riding lesson. At once he comes to me, elbowing his little sister to one side.

'Be careful with Her Grace,' I remind him. She giggles; she is a robust little beauty.

'But where is the Spanish princess?' he demands. 'Why is she not here?'

'Because she's still on her way,' I say, offering Princess Mary a brightly coloured ball. She takes it and carefully tosses it up and catches it. 'Princess Katherine has to make a progress through the country so that people can see her, and then you will ride out to greet her and escort her into London. Your new suit is ready, and your new saddle.'

'I hope I do it right,' he says earnestly. 'I hope that my horse behaves, and that I make my mother proud.'

I put my arm around him. 'You will,' I assure him. 'You ride beautifully, you will look princely, and your mother is always proud of you.'

I feel him square his little shoulders. He is imagining himself in a cloth-of-gold jacket, high up on his horse. 'She is,' he says with the vanity of a well-loved little boy. 'I'm not the Prince of Wales, I'm only a second son, but she is proud of me.'

'What about Princess Mary?' I tease him. 'The prettiest princess in the world? Or your big sister, Princess Margaret?'

'They're just girls,' he says with brotherly scorn. 'Who cares about them?'

I am watching to make sure that the queen's new gowns are properly powdered, brushed, and hung in the wardrobe rooms when Elizabeth comes in and closes the door behind her. 'Leave us,' she says shortly to the mistress of the robes, and by this I know that something is very wrong, for the queen is never abrupt with the women who work for her.

'What is it?'

'It's Edmund. Cousin Edmund.'

My knees go weak at the mention of his name. Elizabeth pushes me onto a stool, and goes to the window and throws it open so that cool air comes into the room and my head steadies. Edmund is a Plantagenet like us. He is my aunt's son, Duke of Suffolk, and high in the king's favour. His brother was a traitor, leading the rebels against the king at the battle of Stoke, killed on the battlefield; but in utter contrast Edmund de la Pole has always been fiercely loyal, the Tudor king's right-hand man and friend. He is an ornament to the court, the leader of the jousters, a handsome, brave, brilliant Plantagenet duke, a joyous signal to everyone that York and Tudor live alongside each other as a loving royal family. He is a member of the innermost royal circle, a Plantagenet serving a Tudor, a collar that has been turned, a flag that billows the other way, a new rose of red and white, a signpost for all of us.

'Arrested?'

'Run away,' she says shortly.

'Where?' I ask, horrified. 'Oh God. Where has he gone?'

'To the Holy Roman Emperor Maximilian, to raise an army against the king.' She chokes as if the words are sticking in her throat, but she has to ask me. 'Margaret, tell me – you knew nothing of this?'

I shake my head, I take her hand, I meet her eyes.

'Swear it,' she demands. 'Swear it.'

'Nothing. Not a word. I swear it. He did not confide in me.'

We are both silent as we think of those that he usually does confide in: the queen's brother-in-law, William Courtenay, our cousin Thomas Grey, our cousin William de la Pole, my second cousin George Neville, our kinsman Henry Bourchier. We are a well-recorded, well-known network of cousins and kinsmen tightly interwoven by marriage and blood. The Plantagenets spread across all England, a thrusting, courageous, seemingly endless family of ambitious boys, warrior men and fertile women. And against us – only four Tudors: one old lady, her anxious son, and their heirs Arthur and Harry.

'What's going to happen?' I ask. I get to my feet and walk across the room to close the window. 'I'm all right now.'

She stretches out her arms to me and we hold each other close for a moment, as if we were still young women waiting for the news from Bosworth, filled with dread.

'He can never come home,' she says unhappily. 'We'll never see Cousin Edmund again. Never. And the king's spies are certain to find him. He employs hundreds of watchers now, wherever Edmund is, they'll find him . . .'

'And then they'll find everyone that he has ever spoken with,' I predict.

'Not you?' she confirms again. She drops her voice to a whisper. 'Margaret, really – not you?'

'Not me. Not one word. You know I am deaf and dumb to treason.'

'And then either this year, or the next, or the year after, they will bring him home and kill him,' she says flatly. 'Our cousin Edmund. We'll have to watch him walk to the scaffold.'

I give a little moan of distress. We grip hands. But in the silence, as we think of our cousin and the scaffold on Tower Hill, we both know that we have already survived even worse than this.

I do not stay for the royal wedding but go ahead of the young couple to Ludlow to make sure that the place is warm and comfortable for their arrival. As the king smilingly greets all his Plantagenet kinsmen with excessive, cloying affection I am glad to be away from the court for fear that his charming conversation should delay me in the hall while his spies search my rooms. The king is at his most dangerous when he appears happy, seeking the company of his court, announcing amusing games, urging us to dance, laughing and strolling around the banquet while outside, in the darkened galleries and narrow streets, his spies do their work. I may have nothing to hide from Henry Tudor; but that does not mean that I want to be watched.

In any case, the king has ruled that the young couple shall come to Ludlow after their wedding, without delay, and I must get things ready for them. The poor girl will have to dismiss most of her Spanish companions and travel cross-country in the worst winter weather to a castle nearly two hundred miles from London and a lifetime away from the comfort and luxury of her home. The king wants Arthur to show his bride, to impress everyone along the road with the next generation of the Tudor line. He is thinking of ways to establish the power and glamour of the new throne: he is not thinking of a young woman, missing her mother, in a strange land.

LUDLOW CASTLE, WELSH MARCHES, WINTER 1501

I have the Ludlow servants turn the place upside down and scour the floors and brush the stone walls and then hang the rich, warm tapestries. I have carpenters rehang the doors to try to prevent draughts. I buy a huge new barrel sawn in half from the wine merchants to serve the princess as a bath; the queen my cousin writes to me that the Infanta expects to bathe daily, an outlandish habit that I hope she will give up when she feels the cold winds that buffet the towers of Ludlow Castle. I have new curtains made and lined for the bed that is to be hers – and we hope the prince will find his way to it every night. I order new linen sheets from the drapers in London and they send me the best, the very best that money can buy. I scour the floors and put down fresh strewing herbs so that all the rooms smell hauntingly of midsummer hay and meadow flowers. I sweep the chimneys so that her fires of applewood can burn brightly, I demand from the countryside all around the little castle the finest of food: the sweetest honey, the best-brewed ale, the fruits and vegetables that have been stored since harvest, the barrels of salted fish, the smoked meats, the great rounds of cheese that this part of the world makes so well. I warn them I will need a constant supply of fresh game, and that they will have to kill their beasts and chickens to serve the castle. I have all of my hundreds of servants, all of my dozen heads of house-hold ensure that their division is as ready as it can be; and then I wait, we all wait, for the arrival of the couple who are the hope and light of England, and who are to live under my care, learn to be Prince and Princess of Wales, and conceive a son as soon as possible.

I am looking across the muddled thatched roofs of the little town to the east, hoping to see the bobbing standards of the royal guard coming down the wet, slippery track towards the Gladford gate, when I see instead a single horseman, riding fast. I know at once that this is bad news: my first thought is for the safety of my Plantagenet kinsmen, as I throw on my cape and hurry down to the castle gateway so that I am ready, heart pounding, as he trots up the cobbled road from the broad main street and jumps off before me, kneels and offers me a sealed letter. I take it and break the seal. My first fear is that my rebel cousin Edmund de la Pole has been captured, and named me as a fellow conspirator. I am so frightened that I can't read the scrawled letters on the page. 'What is it?' I say shortly. 'What news?'

'Lady Margaret, I am sorry to tell you the children were very ill when I left Stourton,' he says.

I blink at the crabbed writing and make myself read the short note from my steward. He writes that nine-year-old Henry has been taken ill with a red rash and fever. Arthur, who is seven years old, continues well, but they are afraid that Ursula is ill. She is crying and seems to have a headache and she certainly has a fever as he writes. She is only three years old, a dangerous time for a child emerging from babyhood. He does not even mention the baby, Reginald. I have to assume that he lives and is well in the nursery. Surely, my steward would have told me if my baby was already dead?

'Not the Sweat,' I say to the messenger, naming the new illness that we all fear, the disease that followed the Tudor army and nearly wiped out the City of London when they assembled to welcome him. 'Tell me it's not the Sweat.'

He crosses himself. 'I pray not. I think not. No-one had . . .' He breaks off. He means to say that no-one had died – proof that it is not the Sweat, which kills a healthy man in a day, without warning. 'They sent me on the third day of the oldest boy's illness,' he says. 'He had lasted three days as I left. Maybe he continues . . .'

'And the baby Reginald?'

'Kept with his wet nurse at her cottage, away from the house.'

I see my own fear in his pale face. 'And you? How are you, sirrah? No signs?'

Nobody knows how sickness travels from one place to another. Some people believe that messengers carry it on their clothes, on the paper of the message, so that the very person who brings you a warning brings your death as well.

'I'm well, please God,' he says. 'No rash. No fever. I would not have come near you otherwise, my lady.'

'I'd better go home,' I say. I am torn between my duty to the

Tudors and my fear for my children. 'Tell them in the stable I'll leave within the hour, and that I'll need an escort and a spare riding horse.'

He nods and leads his horse through the echoing archway and turns into the stable yard. I go to tell my ladies to pack my clothes and that one of them will have to ride with me in this wintry weather, for we have to get to Stourton; my children are ill and I must be with them. I grit my teeth as I rap out orders, the number of men in the guard, the food we will have to carry with us, the oiled cape I want strapped on my saddle in case of rain or snow, and the one that I will wear. I don't let myself think about the destination. Above everything, I don't let myself think about my children.

Life is a risk, who knows this better than me? Who knows more surely that babies die easily, that children fall ill from the least cause, that royal blood is fatally weak, that death walks behind my family the Plantagenets like a faithful black hound?

STOURTON CASTLE, STAFFORDSHIRE, WINTER 1501

I find my home in a state of feverish anxiety. All three of the children are ill; only the baby, Reginald, is not sweating nor showing a red rash. I go to the nursery at once. The oldest, nine-year-old Henry, is sleeping heavily in the big four-poster bed, his brother Arthur curled up beside him, and a few paces away my little girl Ursula tosses and turns in her truckle bed. I look at them and I feel my teeth grit.

At my nod, the nursemaid turns Henry onto his back and lifts his nightgown. His chest and belly are covered with red spots, some of them merging into one another, his face is swollen with the rash and behind his ears and on his neck there is no normal skin at all. He is flushed and sore all over.

'Is it the measles?' I ask her shortly.

'That, or the pox,' she says.

Dozing beside Henry, Arthur cries a little when he sees me and I lift him from the hot sheets and sit him on my knee. I can feel his small body is burning hot. 'I'm thirsty,' he says. 'Thirsty.' The nurse gives me a cup of small ale and he drinks three gulps and then pushes it away. 'My eyes hurt.'

'We kept the shutters closed,' the nursemaid says quietly to me. 'Henry complained that the light hurt his eyes, so we closed them. I hope we did right.'

'I think so,' I say. I feel such dread at my own ignorance. I don't know what should be done for these children, nor even what is wrong with them. 'What does the doctor say?'

Arthur leans back against me, even the nape of his neck is hot under my kiss.

'The doctor says that it is probably the measles and that, God willing, they will all three recover. He says to keep them warm.'

We are certainly keeping them warm. The room is stifling, a fire in the grate and a glowing brazier under the window, the beds heaped with covers and all three children sweating, flushed with heat. I put Arthur back in his hot sheets and go to the little bed where Ursula is lying limp and silent. She is only three, she is tiny. When she sees me, she raises her small hand and waves, but she does not speak or say my name.

I round with horror on the nursemaid.

'Her mind hasn't gone!' she exclaims defensively. 'She's just wandering because of the heat. The doctor said that if the fever breaks she will be well. She sings a little and she whimpers a little in her sleep, but she hasn't lost her mind. At any rate, not yet.'

I nod, trying to be patient in this overheated room with my children lying around like drowned corpses on a strand. 'When does the doctor come again?'

'He'll be on his way now, your ladyship. I promised I'd send for him as soon as you arrived, so that he could talk with you. But he swears that they will recover.' She looks at my face. 'Probably,' she adds.

'And the rest of the household?'

'A couple of page boys have it. One of them was sick before Henry. And the kitchen maid who looks after the hens has died. But no-one else has taken it yet.'

'And the village?'

'I don't know about the village.'

I nod. I will have to ask the doctor about that, all sickness on our lands is my responsibility. I will have to order our kitchen to send out food to cottages where there is illness, I will have to make sure that the priest visits them, and that when they die they have enough money for the grave-diggers. If not, I will have to pay for a grave and a wooden cross. If it gets worse I will have to order that they dig plague-pits to bury the bodies. These are my obligations as the lady of Stourton. I have to care for everyone in my domain, not just my children. And as usual – as is always the case – we have no idea what causes the illness, no idea what will cure it, no idea when it will pass on to some other poor blighted village and kill people there.

'Have you written to my lord?' I ask.

My steward, waiting on the threshold of the open door, replies for her. 'No, my lady, we knew he was travelling with the Prince of Wales but we didn't know where they were on the road. We didn't know where to write to him.'

'Write in my name, and send it to Ludlow,' I say. 'Bring it to me before you seal and send it. He will be at Ludlow within a few days. He might even be there now. But I will have to stay here until everyone is well again. I can't risk taking this illness to the Prince of Wales and his bride, whether it is the measles or the pox.'

'God forbid,' the steward says devoutly.

'Amen,' the nursemaid replies, praying for the prince even while her hand is on my son's hot red face, as if no-one ever matters more than a Tudor.

STOURTON CASTLE, STAFFORDSHIRE, SPRING 1502

I spend more than two months with my children at Stourton while they slowly, one after another, lose the heat from their blood, the spots from their skin, and the pain from their eyes. Ursula is the last to improve, and even when she is no longer ill she is quick to tire and moody, and she shades her eyes from the light with her hand. There are a few people sick in the village and one child dies. There is no Christmas feasting and I ban the village from coming to the castle for their twelfth-night gifts. There is much complaining that I have refused to give out food and wine and little fairings, but I am afraid of the sickness in the village and terrified that if I let the tenants and their families come to the castle they will bring disease with them.

Nobody knows what caused the illness, nobody knows if it has gone for good, or will return with the hot weather. We are as helpless before it as the cattle herd before a murrain; all we can do is suffer like lowing cows and hope that the worst of it passes us by. When finally the last man is up and about and the village children back to work I am so deeply relieved that I pay for a Mass in the village church, to give thanks that the illness seems to have passed us by for now, that we have been spared in this hard winter season, even if this summer the warm winds bring us the plague.

Only when I have stood at the front of the church and seen it filled with a congregation no thinner, no dirtier, no more desperate-looking than usual, only when I have ridden through the village and asked at each ramshackle door if they are all well, only when I have confirmed the health of everyone in our household from the boys who scare the birds from the crops to my head steward, only then do I know it is safe to leave my children, and go back to Ludlow.

The children stand at the front door to wave goodbye, the nursemaid holds my baby Reginald in her arms. He smiles at me and waves his fat little hands. He calls: 'Ma! Ma!' Ursula holds her hands cupped over her eyes to shield them against the morning sunlight. 'Stand properly,' I say to her, as I swing up into the saddle. 'Put your hands down at your sides, and stop scowling. Be good children, all four of you, and I will come home to see you soon.'

'When will you come?' Henry asks.

'In the summer,' I say to pacify him; in truth, I don't know. If Prince Arthur and his new bride make a summer progress with the royal court then I can come back to Stourton for all of the summer. But while they stay at Ludlow, under the protection of my husband, I have to be there too. I am not only a mother to these children; I have other duties. I am the lady of Ludlow and the guardian of the Prince of Wales. And I must play these parts perfectly, so that I can hide what I was born to be: a girl of the House of York, a white rose.

I blow them a kiss, but already my mind is away from them and on the road ahead. I nod to the Master of Horse and our little cavalcade, half a dozen men at arms, a couple of mules with my goods, three ladies in waiting on horseback, and a gaggle of servants, starts the long ride to Ludlow where I shall meet, for the first time, the girl who will be the next Queen of England: Katherine of Aragon.

LUDLOW CASTLE, WELSH MARCHES, MARCH 1502

I am greeted by my husband in his rooms. He is working with two clerks and papers are spread all over the great table. As I come in, he waves them away, pushes back his chair and greets me with a kiss on both cheeks. 'You're early.'

'The roads were good.'

'All well at Stourton?'

'Yes, the children are better at last,' I say.

'Good, good. I had your letter.' He looks relieved; he wants sons and healthy heirs like any man, and he is counting on our three boys to serve the Tudors and advance the family fortunes. 'Have you dined, my dear?'

'Not yet, I'll dine with you. Shall I meet the princess now?'

'As soon as you are ready. He wants to bring her to you himself,' he says, going back to sit down behind the table. He smiles at the thought of Arthur as a bridegroom. 'He's very keen that he should make the introduction. He asked me if he could bring her to you alone.'

'Very well,' I say drily. I have no doubt that Arthur has considered that introducing me to the young lady whose parents demanded my brother was killed before they would send her to England is a task that should be handled carefully. Equally, I know that this idea will not have crossed the mind of my husband.

I meet her as Arthur wishes, without ceremony, alone in the presence chamber of the Castle Warden of Ludlow, a great wood-panelled room immediately below her own apartment. There is a good fire in the grate and rich tapestries on the walls. It is not the glorious palace of the Alhambra; but equally it is nothing poor or shameful. I go to the hammered metal mirror and I adjust my headdress. My reflection looks dimly back at me, my dark eyes, pale clear skin, and pretty rosebud mouth – these are my best features. My long Plantagenet nose is my greatest disappointment. I straighten my headdress and feel the pins pull in my thickly coiled auburn hair, and then I turn from the mirror as a vanity that I should despise, and wait by the fireside.

In a few moments I hear Arthur's knock on the door and I nod to my lady in waiting who opens it and steps outside as Arthur comes in alone, bobs a swift bow to me as I curtsey to him and then we kiss each other on both cheeks.

'Are all three of them quite well?' he asks. 'And the baby?'

'Thanks be to God,' I say.

He crosses himself quickly. 'Amen. And you didn't take it?'

'It was surprising how few people took it this time,' I say. 'We were very blessed. Just a couple of people in the village and only two deaths. The baby showed no signs at all. God is merciful indeed.'

He nods. 'May I bring the Princess of Wales to you?'

I smile as he says her title with such care. 'And how do you like being a married man, Your Grace?'

The quick flush on his cheek tells me that he likes her a lot and is embarrassed to own it. 'I like it well enough,' he says quietly.

'You deal well together, Arthur?'

The red in his cheek deepens and spreads to his forehead. 'She is . . .' He breaks off. Clearly there are no words for what she is.

'Beautiful?' I suggest.

'Yes! And . . .'

'Pleasing?'

'Oh yes! And . . .'

'Charming?'

'She has such . . .' he starts and falls silent.

'I had better see her. Clearly she is beyond describing.'

'Ah Lady Guardian, you are laughing at me but you will see . . .'

He goes outside to fetch her. I had not realised we were keeping her waiting, and I wonder if she will be offended. After all, she is an Infanta of Spain and raised to be a very grand woman indeed.

As the heavy wooden door opens I get to my feet and Arthur brings her into the room, bows and steps out. He closes the door. The Princess of Wales and I are quite alone.

My first thought is that she is so slight and so dainty that you would think her a portrait of a princess in stained glass, not a real girl at all. She has bronze-coloured hair tucked modestly under a heavy hood, a tiny waist cinched in by a stomacher as big and heavy as a breastplate, and a high headdress draped in priceless lace, which falls to either side and shields her as if she might wear it down over her face like an infidel's veil. She curtseys to me with her eyes and face downturned, and only when I take her hand and she glances up can I see that she has bright blue eyes and a shy pretty smile.

She is pale with anxiety as I deliver my speech in Latin, welcoming her to the castle, and apologising for my previous absence. I see her glance around for Arthur. I see her bite her lower lip as if to summon courage, and plunge into words. At once she speaks of the one thing that I would willingly never hear, especially from her.

'I was sorry for the death of your brother, very sorry,' she says.

I am quite astounded that she should dare to speak to me of this at all, let alone that she should do so with frankness and compassion.

'It was a great loss,' I say coolly. 'Alas, it is the way of the world.'

'I am afraid that my coming . . .'

I cannot bear for her to apologise to me for the murder that was done in her name. I cut her off with a few words. She looks at me, poor child, as if she would ask how she can comfort me. She looks at me as if she is ready to fall at my feet and confess it as her fault. It is unbearable for me that she should speak of my brother. I cannot hear his name on her lips, I cannot let this conversation continue or I will break down and weep for him in front of this young woman whose coming caused his death. He would be alive but for her. How can I speak calmly of this?

I put out my hand to her to keep her at a distance, to silence her, but she grasps it, and makes a little curtsey. 'It's not your fault,' I manage to whisper. 'And we must all be obedient to the king.'

Her blue eyes are drowned in tears. 'I am sorry,' she says. 'So sorry.'

'It's not your fault,' I say, to stop her saying another word. 'And it was not his fault. Nor mine.'

And then, strangely, we live together happily. The courage that she showed when she faced me and told me that she was sorry for my grief and that she would have wanted to prevent it, I see in her every day. She misses her home terribly, her mother writes only rarely, and then briefly. Katherine is little more than a motherless child in a strange land, with everything to learn: our language, our customs, even our foods are foreign to her, and sometimes, when we sit together in the afternoon, sewing, I divert her by asking her about her home.

She describes their palace, the Alhambra, as if it were a jewel set in a lining of a green garden, placed in the treasure chest of the castle of Granada. She tells me of the icy water that flows in the fountains in the courtyards piped from the mountains of the high sierra, and of the burning sun that bakes the landscape to arid gold. She tells me of the silks that she wore every day, and of the languid mornings in the marble-tiled bath house, of her mother in the throne room dispensing justice and ruling the kingdom as an equal monarch with her father, and of their determination that their rule and the law of God should stretch throughout Spain.

'This must all feel so strange to you,' I say wonderingly, looking out of the narrow window to where the light is draining from the dark wintry landscape, the sky going from ash grey through slate grey, to soot grey. There is snow on the hills and the clouds are rolling up the valley, as a scud of rain hammers against the little panes of glass in the window. 'It must seem like another world.'

'It is like a dream,' she says quietly. 'You know? When everything is different, and you keep hoping and hoping to wake?'

Silently, I assent. I know what it is like to find that everything has changed and you cannot get back to your earlier life.

'If it were not for Arth ... for His Grace,' she whispers and lowers her eyes to her sewing, 'if it were not for him, I would be most unhappy.'

I put my hand over hers. 'Thank God that he loves you,' I say quietly. 'And I hope that we can all make you happy.'

At once she looks up, her blue eyes seeking mine. 'He does love me, doesn't he?'

'Without any doubt,' I smile. 'I have known him since he was a baby and he has a most loving and generous heart. It is a blessing that you two should come together. What a king and queen you will make, some day.'

She has the dazzled look of a young woman very much in love.

'And are there any signs?' I ask her quietly. 'Any signs of a child? You do know how to tell if a baby is coming? Your mother or your duenna has talked to you?'

'You need say nothing; my mother told me all about it,' she says with endearing dignity. 'I know everything. And there are no signs yet. But I am sure that we will have a child. And I want to call her Mary.'

'You should pray for a son,' I remind her. 'A son and call him Henry.'

'A son named Arthur, but first a girl called Mary,' she says, as if she is certain already. 'Mary for Our Lady who brought me safely here and gave me a young husband who could love me. And then Arthur for his father and the England that we will make together.'

'And how will your country be?' I ask her.

She is serious, this is no childish game to her. 'There will be no fines for small offences,' she says. 'Justice should not be used to force people into obedience.'

I give the smallest nod of my head. The king's rapacity in fining his noblemen, even his friends, and binding them over with tremendous debts is eating away at the loyalty of his court. But I cannot discuss it with the king's heir.

'And no unjust arrests,' she says very quietly. 'I think your cousins are in the Tower of London.'

'My cousin William de la Pole has been taken to the Tower, but there is no charge read against him,' I say. 'I pray that he has nothing to do with his brother Edmund, a rebel who has run away. I don't know where he is, nor what he is doing.'

'Nobody doubts your loyalty!' she reassures me.

'I make sure they don't,' I say grimly. 'And I rarely speak to my kinsmen.'

LUDLOW CASTLE, WELSH MARCHES, APRIL 1502

Arthur tries his best, we all try to keep her spirits up but it is a long cold winter for her in the hills on the borders of Wales. He promises her everything but the moon itself: a garden to grow vegetables, deliveries of oranges for her to make a sort of preserve that they love to eat in Spain, oil of roses for her hair, fresh lilies – he swears that they will bloom even here. We constantly assure her that the warm weather will come soon, and that it will be hot – not as hot as Spain, we say cautiously, but hot enough to walk outside without being wrapped in layer after layer of shawls and furs, and for certain, one day there will be an end to the unceasing rain, and the sun will rise earlier into a bright sky, and the night will come later, and she will hear nightingales.

We swear to her that May will be sunny, and we tell her the silly plays and games of May Day: she will open her window at dawn and be greeted with a carol, all the handsome young men will leave peeled wands at her door, and we will crown her Queen of the May and we will teach her how to dance around a maypole.

But, despite our plans and our promises, it is not like that. May is not like that at all. Perhaps it never could have been what we promised; but it was not the weather that failed us, nor the easily invoked joy of a court cooped up for months, it was not the blossoms, nor the fish spawning in the river; the nightingales came and sang, but nobody listened – it was a disaster which none of us could have imagined.

'It's Arthur,' my husband says to me, forgetting the prince's many titles, forgetting to knock on my bedroom door, bursting in, scowling with worry. 'Come at once, he's sick.'

I am seated before my mirror, my maid in waiting behind me plaiting my hair, with my headdress ready on the stand and my gown for the day hung on the carved wood cupboard door behind her. I jump to my feet, tweaking the plait from her hand, throw my cape over my nightgown and hastily tie the cords. 'What's the matter?'

'Says he's tired, says he aches as if he had an ague.'

Arthur never complains of illness, never sends for the physician. The two of us stride from my room down the stairs and across the hall to the prince's tower and up to his bedroom at the top. My husband pants up the winding stair behind me as I run up the stone steps, round and round, my hand on the cool stone pillar at the centre of the spiral.

'Have you called the physician to him?' I throw over my shoulder.

'Of course. But he's out somewhere. His servant has gone into town to look for him.' My husband steadies himself, one hand against the central stone pillar, one hand on his heaving chest. 'They won't be long.'

We reach Arthur's bedroom door and I tap on it and go in without waiting for a response. The boy is in bed; his face has a sheen of sweat over it. He is as white as his linen, the ruffled collar of his nightshirt lying against his young face without contrast.

I am shocked but I try not to show it. 'My boy,' I say gently, my voice as warm and as confident as I can make it. 'Are you not feeling well?'

He rolls his head towards me. 'Just hot,' he says through cracked lips. 'Very hot.' He gestures to his menservants. 'Help me. I'll get up and sit by the fire.'

I step back and watch them. They turn back the covers and throw his robe around his shoulders. They help him from the bed. I see him grimace as he moves, as if it hurts him to take the two steps to the chair, and when he gets to the fireside he sits down heavily, as if he is exhausted.

'Would you fetch Her Grace the princess for me?' he asks. 'I must tell her I cannot ride out with her today.'

'I can tell her myself . . .'

'I want to see her.'

I don't argue with him, but go down the stairs of his tower, across the hall, and up the stairs of her tower to her rooms and ask her to come to her husband. She is at her morning studies, reading English, frowning over her book. She comes at once, smiling and expectant; her duenna, Doña Elvira, follows with one fierce look at me, as if to ask: What is wrong? What has gone wrong in this cold, wet country now? How have you English failed again?

The princess follows me through Arthur's great presence chamber where there are half a dozen men waiting to see the prince. They bow as she goes by and she walks through with a little smile to right and left, a gracious princess. Then she enters into Prince Arthur's bedroom and the brightness drains from her face.

'Are you ill, my love?' she asks him at once.

He is hunched in his chair at the fireside; my husband, agonised as an anxious hound, stands behind him. Arthur puts out his hand to stop her coming any closer, murmuring so low that I cannot hear what he says. She turns at once to me and her face is shocked.

'Lady Margaret, we must call the prince's physician.'

'I have sent my servants to find him already.'

'I don't want a fuss,' Arthur says immediately. From childhood he has hated being ill and being nursed. His brother Harry revels in attention, and loves to be ill and cosseted; but Arthur always swears there is nothing wrong.

There is a tap on the door and a voice calls out: 'Dr Bereworth is here, Your Grace.'

Doña Elvira takes it upon herself to open the door and as the doctor comes in, the princess goes towards him with a ripple of

Latin questions too quick for him to understand. He looks to me for help.

'His Grace is unwell,' I say simply. I step back and he sees the prince rise from his chair, staggering with the effort, all colour drained from his face. I see the doctor recoil when he sees Arthur and from his aghast look I instantly know what he is thinking.

The princess speaks urgently to her duenna, who replies in rapid muttered Spanish. Arthur looks from his young bride to his doctor, his eyes hollow, his skin yellowing from one hour to another.

'Come,' I say to the princess, taking her by her arm and leading her out of the bedchamber. 'Be patient. Dr Bereworth is a very good doctor and he has known the prince from childhood. It's probably nothing to worry about at all. If Dr Bereworth is concerned we'll send for the king's own physician from London. We'll soon have him well again.'

Her little face is downcast, but she lets me press her into a window seat in the presence chamber and she turns her head and looks out at the rain. I wave the crowd of petitioners out of the presence chamber and they leave, reluctantly bowing, glancing at the still figure in the window seat.

We wait in silence until the doctor reappears. I can just see as he closes the door that Arthur has returned to his bed and is lying back against the pillows.

'I think he should be left to sleep,' the doctor says.

I go to him. 'It's not the Sweat,' I mutter to him urgently, daring him to contradict me, glancing back at the frozen young woman in the window seat. I realise that I am not asking him for his opinion, I am forbidding him to name our greatest fear. 'It's not the Sweat. It can't be.'

'Your ladyship, I can't say.'

He is terrified to say. The Sweat kills within a night and a day, taking the old and the young, the healthy and the frail without distinction. It is the curse that the king trailed behind him when he marched into his kingdom with his army of mercenaries who brought it from the gutters and prisons of Europe. It is Henry

Tudor's blight on the English people and in the first months after the battle people said that it proved that his line would not prosper; they said that the reign which had begun in labour would end in Sweat. I wonder if this was a prediction laid on our young prince, I wonder if his fragile life is doubly cursed?

'Please God, it's not the Sweat,' the doctor says.

The princess comes across to him and speaks slowly in Latin, desperate to have his opinion. He assures her that it is nothing more than a fever, that he can administer a draught and the prince's temperature will come down. He speaks soothingly to her, and goes, leaving me to persuade the princess that she cannot watch over her husband as he sleeps.

'If I leave him now, do you swear to me that you will stay with him, all the time?' she pleads.

'I'll go back in now, if you will walk outside and then go to your room and read or study or sew.'

'I'll go!' she says, instantly obedient. 'I'll go to my rooms if you will stay with him.'

The duenna, Doña Elvira, exchanges a level look with me and then follows her charge from the room. I go to the prince's bedside, conscious that I have now sworn to both his wife and his mother that I will watch over him, but that my watching may be of little use if the young man who is so white and restless in the great curtained bed is the victim of his father's disease and his mother's curse.

The day goes by with painful slowness. The princess is obedient to her word and walks in the garden and studies in her rooms and sends every hour to ask how her husband does. I reply that he is resting, that his fever is still high. I don't tell her that he is getting worse and worse, he is rolling around in feverish dreams, we have sent for the king's own doctor from London and that I am sponging his forehead, his face and his chest with wine vinegar and icy water but nothing makes him cool.

Katherine goes to the circular chapel in the courtyard of the castle and prays on her knees for the health of her young husband. Late at night, I look down from the window in Arthur's tower and I see her bobbing candle in the darkened courtyard and the train of women following her from the chapel to her bedroom. I hope that she can sleep as I turn back to the bed and the boy who is burning up with fever. I put some cleansing salts on the fire and watch the flames burn blue. I take his hand and feel the sweat in his hot palms and his pulse hammering under my fingertips. I don't know what to do for him. I don't know what there is to do for him. I fear that there is nothing that anyone can do for him. In the cold long darkness of the night I begin to believe that he will die.

I eat my breakfast in his room but I have no appetite. He is wandering in his mind and will neither eat nor drink. I have the grooms of the bedchamber hold him while I force the cup against his mouth and pour small ale down his throat until he chokes and splutters and swallows, and then they lie him back on the pillow and he throws himself around in the bed, hot, and getting hotter.

The princess comes to the door of his presence chamber and they send for me. 'I shall see him! You will not prevent me!'

I close the door behind me and confront her white-faced determination. Her eyes are shadowed like bruised violets; she has not slept all night. 'It may be a grave illness,' I say, not naming the greatest fear. 'I cannot allow you to go to him. I should be failing in my duty if I let you go to him.'

'Your duty is to me!' shouts the daughter of Isabella of Spain, driven to rage by her fear.

'My duty is to England,' I say to her quietly. 'And if you are carrying a Tudor heir in your belly then my duty is to that child as well as to you. I cannot allow you to go closer than to the foot of the bed.'

At once she almost collapses. 'Let me go in,' she pleads. 'Please, Lady Margaret, just let me see him. I will stop where you say, I will do as you command, but for Our Lady's sake, let me see him.'

I take her in, past the waiting crowds who call out a blessing, past the trestle table where the doctor has set up a small cabinet with herbs and oils and leeches crawling in a jar, through the double doors to the bedroom where Arthur is lying, still and quiet, on the bed. He opens his dark eyes as she comes in, and the first words he whispers are, 'I love you. Don't come closer.'

She takes hold of the carved post at the foot of the bed, as if to stop herself from climbing in beside him. 'I love you too,' she says breathlessly. 'You will be well?'

He just shakes his head and, in that terrible moment, I know that I have failed in my promise to his mother. I said that I would keep him safe, and I have not. From a wintry sky, from an east wind – who knows how? – he has taken the curse of his father's disease, and My Lady the King's Mother will be punished by the curse of the two queens. She will pay for what she did to their boys, and see her grandson buried and, no doubt, her son also. I step forward and take hold of the princess by her slight waist and draw her to the door.

'I shall come back,' she calls to him as she takes unwilling steps away from him. 'Stay with me; I will not fail you.'

All day we fight for him, as arduously if we were infantrymen bogged down in the mud of Bosworth Field. We put scalding plasters on his chest, we put leeches on his legs, we sponge his face with icy water, we put a warming pan under his back. As he lies there, white as a marble saint, we torment him with every cure that we can think of, and still he sweats as if he is on fire, and nothing breaks his fever.

The princess comes back to him as she promised to do and this time we tell her that it is the Sweat and she may go no closer to him than the threshold of his room. She says that she has to speak with him privately, orders us all from the room and stands on tiptoe, holding the door jamb, calling across the herb-strewn floor to him. I hear a quick exchange of vows. He asks for a promise from her, she agrees but begs him to get well. I take her arm.

'For his own good,' I say. 'You have to leave him.'

He has raised himself up on one elbow and I catch a glimpse of his deathly determined face. 'Promise,' he says to her. 'Please. For my sake. Promise me now, beloved.'

She cries out, 'I promise!' as if the words are torn from her, as if she does not want to grant him his last wish, and I pull her from the room.

The bell tolls six. Arthur's confessor gives him extreme unction and he lies back on his pillow and closes his eyes. 'No,' I whisper. 'Don't let go, don't let go.' I am supposed to be praying at the foot of the bed, but instead I have my hands clenched in fists pressing into my wet eyes and all I can do is whisper 'No'. I cannot remember when I last left the room, when I last ate or when I last slept, but I cannot bear that this prince, this supremely beautiful and gifted young prince, is going to die – and in my care. I cannot bear that he should give up his life, this beautiful life so full of promise and hope. I have failed to teach him the one thing I most truly believe: that nothing matters more than life itself, that he should cling on to life.

'No,' I say. 'Don't.'

Prayers cannot stop him slipping away, the leeches, the herbs, the oils, and the charred heart of a sparrow tied on his chest cannot hold him. He is dead by the time the bell strikes seven. I go to his bedside and straighten his collar, as I used to do when he was alive, and close his dark, unseeing eyes, pulling the embroidered coverlet straight across his chest as if I were tucking him up for the night, and I kiss his cold lips. I whisper: 'God bless you. Goodnight, sweet prince,' and then I send for the midwives to lay him out and I leave the room.

To Her Grace the Queen of England

  Dear Cousin Elizabeth,

  They will have told you already, so this is a letter between us: from the woman who loved him as a mother, to the mother who could not have loved him more. He faced his death with courage, as the men of our family do. His sufferings were short and he died in faith.

  I do not ask you to forgive me for failing to save him because I will never forgive myself. There was no sign of any cause but the Sweat and there is no cure for that. You need not reproach yourself, there was no sign of any curse on him. He died like the beloved brave boy he was from the disease that his father's armies unknowingly brought into this poor country.

  I will bring his widow, the princess, to you in London. She is a young woman with a broken heart. They had come to love one another and her loss is very great.

  As is yours, my dear.

  And mine.

  Margaret Pole

LUDLOW CASTLE, WELSH MARCHES, SUMMER 1502

The queen, my cousin, sends her private litter for the widow to make the long journey to London. Katherine travels shocked and mute, and every night on the road goes to bed in silence. I know she prays that she will not wake in the morning. I ask her, as I am bound to do, whether she thinks she might be with child and she shakes with rage at the question as if I am intruding on the privacy of her love.

'If you are with child, and that child is a boy, then he will be the Prince of Wales and much later King of England,' I say to her gently, ignoring her tremulous fury. 'You would become a woman as great as Lady Margaret Beaufort who created her own title: My Lady the King's Mother.'

She can hardly bring herself to speak. 'And if I am not?'

'Then you are the Dowager Princess, and Prince Harry becomes the Prince of Wales,' I explain. 'If you have no son to take the title then it goes to Prince Harry.'

'And when the king dies?'

'Please God, that day is long coming.'

'Amen. But when it does?'

'Then Prince Harry is king and his wife – whoever she is – will be queen.'

She turns away from me and goes to the fireplace but not before I see the swift expression of scorn that crosses her face at the mention of Prince Arthur's little brother. 'Prince Harry!' she exclaims.

'You have to accept the position in life that God gives you,' I remind her quietly.

'I do not.'

'Your Grace, you have suffered a great loss, but you have to accept your fate. God requires us all to accept our fate. Perhaps God commands that you are resigned?' I suggest.

'He does not,' she says firmly.

WESTMINSTER PALACE, LONDON, JUNE 1502

I leave the Dowager Princess of Wales, as she is now to be called, at Durham House on the Strand and I go to Westminster where the court is in deep mourning. I walk through the familiar halls to the queen's rooms. The doors stand open to her presence chamber which is crowded with the usual courtiers and petitioners but everyone is subdued and talking quietly, and many are wearing black trim on their jackets.

I pass through, nodding to one or two people that I know; but I don't stop. I don't want to talk. I don't want to have to say, yet again: 'Yes. It is a very sudden disease. Yes, we did try that remedy. Yes, it was a terrible shock. Yes, the princess is heartbroken. Yes, it is a tragedy that there is no child.'

I tap on the inner door and Lady Katherine Huntly opens it and looks at me. She is the widow of the pretender who was executed with my brother and there is no great love lost between us. She steps back and I go by her without a word.

The queen is kneeling before her prie-dieu, her face turned up to the golden crucifix, her eyes closed. I kneel beside her and I bow my head and pray for the strength to talk to our prince's mother about the loss of him.

She sighs and glances at me. 'I have been waiting for you,' she says quietly.

I take her hands. 'I am sorrier than I can say.'

'I know.'

We kneel, hand-clasped in silence, as if there is nothing more that needs saying. 'The princess?'

'Very quiet. Very sad.'

'There's no chance that she could be with child?'

'She says not.'

My cousin nods as if she were not hoping for a grandchild to replace the son she has lost.

'Nothing was left undone . . .' I begin.

She puts her hand gently on my shoulder. 'I know you will have cared for him as you would have cared for your own,' she says. 'I know you loved him from babyhood. He was a true York prince, he was our white rose.'

'We still have Harry,' I say.

'Yes.' She leans on my shoulder as she rises to her feet. 'But

Harry wasn't raised to be Prince of Wales, or king. I've spoiled him, I'm afraid. He's flighty and vain.'

I am so surprised to hear her say so much as one word against her beloved son that for a moment I cannot answer her. 'He can learn ...' I stumble. 'He will grow.'

'He'll never be another Prince Arthur,' she says, as if measuring the depth of her loss. 'Arthur was the son that I made for England. Anyway,' she continues. 'God be praised, I think I am with child again.'

'You are?'

'It's early days yet, but I pray so. It would be such a comfort, wouldn't it? Another boy?'

She is thirty-six, she is old for another childbirth. 'It would be wonderful,' I say, trying to smile. 'God's favour to the Tudors, mercy after sacrifice.'

I go with her to the window and we look out at the bright gardens and the people playing at bowls on the green below us. 'He was such a precious boy, coming as he did, so early in our marriage, like a blessing. And he was such a happy baby, d'you remember, Margaret?'

'I remember,' I say shortly. I won't tell her that my sorrow is that I feel I have forgotten so much, that his years with me have just slipped through my fingers as if they were nothing more than uneventful sunny days. He was such a happy boy, and happiness is not memorable.

She does not sob, though she constantly brushes tears from both of her cheeks with the back of her hands.

'Will the king send Harry to Ludlow?' I ask. If my husband has to be guardian to another prince then I will have to care for him too, and I don't believe I can bear to see another boy, not even Harry, in Prince Arthur's place.

She shakes her head. 'My Lady forbids it,' she says. 'She says he is to stay with us, at court. He will be educated here and trained for his new calling under her eye, under our constant supervision.'

'And the Dowager Princess?'

'She will go home to Spain, I suppose. There's nothing for her here.'

'Nothing, poor child,' I agree, thinking of the white-faced girl in the big palace.

I visit Princess Katherine before I go home to Stourton Castle. She is very young to be left all alone with no-one but paid companions – her strict duenna and her ladies in waiting, her confessor and her servants – in the beautiful palace with great terraced gardens leading down to the river. I wish they would take her into the queen's rooms at court and not leave her here, to run her own household.

She has grown more beautiful in the months of mourning, her pale skin luminous against the bronze of her hair. She is thinner and it makes her blue eyes seem larger in her heart-shaped face.

'I have come to say goodbye,' I tell her with forced cheerfulness. 'I am going to my home at Stourton and I expect you will soon be on your way back to Spain.'

She looks around as if to make sure that we are not overheard; but her ladies are at a distance, and Doña Elvira does not speak English.

'No, I'm not going home,' she says with quiet determination.

I wait for an explanation. She gives me a swift, mischievous smile that brightens the gravity of her sad face. 'I am not,' she repeats. 'So there's no need to look at me like that. I'm not going.'

'There's nothing for you here any more,' I remind her.

She takes my arm so that she can speak very low as we walk down the length of the gallery, away from the ladies, with the slap of our slippers on the wooden floor hiding the sound of our words.

'No, you are wrong. There is something here for me. I made a promise to Arthur on his deathbed, that I would serve England as I had been born and raised to do,' she says quietly. 'You yourself heard him say, "Promise me now, beloved" – they were his last words to me. I will keep that promise.'

'You can't stay.'

'I can, and in the most simple way. If I marry the Prince of Wales I become Princess of Wales once more.'

I am stunned into silence, then I find my voice. 'You can't want to marry Prince Harry.' I state the obvious.

'I have to.'

'Was this your promise to Prince Arthur?'

She nods.

'He can't have meant you to marry his little brother.'

'He did. He knew it would be the only way that I would be Princess of Wales and Queen of England, and he and I had many plans, we had agreed many things. He knew that the Tudor rule of England is not as the Yorks had ruled. He wanted to be a king from both houses. He wanted to rule with justice and compassion. He wanted to win the respect of the people, not coerce them. We had plans. When he knew he was dying he still wanted me to do as we had planned – even though he could not. I shall guide Harry and teach him. I will make him into a good king.'

'Prince Harry has many strengths.' I try to choose my words. 'But he is not, and he will never be, the prince we have lost. He is charming, and energetic, he is brave as a little lion cub and ready to serve his family and his country . . .' I hesitate. 'But he is like enamel, my dear. He shines on the surface, he sparkles; but he's not pure gold. He's not like Arthur – who was true, through and through.'

'Even so, I will marry him. I will make him better than he is.'

'Your Grace, my dear, his father will be looking for a great match for him, another princess. And your parents will be looking for a second marriage for you.'

'Then we solve two problems with one answer. And besides, this way the king avoids paying my widow's allowance. He'll like that. And he'll get the rest of my dowry. He'll like that. And he keeps an alliance with Spain which he wanted so much that he . . .' She breaks off.

'He wanted it so much that he killed my brother for it.' I finish the sentence quietly. 'Yes, I know. But you are not the Spanish Infanta any more. You have been married. It's not the same. You are not the same.'

She flushes. 'It will be the same. I shall make it be the same. I shall say that I am a virgin, and that the marriage was not consummated.'

I gasp. 'Your Grace, nobody would ever believe you . . .'

'But nobody will ever ask!' she declares. 'Who would dare to challenge me? If I say such a thing, it must be so. And you will stand as my friend, won't you, Margaret? Because I am doing this for Arthur and you loved him as I did? If you don't deny what I say, then no-one will question it. Everyone will want to think that I can marry Harry, nobody is going to question servants and companions for gossip. None of my ladies would answer a question from an English spy. If you don't say anything, nobody else is going to.'

I am so astounded by this jump from heartbreak into conspiracy that I can only gasp and look at her. Her face is completely determined, her jaw set.

'Believe me, you cannot do this.'

'I am going to do this,' she says grimly. 'I promised. I am going to do this.'

'Your Grace, Harry is a child . . .'

'Don't you think I know that? It's to the good. It's why Arthur was so determined. Harry has to be trained. Harry will be guided by me. I will advise him. I know he's a vain, spoiled little boy. But I am going to make him into the king that he has to be.'

I am about to argue but suddenly I see her as the queen she may become. She will be formidable. This girl was raised to be Queen of England from the age of three. It seems she will be Queen of England however the luck runs against her.

'I don't know what's the right thing to do,' I say uncertainly. 'If I were you . . .'

She shakes her head, smiling. 'Lady Margaret, if you were me you would go home to Spain and hope to live your life in quiet safety, because you have learned to keep your distance from the throne, you were raised in fear of the king, any king. But I was raised to be Princess of Wales and then Queen of England. I have no choice. They called me the Princess of Wales from the cradle! I can't just change my name now and hide from my destiny. I have to do what I promised to Arthur. You have to help me.'

'Half the court saw you put to bed together on your wedding night.'

'I'll say that he was incapable if I have to.'

I gasp at her determination. 'Katherine! You would never shame him?'

'It's no shame to him,' she says fiercely. 'It is a shame on anyone who asks me. I know what he was to me and what I was to him. I know how he loved me and what we were to each other. But nobody else need know. Nobody else will ever know.'

I see her passion for him still. 'But your duenna . . .'

'She'll say nothing. She doesn't want to go back to Spain with spoiled goods and a half-spent dowry.'

She turns to me and smiles her fearless smile, as if it will be easy. 'And I'll have a son with Harry,' she promises. 'Just as Arthur and I hoped. And a girl called Mary. Will you look after my children for me, Lady Margaret? Don't you want to care for the children that Arthur wanted me to have?'

I would have been wiser to say nothing, though I should have told her that women have to change their names and silence their own wills, though I could have told her that destinies are for men. 'Yes,' I say reluctantly. 'Yes. I do want to care for the children you promised him. I do want to be Mary's governess. And I'll never say anything about you and Arthur. I knew nothing for sure, I was not even there at your wedding night, and if you are truly determined, then I will not betray you. I will have no opinion.'

She bows her head, and I realise that she is deeply relieved at my decision. 'I am doing this for him,' she reminds me. 'For love of him. Not for my own ambition, not even for my parents. He asked it of me, and I am going to do it.'

'I'll help you,' I promise her. 'For him.'

STOURTON CASTLE, STAFFORDSHIRE, AUTUMN 1502

But there is little I can do for her. I am no longer the wife of the guardian of the Prince of Wales, because there is no longer a court for the Prince of Wales or a Welsh household. The new prince – Harry – is declared to be too precious to be sent away. While my cousin the queen grows big with a child which everyone says must be a boy, their only living heir, Harry, is raised at Eltham Palace near Greenwich with his sisters Margaret and Mary, and though he is a sturdy, strong eleven-year-old, old enough to take up his duties as a royal heir, old enough to have his own council and learn from them to make careful judgements, My Lady the King's Mother demands that he be kept at home like his sisters, the adored and indulged lord of the nursery kingdom.

He has the best of tutors, the finest musicians and the best horsemen to teach him all the arts and skills of a young prince. My cousin his mother ensures that he is a scholar and tries to teach him that a king cannot have everything his own way; but My Lady insists that he must never be exposed to any danger.

He must never go near a sick person, his rooms must be constantly cleaned, he must be attended always by a physician. He must ride wonderful horses but they must be broken by his horsemaster and guaranteed safe for their most precious rider. He can ride at the quintain, but he may never face an opponent in the joust. He can row on the river but never if it looks like rain. He can play tennis, though nobody ever beats him, and sing songs and make music, but he must never be overexcited or flushed too hot, or strain himself. He is not taught to rule, he is not even taught to rule himself. The boy, already indulged and spoiled, is now the only Tudor stepping stone to the future. If they were to lose him they would lose everything they have fought and plotted and worked for. Without a son and heir to follow the Tudor king there is no Tudor dynasty, no House of Tudor. With the death of his brother, Harry is now the only son and heir. No wonder they wrap him in ermine and serve him off gold.

They cannot see him take a step without being dizzily aware that he is their only boy. The Tudor family is so few: our queen facing the ordeal of childbirth, a king who is plagued with quinsy and cannot draw a breath without pain, his old mother, two girls and only one boy. They are few and they are fragile.

And nobody remarks it, but we Plantagenets in the House of York are so many. They call us the demon's brood and indeed we breed like the devil. We are rich in heirs, headed by my cousin Edmund, gaining followers and power all the time at the court of the Emperor Maximilian, his brother Richard, and scores of kinsmen and cousins. Plantagenet blood is fertile; they named the family for the *planta genista*, the broom shrub, which is never out of flower, which grows everywhere, in the most unlikely soil, which can never be uprooted and even when it is burned out will thrive and grow again the very next spring, yellow as gold though it is rooted in the blackest charcoal.

They say that when you behead one of the Plantagenets there is another that springs up, fresh in the green. We trace our line back to Fulk of Anjou, husband to a water goddess. We always bear a dozen heirs. But if the Tudors lose Harry they have nothing to replace him with but the baby my cousin carries low and heavy in her belly that drains her face of colour and makes her sick every morning.

Since Prince Harry is so rare, since he is their singular precious heir, he has to be married and they succumb to the temptation of Spanish wealth, Spanish power and the convenience of Katherine, obedient and helpful, waiting for the word in her London palace. They promise Harry in marriage to her, and so she has her way. I laugh out loud when my husband comes back from London and tells me the news, and he looks at me curiously, and asks me what is so amusing.

'Just say it again!' I demand.

'Prince Harry has been betrothed to the Dowager Princess of Wales,' he repeats. 'But I don't see what's so funny about that.'

'Because she had set her heart on it, and I never thought that they would consent,' I explain.

'Well, I'm surprised that they did. They've got to get a dispensation and negotiate a settlement, and then they can't marry for years. I'd have thought that nothing but the best would have been good enough for Prince Harry. Not his brother's widow.'

'Why not, if the marriage was never consummated?' I venture.

He looks at me. 'That's what the Spanish are saying, it's all around court. I didn't contradict it, though I had eyes in my head at Ludlow. I don't know the truth of it and I didn't know what to say.' He looks sheepish. 'I didn't know what My Lady the King's Mother would want to hear. Until she tells me, I'll say nothing.'

STOURTON CASTLE, STAFFORDSHIRE, FEBRUARY 1503

Elizabeth, my cousin the queen, prayed that she was carrying another boy, prayed that the curse she had recited as a young woman of seventeen was nothing but words on the cold wind, prayed that the Tudor line would not die out. But she was brought to bed and she had a girl, a worthless girl, and it cost her her life, and the baby died too.

'I am sorry,' my husband says gently to me, the letter sealed with black wax trailing black satin ribbons in his hand. 'I am sorry. I know how much you loved her.'

I shake my head. He does not know how much I loved her, and I cannot tell him. When I was a little girl and my world was all but destroyed by the Tudor victory she was there, pale and afraid like me but determined that we Plantagenets would survive, determined that we would share in the Tudor spoils, determined that we would lead the Tudor court, determined that she would be queen and that the House of York would still rule England even if she had to marry the invader.

When I was sick with fear and utterly at a loss as to how I would keep my brother safe from the new king and his mother, it was Elizabeth who reassured me, who promised me that she and her mother would guard us. It was Elizabeth who barred the way of the yeomen of the guard when they came to arrest my little brother Teddy and Elizabeth who swore that they should not take him. It was Elizabeth who spoke to her husband time after time, begging him for Teddy's release, and it was Elizabeth who held me and cried with me when, finally, the king brought himself to do that one terrible act, and kill my brother Teddy for the crime of being Edward Plantagenet, for carrying his name, our name, the name that Elizabeth and I shared.

'Will you come with me to her funeral?' Richard asks.

I don't know that I can bear it. I buried her son, and now I have to bury her. One died of the Tudor disease, the other of Tudor ambition. My family is paying a high price to keep the Tudors safe on their throne.

'They want you there,' he says shortly, as if that simply settles the matter.

'I'll come,' I say; because it does.

WESTMINSTER PALACE, LONDON, SPRING 1503

My Lady the King's Mother rules how the funeral of a queen is to be done, as she rules all the great ceremonials of this great court. Elizabeth's coffin is drawn through the streets of London by eight black horses, followed by two hundred paupers carrying lit candles. Dressed in black, I follow the coffin with her ladies, while the gentlemen of the court ride behind us, robed and hooded in black, through streets that are blazing with torches and filled with mourners, all the way to Westminster Abbey.

London turns out for the York princess. London has always loved the Yorks and as I go by, following her coffin, there is a whisper that follows me down the cobbled street, 'À Warwick', like a blessing, like an offer. I keep my eyes and head down, as if I cannot hear my grandfather's battle cry.

The king is not here; he has gone upriver to the beautiful palace that he built for her, Richmond; gone into the privy chamber at the heart of the palace and closed the door, as if he cannot bear to live without her, as if he dare not look to see what friends he has left, now that the princess of the House of York has gone. He always swore that she did not bring him England, he took it on his own account. Now she is gone, he can see what his own account really is: what friends he has, what he holds without her; he can see how safe he feels among her people.

He does not come out from darkness and solitude till the middle of spring, and then he is still wearing black for her. My Lady, his mother, commands that he ends his solitary mourning, nurses him back to health, and Sir Richard and I are at court at her bidding, seated among the knights and their ladies in the great dining hall. To my surprise the king walks down the length of the room, and when I rise to curtsey to him he leads me away from the ladies' table to an alcove at the back of the great hall.

He takes both my hands in his own. 'You loved her as I did, I know. I can't believe that she is gone,' he says simply.

He looks like a man injured beyond recovery. His face is engraved with new lines of suffering; his grey complexion shows that he is exhausted by grief. The sagging skin under his eyes shows a man who has wept for night after night instead of sleeping, and he stands a little bent, as if to ease the pain in his chest. 'I can't believe it,' he repeats.

I have no words of comfort because I share his loss, and I am still bewildered at the suddenness of her going. All my life my cousin Elizabeth has been with me, a constant loving presence. I cannot understand that she is here no longer. 'God is . . .'

'Why would God take her? She was the best queen that England could have had! She was the best wife that I could have had.'

I say nothing. Of course she was the best queen that England could have had; she was from England's own royal family that ruled long before he stumbled ashore at Milford Haven. She did not come in with a diseased army, and take her crown from a thorn bush; she was our own, born and bred an English princess. 'And my children!' he exclaims, looking over to them.

Harry was placed at his father's side for dinner, and he sits now beside the empty throne, his face turned down to his plate, eating nothing. For him it has been the worst blow a child can suffer; I wonder if he will ever recover. His mother loved him with a steady calmness that his grandmother's passionate favouritism could not overthrow. Elizabeth saw him for what he was – a highly talented and charming little boy – and yet kept before him a picture of what he must be: the master of himself. Just by walking into his nursery she showed him that it is not enough to be the centre of attention; every prince has that from birth. Instead, she required that he be true to himself, that he curb his boastful vanity, that he learn to put himself in others' shoes, that he practise compassion.

His sisters Margaret and Mary, terribly lost without her, are seated beside their grandmother, My Lady the King's Mother, and Katherine the Spanish princess is beside them. She feels my gaze on her and she looks up and gives me a swift, inscrutable smile.

'At least they had their childhood with her,' I say. 'A mother who truly loved them. At least Harry had his childhood safe in his mother's love.'

He nods. 'At least they had that,' he says. 'At least I had my years with her.'

'It's a grave loss for the Dowager Princess too,' I observe carefully. 'The queen was very tender towards her.'

He follows my gaze. Katherine is seated in a place of honour but the young princesses are not talking to her as sisters should. Thirteen-year-old Margaret has turned her shoulder and is whispering with her little sister Mary, their heads close together. Katherine looks lonely at the high table, as if she is there on sufferance. As I look closely, I see that she is pale and anxious, occasionally glancing down the table to where Harry stares blindly at his plate, as if she would like to catch his eye.

'She's more beautiful every time she comes to court,' he says quietly, his eyes on her, unaware that this grates on me as an insult on pain. 'She's growing into real beauty. She was always a pretty girl but now she is becoming a remarkable young woman.'

'Indeed,' I say stiffly. 'And when is her marriage to Prince Harry to take place?'

The look that he slides sideways makes me shiver, as if a cold draught had suddenly blown into the room. He looks roguish, like Prince Harry does when he has been caught stealing pastries from the kitchen, excited and apologetic all at once, knowing that he is naughty, hoping that he can charm his way out of trouble, aware that no-one can deny him anything.

'It's too soon.' I see him decide not to tell me what has made him smile. 'It's too soon for me to say.'

My Lady the King's Mother calls me to her private rooms before Sir Richard and I leave for Stourton. Her rooms are crowded with people seeking favours and help. The king has started to fine people heavily for small misdemeanours and many people go to My Lady for mercy. Since she works with him on the royal account books and revels in the profit of fines, most petitioners come away unsatisfied, many of them poorer than before.

My Lady knows well enough that her son will only hold England if he can always put an army in the field, and that armies eat treasure. She and her son are at constant work on a war chest, saving funds against the rebellion that they fear will come.

She beckons me to her side with a quick gesture and her ladies tactfully rise up from their seats and move away, so that we can talk in private.

'You were at Ludlow Castle with the young couple, the prince and princess?' My Lady remarks without preamble.

'Yes.'

'You dined with them every day?'

'Almost every day. I was not there when they arrived, but after that, I lived there with them.'

'You saw them together, as husband and wife.'

I have a chilly realisation that I do not know where this line of questioning is going, and that My Lady always talks for a purpose.

'Of course.'

'And you never saw anything that would suggest to you that they were not married in thought and word and deed.'

I hesitate. 'I dined with them every night in the great hall. I saw them in public. They were a devoted young couple in public,' I say.

She pauses, her gaze as hard as a fist at my face. 'They were wedded and bedded,' she states flatly. 'There can be no doubt.'

I think of Arthur wresting the promise from the princess, his deathbed promise, that she would marry again and be Queen of England. I think that this was his plan and his wish. I remember that I would have done anything for Arthur, I think I would still do anything for him.

'Of course I cannot know what occurred in Her Grace's bedchamber,' I say. 'But she told me, and others, that the marriage had not been consummated.'

'Oh, you say that, do you?' My Lady remarks as if it is a matter of cold interest.

I take a breath. 'I do.'

'Why?' she asks. 'Why say such a thing?'

I try to shrug, although my shoulders are too stiff to move. 'It's just what I observed. Just what I heard.' I try to speak casually, but I am breathless.

She rounds on me so fiercely that I flinch from her furious face.

'What you observed! What you heard! It is what you have made up, between the three of you, her duenna, the Spanish Infanta, and you, you three wicked women, for the downfall of my house and the destruction of my son! I know it! I know you! I wish she had never come to this country! She has brought us nothing but grief!'

A silence falls; everyone is staring at me in horrified speculation at what I have done to upset My Lady. I drop to my knees, my heart hammering in my ears. 'Forgive me, Your Grace. I have done nothing, I would never do anything against you or your son. I don't understand?'

'Tell me one thing,' she spits. 'You know for a fact, don't you, that Prince Arthur and the Dowager Princess were lovers? You saw the unmistakable signs of their bedding. Under your roof he was conducted to her room once a week, was he not? I had ordered it, and it was done? Or are you telling me that you disobeyed me and they were not put together every week?'

I can hardly speak. 'You were obeyed,' I whisper. 'Of course, I obeyed you. He was taken to her room every week.'

'So,' she says, a little pacified. 'So. You admit this much. He went to her room. We know this. You don't deny this.'

'But whether they were lovers or not, I cannot tell,' I say. My voice is so small that I fear she will not hear me and from somewhere I shall have to find the courage to speak again.

But her hearing is acute, her understanding like a trap. 'So. You are supporting her,' she says. 'Supporting her ridiculous claim that her husband was incapable over four months of marriage. Though he was young and healthy and she was his wife. Though she never said anything to anyone at the time. Though she never complained. She never even mentioned it.'

I have promised Princess Katherine my help and I am bound to her. I loved Arthur and I heard him whisper to her: 'Promise!' I stay on my knees and I keep my head down and I pray for this ordeal to pass.

'I cannot tell,' I repeat. 'She told me that there was no chance that she was with child. I understood her to be saying that they were not lovers. That they had never been lovers.'

Her rage has passed; the colour drains from her face, she is white as if she might faint. A lady steps forward to support her and then falls back before her fierce glare.

'Do you know what you are doing, Margaret Pole?' My Lady demands of me, her voice like ice. 'Do you really know what you are saying?'

I sit back on my heels, finding that I am holding my hands together under my chin, as if I am praying for mercy. I shake my head. 'Forgive me, Your Grace, I don't know what you mean.'

My Lady leans forward and hisses in my ear so that no-one else can hear. She is so close that I can feel her malmsey breath on my cheek. 'You are not getting your little friend married to Prince Harry, if that was your plan. You are putting that little Spanish whore in the bed of her father-in-law!'

The word 'whore' from the mouth of My Lady is as shocking as the idea. 'What? Her father-in-law?'

'Yes.'

'The king?'

'My son, the king.' Her voice quavers with frustrated passion. 'My son, the king.'

'He wants to marry the Dowager Princess now?'

'Of course he does!' Her voice is grindingly low and I can feel the heat of her rage against my hair, against my ear. 'Because that way he doesn't have to pay her widow's jointure, that way he keeps the dowry she brought and he can demand the rest, that way he keeps an alliance with Spain against our enemy, France. That way he gets himself a cheap wedding with a princess who is here in London already and from her he gets a new baby, another son and heir. And that way' – she breaks off to pant like a hunted dog – 'that way he takes the girl in sinful lust. In a sinful, incestuous lust. She has tempted him with her bold, wicked eyes. She has inflamed him with her dancing, she walks with him, she whispers with him, she smiles at him and curtseys when she sees him, she tempts him, she will take him down to hell.'

'But she is betrothed to Prince Harry.'

'You tell her that, while she hangs on his father's arm and rubs herself against him!'

'He can't marry his daughter-in-law,' I say, utterly bemused.

'Fool!' she snaps. 'He needs only a dispensation from the Pope. And he will get that if she continues to say, as she constantly says, that the marriage was never consummated. If her friends support her, as you are doing. And her lie – for I know it is a lie – plunges my son into sin and my house into ruin. This lie will destroy us. And you are telling it for her. You are as bad as she. I will never forget this. I will never forgive this. I will never forgive you!'

I can say nothing but gape at her.

'Speak!' she commands me. 'Say that she was wedded and bedded.'

Dumbly, I shake my head.

'If you do not speak, it will be the worse for you,' she warns me.

I bow my head. I say nothing.

STOURTON CASTLE, STAFFORDSHIRE, AUTUMN 1504

I am with child again and I choose to stay at Stourton Castle while my husband rules Wales from Ludlow. He comes home to see me and is pleased with my care of our lands and our home and the education of my children.

'But we have to be careful with money,' he reminds me. We are seated together in the steward's room at Stourton, the rent books spread around us. 'We have to take every care, Margaret. With four children and another on the way we have to guard our little fortune. They're all going to need a place in the world and Ursula will need a good dowry.'

'If the king would only grant you some more lands,' I say. 'God knows you serve him well. Every time you make a judgement in court you send the fine to him. You must earn him thousands of pounds and you never keep back a penny. Not like the others.'

He shrugs. He is no courtier, my husband. He has never gone to the king for money, he has only ever been paid the smallest sum that the Tudors thought he would accept. And besides, there is more and more going into the royal coffers and less and less coming out. Henry Tudor paid off everyone who served him at Bosworth in the early years of his reign, and ever since he has been clawing back the lands he so generously granted in those first heady days. Every traitor finds his family home is forfeit, every minor criminal finds himself laden with demands to pay a fine. Even the smallest of offences come with a great demand for payment, and everything – from the salt on the table to the ale in the inn – is taxed.

'Perhaps you can speak to My Lady when we next go to court,' I suggest. 'Everyone else is better rewarded than you.'

'Can't you ask her?'

I shake my head. I have never told my husband of the terrible scene in My Lady's rooms. I think that she got her way – I have heard no more talk of the king marrying the Dowager Princess – but she will never forget or forgive that I did not write a witness account to her dictation.

'I'm no great favourite,' I say shortly. 'Not with my cousin Edmund going round Europe, raising an army against them. Not with two other cousins, William de la Pole still in the Tower and William Courtenay just arrested.'

'They're not charged with anything,' he points out.

'They're not freed either.'

'Then can't you cut the costs here?' Sir Richard asks me irritably. 'I don't like to go to her. She is not an easy woman to ask.'

'I try. But as you say, we have four children and another on the way. They all have to have horses and tutors. They all have to be fed.'

We look at each other in mutual impatience. I think: this is so unfair! He can have no criticism of me. He married me, a young woman of royal birth, and I have given him children – three of them sons – and I have never boasted of my name or my lineage. I have never reproached him for bringing me down to be the wife of a small knight when I was born all but a princess and an heiress to the Warwick fortune. I have never complained that he made no attempt to get my title or my fortune restored, I have played the part of Lady Pole and managed his two little manors and a castle, and not the thousands on thousands of acres that were mine by right.

'We'll raise the rents for all the tenants,' he says shortly. 'And we'll tell them they have to increase what they send to the house from their own farms.'

'They can barely pay at the moment,' I observe. 'Not with the king's new fines and the new royal service.'

He shrugs. 'They'll have to,' he says simply. 'The king requires it. These are hard times for everyone.'

I go into my confinement thinking how hard the times are, and wondering why this should be. Our York court was notoriously rich and wasteful, with an unending annual round of entertainments and parties, hunts, jousts, and celebrations. I had ten royal cousins and they were all magnificently dressed and equipped, and married well. How can it be that the same country that poured gold into the lap of Edward IV and dispersed it to an enormous family cannot find enough money to pay the fines and taxes of one man: Henry Tudor? How can it be that a royal family of only five people can need so much money when all the Plantagenets and the Rivers affinity made merry on so much less?

My husband says he will stay at Stourton Castle during my confinement to greet me when I come out. I cannot see him when I am confined, of course, but he sends me cheering messages telling me that we have sold some of the hay crop, and that he has had a pig killed and salted down for the christening party for our baby.

One evening he sends me a short handwritten note.

I have taken a fever and am resting in my bed. I have ordered the children not to see me. Be of good cheer, wife.

I feel nothing but irritation. There will be no-one to watch the steward check the Michaelmas rents, nor to take the apprenticeship fees from the young people who start work this quarter. The horses will start eating the stored hay and there will be no-one to make sure they are not overfed. We cannot afford to buy in hay, we have to parcel it out throughout the winter. There is nothing I can do about this but curse our bad luck that has me confined and my husband sick at such a time. I know our steward, John Little, is an honest man, but the feast of Michaelmas is one of the key times for the profitable running of our lands and if neither Sir Richard nor I is leaning over his shoulder and watching every number he writes, he is bound to be more careless or worse, more generous to the tenants, forgiving them bad debts, or letting unpaid rents run on.

Two nights later I get another note from Sir Richard.

Much worse, and sending for the doctor. But the children are in good health, God willing.

It is unusual for Sir Richard to be ill. He has been on one campaign after another for the Tudors, ridden out for them in all weather over three kingdoms and a principality. I write back:

Are you very ill? What does the doctor say?

I get no reply from him, and the next morning I send my lady in waiting Jane Mallett to my husband's groom of the bedchamber to ask if he is well.

As soon as she comes into my confinement chamber I can tell from her shocked face that it is bad news. I put my hand over the swell of my belly where my baby is packed as tight as herring in a barrel. I can feel its every move inside my straining belly and suddenly it goes still too, as if it is listening, like me, for bad news.

'What's the matter?' I ask, my voice hard with worry. 'What's the matter that you look so pale? Speak up, Jane, you are frightening me.'

'It's the master,' she says simply. 'Sir Richard.'

'I know that, fool! I guessed that! Is he very ill?'

She drops a curtsey, as if deference can soften the blow. 'He's dead, my lady. He died in the night. I am so sorry to be the one to tell you . . . he's gone. The master's gone.'

It makes it so much worse being in confinement. The priest comes to the door and whispers words of consolation through the crack, as if his vows of celibacy will be all overthrown if he sees my tear-stained face. The physician tells me it was a fever that overcame Sir Richard's great strength. He was a man of forty-six, a good age, but he was powerful and active. It was not the Sweat and not the pox and not the measles and not the ague and not St Anthony's fire. The doctor gives me such a long list of things that the disease was not that I lose patience and tell him he can go and send me the steward; and I command him, in a whisper through the door, to make sure everything is done that should be done, that Sir Richard is laid in his coffin on the chancel steps of Stourton church and proper watch is kept. The bell must be tolled and all the tenants given a grant of money, mourners must have black cloth, and Sir Richard must be buried with all the dignity that he should have – but as cheaply as possible.

Then I write to the king and to his mother, My Lady, and tell them that their honourable servant, my husband, has died in their service. I do not point out to them that he leaves me all but penniless with four children of royal blood to raise on nothing, and an unborn child on the way. My Lady the King's Mother will understand that well enough. She will know that they have to help me with an immediate grant of money, and then the gift of some more land for me to keep myself, and my children, now that we do not have the fees from his work in Wales or from his other posts. I am their kinswoman, I am of the old royal house, they have no choice but to make sure I can live with dignity and feed and clothe my children and my household.

I send for my two oldest children, my boys, the boys that I will have to raise alone. I will let the Lady Governess tell Ursula and Reginald that their father has gone to heaven. But Henry is twelve and Arthur ten, and they should know from their mother that their father is dead and from now on there is no-one but our-selves; we will have to help one another.

They come in very quiet and anxious, looking around at the shadowy confinement chamber with the superstitious anxiety of growing boys. It is only my bedroom where they have been a hun-dred times, but now there are tapestries over the windows to shut out the light and the damp, there are small fires in the grates at either end of the room, and there is the haunting smell from the herbs that are said to be helpful in childbirth. Against the wall a candle burns before a silver-framed icon of the Virgin Mary and the communion wafer is on display in a monstrance. There is a small bed for birthing set at the foot of my big canopied bed, and the ominous ropes tied to the two bottom posts for me to haul against when my time comes, a lathe of wood for me to bite, a holy girdle to tie around my waist. They take all this in with round, frightened eyes.

'I have some bad news for you both,' I say steadily. There is no point trying to break such a thing to them gently. We are all born to suffer, we are all born to loss. My boys are the sons of a house that has always dealt liberally in death, both in giving and receiving.

Henry looks at me anxiously. 'Are you ill?' he asks. 'Is the baby all right?'

'Yes. It's not bad news about me.'

Arthur knows at once. He is always quick to understand, and quick to speak. 'Then it's Father,' he says simply. 'Lady Mother, is my father dead?'

'Yes. I am very sorry to tell you,' I say. I take Henry's cold hand in my own. 'You are now the head of this family. Make sure that you guide your brothers and sister well, protect our fortune, serve the king and avoid malice.'

His dark eyes well up with tears. 'I can't,' he says, his voice quavering. 'I don't know how to.'

'I can do it,' Arthur volunteers. 'I can do it.'

I shake my head. 'You can't. You're the second son,' I remind him. 'It's Henry who's the heir. Your task is to help and support him, defend him if you have to. And you can do everything, Henry. I will advise and guide you, and we will find a way to advance this family in wealth and greatness – but not too far.'

'Not too far?' Arthur repeats.

'Great under the great king,' Henry says, showing, just as I thought, that he is old enough to do his duty and wise enough already to know that we want to prosper – but not enviably so.

Only then, after my boys have wept a little and gone, do I have time to kneel before my prie-dieu and grieve for the loss of my husband and pray for his immortal soul. I cannot doubt that he will go to heaven though we will have to find the money from somewhere to have Masses said. He was a good man, loyal as a dog to the Tudors, faithful as a dog to me. Kind, as a strong man of few words is often kind to his children and servants and tenants. I never could have fallen in love with him; but I was always grateful to him and glad of his name. Now that he is dead and I will never see him again, I know that I will miss him. He was a comfort and a shield and a kind husband – and these qualities are rare.

He gave me his name, and death does not take it away from me. Now I am Lady Margaret Pole the widow, as I once was Lady Margaret Pole the wife. But the important thing is that his name is not buried with him. I can keep it. I can hide my true self behind it; even in death he will keep me safe.

I give birth to a baby boy – a son who will never know his father. In the weak moments after they put him in my arms I find I am crying over his little downy head. This is the last gift my husband will ever give me, this is the last child I will ever have. This is my last chance to love an innocent who depends on me, as I loved my brother who depended on me. I kiss his damp little head and I feel his pulse flutter. This is my last, my most precious child. Pray God I can keep him safe.

I come out of confinement to pray at the new memorial that bears the name *Sir Richard Pole* set under a window at our little church. The king sends me a gift of one hundred and fifty-seven nobles for funeral clothes for me and for all the tenants, which – managed carefully – also pays for the feast after the funeral and goes a long way to paying for the memorial stone too. I call our steward John Little to me, to tell him that I am pleased with what he has done.

'And His Grace the king has sent permission for you to borrow one hundred and twenty nobles from your son's estate,' he says. 'So we will get through Christmastide, at least.'

'One hundred and twenty nobles?' I repeat. It is a help; but it is hardly a princely gift. It is not generous. The Tudors will have to do more than this if they are to keep us warm.

In the meantime, all the money goes the wrong way: from us to them. My boys must become royal wards since their father died while they are still children. This is a disaster for me and for the family. All of the earnings of the estate will go to the king, poured into the royal treasury until my son is a man and can inherit his own – or whatever is left of it after it has been bled by the king's treasury. If the king wants to cut down every standing tree for timber he can do so. If he wants to butcher every cow in the field no-one can prevent him. All that I can take is my widow's dower, a third of the rents and profits – only one hundred and twenty nobles, for a whole year! King Henry is offering me a loan from what was once all mine; I can't feel grateful.

'One hundred and twenty nobles only takes us to Christmas-tide. And what happens after that?' I ask my steward.

He just looks at me. He knows that he is not expected to have an answer to this. He knows that I have no answer. He knows there is none.

STOURTON CASTLE, STAFFORDSHIRE, SPRING 1505

Christmas comes and goes with no feast for the tenants, and Twelfth Night goes by with only the smallest of gifts for the children. I announce that we are still mourning the loss of my husband but they mutter in the village that it is not how things should be done, and it was better in the old days when the gentle knight Sir Richard ordered a good feast for the household and all the tenants, and remembered that these are the cold and hungry months and that a good dinner is helpful for people with many mouths to feed, and free firewood should be sent out too.

Geoffrey the baby thrives with his wet nurse but I find I am wondering when he can be weaned from her, as she is such an extra expense in the nursery. I cannot let the boys' tutor go – these are my father's grandsons, the grandsons of George, Duke of Clarence, the best-read nobleman of an exceptional court; these are Warwick children, they have to be able to read and write in three languages at least. I cannot let this family slide down into ignorance and dirt; but teaching and cleanliness are terribly expensive.

We have always lived off the produce from the home farm and we sell some of our surplus at the local markets. We make cheeses and butter, we harvest fruit, and salt down meat. Our spare food we send to the local market for sale, any extra grain I sell to the miller, and hay and straw I sell to a local merchant. The mills on the river pay me a fee every time they grind, the local potters pay me for firing their wares in my kiln, and I sell wood from the forest.

But the tail-end of winter is the worst time of year; our horses are eating our summer crop of hay and there is no extra to sell, the beasts are eating the straw and if they finish it before the spring grass comes, they will have to be killed for meat and then I have no livestock. Once the household has been fed there is no surplus food left to sell for cash; indeed, we rely on the tenants giving us our share of their crops, as we cannot grow enough on our own fields.

Princess Katherine writes to condole with me on the loss of my husband. She too has suffered a terrible loss. Her mother wrote to her rarely, and seldom with any warmth, but Katherine never stopped looking for her letters, and missed her every day. Now Isabella of Spain is dead, and Katherine will never see her mother again. Even worse than this, the death of her mother means that her father no longer jointly rules all of Spain, but only his own kingdom of Aragon. His wealth and position in the world have been halved, worse than halved, and his oldest daughter Juana has inherited the throne of Castile from her mother. Katherine is no longer the daughter of the monarchs of Spain, she is the daughter of mere Ferdinand of Aragon – a very different prospect. I am not surprised to read that Prince Harry and his father no longer visit her as they used to do. She survives on little gifts of money from the king and sometimes they are less than she expected, and sometimes the royal exchequer forgets to pay altogether. The king is insisting that her full dowry must be paid by Spain to him before the marriage to Prince Harry can go ahead, and in riposte Katherine's father Ferdinand is demanding that her widow's jointure be paid by the king to her, in full and at once.

Will you write for me to My Lady and ask her if I can come to court? Will you tell her that I am sorry but I cannot seem to manage my household bills and that I am lonely and unhappy here? I want to live in her rooms as her granddaughter, as I should.

I reply and tell her that I am a widow, as she is, and that I too am struggling to pay my way in the world. I say that I am sorry, but I have no influence over My Lady. I will write to her, but I doubt she will be kind to Katherine at my bidding. I don't say that My Lady said she would never forgive me for refusing to bear witness against Katherine, and that I doubt any word from me, any word from anyone, would make her act kindly to the princess.

Katherine replies quite cheerfully that her duenna, Doña Elvira, is so bad-tempered that she sends her out to the market to haggle with traders and her angry broken English wins them bargains. She writes this as if it is funny and I laugh aloud when I read her letter and tell her about the quarrel I have with the farrier about the cost of horseshoes.

It is not grief that will deprive me of my wits but hunger. I go round the kitchen under the pretence that there must be no waste; but really I am getting so low that I shall start licking the spoons and scraping the pots.

I turn away as many as I can of the household staff as soon as we get to the end of the quarter at Lady Day. Some of them cry as they leave and I have no quit-money to give them. Those who are left have to work harder and some of them don't know how the work is done. The kitchen maid now has to lay the fire and sweep the grate in my room and she constantly forgets to bring the wood or spills the ash. It's heavy work for her and I see her struggle with the log basket and I look away. I put myself in charge of the dairy and learn to make cheese and skim milk and send the dairymaid back to her family. I keep the boy in the malthouse but I learn to make ale. My son Henry has to ride out in the fields with the steward and watch them sowing the seed. He comes home afraid that they are scattering it too thickly, that the carefully measured scoops of grain are not covering the ground.

'Then we'll have to buy more somehow,' I say grimly. 'We have to have a good crop or there will be no bread next winter.'

As the evenings get lighter I give up using wax candles alto-gether, and tell the children they must do all their studying before dusk. We live in the guttering shadows and stink of the rush lights and the tallow drips on the floors. I think that I will have to marry again, but no man of any wealth or position would consider me, and My Lady will not order one of her relations to the task this time. I am a widow of thirty-one years with five young children and growing debts. When I remarry I will lose all rights over the estates, as they will all go to the king as Henry's guardian, so I would come to a new husband as a pauper. Very few men would see me as a desirable wife. No man who wants to prosper at the Tudor court would marry a widow with five children of Plantagenet blood. If My Lady the King's Mother will not make a marriage for me with someone that she can command, then I cannot see how to raise my children and feed myself.

STOURTON CASTLE, STAFFORDSHIRE, SUMMER 1505

It all comes back to her. It all comes back to her favour and her influence. In the summer I realise that however good the harvest, however high the price of wheat, we will not make enough to get through another winter. I am going to have to raise the money to go to London and ask her for help.

'We could sell Sir Richard's warhorse?' my steward John Little suggests.

'He's so old!' I exclaim. 'Who would want him? And he served Sir Richard so well for so long!'

'He's no use to us,' he says. 'We can't use him on the plough, he won't go between the shafts. I might get a good price for him in Stourbridge. He's well-known as Sir Richard's horse, people know he's a good horse.'

'Then everyone will know that I can't afford to keep him,' I protest. 'That I can't afford to keep him for Henry to ride.'

The steward nods, his eyes on his boots, not looking at me. 'Everyone knows that already, my lady.'

I bow my head at this new humiliation. 'Take him then,' I say.

I watch the big horse being saddled up. He lowers his proud head for the bridle and stands still while they tighten the girth. He may be old, but his ears come forward when the steward steps off the mounting block to swing a leg over his back and sit in the saddle. The old warhorse thinks he is riding out to battle once more. His neck arches, and he paws the ground as if he is eager to go to work. For a moment I nearly cry out: 'No! Keep him! He's our horse, he's served my husband well. Keep him for Henry.'

But then I remember that there is nothing to feed him unless I can get help from My Lady the King's Mother in London, and that the price of the horse will pay for my journey.

We take our own horses and we stay in the guest houses of the nunneries or abbeys along the way. They are positioned along the road to help pilgrims and wayfarers and I am comforted every time I see a bell tower on the horizon and know there is a place of refuge, every time I step into a clean lime-washed room and feel the sense of holy peace. One night there is nowhere to go but an inn, and I have to pay for myself, for my lady companion, and for the four men at arms. I have spent nearly all my money by the time we see the spires of London coming out of the afternoon mist and hear the dozens of bells tolling for Nones.

WESTMINSTER PALACE, LONDON, SUMMER 1505

The court is at Westminster, which is a blessing for me because there are always extra rooms in the huge rambling palace. Once I used to sleep in the best room, in the bed of the queen to keep her company through the night; now I am allotted a small room, far away from the great hall. I note how quickly and accurately the steward of the household observes the fall in my fortunes.

This palace is like an enclosed village, set inside its own great walls inside the city of London. I know all the twisting alleyways and the little walled gardens, the backstairs and the hidden doorways. This has been my home since childhood. I wash my face and hands and pin on my hood. I brush the dust from my gown and hold my head high as I walk through the little cobbled streets to the great hall and the queen's rooms.

I am just about to cross the queen's gardens when I hear someone call my name, and I turn to see Bishop John Fisher, confessor to My Lady, and an old acquaintance of mine. When I was a little girl he used to come to Middleham Castle to teach us our catechism and hear our confessions. He knew my brother Teddy as a small boy, as the heir to the throne, he taught me the psalms when the name in my psalter was Margaret Plantagenet, and I was niece to the King of England.

'My lord bishop!' I exclaim, and I drop a little curtsey, for he has become a great man under the pious rule of My Lady.

He makes the sign of the cross over my head, and bows as low to me as if I were still the heiress to the royal house. 'Lady Pole! I am sorry for your loss. Your husband was a fine man.'

'He was indeed,' I say.

Bishop Fisher offers me his arm and we walk side by side on the little path. 'It is rare that we see you at court, my daughter?'

I am about to say something light-hearted about wanting to

buy new gloves when something in his friendly, smiling face makes me want to confide in him.

'I have come for help,' I say honestly. 'I am hoping that My Lady will advise me. My husband left me with next to nothing, and I cannot manage on my dower rents.'

'I am sorry to hear it,' he says simply. 'But I am sure she will hear you kindly. She has many worries and much work, God bless her; but she would never neglect one of her family.'

'I hope so,' I say. I am wondering if there is any way in which I can ask him to plead my case with her, when he gestures towards the open doors of the gallery before her presence chamber. 'Come on,' he urges me. 'I'll go in with you. There's no time like the present, and there are always many people waiting to see her.'

We walk together. 'You will have heard that your former charge, the Dowager Princess of Wales, is to go home to Spain?' he asks me quietly.

I am shocked at the news. 'No! I thought she was betrothed to marry Prince Harry.'

He shakes his head. 'It's not widely known, but they cannot agree the terms,' he says. 'Poor child, I think she is very lonely in her big palace with no-one but her confessor and her ladies. Better for her to go to her home than live alone here, and My Lady does not wish her to come to court. But this is between the two of us. I don't know that they have even told her yet. Will you go to see her while you are in London? I know she loves you very much. You might advise her to accept her destiny gladly and with grace. I truly think that she would be happier at home than waiting and hoping here.'

'I will. I am so sorry!'

He nods. 'It's a hard life she has had. Widowed so young and now having to go home again a widow. But My Lady is guided by her prayers. She thinks it is God's will that Prince Harry should marry another bride. The Dowager Princess is not for him.'

The guards stand aside for the bishop and open the doors to the presence chamber. It is crowded with petitioners; everyone wants to meet My Lady and ask her for one favour or another. All of the business of being the queen has fallen on her shoulders, and she has her own great lands to manage too. She is one of the king-dom's wealthiest landowners, by far the wealthiest woman in England. She has endowed colleges and chantries and built hos-pitals, churches, colleges and schools, and all of them send representatives to report to her or to ask for her favour. I look around the room and calculate that there are about two hundred people waiting to see her. I am one of very, very many.

But she singles me out. She comes into the room from chapel, with her ladies walking two abreast behind her, carrying their missals as if they were a small exclusive convent of nuns, and she looks around with her sharp, observing gaze. She is more than sixty years old now, deeply lined and unsmiling, but her head is erect under her heavy gable hood, and though she leans on one of her ladies as she walks through the room, I suspect that she does this for show; she could walk equally well on her own.

Everyone curtseys or bows to her as low as if she were the queen whose rooms she occupies. I sink down but I keep my head up and smiling: I want her to see me. I catch her eye and when she stops before me I kiss the hand she holds out to me, and when she gestures that I may rise up and she leans forward, I kiss her soft old cheek.

'Dear Cousin Margaret,' she says coolly, as if we had parted as good friends only yesterday.

'Your Grace,' I reply.

She nods that I am to walk beside her. I take the place of her lady in waiting and she leans on my arm as we walk through the hundreds of people. I note that I am being publicly honoured with her attention.

'You have come to see me, my dear?'

'I am hoping for your advice,' I say tactfully.

The beak-like nose turns to me, her hard eyes scan my face. She nods. She knows full well I do not need advice but that I am desperately short of money.

'You have come a long way for advice,' she observes drily. 'Is everything all right at your home?'

'My children are well and ask for your blessing,' I say. 'But I cannot manage on my dower. I have only a small income now that my husband is dead, and I have five young children. I do the best I can, but there is only a little land at Stourton and the estates at Medmenham and Ellesborough only pay fifty pounds a year in rents, and of course I only get a third of that.' I am anxious not to sound as if I am complaining. 'It is not enough to pay my bills,' I say simply. 'Not to keep the household.'

'Then you will have to reduce your household,' she advises me. 'You are not a Plantagenet now.'

To use my name to me in public, even so low that no-one can hear, is to threaten me.

'I have not heard that name in years,' I say to her. 'And I have never lived like that. I have reduced my household. I want only to live as the widow of a loyal Tudor knight. I don't look for anything grander than that. My husband and I were proud to be your humble servants, and to serve you well.'

'Would you like your son to come to court? To be a companion to Prince Harry?' she asks. 'Would you like to be a lady in waiting to me?'

I can hardly speak; this is a solution that I had not dreamed of. 'I would be honoured . . .' I stammer. I am amazed that she should suggest such a favour. This would resolve all my difficulties. If I could get Henry into Eltham Palace he would have the best education in the world; he would live like a prince, with the prince himself. And a lady in waiting gets a fee for her services, is awarded posts when they fall vacant, is tipped for the smallest of tasks, bribed by strangers coming to court. A lady in waiting gets gifts of jewels and gowns, a purse of gold at Christmas, her keep and that of her household, her horses stabled for free, her servants fed in the royal hall. The thought of dining out of the royal kitchens with my horses in the royal stables eating Tudor hay is like the promise of release from a prison of worry.

Lady Margaret sees that hope illuminates my face. 'It is possible,' she concedes. 'After all, it is suitable.'

'I would be honoured,' I said. 'I would be delighted.'

A smartly dressed man steps before us and bows. I scowl at him; this is my time with My Lady. She is the source of all wealth and patronage, she and her son, the king, own everything. This is my only time and my only chance, nobody is going to interrupt us if I can help it. To my surprise, Bishop Fisher puts a hand on the gentleman's arm before he can present his petition, and draws him away with a quiet word.

'I have to ask you a question that I asked you once before,' Lady Margaret says quietly. 'It is about your time at Ludlow, with the Prince and Princess of Wales.'

I can feel myself growing cold. John Fisher has just told me that they are planning to send Katherine home to Spain. If that is the case, why would they care whether the marriage was consummated or not? 'Yes?'

'We are troubled by a small matter, a legal question, for the dispensation of her first marriage. We have to ensure that we get the right wording of the dispensation so that our dear Katherine can marry Prince Harry. It is in the interest of the princess that you tell me what I need to know.'

I know that this is a lie. Lady Margaret wants to send her home.

'The marriage between Prince Arthur and the princess was consummated, was it not?' The grip on my arm tightens as if she would squeeze a confession from the marrow of my bones. We have reached the end of the room but instead of turning to stroll back again through the crowd of petitioners she nods to her liveried servants on the double doors to throw them open, and we pass through into her private rooms and the doors close behind us. We are alone; nobody can hear my answer but her.

'I cannot say,' I say steadily though I find I am frightened of her, here in this empty room with guards on the doors. 'Your ladyship, I told you, my husband took the prince to her bedchamber; but she told me that he was not able.'

'She said that. I know what she said.' There is a grating impatience in her voice, but she manages a smile. 'But, my dear Margaret, what do you believe?'

More than anything else I believe that this is going to cost me my post as lady in waiting and my son his education. I rack my brains to think of something I can say to satisfy her that will not betray the princess. She is waiting, hard-faced. She will be satisfied with nothing but the words she wants to hear. She is the most powerful woman in England and she will insist that I agree with her. Miserably, I whisper: 'I believe Her Grace the Dowager Princess.'

'She thinks that if she is a virgin untouched, we will marry her to Prince Harry,' My Lady says flatly. 'Her parents asked for a dispensation from the Pope and told him the marriage was not consummated. He gave them a dispensation that leaves it deliberately unclear. It is typical of Isabella of Castile to get a document that can be read any way she wants. Even after death she tricks us. Apparently her daughter is not to be challenged. She must not even be questioned. She thinks that she can walk into our family, walk into our house, walk into these very rooms – my rooms – and make them her own. She thinks to take the prince and everything away from me.'

'I am sure Prince Harry will be well-suited . . .'

'Prince Harry will not choose his bride,' she declares. 'I shall choose her. And I will not have that young woman as my daughter-in-law. Not after this lie. Not after her attempt to seduce the king in the very first days of his grief. She thinks that because she is a princess born and bred she can take everything that I have won, everything that God has given to me: my son, my grandson, my position, my whole life's work. I spent the best years of my life bringing my son to England, keeping him safe. I married to give him allies, I befriended people that I despised for his sake. I stooped to . . .' She breaks off as if she does not want to remember what she stooped to do. 'But she thinks she can walk in here with a lie in her mouth because she is a princess of royal blood. She thinks she is entitled. But I say that she is not.'

I realise that when Katherine marries Prince Harry she will precede My Lady in every procession, every time they go to Mass or to dinner. She will have these very rooms, she will command the best gowns from the royal wardrobes, she will outrank the king's mother, and if the court follows the tastes of the king – and courts always do – then they will empty out from My Lady's rooms and flock to the pretty young princess. Princess Katherine will not step back and yield to My Lady as my cousin the queen yielded to her. Katherine has grit. If she ever becomes Princess of Wales then she will make My Lady give her precedence, every-where, in everything. She will wrest her dues from this possessive old woman and repay her enmity.

'I have told you everything I know,' I say quietly. 'I am yours to command, My Lady.'

She turns her back on me, as if she does not care to see my white face and my pleading eyes. 'You have a choice,' she says shortly. 'You can be my lady in waiting and your son can be a companion to Prince Harry. You will be generously paid and there will be gifts and grants of land. Or you can support the Dowager Princess in her monstrous lie and her disgusting ambition. It is your choice. But if you collude in tempting the Prince of Wales, our prince, our only prince, into marriage with that young woman, then you will never come to court for as long as I live.'

I wait until dusk before I go to visit Princess Katherine. I go on foot with one lady companion and a manservant, and my stew-ard leads the way with a cudgel in his hand. The beggars are everywhere in London nowadays, desperate men driven from their farms by higher rents, made homeless when they could not pay fines, made paupers by the king's taxes. Some of my own ten-ants may be sleeping in the doorways of the London churches and begging for food.

I walk with my hood pulled over the betraying bronze of my hair, and I look all around me in case we are being followed. There are more spies in England than there have ever been before, as everyone is paid to report on their neighbour, and I would rather that My Lady did not know that I am visiting the home of the princess that she calls 'that young woman'.

There is no light burning at her doorway, and it takes a long time for anyone to respond to the quiet tap that my steward makes on the double wooden doors. There is no guard to open them but only a page boy who leads us across the cold great hall and knocks on the door of what used to be the grand presence chamber.

One of Katherine's remaining Spanish ladies peeps around the door and, seeing me, straightens up, brushes down her gown, sweeps a curtsey and leads me through the echoing presence chamber and into the privy chamber where a small group of ladies huddle around a mean fire.

Katherine recognises me as soon as I put back my hood, jumps up with a cry and runs towards me. I am about to curtsey but she flings herself into my arms and hugs me, kisses me on one cheek and then the other, leans back to study my face, and then hugs me again.

'I have been thinking and thinking of you. I was so sorry when I heard of your loss. You will have had my letters? I was so sorry for you, and for the children. And for the new baby! A boy, God bless him! Is he thriving? And you? Could you get the price of horseshoes down?'

She draws me towards the light of the single sconce of wax candles, so that she can look into my face.

'Santa Maria! But you are so thin, and my dear, you look so weary.'

She turns and shoos away her ladies from the fireside seats. 'Go. All of you. Go to your bedrooms. Go to bed. Lady Margaret and I will talk alone.'

'To their bedrooms?' I query.

'There's not enough firewood for a fire anywhere but here and the kitchen,' she says simply. 'And they're all too grand to sit in the kitchen. So if they don't sit here, they have to go to bed to keep warm.'

I look at her in disbelief. 'They are keeping you so short of money that you cannot have a fire in the bedrooms?'

'As you see,' she says grimly.

'I have come from Westminster,' I say, taking a stool beside her chair. 'I had a terrible conversation with My Lady.'

She nods, as if this does not surprise her.

'She questioned me as to your marriage with . . .' Even now, three years on, I cannot easily say his name. 'With our prince,' I amend.

'She would do. She is very much against me.'

'Why, do you think?' I ask curiously.

She slides her mischievous girl's smile towards me. 'Oh, was she such a loving mother-in-law to your cousin the queen?' she asks.

'She was not. We were both terrified of her,' I admit.

'She's not a woman who enjoys the company of women,' she remarks. 'With her son a widower and her grandson unmarried she's mistress of the court. She doesn't want a young woman coming in and being merry and loving and happy, making it a true court of learning and elegance and pleasure. She's not even very kind to her granddaughter Princess Mary because she's so very pretty. She's always telling her that looks mean nothing and that she should strive for humility! She doesn't like pretty girls, she doesn't like rivals. If she lets Prince Harry marry at all it will be to a young woman that she can command. She'll marry him off to a child, someone who can't even speak English. She doesn't want someone like me who knows how things should be done, and will see they are done and the kingdom put to rights. She doesn't want anyone at court who will try to persuade the king to rule as he should.'

I nod. It is exactly what I have been thinking.

'She tries to keep you from the court?'

'Oh, she succeeds, she is triumphant.' She gestures at the threadbare hangings of the room and the gaps on the walls where the frames for rich tapestries are bare. 'The king doesn't pay my allowance, he makes me live off the things that I brought with me from Spain. I have no new gowns, so when they invite me to court I look ridiculous in Spanish fashions that are darned all over. My Lady hopes to break my will and force me to ask my father to take me home. But even if I were to ask him, he would not have me back. I am trapped here.'

I am horrified. The two of us have fallen from such prosperity to such poverty in such a short time. 'Katherine, what will you do?'

'I'll wait,' she says with quiet determination. She leans close to me and puts her mouth to my ear. 'He is forty-eight, he's in poor health, he can hardly breathe for the quinsy. I'll wait.'

'Don't say another word,' I say nervously. I glance towards the closed door and at the shadows on the walls.

'Did My Lady ask you to swear that Arthur and I had been lovers?' she asks me bluntly.

'Yes.'

'What did you answer?'

'At first I told her that I had seen no signs of it, and that I couldn't say.'

'What did she say?'

'She promised me a place at court and a place for my son and the money that I need if I would tell her what she wants to hear.'

She hears the anguish in my voice, takes my hand and looks at me steadily with her level blue gaze. 'Oh Margaret, I can't ask you to be poor for me. Your sons should be at court, I know that. You don't have to defend me. I release you from your promise, Margaret. You can say what you wish.'

I am due to ride home but I go in my riding dress once more to the queen's rooms where My Lady is listening to a psalm being read before going to dinner in the great hall at Westminster.

She sees me the moment I come quietly into the room, and when the psalm is finished she beckons me to her side. Her ladies fall back and pretend to be looking at each other's neat head-dresses. Clearly, after yesterday's meeting, they know that she has quarrelled with me and they think I have come to surrender.

She smiles at me. 'Ah, Lady Margaret. Can we can make our arrangements for you to come to court?'

I take a breath. 'I should be very glad to come to court,' I say.

'I should be very glad for my son to go to Prince Harry at Eltham Palace. I beg of you, My Lady, to favour him with that. For the sake of his father, your half-cousin who loved you so well. Let Sir Richard's son be raised as a nobleman. Let your little kinsman come to you, please.'

'I will, if you will serve me in this one thing,' she says steadily. 'Tell me the truth, and you will be saving us, your family, from a dishonourable bride. Tell me something that I can take to my son, the king, and prevent him marrying the Spanish liar to our innocent boy. I have prayed over this and I am certain. Katherine of Aragon will never marry Prince Harry. You must be loyal to me, the mother of the king, and not to her. I warn you, Lady Margaret, take care what you say. Fear the consequences! Think very carefully before you consult your own will.'

She glares at me, her dark eyes boggling, as if to ensure that I understand the threat she promises, and at once I have a contrary reaction. My fear dissolves when she bullies me. I could almost laugh at her words. Fool that she is! Wicked old cruel fool that she is! Has she forgotten who I am, when she threatens me like this? Before God, I am a Plantagenet. I am a daughter of the House of York. My own father broke sanctuary, murdered a king, and was killed by his own brother. My mother followed her father into rebellion and then changed sides and waged war with her husband against him. We are a house of men and women who always follow our own wills; we cannot be made to fear consequences. If you show us danger we will always, *always* go towards it. They call us the demon's brood for our devilish wilfulness.

'I cannot lie,' I say to her quietly. 'I don't know if the prince was able with his wife or not. I never saw any signs. She told me, and I believed her, that they were not lovers. I believe her to be a virgin as she was when she came to this country. I believe that she can marry any suitable prince that her father approves. Myself, I think she would make a very good wife to Prince Harry, and a very good Queen of England.'

Her face grows dark and I can see a vein pulse at her temple, but she says nothing. With a quick, angry gesture she beckons her ladies to line up behind her. She is going to lead them into dinner, and I will not be eating at the high table ever again.

'As you wish.' She spits out the words as if they were venom. 'I do hope that you can manage on your widow's jointure, Lady Margaret Pole.'

I drop into a deep curtsey. 'I understand,' I say humbly. 'But my son? He is a royal ward, he is the son of your half-cousin, he is a fine boy, Your Grace . . .'

She sweeps past me without a word and all her ladies follow. I stand up to watch them go. I have had my moment of pride, I have charged down my own Ambion Hill to Bosworth Field and found nothing but defeat. And now I don't know what I am going to do.

STOURTON CASTLE, STAFFORDSHIRE, AUTUMN 1506

For another year I do everything I can to wring more money out of my lands. When the gleaners go into the field I confiscate a cup of grain from every basket, breaking the usual rules and upsetting all the older people in the village. I pursue poachers of game into the manor courts, and shock them by demanding cash fines for the minor thieving that they had done since childhood. I forbid the tenants from taking any living thing from the land – even rabbits, even old eggs that the hens have laid away – and I hire a game keeper to prevent them taking trout from my rivers. If I catch a child taking eggs from the nests of wild ducks I fine his parents. If I find a man in the woods with a faggot of kindling and a single twig that is too thick, I take the whole load off him and fine him too. I would fine the birds for flying in the air over my fields or the cocks for crowing if they could pay.

The people are so poor it goes against the grain to take from them. I find I am starting to count the eggs that I can expect from a woman who has only six hens. I demand our share of honey from a man who has only one hive and has been storing the honeycombs since summer. When Farmer Stride butchers a cow that has fallen in a ditch and broken her neck I demand every ounce of my share of the meat, I demand tallow from her fat and some of her hide for shoe leather. I am no good lord to him, I am grasping during his disaster, making a bad time worse for him, as the royal treasury is grasping in mine.

I send the men of my household out after deer, after pheasant, after heron, moorhen, anything that we might eat. The rabbit catcher has to bring in more coneys from the warren, the boy who empties the dove nests learns to expect me at the foot of his ladder. I become terrified that people are stealing from me, and I start to steal from them as I insist on my dues and more.

I am becoming the sort of landlord I despise; we are becoming a family whose tenants hate them. My mother was the richest heiress in England, my father was brother to the king. They kept followers, retainers and adherents by constant open-handed generosity. My grandfather fed everyone in London who chose to come to his door. Any man could come at dinnertime and go away with as much meat as he could spear on the blade of his dagger. I am their heir, but I betray their traditions. I think I have become half-mad with worry about money, the ache of fear in my belly is sometimes anxiety and sometimes hunger, and I have become so tormented that I can no longer tell which is which.

I am leaving church one day when I hear one of the village elders complaining to the priest and begging him to intervene. 'Father, you must speak to her. We can't pay our dues. We don't even know what's owed. She's looked at every tenancy going back years and found new fines. She's worse than a Tudor, she's worse than the king for looking through the laws and turning them to her advantage. She's starving us.'

In any case, it is not enough. I cannot buy my boys new riding boots, I cannot feed their horses. I struggle on for a year trying to deny that I am borrowing from myself, robbing my own tenants, stealing from the poor, but then I realise that all of my shabby attempts have failed.

We are ruined.

Nobody will help me. My widowhood is against me, my poverty is against me and my name is against me. Worst of all, the king's mother is against me and no-one will dare to help me. Two of my cousins are still imprisoned in the Tower; they cannot help me. Only my kinsman George Neville replies to the dozens of letters that I send out. He offers to raise my oldest boys at his home, and I will have to send Henry and Arthur away with the promise that I will fetch them as soon as I can, that they will not be in exile forever, that something will happen to bring us back together again, to restore us to our home.

Like a losing gambler I tell them that good times will come soon, but I doubt either of them believes me. My steward, John Little, takes them to Cousin Neville's house, Birling Manor in Kent, on the last of the horses, John mounted on the big plough horse, Henry on his hunter, and Arthur on his outgrown pony. I try to smile and wave to them, but the tears are blinding me and I can hardly see them – just their white faces and their big frightened eyes, two boys in shabby clothes, riding away from their home, with no idea of their destination. I don't know when I will see them again, I will not watch and guard their childhood as I hoped to do. I will not raise them as Plantagenets. I have failed them as their mother and they will have to grow up without me.

Ursula, at eight too little to be sent away to a great household, has to stay with me, and Geoffrey at nearly two is my baby. He has only just learned to walk, does not yet speak, and is clingy and anxious, quick to tears and fearful. I cannot let Geoffrey go. He has suffered already, born into a house of mourning, fatherless from the day of his birth. Geoffrey will stay with me, whatever it costs me; I cannot be parted from him, his only word is 'Mama'.

But my boy Reginald, the bright, happy, cheeky boy, has to be found a place. He is too young to go as a squire into a household, and I have no kinsmen with children who will take him into their nursery. The friends I used to know in the Marches or Wales are well aware that I am not invited to court nor paid a pension. They rightly take this to mean that the Tudors do not look kindly on me. I can think of only one man, too unworldly to calculate the danger of helping me, too kind to refuse. I write to My Lady's confessor, Bishop Fisher:

Dear Father,
I hope you can help me, for I have nowhere else to turn. I cannot pay my bills, nor keep my children at home.
I have been forced to send my two oldest boys to my cousin Neville; but I would like to find a place in a good religious house for my little son Reginald. If the Church insists, I will give him to God. He is a clever boy, quick-witted and lively, perhaps even a spiritual boy. I think he will serve God well. And anyway, I cannot keep him.
For myself and my two younger children I hope to find refuge in a nunnery where we can live on the small income that I have.
Your daughter in Christ,
Margaret Pole

He writes back at once. He has done more than I had asked of him – he has found a place for Reginald, and a refuge for me. He says I may stay at Syon Abbey, one of my family's favourite religious houses opposite the old Sheen Palace. The abbey is commanded by a Mother Abbess and attended by about fifty nuns, but they often take noble visitors and I can live there with my daughter and Baby Geoffrey. When Ursula is of age she can become a novice and then a nun in the order and her future will be secure. At the very least there will be food on the table and a roof over our heads for the next few years.

Bishop Fisher has found Reginald a place in the brother house to the abbey – Sheen Priory, a monastery of the Carthusian Order. He will be only a few miles from us, across the river. If I were to be allowed a candle to set in my window he would see the glow of the light and know I was thinking of him. We may be allowed to hire a boatman to row across the river to see him on feast days. We will be separated by the discipline of the religious houses, and by the wide, wide river, but I will be able to see the chimneys of the priory that houses my son. There is every reason for me to be delighted with such a generous solution to my difficulties. My son will be provided for in one house, and the other children and I will have a roof over our heads almost within sight of him. I should be joyous with relief.

Except, except, except . . . I slide to my knees on the floor and I pray to Our Lady to save us from this refuge. I know with complete conviction this is not the right place for Reginald, my clever, bright, chattering boy. The Carthusians are an order of silent hermits. Sheen Priory is a place of unbroken silence of the strictest of religious discipline. Reginald, my merry little boy who is so proud of learning to sing in a round, who loves to read aloud, who has learned some riddles and jokes and loves to tell them slowly, with intense concentration, to his brothers: this bright, talkative child will have to serve the monks who live like hermits in individual cells, each one praying and working alone. There is not one word spoken in the priory, except for Sundays and feast days. Once a week, the monks take a walk together and then they may talk in quiet tones, among themselves. The rest of the time they are in prayerful silence, each one alone with his thoughts with his own struggle with God, alone in his cell, enclosed by high walls, listening only to the sound of the wind.

I cannot bear to think of my chattering, high-spirited son silenced in a place of such holy discipline. I try to reassure myself that God will speak to Reginald in the cold quietness, and call him to a vocation. Reginald will learn to be silent, just as he learned to talk. He will learn to value his own thoughts and not laugh or dance or sing or caper and play the fool for his big brothers. Again and again I assure myself that this is a great opportunity for my bright boy. But I know in my heart that if God fails to call this little boy to a lifetime of holy service then I will have put my bright, loving boy in a wordless prison for life.

I dream of him locked in a tiny cell, and I wake with a start and cry out his name. I rack my brains to think of something else that I can do with him. But I do not know anyone who would take him as a squire, and I have no money to swear him as an apprentice, and besides – what could he do? He is a Plantagenet – I cannot have him trained up to be a cobbler. Shall an heir to the House of York stir the mash for a brewer? Would I be a better mother if I sent him to learn oaths and blasphemy running errands in an inn, than prayer and silence with a devout order?

Bishop Fisher has found him a place, a safe place and one where they will feed and educate him. I have to accept it. I can do nothing more for him. But when I think of my light-hearted son in a place where the only sound is the ticking of the clock, telling the hours to the next service of liturgy, I cannot stop my eyes blurring with tears.

It is my duty to destroy my home and my family, which I created so proudly as the new Lady Pole. I order all the household servants and the grooms into the great hall and I tell them that we have fallen on hard times and that I release them from service. I pay them their wages up to that day; I can offer no more though I know that I am flinging them into poverty. I tell the children that we have to leave our home and I try to smile and suggest that it is an adventure. I say it will be exciting to live elsewhere. I close down the castle at Stourton where my husband brought me as a bride, and where my children were born, leaving only John Little to serve as a bailiff and collect the rents and fees. Two thirds he has to send to the king, one third he will send to me.

We ride away from our home, Geoffrey in my arms as I ride pillion behind John Little, Ursula on the little pony and Reginald tiny on his brother's old hunter. He rides well; he has his father's way with horses and people. He will miss the stables and the dogs and the cheerful noise of the farmyard. I cannot bring myself to tell him his destination. I keep thinking that when we are on the road, he will ask me where we are going and I will find the courage to tell him that we have to part: Ursula and Geoffrey and I to one religious house and he to another. I try to fool myself that he will understand that this is his destiny – not what we might have chosen, yet now inevitable. But trustingly, he does not ask me. He assumes we will stay together; it does not occur to him that he might be sent away.

He is subdued at leaving his home, while little Geoffrey is excited by the journey and Ursula starts brightly and then starts to whimper. Reginald never asks me where we are going, and then I start to imagine that somehow he already knows, and that he wants to avoid the conversation as I do.

Only on the very last morning, as we are riding on the towpath beside the river towards Sheen, do I say: 'We'll soon be there. This will be your new home.'

He looks up at me from his little pony. 'Our new home?'

'No,' I say shortly. 'I am going to stay nearby, just a little way across the river.'

He says nothing, and I think perhaps he has not understood.

'I have often lived apart from you,' I remind him. 'When I had to go to Ludlow, and I left you at Stourton.'

He turns his wide-eyed face towards me. He does not say, 'But then I was with my brothers and sister and with all the people I had known all my life, my nurse in the nursery, my tutor who taught my brothers and me.' He just looks at me, uncomprehending. 'You will not leave me alone?' he finally asks. 'In a strange place? Mother? You will not just leave me?'

I shake my head. I can hardly trust myself to speak. 'I will visit you,' I whisper. 'I promise.'

The high towers of the priory come into sight, the gate opens and the prior himself comes out to greet me, takes Reginald by the hand and helps him down from the saddle.

'I will come and see you,' I promise from high on my horse, looking down at the golden crown of his bowed head. 'And you will be allowed to visit me.'

He looks very small as he stands beside the prior. He does not pull away or show any defiance but he turns up his pale face and he looks at me with his dark eyes and he says clearly: 'Lady Mother, let me come with you and my brother and sister. Don't leave me here.'

'Now, now,' says the prior firmly. 'Let's have no words from children who should always be silent before their elders and betters. And in this house, you will only speak when you are ordered to do so. Silence, holy silence. You will learn to love it.'

Obediently Reginald folds his lower lip under his teeth, and says not another word; but still he looks at me.

'I shall visit you,' I say helplessly. 'You will be happy here. It is a good place. You will serve God and the Church. You will be happy here, I am sure.'

'Give you good day.' The prior hints me away. 'Better done quickly, since it has to be done.'

I turn my horse's head and I look back at my son. Reginald is only six; he looks very small beside the prior. He is pale with fear. Obediently he says nothing, but his little mouth forms the silent word: 'Mother!'

There is nothing I can do. There is nothing I can say. I turn my horse's head, and I ride away.

SYON ABBEY, BRENTFORD, WEST OF LONDON, WINTER 1506

My boy Reginald has to learn to live among shadows and silence and so do I. Syon Abbey, run by the Bridgettine Order, is not a silent one; the sisters even go into London to teach and to pray, but I live among them as if I were sworn dumb, like my little boy. I cannot speak of my resentment and my bitterness, and I have nothing to say which is not resentful and bitter.

I will never forgive the Tudors for this heartbreak. They have waded to the throne through the blood of my kinsmen. They pulled my uncle Richard from the mud of Bosworth Field, stripped him naked, slung him over his own saddle and then threw him into an unmarked grave. My own brother was beheaded to reassure King Henry, my cousin Elizabeth died trying to give him another son. They married me to a poor knight to bring me low, and now he is dead and I am lower than I imagined a Plantagenet could sink. All this – all this! – to legitimise their claim to a throne which in any case they took by conquest.

And clearly, the Tudors take little joy in their triumph and our subjection. Since the death of his wife, our princess, the king is uncertain of his court, anxious about his subjects and terrified by us Plantagenets of the House of York. For years he has poured money into the pockets of the Emperor Maximilian, paying him to betray my cousin, Edmund de la Pole, the York claimant to the throne of England, and send him home to his death. Now I learn that the deal has been done. The emperor takes the money and promises Edmund that he will be safe, showing him the letter of safe conduct from the king, signed in his own hand. It is a guarantee that Edmund can come home. Edmund believes the assurances of Henry Tudor, he trusts the word of an ordained king. He sees the signature, he checks the seal. Henry Tudor swears he will have safe passage and an honest welcome. Edmund is a Plantagenet; he loves his country, he wants to come home. But the moment he walks under the portcullis of Calais Castle he is arrested.

This starts a chain of accusations that tears through my kinsmen like scissors through silk, and now I am on my knees praying for their lives. My cousin William Courtenay, already under arrest, is now charged with treasonous plotting. My kinsman William de la Pole in the Tower is questioned harshly in his cell. My cousin Thomas Grey falls under suspicion, for nothing more than dining with Cousin Edmund, years ago, before he fled from the country. One after another the men of my family disappear into the Tower of London, forced to endure solitude and fear, persuaded to name other dinner guests, and held in that dark keep, or secretly sent overseas to Calais Castle.

SYON ABBEY, BRENTFORD, WEST OF LONDON, SPRING 1507

I write to my sons Henry and Arthur to ask them how they are, and if they are studying and learning. I dare not trespass on the generosity of the abbey by inviting them here; the sisters cannot welcome two energetic young men into their quiet cloisters and anyway I cannot pay for their journey.

I see my little boy Reginald only once every three months, when they send him across the river to me by a hired rowing boat. He comes as he is commanded, cold and huddled in the prow of the little wherry. He can only stay for one night and then he has to go again. They have taught him to be silent, they have taught him very well; he keeps his eyes down and his hands at his side. When I run to greet him and hug him closely, he is stiff and unwilling, as if my lively, talkative son is dead and buried and all I have left to hold is this cold little headstone.

Ursula, nearly nine years old, seems to grow every day, and I let down the hems of her second-hand gowns again and again. Two-year-old Geoffrey's toes are pressed up against the front of his little boots. When I put him to bed at night I stroke his feet and pull his toes as if I can stop them growing twisted and cramped. The rents from Stourton are collected and faithfully sent to me but I have to hand them to the abbey for our keep. I don't know where Geoffrey will go when he is too old to stay here. Perhaps both he and Ursula will have to be sworn to the Church like their brother Reginald, and disappear into silence. I spend hours on my knees praying to God to send me a sign, or send me some hope, or simply send me some money; sometimes I think that when my last two children are safely locked up inside the Church, I will tie a great sack of stones to my belt and walk into the cold deeps of the River Thames.

SYON ABBEY, BRENTFORD, WEST OF LONDON, SPRING 1508

I kneel at the chancel steps and look up at the statue of the crucified Christ. I feel as if I have been walking the road of sorrows
of the Plantagenets, a Via Dolorosa, just like He did, for two long
years.

Then the danger comes a step closer to me: the king arrests my
cousin Thomas Grey, and my cousin George Neville, Lord
Bergavenny, who is keeping my two boys, Henry and Arthur.
George leaves my boys at his home in Kent and enters the Tower,
where people have started to whisper that the king himself visits
nightly to oversee the torture of the men he suspects. The pedlar
who comes to the door of the abbey with chapbooks and rosaries
for sale tells Porteress Joan that in the City they are saying that the
king has become a monster who likes to hear the cries of pain. 'A
Mouldwarp.' He whispers the old word for a cursed mole who
works in darkness among dead and buried things, who under-
mines his own pastures.

I am desperate to send for my boys, to take them away from the
household of a man who has been arrested as a traitor. But I do
not dare. I am afraid to draw attention to myself, almost in seclusion, almost in hiding, almost in sanctuary. I must not alert the
Tudor spy system to Reginald, kept in silence at the Charterhouse
at Sheen, Ursula and I hidden by our devotions at Syon, or
Geoffrey, the most precious of them all, clinging to my side as the
nuns know that there is nowhere that he can go, that even a child
of three years old cannot be allowed out into the world, since
there is no doubt that Henry Tudor, scenting Plantagenet blood,
will sniff him out.

This is a king who has become a dark mystery to his people.
He's not like the kings of my house – open, joyful sensualists
who ruled by agreement and made their way by charm. This

king spies on his people, imprisons them on a word, tortures them so they accuse and counter-accuse each other and, when he has evidence of treason, amazingly he forgives them, releasing them with a pardon, but burdened by fines so terrible that they will never be free of service to him, not through half a dozen generations. This is a king driven by fear, and ruled by greed.

My second cousin George Neville, my boys' guardian, comes out of the Tower tight-lipped about a limp which looks as if his leg has been broken and left to set crooked, poorer by a fortune, but free. My other cousins are still imprisoned. George Neville tells no-one what agreement he made inside those damp walls; silently he pays the king half of his income every quarter and never complains. He has fines so heavy that twenty-six of his friends have to serve as guarantors, and he is forbidden ever to go home to his beloved house in Kent, or to Surrey, Sussex, or Hampshire. He is an exile in his own country though he has been charged with nothing, and nothing has been proved against him.

None of the men who were arrested with him ever speaks of the contracts that each of them signed with the king in the darkened rooms underneath the Tower where the walls are thick and the doors are bolted and only the king stands in the corner of the chamber as his headsman turns a lever on the rack and the ropes bite tight. But people say that their agreements for huge debts are signed in their own blood.

My cousin George writes to me briefly.

You can safely leave your boys with me, they did not fall under any suspicion. I am a poorer man than I was, and banned from my home; but I can still house them. Better leave them with me until the fuss dies down. No point in having them lead people to you. You had better stay quietly there. Speak to no-one and trust no-one. These are hard times for the white rose.

I burn the letter and I do not reply.

SYON ABBEY, BRENTFORD, WEST OF LONDON, SPRING 1509

The king grows more mistrustful every year, retreating into the inner rooms of his palaces to sit with his mother, refusing to allow any strangers over the threshold, doubling the numbers of the yeomen of the guard who stand at his door, going endlessly, endlessly, through his book of accounts, binding men who were already loyalists to keep the peace with massive fines, taking their lands as sureties for good behaviour, asking them for good-will gifts, interfering with court cases and taking the fees. Justice itself can now be bought with a payment to the king. Safety can be bought with a fee to his treasury. Words can be written in the accounts for the price of a gift to the right servant, or erased for a bribe. Nothing is certain but that money offered to the royal treasury can buy anything. I believe that my cousin George Neville is all but ruined, paying for his freedom every quarter; but nobody dares to write and tell me so. I receive occasional letters from Arthur and Henry and they do not mention the arrest of their host and his return, a broken man, barred from the home that was his pride. They are only sixteen and fourteen years old but already they know that the men of our house should stay silent. They were born into the most talented, intellectual, questioning family in England, and they have been taught to hold their tongues for fear that they be cut out. They know that if you are of Plantagenet blood you should have been born dumb and deaf too. I read their innocent letters and I burn them on reading. I do not dare to keep even these, my boys' good wishes. None of us dares to own anything.

A widow for four years, with no prospect of help, barely enough money to eat, no roof to put over my children's heads, no dowry for my daughter, no brides for my sons, no lover, no friends, no chance of re-marriage since I never even see a man who is not a priest, I go on my knees eight hours a day every day alongside the nuns to observe the liturgy of the hours, and I watch my prayers change.

In the first year I prayed for help, in the second year for release. By the end of the third year I am praying for the death of King Henry and the damnation of his mother and the return of my House of York. In the silence I have grown into a bitter rebel. I damn the Tudors to hell and I come to hope that the curse that my cousin Elizabeth and her mother laid on them rings true, down through the long years to the end of the Tudors and the destruction of their line.

SYON ABBEY, BRENTFORD, WEST OF LONDON, APRIL 1509

I have the news first from the old porteress at the abbey who comes to the door of my cell and throws it open without knocking. Ursula is in her truckle bed and does not stir but Geoffrey sleeps in my narrow bed, held in my arms, and he pops up his little head as Joan bangs into the room and says: 'The king is dead. Wake up, my lady. We are free. God is merciful. He has blessed us. God has saved us. The curse of the Red Dragon has passed over us. The king is dead.'

I was dreaming that I was in the court of my uncle Richard at Sheriff Hutton and my cousin Elizabeth was dancing with him in a swirl of gold and silver brocade. I sit up at once and say to her: 'Hush. I won't hear it.'

Her old wizened face is cracked open with a smile. I have never seen her beam before. 'You'll hear this!' she says. 'And anyone can say it, and anyone can hear it. For the spymaster is dead and the spies are thrown out of employment. The king is dead and the bonny, bonny prince has come to his throne just in time to save us all.'

Just then the bell of the abbey starts to toll, a steady, deep, sonorous note, and Geoffrey scrambles to his knees and says: 'Hurrah! Hurrah! Is Henry to be king?'

'Of course,' the old woman says, catching at his little hands and dancing him on the bed. 'God bless him and the day he comes to the throne.'

'My brother Henry!' Geoffrey squeaks. 'King of England!'

I am so horrified by this innocent speaking of treason that I snatch him to me, put my hand over his mouth and turn to her in an agonised appeal for her silence. But she just shakes her head at him and laughs at his pride. 'By rights – yes,' she says boldly. 'It should be your brother Henry. But we have a bonny Tudor boy to come after the old sweat master and Prince Harry Tudor will take the throne and the spies and the taxmen will be gone.'

I jump out of bed and start to pull on my clothes.

'Will she send for you?' Joan the porteress asks me, swinging Geoffrey from the bed, and letting him dance around her. Ursula rises up and rubs her eyes and says: 'What's happening?'

'Who?' I am thinking of My Lady the King's Mother, who has buried her grandson and will now bury her son, just as Elizabeth's curse foretold. She will be a broken woman. She will believe, as I do, that the Tudors signed their own death warrant when they killed our princes in the Tower. She will think, as I do, that they are accursed murderers.

'Katherine, Dowager Princess of Wales,' Joan says simply. 'Won't he marry her and make her Queen of England as he promised to do? Won't she send for you, her dearest friend? Won't you be able to have your children with you at court and live as you were born to? Won't it be like a miracle for you, like the stone rolling from the tomb and letting you all out?'

I stop short. I am so unaccustomed to hope that I hardly know what to say. I had not even thought of this.

'He might,' I say wonderingly. 'He might marry her. And she might send for me. You know, if he does – she will.'

It is like a miracle, a release as powerful as spring after a cold, grey winter. It comes in springtime and ever after when I see the hawthorn blossom making the hedges as white as snow, or the daffodils leaning over in the wind, I think of that spring when the old Tudor king was dead and the Tudor boy took the throne and made everything right.

He had told me in his nursery that to be a king was a holy duty. I thought of him then as a lovable little braggart: a boy spoiled by doting women, a loving boy of good intentions. Yet who would have thought that he would have leapt up to defy the mean old man, to take Katherine as his betrothed wife, to declare himself king and ready to marry her in one breath? It was the first thing he did, this boy of seventeen, the very first thing that he did. Just like my uncle King Edward, he took the throne and he took the woman he loved. Who would have thought that Harry Tudor had the courage of a Plantagenet? Who would have thought he had the imagination? Who would have thought he had the passion?

He is his mother's son; that can be the only explanation. He has her love and her courage and her bright optimism, which is the nature of our family. He is a Tudor king but he is a boy of the House of York. In his joy and his optimism, he is one of ours. In his willing grasping of power, in his quick execution: he is one of ours.

Katherine the princess sends for me with a short note that bids me come to the house of Lady Williams. where I will find rooms waiting for me suitable for a noblewoman of my station. Then I am to come at once to the Palace of Westminster, go straight to the wardrobe rooms, pick out half a dozen gowns and attend her, richly dressed, as her first lady in waiting. It is my release. I am free. It is my restoration.

I leave the children at Syon while I go downriver to London. I dare not take them with me yet; I feel as if I have to make sure that we are safe, to see that we are truly free before I dare summon them to be with me.

London does not look like a city which has lost a king. It is not a capital in mourning; it is a city mad with joy. They are roasting meat at the street corners, they are sharing ale out of the windows of the brewhouses. The king has not been buried long, the prince is not yet crowned but the place is elated. They are opening the debtors' prisons and men are coming out who had thought they would never see daylight again. It is as if a monster has died and we are freed from the grip of a bad spell. It is like waking from a nightmare. It is like spring after a long, long winter.

Dressed in my new gown of pale Tudor green, wearing a gable hood as heavy as that of the princess, I walk into the presence chamber of the King of England and see the prince, not on his throne, not standing in a stiff pose under the cloth of estate as if he were the portrait of majesty, but laughing with his friends strolling around the room, with Katherine at his side, as if they were a pair of lovers, enchanted with each other. And at the end of the room, seated on her chair with a circle of silent ladies all around her, a priest on either side for support, is My Lady, wearing deepest black, torn between grief and fury. She is no longer My Lady the King's Mother – the title that gave her so much pride is buried with her son. Now, if she chooses it, she can be called My Lady the King's Grandmother, and by the thunderous look on her face she does not choose it.

ENGLAND, 1509

For the commons of England it is a merciful release from hardship. For the lords it is an escape from tyranny. For the people of my family and my house it is the miraculous lifting of a death sentence. Anyone with Plantagenet blood or affinity to York has been living on licence, achingly aware that at any moment the king might revoke permission and there would be a knock on the door from the green-and-white-liveried yeomen of the guard and a swift trip in their unmarked barge to the watergate of the Tower. The great portcullis would slide up, the barge would enter – and the prisoner would never come out again.

But now we do come out. William Courtenay emerges from the Tower with a royal pardon, and we pray that William de la Pole will be out soon. My cousin Thomas Grey is released from Calais castle and comes home. Disbelievingly, like householders slowly opening their painted doors after plague has passed through a village, we all start to emerge. Cousins come to London from their distant castles hoping it is safe to be seen at court again. Kinsfolk that have not written for years now dare to send a message, sharing family news, telling of the birth of babies and the death of members of the family, asking, fearfully, how is everyone else? Has anyone seen such a man? Does anyone know if a distant cousin is safe abroad? The death-like grip of the old king on every one of us is suddenly released. Harry the prince has not inherited his father's fearful suspicions; he dismisses the spies, he cancels the debts, he pardons the prisoners. It feels as if we can all come out, blinking into the light.

Servants and tradesmen who have avoided me since the death of my husband and my fall from favour come to me in their dozens to offer their services now that my name is no longer written somewhere, on some list, with a question mark beside it.

Slowly, hardly able to believe my luck, like the rest of the country I find I am safe. I seem to have survived the dangerous twenty-four years of the first Tudor reign. My brother died on King Henry's scaffold, my husband in his service, my cousin in childbed trying to give him another heir; but I have survived. I have been ruined, I have been heartbroken, I have been estranged from all but two of my children and lived in hiding with them, but now I can emerge, half-blinded, into the sunlight of the young prince's summer.

Katherine, once a widow as poor as me, soars upward into the sunshine of the Tudor favour like a kestrel spreading her russet wings in the morning light, her debts excused, her dowry forgotten. The prince marries her, in haste, in private, in the delight of passion finally expressed. Now he says he has loved her in silence and at a distance for all this time. He has been watching her, he has been desiring her. Only his father, only his grandmother, My Lady, enforced his silence. The ambiguous papal dispensation for this marriage that Katherine's mother cunningly provided so long ago makes the marriage legal beyond question; nobody asks about her first husband, nobody cares, and they are wedded and bedded in days.

And I take my place at her side. Once again I have the right to draw the finest velvets from the royal wardrobe, I help myself to ropes of pearls and gold and jewels from the royal treasury. Once again, I am the senior lady in waiting to the Queen of England and I follow nobody but a Tudor into dinner. Katherine's new husband, King Henry – Henry VIII as we all delightedly remind ourselves – pays me a grant of a hundred pounds a year the moment that I arrive at court, and I settle my debts: to my faithful steward John Little at Stourton, to my cousins, to the nuns at Syon, to Reginald's priory. I send for Henry and Arthur, and the king offers them a place in his household. The king speaks highly of an education in the new learning, and orders that Reginald shall be well taught in his monastery; he will come to court as a philosopher and a scholar. I keep my boy Geoffrey and Ursula in the queen's rooms for now, but soon I will send them home, and they can live again in the country and be raised as Plantagenet heirs should be.

I even receive a proposal of marriage. Sir William Compton, the young king's dearest friend and companion in his revels and jousting, asks me, humbly on his knees, with his smiling eyes looking boldly up at me, if I would consider him as a husband. His bowed knee indicates that I could have the ruling of him, his warm hand holding mine suggests that this might be pleasurable. I have lived as a nun for nearly five years; the thought of a handsome man between good linen sheets cannot help but make me pause for a moment and look into William's brown smiling eyes.

It takes me only one minute to decide, but to serve his urgent sense of his own dignity as a man come from next to nowhere, I spin it out for a couple of days. Thank God that I do not need his newly minted name, I don't have to hide my name now. I don't need the royal favour that he carries. My own popularity at court is high, and only grows as the young king turns to me for advice, for stories of the old days, for my memories of his mother. I tell him of the fairy tale Plantagenet court and I see that he longs to recreate our reign. So I do not need Compton's newly built house; I am so restored, I have such great prospects, that the king's favourite thinks me an advantageous match. Gently, I tell him no. Graciously, courteously, he expresses his disappointment. We conclude the passage like two skilled performers skating through the steps of an elegant dance. He knows that I am at the height of my triumph, I am his equal, I don't need him.

A tide of wealth and prosperity flows out of the open doors of the treasury. Incredulously, they throw open cupboards, boxes and chests in every royal house, and everywhere they find plate and gold, jewels and fabrics, carpets and spices. The old king took his taxes and fines in money and goods, indiscriminately sucking in household furnishings, tradesmen's stores, even the tools of apprentices, impoverishing the poor. The new king, the young Henry, gives back to innocent people what his father stole from them, in a festival of redress. Unjust fines are repaid from the exchequer, noblemen are restored to their lands, my kinsman George Neville who guarded my sons is released from his crippling debts and given the post of Chief Larderer, a patron to thousands, the master of hundreds, a royal fortune at his disposal just waiting to be spent on good things. He is high in the king's favour, Henry admires him, calls him a kinsman and trusts him. Nobody mentions his ill-set leg; he is allowed to go to any, to all of his beautiful homes.

His brother, Edward Neville, is a favourite and serves in the king's bedchamber. The king swears that Edward is the very match of him, calls him to stand beside him, to compare heights and the colour of their hair, assures my cousin that they could be mistaken for brothers, that he loves us all as his brothers and sisters. He is warm to all my family – Henry Courtenay of Devon, my cousin Arthur Plantagenet, the de la Poles, the Staffords, the Nevilles, all of us – as if he were seeking his mother in our smiling, familiar faces. Slowly, we return to where we were all born to be, at the centre of power and wealth. We are the king's cousins, there is no-one closer to him.

Even My Lady the old King's Mother is rewarded with the return of her palace of Woking, though she does not live to enjoy it for long. She sees her grandson crowned and then she takes to her bed and dies. Her confessor, dear John Fisher, preaches the eulogy at her funeral and describes a saint who spent her life in the service of her country and her son, who laid down her work only when it was done. We listen in polite silence but, truth be told, she is little mourned; most of us experienced her family pride more than her cousinly love. And I am not the only one who secretly thinks that she died of fatal pique, in fear that her influence had run out, and so that she would not have to see our Queen Katherine looking beautiful and making merry in the rooms where the old woman had ruled so meanly for so long.

God is blessing the new generation, and we care nothing for those who have gone. Queen Katherine conceives a child almost at once, during the carefree days of the summer progress, and announces her happy state before Christmas, at Richmond Palace. For a moment, in that season of celebration, in a constant rush of entertainments, I start to think that my cousin's curse is forgotten and that the Tudor line will inherit my family's luck and be as sturdy and prolific as we have always been.

RICHMOND PALACE, WEST OF LONDON, SPRING 1510

It is a bad night for her when she loses the baby, and then worse days follow. The fool of a physician tells her and, even worse, assures the king that she was carrying twins, and there is another healthy baby in her belly. She may have had an agonising miscarriage, but there is no cause for dismay: she is still carrying an heir, there is a Tudor boy, waiting to be born.

This is how we learn that the young king likes to hear good news, indeed he insists on hearing good news, and in the future it may take some courage to force the truth on him. An older man, a more thoughtful man, would have questioned such an optimistic doctor; but Henry is eager to believe that he is blessed, and joyfully continues to celebrate his wife's pregnancy. At the Shrove Tuesday feast he walks all around the diners proposing toasts to the queen and the baby that he thinks she is carrying in her swollen womb. I watch him, incredulously. This is the first time that I see that his sickly father and his fearful grandmother have instilled in him an absurd devotion to physicians. He listens to anything they say. He has a deep, superstitious terror of illness, and he longs for cures.

GREENWICH PALACE, LONDON, SPRING 1510

Obediently, Katherine goes into confinement at Greenwich Palace, and as her swollen belly slims down to nothing, she waits with grim determination, knowing that there is going to be no birth. When her time is over and she has nothing to show for it, she bathes like a Spanish princess, in jug after jug of boiling-hot water with rose oil and the finest of soap, dresses in her best gown, and summons her courage to come out and face the court, looking like a fool. I stand beside her like a fierce guardian, my eyes raking the room, daring anyone to comment on her long pointless absence and now her surprise reappearance.

Her bravery is poorly rewarded. She is greeted without sympathy, for nobody is much interested in the return to court of a childless bride. Something far more intriguing is going on; the court is agog with scandal.

It is William Compton, my former suitor, who seems to have comforted himself by flirting with my second cousin, Anne, one of the two beautiful sisters of the Duke of Buckingham, newly married to Sir George Hastings. I failed to see this foolish affair develop as I was absorbed in Katherine's grief, and I am sorry to learn that matters have gone so far that my cousin Stafford has had high words with the king at the insult to his family, and taken her away from court.

This is madness from the duke, but typical of his prickly sense of pride. There is no doubt in my mind that his sister will have been guilty of almost any indiscretion; she is the daughter of Katherine Woodville, and like most Woodville girls she is outstandingly beautiful and wilful. She is unhappy with her new husband, and he will apparently allow any misdemeanour. But then, as the court continues to whisper of nothing else, I begin to think that there must be more to this than a courtier's escapade, an episode of courtly lovemaking, play-acting desire which went beyond the rules. Henry, who is normally pompous about the rules of courtly love, seems to side with Compton, who declares himself insulted by the duke. The young king flies into a rage, orders Buckingham to stay away from court, and goes everywhere arm in arm with Compton who looks both sheepish and rakish all at once, like a young tup in a lush field full of ewes.

Whatever has been taking place here seems to be more troubling than William Compton playing fast and loose with the duke's sister. There must be some reason that the king supports his friend and not the cuckolded husband; there must be some reason that the duke is disgraced but the seducer is in favour. Someone is lying, and someone is hiding something from the queen. The ladies of her household are no use, they are not going to tell tales. My cousin Elizabeth Stafford maintains an aristocratic discretion since it is her kinswoman who is the centre of the scandal, Lady Maud Parr says she knows nothing more than common gossip.

Katherine sends for the books of the household and sees that while she was confined, waiting for a baby that she knew was long gone, the court was making merry and it was Anne Hastings who was Queen of the May.

'What is this?' she asks me, pointing at the payment for a choir to sing under Anne's window on May Day morning. 'What is this?' – the wardrobe accounts for Anne's costume in a masque.

I say I don't know; but I can read the accounts as well as she can. What I see, what I know she sees, what anyone would see, is a small fortune from the royal treasury being spent for the amusement of Anne Hastings.

'Why would the royal household pay for William Compton's choir for Lady Anne?' she asks me. 'Is this usual, in England?'

Katherine is the daughter of a king whose philandering was well known. She knows that a king can take lovers as he wishes, that there can be no complaint, least of all from his wife. Queen Isabella of Spain broke her heart over the love affairs of her husband, and she was as royal as he was, no mere wife crowned as a favour, but a monarch in her own right. Even so, he never mended his ways. Isabella suffered hell's own torments of jealousy and her daughter Katherine saw it, and resolved that she would never feel such pain. She did not know that this young prince who told her that he loved her, that he had waited for her for years, would turn out like this. She did not imagine that while she was in the dark loneliness of confinement, knowing that she had lost her baby and that nobody would let her grieve, her young husband was starting a flirtation with her own lady in waiting, a young woman in her service, in her rooms, a kinswoman of mine, a friend.

'I'm afraid that it's what you're thinking,' I say bluntly to her, telling her the worst and getting it over with. 'William Compton pretended to court Anne; everyone saw them together, everyone knew they were meeting. But he was a shield. All the time she was meeting with the king.'

It is a hard blow for her, but she takes it like a queen.

'And there's worse than this,' I say. 'I'm sorry to have to tell you of it.'

She takes a breath. 'Tell me. Tell me, Margaret, what can be worse than this?'

'Anne Hastings told one of the other ladies in waiting that it was not a flirtation, not a May Day courting, over and forgotten in one day.' I look at her pale face, the folded resolute line of her mouth. 'Anne Hastings said that the king had made promises.'

'What? What could he promise?'

I ignore protocol and sit beside her and put my arm around her shoulders as if she were still a homesick princess and we were back at Ludlow. 'My dear . . .'

For a moment she lets her head droop and rests it on my shoulder and I tighten my grip. 'You'd better tell me, Margaret. I had better know everything.'

'She says that he swore he was in love with her. She told him that her vows could be annulled and, more importantly, she said that his were invalid. They spoke of marriage.'

There is a long, long silence. I think, please God she does not become queenly and leap to her feet and rage at me for bringing her such bad news. But then I feel her soften, her whole body yields, and she turns her hot face with her cheeks wet with tears to my neck, and I hold her while she cries like a hurt girl.

We are silent for a long time, then she pulls back and rubs her eyes roughly with her hands. I give her a handkerchief and she wipes her face and blows her nose.

'I knew it,' she sighs as if she is weary to her very bones.

'You knew?'

'He told me some of this last night, and I guessed the rest. God forgive him: he told me he was confused. He told me that when he bedded her she cried out in pain and said that she could not bear it. He had to take her gently. She told him that a virgin bleeds when it is her first time.' She makes a little face of disgust, of derision. 'Apparently she bled. Copiously. She showed him all that, and convinced him that I was no virgin on our wedding night, that my marriage to Arthur had been con-summated.'

She holds herself very still and then she gives a deep shudder. 'She suggested to him that his marriage to me is invalid, because I was wedded and bedded by Arthur. That in the sight of God, I will always be Arthur's wife, and not Henry's. And God will never give us a child.'

I am aghast. I look at her blankly. I have no words to defend our secret, I can only marvel at this nonchalant unravelling of our old plot.

'She's a married woman herself,' I say flatly. 'She's been mar-ried twice.'

Katherine finds a mournful smile at my incredulity.

'She's put it into his head that our marriage is against the will of God and that is why we lost the baby. She told him that we will never have a child.'

I am so appalled that I can only reach for her again. She takes my hand, pats it and puts it aside.

'Yes,' she says thoughtfully. 'Cruel, isn't she? Wicked, isn't she?'

And when I don't reply, she says: 'This is serious. She told him that my belly was swollen but since there was no child, it was a message from God that there will never be one. Because the marriage is against the word of God. That a man should not marry his brother's widow, and if he does their marriage will be without issue. It's written in the Bible.' She smiles without humour. 'She quoted Leviticus to him. "And if a man shall take his brother's wife it is an unclean thing: he hath uncovered his brother's nakedness: they shall be childless".'

I am quite stunned at Anne Hastings' sudden interest in theology. Someone has prepared her to whisper this poison into Henry's ear. 'The Pope himself gave a dispensation,' I insist. 'Your mother arranged it! Your mother made sure that the dispensation provided, whether you had been bedded by Arthur or not. She made sure of it.'

She nods. 'She did. But Henry has been filled with fears by that old grandmother of his. She quoted Leviticus to him before we were married. His father lived in terror that his luck would not hold. And now this Stafford girl turns his head with lust, and tells him it is God's will that I should lose a baby and that another should disappear from my womb. She says our marriage is cursed.'

'It doesn't matter what she says.' I am furious with the wicked girl. 'Her brother has taken her from court, you need never have her back in your service. For God's sake – she has a husband of her own! She is married and cannot get free! She can't marry the king! Why cause all this trouble? And Henry cannot really believe that she is a virgin! She's been married twice! Are they mad to talk like this?'

She nods. She is thinking, not railing against her circumstances, and I suddenly realise this must be the woman that her mother was, a woman who in the middle of a disaster could assess her chances, look at the odds, and plan. A woman who, when her camp of tents burned down, built a besieging camp of stone.

'Yes, I think we can get rid of her,' she says thoughtfully. 'And we'll have to make peace with her brother the duke and get him back to court, he's too powerful to be an enemy. The old Lady

Mother is dead, she can't frighten Henry any more. And we have to silence this talk.'

'We can,' I say. 'We will.'

'Will you write to the duke?' she asks. 'He's your cousin, isn't he?'

'Edward is my second cousin,' I specify. 'Our grandmothers were half-sisters.'

She smiles. 'Margaret, I swear you're related to everyone.'

I nod. 'I am. And he'll come back. He's loyal to the king and he's fond of you.'

She nods. 'He's not my danger.'

'What do you mean?'

'My father was famous for his philandering; everyone knew, my mother knew. But everyone knew that the women were his pleasure; nobody every spoke of love.' She makes a little face of disgust, as if love between a king and a woman is always disreputable. 'My father would never have spoken of love to anyone but his wife. Nobody ever doubted his marriage, nobody ever challenged my mother, Queen Isabella. They were married in secret without a papal dispensation at all – their marriage was the most uncertain one in the world, but nobody ever thought that it would not last until death. My father bedded dozens of other women, probably hundreds. But he never said one word of love to any one of them. He never let anyone think for even a moment that there was any other possible wife for him, any other possible Queen of Spain but my mother.'

I wait.

'It is my husband who is my danger,' she says wearily, her face a hard mask of beauty. 'A young fool, a spoiled fool. He should be old enough now to take a lover without falling in love. He should never allow anyone to question our marriage. He should never think for a moment that it might be set aside. To do that is to destroy his own authority as well as mine. I am Queen of England. There can only be one queen. There can only be one king. I am his wife. We were both crowned. That should never be questioned.'

'We can make sure that this never goes further,' I suggest.

She shakes her head. 'The worst damage has already been done,' she says. 'A king who speaks of love to anyone but his wife, a king who questions his marriage is a king who rocks the foundations of his own throne. We can stop this nonsense going further, but the damage was done when it entered his stupid head.'

We sit in silence for long moments, thinking about Henry's handsome golden head. 'He married me for love,' she observes wearily, as if it were a long time ago. 'It was not an arranged marriage, it was one of love.'

'It's a bad precedent,' I say, the daughter of an arranged marriage, the widow of an arranged marriage. 'If a man marries for love, does he think he can get the marriage annulled when he loves no more?'

'Does he not love me any more?'

I cannot answer her. It is such a painful question from a woman who was so deeply loved by her first, dead husband, who would never have bedded another woman and spoken of love to her.

I shake my head because I don't know. I doubt that Henry himself knows. 'He's young,' I say. 'And impulsive. And powerful. It's a dangerous combination.'

Anne Hastings never comes back to court; her husband packs her off to a nunnery. My cousin Edward Stafford, the Duke of Buckingham, her brother, recovers his good temper and rejoins us. Katherine wins Henry back to her side and they conceive another child, the boy that is to prove that God smiles on their marriage. The queen and I behave as if her realisation that her husband is a fool had never happened. We don't conspire in this. We don't have to discuss it. We just do it.

RICHMOND PALACE, WEST OF LONDON, JANUARY 1511

We are blessed, we are redeemed, and Katherine in particular is saved. She gives the king a Tudor son and heir and overturns in one act the rumours that were growing about the curse that sits on the Tudor family, the questioning of the marriage.

I have the honour to go to the young king and tell him that he is father to a boy and I find him exultant among the young men of his court who drink to his great triumph. Katherine, confined in her rooms, leaning on the pillows in the great bed of state, is exhausted and smiling when I return.

'I did it,' she says quietly to me as I lean to kiss her cheek.

'You did it,' I confirm.

The next day, Henry sends for me. I find his rooms still crowded with men shouting congratulations and drinking the health of his son. Above the noise and the cheering he asks me if I will be the prince's Lady Governess, and set up his household and appoint his staff and raise him as heir to the throne.

I put my hand on my heart and I curtsey. When I come up, Henry the boy pitches into my arms and I hug him in our shared joy. 'Thank you,' he says. 'I know you will guard him and raise him and govern him as if you were my mother.'

'I will,' I say to him. 'I know just how she would have wanted it done, and I will make everything right.'

The baby is christened at the chapel of the Observant Friars at Richmond; he is to be Henry, of course. He will be Henry IX one day, God willing, and he will rule over a country which will have forgotten that once the rose of England was pure white. His Lady Mistress is appointed and his wet nurse, he sleeps in a cradle of gold, he is swaddled in the finest of linen, he goes everywhere carried breast-high, with two yeomen of the guard preceding his nurse and two behind. Katherine has him brought to her rooms every day, and while she rests in bed she has him laid beside her, and when she sleeps she has his little cradle put at the head of her bed.

Henry goes on a pilgrimage to give thanks. Katherine is churched and rises up from her bed, takes one of her hot Spanish baths, and returns to her court, glowing with pride in her youth and fertility. Not a girl in her train, not a lady in her rooms hesitates for one moment before bowing low to this triumphant queen. I don't believe there is a woman in the country who does not share her joy.

WESTMINSTER PALACE, LONDON, SPRING 1511

The king, returned from pilgrimage to Walsingham where he gave thanks to Our Lady, or perhaps, in truth, told Her of his achievement, sends for me to come to the jousting arena. My son Arthur comes with a smile and says I am not to tell anyone that I am going to watch a practice for the joust to celebrate the birth of the prince, but to slip quietly away from the queen's rooms.

Indulgently, I go to the arena and, to my surprise, I find that Henry is alone, riding a great grey war charger round and round in careful circles, first one way then the other. Henry waves me to sit in the royal box, and I take the seat that his mother would have taken and know, for I know him so well, that he wants me there, watching over him, as she and I once watched him practise on his pony.

He brings the horse right up to the balcony and shows me that it can bow, one foreleg extended, one foreleg tucked back. 'Hold up a glove or something,' he says.

I take a kerchief from my neck and hold it up. Henry goes to the other side of the arena and shouts: 'Drop!' As it falls he spurs forward and catches it in his hand, riding around the arena holding it high above his head like a flag.

He pulls up before me, his bright blue eyes fixed on my face.

'Very good,' I say approvingly.

'And there's this,' he says. 'Don't be frightened. I know what I'm doing.'

I nod. He turns the horse sideways to my view and makes it rear and then buck, forelegs up then back legs kicking, in a fantastic display. He changes his seat slightly and the horse leaps above the ground, as the Moorish horses do, all legs in the air at once as if it were flying, and then it trots on the spot, raising one leg proudly high and then another. He really is a remarkable rider; he sits completely and beautifully still, holding the reins tightly, his whole body moulded to the horse, alert, relaxed, at one with the great muscled animal.

'Get ready,' he warns me, and then he swings the horse round and it rears up, terribly high, its head as high as me in the royal box built over the arena, and it crashes its front hooves onto the wall of the box, springs back again and drops down.

I nearly scream with fright, and then I jump to my feet and applaud. Henry beams at me, loosens the reins, pats the horse's neck. 'Nobody else can do that,' he remarks breathlessly, bringing the horse closer, watching me for my reaction. 'Nobody in England can do that but me.'

'I should think not.'

'You don't think it's too loud? Will she be frightened?'

Katherine once stood with her mother to face a charge of enemy Arab cavalry, the fiercest horsemen in the world. I smile. 'No, she'll be very impressed, she knows good horsemanship.'

'She'll never have seen anything like this,' he claims.

'She will,' I contradict him. 'The Moors in Andalusia have Arab horses, and they ride wonderfully.'

At once the smile is wiped from his face. He turns a furious look on me. 'What?' he demands icily. 'What do you say?'

'She will understand how great is your achievement,' I say, the words tumbling out in my haste to redress the offence. 'For she knows good horsemanship from her home in Spain, but she will never have seen anything like this. And no man in England can do this. I have never seen a better horse and rider.'

He is uncertain, and pulls on the rein; the horse, sensing the change of his mood, flicks his ear, listening.

'You are like a knight of Camelot,' I say hastily. 'Nobody will have seen anything like it since the golden age.'

He smiles at that, and it is almost as if the sun comes out and birds start to sing. 'I am a new Arthur,' he agrees.

I ignore the pang I feel at the casual use of the name of the prince we loved, whose little brother is still striving to better him. 'You are the new Arthur of the new Camelot,' I repeat. 'But where is your other horse, Your Grace? Your lovely black mare?'

'She was disobedient,' he throws over his shoulder as he rides out of the ring. 'She defied me. She would not learn from me.'

He turns and gives me his most charming smile, all sunshine once again. I think that he is the most adorable young man as he says lightly: 'I sent her for baiting. The hounds killed her. I can't bear disloyalty.'

It is the greatest joust that I have ever seen, that England has ever seen. The king is everywhere, no scene is complete without him in a new costume. He leads the procession of the Master of the Armoury, the trumpeters, the courtiers, the heralds, the court assistants, the poets, the singers and at last, the long line of jousters. Henry has announced a tournament in which he will take on all comers.

He rides his great grey warhorse and he wears cloth of gold, interleaved with the richest blue velvet, gleaming in the bright spring sunshine as if he were a king newly minted. All over his jacket, his hat, his riding breeches, his trappings are sewn little gold 'K's as if he wants to show the world that he is hers, that she has set her initial all over him. Above his head is the standard he has chosen for this day: *Loyall*. His tournament name is *Coeur Loyall*, Henry is Sir Loyal Heart and as Katherine glows with pride he rides his horse around the ring and shows the tricks that he practised before me, a perfect prince.

We all share her joy, even the girls who would welcome the attentions of the perfect prince themselves. Katherine sits in a throne with the sunlight shining through the cloth of gold canopy making her skin rosy and golden, smiling on the young man that she loves, knowing that their first child, their son, is safe in his golden cradle.

But only ten days later, they go to pick him up and he is cold, and his little face is blue, and he is dead.

It is as if the world has ended. Henry withdraws to his rooms; the queen's rooms are stunned and silent. All of the words of comfort that can be given to a young woman who has lost her first child dissolve on the tongue in the face of Katherine's bleak horror. For day after day no-one says anything to her. There is nothing to say. Henry falls into silence, and won't speak of his lost child; he does not attend the funeral or the Mass. They cannot comfort each other, they cannot bear to be together. This loss in their new marriage is so terrible that Henry cannot comprehend it, cannot try to comprehend it. A darkness spreads over the court.

But even in grief, Katherine and I know that we have to be watchful, all the time. We have to wait for the next girl that Henry takes to his bed, who will wind her arms around his neck and whisper in his ear that look! see! God does not bless his marriage. It has only been twenty months and yet there have been three tragedies: one miscarriage, one child vanished clear away from the womb, one baby dead in its cradle. Is this not proof, building, growing proof, that the marriage is against the will of God, but she – a virgin of healthy English stock – might give him a son?

'And which of my ladies in waiting should I suspect?' Katherine asks me bitterly. 'Who? Who should I watch? Lady Maud Parr? She's a pretty woman. Mary Kingston? Lady Jane Guildford? Lady Elizabeth Boleyn? She's married of course but why should that prevent her seducing the king? You?'

I am not even offended by her outburst. 'The queen has to be served by the most beautiful and wealthiest ladies of the kingdom,' I say simply. 'It's how a court works. You have to be surrounded by beautiful girls, they are here to find a husband, they are determined to shine, they are bound to catch the eye of the courtiers and the king.'

'What can I do?' she asks me. 'How can I make my marriage unassailable?'

I shake my head. We both know that the only way she can prove that God has blessed her marriage is to give birth to a live son. Without him, without that little saviour, we are all waiting for the moment that the king starts to interrogate God.

WESTMINSTER PALACE, LONDON, SPRING 1512

The king, as he emerges from his grief for his baby, is good to me, and I am advised that I should apply for the return of my brother's fortune and lands. I should even ask for the return of my family title. Having spent my life pretending that my name was nothing and my fortune was lost, I am bidden to claim them both.

It is a heady experience, like coming out of the cold nunnery to the springtime court once again, like coming out of darkness, blinking into light. I list the great fortune that my brother lost when this king's father tore him from the schoolroom and bundled him into the Tower. I name the titles that I commanded when I walked away from them down the aisle to marry a lowly Tudor knight. Tentatively, at first, as if I am taking a great risk, I state my great name, estimate my great fortune, and say that it was my own, all my own, that the Tudors wrongly took it from me, and that I want it back.

I think of my angry prayers in Syon Abbey and I put my temper to one side and write a careful petition to the king, framing my request in such a way that it is no criticism of that grasping tyrant, his father, but a measured claim for what is my own. A claim for my sons that they should have what is ours. I want to be restored to my greatness, I want to be a Plantagenet again. Apparently, the time has come that I can be a Plantagenet. Apparently, at last, I can be myself.

Amazingly, the king grants it. Freely, generously, sweetly, he grants me everything that I ask, and tells me that since I am by birth and by disposition one of the greatest ladies of the kingdom I should enjoy the greatest fortune. I am to be what I was born to be: Margaret Plantagenet, as wealthy as a princess of York.

I ask the queen for permission to be away from court for the night. 'You want to tell your children,' she smiles.

'This changes everything for us,' I say.

'Go,' she says. 'Go to your new house and meet them there. I am glad that you have justice, at last. I am glad that you are Margaret Plantagenet once more.'

'Countess of Salisbury,' I say, sweeping her a deep curtsey. 'He has given me my family title, in my own right. I am Countess of Salisbury.'

She laughs with pleasure and says: 'Very grand. Very royal. My dear, I am glad for you.'

I take Ursula, who is now a tall girl of thirteen years, and her younger brother Geoffrey in the royal barge down the river to L'Erber, the beautiful Plantagenet palace on the riverside, near to the Tower, that the king has returned to me. I make sure that the fire is lit in the grand hall and the flames are burning in the sconces so that when my boys come in, the place is warm and welcoming, and my new household can see, lit as brightly as players in a pageant, these York boys coming into their own.

I wait for them, standing before the huge fire of wood in the great hall, Ursula at my side, seven-year-old Geoffrey's hand in mine. Henry comes in first, as he should, kneels for my blessing and kisses me on both cheeks then steps aside for his brother Arthur. Side by side they kneel before me, their height and their strength obscured by their deference. These are boys no longer, they are young men. I have missed five, nearly six years of their lives, and no-one, not even a Tudor king, can restore that to me. This is a loss that can never be made up.

I raise Henry to his feet and I smile at my pride as he goes up and up. He is a tall, well-built young man of nearly twenty. He overtops me by a head, and I can feel the strength in his arms. 'My son,' I say, and I clear my throat so that my voice does not tremble. 'My son, I have missed you, but we are returned to one another now, and to our place in the world.'

I raise Arthur and kiss him too. At seventeen he is nearly as tall as his older brother, and broader, stronger. He is an athlete, a great rider. I remember that my cousin George Neville – Lord Bergavenny – promised me that he would make this boy into a great sportsman: 'Put him at the king's court and they will fall in love with him for his courage at the joust,' he told me.

Next in line, Reginald rises to his feet as I step towards him but though I hold him close he does not put his arms around me, he does not cling to me. I kiss him and I step back to look at him. He is tall and lean, with a narrow face as sensitive and mobile as a girl's, his brown eyes very wary for an eleven-year-old, his mouth firm as if closed by enforced silence. I think he will never forgive me for leaving him at the monastery. 'I am sorry,' I say to him. 'I didn't know how to keep you safe, I didn't even know how to feed you. I thank God that you are restored to me now.'

'You kept the others safe enough,' he says shortly, his voice unreliable, sometimes a boyish treble and sometimes cracking and going low. He glances at Geoffrey at my side, who tightens his grip on my hand when he hears the hostility in his brother's voice. 'They didn't have to live like silent hermits, alone among strangers.'

'Come now!' Henry surprisingly interrupts his brother. 'We are together again now! Our Lady Mother has won back our fortune and our title. She has rescued us from a lifetime of hardship. What's done is done.'

Ursula comes close to me, as if to defend me from Reginald's resentment, and I hold her to my side. 'You're right,' I say to Henry. 'And you're right to command your brother. You are the man of the family, you will be Lord Montague.'

He flushes with pleasure. 'I am to have the title? They give me your title too? I am to carry your family name?'

'Not yet,' I say. 'But you will have it. I shall call you Son Montague from now on.'

'Are we all to call him Montague and not Henry?' Geoffrey pipes up. 'And do I have a new name too?'

'Surely you'll be an earl at the very least,' Reginald remarks unpleasantly. 'If they don't find a princess for you to marry.'

'And will we live here now?' Ursula asks, looking round the great hall with the high painted beams and the old-fashioned fire-place in the centre of the room. She has learned a taste for good things and the life of the court.

'This will be our London house but we'll stay at court,' I tell her. 'You and I in the queen's chambers, your brother Geoffrey as the queen's page. Your brothers will continue to serve the king.'

Montague beams, Arthur clenches a fist. 'Just what I was hoping for!'

Reginald's face lights up. 'And me? Am I to come to court too?'

'You're lucky,' I tell him. 'Reginald is to go to the university!' I announce to the others, as his smile dies.

'The king himself has offered to pay your fees,' I tell him. 'You are fortunate in his favour. He is a great scholar himself, he admires the new learning. It is a great privilege. I have told him you were studying with the Carthusian brothers and so he is giving you a place at Magdalen College, Oxford. This is a great favour.'

He looks down at his feet, his dark eyelashes shielding his eyes, and I think he may be struggling not to cry. 'So I have to live away from home again,' he observes, his voice very small. 'While you are all at court. All of you together.'

'My son, it is a great privilege,' I say, a little impatiently. 'If you have the king's favour and rise through the Church who knows where you might end?'

He looks as if he might argue, but his brother interrupts him. 'Cardinal!' Montague exclaims, ruffling his hair. 'Pope!'

Reginald cannot even find a smile for his brother. 'And now you are laughing at me?'

'No! I mean it!' Montague replies. 'Why not?'

'Why not?' I agree. 'Everything is restored to us, everything is possible.'

'And what do we have?' Arthur asks. 'Exactly? Because if I am to serve the king I shall need to buy a horse, and a saddle and armour.'

'Yes, what has he given us?' Montague asks. 'God bless him for putting everything to right. What have we got?'

'Only what was our own, returned to us,' I say proudly. 'I petitioned the king for what was rightfully mine, the title and the lands that were taken from me when my brother was wrongfully executed. He agreed that my brother was no traitor, so he is restoring our fortune. It's justice, not charity.'

The boys wait, like children waiting for New Year gifts. All their lives they have known of the shadowy existence of an uncle whose name must not be mentioned, of a past so glorious that we had to conceal it, of wealth so great that we could not bear to discuss what had been lost. Now it is as if their mother's dream is proven real.

I take a breath. 'I have the earldom back,' I say. 'My family name, my title is restored to me. I shall be Countess of Salisbury.'

Montague and Arthur, who understand the scale of this

privilege, look astounded. 'He gives you, a woman, an earldom?' Montague asks.

I nod. I know that I am beaming, I cannot hide my joy. 'In my own right. And the lands. All my brother's lands are returned to us.'

'We're rich?' Reginald suggests.

I nod. 'We are. We're one of the richest families in the whole kingdom.'

Ursula gives a little gasp and clasps her hands together.

'This is ours?' Arthur confirms, looking round. 'This house?'

'It was my mother's house,' I say proudly. 'I shall sleep in her great chamber, where she lay with her husband, the king's brother. It's as big a palace as any in London. I can just remember it, when I was a little girl. I can remember living here. Now it is mine again, and you shall call it home.'

'And what country houses?' Arthur asks eagerly.

I see the avidity in his face, and I recognise my own greed and excitement. 'I'm going to build,' I promise him. 'I'm going to build a great house of brick, a castle fitted out as richly as any palace, at Warblington in Hampshire. It'll be our biggest house. And we'll have Bisham, my family house, in Berkshire, and this house in London, and a manor at Clavering in Essex.'

'And home?' Reginald asks. 'Stourton?'

I laugh. 'It's nothing compared with these,' I say dismissively. 'A little place. One of our many other houses. We have dozens of houses like Stourton.' I turn to Montague. 'I shall arrange a great marriage for you, and you shall have a house and lands of your own.'

'I'll marry,' he promises. 'Now that I have a name I can offer.'

'You'll have a title to offer your bride,' I promise him. 'Now I can look around and find someone suitable. You have something to bring to a marriage. The king himself calls me "cousin". Now we can look for an heiress whose fortune will match yours.'

He looks as if he might have a suggestion, but he smiles and keeps it to himself for the moment.

'I know who,' Arthur teases him.

At once, I am alert. 'You can tell me,' I say to Montague. 'And if she is wealthy and well-bred I will be able to arrange it. You can take your pick. There's not a family in the kingdom who would not think it an honour to be married into ours, now.'

'You've gone from pauper to princess,' Reginald says slowly. 'You must feel as if God has answered your prayers.'

'God has sent me nothing more than justice,' I say carefully. 'And we must, as a family, give thanks for that.'

Slowly, I become accustomed to being wealthy again, as I had to become accustomed to being poor. I order builders into my London home, and they start to transform L'Erber from the great palace that it is into an even more imposing house, paving the forecourt, carving beautiful wooden panels for the great hall. At Warblington I commission a castle, with a moat and a draw-bridge and a chapel and a green, everything just as my parents would have had, just like Middleham Castle in my childhood, when I had known I was born for greatness and never dreamed that it could all disappear overnight. I build the equal of any castle in the land, and I create beautiful guest rooms for when the king and court come to stay with me, their great subject in her own great castle.

Everywhere I put my coat of arms, and I have to confess every day to the sin of pride. But I don't care. I want to declare to the world: 'My brother was no traitor, my father no traitor either. This is an honourable name, this is a royal standard. I am the only countess in England holding a title in my own right. Here is my stamp upon my many houses. Here am I. Alive – no traitor. Here am I!'

My boys enter court life like the princes they are. The king immediately takes to Arthur for his courage and skill at the joust. My kinsman George Neville served my sons well when he brought them up and taught them everything they needed to know to be popular courtiers. Montague is easy and elegant in the royal rooms, Arthur is one of the bravest jousters at a court that cares for nothing more than bravery. He is one of the few men who dare ride against the king, one of the very, very few who can beat him. When Arthur unseats the King of England, he flings himself off his own horse, brushing past pages to help Henry to his feet, and Henry bellows with laughter and holds Arthur in his arms. 'Not yet, Cousin Plantagenet! Not yet!' he shouts and they roar together as if a fallen king is a great joke, and a Plantagenet standing over an unseated Tudor can only be a fine, comradely jest.

Reginald studies at the university, Ursula serves beside me in the queen's rooms at court, Geoffrey stays at the nursery rooms in L'Erber with his tutors and companions and sometimes comes to court to serve the queen. I cannot bring myself to send him away to the country, not after the grief of losing my older boys, not after the lasting pain of Reginald's exile. This boy, my youngest boy, my baby, I will keep at home. I swear I will have him by my side until he is married.

The king is desperate to go to war and determined to punish the French for their advances in Italy, determined to defend the Pope and his lands. In the summer my cousin Thomas Grey, Marquis of Dorset leads an expedition to take Aquitaine but can do nothing without the support of the queen's father, who refuses to play his part in their joint battle plans. Thomas is blamed for this and for the misconduct of his troops, and a shadow falls, once again, over his reputation as a Tudor supporter and our family.

'The fault is not in your cousins, Your Grace, but in your father-in-law,' the blunt-spoken northern lord Tom Darcy tells the king. 'He did not support me when I went on crusade. He has not supported Thomas Grey. It is your ally, not your generals, who is at fault.'

He sees me watching him, and he gives me a small wink. He knows that all my family fear the loss of Tudor favour.

'You might be right,' Henry says sulkily. 'But the Spanish king is a great general and Thomas Grey is certainly not.'

WESTMINSTER PALACE, LONDON, SUMMER 1513

Not even such a set-back can permenantly diminish the king's enthusiasm for a war against France, driven on by his conscience which assures him that he is defending the Church and by the promise of the title 'King of France'. The Pope is clever enough to know that Henry longs to win back the title that other English kings have lost, and show himself as a true king and a leader of men.

This summer the court and my boys can think of nothing but harnesses and armour, horses and provisions. The king's new advisor Thomas Wolsey proves to be uniquely able to get an army on the move, ordering the goods where they are needed, controlling the mustering of troops, commanding the smiths to forge pikes and the saddlers to make jackets of leather. The detail, the constant orders about transport, supplies and timing – which no nobleman can be bothered to follow – is all that Wolsey thinks about, and he thinks about nothing else.

The ladies of the queen's chamber sew banners, keepsakes and special shirts made from tough cloth to wear under chain mail; but Katherine, herself the daughter of a fighting queen, raised in a country at war, meets with Henry's commanders and talks to them about provisions, discipline, and the health of the troops they will take to invade France. Only Wolsey understands her concerns, and she and the almoner are often closeted together, discussing routes for the march, provisions along the way, how to establish lines of messengers and how one commander can communicate with another and be persuaded to work together.

Thomas Wolsey treats her with respect, observing that she has seen more warfare than many of the noblemen at court, since she was raised at the siege of Granada. The whole court treats her with a secret smiling pride, for everyone knows that she is with child again, her belly starting to grow hard and curved. She walks everywhere, refusing to ride, resting in the afternoons, a plump, shining confidence about her.

CANTERBURY, KENT, JUNE 1513

We set off for the coast with the army, travelling slowly through Kent and stop at Canterbury, at the glorious shrine, dripping in gold and rubics, of Thomas Becket, where we pray for victory for England.

The queen takes my hand as I kneel to pray beside her, and passes me her rosary, pressing it into my hand.

'What's this?' I whisper.

'Hold it,' she says. 'While I tell you something bad. I have to tell you something that will distress you.'

The sharp ivory crucifix digs into my palm like a nail. I think I know what she has to tell me.

'It's your cousin Edmund de la Pole,' she says gently. 'I am sorry, my dear. I am so sorry. The king has ordered that he be put to death.'

Even though I am expecting this, even though I have known it must come, even though I have waited for this news for years, I hear myself say: 'But why? Why now?'

'The king could not go to war leaving a pretender in the Tower.' I can tell from the guilt in her face that she remembers the last pretender to the Tudor throne was my brother, killed so that she would come to England and marry Arthur. 'I am so sorry, Margaret. I am so sorry, my dear.'

'He's been imprisoned for seven years!' I protest. 'Seven years and there has been no trouble!'

'I know. But the council advised it too.'

I bow my head as if in prayer, but I can find no words to pray for the soul of my cousin, dead under a Tudor axe, for the crime of being a Plantagenet.

'I hope you can forgive us?' she whispers.

Under the soaring chant of the Mass I can hardly hear her. I grip her hand. 'It's not you,' I say. 'It's not even the king. It's what anyone would do to rid themselves of a rival.'

She nods, as if she is comforted; but I put my head in my hands and know that they have not rid themselves of Plantagenets. It is impossible to be rid of us. My cousin Edmund's brother, Richard de la Pole, his heir, now the new pretender, has run away from England and is somewhere in Europe, trying to raise an army; and after him, there is another and another of us, unending.

DOVER CASTLE, KENT,
JUNE 1513

The queen says goodbye to her husband at Dover Castle and he honours her with the title of Regent of England – she will rule this country with the authority of a crowned king. She is a monarch of England, a woman born to rule. He gently rests his hand on her belly and asks her to keep his country and his baby safe until he returns.

I can think of nothing but my boys, especially my son Montague, whose duty will keep him at the king's side and whose honour will take him into the heart of any battle. I wait till his warhorse is loaded on the ships and he comes to me and bends his knee for my blessing. I am determined to say a smiling good-bye, and try to hide my fear for him.

'But take care,' I urge.

'Lady Mother, I am going to war. I am not supposed to take care. It would be a very poor war if we all rode out taking care!'

I am twisting my fingers together. 'Take care with your food at least, and don't lie on wet ground. Make sure that your squire always puts a leather cloak down first. And never take your helmet off if you are anywhere near . . .'

He laughs and takes my hands in his own. 'Lady Mother, I will come home to you!' He is young and light-hearted and thinks that he will live forever, and so he promises the thing that in truth he cannot: that nothing will ever hurt him, not even on a battle-field.

I snatch at a breath. 'My son!'

'I'll make sure Arthur is safe,' he promises me. 'And I'll come home safe and sound. Perhaps I shall capture French prisoners for ransom, perhaps I shall come home rich. Perhaps I shall win French lands and you will be able to build castles in France as well as England.'

'Just come home,' I say. 'Not even new castles matter more than the heir.'

He bends his head for my blessing and I have to let him go.

The war goes better than anyone dreams possible. The English army, under the king himself, take Therouanne, and the French cavalry flee before them. My son Arthur writes to me that his brother has ridden like a hero and has been knighted by the king, for his bravery in battle. My son Montague is now Sir Henry Pole – Sir Henry Pole! – and he is safe.

RICHMOND PALACE, WEST OF LONDON, SUMMER 1513

It is encouraging news for us in London; but far graver things are happening at home than the easy progress of the king's campaign. Almost as soon as Henry's fleet set sail, and despite the fact that the King of Scotland is sworn to a sacred permanent peace sealed by his marriage to an English princess, our own Princess Margaret, the king's sister, James IV of Scotland invades, and we have to defend the kingdom with our army in France and our king playing at commander overseas.

The only man left in England able to command is Thomas Howard, Earl of Surrey, the old dog of war that Henry left behind for his queen to deploy as she thinks best. The seventy-year-old warrior and the pregnant queen take over the presence chamber at Richmond and instead of sheets of music and plans of dances spread on the table, there are maps of England and Scotland, lists of musters, and the names of landlords who will turn out their tenants for the queen's war against Scotland. The queen's ladies go through their household men and report on their border castles.

Katherine's early years with her parents who fought for every inch of their kingdom show in every decision she and Thomas Howard make together. Though everyone left in England complains that they are guarded by an old man and a pregnant woman, I believe that these two are better commanders than those in France. She understands the dangers of a battle ground and the deploying of a troop as if it were the natural business of a princess. When Thomas Howard musters his men to march north they have a battle plan that he will attack the Scots in the north, and she will hold a second line in the Midlands, in case of his defeat. It is she who defies her condition to ride out to the army on a white horse, dressed in cloth of gold, and bawls out a speech to tell them that no nation in the world can fight like the English.

I watch her, and I can hardly recognise the homesick girl who cried in my arms at Ludlow. She is a woman indeed, she is a queen. Better than that, she is a queen militant, she has become a great Queen of England.

WESTMINSTER PALACE, LONDON, AUTUMN 1513

Their battle plan is astoundingly successful. Thomas Howard sends her the bloodstained coat of James IV. The king's own brother-in-law and fellow monarch is dead, we have widowed Princess Margaret and made her a dowager queen with a seventeen-month-old baby in her arms, and Scotland is ours for the taking.

Katherine is filled with bloodthirsty delight, and I laugh as she dances round the room, singing a battle song in Spanish. I take her hands and beg her to sit, be still and be calm; but she is completely her mother's daughter, demanding that the head of James of Scotland be sent to her, until we persuade her that an English monarch cannot be so ferocious. Instead she sends his bloodstained coat and torn banners to Henry in France, so that he shall know she has guarded the kingdom better than any regent has ever done before, that she has defeated the Scots as no-one has ever done before, and London celebrates with the court that we have a heroine queen, a queen militant, who can hold the kingdom and carry a child in her womb.

She is taken ill in the night. I am sleeping in her bed and I hear her moan before the pain breaks through her sleep. I turn and raise myself up on one elbow to see her face, thinking that she is having a bad dream, and that I will wake her. Then I feel under my bare feet the wetness in the bed, and I flinch from the sensation, jump out of bed, pull back the sheets, and see my own nightgown is red, terribly stained with her waters.

I tear to the door and fling it open, screaming for her ladies and for someone to call the midwives and the physicians, and then come back to hold her hands as she groans as the pains start to come.

It is early, but it is not too early; perhaps the baby will survive this sudden urgent, fearful rush. I hold Katherine's shoulders as she leans forward and then I sponge her face as she leans back and gasps with relief.

The midwives shout for her to push, and then suddenly they say, 'Wait! Wait!' And we hear, we all can hear, a tiny gurgling cry.

'My baby?' the queen asks wonderingly, and then they lift him, his little legs writhing, the cord dangling, and rest him on her slack, quivering belly.

'A baby boy,' someone says in quiet wonderment. 'My God, what a miracle,' and they cut the cord and wrap him tightly and then fold the warmed sheets across Katherine and put him into her arms. 'A baby boy for England.'

'My baby,' she whispers, her face alight with joy and love. She looks, I think, like a portrait of the Virgin Mary as if she held the grace of God in her arms. 'Margaret,' she says in a whisper. 'Send a message to the king . . .'

Her face changes, the baby moves just slightly, his back arches, he seems to choke. 'What's the matter?' she demands. 'What's the matter with him?'

The wet nurse who was coming forward, undoing the front of her gown, rears back as if she is suddenly afraid to touch the child. The midwife looks up from the bowl of water and the cloth and lunges for him, saying, 'Slap him on the back!' as if he has to be born and take his first breath all over again.

Katherine says: 'Take him! Save him!' and bounds forward in the bed, thrusting him out to the midwife. 'What's wrong with him? What's the matter?'

The midwife clamps her mouth over his nose and mouth, sucks and spits black bile on the floor. Something is wrong. Clearly, she does not know what to do, nobody knows what to do. The little body retches, a pool of something like oil spills from his mouth, from his nose, even from his closed eyes where little dark tears run down the tiny pale cheeks.

'My son!' Katherine cries.

They upend him like a drowned man from the moat, they slap him, they shake him, they put him over the nurse's knees and pound his back. He is limp, he is white, his fingers and little toes are blue. Clearly he is dead and slapping will not return him to life.

She falls back on the bed, she pulls the covers over her face as if she wishes she were dead too. I kneel at the side of the bed and reach for her hand. Blindly she grips me; 'Margaret,' she says from under the covers as if she cannot bear that I should see her lips framing the words. 'Margaret, write to the king and tell him that his baby is dead.'

As soon as the midwives have cleared up and gone, as soon as the physicians have given their opinion, which is nothing of any use, she herself writes to the king and sends the news by Thomas Wolsey's messengers. She has to tell Henry, the homecoming conqueror in his moment of triumph, that although he has won proof of his valour; there is no proof of his potency. He has no child.

We wait for his return; she is bathed and churched and dressed in a new gown. She tries to smile, I see her practise before a mirror, as if she has forgotten how to do it. She tries to seem joyful for his victory, glad of his return, and hopeful for their future.

He does not look closely enough to observe that she is only pretending to joy. She plays a masque of delight for him and he barely glances her way, he is so full of stories of the battle and the capture of villages. Half of his court have been awarded their spurs, you would think he had taken Paris and been crowned in Rheims; but nobody mentions that the Pope has not given him the promised title of 'Most Christian King of France'. He has ridden so far, and done so much, and won next to nothing.

To his queen he shows a sulky resentment. This is their third loss and this time he seems more puzzled than grieved. He cannot understand why he, so young, so handsome, so beloved, and this year so triumphant, should not have a child for every year of his marriage, like the Plantagenet king Edward. By this accounting he should have four children by now. So why is his nursery empty?

The boy who had everything that a prince might want, the young man who came to his throne and his bride in the same year, acclaimed by his people, cannot understand that something should go so wrong for him. I watch him and see him puzzling over disappointment, as a new and disagreeable experience. I see him seeking out the men who were with him in France to relive their triumphs, as it to assure himself that he is a man, the equal of any, superior to all; and then again and again, his glance goes to the queen as if he cannot understand how she, of the whole world, will not give him what he wants.

GREENWICH PALACE, LONDON, SPRING 1514

The court can think of nothing but when they can go to war against France again. Thomas Howard's triumph against the Scots is not forgotten – he is rewarded with the restoration of his dukedom of Norfolk. I see him coming towards us, with his dogged limp, as the queen and I and her ladies are walking beside the river one icy spring afternoon and he smiles at me and bows low to her.

'It seems I too am restored,' he says bluntly, falling in beside me. 'I am myself again.' He is no courtier, the old soldier, but he is a good friend and the most loyal subject in the kingdom. He was a henchman of my uncle King Edward, and a faithful commander for my uncle King Richard. When he asked for pardon from Henry Tudor he explained that he had done no wrong but served the king. Whoever sits on the throne has Howard's loyalty; he is as uncomplicated as a mastiff.

'He has made you duke again?' I guess. I glance towards his wife, Agnes. 'And my lady will be a duchess?'

He bows. 'Yes, Countess,' he says with a grin. 'We all have our coronets back.'

Agnes Howard beams at me.

'I congratulate you both,' I say. 'This is a great honour.' It is true. This raises Thomas Howard to be one of the greatest men in the kingdom. Dukes are only inferior to the king himself; only Buckingham – a duke with royal blood – is greater than Norfolk. But the new duke has gossip for me that takes the shine off his triumph. He catches my arm and takes a halting step beside me. 'You'll have heard that he's going to ennoble Charles Brandon too?'

'No!' I am genuinely scandalised. The man has done nothing but seduce women and amuse the king. Half the girls of the court are in love with him, including the king's youngest sister, Princess Mary, though he is nothing more than a handsome rogue. 'Why? What has he ever done to earn it?'

The old man's eyes narrow. 'Thomas Wolsey,' he says shortly.

'Why would he favour Brandon?'

'It's not that he loves Charles Brandon so much, but he wants a power to set against that of Edward Stafford, Duke of Buckingham. He wants a friend in power to help pull the great duke down.'

I take this in, glancing forward to see that the queen is out of earshot. 'Thomas Wolsey is growing very great,' I observe disap-provingly. 'And that from very small beginnings.'

'Since the king stopped taking the queen's advice he is prey to any clever talker who can put an argument together,' the duke says scathingly. 'And this Wolsey has nothing to boast of but a library of books, and the mind of a goldsmith. He can tell you the price of anything, he can tell you the names of every town in England. He knows the bribe for every member of parliament and every secret that they hide. Anything that the king desires, he can get for him, and now he gets it for him before the king even knows that he wants it. When the king listened to the queen we knew where we were: friends with Spain, enemies with France, and ruled by the nobility. Now that the king is advised by Wolsey we have no idea who is our friend or our enemy, and no idea where we're going.'

I glance ahead, to where the queen is leaning on Margery Horsman's arm. She looks a little weary already, though we have only walked for a mile.

'She used to keep him steady,' Howard grumbles in my ear. 'But Wolsey gives him whatever he wants and urges him on to want more. She's the only one that can say no to him. A young man needs guidance. She has to take back the reins, she has to guide him.'

It is true that the queen has lost her influence with Henry. She won the greatest battle that England has ever seen against the Scots but he cannot forgive her for losing the child. 'She does all that she can,' I say.

'And d'you know what we are to call him?' Howard growls.

'Call Thomas Wolsey?'

'Bishop it is now. Bishop of Lincoln, no less.' He nods at my surprise. 'God knows what that's worth to him annually. If she could only give him a son we would all be the richer for it. The king would attend to her if she gave him an heir. It's because she fails in this one thing that he cannot trust her in anything else.'

'She tries,' I say shortly. 'No woman in the world prays more for the blessing of a son. And perhaps . . .'

He raises a craggy eyebrow at my discreet hint.

'It's very early days,' I say cautiously.

'Please God,' he says devoutly. 'For this is a king without patience, and we cannot afford to wait long.'

ENGLAND, SUMMER 1514

The queen grows big with her child, riding in a litter drawn by two white mules when we go on progress. Nothing is too luxurious for this most important pregnancy.

Henry no longer comes to her bedroom at night. Of course, no good husband beds his wife during her pregnancy; but neither does he come to her for conversation or advice. Her father is refusing to go to war in France again, and Henry's fury and disappointment with Ferdinand of Aragon overflows onto Ferdinand's daughter. Even the marriage planned for Henry's little sister Princess Mary with Archduke Charles is overthrown as England turns from Spain and all things Spanish. The king swears that he will take advice from no foreigner, that no-one knows better than he what good English people desire. He scowls at the queen's Spanish ladies and pretends he cannot understand them when they bid him a courteous good morning. Katherine herself, her father, her country, are publicly insulted by her husband as she sits very still and very quietly under the cloth of estate and waits for the storm to pass, her hands folded on her rounded belly.

Henry loudly declares that he will rule England without advice or help from anyone, but in fact he does nothing; everything is read, studied and considered by Wolsey. The king barely glances at documents before scrawling his name. Sometimes he cannot even find the time to do that, and Wolsey sends out a royal command under his own seal.

Wolsey is an enthusiast for peace with the French. Even the king's current mistress is a French woman, one of Princess

Mary's maids of honour, a young woman very ill-suited for a decent court, a notorious whore from the French court. The king is dazzled by her reputation for wickedness, and seeks her out, following her around court as if he were a young hound and she a bitch in season. Everything French is in fashion, whores and ribbons and alliances alike. It seems that the king has forgotten all about his crusade and is going to ally with England's traditional enemy. I am not the only sceptical English subject who thinks that Wolsey is planning to seal the peace with a marriage – Henry's sister Princess Mary, the daintiest princess that ever was, will be sacrificed like a virgin chained on a dragon's rock to the old French king.

I suspect this; but I don't tell Katherine. I will not have her worried while she is carrying a child, perhaps even carrying a son. Fortune tellers and astrologists constantly promise the king that this time a son will be born who is certain to live. For sure, every woman in England prays that this time Katherine will be blessed and give the king his heir.

'I doubt that Bessie Blount prays for me,' she says bitterly, naming the new arrival at court whose childish blonde prettiness is much admired by everyone, including the king.

'I am certain that she does,' I say firmly. 'And I'd rather have her as the centre of attention than the French woman. Bessie loves you, and she is a sweet girl. She can't help it if the king favours her above all your other ladies. She can hardly refuse to dance with him.'

But Bessie does not refuse. The king writes her poems and he dances with her in the evenings; he teases her and she giggles like a child. The queen sits on her throne, her belly heavy, determined to rest and be calm, beating the time of the music with her heavily ringed hand, and smiles as if she is pleased to see Henry, flushed with excitement, dancing like a boy, while all the courtiers applaud his grace. When she makes the signal to leave, Bessie withdraws with the rest of us, but it is common knowledge that she sneaks back to the great hall with some of the other ladies in waiting and that they dance till dawn.

If I were her mother, Lady Blount, I should take her away from court, for what can a young woman possibly hope to gain from a love affair with the king but a season of self-importance and then a marriage to someone who will accept a royal cast-off? But Lady Blount is faraway in the west of England, and Bessie's father, Sir John, is delighted that the king admires his girl, foreseeing a river of favours, places and riches flowing in his direction.

'She is better-behaved than some would be,' I remind Katherine quietly. 'She asks for nothing, and she never says a word against you.'

'What word could she say?' she demands with sudden resentment. 'Have I not done everything a wife could do, did I not defeat Scotland while he was not even in the country? Have I not worked at the ruling of the kingdom when he cannot be bothered? Do I not read the papers from the council so that he is free to go out hunting all day? Do I not constantly choose my words to try to keep the treaty with my father when Henry would break his oath every day? Do I not sit quietly and listen while he abuses my father and my own countrymen as liars and traitors? Do I not ignore the shameful French mistress and now the new flirtation with Mistress Blount? Do I not do everything, *everything* I can, to prevent Thomas Wolsey from forcing us into an alliance with the French which will be the ruin of England my home, and Spain my motherland?'

We are both silent. Katherine has never spoken against her young husband before. But he has never before been so openly guided by his vanity and selfishness.

'And what does Bessie do that is so charming?' Katherine demands angrily. 'Write poems, compose music, sing love songs? She is witty, she is talented, she is pretty. What does this matter?'

'You know what you have not done,' I say gently. 'But you will put that right. And when he has a child he will be loving and grateful and you can bring him back into alliance with Spain, out of Thomas Wolsey's pocket and away from Mistress Blount's smiles.'

She puts her hand on her belly. 'I am doing that now,' she says. 'This time I will give him a son. God Himself knows that everything depends on it, and He will never forsake me.'

GREENWICH PALACE, LONDON, AUTUMN 1514

But three months before the baby is due, we have bad news from Scotland where the king's sister, the widowed Queen Margaret, has been fool enough to marry a fool at her court: the handsome Archibald Douglas, the Earl of Angus. In one stroke she loses her right to be regent and the care of her two-year-old son and heir, and his baby brother who is only six months old. The honeymooners hide in Stirling Castle with the babies, and the new regent of Scotland, John Stewart, the second Duke of Albany, takes power.

Henry and the whole of the north of England are anxious that Albany will make alliances with the French and turn on England. But, before the Scots can make an alliance with the French, we have beaten them to it. Henry has decided that his friendship with France will be sealed by the marriage of his little sister Princess Mary and the queen has to see her sister-in-law married to the king that she regards as an enemy of herself, her father, and both her countries.

Princess Mary is bitterly opposed to this match – the French king is nearly old enough to be her grandfather – and she comes crying into the queen's private rooms, whispering that she is in love with Charles Brandon and that she has begged the king to allow her to marry him. She asks the queen to take her part and persuade Henry that his sister can marry for love as he did.

Katherine and I share a glance over the bowed red-gold head, as the young princess cries with her face in the queen's lap. 'You are a princess,' Katherine says steadily. 'Your destiny brings great riches and power; but you were not born to marry for love.'

Henry revels in this opportunity to be dominant and kingly. I can almost see him admiring his own statesmanlike determination as he rises above the complaints of his wife and his sister and proves to them that as a man and a king he knows best. He ignores both the furiously bargaining princess and the dignified protests of his wife. He sends Princess Mary to France with a noble entourage of ladies and gentlemen of the court; my son Arthur with his growing reputation for jousting and dangerous sports is among them.

Carefully, the queen suggests that Bessie Blount might go with Princess Mary to France, and the princess at once asks pretty Bessie would she not like the chance of seeing the French court? Princess Mary knows well enough that her sister-in-law the queen would go into her confinement with a lighter heart if Bessie were not dancing with the king while she is in labour. But instantly Bessie's father refuses the honour offered to his daughter, and we know that he is obeying the king. Bessie is not to leave court.

I catch hold of her arm when I am on my way to Katherine's darkened room one day and Bessie, dressed for hunting, is running in the opposite direction.

'Bessie!'

'I can't stop, your ladyship!' she says hurriedly. 'The king is waiting for me. He has bought me a new horse and I have to go and see it.'

'I won't keep you,' I reply. Of course, I cannot keep her. No-one can exert any authority over the king's chosen favourite. 'But I wanted to remind you to say nothing against the queen. She is anxious in her confinement, and everyone gossips so. You won't forget, will you, Bessie? You wouldn't want to hurt Queen Katherine?'

'I'd never hurt her!' she flares up. 'All of us maids in waiting love her, I'd do anything to serve her. And my father told me especially to say nothing to worry the king.'

'Your father?' I repeat.

'He told me, if the king ever said anything to me, that I was to say nothing about the queen's health, but only to remark that we come from fertile stock.'

'Fertile stock?'

'Yes,' she says, pleased at remembering her father's instruction.

'Oh, did he?' I say furiously. 'Well, if your father wants a nameless bastard in his house then it's his concern.'

Bessie flushes, the quick tears coming to her eyes as she turns away from me. 'I am commanded by my father and the King of England,' she mutters. 'There's no point scolding me, your ladyship. It's not as if I can choose.'

DOVER CASTLE, KENT, AUTUMN 1514

The court turns out to escort the princess to Dover and see her party set sail. After waiting for the storms to die down, finally the horses and carts with Mary's enormous wardrobe, furniture, goods, carpets and tapestries lumber on board and finally the young princess and her ladies walk up the gangplank and stand like fashionably dressed martyrs on the poop deck and wave to those of us who are lucky enough to stay in England.

'This is a great alliance I have made,' Henry declares to the queen, and all his friends and courtiers nod. 'And your father, Madam, will regret the day that he tried to play me for a fool. He will learn who is the greater man. He will learn who will be the maker and breaker of the kingdoms of Europe.'

Katherine lowers her eyes so that he cannot see the flash of her temper. I see her grip her hands together so tightly that the rings are biting into her swollen fingers.

'I do think, my lord . . .' she begins.

'There is no need for you to think,' he overrules her. 'All you can do for England is give us a son. I have the command of my country, I do the thinking; you shall have the making of my heir.'

She sweeps him a curtsey, she manages a smile. She manages to avoid the avid gaze of the court who have just heard a princess of Spain reprimanded by a Tudor, and she turns to walk back towards Dover Castle. I go half a step behind her. When we are in the lee of the wall that overlooks the sea, she turns and takes my arm as if she needs the support.

'I am sorry,' I say inadequately, flushing for his rudeness.

She gives a little shrug. 'When I have a son . . .' she says.

GREENWICH PALACE, LONDON, AUTUMN 1514

The king is remodelling the palace of Greenwich on a grand scale. It was my cousin's, his mother's, favourite palace and I am walking with this queen where I walked with her predecessor, on the gravelled paths which run alongside the great expanse of the river, when the queen pauses and puts her hand to her belly as if she felt something deeply, powerfully move.

'Did he give you a great kick?' I ask, smiling.

She doubles up, folding like a paper queen, and blindly reaches out a hand for me. 'I have a pain. I have a pain.'

'No!' I say, and take her hand as her legs give way and she goes down. I drop to my knees beside her as her ladies come running. She looks up at me, her eyes black with fear and her face as white as one of the sails of the ships on the river, and she says: 'Say nothing! This will pass.'

At once I turn to Bessie, and to Elizabeth Bryan. 'You heard Her Grace. You two say nothing, and let's get her inside.'

We are about to lift her when she suddenly screams loudly, as if someone has run her through with a spear. At once, half a dozen yeomen of the guard dash to her, but skid to a halt when they see her on the ground. They dare not touch her, her body is sacred. They are at a loss as to what they should do.

'Fetch a chair!' I snap at them, and one runs back. They come from the palace with a wooden chair with arms and a back and we ladies help her into it. They carry the chair carefully to the palace, the beautiful palace on the river where Henry was born, the lucky palace for the Tudors, and we take her into the darkened room.

It is only half-prepared, since she is more than a month before her time, but she goes into labour despite the rules in the great book of the court. The midwives look grim; the housemaids rush in with clean linen, hot water, tapestries for the walls, carpets for the tables, all the things that were being made ready but are suddenly needed now. Her pains come long and slow, as they prepare the room around her. A day and a night later the room is perfect, but still the baby has not been born.

She leans back on the richly embroidered pillows and scans the bowed heads of her ladies as they kneel in prayer. I know that she is looking for me and I stand up and go towards her. 'Pray for me,' she whispers. 'Please, Margaret, go to the chapel and pray for me.'

I find myself kneeling beside Bessie, our hands gripped on the chancel rail. I glance sideways, and see her blue eyes are filled with tears. 'Pray God that it is a boy and comes soon,' she whispers to me, trying to smile.

'Amen,' I say. 'And healthy.'

'There is no reason, is there, Lady Salisbury, why the queen should not have a boy?'

Stoutly, I shake my head. 'No reason at all. And if anyone ever asks you, if anyone at all ever asks you, Bessie, you owe it to Her Grace to say that you know of no reason why she should not have a healthy son.'

She sits back on her heels. 'He asks,' she confides. 'He does ask.'

I am appalled. 'What does he ask?'

'He asks if the queen talks privately to her friends, to you and to her ladies. He asks if she is anxious about bearing a child. He asks if there is some secret difficulty.'

'And what do you tell him?' I ask. I am careful to keep the burn of anger out of my voice.

'I tell him I don't know.'

'You tell him this,' I say firmly. 'Tell him that the queen is a great lady – that's true, isn't it?'

Pale with concentration, she nods.

'Tell him that she is a true wife to him – that's true, isn't it?'

'Oh yes.'

'And that she serves the country as queen and serves him as a loving partner and helpmeet. He could have no better woman at his side, a princess by birth and a queen by marriage.'

'I know she is. I do know.'

'Then, if you know so much, tell him that there is no doubt that their marriage is good in the sight of God as it is before us all, and that a son will come to bless them. But he has to be patient.'

She gives a pretty little moue with her mouth and a shrug of her shoulders. 'You know, I can't tell him all that. He doesn't listen to me.'

'But he asks you? You just said that he asks you!'

'I think he asks everyone. But he doesn't listen to anyone, except perhaps the Bishop Wolsey. It's natural that he should, my lord being so wise and knowing the will of God and everything.'

'At any rate, don't tell him that his marriage is invalid,' I say bluntly. 'I would never forgive you, Bessie, if you said something like that. It would be wicked. It would be a lie. God would never forgive you for such a lie. And the queen would be hurt.'

Fervently, she shakes her head and the pearls on her new head-dress bob and shine in the candlelight. 'I never would! I love the queen. But I can only tell the king what he wants to hear. You know that as well as I.'

I go back into the confinement chamber and stay with Katherine through her labour until the pains come faster and faster and she hauls on a knotted cord and the midwives throw handfuls of pepper in her face to make her sneeze. She is gasping for breath, the tears pouring down her face, her eyes and nostrils burning with the harsh spice, as she screams in pain and with a rush of blood the baby is born. The midwife pounces on him, hauls him out like a wriggling fish, and cuts the cord. The rocker enfolds him in a pure linen cloth and then a blanket of wool, and holds him up for the queen to see. She is blinded with tears and choking with the pepper and with the pain. 'Is it a boy?' she demands.

'A boy!' they tell her, in a delighted chorus. 'A boy! A live boy!'

She reaches out to touch his little clenched fists, his kicking feet, though this time, she is afraid to hold him. But he is strong: red in the face, hollering, loud as his father, as self-important as a Tudor. She gives an amazed, delighted little laugh, and holds out her arms. 'He is well?'

'He is well,' they confirm. 'Small, because he is early, but well.'

She turns to me and gives me the great honour: 'You shall tell the king,' she says.

I find him in his rooms, playing cards with his friends Charles Brandon, William Compton and my son Montague. I am announced just ahead of a scramble of courtiers who were hoping to gather the news from the maids at the doorway and get to him with the first tidings, and he knows at once why I have come to him. He leaps to his feet, his face bright with hope. I see once more the boy I knew, the boy who always hovered between boasting and fearfulness. I curtsey and my beam, as I rise up, tells him everything.

'Your Grace, the queen has been brought to bed of a bonny boy,' I say simply. 'You have a son, you have a prince.'

He staggers, and puts his hand on Montague's shoulder to steady himself. My own son supports his king and is the first to say: 'God bless! Praise be!'

Henry's mouth is trembling, and I remember that despite his vanity he is only twenty-three, and his ostentation is a shield over his fear of failure. I see the tears in his eyes and realise he has been living under a terrible dread that his marriage was cursed, that he would never have a son, and that right now, as people outside the room cheer at the news and his comrades slap him on the back and call him a great man, a bull of a man, a stallion of a man, a man indeed, he is feeling the curse lifting from him.

'I must pray, I must give thanks,' he stammers, as if he does not know what he is saying, he does not know what he should say. 'Lady Margaret! I should give thanks, shouldn't I? I should have a Mass sung at once? This is God's blessing on me, isn't it? Proof of His favour? I am blessed. I am blessed. Everyone can see that I am blessed. My house is blessed.'

Courtiers crowd around him. I see Thomas Wolsey elbowing his way through the young men, and then sending a message for the cannons to fire and all the church bells in England to peal, and a thanksgiving Mass to be said in every church. They will light bonfires in the streets, they will serve free ale and roast meats, and the news will go out all around the kingdom that the king's line is secure, that the queen has given him a son, that the Tudor dynasty will live forever.

'She is well?' Henry asks me over the babble of comment and delighted congratulation. 'The baby is strong?'

'She is well,' I confirm. No need to tell him that she is torn, that she is bleeding terribly, that she is almost blinded by the spices they threw in her face and exhausted by the labour. Henry does not like to hear of illness; he has a horror of physical weakness. If he knew the queen was ripped and bleeding he would never bring himself to her bed again.

'The baby is lusty and strong.' I take a breath and I play my strongest card for the queen. 'He looks just like you, sire. He has hair of Tudor red.'

He gives a shout of joy and at once he is jumping round the room like a boy, pounding men on the back, embracing his friends, ebullient as a young tup in the meadow.

'My son! My son!'

'The Duke of Cornwall.' Thomas Wolsey reminds him of the title.

Someone brings in a flask of wine and slops it into a dozen cups. 'The Duke of Cornwall!' they bellow. 'God bless him! God save the king and the Prince of Wales!'

'And you will watch over the nursery?' Henry calls over his shoulder to me. 'Dear Lady Margaret? You will care for and guard my son? You are the only woman in England I would trust to raise him.'

I hesitate. I was to be Lady Governess to the first son, and I am afraid to undertake this again. But I have to consent. If I do not, it looks as if I doubt my abilities, it looks as if I doubt the health of the child that they are putting into my keeping. All the time, every day of our lives, every minute of every day, we have to act as if nothing is wrong, as if nothing can go wrong, as if the Tudors are under the exceptional blessing of God.

'You could not choose more tender care,' my son Montague says quickly as I hesitate. He gives me a look as if to remind me that I must respond, and promptly.

'I am honoured,' I say.

The king himself presses a goblet of wine into my hand. 'Dear Lady Margaret,' he says. 'You will raise the next King of England.'

And so it is me the nurse calls first, when she lifts the little baby from his golden enamelled crib and finds that he is blue and lifeless. They were in the room next door to the queen's bedroom; the nursemaid was sitting beside the cradle, watching him, but she had thought that he was very quiet. She put her hand on his soft head and felt no pulse. She put her fingers down inside his lawn nightgown and found him still warm. But he was not breathing.

He had just stopped breathing, as if some old curse had gently rested a cool hand over his little nose and mouth, and made an end to the line that killed the princes of York.

I hold the lifeless body as the nurse weeps on her knees before me, crying over and over again that she never took her eyes off him, he made not a sound, there was no way of knowing that anything was wrong – and then I put him back into his ornate crib as if I hope that he will sleep well. Without knowing what to say, I walk through the adjoining door between the nursery and the confinement room where the queen has been washed and bandaged and dressed in her nightgown, ready for the night.

The midwives are turning down the fresh sheets on the big bed, a couple of ladies in waiting are seated beside the fire, the queen herself is praying at the little altar at the corner of the room. I kneel beside her and she turns her face to me and sees my expression.

'No,' she says simply.

'I am so sorry.' For a terrible moment I think I am going to vomit, I am so sick to my belly and so filled with horror at what I have to say. 'I am so sorry.'

She is shaking her head, wordlessly, like an idiot at the fair. 'No,' she says. 'No.'

'He is dead,' I say very quietly. 'He died in his cradle while he was sleeping. Just a moment ago. I am so sorry.'

She goes white and sways backwards. I give a shout of warning and one of her ladies, Bessie Blount, catches her as she faints. We pick her up and lie her on the bed and the midwife comes to pour a bitter oil onto a cloth and clamps it to her nose and mouth. She chokes and opens her eyes and sees my face. 'Tell me it's not true. Tell me that was a terrible dream.'

'It's true,' I say, and I can feel my own face is wet with tears. 'It's true. I am so sorry. The baby is dead.'

On the other side of the bed I see Bessie's aghast face as if her worst fears have been confirmed, as she slides to her knees and bows her head in prayer.

The queen lies in her glorious bed of state for days. She should be dressed in her best, reclining on golden pillows, receiving gifts from godparents and foreign ambassadors. But nobody comes, and in any case, she would not see them. She turns her face into her pillow and lies in silence.

I am the only one who can go to her and take her cold hand and say her name. 'Katherine,' I whisper as if I am her friend and not her subject. 'Katherine.'

For a moment I think she will stay mute, but she moves a little in the bed and looks at me over her hunched shoulder. Her face is etched with pain; she seems far older than her twenty-eight years, she is like a fallen statue of sorrow. 'What?'

I pray for a word of encouragement to come to me, for a message of Christian patience, for a reminder that she has to be brave as her mother, that she is a queen and has a destiny laid on her. I think perhaps I might pray with her, or cry with her. But her face like white Carrara marble is forbidding, as she waits for me to find something to say as she lies there, curled up, clenched around her grief.

In the silence I understand that there are no words to comfort her. Nothing can be said that would bring her comfort. But still, there is something that I have to tell her. 'You've got to get up,' is all I say. 'You can't stay here. You've got to get up.'

Everyone wonders, but no-one speaks. Or perhaps: everyone wonders, but no-one speaks just yet. Katherine is churched and returns to the court and Henry greets her with a sort of coolness that is new to him. He was raised to be a boisterous boy, but she is teaching him sorrow. He was a boy confident of his own good luck, demanding of good fortune, but Katherine is teaching him doubt. Man and boy he has striven to be the best at everything he does; he has delighted in his own strength, ability and looks. He cannot bear failure in himself or in anyone near him. But now he has been disappointed by her, he has been disappointed by her dead sons, he has even been disappointed by God.

GREENWICH PALACE, LONDON, CHRISTMAS 1514

Bessie Blount goes everywhere with the king, all but hand in hand as if they were a young husband and his pretty wife. The Christmas festivities take place with a silent queen presiding over it all like one of the statues that the court delightedly shapes out of the thick snow in the white gardens. She is a perfect version of the queen, in all her finery, but cold as ice. Henry talks to his friends seated on his left at his dinner, and often he steps down from the dais and strolls around the hall with his easy, cheerful manner, speaking to one man and another, spreading the royal favour and greeted at every table with laughter and jokes. He is like the most handsome actor in a masque, drawing admiration everywhere he goes, playing the part of a handsome man, beloved by everyone.

Katherine sits still on her throne, eating almost nothing, showing an empty smile that fails to illuminate her hollow eyes. After dinner they sit side by side on their thrones to watch the entertainments and Bessie stands beside the king and leans in to hear his whispered comments, and laughs at everything he says, every single thing that he says, in a ripple of girlish laughter as meaningless as birdsong.

The court puts on a Christmas pageant and Bessie is dressed as a lady of Savoy in a blue gown with her face masked. In the dance, she and her companions are rescued by four brave masked knights, and they all dance together, the tall red-headed masked man dancing with the exquisitely graceful young woman. The queen thanks them for a delightful entertainment, and smiles and gives out little gifts, as if there is nothing that can give her more pleasure than seeing her husband dance with his mistress to the acclaim of a drunken court.

GREENWICH PALACE, LONDON, SPRING 1515

My son Arthur and the young Princess Mary do not stay long in France. Only two months after the wedding of the most beautiful princess in Christendom to the oldest king, Louis of France is dead and Princess Mary is now Dowager Queen. The English wedding party have to stay in France until they are certain that she is not with child – the scandalmongers say gleefully that she cannot be pregnant since the old king killed himself in the attempt – and then they all have to wait a few weeks longer; for the little madam has married Charles Brandon sent by the king to fetch her home, and they have to beg the king's pardon before they can return.

She was always a self-willed child, as passionate and headstrong as her brother. When I hear that she has married for love, against the wishes of the king, I smile, thinking of her mother, my cousin Elizabeth, who also fell in love and swore she would marry her choice, and of her mother who married in secret for love, and of her mother before her who was a royal duchess and married her dead husband's squire and caused a scandal. Princess Mary comes from three generations of women who believed in pleasing themselves.

Henry has been outwitted by the pair of them or perhaps, more truly, the two men were outwitted by the young woman.

Henry knew that she was head over heels in love with Charles Brandon and made his friend promise that he would escort her safely home as a widow and not dream of speaking to her of love – but as soon as Charles arrived from England, she wept and swore that she would marry him or go into a convent. Between hot tears and temper she completely seduced him, and made him marry her.

She has wrong-footed her brother too, as he cannot blame her for holding him to his word. When he insisted on the French marriage she agreed that she would marry his choice for her first husband if she might choose her second – and now she has done so. Henry is furious with her, and with his dear friend Charles, and there are many who say that Brandon is guilty of high treason for marrying a princess without permission.

'He should be beheaded,' old Thomas Howard says bluntly. 'Better men than he, far better, have gone to the block for far less. It's treason, isn't it?'

'I don't think this is a king for executions,' I say. 'And thank God for it.'

It is true. Unlike his father, Henry is a king neither for the Tower nor the block, and he craves the love and admiration of his court. Quickly, he forgives both his beloved young sister and his oldest friend, as they return to court in triumph and plan a second, public wedding in May.

It is one of the few happy events this spring, when the king and the queen are united in their affection for his naughty pretty sister, and their joy in her return to court. Apart from this, they are cool with each other and Princess Mary, the Dowager Queen of France, finds the court much changed.

'Does he not take the queen's advice at all?' she asks me. 'He never comes to her rooms like he used to do.'

I shake my head and nip off a thread from my sewing.

'Does he listen to no-one but Thomas Wolsey now?' she persists.

'No-one but Thomas Wolsey, Archbishop of York,' I say. 'And the archbishop, in his wisdom, favours the French.'

The archbishop has taken the place of the queen in Henry's private councils; he has taken the place of all the other advisors in the council chambers. He works so hard that he can gobble up the places and fees of a dozen men, and while he goes between offices and treasure rooms Henry is free to play at falling in love and the queen can do nothing but smile and pretend that she does not mind.

The king still visits Katherine's bed from the continuing need for an heir, but he takes his pleasure elsewhere. Katherine's praise means less to him now that she is no longer the beautiful widow of his older brother, the woman he was forbidden to marry. He thinks less of her father since he failed against France, he thinks less of her for not giving him an heir. They are still side by side at every dinner, of course she is honoured as Queen of England at every great event, but he is Sir Loyal Heart no longer, and everyone can see it now, not just the alert ladies of the queen's rooms and their opportunistic families.

GREENWICH PALACE, LONDON, MAY 1515

I don't like Charles Brandon; even on his official public wedding day to our Princess Mary I cannot warm to him, but that is the fault of my caution. When I see a man that everyone adores, whose ascent to the highest places in the land has been like an upward flying spark, I always wonder what he will do with all this heat and light, and whose thatch will he burn down?

'But at least this is a marriage for love for our Princess Mary,' the queen says to me as I stand behind her, holding her coronet as the lady in waiting pins her hair. It is still the rich auburn that Prince Arthur loved with just a few threads of grey.

I smile at her. 'On her side certainly there is love; but you are making the assumption that Charles Brandon has a heart.'

She shakes her head at me in smiling reproof, and the lady snatches at a falling pin. 'Oh, sorry,' the queen says and sits still. 'I see that you are not in favour of love, Lady Margaret,' she smiles. 'You have become a cold old widow.'

'I am indeed,' I say cheerfully. 'But the princess – I mean the Dowager Queen of France – has enough heart for both of them.'

'Well, I for one am glad to have her back at court,' Katherine says. 'And I'm glad that the king has forgiven his friend. They're such a handsome couple.' She slides a sidewise smile at me. Katherine is never a fool. 'The Archbishop of York, Thomas Wolsey, was in favour of the match?' she confirms.

'He was indeed,' I say. 'And I am sure Charles Brandon is grateful for his support. And I am sure it will cost him.'

She nods in silence. The king is circled by favourites like wasps around a tray of jam tarts, set on a windowsill to cool. They have to outdo each other in buzzing compliments. Wolsey and Brandon are united against my cousin the Duke of Buckingham; but every lord in the land is jealous of Wolsey.

'The king is loyal to his friends,' she observes.

'Of course,' I agree. 'He was always a most sweet-tempered boy. He never bears a grudge.'

The wedding feast is a joyous one. Mary is a favourite of everyone at court and we are glad to have her back with us, though we are all anxious as to the health and safety of her sister Margaret in Scotland. Since Margaret was widowed, and re-married a man that the Scots lords cannot accept, we all wish that she too would come home to safety.

My son Arthur comes to find me during the dancing, kisses me on both cheeks and kneels for my blessing.

'Not dancing?' I ask.

'No, for I have someone to meet you.'

I turn to him. 'No trouble?' I say quickly.

'Merely a visitor to court who wants to see you.'

He winds his way through the dancers with a smile to one and the touch of an arm to another, through an arched door and into an inner room. I go through, and there is the last person I would have expected to see: my boy Reginald, lanky as a colt, his wrists showing at the cuffs of his jacket, his boots scuffed and his shy smile. 'Lady Mother,' he says, and I put my hand on his warm head and then hold him as he springs up. 'My boy!' I say in delight. 'Ah, Reginald!'

I hold him in my arms but I feel the tension in his shoulders. He never embraces me as my two older boys do, he never clings to me like his younger brother Geoffrey. He was taught to be a diffident child; now, at fifteen years old, he is a young man made by a monastery.

'Lady Mother,' he repeats, as if he is testing the words for meaning.

'Why are you not at Oxford?' I release him. 'Does the king know you are here? Do you have permission to be away?'

'He's graduated, Lady Mother!' Arthur reassures me. 'He need not go back to Oxford ever again! He's done very well. He's completed his studies. He's triumphant. He's regarded as a very promising scholar.'

'Are you?' I ask him doubtfully.

Shyly, he ducks his head. 'I am the best Latinist in my college,' he says quietly. 'They say the best in the town.'

'That's the best in England!' Arthur declares exuberantly.

The door behind us opens, and a gust of music comes in with Montague, Geoffrey at his side. Ten-year-old Geoffrey bounds towards his older brother like an excited child and Reginald fends him off and embraces Montague.

'He debated for three days on the nature of God,' Arthur tells me. 'He's much admired. Turns out our brother is a great scholar.'

I laugh. 'Well, I am glad of it,' I say. 'And so what now, Reginald? Has the king commanded you? Are you to join the Church? What does he want you to do?'

Reginald looks at me anxiously. 'I have no calling for the Church,' he says quietly. 'So I hope you will allow me – Lady Mother . . .'

'No calling?' I repeat. 'You have lived behind the walls of an abbey since you were six years old! You have spent almost all your life as a churchman. You have been educated as a churchman. Why would you not take orders?'

'I have no vocation,' he repeats.

I turn to Montague. 'What does he mean?' I demand. 'Since when did a churchman have to be called by God? Every bishop in the land is there for the convenience of his family. Obviously he has been educated for the Church. Arthur tells me that he is well-regarded. The king himself could not have done more for him. If he takes holy orders he can be given the livings that come with our great estates and he will, no doubt, be made a bishop. And he could rise, perhaps even become an archbishop.'

'It's a matter of conscience.' Arthur interrupts his brother's answer. 'Really, Lady Mother . . .'

I go to the chair at the head of the table, seat myself and look down the long polished surface at my boys. Geoffrey follows me, and stands behind my chair looking gravely at his older brothers, as if he is my page boy, my little squire, and they are supplicants to the two of us. 'Everyone in this family serves the king,' I say flatly. 'That's the only way to wealth and power. That is safety as well as success. Arthur, you are a courtier, one of the best jousters in the court, an ornament to the court. Montague, you have won your place as a server of the body, the best position at court, and you are rising in favour; you will be a senior advisor, I know. Geoffrey will go into the king's rooms when he is a little older and will serve the king as well as any one of you. Ursula will marry a nobleman, link us to the greatest family we can obtain, and continue our line. Reginald here will be a churchman and serve the king and God. What else is possible? What else can he do?'

'I love and admire the king,' Reginald says quietly. 'And I am grateful to him. He has offered me the deanship of Wimborne Minster, a valuable place. But I don't have to take holy orders to get it, I can be a dean without being ordained. And he says he will pay for me to study abroad.'

'He does not insist you take your vows?'

'He does not.'

I am surprised. 'This is a sign of great favour,' I say. 'I would have thought he would have demanded it of you, after all he has done for you.'

'The king has read one of Reginald's essays,' Arthur explains. 'Reginald says that the Church should be served by no-one but men who have heard the call of God, not men that hope to rise in the world by using the Church as their ladder. The king was very impressed. He admires Reginald's logic, his judgement. He thinks he is both inspired and educated.'

I try to conceal my surprise at this son of mine who seems to have become a theologian rather than a priest. I cannot force him to take his vows at this stage in his life, especially if the king is willing to patronise him as a lay scholar. 'Well, so be it,' I agree. 'Very well for now. Later on, you will have to take holy orders to rise through the Church, Reginald. Don't think that you can avoid that. But for the time being you can take the deanship and study as you wish, since His Grace approves.' I glance at Montague. 'We'll collect the fees for him,' I say. 'We'll pay him an allowance.'

'I don't want to go abroad,' Reginald says very quietly. 'If you will allow me, Lady Mother, I would like to stay in England.'

I am so shocked, that for a moment I say nothing, and Arthur speaks into the silence. 'He has never lived with us since he was a child, Lady Mother. Let him study at Oxford and live at L'Erber, and spend his summers with us. He can join us when we are on progress, and when we go to Warblington or Bisham he can come with us. I am sure the king would allow it. Montague and I could ask it for Reginald. Now that he has completed his degree surely he can come home?'

Reginald, the boy I could not afford to feed or house, looks directly at me. 'I want to come home,' he says. 'I want to live with my family. It's time. It's my turn. Let me come home. I have been away from all of you for so long.'

I hesitate. To gather my family together again would be the greatest triumph of my return to wealth and favour. To have all my sons under my roof and see them working for the power and strength of our family is my dream. 'It's what I want,' I tell him. 'I have never told you, I never *will* tell you how much I missed you. Of course. But I shall have to ask the king,' I say. 'None of you will ask him. I shall ask the king and if he agrees, then that would be my dearest wish.'

Reginald flushes like a girl and I see his eyes grow suddenly dark with tears. I realise that though he may be a scholar of brilliance and promise he is still only fifteen – a boy who never had a childhood. Of course he wants to live with us all. He wants to be my beloved son once more. We have found our home again, he wants to be with us. It is right that he should be with us.

RICHMOND PALACE, WEST OF LONDON, JUNE 1515

The return of our Princess Mary as Dowager Queen of France brings an energy and beauty to a court where joy had been wearing thin. She runs in and out of the queen's rooms to show her the swirl of a new gown, or to bring a book of the new scholarship. She teaches the queen's ladies the dances that are fashionable in France, and the presence of her entourage brings all the king's young men, and the king himself, into the queen's rooms to sing and play and flirt and write poetry.

It brings the king back into his wife's company and he discovers again the charm and wit that are naturally hers. He realises once more that he is married to a beautiful, educated, amusing woman, and he is reminded that Katherine is a true princess: beautiful, admired, the finest woman at the court. Compared to the girls who throw themselves at his attention, Katherine simply shines. As the summer becomes warmer and the court starts to go boating on the river and eating dinner in the lush fields around the city of London, the king comes often to Katherine's bed and though he dances with Bessie Blount, he sleeps with his wife.

In these sunny days I take the chance to ask the king if Reginald may stay in England.

'Ah Lady Margaret, you have to say goodbye to your boy, but not for long,' he says pleasantly enough. I am walking beside him on the way back from the bowling green. Ahead of us are some of the queen's ladies dawdling along with much affected laughter and playfulness, hoping that the king notices them.

'Every kingdom in Europe is taken up with the new learning,' Henry explains. 'Everyone is writing papers, drawing plans, inventing machines, building great monuments. Every king, every duke, the lowliest lord wants scholars in his house, wants to be a patron. England needs scholars just as much as Rome does. And your son, they tell me, will be one of the greatest.'

'He is pleased to study,' I say. 'Truly, I think he has a gift. And he is grateful to you for sending him to Oxford. We all are. But surely, he can be a scholar for you at Westminster as well as anywhere else, and he can live at home.'

'Padua,' the king rules. 'Padua is where he must go. That's where everything is happening, that's where all the greatest scholars are. He needs to go there and learn all that he can, and then he can come home to us and bring the new learning to our universities, and publish his thoughts in English. He can translate the great texts that they are writing into English so that English scholars can study them. He can bring their scholarship to our universities. I expect great things of him.'

'Padua?'

'In Italy. And he can find and buy books for us and manuscripts, and translate them. He can dedicate them to me. He can found a library for me. He can direct Italian scholars to our court. He will be my scholar and servant in Padua. He will be a shining light. He will show Christendom that here in England we too are reading and studying and understanding. You know I have always loved scholarship, Lady Margaret. You know how impressed Erasmus was with me when I was just a boy! And all my tutors remarked that when I entered the Church I would be a great theologian. And a linguist too. I still write poetry, you know. If I had had the chances that Reginald has before him I don't know what I might have been. If I had been raised as he has been, as a scholar, I would want to do nothing but study.'

'You've been very good to him.' I cannot shift the king from the flattering picture of his court as a centre of the new learning and Reginald as his ambassador to an admiring world. 'But surely he need not go at once?'

'Oh, as soon as possible, I would think,' Henry says grandly. 'I will pay him an allowance and he has his fees from . . .' He turns, and Thomas Wolsey, who has been walking behind us and clearly listening, says: 'Wimborne Minster.'

'Yes, that's it. And there will be other livings he can have, Wolsey will see to it. Wolsey is so clever at giving men places and matching them to their needs. I want Reginald to be our representative; he must look like a well-regarded scholar in Padua and live like one. I am his patron, Lady Margaret, his position reflects my own scholarship. I want the world to know that I am a thoughtful man at the forefront of the new learning, a scholar-king.'

'I thank you,' I say. 'It is just that we, his family, wanted to have him home with us for a while.'

Henry takes my hand and tucks it in the crook of his arm. 'I know,' he says warmly. 'I miss my mother too, you know. I lost her when I was younger than Reginald is now. But I had to bear it. A man has to go where his destiny calls him.'

The king strolls with my hand tucked under his arm. A pretty girl goes by and flashes a radiant smile at him. I can almost feel the burn of Henry's interest as she curtseys, her fair head lowered.

'All the ladies seem to have changed their hoods,' Henry remarks. 'What is this fashion that my sister has brought in? What are they wearing these days?'

'It's the French hood,' I say. 'The Dowager Queen of France brought it back with her. I think I shall change too. It's a lot lighter and easier to wear.'

'Then Her Grace must wear them,' he says. He draws me a little closer. 'She is well, do you think? We might be lucky this time? She tells me she has missed her course.'

'It's very early days, but I hope so,' I say steadily. 'I pray so. And she prays every day for the blessing of a child, I know.'

'So why does God not hear us?' he asks me. 'Since she prays every day, and I pray every day, and you do too? And half of England as well? Why would God turn his face away from my wife and not give me a son?'

I am so horrified at him speaking this thought aloud to me, with Thomas Wolsey within earshot, that my feet stumble as if I am wading in mud. Henry slowly turns me to face him and we stand still. 'It's not wrong to ask such a question,' he insists, defensive as a child. 'It's not disloyal to Her Grace whom I love and always will. It's not to challenge God's will, so it's not heretical. All I am saying is: why can any fat fool in a village get a son and the King of England cannot?'

'You might have one now,' I say weakly. 'She might be carrying your son right now.'

'Or she might have one that dies.'

'Don't say that!'

He shoots a suspicious glance at me. 'Why not? D'you fear ill-wishing now? Do you think she is unlucky?'

I choke on my words. This young man asks me do I believe in ill-wishing when I know for a fact that his own mother cursed his father's line, and I remember very clearly going down on my knees and praying God to punish the Tudors for the harm they have done to me and mine. 'I believe in God's will,' I say, avoiding the question. 'And no woman as good and as dear and as holy as the queen could be anything but blessed.'

He is not comforted; he looks unhappy, as if I have not said enough for him. I cannot think what more he could want to hear. '*I* should be blessed,' he reminds me as if he were still a spoiled boy in a nursery that revolved around his childish will. 'It is me that should be blessed. It can't be right that I cannot have a son.'

ENGLAND, SUMMER 1515

The court goes on progress to the west, the queen travelling with them in a litter so that she does not get too tired. The king, eager as a boy, gets up at dawn every morning to go hunting, and comes back to wherever we are staying, shouting that he is starving! Starving to death! The cooks serve a huge breakfast at midday, sometimes in the hunting field where they put up a village of tents as if we were on campaign.

Thomas Wolsey travels with us, always riding a white mule as did the Lord, but his modest mount is tacked-up in the best leather of cardinal red which I don't believe was the preference of Jesus. The clerk from humble beginnings has made the greatest jump that any churchman can make, and now has a cardinal's hat and is preceded everywhere by a silver cross and a household in full livery.

'The greatest ascent possible, unless he can persuade them to make him Pope,' the queen whispers through the curtains of her litter as I ride alongside her.

I laugh, but I cannot help but wonder what answer the cardinal would make if the king asked him why God did not bless him with a son. A churchman – so near to Rome, so well-read, so high in the Church – must surely have an answer for the master who raised him up just because he could answer any question. I am certain that Henry will ask him. I am certain that his answer will be what Henry wants to hear; and I do wonder what that is.

WESTMINSTER PALACE, LONDON, AUTUMN 1515

At last we hear from Scotland. The king's sister the dowager queen Margaret has escaped from the country that she so markedly failed to rule and collapsed in a northern castle to give birth to a little girl, to be called Lady Margaret Douglas. God help the child, for her mother is in exile and her father has run back to Scotland. The dowager queen will have to make her way south to safety with her brother, and Queen Katherine sends her everything she could want for the journey.

GREENWICH PALACE, LONDON, SPRING 1516

We are preparing the queen's rooms for her confinement. Her ladies watch while the servants hang the rich tapestries from wall to wall, blotting out all light from the windows, and supervise the arranging of the gold and silver cups and plates in the cupboards. They will not be used by the queen, who will eat off her usual gold plates, but every confinement chamber has to be richly stocked to honour the prince who will be born here.

One of the ladies, Elizabeth Bryan now Carew, oversees the making of the huge bed of state with creamy white linen sheets, and the overlaying of the rich velvet spreads. She shows these careful preparations to the girls who are newly come to court; they have to know the correct rituals for the confinement of a queen. But it is no novelty to Bessie Blount and the other ladies and we go about our work quietly, without excitement.

Bessie is so subdued that I stop to ask her if she is well. She looks so troubled that I draw her into the queen's private chamber, and the dipping flame of the candle on the little altar throws her face alternately into golden light and shadows.

'It just feels like a waste of time for us, and grief for her,' she says.

'Hush!' I say instantly. 'Take care what you say, Bessie.'

'But it's obvious, isn't it? It's not just me saying it. Everyone knows.'

'Everyone knows what?'

'That she will never give him a child,' Bessie whispers.

'Nobody can know that!' I exclaim. 'Nobody can know what will happen! Perhaps this time she will give birth to a strong, bonny boy and he will be Henry Duke of Cornwall and grow to be Prince of Wales, and we will all be happy.'

'Well I hope so, I'm sure,' she replies obediently enough; but her eyes slide away from me, as if the words in her mouth mean nothing, and in a moment she slips through the arched doorway and is gone.

As soon as the rooms are prepared, the queen goes into confinement, her lips folded in a grim line of determination. I go into the familiar shadowy rooms with her and, cravenly, I confess to myself that I don't think I can bear to go through another death. If she has another son, I don't think that I can find the courage to take him into my care. My fears have become so great that they have quite drowned out any hopes. I have become convinced that she will give birth to a dead child, or that any baby she has will die within days.

I feel only more gloomy when the king calls me to his side after Prime one morning, and walks with me in the early morning darkness back to the shadowy confinement chamber. 'The queen's father, King Ferdinand, has died,' he says to me shortly.

'I don't think we should tell her while she's in confinement. Do you?'

'No,' I say instantly. There is an absolute rule that a queen in confinement should be kept from bad news. Katherine adored her father, though nobody can deny that he was a hard master to his little daughter. 'You can tell her after the birth. She must not be distressed now.'

'But my sister Margaret went into confinement in fear of her life from the rebels,' he complains. 'She barely got over the border to take refuge. And yet she had a healthy girl.'

'I know,' I say. 'Her Grace the Queen of Scotland is a brave woman. But nobody could doubt the courage of our queen.'

'And she is well?' he asks, as if I am a physician, as if my assurance counts for anything.

'She is well,' I say stoutly. 'I am confident.'

'Are you?'

There is only one answer that he wants to hear. Of course I say it: 'Yes.'

I try to act as if I am confident as I greet her brightly every morning and kneel beside her at the grille where the priest comes three times a day to pray. When he asks for God's blessing on the fertility of the mother and the health of the baby I say 'Amen' with conviction, and sometimes I feel her hand creep into mine as if she seeks assurance from me. I always take her fingers in a firm grip. I never allow a shadow of doubt in my eyes, never a hesitant word from my mouth. Even when she whispers to me: 'Sometimes, Margaret, I fear that there is something wrong.'

I never say: 'And you are right. What you fear is a terrible curse.' Instead always I look her in the eye and declare: 'Every wife in the world, every woman that I know has lost at least one baby and gone on to have more. You come from a fertile family and you are young and strong, and the king is a man among men. Nobody can doubt his vigour and his strength, nobody can doubt that you are fertile as your emblem, the pomegranate. This time, Katherine, this time I am certain.'

She nods. I see her staunch little smile as she enforces confidence on herself. 'Then I will be hopeful,' she says. 'If you are. If you really are.'

'I am,' I lie.

It is an easier birth than the last one, and when the midwives cry out that they can see the little bloody crown of the head, and Katherine clutches at my arm, I have a moment when I think, perhaps this is a strong baby? Perhaps all will be well.

I grip her hand and tell her to wait, and then the midwives exclaim that the baby is coming, and that she must push. Katherine grits her teeth and holds back a groan of pain. She believes – some devout fool has told her – that a queen does not cry out in childbirth, and her neck is straining like the bough of a twisted tree in the effort to hold herself regally silent, as hushed as the Virgin Mary.

Then there is a cry, a loud complaining bawl, Katherine gives a hoarse sob and everyone is exclaiming that the baby is here. Katherine turns a frightened face to me and says: 'He lives?'

There is another flurry of activity, her face contorts with pain and the midwife says: 'A girl. A girl, a live girl, Your Grace.'

I am almost sick with disappointment for the queen, but then I hear the baby cry, a good loud shout, and I am overwhelmed at the thought that she lives, that there is a live child, a live child in this room that has seen so many deaths.

'Let me see her!' Katherine says.

They wrap her in scented linen and pass her to her mother, while the midwives busy themselves, and Katherine sniffs at the damp head as if she were a cat in a basket with a litter of kittens, and the baby stops crying and snuffles against her mother's neck.

Katherine freezes and looks down. 'Is she breathing?'

'Yes, yes, she's just hungry,' one of the midwives pronounces, smiling. 'Will you give her to the wet nurse, Your Grace?'

Reluctantly, Katherine hands her over to the plump woman. She does not take her eyes off the little bundle for one moment.

'Sit beside me,' she says. 'Let me watch her feed.'

The woman does as she is ordered. This is a new wet nurse, I couldn't bear to have the same woman who had fed the previous baby. I wanted everything new: new linen, new swaddling bands, new cradle, new nurse. I wanted nothing to be the same, so I am dreading what happens now, as the queen turns to me and says gravely: 'Dear Margaret, will you tell His Grace?'

This is no honour any more, I think, as I go slowly from the overheated room and step into the cold hall. Unbidden, my son Montague is waiting for me outside. I am so relieved to see him that I could weep. I take his arm.

'I thought you might want someone to walk with?' he asks.

'I do,' I say shortly.

'The baby?'

'Alive. A girl.'

He purses his lips at the thought that we may have to tell the king disagreeable news, and we walk swiftly in silence, down the hall together to the king's private rooms. He is waiting, Cardinal Wolsey at his side, his companions quiet and anxious. They do not wait with excitement and confidence any more, cups filled in their hands ready for a toast. I see Arthur among them and he nods to me, his face pale with anxiety.

'Your Grace, I am happy to tell you that you have a daughter,' I say to King Henry.

There is no mistaking the joy that leaps into his face. Anything, as long as he has got a live child on his queen. 'She is well?' he demands hopefully.

'She is well and strong. I left her at the wet nurse's breast and she is feeding.'

'And Her Grace?'

'She is well. Better than ever before.'

He comes towards me and takes my arm to speak quietly to me, so that no-one, not even the cardinal following behind, can hear. 'Lady Margaret, you've had many children . . .'

'Five,' I reply.

'All live births?'

'I lost one in the early months, once. It's usual, Your Grace.'

'I know. I know. But does this baby look strong? Can you tell? Will she live?'

'She looks strong,' I say.

'Are you sure? Lady Margaret, you would tell me if you had doubts, wouldn't you?'

I look at him with compassion. How will anyone ever find the courage to tell him anything that does not please him? How will this indulged boy ever learn wisdom in manhood if nobody ever dares to say no to him? How will he learn to judge a liar from a true man if everyone, even the truest, cannot speak a word to him that is not good news?

'Your Grace, I am telling you the truth: she looks well and strong now. What will become of her only God can say. But the queen has been safely delivered of a bonny girl, and they are both doing well this afternoon.'

'Thank God,' he says. 'Amen.' He is deeply moved, I can see it. 'Thank God,' he says again.

He turns to the waiting court. 'We have a girl!' he announces. 'Princess Mary.'

Everyone cheers; no-one reveals the slightest anxiety. No-one would dare to show the slightest doubt. 'Hurrah! God save the princess! God save the queen! God save the king!' they all say.

King Henry turns back to me with the question that I am dreading. 'And will you be her Lady Governess, my dear Lady Margaret?'

I cannot do it. I really cannot do it this time. I cannot once again lie sleepless, waiting for the gasp of shock from the nursery and the noise of running feet and the knock on my door, the white-faced girl crying that the baby has just stopped breathing, for no reason, for no reason at all, and will I come and see? And who will tell the queen?

My son Montague meets my eyes and nods. He need do nothing more to remind me that we all have to endure things we would prefer to avoid, if we are to keep our titles and our lands and our favoured place at court. Reginald has to go far away from his home, Arthur has to smile and play tennis when his back is wrenched from jousting, he has to climb back on a horse which has thrown him and laugh as if he has no fear. Montague has to lose at cards when he would rather not bet, and I have to watch over a baby whose life is unbearably uncertain.

'I shall be honoured,' I say and I make my face smile.

The king turns to Lord John Hussey. 'And will you be her guardian?' he asks him.

Lord John bows his head as if overwhelmed by the honour, but when he looks up he meets my eye, and I see in his face my own silent dread.

We christen her quickly, as if we don't dare to wait, in the chapel of the Observant Friars nearby, as if we don't dare to take her further afield in the cold wintry air. And she is confirmed in her faith in the same service, as if we can't be sure she will live long enough to make her own vows. I stand sponsor for her confirmation, taking her vows for her as if they will make her safe when the plague winds blow, when the sickly mists rise from the river, when the cold gales rattle the shutters. When I take the holy oil on my forehead and the candle in my hand I cannot help but wonder if she will live long enough for me to tell her that she was confirmed in the faith of the Church and that I stood proxy for her and prayed desperately for her little soul.

Her godmother, my cousin Catherine, carries her down the aisle, and hands her at the church door to the other godmother, Agnes Howard, Duchess of Norfolk. As the ladies file by, each one dipping a little curtsey to the royal baby, the duchess hands her back to me. She is not a sentimental woman, she does not love to hold a baby; I see her brisk nod at her stepdaughter Lady Elizabeth Boleyn. Gently, I put the little princess in the arms of her Lady Mistress,

Margaret Bryan, and I walk alongside her, wrapped in ermine against the cold wind blowing down the Thames valley, yeomen of the guard around me, the cloth of estate carried over our regal heads, and all the ladies of the baby's nursery following me.

It is a moment of greatness for me, even grandeur. I am Lady Governess of the royal baby and heir, I should be relishing this moment. But I can't revel in it. All I can do, all I want to do, is to go on my knees and pray that this baby lives longer than her poor little brothers.

ENGLAND, SUMMER 1517

The sweating sickness comes to London. The Dowager Queen of Scotland, Margaret, hopes to avoid it by travelling north, returning to her own country to rejoin her husband and son. As soon as she leaves, the king orders that the court pack up and go to Richmond, further away from the dirt and the smells and the low-lying mists of the city.

'He's gone on ahead with just a riding court,' my son Montague tells me, leaning on the doorway of my room and watching my maids go one way and another, packing all of our goods into travelling chests. 'He's terrified.'

'Hush,' I say cautiously.

'It's no secret that he's sick with fear.' Montague steps inside and closes the door behind him. 'He'd admit it himself. He has a holy terror of all diseases but the Sweat is his particular dread.'

'No wonder, since it was his father who brought it in, and it killed his brother Arthur,' I remark. 'They called it the Tudor curse even then. They said that the reign had begun in sweat and would end in tears.'

'Well, please God they were wrong,' my son says cheerfully. 'Will the queen come with us today?'

'As soon as she's ready. But she's making a pilgrimage to pray at Walsingham later in the month. You won't see her change her plans for the Sweat.'

'No, she doesn't imagine herself dying with every cough,' he says. 'Poor lady. Is she going to pray for another child?'

'Of course.'

'She still hopes for a boy?'

'Of course.'

Reports of the disease grow worse, and worse still in the telling. It is the most terrifying of sicknesses because of its speed. A man at dinnertime, reporting to his household that he is well and strong, and that they are lucky to have escaped, will complain of a headache and heat in the evening and will be dead by sunset. Nobody knows why the disease goes from one place to another, nor why it takes one healthy man but spares another. Cardinal Wolsey takes the disease and we are all prepared to hear of his death, but the cardinal survives it. Henry the king is not comforted by this; he is completely determined to escape even the breath of it.

We stay at Richmond and then one of the servers takes ill. Henry is at once plunged into terror at the thought that a boy under the wing of death handed him his meat; he thinks of the poor victim as an assassin. The whole court packs up to leave. Every head of each service is told to go through his staff and examine each one minutely, demand of every man if he has any symptoms, any heat, any pain, any faintness. Of course, everyone denies that he is ill – nobody wants to be left behind with the dying page boy at Richmond; and besides, the disease comes on so fast that by the time everyone has sworn to good health, the first of them could be taking to their beds.

We rush downriver to Greenwich where the clean air smells of salt from the sea, and the king insists that the rooms are swept and washed daily and that no-one comes too close to him. The king, who is supposed to be blessed with a healing touch, will let no-one come near him at all.

He is distracted from his fears by the Spanish, who send an embassy hoping for an alliance against France, and under their urbane scrutiny we pretend for weeks that there is nothing wrong, that the kingdom is not dogged by sickness and that our king is not terrified. As ever with the king, when he is meeting with the Spanish he prizes his Spanish wife more highly, so he is kind and attentive to the queen, listening to her advice, admiring her elegant conversation with the emissaries in their language, coming to her bed at night, resting in her clean sheets. Her dear friend Maria de Salinas has married an English nobleman, William Willoughby, and there are compliments about the natural love between the two countries. There are feasts and celebrations and jousts, and for a brief while it is like the old days; but after the Spanish visitors ride away we hear of sickness in the village of Greenwich, and the king decides that he would be safer at Windsor Castle.

This time, he shuts down the court altogether. Only the queen, a small riding court of the king's friends, and his personal doctor are allowed to travel with them. I go to my own house at Bisham and pray that the Sweat passes us by in Berkshire.

But death follows the Tudor king, just as it followed his father. The pages who serve in his bedchamber take the illness and when one of them dies, the king is certain that death is tracking him like a dark hound. He goes into hiding, leaves all his servants behind, abandons his friends and, taking only the queen and his doctor, travels from one house to another like a guilty man seeking sanctuary.

He sends outriders ahead, wherever he plans to go, and the king's doctor interrogates his hosts, asking if anyone is ill in the house, or if the Sweat has passed them by. Henry will only go to a house where he is assured that everyone is well, but even so, time and again, he has to order that the horses be saddled and they rush on, because a lady's maid complained of the heat at noon, or a child was crying with toothache. The court loses its dignity and its elegance careering from one house to another, leaving furniture, linen, even silverware behind in the confusion. The king's hosts cannot prepare for him, and when they have ordered in costly food and entertainment he declares that it is not safe, and he cannot stay. While other people rest at home, try to avoid travel, discourage strangers, and quietly, trustingly, put their faith in God, the king roams the countryside demanding safety in a dangerous world, trying to get a guarantee in an uncertain realm, as if he fears that the very air and streams of England are poison to the man whose father claimed them against their will.

In London, a leaderless city plagued with illness, the apprentices take to the streets in running riots, demanding to know: Where is the king? Where is the Chancellor? Where are the Lord Mayor and the City fathers? Is London to be abandoned? How far will the king run? Will he go to Wales? To Ireland? Beyond? Why does he not stand alongside his people and share their troubles?

The common people – fainting as they walk behind the plough, resting their burning heads on their workbenches, the brewers dropping down their malting spoons and saying they have to rest, the spinners lying down with a fever and not getting up – the common people take against the young king that they had adored. They say that he is a coward, running away from the sickness that they cannot escape, fearful of the disease that carries his name. They curse him, saying that his Tudor father brought in death and now the son abandons them to its pains.

BISHAM MANOR, BERKSHIRE, SUMMER 1517

Released from court by the king's flight, I am not required to care for Princess Mary, who is safe and well in her nursery. I can take the summer to myself, working on my own buildings, my own lands, my own farms, my own profit and – at long last – the marriage of my son Montague.

Now that we have our fortune and our name restored he is the most eligible bachelor in England. I will match him only to a great heiress whose fortune will enhance ours, or to a girl with a great name. Of course, I don't have to look very far. Montague spent his childhood in the nursery of my cousin George Neville, Lord Bergavenny, and was with his cousin Jane almost every day. The boys were educated together as young noblemen should be, they did not share lessons with the daughters of the house; but he saw her at dinner, at church, and at the great feast days and holidays. When the dancing master came they were paired together, when the lute master played they sang duets. When the household went hunting she followed his lead over hedges and stiles. He was thoughtlessly fond of her, as young boys can be, and she set her heart on him, as silly young girls will.

When they grew older, living in the same household, travelling from one great palace to another, she emerged from the schoolroom and he saw her make that transformation, almost alchemical, from a little girl, a playmate, an uninteresting creature, rather like an inferior brother, into a young woman: a thing of mystery, a beauty.

It is Montague who asks me what I think of a match between him and Jane. He does not demand it like a fool, for he knows what is due to his name. He suggests it, cautiously, and tells me that he likes her better than any other young woman he has seen at court.

I ask: 'Better than Bessie Blount?' who is popular with all the young men of the court for her sweetness and radiant beauty.

'Better than anyone,' he says. 'But it is for you to judge, Lady Mother.'

I think it a happy ending to a hard story. Without the help of her father, my cousin, I could not have fed my children. Now, I am happy that he should profit from his loyalty and care for me and my family by making his daughter Lady Pole, with a jointure of two hundred pounds for now and the prospect of my fortune and title after my death. In marrying my son she nets herself a great title and vast lands. And she is an heiress in her own right, she will bring a fortune as her dowry, and on the death of my cousin George she will inherit half of his wealth. My cousin George Neville is growing old and he has only two girls; it happens that Montague's fancy has lit on a great heiress and hers on him.

Their children will be Plantagenets from both sides, doubly royal, and will be ornaments to the Tudor court and supporters of their Tudor cousins. Without a doubt they will have handsome children. My son is a tall, good-looking young man of twenty-five, and his bride matches him, her fair head coming up to his shoulder. I hope she is fertile, but as my cousin George says as he signs the detailed marriage contract: 'I think we can be confident – eh, Cousin? No Plantagenets ever failed to make a son.'

'Hush,' I say without thinking as I put sealing wax into the candle flame and impress it with the insignia on my ring, the white rose.

'Actually, the king remarks on it himself. He asks everyone why a man as lusty and strong and handsome as himself should not have a son in the nursery by now. Three or four sons in the nursery by now. What do you think? Is it some weakness in the queen? She comes from good breeding stock, after all. What can be wrong? Can it be that the marriage is not blessed?'

'I won't hear of it.' I make a gesture with my hand as if to halt an army of whispers. 'I won't hear of it, and I won't speak of it. And I tell all her ladies that they are not to discuss it. Because if it were to be true: what would happen? She's still his wife, baby or no baby, she's still Queen of England. She bears all the pain and sorrow of their losses, must she bear the blame as well? To gossip about it and to slander her can only make it worse for her.'

'Would she ever step aside?' he asks very softly.

'She can't,' I say simply. 'She believes that God called her to be Queen of England and made great and terrible changes so that she took the crown beside the king. She has given him a princess, and God willing they will have a son. Otherwise, what are we saying? That a marriage should end because a man does not have a son in eight years? In five years? Is a wife to be a leasehold that he can cancel on quarter day? It is "in sickness and in health, till death us do part", it is not "until I have doubts".'

My cousin smiles. 'She has a staunch defender in you,' he says.

'You should be glad of it.' I gesture at the contract. 'Your daughter will marry my son and they will swear to be parted only by death. Only if marriage lasts without doubt till death can your daughter, or any woman, be sure of her future. The queen would not overthrow the safety of every woman in England by agreeing that a husband can put a wife aside at will. She would be no good queen to the women of England if she did that.'

'He has to have an heir,' he points out.

'He can name his heir,' I point out. I allow myself the smallest of smiles. 'After all, there are heirs,' I say. My cousin's daughter is marrying one of them, my son Montague. 'There are many heirs.'

My cousin is silent for a moment as he thinks of how close we are to the throne. 'The return of the Plantagenets,' he says very quietly. 'Ironic, if after all this it should come back to one of us.'

WARBLINGTON CASTLE, HAMPSHIRE, SPRING 1518

Christmas comes and goes; but the king does not return to his capital city, nor does he summon the court to his feast. I visit the baby princess in her nursery at Greenwich and find the palace free from any disease and the little girl chattering and playing and learning to dance.

I spend a happy week with Mary, hand-clasped, obeying her imperious demands to dance up and down the long galleries, while it grows colder and colder and finally snows outside the windows that overlook the river. She is an adorable child, and I leave her with a pile of gifts and the promise to return soon.

The queen writes that they have moved to Southampton, so they can buy provisions that come in from the Flanders merchants; the king does not want English goods, fearing that they are contaminated. He will not let his hosts' servants go to the town market.

We see no-one but the king's closest friends that he cannot do without. The king will not even receive letters from the City for fear of the disease. Cardinal Wolsey writes to him on special paper from Richmond Palace and is living there, ruling like a king himself. He hears pleas from all over the country and decides on them in the royal presence chamber, seated on a throne. I have urged the king to return home to Westminster and open the court for Easter but the cardinal is firmly against me, and the king listens to no-one else. The cardinal fills his letters with warnings of disease and the king thinks it safer to stay away.

I burn the queen's letter to me, from the old habit of caution, but her words stay with me. The thought of the court of England, my family's court, hiding like outlaws from the natural lords and advisors, living near a port so they can buy food from foreigners rather than honest fare in the English markets, taking advice only from one man, and he not a Plantagenet, not even a duke, nor a lord, but a man dedicated to his own rise, troubles me very deeply as I celebrate the turn of the year at the heart of my newly built home, and ride around the fields where my people are walking behind the plough, and the ploughshare is turning over the rich earth.

I would not choose to live anywhere but on my own lands, I would not eat anything that we have not grown. I would not be served by anyone but my own people. I am a Plantagenet born and bred in the heart of my country. I would never willingly leave. So why does the king, whose father spent his life trying to get to England and risked his life to win it, not feel this deep, loving connection to his kingdom?

BISHAM MANOR, BERKSHIRE, EASTER 1518

We celebrate the feast of Easter at Bisham, with just our family. The royal court, still closed to everyone but Henry's inner circle and the cardinal, is now travelling near Oxford. I begin to wonder if they will ever come home to their capital city.

The cardinal is trusted with all the business of the realm, as no-one can see the king; he will not even receive documents. Everything goes to Wolsey and his ever-expanding household. His clerks write the royal letters, his surveyors know the price of everything, his advisors judge how things should be, and his favourite, Thomas More, who has risen to be the trusted go-between for king and cardinal, is now given the huge responsibility of the health of the court. He commands that any household in the kingdom with a sick member has to show a bundle of hay at the door so that anyone can see the sign and keep away.

People complain that the lawyer More is persecuting the poor by marking them out, but I write to the young lawyer to thank him for his care of the king and when I hear that he is ill himself, I send him a bottle of oils of my own distilling which are said to reduce fever.

'You're very generous,' my son Montague observes as he sees the carrier take a basket of precious medicines directed to Thomas More at Abingdon, near Oxford. 'I didn't know that More was a friend of ours?'

'If he's the favourite of the cardinal then he'll be close to the king,' I say simply. 'And if he's close to the king then I would want him to think kindly of us.'

My son laughs. 'We're safe now, you know,' he points out to me. 'Perhaps everyone had to buy the friendship of the court in the old days, when the old king was on the throne, but Henry's advisors are no threat to us. No-one would turn him against us now.'

'It's a habit,' I admit. 'All my life I have lived on the favour of the court. I know no other way to survive.'

Since none of us is invited to the tiny court that is allowed to live with the king, my kinsmen the Nevilles and the Staffords come to stay for a sennight to celebrate the end of Lent and the festival of Easter. The Duke of Buckingham, Edward Stafford, my second cousin, brings with him his son, Henry, sixteen years old and a bright, charming boy. My boy Geoffrey is only three years his junior and the two cousins take a liking to each other and disappear for a whole day at a time, riding at the ring in the jousting arena, hawking, even fishing in the cold water of the Thames and bringing home a fat salmon which they insist on cooking themselves in the kitchen, to the outrage of the cook.

We indulge their pride, and have trumpeters announce the arrival of the dish in the dining room, where it is carried shoulder-high in triumph, and the three hundred people of our combined households who sit down to dinner in my great hall rise to their feet and applaud the noble salmon and the grinning young fishermen.

'Have you heard when the court will return?' George Neville asks Edward Stafford when dinner is over and we cousins and our boys are seated in my private chamber and at ease with wine and sweetmeats before the fire.

His face darkens. 'If the cardinal has his way, he will keep the king apart from his court forever,' he says shortly. 'I am ordered not to come to him. Banned from court? Why would such a thing be? I am well, my household is well. It's nothing to do with illness, it is that the cardinal fears the king will listen to me – that's why I am barred from attending on him.'

'My lords,' I say carefully. 'Cousins. We must watch our words.'

George smiles at me and puts his hand over mine. 'You're always cautious,' he says. To the duke he nods. 'Can't you just go to the king, even without permission, and tell him that the cardinal is not serving his interests? Surely, he'd listen to you. We're a great family of the realm, we have nothing to gain by causing trouble, he can trust our advice.'

'He doesn't listen to me,' Edward Stafford says irritably. 'He doesn't listen to anyone. Not to the queen, not to me, not to any of the great men of the realm who carry blood as good or better than his, and who know as well as he does, or better, how the kingdom should be ruled. And I cannot just go to him. He won't admit anyone to his court unless he is assured that they are not carrying disease. And who do you think is judge of that? Not even a doctor – the cardinal's new assistant, Thomas More!'

I nod to my sons, Montague and Arthur, to leave the room. It may be safe to speak against the cardinal; there are very few lords of the land who do not speak against him. But I would rather my sons didn't hear it. If anyone ever asks them, they can truthfully say that they heard nothing.

They both hesitate to go. 'Nobody could doubt our loyalty to the king,' Montague says for both of them.

The Duke of Buckingham gives a reluctant laugh, more like a growl. 'Nobody had better doubt mine,' he says. 'I have breeding as good as the king himself, better in fact. Who believes in loyalty to the throne more than a royal? I don't challenge the king. I never would. But I do question the motives and the advancement of that damned butcher's son.'

'I think, Lord Uncle, that the cardinal's father was a merchant?' Montague queries.

'What difference does that make to me?' Buckingham demands. 'Tinker or tailor or beggar? Since my father was a duke and his grandfather was a duke, and my great-great-great-great-grandfather was King of England?'

BISHAM MANOR, BERKSHIRE, SUMMER 1518

The king's Knight Harbinger rides up to my front door, with half a dozen yeomen of the guard riding with him, glances at the new stonework that shows my proud crest over the door of my old family home, and dismounts. His eyes travel over the newly renovated towers, the handsome retiled roofs, the meadows that run down to the wide river, the well-tilled fields, the haystacks, the gold of the wheat and the rich greenish shimmer of the barley in the fields. He counts – I know without even seeing the greed in his eyes – the wealth of my fields, the fatness of my cattle, the prosperity of this rolling vast expanse of lush countryside that I own.

'Good day,' I say, stepping out of the great door in my riding gown, a plain hood on my head, the very picture of a working landlord with great lands in her stewardship.

He bows very low, as he should. 'Your ladyship, I am sent from the king to say that he will come to stay with you for eight nights, if there is no illness in the village.'

'We are all well, thanks be to God,' I reply. 'And the king and court will be welcome here.'

'I see that you can house them,' he says, conceding the grandeur of my house. 'We've been in much more modest quarters recently. May I speak to the steward of your household?'

I turn and nod and James Upsall steps forward. 'Sir?'

'I have a list of rooms required.' The Knight Harbinger pulls a rolled scroll of paper from an inner pocket in his jacket. 'And I shall have to see every one of your stable lads and household servants. I have to see for myself that they are well.'

'Please assist the Knight Harbinger,' I say calmly to Upsall, who is bristling at this high-handed treatment. 'When will His Grace the King arrive?'

'Within the week,' the Harbinger replies, and I nod as if this is an everyday matter to me, and go quietly into my house, where I pick up my gown and run to tell Montague and Jane, Arthur and Ursula, and especially Geoffrey, that the king himself is coming to Bisham and everything must be absolutely perfect.

Montague himself rides out with the waymarkers and sets up the signs on the road to make sure that the scurriers who go ahead of the court cannot possibly get lost. Behind them will come yeomen of the guard, making sure that the countryside is safe and that there is no point where the king might be ambushed, or attacked. They come into the stables and dismount from their sweating horses and Geoffrey, who has been on faithful lookout all the morning, comes running to tell me that the guards are here so the court cannot be far behind.

We are ready. My son Arthur, who knows the king's tastes better than any of us, has ordered musicians and rehearsed them; they will play after dinner for dancing. He has arranged the loan of good horses for hunting from all our neighbours, to supplement the full stable of hunters that will come with the court. Arthur has warned our tenants that the king will ride all over their fields and woodland and any damage to crops will be settled up when the visit is over. They are strictly forbidden to complain before then. The tenants have been primed to cheer the king and shout blessings whenever they see him; they may not present complaints or requests. I have sent my steward to every local market to buy up delicacies and cheeses, while Montague sends his own man to London to raid the cellar at L'Erber for the best wines.

Ursula and I set the groom of the ewery to bring out the very best of linen for the two best bedrooms, the king's room on the west side of the building and the queen's at the east. Geoffrey runs errands from one room to another, from one tower to another, but even he, in his boyish glee, is not more excited than I that the King of England will sleep under my roof, that everyone will see that I am restored to my place, in the home of my forefathers, and that the King of England is a visiting friend.

It is odd that the best part of it, the best moment – after all the work of preparation and the boastful joy – is when Geoffrey stands by my side as I help Katherine out of her litter and see her face radiant, and she clings to me as if she were my little sister and not my queen, and whispers in my ear: 'Margaret! Guess why I am in a litter and not riding?'

And when I hesitate, afraid to say what I am suddenly, wildly hoping, she laughs aloud and hugs me again. 'Yes! Yes! It's true. I am with child.'

It is clear they have been happy together, away from the court, the place-servers and flatterers banned from the king's presence. She has been attended by only a few of her ladies – no flirtatious girls. For a full year they have lived like a private couple with only a handful of friends and companions. Henry has been starved of the constant flood of attention and praise and it has done him good. In the absence of others they have enjoyed each other's company. Whenever Henry pays attention to Katherine she blooms under the warmth of his affection, and he discovers again the steady wisdom and the genuine learning of the charming woman that he married for love.

'Except I am afraid the king is neglecting his rule,' she says.

'Neglecting?'

Nobody could be a better judge of monarchy than Katherine of Aragon; she was raised to believe that ruling a kingdom is a holy duty to pray for last thing at night, and think of as you wake. When Henry was a little boy, he felt the same but he has grown to be casual with the work of kingship. When the queen was regent for England she met with her councillors every day, consulted the experts, took advice from the great lords and read and signed every single document that was released from the court. When Henry came home he devoted himself to hunting.

'He leaves all the work to the cardinal,' she says. 'And I am afraid that some of the lords may feel that they have been ignored.'

'They have been ignored,' I say bluntly.

She lowers her eyes. 'Yes, I know,' she concedes. 'And the cardinal is well rewarded for his work.'

'What is he getting now?' I demand. I can hear the irritation in my own voice. I smile, and touch her sleeve. 'Forgive me, I too think that the cardinal rules too widely and is paid too much.'

'Favourites are always expensive,' she smiles. 'But this new honour will cost the king little. It is from the Holy Father. The cardinal is to be made a papal legate.'

I gasp. 'A papal legate? Thomas Wolsey is to rule the Church?'

She raises her eyebrows and nods.

'No-one above him but the Pope?'

'No-one,' she observes. 'At least he is a peacemaker. I suppose we should be glad of that. He is proposing a peace between us and France and the marriage of my daughter to the Dauphin.'

With quick sympathy I put my hand on hers. 'She's only two,' I say. 'That's a long way off. It might never happen; there is certain to be a quarrel with France before she has to go.'

'Yes,' she concedes. 'But the cardinal – forgive me, His Lordship the Papal Legate – always seems to get what he wants.'

Everything goes smoothly on the royal visit. The king admires the house, enjoys the hunting, gambles with Montague, rides with Arthur. The queen walks around the grounds with me, smilingly praises my presence chamber, my privy chamber, my bedroom. She recognises the joy that I take in my house, and in the knowledge that I have all my other houses returned to me. She admires my treasure room and my records room and understands that the running of this, my kingdom, is my pride and my joy.

'You were born for a great place,' she says. 'You must have had a wonderful year, organising a wedding and getting everything just as you want it here.'

When the court moves on, they will take Arthur with them. The king swears that no-one can keep up with him in the hunting field like Arthur.

'He is to make me a gentleman of the privy chamber.' Arthur comes to my room on the last night.

'A what?'

'It's a new order of the household that the king is making. All his best friends, just as we are now, but we are to be attached to the privy chamber – just like the King of France has his gentlemen. Henry wants to do whatever the King of France does. He wants to rival him. So we are to have a privy chamber and I am to be one of the very, very few gentlemen.'

'And what will your duties be?'

He laughs. 'As now, I think. To be merry.'

'And drink too much,' I supplement.

'To be merry and drink too much, and flirt with ladies.'

'And lead the king into bad ways?'

'Alas, Lady Mother, the king is a young man, and every day he seems younger. He can lead himself into bad ways, he doesn't need me as his waymarker.'

'Arthur, my boy, I know you can't stop him, but there are some young ladies who would be happy to break the heart of his wife. If you could steer him away from them . . .'

He nods. 'I know. And I know how dear she is to you, and God knows that England could not have a better queen. He would never do anything disrespectful; he loves her truly, it is just . . .'

'If you can keep the king to light pleasures, with women who remember that courtly love is a game, and that it should be played lightly, you would be doing the queen and the country a service.'

'I would always want to serve the queen. But not even William Compton, not even Charles Brandon can lead the king.' Arthur's face lightens with laughter. 'And, Mother, nothing can stop him from falling in love. It is quite ridiculous! He is the oddest mixture of lust and primness. He will see a pretty girl, a laundress in a dye shop, and he could have her for a penny. But instead he has to write a poem to her and speak words of love before he can do an act that most of us would finish and be done with in minutes on the drying green, hidden by the wet sheets.'

'Yes, and it's this that troubles the queen,' I say. 'The words of love, not the penny, not the business of minutes.'

'That's the king for you,' Arthur shrugs. 'He doesn't want the momentary pleasure, he wants words of love.'

'From a laundress in a dye shop?'

'From anyone,' Arthur says. 'He is chivalric.'

He says it as if it were an affliction, and I have to laugh.

I bid the court farewell and I don't travel with them. Instead I go to London and visit the Princess Mary for a few weeks and then on to the silk merchants, for I have much to buy. My daughter Ursula is to be married from home this autumn. I have won for her a truly great marriage and I will celebrate it as my own triumph as well as her happiness. She is to marry Henry Stafford, the son and heir of my cousin Edward, the Duke of Buckingham. She will be a duchess and one of the greatest landowners in England. We will make a new link to our cousins, the greatest ducal family in the land.

'He's a child,' she says shortly when I tell her the news. 'When he was here at Easter he was Geoffrey's little playmate.'

'He's seventeen, he's a man,' I say.

'I'm twenty years old!' she exclaims. 'I don't want to marry one of Geoffrey's little friends. Mother, how can I? How can I marry my younger brother's playmate? I will look like a fool.'

'You'll look like an heiress,' I say. 'And later on, in good time, you'll look like a duchess. You will find that a great compensation for anything you feel now.'

She shakes her head; but she knows that she has no choice, and we both know that I am right. 'And where will we live?' she asks sulkily. 'Because I can't live here with Geoffrey, and see the two of them running out to play every morning.'

'He's a young man. He will grow out of play,' I say patiently. 'But in any case you will live with the duke, his father, who will bring you to court to live in the Buckingham rooms there. I will see you there and you will continue to serve the queen when you are at court. But you'll go into dinner practically on her heels. You will outrank almost every other woman but the royal princesses.'

I see her face warm to the thought of that, and I hide a smile. 'Yes, think of it! You'll have a greater title than mine. You'll go ahead of me, Ursula.'

'Oh, will I?'

'Yes. And when you're not at court, you will live at one of His Grace's houses.'

'Where?' she asks.

I laugh. 'I don't know which one. At any one of his twelve castles, I suppose. I have provided well for you, Ursula, I have provided for you outstandingly well. You will be a wealthy young woman on your wedding day, even before your father-in-law dies, and when he does, your husband will inherit everything.'

She hesitates. 'But will the duke wait on the king any more? I thought Arthur said that it is always the papal legate who advises the king now, not the lords.'

'The Duke of Buckingham will attend court,' I assure her. 'No king can rule without the support of the great lords, not even with Thomas Wolsey doing all the work. The king knows that, his father knew that. The king will never quarrel with his great lords, that is the way to divide the country. The duke has such great lands, and so many men under his command, so many faithful tenants, that no-one can rule England without him. Of course he will go to court as one of the greatest lords of the land, and you will be respected everywhere as his daughter and the next Duchess of Buckingham.'

Ursula is no fool. She will disregard the childishness of her new husband for the riches and position that he can bring to her. And she understands something more: 'The Stafford family are directly descended from Edward III,' she observes. 'They are of royal blood.'

'No less than us,' I agree.

'If I were to have a son he would be Plantagenet on both sides,' she points out. 'Royal on both sides.'

I shrug. 'You are of the old royal family of England,' I say. 'Nothing can change that. Your son will inherit royal blood. Nothing can change that. But it is the Tudors who are on the throne, the queen is with child, if she has a boy then he is a Tudor prince – and nothing can change that either.'

I don't object to improving myself through the rise of a daughter who will be a duchess one day, because, for the first time, I have a moment's doubt about my own position at court. From the very first moment that he came to the throne, the king has done nothing but single me out for favour: raising me, restoring me to my family lands, giving me the greatest of titles, seeing that I have the best rooms at court, encouraging the queen to appoint me as a principal lady and, of course, trusting me with the future guidance and education of the princess. He could do nothing more to show to the world that I am a favoured royal kinswoman. I am one of the wealthiest lords of the country, I am by far the wealthiest woman, and the only one with a title and lands in my own right.

But some sort of shadow has fallen, though I cannot tell why. The king is less free with his smiles, less pleased to see us – me and all my wider family. Arthur remains his favourite, Montague is still in the inner circle but all the older cousins – the Duke of Buckingham, George Neville, Edward Neville – are slowly being edged out of the king's privy chamber to join the less favoured guests in the presence chamber outside.

The riding court that the king lived with for his year of exile during the Sweat has become his inner circle, a private ring of friends all his age and younger. They even have a name for themselves: they call themselves the 'minions' – the king's boon companions.

My cousins, especially Edward Stafford, Duke of Buckingham, and George Neville, are too old and too dignified to act like fools to amuse the king. There is an incident when the young men ride their horses up the stairs of the palace and canter round the presence chamber; this is supposed to be the best sport. Someone balances a jug of water over a door, and an ambassador coming on a state visit is drenched. They ambush the kitchen in a miniature military raid and capture dinner and ransom it back to the court, who have to eat it cold after the roasted meats have been speared and thrown hand to hand; nobody thinks this is funny but the young men themselves. They go into London and charge through a market and overturn the stalls, breaking the goods and spoiling the wares, they drink themselves to a standstill and vomit in the fireplaces and they pester the women servants of the court till there is not one honest woman left in the dairy.

Of course, my older kinsmen are excluded from such sports but they say that it is more serious than high spirits and young men at play. While Henry roisters with the minions, all the work of the kingdom is done by his smiling helper, Cardinal Wolsey. All the gifts and privileges and high-paying places pass through the cardinal's soft, warm hands, and many of them slide up his capacious red sleeves. Henry is in no hurry to invite grave older councillors back into his presence to question his increasing enthusiasm for another handsome young king, Francis of France, and will not hear anything about the increasing folly and extravagance of his friends.

So I am anxious he is thinking of me as one of the dull old people, and I am worried when he tells me one day that he thinks his grant to me of some of my manors in Somerset was a mistake – for they should really belong to the Crown.

'I don't think so, Your Grace,' I say at once. I glance around the young men and see my son Montague's head come up to listen, as I contradict the king.

'Sir William seems to think so,' Henry drawls.

Sir William Compton, my former suitor, gives me one of his most seductive smiles. 'Actually, they are crown lands,' he rules. Apparently he has become an expert. 'And three of them belong to the duchy of Somerset. Not to you.'

I ignore him, and turn to the king. 'I have the documents which show that they are, and always have been, in my family. Your Grace was good enough to return my own to me. I have only what is rightfully mine.'

'Oh, the family!' Sir William yawns. 'My God, that family!'

I am stunned for a moment, I don't know what to say or think. What does he mean by such a remark? Does he mean that my family, the Plantagenet family of England, are not deserving of the greatest respect? My young cousin Henry Courtenay raises his eyebrows at the insult and stares at William Compton, his hand drifting to where his sword would be, on his empty belt.

'Your Grace?' I turn to the king.

To my relief he makes a little gesture with his hand and Sir William bows, smiles, and withdraws.

'I'll have my steward look into it,' Henry says simply. 'But Sir William is quite sure that they are my lands and you have them in error.'

I am about to say, as I would be wise to say: *Oh! let me return them to you at once, now, without delay, whether they are mine by right or not* – that would be the work of a good courtier. Everything belongs to the king, we hold our fortunes at his pleasure, and if I give them to him at the first moment of asking, he might return something else to me later.

I am just about to dispossess myself when I see a quick, sly smile on Sir William's face as he turns away from my son Montague. It's a gleam of triumph between the man who knows that he is the absolute favourite, allowed all sorts of liberties, guilty of all sorts of indiscretions, to another who is younger, steadier, and a better man by far. And I feel a stubbornness rise up in me as I think I will not give my son's inheritance away because this popinjay thinks that it is not mine. It is mine. These are my family lands. I had to endure poverty without them and it was hard for me to win them back, I am damned if I am going to give them away at the bidding of such as William Compton, to a king like Henry who I watched dance around the nursery snatching his sister's moppets and refusing to share.

'I shall ask my steward Sir Thomas Boleyn to look into it and inform Sir William,' I say coolly. 'But I am certain that there is no mistake.'

I am walking away from the king's privy chamber, with a couple of my ladies in waiting, going towards the queen's rooms, when Arthur catches me up and takes my arm so that he can speak quietly, and no-one else can hear.

'Lady Mother – just give him the lands,' he says shortly.

'They are mine!'

'Everyone knows it. Doesn't matter. Just give them to him. He doesn't like to be crossed and he doesn't like to have work to do. He won't want to read a report, he doesn't want to make a judgement. Most of all he doesn't want to have to write anything and sign it.'

I stop and turn to him. 'Why would you advise me to give away your brother's inheritance? Where would we be if I had not dedicated my life to winning back what is ours?'

'He is the king, he's accustomed to having his own way,' Arthur says briefly. 'He gives Wolsey an order, sometimes he gives him nothing more than a nod, and it's done. But you and my uncle Stafford, and my uncle Neville – you all argue with him You expect him to act within a set of rules, of traditions. You expect him to explain any change. You hold him to account. He doesn't like it. He wants to be a power that is not disputed. He really can't bear being challenged.'

'They are my lands!' I have raised my voice and I glance around and then speak more quietly. 'These are my family lands that I own by right.'

'My cousin the duke would say that we own the throne by

right,' Arthur hisses. 'But he would never say it out loud before the king. We own these lands, we own the whole of England by right. But we never say such a thing, or even suggest it. Give him back the lands. Let him see that we think we have no rights, that we claim no rights, that we are nothing but his humblest subjects. That we are glad to receive only what he freely gives us.'

'He's the King of England,' I say impatiently. 'I grant you that. But his father got the throne by conquest and, some would say, treachery on the battlefield. He only held it by the skin of his teeth. He did not inherit it, he's not of the old royal blood of England. And young Henry is first among equals, he is not above us, he's not above the law, he's not above challenge. We call him "Your Grace", as we would call any duke, as we call your cousin Stafford. He is one of us, honoured; but not above us. He is not beyond challenge. His word is not that of God. He's not the Pope.'

WESTMINSTER PALACE, LONDON, NOVEMBER 1518

In November the court moves to Westminster and together the queen and I plan her confinement, ordering her favourite bed to be moved into the great chamber and choosing the tapestries which will hang over the windows, blocking out the disturbing daylight.

We are going to use the birthing bed where she had Princess Mary. I even have the same linen ready. Without saying anything, we both hope that it will bring us luck. She is busy and happy and confident, her belly curved like a fat cauldron, nearing her eighth month. We are standing side by side, considering a space in the room where we plan to place a great dresser to show her golden

plates, when she suddenly stops and pauses, as if she has heard
something, a whisper of unease.

'What is it?'

'Nothing, nothing.' She is uncertain. 'I just felt . . .'

'Should you sit down?'

I help her to her chair and she sits gingerly.

'What did you feel?'

'I felt . . .' she begins, and then she suddenly scoops the skirts
of her gown towards her, as if she would hold the baby inside her
womb by sheer force. 'Get the midwives,' she says very low and
quiet, as if she is afraid that someone might hear. 'Get the midwives, and close the door. I'm bleeding.'

We rush hot water and towels and the cradle into the room,
while I send a message to the king that the queen has gone into
labour, weeks early of course, but that she is well and we are
caring for her.

I dare to hope; little Mary is flourishing in her nursery, a
healthy clever two-year-old, and she came early. Perhaps this will
be another frighteningly small baby who will surprise us all by
strength and tenacity. And if it were to be a tough little boy . . .

It is all that we think about, and nobody says it aloud. If the
queen were to have a boy, even at this late stage of her life, even
though she has lost so many, she would be triumphant.
Everyone who has whispered that she is weak or infertile or
cursed would look a fool. The grand newly made papal legate
Wolsey himself would take second place to such a wife who had
given her husband the one thing that he lacks. The girls who
accompany the queen when she dines with the king, or walks
with him or plays cards with him, always with their eyes modestly downturned, always with their hoods pushed back to show
their smooth hair, always with their gowns pulled down in front
to show the inviting curve of their breasts, those girls will find
that the king only has eyes for the queen – if she can give him a
son.

At midnight she goes into full labour, her gaze fixed on the
holy icon, the communion wafer in the monstrance on the altar

in the corner of the room, the midwives pulling on her arms and shouting at her to push, but it is all over too quickly, and there is no little cry, just a small creature, hardly visible in a mess of blood and a rush of water. The midwife picks up the tiny body, shrouds it from the queen's sight in the linen cloth that was supposed to be used to swaddle a lusty son, and says: 'I am sorry, Your Grace, it was a girl, but she was already dead inside you. There's nothing here.'

I don't even wait for her to ask me. Wearily she turns to me and silently gives me a nod to send me on my errand, her face twisted with grief. Wearily, I get to my feet and go from the confinement chamber, down the stairs, across the great hall and up the stairs to the king's side of the palace. I dawdle past the guards who raise their pikes in a salute to let me through, past a couple of courtiers who drop into a bow and stand aside to let me by, through the outer doors of the presence chamber, through the whispering, staring crowds who are waiting and hoping to see the king. A silence falls all around as I enter the room. Everyone knows what my errand is, everyone guesses that it is bad news from my stony face, as I walk through the doors of the privy chamber, and there he is.

The king is playing at cards. Bessie Blount is his partner, there is another girl on the other side of the table, but I can't even be troubled to look. I can see from the pile of gold coins before Bessie that she is winning. This new inner court of friends and intimates, dressed in French fashions, drinking the best wine in the early morning, boisterous, noisy, childish, looks up when I come into the room, reads with perfect accuracy the defeat in my face and the droop of my shoulders. I see, I cannot miss, the avid gleam of some who scent heartbreak and know that trouble brings opportunity. I can hear, as the hubbub of the room drops to silence, someone tut with impatience as they see I have brought bad news again.

The king throws down his cards and comes quickly towards me as if he would silence me, as if he would keep this as a guilty, shameful secret. 'Is it no good?' he asks shortly.

'I am sorry, Your Grace,' I say. 'A girl, stillborn.'

For a moment his mouth turns down as if he has had to swallow something very bitter. I see his throat clench as if he would retch. 'A girl?'

'Yes. But she never breathed.'

He does not ask me if his wife is well.

'A dead baby,' is all he says, almost wonderingly. 'It is a cruel world for me, don't you think, Lady Salisbury?'

'It is a deep sorrow for you both,' I say. I can hardly make my lips frame the words. 'The queen is very grieved.'

He nods, as if it goes without saying, almost as if she deserves sorrow; but he does not.

Behind him, Bessie rises up from the table where they were playing cards while his wife was labouring to give birth to a dead child. Something about the way she turns attracts my attention. She averts her face and then she steps backwards, almost as if she were trying to slip away and avoid my notice, as if she were hiding something.

Unseen, she curtseys to the king's back and steps away, leaving her winnings as if she has quite forgotten them, and then, as she turns to sidle through the opening door, I see the curve of her belly against the ripple of the rich fabric of her gown. I see that Bessie Blount is with child, and I suppose that it is the king's.

WESTMINSTER PALACE, LONDON, WINTER 1518

I wait until the queen is ready to return to court, her grief forced down, churched, bathed and dressed. I think I will try to speak to her in the morning after Matins, as we walk back from her chapel.

'Margaret, do you not think that I can see that you are waiting to speak to me? Don't you think after all these years I can read you? Are you going to ask to go home and get your handsome boy Arthur married?'

'I will ask you that,' I agree. 'And soon. But I don't need to talk to you about it now.'

'What then?'

I can hardly bring myself to wipe the smile from her face when she is trying so hard to be merry and carefree. But she does not know quite how carefree and merry the court has become.

'Your Grace, I am afraid I have to tell you something which will trouble you.' Maria de Salinas, now Countess Willoughby, steps to her side and looks at me as if I am a traitor to bring distress to a queen who has already suffered so much.

'What now?' is all she says.

I take a breath. 'Your Grace, it is Elizabeth Blount. While you were in confinement she was with the king.'

'This is old news, Margaret.' She manages a careless laugh. 'You're a very poor gossip to bring me such an ancient scandal. Bessie is always with the king when I am with child. It's a sort of fidelity.'

Maria says a word under her breath and turns her face away.

'Yes, but – what you don't know is that now she is with child.'

'It is my husband's child?'

'I suppose so. He hasn't owned it. She's not drawing any attention to herself except that her gowns are growing tight across her belly. She didn't tell me. She is making no claims.'

'Little Bessie Blount, my own lady in waiting?'

Grimly, I nod.

She does not cry out, but turns from the gallery into an oriel window, and puts Maria's supporting hand aside with one little gesture. She looks out of the small panes of glass at the water meadows that are grey with sheets of ice and driven snow. She looks towards the cold river, seeing nothing but a memory of her mother, sobbing, face down on her pillows, breaking her heart over the infidelity of her husband, the King of Spain.

'That girl has been with me since she was twelve years old,' she says wonderingly. She finds a hard little laugh. 'Clearly, I cannot have taught her very well.'

'Your Grace, it was impossible for her to refuse the king,' I say quietly. 'I don't doubt her affection for you.'

'It's no surprise,' she says levelly, as if she were as cold as the flowers of frost on the window panes.

'No, I suppose not.'

'Does the king seem very pleased?'

'He has said nothing about it. And she's not here now. She – Bessie – withdrew from court as soon as she . . . as soon as it . . .'

'As soon as everyone could see?'

I nod.

'And where has she gone?' the queen asks without much interest.

'To a house, the Priory of St Lawrence, in the county of Essex.'

'She won't be able to give him a child!' Maria suddenly bursts out passionately. 'The child will die, for sure!'

I gasp at her words that sound like a curse. 'It cannot be any fault of the king that we have only Princess Mary!' I correct her instantly. To say anything else is to speak against the king's potency and health. I turn to my friend, the queen. 'And no fault of yours either,' I say very low. 'It must be God's will, God's will.'

The queen turns her head to look at Maria. 'Why would Bessie, so young and so healthy, not give him a child?'

'Hush, hush,' I whisper.

But Maria answers: 'Because God could not be so cruel to you!'

Katherine crosses herself and kisses the crucifix that hangs from coral rosary beads at her waist. 'I think that I have suffered greater sorrows than the birth of a bastard to little Bessie,' she says. 'And anyway, don't you know that the king will lose all interest in her now?'

GREENWICH PALACE, LONDON, MAY 1519

My cousins and the other lords of the kingdom, Thomas Howard, the old Duke of Norfolk, and his son-in-law, my steward, Sir Thomas Boleyn, meet in private with the king and papal legate Wolsey and explain that the behaviour of the wilder young men of the court reflects badly on us all. Henry, who loves the excitement and the laughter of his comrades, will hear nothing against his friends, until the older men tell him that the young courtiers on a diplomatic visit made fools of themselves in France, in front of King Francis himself.

This strikes home. Henry is still the boy who looked up to his brother Arthur, who longed to be his equal, who toddled after him on chubby legs and shouted for a horse as big as his brother's. Now he sees a new version of a glorious prince in Francis of France. He sees in him a model of elegance and style, and he wants to be like him. King Francis has a small inner circle of friends and advisors who are sophisticated and witty and highly cultured. They don't play pranks and jokes on each other, they don't cheat at cards and drink themselves sick. Henry is fired with the ambition to have a court as cosmopolitan and elegant as the French.

For once, the cardinal and the councillors are united, and they persuade Henry that the minions must go. Half a dozen of them are sent from court and told not to return. Bessie Blount has retired for her confinement and nobody even mentions her. Some of the better-behaved young courtiers, including my son Arthur and my heir Montague, are retained. The court is purged of its wilder element but my family, with our good breeding and good training, stay in place. The cardinal even remarks to me that he is glad that I visit the Princess Mary with such regularity, that she must learn from me as a model of decorum.

'It's no hardship to spend time with her,' I say, smiling. 'She is a beautiful child; it is a real pleasure to play with her. And I am teaching her letters, and how to read.'

'She could have no better Lady Governess,' he says. 'They tell me that she runs to greet you as if you were a second mother.'

'I could not love her more if she were my own,' I say. I have to stop myself repeating how bright she is, and how clever, how prettily she dances and what a good voice she has.

'Well, God bless you both,' the cardinal says airily, waving his fat fingers in a cross over my head.

WARBLINGTON CASTLE, HAMPSHIRE, JUNE 1519

I leave the newly sober and composed court to go to my favourite house and plan Arthur's marriage. It is a very good one. I would not throw my popular son Arthur away on anyone but a well-born heiress. His wife will be Jane Lewknor, the only daughter – and so the sole heiress – of a Sussex knight, a good old family and one that has amassed a fortune. She was married before and brings a good fortune from that marriage too. She has a daughter, living with her guardian, so I know she is fertile. Best of all, for Arthur, at court among the king's friends who are ready, at the drop of a glove, to write a poem about Beauty and Unattainable Virtue, she is fair-haired, grey-eyed and lovely but no fool; she will not write love poems in reply. And she is educated and well-mannered enough to serve the queen. Altogether, she is an expensive asset for the family to buy, but I think she will serve us well.

PENSHURST PLACE, KENT, JUNE 1519

The king is honouring my cousin Edward Stafford, Duke of Buckingham, with another visit to Penshurst Place, and Cousin Edward begs me to come, bring the newly-weds, and help entertain the king. It is a great moment for my cousin, but an even greater event for my daughter Ursula who finds, as I promised her, that being married to little Henry Stafford brings rewards. She stands beside her mother-in-law, Duchess Eleanor, to greet the King of England and his court and everyone tells me that she will be the most delightful duchess one day.

I expect a magnificent show but even so, I am amazed at my cousin's lavish hospitality. Every day there is a hunt and an entertainment and a picnic in the woods. There are masques and one day a bull-baiting, a fight with dogs and a bear-baiting with a magnificent beast that goes on for three hours. The duke has prepared the costumed dances and disguisings that the king loves, and commissioned music and performances. There are satirical plays that mock the ambition of Charles of Castile, who has just squandered a fortune buying the position of Holy Roman Emperor. Our king Henry, who hoped for the title for himself, laughs so hard that he nearly weeps when the play accuses Charles of greed and hubris. The queen listens to the abuse of her nephew with a tolerant smile, as if it were nothing at all to do with her.

We are awakened some mornings by a choir singing under our windows, another day boatmen call us from the lake and we row for pleasure with musicians on the boats and then gather for a tremendous regatta. The king wins the race, battling his way through the water, his face red with effort, his shoulder and chest muscles standing out under his fine linen shirt, just as he wins at cards, at tennis, at horse-racing, at wrestling, and of course at the great joust which my cousin the duke stages for the entertainment of the court and to show the skill and courage of the king and his friends. Everything is designed for the king's entertainment and amusement, not a moment of the day passes without some fresh extravagance, and Henry revels in it all, the winner of every game, a head taller than any man, as undeniably handsome as a carved statue of a prince, his hair curled, his smile wide, his body like a young god's.

'You've spent a fortune on giving the king the best visit of the year,' I observe to my cousin. 'This has been your kingdom.'

'As it happens, I have a fortune,' he replies nonchalantly. 'And this is my kingdom.'

'You have succeeded in persuading the king that this is the most beautiful and well-ordered house in England.'

He smiles. 'You speak as if that were not a triumph. For me, for my house, for my name. For your daughter too, who will inherit it all.'

'It's just that from boyhood, the king has never admired something without wanting it for himself. He's not given to disinterested joy.'

My cousin tucks my hand in the crook of his elbow and walks me past the warm sandstone walls of his lower garden towards the archery butts where we can hear the court exclaiming at the contest, and their ripple of applause at a good shot. 'You are kind to caution me, Cousin Margaret; but I don't need a warning. I never forget that this is a king whose father had nothing, who came into England with little more than the clothes on his poor back. Every time his son sees a landowner like you or me whose rights go back to Duke William of Normandy, or even earlier, he feels a little gnaw of envy, a little shiver of fear that he has not enough, that he is not enough. He wasn't raised like us, in a family who knew that their place was the greatest in England. Not like you and me, born noble, raised as princes, safe in the greatest buildings in England, looking out at the widest fields. Henry was born the son of a pretender. I think he will always feel unsteady on such a new throne.'

I press his arm. 'Take care, Cousin,' I advise. 'It's not wise for anyone, especially for those of us who once owned that throne, to speak of the Tudors as newcomers. Neither of us was raised by our father.'

The duke's father was executed for treason against King Richard, mine for treason against King Edward. Perhaps treason runs in our veins with the royal blood and it would be wise to make sure that no-one remembers it.

'Oh, it's not polite,' he concedes. 'It's true, of course. But not polite in me, as a host. But I think I have shown him what I wanted him to see. He has seen how a great lord of England lives. Not riding his horse up the stairs like a child, not throwing eggs at his tenants, not fooling like an idiot and playing all day, not promising love to ale-house maids, and sending a well-born mistress into hiding to bear a child as if one was ashamed of dirty doings.'

I can't argue with that. 'He is contradictory. He always was.'

'Vulgar,' the duke says under his breath.

We come to the outskirts of the courtiers and people turn and bow low to us, standing back so that we can see the king, who is just about to draw the bow. Henry is like a beautifully wrought statue of an archer, poised, his weight a little back, his body a long, lean line from curly russet head to outstretched leg. We stand in attentive silence as His Grace bends the heavy longbow, pulls back the string, takes careful aim and gently releases the arrow.

It flies through the air with a hiss and clips the central bull in the target, not mid-centre, but just on the edge, close – not perfect, but very close. Everyone bursts into enthusiastic applause; the queen smiles and takes up a little gold chain, ready to award it to her husband.

Henry turns to my cousin. 'Could you do better?' he shouts triumphantly. 'Could anyone do better?'

I grip the duke's hand before he can step forward and take up a bow and arrow. 'I am very sure he cannot,' I say, and the duke smiles and says: 'I doubt that anyone could outshoot Your Grace.'

Henry gives a little crow of delight and then kneels before the queen, looking up at her and beaming as she bends down to put the gold chain of victory around his neck. She kisses him on the mouth, and he puts up his hands and gently holds her face for a moment, as if he were in love with her, or at any rate, in love with the picture that they make: the young handsome man on his knee to his wife, his thick copper hair curling under her caress.

That night there is a masque, performed in the new way, with the actors coming in disguised, playing a scene and then inviting members of the court to dance with them. The king is wearing a mask over his face and a great hat, but everyone knows him at once by his height, and by the deference of the players around him. He is delighted when we all pretend that we think he is a stranger and are amazed at the grace of his dancing, and his charm. When the players break from their circle and mingle with the court, all the ladies in waiting flutter as he comes near to them. He chooses Elizabeth Carew to dance. Now that Bessie is away, there is an opportunity for another pretty girl who cares more for gifts than her good name.

I am standing behind the queen's chair when I see a small disturbance at the end of the great hall, through the heat haze of the central fire, which the duke has proudly retained here at Penshurst, keeping the old ways in his grand hall. Someone is talking urgently to one of Cardinal Wolsey's men and then the message is passed from one to another down the hall, until it reaches the lawyer Thomas More, who leans over the fat red shoulder and whispers in the attentive ear.

'Something has happened,' I say quietly to the queen.

'Find out,' she replies. I step back from her chair into the shadows of the hall and go – not to the cardinal, who has kept his seat and his bland smile, beating time to the dance as if he has heard nothing – but out of the great hall and across the courtyard, where the stable boy is holding the messenger's steaming horse, and another is taking off the sweaty saddle.

'He looks hot,' I remark, walking past as if on my way to somewhere else.

They both bow low to me. 'Nearly foundered,' complains one lad. 'I wouldn't ride a beauty like this so hard.'

I hesitate and pat the horse's damp neck. 'Poor boy. Did he have to come far?'

'From London,' the lad says. 'But the messenger is in a worse state – he rode all the way from Essex.'

'That is a long way,' I agree. 'It'll be for the king, then.'

'It is. But worth the effort. He said he would get a gold noble at the very least.'

I laugh. 'Well, you will have to reward the poor horse,' I say, and stroll past.

I turn as soon as I am out of sight and walk through the little courtyard at the side of the great hall, entering through the side door with a nod to the guards. I find Thomas More at the back of the hall, watching the dancing. He smiles and bows to me.

'So Bessie Blount has a boy,' I assert.

He has not been long enough at court to learn to veil his honest brown eyes. 'Your ladyship . . . I cannot say,' he stammers.

I smile at him. 'You don't need to say,' I tell him. 'Indeed, you didn't say,' and I return to my place beside the queen before anyone notices that I have gone.

'It's news from Bessie Blount,' I say to her. 'Compose yourself, Your Grace.'

She smiles and leans forward to clap her hands in time with the music as the king steps into the centre of the circle, puts his hands on his hips and dances a rapid jig, his feet pounding the ground.

'Tell me,' she says over the shouts of applause.

'She must have had a boy,' I say. 'The messenger was counting on a reward. The king would only pay for news of a boy. And Wolsey's man Thomas More did not deny it. He'll never make a courtier, that man, he can't lie at all.'

Her fixed smile never wavers. Henry twirls around at the burst of applause that greets the end of his dance and sees his wife jumping to her feet in her pleasure at his performance. He bows to her and leads another girl into the ring.

She sits down again. 'A boy,' she says flatly. 'Henry has a live son.'

GREENWICH PALACE, LONDON, SPRING 1520

Bessie's boy survives the first few months, though none of us ladies in the queen's rooms who have buried the half-formed bodies of Tudor princes would give thruppence for his survival. Of course nobody can say anything, but there has grown at court a wordless sense that the king cannot get boys, or, if he gets them, a woman cannot raise them. They call the poor little bastard Henry, as if we had not already buried two babies with that name. They give him the surname Fitzroy, as the king acknowledges his by-blow. Bessie is granted an allowance to raise her boy, and he is generally known, widely known, as the king's own son. There's no doubt in my mind that the man who publicly stands as his godfather, Cardinal Thomas Wolsey, encourages the gossip that spreads across the kingdom, naming the boy as the king's own in order that everyone shall hear that the king can sire a sturdy little son, and that he has done so.

Bessie comes out of confinement and finds herself promptly churched and married off to Cardinal Wolsey's ward, young Gilbert Tailboys, whose father is so weak in the head that he cannot protect his son from a wife who is used goods. Just as the queen foresaw, the king does not return to his former lover, as if birth has given him a distaste for her. As he matures the king seems to be developing a taste for either notorious beauties or unspoiled girls.

Queen Katherine says nothing: nothing about Bessie, nothing about Henry Fitzroy, nothing about Mary Boleyn, the daughter of my steward Sir Thomas, who now comes to court from France, and attracts attention for her fair prettiness. She is an inconsequential little thing, newly married to William Carey who seems to enjoy the court's admiration of his charming wife. The king singles her out, asks her to dance, promises her a good horse of her very own. She laughs at his pleasantries, admires his music, and clasps her hands in delight like a pretty child when she sees the horse. She plays the part of an innocent, and the king likes to spoil her.

'Better for me that he amuses himself with a wife rather than a maid,' the queen remarks quietly. 'It feels less . . .' She chooses her word '. . . injurious.'

'Better for us all,' I reply. 'If he has her, and gives her a son, then the bastard will be put in the Carey cradle, named Henry Carey, and we won't have another Henry Fitzroy.'

'D'you think she will have a boy as well?' she asks me with a sad little smile. 'You think Mary Boleyn can carry a Tudor boy? Birth him live? Raise him? You think that it is only I who cannot give the king a son?'

I take her hand, but I cannot look her in the eyes and see her pain. 'I didn't mean to say that, because I don't know, Your Grace. No-one can know.'

What I do know as the Lenten lilies come out along the river-bank and the blackbirds start to sing at dawn, which comes earlier every day, is that the king is certain to bed Mary Boleyn, for the affair has gone beyond little gifts – he is writing poetry. He hires a choir to sing under her window on May Day morning and the court crowns her Queen of the May. Her family – my steward Sir Thomas and his wife Elizabeth, daughter of the old Duke of Norfolk – see their pretty daughter in a new light, as a step to wealth and position, and like a pair of cheerful bawds wash her and dress her and bejewel her and present her to the king as if she were a fat little pigeon ready for the pie.

THE FIELD OF THE CLOTH OF GOLD, FRANCE, SUMMER 1520

The pinnacle of Thomas Wolsey's strategy is to be a meeting with Francis of France, a campaign of peace with tents, horses, and an invading army of courtiers bright in their new clothes, thousands upon thousands of guardsmen and groomsmen and equerries, the ladies of both courts dressed like queens, and the two queens themselves constantly changing into fresh gowns with jewel-encrusted headdresses. Wolsey plans, commissions and builds an extraordinary temporary town, set in a valley outside Calais, with a castle of fairy-tale beauty thrown up like a dream, overnight, and at the heart of it is our prince, on show like some beautiful rarity, in a setting of his advisor's making.

They call it the Field of the Cloth of Gold, for the canopies and the standards and even the tents gleam with real gold thread, and the damp fields around Calais become the dazzling centre of Christendom. Here the two greatest kings come together in a competition of beauty and strength, swearing peace, a peace that will last forever.

Henry is our golden king, as dashing and handsome and stylish as the King of France, extravagant as his father could never have been, generous in his politics, sincere in his quest for peace: everyone in his train is proud of him. And at his side, rejuvenated, beautiful, taking her place on the greatest stage in Christendom, is my friend the queen, and I am glowing with pride for her, and for them both, for the long struggle they have had to get to peace with France, prosperity in England, and a settled loving accord with each other.

It does not matter to me or to the queen that all of her ladies fold into a curtsey, almost a swoon, when the king – either king – comes by. It does not matter to me that Francis of France kisses every one of the queen's ladies except old Lady Eleanor, the Duchess of Buckingham, Ursula's fierce mother-in-law. Katherine and Queen Claude of France strike up an immediate friendship and understanding of each other. They are both married to handsome young kings; I imagine they share more difficulties than they discuss.

My sons Montague and Arthur shine in these two hotly competitive courts, Geoffrey is at my side, learning courtly manners at this, the greatest event that the world will ever see, Ursula is in attendance on the queen though she will have to go into confinement in the autumn, and one afternoon, without warning, my son Reginald comes into my private room on the queen's side of the castle, and kneels at my feet for my blessing.

I am breathless with surprise. 'My boy! Oh! My boy, Reginald.'

I raise him up and kiss him on both cheeks. He is taller than me and he has filled out; he is a handsome young man now, strong and serious, twenty years old. He has thick brown hair and dark brown eyes. Only I can see in his face the little boy that he was. Only I remember leaving him at Sheen Priory, when his lip trembled but they told him he could not speak to ask me to stay.

'Are you allowed to be here?' I ask.

He laughs. 'I am not sworn to an order,' he reminds me. 'I am not a child at school. Of course I can be here.'

'But the king . . .'

'The king expects me to study throughout Christendom. I often travel from Padua to visit a library or a scholar. He expects that. He pays for it. He encourages it. I wrote to him to tell him I would come here. I am to meet with Thomas More. We have written so much to each other and we have promised ourselves an evening of debate.'

I have to remember that my boy is now a respected theologian, a thinker, who talks with the greatest philosophers of the age. 'What will you discuss with him?' I ask. 'He's become an important man at court. He's now the king's own secretary, he writes the important letters and he leads many of the discussions about peace.'

He smiles. 'We're going to talk about the nature of the Church,' he says. 'That's what we're all talking about these days. About whether a man's conscience can teach him, or whether he is bound to rely on the teachings of the Church.'

'And what do you think?'

'I believe that Christ formed the Church to teach us, the liturgy is our lesson, and the priests and the clergy translate God to us, just as we scholars translate the teaching of Christ from Greek. There is no better guide than the Church that Christ Himself gave to us. A single man's imperfect conscience can never be superior to centuries of tradition.'

'And what does Thomas More think?'

'Mostly the same,' he says negligently, as if the subtle shades of theology are not worth discussing with his mother. 'And we cite authorities, and counter each other's arguments. You wouldn't be interested, it's quite detailed.'

'And will you be ordained?' I ask eagerly. Reginald cannot rise unless he takes holy orders, and he has been trained to lead the Church.

He shakes his head. 'Not yet,' he says. 'I don't feel that I have been called.'

'But surely, your own conscience cannot be your guide! You just said, a man must be guided by the Church.'

He laughs and nods his approval. 'Lady Mother, you are a rhetorician, I should take you with me to meet Erasmus and More. You're right. A man's conscience cannot be his guide if it is opposed to the teaching of the Church. A man cannot set himself up against his master, the Church. But the teaching of the Church itself tells me that I must wait and study until the time is right for me to be called. Then, if I am called, I will answer. If the Church requires my obedience I must serve it, as must every man, even a king.'

'And be ordained,' I press.

'Haven't I always done what you order?'

I nod. I don't want to hear that impatient tone.

'But if I am ordained I will have to serve wherever the Church sends me,' he points out. 'What if I am sent to the East? Or to the Russias? What if they send me so far away that I can never come home?'

I cannot say to this young man that the service of one's family often means that one cannot live at the heart of the family. I left him when he was a baby, to care for Arthur Tudor, and I won't attend Ursula's lying-in if the queen needs me at her side. 'Well, I hope that you will come home,' I say inadequately.

'I would want to,' is all he replies. 'I feel that I hardly know my family at all, and I have been away a long time.'

'When you have finished your studies . . .'

'Do you think the king will invite me to court and have me work for him there? Or perhaps teach at the universities?'

'I do. It's what I hope for. Whenever I can, I mention you. And Arthur keeps you in his mind. Montague too.'

'You mention me?' he asks with a slight sceptical smile. 'You find time to mention me to the king, among all the favours you request for your other boys, for Geoffrey?'

'This is a king who commands all the places and all the favours,' I say shortly. 'Of course I mention you. I mention all of you. I can hardly do more.'

Reginald stays the night and dines with the lords and his brothers. Arthur comes to see me after dinner and says that Reginald was good company, very knowledgeable and able to explain the new learning that is sweeping Christendom clearly and critically. 'He would make a wonderful tutor for the Princess Mary,' he says. 'Then he could come home.'

'Princess Mary's tutor? Oh, what a good idea! I'll suggest it to the queen.'

'You will live with the princess as her governess next year,' he considers. 'When would she be old enough for a tutor?'

'Perhaps six or seven?'

'Two years' time. Then Reginald could join you.'

'And the two of us could guide her and teach her,' I say. 'And if the queen were to give birth to a prince' – neither of us remark how unlikely that seems to be – 'then Reginald could teach him too. Your father would have been so proud to see his son as the tutor of the next King of England.'

'He would have been.' Arthur smiles at the memory of his father. 'He was proud of anything we did well.'

'And how are you, my son? You must have ridden miles with the kings. Every day they go out for sport or riding or races.'

'I'm well enough,' Arthur says, though he looks weary. 'Of course, keeping up with the king is sometimes more like work than play. But I'm a little troubled, Lady Mother. I am quarrelling with Jane's father, and so she is displeased with me.'

'What's happened?'

Arthur tells me that he has tried to persuade Jane's father to hand over his lands so that my son can be responsible for the military service that goes with ownership. Arthur is going to inherit them anyway; there is no reason for the old man to hold them now and be responsible for raising the tenants if there should be a call to war. 'He really cannot serve the king,' he says, aggrieved. 'He's too old and too frail. It was a fair offer to help him. And I offered to pay rent as well.'

'You were quite right,' I say. Nothing that adds to Arthur's landholdings could be wrong for me.

'Well, he has complained to Jane, and she thinks I am trying to steal her inheritance before his death, borrowing dead man's shoes, and she has broken a storm over my poor head. And now he has complained to our cousin Arthur Plantagenet, and to our kinsman the old Earl of Arundel, and now they are threatening to complain of me to the king. They're suggesting that I am trying to cheat the old fool out of his lands! Robbing my own father-in-law!'

'Ridiculous,' I say loyally. 'And anyway, you have nothing to fear. Henry won't listen to a word against you. Not from your own cousins. Not now. Not while he wants England to win at the jousting.'

L'ERBER, LONDON, SPRING 1521

The king's favour to my son Arthur continues. Arthur is at the centre of the sporting, gambling, drinking, whoring court. All the young men, noisy and disrespectful, who had been banned from court, have come back, one at a time, forgetting that they were prohibited and that the king was supposedly reformed. Henry does not check or reprimand them; he likes to be among them, as wild as them, as free as them. Arthur tells me that the king will let a word or a jest go by that challenges his very majesty, while my cousin the Duke of Buckingham rages that the court is more like a taproom than a place of grandeur and complains that Wolsey has brought the manners of Ipswich to Westminster.

Since they have come back from the Field of the Cloth of Gold they are worse than ever, filled with joy at their triumph, conscious of their youth and beauty like never before. It is a court of young people, raging with desire and zest for life, with no-one to halt or control them.

The queen's ladies, delighted to return to England away from the hotly competitive French court, flaunt their French fashions and practise their French dances. Some of them have even assumed French accents that I find ridiculous, but are generally regarded as very sophisticated – or as they would say themselves: *très chic*. The most exotic and certainly the vainest of them all is Anne Boleyn, sister to Mary and George who, thanks to her father's charm, has spent her childhood at the French royal courts and quite forgotten any English modesty that she might have had. With her return from France we now have Sir Thomas' full family at court: George Boleyn, his son who has served the king for almost all of his life; Elizabeth, his wife, and his newly married daughter Mary, who both serve with me in the queen's rooms.

My cousin the Duke of Buckingham is increasingly excluded from this French-mad, fashion-mad court, and he is more protective of his family dignity, for my daughter Ursula has given him a grandson, and there is a new little Henry Stafford whose cradle linen is all embroidered with ducal strawberry leaves, and the duke is proud of another generation bearing royal blood.

There is one truly terrible moment when the king, washing his hands in a golden bowl before his dinner, steps to his throne under his cloth of estate and sits as the cardinal summons the server to his side, and dips his own fingers into the same gold bowl, into the king's water. My cousin the duke bellows and knocks the bowl down, splashing water over the long red robes, raging like a madman. Henry turns at the noise, looks over his shoulder, and laughs as if it does not matter.

My cousin says something furious about how the dignity of the throne should not be usurped by upstarts and Henry's laugh stops short as he looks at my cousin. He looks at him with a long, level look as if he is thinking about something other than the spinning golden bowl which throws flashes of reflected light on the king's riding boots, the cardinal's splashed robe, my cousin's stamping feet. For a moment, we all see it: at the word 'upstart' Henry has the guarded, suspicious expression of his father.

I take leave from court for many of the days of this spring. I divide my time between supervising work on my London house, L'Erber, and staying with the Princess Mary. My duties as her Lady Governess should not really start until she enters the schoolroom but she is such a clever little girl that I want her to begin lessons early and I love to read her bedtime story, to listen to her sing, to teach her prayers and to dance with her in her rooms as my musicians play.

I am excused from court as the queen does not need me. She is happy in her rooms with her music and her reading, dining every night with the king and watching her ladies dance. She likes to know I am with her daughter, and often visits. The king is absorbed in a new flirtation but it is such a discreet affair that we only guess at it because he is writing love poetry, and every afternoon finds him bending over a blank page, nibbling at the end of his quill. Nobody knows who has caught his fancy this time. Neither the queen nor I can be troubled over the whimsical shifting of Henry's attachments; there are so many girls, and they all smile and blush when the king looks at them, and he makes such a performance of his courtship, almost as if he wanted them to be reluctant. Perhaps one goes to his rooms for a private supper; perhaps she does not come back to the queen's apartment till the early hours. Perhaps the king writes a poem or a new love song. The queen may not like it; but it hardly matters. It makes no real difference to the balance of power at court that is a deathly unstated struggle between the cardinal and the lords, between the cardinal and the queen, for the attention of the king. The girls are a diversion; they make no difference to this.

Besides, the king speaks strongly in favour of the sanctity of the holy sacrament of marriage. His sister Margaret, the Dowager Queen of Scotland, now sees the husband that she chose for love has turned into her enemy, and she wants to replace him in the country, and some say in her bed, with the Duke of Albany, her rival regent. Then we hear even worse. One of the northern lords writes to Thomas Wolsey to warn him bluntly that the king's sister is asking her lover Albany to help her to get a divorce. The old commander predicts that there will be a murder, not an annulment.

Henry is greatly offended at the suggestion of loose behaviour from his sister, and writes to her and her unwanted husband to remind them very grandly that the marriage bond is an indissoluble tie and marriage is a sacrament that no man can put asunder.

'However many laundry maids there may be,' I observe to Montague.

'Marriage is sacred,' Montague agrees with a little smile. 'It cannot be set aside. And someone has to do the washing.'

I have much to do with my London house. The great vine that sprawls across the front is pulling down the masonry and threatening the roof. I have to put up a forest of wooden scaffolding to allow the workmen to get as high as the chimneys to trim the monster, and they take up saws and hatchets to hack through the thick boughs. Of course my neighbours complain that the road is blocked, and next thing I have a letter from the Lord Mayor bidding me keep the roadways clear. I ignore it completely. I am a countess, I can block all the roads in London if I want to.

The gardeners swear to me that this hard pruning will make the vine flower and fruit and I will be bathing in my own wine come the autumn. I laugh and shake my head. We have had such cold, wet weather in the last few years that I fear we will never make wine again in England. I don't think we've had a good summer since my childhood. I seem to remember day after day of riding in glorious weather behind a great king, people coming out to wave and cheer for King Richard. We never seem to have summers like that any more. Henry never makes a long progress through sunshine and acclaim. The golden summers of my childhood have gone; no-one ever sees three suns in the sky any more.

When we take the scaffolding down, I pave the road before my house so that the foul water the scullions throw into the street can run away. I make a great central ditch in the road and tell the lads in the stables that the dung is to be swept out of our courtyard and into the stream and from thence to the river. The stink of the town house is eased, and I am certain that we have fewer rats in the kitchen and the stores. It is obvious to anyone who walks down Dowgate Street that this is one of the greatest houses in London, as grand as a royal palace.

My steward comes to me as I am admiring my new paving stones and says quietly: 'I would have a word with you, your ladyship.'

'Sir Thomas?' I turn to see Boleyn looking anxious at my elbow. 'Is something the matter?'

'I'm afraid so,' he says shortly. He glances round. 'I can't speak here.'

I am reminded, with a sudden pang of fear, of the years where no-one could speak in the street, where they checked the doors of their own houses before they would say a word. 'Nonsense!' I say roundly. 'But we may as well go inside, away from this noise.'

I lead the way into the shadowy hall and turn to the little door on the right. It is the downstairs records room for the steward of the household, so he can observe guests coming and going, receive messengers, and pay bills. There are two chairs, a table, and a double door so that no-one can eavesdrop when he is giving instructions or reprimands. 'There,' I say. 'It's quiet enough here. What's the matter?'

'It's the duke,' he says baldly. 'Edward Stafford, Duke of Buckingham.'

I seat myself in the chair behind the table, gesturing that he can sit opposite. 'You want to speak to me about my cousin?' I ask.

He nods.

I have a sort of dread of what will come next. This is Ursula's father-in-law; my grandson is in the Stafford cradle. 'Go on.'

'He's been arrested. In the Tower.'

Everything is suddenly very still, and quiet. I hear a rapid thudding noise and realise it is the sound of my heart beating, echoing in my ears. 'For what?'

'Treason.'

The one word is like the whistle of an axe in the quiet room. Boleyn looks at me, his pale face filled with dread. I know that I am absolutely impassive, my jaw clamped shut to stop my teeth chattering with fear.

'He was summoned to London, to the king at Greenwich. He was getting into his own barge, going to His Grace, when the captain of the king's yeomen stepped on board with his men and said that they were to go to the Tower. Just like that.'

'What do they say he has done?'

'I don't know,' Sir Thomas begins.

'You do know,' I insist. 'You said "treason". So tell me.'

He moistens his dry lips, swallows. 'Prophesying,' he says. 'He met with the Carthusians.'

This is no crime. I have met with the Carthusians, I worship in their chapels, we all do. They took Reginald into Sheen Priory and educated him, they raised him; they are a good order of religious men. 'Nothing wrong with that,' I say stoutly. 'Nothing wrong with them.'

'They said that they had a prophecy in their library at Sheen which says that people will acclaim the duke as king,' he goes on. 'Parliament will offer him the crown as they did to Henry Tudor.'

I bite my lip and say nothing.

'The duke is supposed to have said that the king was accursed, and that there will be no legitimate son and heir,' Sir Thomas says very quietly. 'He said that one of the queen's ladies spoke of a curse on the Tudors. One of the queen's ladies said that there would be no son.'

'Which lady? Do they have a name? For this indiscreet lady?' I can feel my hands start to tremble and I hold them together in my lap before he sees. I remember that Sir Thomas is the Duke of Norfolk's son-in-law, and it is the Duke of Norfolk as Lord High Steward who will try my cousin for treason. I wonder if Boleyn is here as my steward to warn me, or as the duke's spy to report on me. 'Who would say such a thing? Did your daughters speak of it?'

'Neither would say such a thing,' he says quickly. 'It is the duke's confessor, who has given evidence against him. And his steward, and his servants. Did your daughter ever speak of it?'

I shake my head at the riposte. The duke's steward has stayed at my house; I have prayed with his confessor. My daughter lives with the duke and discusses everything with him. 'My daughter would never hear or repeat such a thing,' I say. 'And the duke's confessor cannot speak against him. He is bound by the oath of the confessional. He cannot repeat what a man says in his prayers.'

'The cardinal now says that he can. It is a new ruling. The cardinal says that a priest's duty to the king is greater than his oath to the Church.'

I am silenced. This cannot be. The cardinal cannot change the rules that protect the confessional, that make a priest as silent as God. 'It is the cardinal gathering evidence against the duke?'

He nods. Exactly. Wolsey is destroying his rival for the king's affection and attention. This has been a long campaign. The splash of water on the robe of cardinal red left a stain that will be blotted out, blood red. Wolsey wants revenge.

'What will happen to the duke?' I don't need to ask because I know. I know the punishment for treason. Who would know better than I?

'If they find him guilty he will be beheaded,' Boleyn says quietly.

He waits while I absorb the information that I know already. Then he says something even worse. 'And, my lady, they are questioning others. They are suspicious that there is a plot. A faction.'

'Who? What others?'

'His family, his friends, his affinity.'

This is my family, these are my friends, this is my affinity. The accused is my cousin and friend, my daughter Ursula is married to his son.

'Who are they questioning, exactly?'

'His cousin and yours, George Neville.'

I take a little breath. 'Is that all?'

'His son, your son-in-law, Henry Stafford.'

Geoffrey's friend, Ursula's husband. I take a little breath. 'Anyone else?'

'Your son Montague.'

I choke. I can hardly breathe. The air in this tiny room is thick, I feel as if the walls are closing in. 'Montague is innocent,' I say stoutly. 'Has anyone named Arthur?'

'Not yet.'

We are intertwined like a plant: the *planta genista* that we are named for. My daughter Ursula is married to the duke's own son. He and I are cousins. My boys were raised in the house of my other cousin, George Neville, who is married to the duke's daughter. My son Montague is married to Cousin George's daughter. We could not be more closely related. It is the way of great families, marriage and intermarriage, working together as one force. This way we keep our wealth inside the families, concentrate our power, join our lands. But looked at with a critical eye, looked at with a suspicious, fearful eye, it gives the impression that we are a faction, a conspiracy.

At once I think of Geoffrey, serving as a page in the queen's rooms. At least his loyalty must be unquestioned. He must be safe. If Geoffrey is safe then I can face anything.

'No word against Geoffrey?' I say flatly.

He shakes his head.

'Will they question me?' I ask.

He turns just slightly away from me, a cold shoulder. 'Yes. They are bound to. If there is anything in the house ...'

'What do you mean?' I am furious with fear.

'I don't know!' he bursts out. 'I don't know! How would I know? I don't hold with prophecies and predictions and long-lost kings. I don't have giants in my family tree, like you Nevilles. I don't have three suns in the sky like you Yorks. I am not descended from a water goddess who comes out of a river to mate with mortals! When your family was founded no-one had ever heard of us. When your uncles were on the throne, mine were quiet City men. I don't know what you might have, what you might have kept from those times – a banner or a standard, a bede roll or letter. Anything that shows your descent, anything that shows your royal blood, any prophecy that you once had the throne and will have it again. But whatever you have, your ladyship, clear it out and burn it. Nothing is worth the risk of keeping.'

The first thing I do is send a message to Geoffrey and tell him to go at once to Bisham and stay there till he hears from me, to speak to no-one and to receive no-one. He is to tell the servants that he is sick, he is to give out that it might be the Sweat. If I know that he is safe then I can fight for my other sons. I send my Master of Horse to the Tower of London to discover who is behind those high grey walls, and what is being said about them.

I send one of my ladies in waiting to Ursula and tell her to take her little son and go to L'Erber and stay there until we know what we should do. I send my page boy to Arthur and say that I am coming to court at once, that I will see him there.

I send for my barge and have them take me downriver. The court is at Greenwich and I sit quietly in my seat at the back of the barge with a couple of my ladies at my side and compose myself to be patient as the high towers come into sight over the tops of the fresh green trees.

The barge ties up at the pier and the rowers make a guard of honour with their oars as I step onshore. I have to wait until they are assembled and ready, and then I walk through them with a smile, controlling my desire to run to the queen's rooms. I walk slowly up the gravelled path and hear the noise from the stables as half a dozen riders come in and shout for their grooms. A guard swings open the private garden door to the queen's stair. I nod my thanks and go up, but I don't hurry, and my breath is steady and my heartbeat regular when I get to the top.

The guards outside her door salute me and stand aside as I go in to see the queen settled in the windowseat, looking out at the garden, a beautifully embroidered linen shirt in her hands, one of her ladies reading from manuscript pages, the others sitting around and sewing. I see the Boleyn girls and their mother, I see Lord Morley's daughter Jane Parker, the Spanish ladies, Lady Hussey, half a dozen others. They rise to curtsey to me as I curtsey to the queen and then she waves them away and I kiss her on both cheeks and sit beside her.

'That's pretty,' I say, my voice light and indifferent.

She raises it up, as if to show me the detail of the black on white embroidery, so no-one can see her lips as she whispers: 'Have they taken your son?'

'Yes, Montague.'

'What's the charge?'

I grit my teeth and manage a false smile, as if we were speaking of the weather. 'Treason.'

Her blue eyes widen, but her face does not change. Anyone looking at us would think she was mildly interested in my news. 'What does this mean?'

'I think it is the cardinal, moving against the duke: Wolsey against Buckingham.'

'I will speak with the king,' she says. 'He must know this is baseless.' She hesitates as she sees my face. 'It is baseless,' she says less certainly. 'Isn't it?'

'They say that he spoke of a curse on the Tudor line,' I tell her, my voice a thread of sound. 'They say that a lady from your rooms spoke of a curse.'

She takes a little breath. 'Not you?'

'No. Never.'

'Is your son accused of repeating this curse?'

'And my cousin,' I confess. 'But, Your Grace, neither my sons, nor my son-in-law, nor my cousin George Neville have ever said or heard a word against the king. The Duke of Buckingham might be intemperate but he is not disloyal. If a great nobleman of this kingdom is going to be charged at the whim of an advisor, a man who is nothing more than one of the king's servants, a man without birth or breeding, then none of us will be safe. There is always rivalry around the throne. But a loss of favour cannot lead to death. My cousin Edward Stafford is tactless; is he to die for it?'

She nods. 'Of course. I will speak with the king.'

Ten years ago, she would have walked at once to his rooms and taken him to one side; a touch on his arm, a quick smile and he would have done what she told him. Five years ago she would have gone to his rooms, given him advice and he would have been influenced by her opinion. Even two years ago she would have waited for him to come to her rooms before dinner and then told him the right thing to do and he would have listened. But now she knows that the king may be talking with the cardinal, he may be gambling with his favourites, he may be walking in the gardens with a pretty girl on his arm, whispering in her ear, telling her he has never, never desired a woman more, that her voice is like music, that her smile is like sunlight, and he has little interest in the opinions of his wife.

'I'll wait till dinner,' she decides.

I sit with the queen until the king comes with his friends to escort her and her ladies to dinner. I plan to greet Arthur with a smile, whisper a warning, and meet with him later. But when the double doors are thrown open and Henry strides into the room, handsome, laughing, and makes his bow to the queen, Arthur does not stroll in behind him.

I curtsey, a smile pinned on my face like a mask, a cold sweat starting to trickle on my spine. They are all there: Charles Brandon, William Compton, Francis Bryan, Thomas Wyatt. Everyone that I can think of is there, none of them missing, all laughing at some private joke that they swear they will tell when it is composed into a sonnet; but no Arthur Pole. My son is missing, and no-one remarks on it.

One of the maids in waiting drops a book that she has been reading, and bends to pick it up. She makes a low curtsey to the king, the book clasped to her bodice, emphasising her love of study and drawing the eye to the warm, inviting skin of her neck and breasts. I see dark hair shining under the French hood and the flash of a gold initial 'B' with three creamy pearl drops tied low at her neck; but the king bows over his wife's hand and does not notice her at all.

The ladies flutter into their order of precedence behind the queen. I see Mary Boleyn jostling, elbows to ribs with Jane Parker, but as I smile at them, though I look everywhere, I do not see my son Arthur, and I do not know where he is tonight.

Thomas More is waiting at the entrance to the dining room as the ladies and gentlemen of the court take their places, his fleshy face downturned, deep in thought. He will be waiting for his master the cardinal; he may be working on the case against my sons.

'Councillor More,' I say politely.

He turns with a start and sees me.

'I am sorry to interrupt your meditations. One of my sons is a scholar and I have seen him deep in thought, just like you. He scolds me if I interrupt him.'

He smiles. 'I would hesitate before I interrupted Reginald's thinking, but you are safe with me. I was daydreaming. But still, he should not scold his mother. A child's obedience is a holy duty.' He smiles, as if he is amused at himself. 'I keep telling my children this. It is true of course, but my daughter accuses me of special pleading.'

'Do you have any news of my other sons, Montague and Arthur?' I ask quietly. 'I don't see Arthur here tonight.'

And then the worst thing happens. He does not look at me with contempt for raising traitors, he does not look at me with anger for trying to plead their case to him. He looks at me with great sympathy, as you would look at a woman who is bereaved. The steady gaze of his dark eyes tells me that he thinks of me as a woman who has lost her sons, whose children are already dead.

'I was sorry to learn that Lord Montague is under arrest,' he says quietly.

'And Arthur? You don't speak of Arthur?'

'Banished from court.'

'Where is he?'

He shakes his head. 'I don't know where he has gone. I would tell you if I knew, your ladyship.'

'Sir Thomas, my son Montague is innocent of anything. Can you speak for him? Can you tell the cardinal that he has done nothing?'

'No, I cannot.'

'Sir Thomas, the king must not be advised that the law is his for the taking. Your master is a great thinker, a wise man, he must know that kings should live under the law, like all their people.'

He nods as if he agrees with me. 'All kings should live under the law; but this king is learning his power. He is learning that he can make the law. And you cannot tell a grown man to show childlike obedience. Once he is a man, can he be a child again? Who will order a king when he is no longer a prince? Who will command a lion when he has learned he is no longer a cub?'

The cardinal sits at the king's left hand at dinner, the queen on the other side. Nobody watching the king's intent conversation with the cardinal and his occasional pleasantry to the queen could doubt who is his principal advisor now. The men talk head to head as if they are alone.

I am seated with the ladies of the queen's household. They chatter among themselves, their gaze always flicking over the king's friends, their voices high and affected, their heads turning this way and that, always trying to exchange a glance with the king, to catch his eye. I want to grab hold of any one of them, shake her for her stupidity, say to her: 'This is not an ordinary night. If you have influence with the king you must use it for my boys. If you dance with him you must tell him that my boys are innocent of anything. If you have been such a foolish slut as to sleep with him then you must whisper to him in bed to spare my boys.'

I grit my teeth and swallow my anxiety. I look up at the king and when he glances towards me I nod my head slightly, like a princess, and I smile at him warmly, full of confidence. His gaze rests on me, indifferently, for a moment, and then he looks away.

After dinner there is dancing, and a play. Someone has composed a masque and then there is a joust of poetry, with people turning lines one after another. It is a cultured, amusing evening and usually I would frame a line or a rhyme to play my part in the court; but this evening I cannot muster my wits. I sit among it all as if I am mute. I am deafened by my fear. It feels like a lifetime before the queen smiles at the king, rises from her chair, curtseys formally to him, kisses him goodnight, and leaves the room, her ladies trailing behind her, one or two of them clearly leaving as a matter of form, but planning to sneak back later.

In her rooms, the queen sends everyone away but Mary Boleyn and Maud Parr, who take off her headdress and her rings. A maid unlaces her gown and sleeves and stomacher, another helps her into her embroidered linen night shift, and she pulls a warm robe around her shoulders and waves them away. She looks tired. I remember that she is no longer the girl who came to England to marry a prince. She is thirty-five years old, and the fairy-tale prince who rescued her from poverty and hardship is now a hardened man. She motions me to sit on a chair beside her at the fireside. We put up our feet on the fender like we used to do at Ludlow, and I wait for her to speak.

'He wouldn't listen to me,' she says slowly, 'You know, I've never seen him like this before.'

'Do you know where my son Arthur is?'

'Sent from court.'

'Not under arrest?'

'No.'

I nod. Please God he has gone to his home at Broadhurst, or to mine at Bisham. 'And Montague?'

'It was as if Henry's father was speaking all over again,' she says wonderingly. 'It was as if his father was speaking through him, as if this Henry has not had years of love and honour and safety. I think he is becoming afraid, Margaret. He is afraid just like his father was always afraid.'

I keep my gaze on the red embers in the grate. I have lived under the rule of a fearful king and I know that fear is a contagion, just like the Sweat. A frightened king first fears his enemies and then his friends and then he cannot tell one from the other until every man and woman in the kingdom fears that they can trust no-one. If the Tudors are returning to terror then the years of happiness for me and for my family are over.

'He cannot fear Arthur,' I say flatly. 'He cannot doubt Montague.'

She shakes her head. 'It's the duke,' she says. 'Wolsey has convinced him that the Duke of Buckingham has foreseen our death, the end of our line. The duke's confessor has broken his vow of silence and told of terrible things, predictions and manuscripts, prophesying and stars in the sky. He says that your cousin the duke spoke of the death of the Tudors and a curse laid on the line.'

'Not to me,' I say. 'Never. And not to my sons.'

Gently she puts her hand over mine. 'The duke spoke with the Carthusians at Sheen. Everyone knows how close your family is to them. Reginald was brought up by them! And the duke is close to Montague, and he is your daughter's father-in-law. I know that neither you nor yours would speak treason. I know. I told Henry so. And I will talk to him again. He will recover his courage, I know that he will. He will come to his senses. But the cardinal has told him of an old curse on the Tudors which said that the Prince of Wales would die – as Arthur died – and the prince who came after him would die, and the line would end with a girl, a virgin girl, and there would be no more Tudors and it would, after all this, all have been for nothing.'

I hear a version of the curse that my cousin Elizabeth the queen once made. I wonder if this is indeed the punishment laid on the murderers of the boys in the Tower. The Tudors killed my brother for sure, killed the pretender for sure, perhaps killed the princes of York. Shall they lose their sons and heirs as we did?

'Do you know of this curse?' my friend the queen asks me.
'No,' I lie.

I send a warning to Arthur by four of my most trusted guardsmen, to each of my three houses, and to Arthur's wife Jane at
Broadhurst. I tell him, wherever he is now, to go to Bisham and
wait there with his brother Geoffrey. If he thinks there is any
danger at all, if any Tudor soldiers arrive in the neighbourhood,
he is to send Geoffrey to Reginald in Padua and then escape himself. I say that I am doing everything I can for Montague. I say
that Ursula is safe with me in London.

I write to my son Reginald. I tell him that suspicion has fallen
on our family and that it is vital he tell everyone that we have
never questioned the rule of the king and never doubted that he
and the queen will have a son and heir who will in time become
Prince of Wales. I add that he must not come home, even if he is
invited by the king and offered safe conduct. Whatever is going to
happen, it is safer for him to stay in Padua. He can be a refuge for
my boy Geoffrey if nothing else.

I go to my bedroom and I pray before the little crucifix. The
five wounds of the crucified Lord show brightly on His pale
painted skin. I try to think of His sufferings, but all I can think is
that Montague is in the Tower, Ursula's husband and father-in-
law imprisoned with him, my cousin George Neville in another
cell, Arthur exiled from court and my boy Geoffrey at Bisham.
He will be frightened, not knowing what he should do.

There is a tap on my bedroom door in the cool greyness of a
spring dawn. It is the queen, returning to her room after Lauds.
She is terribly pale. 'You are dismissed as Mary's governess,' she
says shortly. 'The king told me as we prayed together. He would
listen to no argument. He's gone hunting with the Boleyns.'

'Dismissed?' I repeat, as if I don't understand the word.
'Dismissed from Princess Mary?'

I cannot possibly leave her; she is only five years old. I love her.

I guided her first steps, I trimmed her curls. I am teaching her to read Latin, English, Spanish and French. I kept her steady on her first pony and taught her to hold the reins, I sing with her and I sit beside her when her music master comes to teach her to play the virginal. She loves me, she expects me to be with her. She will be lost without me. Her father cannot, surely cannot say that I am not to be with her?

The queen nods. 'He would not listen to me,' she says wonderingly. 'It was as if he could not hear me.'

I should have thought of this, but I did not. I never thought that he would take me from the care of his daughter. Katherine looks blankly at me.

'She is accustomed to me,' I say weakly. 'Who will take my place?'

The queen shakes her head. She looks frozen with distress.

'I'd better go then,' I say uncertainly. 'Am I to leave court?'

'Yes,' she says.

'I'll go to Bisham, I'll live quietly in the country.'

She nods, her lips trembling. Without another word we move into each other's arms and we cling to each other. 'You will come back,' she promises in a whisper. 'I will see you soon. I will not allow us to be parted. I will get you back.'

'God bless and keep you,' I say, my voice choked up with tears. 'And give my love to Princess Mary. Tell her I will pray for her and see her again. Tell her to practise her music every day. I will be her governess again, I know it. Tell her I will come back. This will all come right. It has to come right. It will be all right.'

It does not come right. The king executes my kinsman Edward Stafford, Duke of Buckingham, for treason, and my friend and kinsman old Thomas Howard, Duke of Norfolk, pronounces the sentence of death with the tears pouring down his face. Right up to the last moment we all expect Henry to grant a pardon, since the duke is his kinsman and was his constant companion; but he does not. He sends Edward Stafford to his death on the scaffold as if he were an enemy and not the greatest duke in the realm, the king's grandmother's favourite, and his own greatest courtier and supporter.

I say nothing in his defence, I say nothing at all. So I too per-haps should be blamed for what we all see this year – the strange shadow that falls over our king. As he turns thirty he becomes harder in the eyes, harder of heart, as if the Tudor curse were not about heirs, but about a darkness that slowly creeps over him. When I pray for the soul of my cousin the Duke of Buckingham, I think that perhaps he was an accidental victim of this coldness where there once was warmth. Our golden prince Henry has always had a weakness: a hidden fear that he is not good enough. My kinsman, with his pride and his untouchable confidence, caught the king on the raw, and this is the terrible outcome.

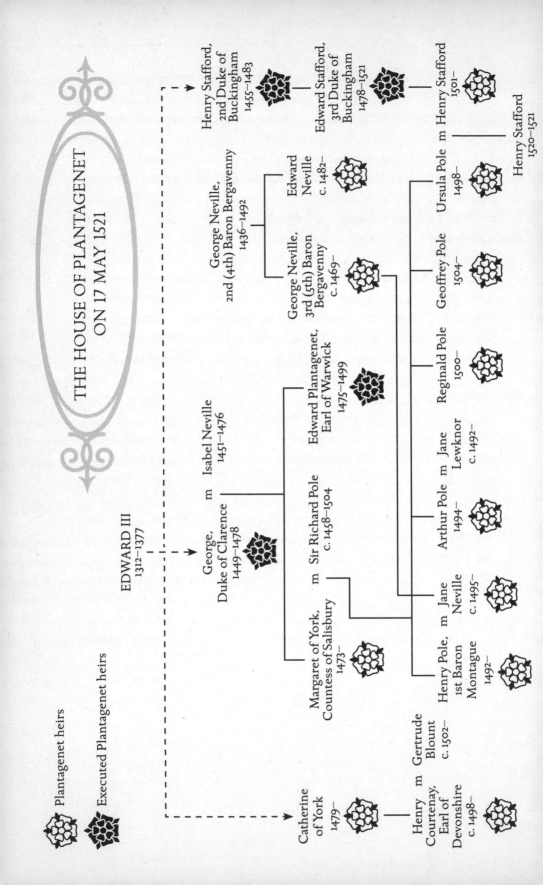

THE HOUSE OF PLANTAGENET ON 17 MAY 1521

Plantagenet heirs

Executed Plantagenet heirs

EDWARD III
1312–1377

George, m **Isabel Neville**
Duke of Clarence 1451–1476
1449–1478

Margaret of York, m **Sir Richard Pole**
Countess of Salisbury c. 1458–1504
1473–

Edward Plantagenet,
Earl of Warwick
1475–1499

Henry Pole, m **Jane Neville**
1st Baron Montague c. 1495–
1492–

Arthur Pole m **Jane**
1494– **Lewknor**
c. 1492–

Reginald Pole
1500–

Geoffrey Pole
1504–

Ursula Pole m **Henry Stafford**
1498– 1501–

Catherine
of York
1479–

Henry m **Gertrude**
Courtenay, **Blount**
Earl of c. 1502–
Devonshire
c. 1498–

George Neville,
2nd (4th) Baron Bergavenny
1436–1492

George Neville, **Baron**
Bergavenny
3rd (5th)
c. 1469–

Edward
Neville
c. 1482–

Henry Stafford, **2nd**
Duke of Buckingham
1455–1483

Edward Stafford,
3rd Duke of
Buckingham
1478–1521

Henry Stafford
1520–1521

BISHAM MANOR, BERKSHIRE, 1521

Our king is not angry for long. He is not like his father the tyrant. The duke is the only one of our family who pays the great price of his life. His son is attainted, he loses his fortune and his duke-dom, but he is released. My son Montague is released, without charge. Henry does not pursue suspicion through the generations, he will not commute a death sentence into a fatal debt. He arrested my son, he banished us all from court in a moment of fear, fear of what we might be saying, or fear of who we are. But he does not pursue us, and once we are out of sight he returns to calmness, he is himself again. I have no doubt that the boy I loved in his childhood will summon me back to his side again. He will let me go back to his daughter.

Once he was a golden prince that we thought could do no wrong. This was folly, too high a standard for any young man to reach. But still he is our Henry, he will come right. He is his mother's son and she was the bravest, steadiest, most loving woman I have ever known. It is not possible that my cousin Queen Elizabeth could have borne and raised a boy who was anything less than loving and trustworthy. I don't forget her. I believe that he will recover.

BISHAM MANOR, BERKSHIRE, 1522

Thinking this, I live quietly, almost invisibly, at my manor at Bisham, secure on my lands, contented with my fortune. I write to no-one and I see only my sons. My cousin George Neville is back at his home at Birling Manor in Kent and he writes nothing to me but the occasional letter with the most anodyne of family news, not even sealing it in case a spy traces its passage and wants to see the contents. I reply that we have grieved at the loss of Ursula's little boy, who died of a fever at less than a year, but that Montague's wife has had a girl and we have named her Katherine for the queen.

My older boys live quietly with their wives in their grand houses. Arthur is nearby with his wife, Jane, at his house at Broadhurst, Montague is only four miles away at Bockmer and we visit each other every month or so. My son Geoffrey I keep at home for these last precious years of his boyhood. I find I am treasuring him even more as he grows stronger and more handsome and reaches manhood. When we sit together in the evening we never lower our voices; even when we are alone and the servants have left, we never say anything about the king, about the court, about the princess that I am not allowed to serve. If anyone is listening at the chimney, under the eaves, at the door, they hear nothing but the ordinary talk of a family. We never even agree upon this pact of silence. It is like an enchantment, like a fairy story, we have become mute as if by magic. A silence has fallen on us; we are so quiet that no-one would bother to listen.

Reginald is safe in Padua. Not only has he completely escaped the king's ill-will but he is in high favour for the help he gave the king and Thomas More as they write a defence of the true faith against the Lutheran heresy. My son helps them with research into scholarly documents held at the library at Padua. I advise Reginald that he keep away from London, however much he, the king, and Thomas More agree on Bible texts. He can study just as well in Padua as in London and the king likes having an English scholar working abroad. Reginald may want to come home, but I am not putting him at risk while there is any shadow over the reputation of our family. Reginald assures me that he has no interest in anything but his studies; yet the duke had no interest in anything but his fortune and his lands and now his wife is a widow and his son disinherited.

Ursula writes to me from a new, modest home in Staffordshire. When I made her marriage I predicted that she would be the wealthiest duchess in England. Never did I think that the great family of the Staffords could be all but ruined. Their title is taken from them, their wealth and their lands quietly absorbed by the royal treasury on the judicious advice of the cardinal. Her great marriage, her wonderful prospects were cut off on Tower Hill with the head of her father-in-law. Her husband does not become Duke of Buckingham, and she will never be a duchess. He is mere Lord Stafford with only half a dozen manors to his name and a yearly income in only hundreds of pounds. She is Lady Stafford and has to turn the panels of her gowns. His name is disgraced and all his fortune is forfeited to the king. She has to manage a small estate and try to make a profit from dry lands when she thought she would never see a ploughshare again, and she has lost her little boy so there is no son to inherit the little that there is left.

BISHAM MANOR, BERKSHIRE, SUMMER 1523

We may be exiled from court but the king still calls on us when he wants outstanding military leaders. Both my boys, Montague and Arthur, are summoned to serve as the king invades France. Montague is appointed captain and Arthur fights so bravely at the forefront on the field of battle that he is knighted and is now Sir Arthur Pole. I think how proud his father would have been, I think how pleased the king's mother would have been, and I am glad that my son has served hers.

BISHAM MANOR, BERKSHIRE, MAY 1524

Nobody from court writes to me; I am in exile, I am in silent disgrace, though everyone knows that I am innocent of anything but bearing my name. Thomas Howard, the old Duke of Norfolk, dies comfortably in his bed and I order a Mass for his soul at the priory, the loyal good friend that he was; but I do not attend his lavish funeral. Katherine the queen sends me a short letter from time to time, a prayer book from her own library, New Year's gifts. She rises and falls in the favour of the king as he enters alliances firstly with and then against Spain. My former pupil, my darling little Princess Mary, is betrothed to marry her kinsman Charles, the emperor, in an alliance against France, then she is to marry her cousin James, the young King of Scotland, then they even say that she will go to France and marry there. I hope that someone stands in my place and tells her not to attach herself to these alliances, not to dream of these young men as lovers. I hope that there is someone teaching her to look at all these ambitions with a steady scepticism. Nothing could be worse for her than to fall in love with the idea of one of these mercenary suitors; they may all come to nothing.

I learn from my Bisham steward, who heard from the drovers who walked our beef cattle to Smithfield, that people are saying the king has a new lover. Nobody is sure which one of the ladies at court has taken the king's unreliable fancy, but then I hear that it is one of the Boleyn girls, Mary Carey, and that she is pregnant and everyone is saying that it is the king's child.

I am glad to hear from a pedlar who comes into the kitchen to sell trinkets to the maids that she has given birth to a girl, and he winks and whispers that while she was in confinement the king took up with her sister Anne. After dinner that night, quietly in my room, Geoffrey suggests that perhaps all Howard girls smell like prey to the king, just as a Talbot hound will prefer the scent of a hare to all else. It makes me giggle, and think with affection of the old Duke of Norfolk, who loved a bawdy joke, but I frown at Geoffrey for disrespect. This family, this boy especially, is never going to say one word against this king.

BISHAM MANOR, BERKSHIRE, JULY 1525

The king creates a duke to replace my cousin that he killed. Bessie's boy, the bastard Henry Fitzroy, is honoured beyond belief. My steward comes back from London and says there was a great procession to the old royal palace of Bridewell and the six-year-old boy was made a duke twice over: Duke of Richmond and Duke of Somerset. Thomas More, the king's new favourite, read out the letters patent.

'I didn't know that you could be two dukes at once,' my steward remarks with a sly smile to me.

'I am sure the king judges rightly,' I say; but inwardly I think that this will have cost my friend the queen a lot of pain, to see a golden-headed Tudor boy kissed by his royal father and draped in ermine.

It is Arthur, Sir Arthur as I now always call him, who gives me my first living grandson, the heir to my name. He names him Henry, as he should, and I send our beautiful gilded cradle to Jane at Broadhurst for the next generation of Plantagenet boys. I am amazed at my own fierce pride at this baby, at my powerful delight at the next generation of our dynasty.

My son Geoffrey was not part of the muster for France, and I made sure that he did not volunteer to go. He is a young man now, nearly twenty-one, and this last son, this most precious child, must be found a wife. I spend more time in considering who would suit Geoffrey than anything else in these years of exile.

She has to be a girl who will run his house for him; Geoffrey has been raised as a nobleman, he has to have a good household around him. She has to be fertile, of course, and well-bred and well-educated, but I don't want a scholar for a daughter-in-law – she should be just well-enough read to raise her children in the learning of the Church. God spare me from a girl running after the new learning and dabbling in heresy as is the fashion these days. She has to be aware that he is a sensitive boy – he's not a sportsman like Arthur nor a courtier like Montague, he is a hand-reared boy, his mother's favourite. Even as a child he knew what I was thinking from just looking into my face, and he still has a sensitivity that is rare in anyone, especially a young nobleman. She must be beautiful; as a young boy with his long blond curls Geoffrey was often mistaken for a pretty girl, and now he has grown to manhood he is as handsome as any man at court. His children will be beauties if I can find a good match for him. She has to be elegant and thoughtful and she has to be proud – she is joining the old royal family of England, there is no greater young man by birth in the country. We may be in half-disgrace at the moment, but the king's mood changed quickly – almost overnight – and is certain to change again. Then we will be restored to royal favour and then she will represent us, the Plantagenets, at the Tudor court, and that is no easy task.

If my youngest son were in his rightful position, present at court, in some good place, heir to the greatest fortune in England, it would be easy to find the right bride for him. But as we are, half-exiled, half-disgraced, half-acknowledged, and with the old lawsuit for my lands that Compton would deny me still running, we are a less attractive family and Geoffrey is not the most eligible bachelor in the land as Montague was. Yet we are fertile – Montague's wife Jane gives birth to another girl, Winifred, so I have three grandchildren now – and fertility is prized in these anxious days.

In the end I choose the daughter of the queen's gentlemen usher, Sir Edmund Pakenham. It's not a great match, but it is a good one. He has no sons, only two well-brought-up daughters, and one of them, Constance, is the right age for Geoffrey. The two girls will jointly inherit their father's fortune and lands in Sussex that run near to my own, so Geoffrey will never be far from home. Sir Edmund is close enough to the queen to know that our friendship remains unshaken, and she will have me back at court as soon as her husband allows. He is gambling on my son being as great a man at court as his brothers were. He thinks, as I do, that Henry was ill advised, that the cardinal played on his fears, his father's fears, and that this will soon pass.

They marry quietly, and the young couple come to live with me at Bisham. It is understood that when I am returned to court I will take Constance with me, that she will serve the queen and no doubt rise in the world. Sir Edmund has faith that he will see me back at court again.

And he is right. As slowly as spring comes to England, I see the royal frost thawing. The queen sends me a gift, and then the king himself, hunting nearby, sends me some game. Then after four years of exile I got the letter I have been expecting.

I am appointed to go, once again, to Ludlow Castle and be companion and governess to the little nine-year-old princess who is to take up the seat and govern the principality. Perhaps soon she will be named Princess of Wales where once there was a beloved prince. I knew it. I knew that Katherine's loving, gentle advice to the king would bring him to a sense of his true self. I knew that as soon as he was in alliance with her homeland he would turn once again to her. I knew that the cardinal would not be in favour forever, and that the prince I had loved as a boy would become what he was born to be: a fair, just, honourable king.

I go at once to meet the princess at Thornbury Castle, and I take my new daughter-in-law Constance with me, to serve the Princess Mary as a lady in waiting. The return of Tudor favour puts us all in our rightful places, back at the heart of the royal court. I show her the beautiful castle at Ludlow with pride as a place where I was once mistress, and I tell her about Arthur and the princess who was his bride. I don't tell her that the young couple were in love, that their passion for each other illuminated the plum-coloured castle. But I do say that it was a happy home, and that we will make it happy again.

THORNBURY CASTLE, GLOUCESTERSHIRE, AUGUST 1525

Nine-year-old Princess Mary arrives on a blazing hot summer's day, riding her own small horse, flanked by two hundred outriders, in her livery of blue and green, and smiling to the people who are massed around the castle gate to see this new princess coming into her own.

I stand in the shadow of the doorway, glad to be out of the heat, ready to welcome her into the castle that I once counted as my daughter Ursula's inheritance. This was a Stafford house; it should have been Ursula's home. The cardinal took it from the duke, and now it is to be used by the princess, and I shall run it as I will run all her houses.

Her retinue is headed by my kinsman Walter Devereux, Baron Ferrers of Chartley. He greets me with a warm kiss on both cheeks and then helps the little princess down from her saddle.

I am shocked at my first sight of her. It has been so long since I have seen her I was imagining her taller, a sturdy Tudor girl like her aunt Margaret, stocky as a pony; but she is tiny, dainty as a flower. I see her pale heart-shaped face in the shadow of the big hood of her cape and think her swamped in adult clothes, too frail for such a costume, for such a force of guards, too slight to be carrying her titles and all our expectations, too young to be taking up her duties and lands. I feel myself swallow with anxiety. She is fragile, like a princess made out of snow, a princess wished into being and only lightly embodied.

But then she surprises me by taking Walter's hand and jumping off her horse like an agile boy, bounding up the steps towards me, and flinging herself into my arms. 'Lady Margaret! My Lady Margaret!' she whispers, her face pressed against me, her head at my breast, her body slight and thin. I hold her close and feel her tremble with relief that she is with me again. I hold her tight and think I should take her by the hand and present her to her household, show her to her people. But I can't bear to turn her away from me. I wrap my arms around her and I don't let go for a long time. This is a child as beloved as any one of my own, a little girl still, and I have missed four years of her childhood and I am glad to have her back into my keeping.

'I thought I would never see you again,' she breathes.

'I knew I would come back to you,' I say. 'And I won't ever leave you again.'

LUDLOW CASTLE, WELSH MARCHES, 1525–1526

She is not a difficult child to raise. She has her mother's sweet temper and all of the Spanish stubbornness, so I introduce her tutors to her, and persuade her to practise music and take exercise. I never command her; this is a daughter of England and Princess of Wales – nobody can command her but her father and mother – but I tell her that her beloved parents have put her in my keeping and will blame me if she does not live well, study like a scholar and hunt like a Tudor. At once she applies herself for love of me. By making her lessons pleasant and interesting and encouraging her to question and consider things, by ensuring that her Master of Horse chooses hunters for her who are eager but obedient, and by having music and dancing in the castle every night it is easy to encourage her to gain the skills that a princess must have. She is an intelligent, thoughtful girl, if anything a little too grave. I cannot help but think that she would be an apt pupil for Reginald, and that it would benefit all our family if he were to become an influence in her life.

In the meantime, her tutor is Dr Richard Fetherston, the choice of her mother and a man that I like on sight. He is tall and brown-haired and he has a quick wit. He teaches Mary Latin with the classic authors, and translations of the Bible; but he also composes silly rhymes for her and nonsense poems. His loyalty to her mother – which we never mention – is, I think, quite unshakeable.

Princess Mary is a passionately loving girl. She counts herself betrothed to her cousin King Charles of Spain, and she pins a brooch which says 'The Emperor' on every gown. Her mother has encouraged this attachment, and spoken of him to her; but this summer we learn that her engagement is to be released and that instead she will marry into the French royal family.

I tell her the news myself and she runs away and locks herself in her room. She is a princess – she knows better than to complain. But she puts the diamond brooch in the bottom of her jewellery box and we have a sulky few days.

Of course, I feel for her. She is nine and she thinks her heart is broken. I brush her beautiful long russet hair as she looks pale-faced into her mirror and tells me that she thinks she will never be happy again. I am not surprised that her betrothal has been broken but I am genuinely shocked when we receive a letter from the cardinal and learn that the king has decided to marry her to a man old enough to be her father, the notoriously loose-living widowed King of France. She dislikes him for these three good reasons and it is my duty to tell her that as a princess of England she has to make up her mind to serve her country with her marriage, and that in this, as in everything else, her father has to be obeyed and that he has the absolute right to place her where he thinks best.

'But what if my mother thinks differently?' she asks me, her dark eyes bright with anger.

I don't allow myself to smile. She draws herself up to her full height, a magisterial four feet, as proud as a Spanish queen. 'Then your mother and your father must agree,' I say steadily. 'And you would not be a good daughter if you presumed to judge them, or to take sides.'

'Well, I shan't like him,' she says stubbornly.

'You will love and respect him as a good and dutiful wife,' I tell her. 'Nobody requires you to like him.'

Her quick wit grasps the humour of this and she rewards me with a peal of ready laughter. 'Oh, Lady Governess! What a thing to say!'

'And anyway you will probably come to like him,' I say comfortingly, pulling her to sit beside me so that she can rest her head on my shoulder. 'Once you marry a man and you have children together and you rule your lands together, you will find in him all sorts of qualities that you admire. And if he is kind to you and a good father to your children, then you will come to love and like him.'

'Not always,' she points out. 'My aunt Margaret, the Dowager Queen of Scotland, turned the cannons of her castle on her own husband and is trying to persuade the Pope to give her a divorce.'

'She's very wrong to do so,' I maintain. 'It is God's will that a woman obey her husband and that their marriage can only be ended by death. And your father has told her so himself.'

'So can it be better to marry for love?' she demands. 'My father the king married my mother for love.'

'He did indeed,' I agree. 'And it was as lovely as a fairy story. But not all of us can have a life like a fairy story. Most of us will not. Your mother was very blessed that the king chose her, and he was honoured with her love.'

'So why does he befriend other ladies?' Mary asks me, her voice lowered to a whisper, though we are quite alone in my private chamber. 'Why does that happen, Lady Margaret?'

'What have you heard?'

'I have seen it myself,' she says. 'His favourite, Mary Boleyn. And I see his son, Bessie Blount's boy, at court. They have made him a duke, he is Duke of Richmond and Duke of Somerset. Nobody else in England is honoured like that. It is too great an honour for a boy born to someone like Bessie. It is too great an honour for a horrid little boy like him.'

'Men, even kings, perhaps especially kings, may love with a free heart, even after their marriage,' I say. I look into her honest, questioning face and I hate the truth that I am telling her. 'Your father, as a king, can do as he pleases, it is his right. The wife of a king, even though she is a queen herself, does not complain to him, does not complain to others. It is not important, it makes no difference. She makes it clear to everyone that it is not important. However many girls there may be, she is still his wife. Your mother is still the queen, however many Bessies and Marys dance at the court or walk behind her into her rooms. They don't trouble her at all. They need not trouble you.'

'And the little double duke?' she asks spitefully.

Since I do not know what the king means by creating such an honour, I dare not advise her. 'You are still the princess,' I say. 'Whatever happens, the queen is still the queen.'

She looks unconvinced, and I am unwilling to tell this young princess that a woman, even a princess, is servant to her father and slave to her husband. 'You know, a husband, any husband, is set by God Himself to rule over his wife.'

She nods. 'Of course.'

'He must do as he pleases. If he imperils his immortal soul a good wife might warn him of this. But she cannot try to take command. She has to live as he wishes. It is her duty as a wife and a woman.'

'But she might mind . . .'

'She might,' I admit. 'But he cannot leave her side, he cannot deny his marriage, he cannot forsake her bed, he cannot deny her title as queen. He may dance and play and write poetry to a pretty girl but that changes nothing. He might give honours and love a bastard son but that changes nothing for the legitimate child of his marriage. A queen is the queen until her death. A princess is born to her coronet and no-one can take it from her. A wife is a wife until her death. Everything else is just pastime and vanity.'

She is a wise girl, this little princess; for we don't talk of this again, and when the couriers from her mother in London also carry gossip into the kitchen that the Boleyn girl has given the king a child, this one a boy, this one named Henry, I order that no-one repeats the story in the hearing of the princess and I tell my daughter-in-law Constance that I will personally beat her into convulsions if I hear that she has allowed anything to be said in Mary's hearing.

My daughter-in-law knows better than to fear my anger, as she knows I love her too dearly to lift a hand to her. But she makes sure that the princess hears nothing of the baby who is called Henry Carey, or of the new flirtation that her father has taken up in place of the old.

Under my guardianship the princess learns nothing more, not even when we go to court at Westminster and Greenwich for Christmas each year, not even when the king commands that we set up a court for the princess in Richmond Palace. I command the ladies as if I were the strictest abbess in the kingdom and there is no gossip spoken around the princess though the main court is beside itself about the king's new flirt, Anne Boleyn, who seems to have taken her sister's place in his favour, though not yet in his bed.

GREENWICH PALACE, LONDON, MAY 1527

I am commanded to bring the princess to court for the celebration of her betrothal into the House of Valois. She is to marry either the French king, or his second son, a little boy of seven years old, the duc d'Orléans, so a completely disorganised and inadequate plan. We arrive at court and Mary flies to her mother's rooms with me running behind her, begging her to walk with dignity, like a princess.

It hardly matters. The queen jumps down from her throne in the presence chamber to embrace her daughter and takes me by the hand to lead us both into her privy chamber so that we can chatter and exclaim, and delight in each other without a hundred people watching.

As soon as the door is closed behind us and mother and daughter have exchanged a ripple of inquiries and answers, slowly the brightness drains from the queen's face, and I see that Katherine is weary. Her blue eyes still shine with pleasure at seeing her daughter; but the skin beneath them is brown and stained, and her face is tired and pale. At the neck of her gown I see a tell-tale rash and I guess that she is wearing a hair shirt beneath her rich clothes, as if her life was not hard enough in itself to mortify her.

I understand at once that she is grieved her precious daughter is to be bundled off to France as part of an alliance against her own nephew, Charles of Spain, and that she blames herself for this, as for everything else that will befall England without an heir. The burden of being a Spanish princess and an English queen is weighing heavily on her. The behaviour of her nephew Charles has made her life in England far worse than it was. He has made promise after promise to the king, and then broken them, as if Henry were not a man dangerously quick to take offence at any threat to his dignity, as if he were not so selfish as to punish his wife for events far beyond her control.

'I have good news, good news: you are not to go to France,' she says, sitting in her chair and pulling Mary onto her lap. 'The betrothal is celebrated but you will not go for years, perhaps two or three. And anything can happen in that time.'

'You don't want me to marry into the House of Valois?' Mary asks anxiously.

Her mother forces a reassuring smile. 'Of course your father will have chosen rightly for you, and we will obey him with a glad heart. But I am pleased that he has said that you are to stay in England for the next few years.'

'At Ludlow?'

'Even better than that! At Richmond. And dear Lady Margaret will live with you, and care for you when I have to go away.'

'Then I am glad too,' Mary says fervently. She looks up into the weary, smiling face. 'Are you well, Lady Mother? Are you happy? Not ill at all?'

'I am well enough,' the queen says, though I hear the strain in her voice and I stretch out a hand to her so that we are linked, one to another. 'I am well enough,' she repeats.

She does not speak to me of her disappointment that her daughter is to marry into the house of her enemy, France; nor of her humiliation that the bastard boy of her former lady in waiting is now Lord of the North, living in the great castle of Sheriff Hutton with a court as grand as that of our princess and commanding the northern marches. Indeed, now he is Lord High Admiral of England though a child of eight.

But she never complains, not of her weariness nor her ill health; she never speaks of the changes of her body, the night-sweats, the nauseating headaches. I go to her room one morning and find her wrapped in sheets stepping out of a steaming bath, a princess of Spain once more.

She smiles at my disapproving face. 'I know,' she says. 'But bathing has never done me any harm and in the nights I am so hot! I dream I am back in Spain and I wake as if I had a fever.'

'I am sorry,' I say. I tuck the linen sheet around her shoulders which are still smooth-skinned and pale as pearls. 'Your skin is as lovely as ever.'

She shrugs as if it does not matter, and pulls up the sheet so I shall not remark on the red weals of flea bites and the painfully raw patches that come from the rubbing of the hair shirt on her breasts and belly.

'Your Grace, you have no sins that would require you to hurt yourself,' I say very quietly.

'It's not for me, it is for the kingdom,' she says. 'I take pain to turn aside the wrath of God from the king and his people.'

I hesitate. 'This can't be right,' I say. 'Your confessor . . .'

'Dear Bishop Fisher wears a hair shirt himself for the sins of the world, and Thomas More does too,' she says. 'Nothing but prayer, passionate prayer, is going to move God to speak to the king. I would do anything.'

That silences me for a moment.

'And you?' she asks me. 'You are well, my dear? Your children are all well? Ursula had a little girl, didn't she? And Arthur's wife is with child, is she not?'

'Yes, Ursula has a daughter named Dorothy and is with child again, and Jane has had a girl,' I say. 'They have called her Margaret.'

'Margaret for you?'

I smile. 'Arthur will inherit his wife's great fortune when her father dies but they would like to see some of my fortune going to my namesake.'

'And they have a boy already,' she says wistfully, and this is the only acknowledgement she makes that her barren marriage with only our little princess has broken her heart, and now it is an old, old sorrow.

But as I go around court and greet my friends and my many cousins, I find that her ladies, indeed everyone at court, seem to know that her courses have stopped and that there will never be any more Tudor babies, girls or boys. Perhaps it will be, in the end, that there are no sons and the line will end with a girl.

The king says nothing about this slow, painful crushing of his hopes, but the favour shown to Bessie Blount's bastard, little Henry Fitzroy, and the honours heaped on him remind everyone that the queen is past the age of childbearing and that, although we have a handsome young Tudor boy visiting court, running down the galleries and calling for his horse in the stables, it is not one that she has carried, and now no-one hopes for anything more from her.

It is Maria de Salinas, now Countess Willoughby, the queen's most loyal friend, who says quietly to me. 'Don't think she is too distressed at this French marriage. She feared far worse.'

'Why, what could be worse for her?' I ask.

We are walking together by the river, as the king has demanded a rowing regatta and the watermen are competing against the noblemen of the court. Everyone is disguised as soldiers or mermen, and it is a pretty scene. I can only tell which team is of noblemen and which watermen by the harsh fact that the watermen win every race and Henry's laughing court collapse over their oars and confess that it is harder work than it looks.

'She fears that the king might order Princess Mary to marry Henry Fitzroy,' she says, and watches as the smile drains from my face. I turn to face her and grip her hand as I feel I am about to faint.

'What?' I think I must have misunderstood her.

She nods. 'It's true. There is a plan that Princess Mary will marry the Duke of Richmond, the bastard.'

'This is an ugly joke,' I say.

Her steady gaze tells me that it is no joke.

'Why would you say such a thing?'

'Because it is true.'

I look around. There is no-one in earshot, but still I draw her hand into my arm and we walk away from the riverbank, where the ladies are cheering their favourites, into the quietness of the lush garden.

'The king would never have thought of such a ridiculous thing.'

'Of course not. The cardinal put it into his head. But now the king thinks of it too.'

I look at her, and I am dumb with horror at what she is saying. 'This is madness.'

'It is the only way he can get his son on the throne of England, without disinheriting his daughter. It's the only way the people would accept Henry Fitzroy as his father's heir. Princess Mary becomes Queen of England, with a Tudor husband at her side.'

'They are half-brother and sister, it is quite horrible.'

'That is what we think. That is what a normal father would think. But this is the king, thinking about who is going to inherit his throne. He would do anything to keep the Tudors on the throne. A princess cannot hold the throne of England. And he could get a dispensation for such a marriage.'

'The Pope would never agree.'

'Actually, the Pope would agree. The cardinal would arrange it.'

'The cardinal has that much influence?'

'Some say he will be the next pope.'

'The queen would never consent.'

'Yes,' Maria says gently, as if finally I have come to an understanding of what she has been trying to say all along. 'Exactly. That is the worst thing. That is the worst thing that might happen. The queen would never consent to it. She would rather die than see her daughter shamed. The queen would fight it. And what do you think will happen if she sets herself against the will of the king? What do you think will happen to her, if she defends her daughter against the command of her husband? What do you think he will do? What is he like, these days, if anyone contradicts him?'

I look at her pale face and I think of my cousin the Duke of

Buckingham who put his head on the block for nothing more than boastful words in the secrecy of the confessional. 'If she opposed him, would he call it treason?' I wonder.

'Yes,' she says. 'Which is why I am glad that the king plans to marry his daughter to our worst enemy, France. Because there was something even worse planned for her.'

My son Arthur, Sir Arthur as I delightedly remind myself to call him, rows in the regatta and beats four other boats before coming in second to a brawny waterman with arms like legs of ham. My son Montague takes bets on the riverbank and wins a purse of gold from the king himself. The happy, noisy court ends the day with a battle of boats with the king's barge leading the charge against a small flotilla of wherries. Anne Boleyn gets herself the part of a figurehead, at the front of the king's boat, gazing out over the water, directing the fire of the bargemen wielding buckets. Everyone gets drenched and the laughing king helps Anne out of the boat and keeps her by him as we all walk back to the palace.

Princess Mary practises her part in the great masque planned to celebrate her betrothal. I go with her to the wardrobe rooms where they are fitting her gown. It is an extraordinarily costly dress, the bodice encrusted with rubies and pearls, the red and white of the Tudor rose, their stems of emeralds, their hearts of yellow diamonds. She staggers at first under the weight of it, but when she stands up she is the most glamorous princess the world has ever seen. She is still slight and small, but her pale skin is flushed with health, her auburn hair is thick and rich, and in this gown she looks like an icon in a valuable shrine.

'We should really be in the treasury for this dress fitting,' I say to her and I see her face light up with pleasure.

'It is more treasure than velvet,' she agrees. 'But see my sleeves!'

They hold out the golden surcoat and she puts it on. The hanging sleeves of the gown are in the new fashion, so long that they almost reach the ground, and she is draped in golden light. They gather her thick hair in a garland of flowers, and capture the mass of flowers and auburn locks in a silver net.

'How do I look?' she asks me, knowing that the answer is 'beautiful'.

'You look like a princess of England and a queen of France,' I tell her. 'You are as beautiful as your mother when she first came to England, but even more richly dressed. You're dazzling, my dear. No-one will look at anyone but you.'

She sweeps me a curtsey. '*Ah, merci, ma bonne mère,*' she says.

At first I am proved right; no-one takes their eyes from our princess. The masque is a great success and the princess and seven ladies emerge from the painted scenery to dance with eight costumed knights, and she is the centre of all attention, dripping in jewels and faultlessly trained. When the masque is over, the French ambassador begs her to honour him with a dance. She takes her place at the head of the set, and on the other side of the room her father lines up with his partner. My friend the queen watches smiling at this official, most important occasion, as her husband dances hand in hand with the commoner Anne Boleyn, his head turned towards her, his eyes on her animated face.

I wait for the signal that the ladies are to withdraw, but the dancing goes on long into the night. Only after midnight does the queen rise from her chair under the cloth of estate and curtsey to the king. He bows to her, with every sign of respect. He takes her hand and he kisses her on both her cheeks. Her ladies and I rise from our stools or reluctantly trail away from the dancing and prepare to leave.

The queen says: 'Goodnight, God bless you,' and smiles at her husband. Princess Mary, her daughter, comes to stand behind her, Mary Brandon, the Dowager Queen of France, comes behind her. I follow them, all the ladies in order of their precedence, we are all ready leave – but Anne Boleyn has not moved.

I feel a moment's horrible embarrassment: she has made a mistake and I, or someone else, had better smooth it over. She has not noticed that we are leaving and she will look a fool, scampering behind us when the queen withdraws. It doesn't matter much, but it's awkward and stupid of her to be inattentive to the time-honoured rituals of the court. I step forward to take her by the arm and curtsey to the queen and sweep her into the train of ladies, to do this young woman the favour of skimming over her error before she is embarrassed by her mistake. But then I see something in the tilt of her head and the gleaming challenge of her smile, and I hesitate.

She stands surrounded by a circle of the most handsome men of the court, the centre of attention in the beautiful arched hall, her dark head crowned by a French hood of deep crimson set with rubies and gold thread. She does not look out of place, she does not look shamed as she should, a lady in waiting who has forgotten her place. Instead, she looks utterly triumphant. She sweeps a shallow curtsey, her red velvet gown spread wide, and she does not hurry to join the queen's train, as she should.

There is a momentary pause, almost an intake of breath, and then the queen looks from her husband to the Boleyn girl as if she realises that something new and strange is happening here. The young woman is not going to withdraw from the hall following the queen, walking behind the superior ladies in order of strict precedence – and since she was born the daughter of a simple knight there are very many of us to precede her. She is not coming at all. In this one act she has changed everything. And the queen is not ordering her. And the king is allowing this.

Katherine gives a little shrug, as if it does not much matter, turns on her heel and walks from the great hall with her head held high. Led by the king's own daughter the princess, the king's sister – a princess by birth and a queen by marriage, his cousins like me born royal, all the other ladies of the court, we all follow the queen in deafening silence. But as we proceed up the broad stairs, we hear Anne's seductive giggle.

I command Montague and Arthur to my rooms at dawn, before breakfast, before Prime, before anyone else in the royal household is stirring.

'You should have told me matters had gone so far,' I say sharply.

Montague checks that the door is tightly closed, and that his sleepy groom is standing outside. 'I couldn't write anything, and besides, I didn't know.'

'You didn't know?' I exclaim. 'She serves as a lady in waiting but goes where she wants, dances with the king and doesn't leave when we do?'

'That's the first time that has happened,' Arthur explains. 'She's never stayed behind before. Yes, she's with him all the time; she goes alone to his rooms, they ride out just the two of them with the rest of us following behind, they sit together and talk or they gamble or they play and sing.' He makes an almost comical grimace. 'Lady Mother, they read books of theology together! What sort of seduction is this? But she's always been discreet before, she's always been like all the others. She's never stayed back like that.'

'So why now?' I demand. 'In front of the French ambassador, and everyone?'

Montague nods at the question. He's more of a politician than his brother. Arthur sees everything because he is all but inseparable from the king, one of the band of his close friends who go everywhere together; but Montague understands better what it means.

'Could it be for that very reason? Perhaps because this was the betrothal of Princess Mary to the French,' he suggests. 'Anne favours the French, she spent years at the French court. She helped to bring this about and they know that. Henry doesn't intend to befriend the Spanish again, they are to be our enemies. The queen – God bless her – is of the enemy. He feels free to offend her. Anne shows that it is her policy which will triumph.'

'What good does it do the king?' I ask crossly. 'To insult the queen before the whole court does nothing but hurt her, and demean himself. And that young woman laughed as we left, I heard her.'

'If it wins him favour with the Lady, he'll do it,' Arthur points out. 'He's beside himself. He'll do anything.'

'What did you call her?'

'I called her the Lady. That's what a lot of them are calling her.'

I could curse like a stable boy with rage. 'For sure they can't call her "Your Grace",' I say sharply. 'Or "Your Ladyship". She's nothing more than a knight's daughter. She wasn't good enough for Henry Percy.'

'She likes anything that makes her stand out,' Arthur pursues. 'She likes to be conspicuous. She likes the king to publicly acknowledge her. She's terrified that everyone will think her nothing more than his whore, just like her sister, just like all the others. She makes him promise, all the time, that this will be different. She's not to be another Bessie, she's not to be another Mary. She's not to be another laundry maid, or the French slut Jehanne. She's got to be special, she's got to be different. Everyone has to see that she is different.'

'The lead hackney,' I say vulgarly.

Montague looks at me. 'No,' he says. 'You have to see this, Lady Mother. It's important. She's more than his latest ride.'

'What more can she be?' I demand impatiently.

'If the queen should die . . .'

'God forbid,' I say instantly, crossing myself.

'Or say: if the queen should retire to live a religious life.'

'Oh, do you think she would?' Arthur asks, surprised.

'No, of course she wouldn't!' I exclaim.

'She might,' Montague insists. 'She might. And really – she should. She knows that Henry has to have a son. Fitzroy isn't enough. Princess Mary isn't enough. The king has to leave a legitimate male heir, not a bastard boy or a girl. The queen knows this, every princess knows this. If she could rise to greatness, if she could act with great generosity she could retire from the marriage, take the veil, then Henry could be free to marry again. She should do that.'

'Oh, is this your opinion?' I ask bitingly. 'The opinion of my son, who owes everything to the queen? Is this the opinion of the young men of the court who have sworn fealty to her?'

He looks awkward. 'I'm not the only one saying it,' he says. 'And many more think it.'

'Even so,' I say flatly. 'Even if she were to choose to join a nunnery – and I swear she would not – that would make no difference to Anne Boleyn. If the queen stepped aside it would only be for the king to marry a princess of Spain or France. The king's whore would still be nothing but a whore.'

'A consort?' Montague suggests.

'A concubine?' Arthur smiles.

I shake my head. 'Are we Mahometans now? In the eyes of God and by the law of the land, there is nothing that girl can be but an adulterous whore. We don't have concubines in England. We don't have consorts. She knows it, and we know it. The best she can get for herself is the right to dance at court after the queen has withdrawn, and a title like the Lady, for those who are too mealy-mouthed to call a whore a whore. Anything else means nothing.'

LUDLOW CASTLE, WELSH MARCHES, SUMMER 1527–1528

I dare not tell Montague to write to me secretly, so everything that I know this summer is learned from tactful pointers in his breezy unsealed letters, or from the gossip at the castle gate from the occasional London tinker or pedlar. Montague writes to me family news: Arthur's new baby, Margaret, is thriving, Ursula is out of confinement and has given the Staffords another boy, another Henry, and then one day he writes with quiet pride to tell me that he too has a son. I take the letter and I kiss it, and hold it to my heart. There will be another Henry Pole, there will be another Lord Montague after my son and I are long gone. This little baby, this Henry, is another step on our family path to greatness from greatness.

He has to be silent about all other news. He can tell me nothing about the queen and the court, he cannot tell me that the king summoned Thomas More to walk in the garden with him at Hampton Court, and among the evening birdsong, and with the scent of the roses on the air, confided that he feared his marriage was invalid. He pronounced that his sister Margaret, the Dowager Queen of Scotland, could not get a divorce from the Pope, but that his marriage was a different case, that God had shown him, so painfully but so vividly in the deaths of his children, that his marriage is not blessed by God. And Thomas, good councillor he is, swallowed his own doubts at the divinity of this revelation, and promised the king that he will form an opinion, a thoughtful legal opinion, on the matter and advise his master.

But Montague's discretion makes no difference, for by the end of the summer, the whole kingdom knows that the king is seeking to end the marriage with his queen. The whole kingdom knows, but there is not one word of it inside the state rooms at Ludlow. I surprise myself at the power of the rule I have established over my household. Nobody speaks ugly gossip to the young woman in my charge and so the princess's world is collapsing around her; and she does not know.

Of course, in the end, I have to tell her. Many times I start; but each time the words simply die in my mouth. It is unreal to me, it is incredible to me, I cannot offer her an account of it, any more than I could seriously tell her the tale of the Lambton Worm as a fact rather than a ridiculous legend. It may be that everyone knows it, but still it is unreal.

And anyway, just as I hope, nothing happens. Or at any rate, we have no certain report that anything has happened. We are so far away from London, in the very distant west, that we get no reliable news. But even out here, we learn that the queen's nephew Charles V of Spain has invaded Rome and captured the Pope and is holding him virtually as a prisoner. This changes everything. Not even our all-persuasive cardinal with his honeyed words is going to be able to convince a pope imprisoned by the Spanish king to rule against the Spanish Queen of England. Any of the king's complicated theological arguments about it being a sin to marry his brother's widow will simply go unheard by the captive Pope. While the Spanish emperor commands the Pope, his aunt, the Spanish Queen of England, is safe. All she has to do is to assert the simple truth: that God called her to marry the King of England, and that there is no reason that the marriage is invalid. And I know she will assert that truth until she dies.

In the very castle where Katherine and Arthur lived as passionate lovers, I say nothing to anyone about the love they shared, or about the promise he drew from her – that if he died, she must still be Queen of England and have a daughter called Mary. I say nothing about the lie that I swore to support. I put it from me as if it were a secret from so long ago that I cannot even remember it. My secret fear is that someone, sooner or later, perhaps the cardinal, perhaps Thomas More, or the cardinal's new servant Thomas Cromwell, another man from nowhere, is going to ask me if Arthur and Katherine were lovers. I am praying that if I continue to study forgetfulness, then I can say in truth that I never knew, and now I cannot remember.

The summer heat comes and brings with it an outbreak of the Sweat, and the queen summons the princess to join her and the king to travel the country far from London. Once again they are going to live privately while the country suffers.

'You are to join them at St Albans,' I say to Princess Mary. 'I will take you there and go to my own house. I daresay you will spend the summer with them.'

'With who?' she asks anxiously. 'Who else will be there?'

Poor child, I think. So she knows. Despite the shield I have put around her, she knows that Anne Boleyn goes everywhere with the king. Her silence about this has not been ignorance, but discretion. But I have good news for her, and I let her see my small, triumphant smile. 'Alas,' I say, lingering over the word till her eyes shine and she gleams in return. 'Alas, I hear that many of the court are ill. The cardinal has retreated to his home with his physician, and Anne Boleyn has gone to Hever. So it will just be a small court. Probably just your father and mother and perhaps one or two attendants, Thomas More who is such a good man attending your father, Maria de Salinas with your mother.'

Her face lights up. 'Just my father and mother?'

'Just them,' I confirm, and I wonder if it would be a sin to pray that the damned whore dies of the disease in Kent.

'And you?' she asks.

I hug her to me. 'I will go to my home at Bisham and make sure that my family and my people are well. It is a terrible illness, I will be needed. Arthur and Jane have had a new baby, I pray that they are well. And I will write to you that we are well, and I will think of you, my darling.'

'And I'll come back to you,' she stipulates. 'When the summer is over. We will be together again.'

'Of course.'

BISHAM MANOR, BERKSHIRE, SUMMER 1528

It is a terrible illness, God forgive England for the sin that has brought it down on us. There are many who say that this was foretold when the first Tudor came. There are many who say that the king cannot get a son and the country cannot enjoy good health.

There are many who fear the present and predict a terrible future and blame it on the Tudor line.

Everyone is talking of a young woman in Kent who has lain as if dead for weeks, and has now come back to life to say that princes should obey the Pope. Now they are calling her a visionary and flocking to hear what else she says. But I don't need a prophetess to tell me that it will be a bad summer. When I had the message from London that men were dying in the streets, falling in the gutters as they were struggling to get to their homes, I knew that it would be a bad year for us all, even for my family, hiding behind the high walls of my great estate. Geoffrey and his wife Constance come to live with me and Arthur sends me his children Henry and Margaret my namesake and the wet-nurse with the baby Mary, with a note to say that the Sweat has come to Broadhurst, he and Jane are both ill, they will pray that they survive it, and will I care for his children as if they were my own?

I pray to God that it passes us by, he writes. *If we are unlucky, Lady Mother, please care for my children, and pray for me as I pray for you – A*

They are a pitiful pair, little Henry and Margaret, who goes by the name of Maggie. They stand, clutching each other's hand, in my great hall and I kneel beside them and gather them into my arms and smile at them with a confidence I don't feel.

'I am so glad you have come to me, for I have much for you to do, work and play,' I promise them. 'And as soon as everyone is well at Broadhurst your mother and father will come here to fetch you and you can show them how much you have grown and what good children you have been this summer.'

I make sure that the house is run with the usual plague-season care. Anything that comes to us from the outside world is washed in vinegar and water. We buy as little food from the market at Bisham as possible; but live off our own lands. Strangers are not welcome, and anyone travelling through the town from London is invited to stay the night at the priory guest house, not in my home. I prepare gallons and gallons of tincture from rosemary and sage and sweet wine, and every servant in the household, every man, woman, and child who dines in the hall or sleeps in the straw, takes a spoonful of it every morning; but I never know if it does any good.

I don't attend the priory church and I forbid my household from going into the warm, dark, stinking place where the incense floats over the stench of the midden and unwashed bodies. Instead I observe the daily liturgy with my own confessor in my own private chapel next to my bedroom and I pray on my knees for hours that this sickness will pass us by. Arthur's two children say their evening and morning prayers in my chapel; I keep them at a distance from the priest, and when he blesses the baby he signs the cross in the air over her precious head.

Especially I pray for Geoffrey, whose slight frame and clear skin make him seem so delicate to my worried inspection. I know that in reality he is strong and healthy, nobody could fail to see the colour in his cheeks or his energy or his joy in life. But I watch him all the time for any signs of a fever, or a headache, or a shrinking from sunlight. His wife Constance is as enduring as her name, stocky as a pony, working hard for me, and I am grateful for her care of her husband. If she did not idolise him, I would hate her.

I begin to think that we will get through this summer with nothing worse than a few deaths in the village and a kitchen boy who was probably sick but ran away to his own home and died there, when Geoffrey taps on the door of my private chapel as I am praying on my knees for the health of all those that I love, Princess Mary, the queen and my children. He puts his golden head into the room.

'Forgive me, Lady Mother,' he says.

I know it must be important if he disturbs me at my prayers. I sit back on my heels and motion him to come in. He crosses himself and kneels beside me. I see his mouth is trembling almost as if he were a little boy again and fighting to hold back tears. Something terrible must have happened. Then I see his hands are clasped tight together and he closes his eyes for a moment as if summoning the help of God to deliver his message, then he turns and looks at me. His dark blue eyes are filled with tears as he takes my cold hand.

'Lady Mother,' he says quietly. 'I have very bad news for you.'

'At once,' I say through cold numb lips. 'Tell me quickly, Geoffrey.' I think, is it the Princess Mary, the girl I love as if she were my own daughter? Is it Montague, my heir and the heir of my royal name? Is it one of the little children, could God be so cruel as to take another Plantagenet boy?

'It's Arthur,' he says and his eyes fill with tears. 'It's my brother. He is dead, Lady Mother.'

For a moment, I cannot hear him. I look at him as if I am deaf and don't know what he is saying. He has to repeat himself. He says again: 'It's Arthur, my brother. He is dead, Lady Mother.'

Arthur's wife Jane is sick also, near to death. She has only one woman at her side, caring for her in her private rooms, so nobody tells her that her husband is dead. The steward of their household is so terrified of the sickness that he has abandoned his duty to his lord and his house and barricaded himself into his own rooms. In his absence the place is falling into complete disorder. There is no-one to arrange things as they should be done, and so my son Montague commands that Arthur's body is to be taken from his unlucky house and brought to our priory and laid in our chapel.

We lay him to rest where the other Plantagenet kings are laid, in our priory at Bisham, and when the church is swept and cleaned and censed, I go with Geoffrey and Constance and we start the prayers for his soul and hear the monks take up the chant.

We walk back to the house, and I look at the great palace that I have renewed, with my family crest above the door, and I think, as bitterly as any sinner, that all the wealth and all the power that

I won back for myself and my children could not save my beloved son Arthur from the Tudor sickness.

BROADHURST MANOR, WEST SUSSEX, SUMMER 1528

Montague and I ride over to Arthur's house at Broadhurst and find the house in chaos and the hay uncut in the fields. The crops are ripening well but the boys who should be scaring the birds are sick or dead, and the village is a silent place with shuttered windows and a bundle of hay at every other door. In the great house it seems everyone has run away. Only one woman is seeing to Jane, and no-one is managing the house, or farming the lands.

'There is no reason why you should do this,' Montague says to me as I stride into the hall and start to give orders to servants who have clearly been sleeping in the unchanged straw and dining out of the larder since the family took to their beds.

'These are Arthur's lands,' I say tersely. 'This is what I made his marriage for. This is the inheritance of his son, Henry. I can't see it go to waste. If Arthur cannot leave a fortune to his children it's as if he never won it by marrying her at all. If he doesn't leave a legacy then what's the point of his life?'

Montague nods. He goes outside to the stables and sees that our horses are turned out into the fields and then tells the bailiff of the estate that, Sweat or no Sweat, he had better get a hay-making gang together tomorrow and start work, or they will die in the winter for lack of forage for the beasts, rather than dying now in the summer of the Sweat.

Between the two of us, we set the house and the land to rights over weeks of work, and then the news comes from London that the illness seems to have burned out. The cardinal himself took the Sweat and yet survived it. God smiles on Thomas Wolsey for a second time. His ways are mysterious, indeed.

'There's no plague in the world that could touch him,' I say grimly. 'No disease is poisonous enough to check that massive frame. What news from Hever?'

'She's survived as well,' Montague says to me, disdaining to name Anne Boleyn as I do. We exchange a look of baffled sorrow, that the Sweat should spare a troublesome slut and yet take Arthur.

'Sir Arthur,' I say out loud.

'God bless him,' Montague says. 'Why him and not the others?'

'God knows best in His wisdom,' I say; but my heart isn't in it.

Jane knows that we are in the house, but we don't go to her rooms for fear of infection, and she doesn't send any message to us, nor ask after her husband.

'I'd think better of her if she asked,' I say irritably to Montague. 'Has it not occurred to her?'

'She may be fighting for her own life,' he says.

He hesitates and then continues. 'You do remember, Lady Mother, that there was provision in the marriage contract for Arthur's early death? The lands that she brought to Arthur as her dowry will revert to her, her future inheritance from her father will go to her, for her to use as she wishes. Her father's fortune will be hers alone, at his death. We get nothing.'

I had not remembered this. The very lands that I have been working this month, the house that I have been repairing will bring me nothing. The contract that I wrote to make my son wealthy gave him nothing but worry, and now there is nothing for our family at all. 'He never stopped his work for these lands,' I say angrily. 'He was prepared to take over their military service and spare her father, he was prepared to command their tenants. He was ready to do everything for them. It was her own father who stood in Arthur's way – old fool. And she supported her father against Arthur.'

Montague bows his head. 'And now nothing,' he observes. 'And all our work this month does nothing for our estate.'

'It serves my grandson Henry; I'm working for Arthur's boy. Thank God that he has been spared. He can come home to his own house, and in the end he'll get everything.'

Montague shakes his head. 'No, because it's his mother's house. His mother inherits, not him. She can leave the lands away from him if she wants.'

The thought of disinheriting a son is so foreign to me that I look aghast. 'She'd never do such a thing!'

'If she marries again?' Montague points out. 'The new husband takes everything.'

I go to the window and look out at the fields that I thought were Arthur's fields, that would go unquestioningly to his son, another Henry Pole.

'And if she doesn't remarry, she'll be a drain on our estate,' Montague adds gloomily. 'We'll have to pay her dower for the rest of her life.'

I nod. I find I cannot think of her as the young woman that I welcomed to my house, that I thought of as another daughter. She failed in her wifely duty when she stood with her father against Arthur, when she took to her bed and let Arthur die alone. Now she sends her children away and lies in bed while her husband's brother and mother save her harvest. For the rest of her life, for as long as she lives, she will be able to draw an income from the estates that I work so hard to sow and reap, to build. The spoiled heiress who took to her bed while her own husband was dying will have the right to live in my house and draw her dower from my rents, her whole life long. She will inherit her father's fortune. I have even promised her lands in my will. Most likely, I will die before her and she will draw my black velvet gown with the black fur trim from my wardrobe and wear it to my funeral.

Jane is on the mend. Her lady in waiting comes to me and tells me, with a low curtsey, that Jane sends her compliments. She has fought the Sweat and won, she will come to dine with us tonight and she is most grateful to us for all we have done for the household.

'Have you told her that her husband is dead?' I ask the woman bluntly.

Her pale strained face tells me that she has not. 'Your ladyship, we did not dare to tell her while she was ill,' she says. 'And then it seemed too late to say it.'

'She hasn't asked?' Montague demands incredulously.

'She's been so very ill.' She excuses her mistress. 'Not really in her right mind, with the fever so hot. I thought perhaps that you ...'

'Tell her to come to my rooms before dinner this afternoon,' I rule. 'I will tell her myself.'

We wait for Lady Arthur Pole in the guest room of this house that was once Arthur's house, but is now hers.

The door is opened for her and she comes into the room leaning on the arm of her lady in waiting, apparently too weak to walk unaided.

'Ah my dear,' I say as kindly as I can manage. 'You do look pale. Sit down, please.'

She manages a curtsey to me and a bow of her head to Montague, who helps her to a chair as I nod to her lady in waiting to leave.

'This is my cousin, Elizabeth,' she says faintly, as if she would keep her.

'You shall sit with us at dinner,' I promise, and the woman takes the hint and goes from the room.

'I have very bad news for you, I am afraid,' I say gently.

'My father?' She blinks.

'Arthur, your husband.'

She gasps. Clearly, she had not even known that he was ill. But surely, when she came out of her chamber and he did not greet her, she must have guessed?

'I thought he had gone to your house with the children! Are they well?'

'Thank God Henry and Maggie were well and merry at Bisham when I left them, the baby Mary, and my son Geoffrey and his wife too.'

She takes this in. 'But Arthur . . .'

'My daughter, I am sorry to tell you that he has died of the Sweat.'

She crumples up, like a piece of dropped cloth. Her head sinks into her hands, her body folds up, even her little feet tuck back under her seat. With her hands over her face she wails out her sorrow.

Montague looks at me, as if to ask: 'What shall I do?' I nod to him to take a seat and wait for this helpless sobbing to cease.

She does not stop. We leave her crying and go into dinner without her. The people of her estate, Arthur's tenants, need to see that we are here, that life will go on, that they are required to do their duty, to work and pay their rents; the household staff need not think they can take a holiday because my son is dead. These lands become Jane's again, but then, God willing, they will be inherited by Arthur's son Henry, so they must be kept in good heart for him. When dinner is over we go back to my rooms and find her red-eyed and pale; but, thank God, she has finally stopped crying.

'I can't bear it,' she says piteously to me, as if a woman can choose what she can or cannot bear. 'I can't bear to be widowed again! I can't bear to live without him. I can't face life as a widow, and I won't ever consider another marriage. I am wedded to him in death as in life.'

'These are early days, you've had a shock,' I say soothingly. But she is determined not to be comforted.

'My heart is broken,' she says. 'I shall come and live at Bisham in my dower rooms. I shall live quite retired. I shall see no-one and never go out.'

'Really?' I bite my tongue on the scepticism in my voice, and say again, more gently: 'Really, my dear? Don't you think you would prefer to live with your father? Don't you want to go home to Bodiam Castle?'

She shakes her head. 'Father would only arrange another marriage for me, I know he would. I will never marry again. I want to be in Arthur's home, I want to always be close to him, nursing my grief. I will live with you and weep for him every day.'

I cannot feel the tenderness of heart that I should. 'Of course, you are distressed now,' I say.

'I am determined,' she says.

I really think she is.

'I will live my life in remembrance of Arthur. I will come to Bisham and never leave. I shall haunt his grave like a sorrowful ghost.'

'Oh,' I say.

I give her a few days to think and pray on this resolution but she doesn't waver. She's determined never to marry again and she has set her heart on the rooms in my house promised to her in her marriage contract. She will have her own little household under my roof, she will no doubt employ her own servants, she will order her meals from my kitchens and she will receive, four times a year, the rents from her dower lands, which I signed away, but never thought that I should pay. I don't see how this is to be borne.

It is Montague, my quiet and thoughtful heir, who comes up with the brilliant solution to prevent the young widow from living with us forever. 'Are you quite sure that you want to be withdrawn from the world?' he asks his sister-in-law one evening, in the small space of time that is available to see her, as she comes out of dinner in the great hall before heading to chapel to pray all night.

'Completely,' she says. She is draped in dark blue, as I am, the colour of royal mourning. Arthur was a boy of the House of Plantagenet; he is mourned like a prince.

'Then I fear that Bisham Manor will be too noisy for you, too busy,' he says. 'The king visits when he is on progress, the whole court comes for weeks during the summer, my mother entertains her family during the winter, the Staffords, the Courtenays, the Lisles, the Nevilles. You know how many cousins we have! The Princess Mary is certain to honour us with a long stay in the summer and she brings her entire court with her. It is not like a private house, not like your lovely house here, it is a palace, a working palace.'

'I don't want to see any of those people,' she says crossly. 'I wish to live completely retired. Perhaps my Lady Mother will give me another property of my own on her lands where I can live in complete peace. I don't want much, just a manor house with a private park would be all I would need.'

Even Montague flinches at this request. 'My Lady Mother has worked hard to put the lands together,' he says quietly. 'I don't think she would parcel them out now.'

'I can't live in a noisy, busy house.' She turns to me. 'I don't want to live in a palace. I want to be as quiet and still as a nun.'

Montague says nothing.

He waits.

I say nothing, I wait too. Slowly we can see a new idea dawning on her.

'What if I were to live at a nunnery?' she asks. 'Or even – what if I were to take my vows?'

'Do you feel you have a calling?' I have to ask her. I think, guiltily, of the queen who has sworn that she could not consider a nunnery unless she knew that God had called her to a religious life, that no man or woman should take their vows unless they know for sure that they have a calling. Anything else is a blasphemy. My son Reginald still refuses to take vows without a calling. He says it is an insult to God Himself.

'I do,' she says with sudden enthusiasm. 'I think I do.'

'And I am sure you do,' Montague, the courtier, says smoothly. 'From the very beginning you said that you wanted to withdraw from the world, that you would never marry again.'

'Exactly,' she says. 'I want to be completely quiet and alone with my grief.'

'Then this is the very best solution,' I say, succumbing without much reluctance to temptation. 'And I shall find you a place in a good house, and I shall pay for your keep.'

She clearly does not realise that when she agrees to be a nun she will return her dower to me, just as if she were remarrying. I will pay out only what it costs to keep her in a nunnery sworn to poverty.

'I think it would be the very best thing,' she says. 'But what about this house and lands? My inheritance? And the fortune that will come to me from my father?'

'You could assign them to Henry, as your heir,' I suggest. 'And I could make him my ward and keep them for him. They need not trouble you at all.'

Carefully, Montague makes sure that he does not exchange a single triumphant glance with me. 'Whatever you wish, sister,' he says respectfully.

I wait to be commanded to open up Richmond Palace for the princess to return to London, but there is no sign of the king coming to the city, and a rumour spreads that he has barricaded himself into a tower so that no unhealthy person can breathe on him. When the citizens hear this, they break off from burying their thousands of dead and laugh with the bitter cackle of a hangman, that their king so brave and showy in the jousting ring should be such a coward before disease.

It is not just Londoners who suffer. My former suitor and lately enemy Sir William Compton dies, and with him I hope dies the dispute over my lands. Anne Boleyn takes the disease and then bounces up from her bed at Hever Castle none the worse for it; but her sister's husband Sir William Carey dies, leaving a luscious and fertile Boleyn girl with two copper-headed father-less children. Here is another healthy bastard boy, here is another red-headed Henry. I cannot help but wonder if the king will look at Mary – the prettier and the warmer of the two, with a Tudor boy and a girl in her nursery – and think to put his wife aside and take Mary Boleyn and her little family and declare them as his own.

Jane takes her vows and becomes a novice at Bisham Priory and I write at once to the newly recovered cardinal to apply for the wardship of my grandson Henry. Wolsey has triumphed over an illness that killed better men than him, and is now well enough to dispose of their heirs. However greedy he is for Henry's inheritance for himself, he surely cannot deny my claim. Who could be more suitable than I to manage my grandson's estates until he reaches his majority?

But I leave nothing to chance. A wealthy ward is a treasure that others will want. I have to promise the cardinal a handsome fee, and this is in addition to the one hundred marks that I pay him anyway every year just for his good will. It will be worth it, if he will only favour my claim. I have lost my beloved son Arthur; I cannot bear it that I should lose his fortune too, and that his son should fail to benefit from the marriage contract I composed.

This is not my only worry in these times. I had hoped that the king's choice to hide from the Sweat with his wife and daughter would have its usual consequence of reminding him what a pleasant companion is his wife of nearly twenty years. But I hear from Montague who visits the small touring court that every day the king writes passionate letters to the absent Boleyn girl, and composes poetry to her dark eyes, and openly yearns for her. Extraordinary though it seems, the court will return to London headed by a king and queen who have clung together through danger, but once they are back in Westminster the king will resume his attempt to get the queen to step aside for a young commoner.

At least my son Geoffrey gives me no cause for concern. Neither he nor Constance take the Sweat and when I go to London they return to their house at Lordington in Sussex.

Geoffrey manages the land so well and is so skilled with his tenants and neighbours that I have no hesitation in giving him the
right to be a member of parliament. The seat of Wilton is in my
gift and I hand it to him.

'You can use this as a stepping stone at court,' I tell him after
dinner, on our last night together before he goes to his home and I
go to court. Constance has tactfully withdrawn, as she knows I love
to be with Geoffrey and free to talk to him about everything. Of all
my boys he is the one that has always been closest to my heart. From
babyhood, he is the one who has never been far from my side.

'Like Thomas More?' he suggests.

I nod. Geoffrey has all of my political skills. 'Exactly so, and
look how far he has risen.'

'But he used to speak against the king and in favour of the
power of parliament,' he reminds me.

'Yes, and there's no need to follow him in that. Besides, once he
became the speaker of parliament he persuaded them to do the
will of the king. You can follow his example in using your speeches
in parliament to draw the attention of people. Let them see you
as thoughtful and loyal. Let the king know that in you he has a
man who can put his case to the parliament, and make friends so
that when you propose something for the king, you will have
influence, and it will be agreed.'

'Or you could just put me at court and I could befriend the
king,' he suggests. 'That's what you did for Arthur and
Montague. You didn't send them to the parliament to study and
speak and persuade people. They just walked into royal favour,
and all they had to do was to be good company for the king, to
entertain him.'

'Those were different times,' I say ruefully. 'Very different.' I
think of my son Arthur and how the king loved him for his
courage and quickness at every game that the court might play.
'It is harder to befriend the king now. Those were more light-
hearted times, when all Arthur had to do was joust and play
games. The king was a happy young man and easy to please.'

RICHMOND PALACE, WEST OF LONDON, AUTUMN 1528

The worst thing about this autumn is that I cannot get news, and if I had any, I could not repeat one word of it to the princess. She knows, of course she knows, that her mother and father are all but estranged, and she probably knows that her father is madly, dangerously in love with another woman – he does nothing to conceal it – and she a woman of such ordinary birth that she was lucky to be a maid in waiting at court, never mind domineering over everyone as an acknowledged favourite. I remember Anne Boleyn, thrilled as a child to serve the Princess Mary in France, and her father's pride when she managed to move into the queen's service. It's almost impossible for me to imagine her as a consort, giving orders to the court, complaining of the great cardinal himself, almost an unofficial queen.

Princess Mary is twelve now, and bright and intelligent as any clever girl, but with a grace and dignity which comes from her breeding and training. I am sure that I judge her rightly. I taught her myself and raised her to know all that a princess should know, to read the minds of subjects and enemies, to think ahead, to plan strategically, to be wise far beyond her years. But how can I prepare her to see the father she adores turn away from the mother she so deeply loves? How can anyone suggest to her that her father truly believes he was not married to her mother, that they have been living in a state of mortal sin for all these years? How can anyone tell her that there is a God in heaven who, observing this, decided to punish a young married couple with the deaths of four baby brothers and sisters? I could not say such a thing to a girl of twelve, not a girl that I love as I love this one, and I make sure that no-one else does either.

It's not hard to keep her ignorant, for we rarely go to dine at court, and nobody now visits us. It takes me a little while to realise that this is another sign of the troubled times. The court of the heir to the throne, however young, is always a bustling, busy, popular place. Even a child like Mary attracts people to her service who know that one day she will be Queen of England, and that her favour should be won now.

But not this autumn. This autumn it grows colder and darker and it seems that every morning there is a dull grey light but no sunshine, there are no riders coming out from London, there are no barges coming quickly up the river, catching the inflowing tide. This autumn we are not popular, not with courtiers, nor advisors. We don't even attract people with petitions and begging letters. I think to myself that we must have sunk very low in the public estimation if we are not even visited by people wanting to borrow money.

Princess Mary does not know why; but I do. There can be only one reason that we live so quietly at Richmond, as if we were in a private house and not a palace. The king must be giving people to understand that she is not the heir to his throne. He must be letting people know, in all the subtle, wordless ways that a king can deploy, that there is good reason that Princess Mary is no longer at her castle in Ludlow ruling Wales, that Princess Mary is no longer betrothed to marry the King of France, nor the King of Spain, that Princess Mary is living at Richmond like a daughter of the House of Tudor, served, supported, and respected but no more important than her bastard half-brother, Bessie Blount's boy.

The courtiers are fluttering around a new attraction like midges around a sweaty face. I learn that much from my dressmaker who comes to Richmond Palace to fit me with a velvet gown in dark red for the winter feasts, telling me proudly that she can barely find the time to make it, as she is fully engaged by all the ladies at Suffolk House in Southwark. I stand on the stool and the dressmaker's assistant pins the hem, as the dressmaker tightens the bodice.

'The ladies at Suffolk House?' I repeat. This is the home of the Dowager Queen of France, Mary, and her utterly worthless husband Charles Brandon. While she has always been dearly loved by the court, I can't imagine why they should be so busy and popular all of a sudden.

'Mademoiselle Boleyn is staying there!' she says delightedly. 'Holding court, and everyone visits, the king daily, and they dance every night.'

'At Suffolk House?' This can only be Charles Brandon's doing. The Dowager Queen Mary would never have allowed the Boleyn girl to hold court in her own house.

'Yes, she has quite taken it over.'

'And the queen?' I ask.

'She lives very quietly.'

'And the plans for the Christmas feast?'

The dressmaker notes in silence that I have not received an invitation. Her arched eyebrows rise a little higher and she tweaks a fold at my waist, as if it is hardly worth making an expensive gown that will never be worn before the king. 'Well,' she remarks, preparing to share scandal. 'I am told that the Lady will have her own set of rooms, right next door to the king, and she will hold court there, to her many, many well-wishers. It will be like two courts in the same palace. But the king and queen will celebrate Christmas together, as always.'

I nod. We exchange one long look and I know that the dressmaker's expression – a sort of grim smile, the natural expression of a woman who knows that her own best years are past – is mirrored on my face.

'Perfect,' she says and helps me down from the stool. 'You know, there's not a woman in England over thirty who does not feel the queen's pain.'

'But the women over thirty will not be asked for their opinions,' I say. 'Who cares what we think?'

I am sitting with my ladies listening to Princess Mary practise on the lute and singing. She has composed the song, which is a reworking of an old reapers' ballad about a merry lad going sowing. I am glad to hear her sing with a lilt in her voice and a smile on her face, and she is looking well; the regular trial of her monthly pains has passed and she has colour in her cheeks and an appetite for her dinner. I watch her, bent over the strings, looking up to sing, and I think what a blessedly pretty girl she is and that the king should go down on his knees and thank God for her, and raise her as a princess who will some day rule England, secure in her position, and confident of her future. He owes that to her, he owes that to England. How can it be that Henry, the boy who was the darling of the nursery, cannot see that here is another Tudor heir as precious and as valuable as he was?

The knock at the door startles all of us and Princess Mary looks up, her fingers still pressed on the strings, as my steward bows, comes into the room and says: 'A gentleman at the gate, your ladyship. Says he is your son.'

'Geoffrey?' I get to my feet with a smile.

'No, I would know the master, of course. He says he is your son from Italy.'

'Reginald?' I ask.

Princess Mary rises and says quietly: 'Oh, Lady Margaret!'

'Admit him,' I say.

The steward nods and steps aside and Reginald, tall, handsome, dark-eyed and dark-haired, comes into the room, takes in everyone in one swift glance and kneels at my feet for my blessing.

I put my hand on his thick dark hair and whisper the words and then he stands taller than me, and bends down to kiss me on both cheeks.

At once I present him to the princess and he sweeps her a deep bow. The colour flushes into her cheeks as she puts out both hands to him. 'I have heard so much about you, and your learning,' she says. 'I have read much of what you have written with such admiration. Your mother will be so happy you are home.'

He throws me a smile over his shoulder, and I see at once the darling little boy that I had to give to the Church, and the tall, composed, independent young man that he has become through years of study and exile.

'You will stay here?' I ask him. 'We are about to go into dinner.'

'I was counting on it!' he says easily. To the princess he says: 'When I miss England I miss my childhood dinners. Does my mother still order a lamb pie with a thick pastry crust?'

She makes a little face. 'I am glad you are here to eat it,' she confides. 'For I disappoint her all the time by not being a hearty eater. And I observe all the fast days. She says I am too rigorous.'

'No, you are right,' he says quickly. 'The fast days are for our observation, both for the good of man and the glory of God.'

'You mean for our good? That it is good to go hungry?'

'For those who go fishing,' he explains. 'If everyone in Christendom ate nothing but fish on Friday then the fishermen and their children would eat well the rest of the week. God's will is always for the greater good of men. His laws are the glory both of heaven and earth. I am a great believer in deeds and faith working together.'

Princess Mary shoots a naughty little smile at me as if to score the point. 'That's what I think,' she says.

'And let us talk about filial obedience?' I suggest.

Reginald throws up his hands in joking protest. 'Lady Mother, I shall obediently come to dinner and you shall command what I eat and what I say.'

It is a talkative and merry meal. Reginald says grace in Greek for the court and listens to the musicians who play as we eat. He talks with the princess' tutor Richard Fetherston, and they share their enthusiasm for the new learning and their belief that Lutheranism is nothing but heresy. Reginald admires the dancing and Princess Mary takes Constance's hand and dances with her ladies before him, as if he were a great visitor. After dinner, I see Mary to her prayers and as she climbs into the big four-poster bed she beams at me.

'Your son is very handsome,' she says. 'And very learned.'

'He is,' I say.

'Do you think my father will appoint him to be my tutor when Dr Fetherston leave us?'

'He might.'

'Don't you wish that he would? Don't you think he would be such a good tutor, so wise and thoughtful?'

'I think he would make you study very hard. He is teaching himself Hebrew right now.'

'I don't mind study,' she assures me. 'It would be an honour to work with a tutor like him.'

'Well, time to go to sleep, anyway,' I say. I am not going to encourage any girlish dreams about Reginald from a young woman who is going to have to marry whoever her father appoints, and who, at the moment, seems to have no prospects at all.

She raises her face for my kiss, and I am moved to deep tenderness by her dainty prettiness and her shy smile.

'God bless you, my little princess,' I say.

Reginald and I go alone to my privy chamber and I tell the servants to set the chairs before the fireside and leave us with a glass of wine, some nuts and dried fruits to talk alone.

'She's delightful,' he says.

'I love her as if she were my own.'

'Tell me the family news, my brothers and sister.'

I smile. 'All well, thank God, though I miss Arthur more than I thought possible.'

'And how is Montague's boy?' he asks with a smile, identifying at once the child who will be my favourite as he will carry our name forward.

'He's well,' I say with a gleam. 'Chattering, running around, strong as any Plantagenet prince. Wilful, cheeky.' I stop myself from listing his latest sayings. 'He's funny,' I tell him. 'He's the image of Geoffrey at his age.'

Reginald nods. 'Well, he has sent for me,' he says without

preamble, knowing that I will understand at once that he means the king. 'It is time for my expensive education and long learning to be of use.'

'It is of use,' I reply instantly. 'He consults your thinking on what is and is not heretical, and I know that you advise Thomas More, and the king relies upon him.'

'You don't need to encourage me,' he says with a small smile. 'I am past the age when I need your approval. I'm not Montague's heir, hopping up to win your favour. I know that I've served the king well at the universities, in my writing to the Pope, and in Padua. But he wants me to come home now. He needs advisors and councillors at court who know the world, who have friends at Rome, who can argue with any of them.'

I draw my shawl around me as if there is a draught in the room to make me shiver, though the logs are banked high and glowing red, and the tapestries are still and warm on the walls. 'You won't advise him to put the queen aside,' I say flatly.

'As far as I know, there are no possible grounds,' he says simply. 'But he can command me to study the books that he has assembled to answer this question – you would be surprised at the size of the library he has collected on this. The Lady too brings him books, and it will be my duty to answer them. Some of them are quite heretical. He allows her to read books that More and I would have banned. Some that are banned. She even brings them to him. I shall explain their errors to him, and defend the Church against these dangerous new ideas. I hope to serve both Church and the king in England. He can request me to consult with other theologians, there can be no harm in that. I should read what authorities he has, and advise him if they make a case. He paid for me to be educated so that I can think for him. I will do that.'

'It harms the queen and the princess to have the marriage questioned at all!' I say angrily. 'The books that question the queen or those that question the Church should be banned, without discussion.'

He bows his head. 'Yes, Lady Mother, I know it is a great harm to a great lady who deserves nothing but respect.'

'She took us out of poverty,' I remind him.

'I know.'

'And I have known her and loved her since she was a girl of sixteen.'

He bows his head. 'I shall study and tell the king my opinion, without fear or favour,' he says. 'But I will do that. It is my duty to do that.'

'And will you live here?' It is a joy to me to see my son, but we have not lived under the same roof since he was a boy of six years old. I don't know if I want the daily company of this independent young man who thinks as he pleases, and has no habit of obedience to his mother.

He smiles, as if he knows this very well. 'I shall go to the Carthusian Brothers at Sheen,' he says. 'I shall live in silence again. And I can visit you. Just as I used to do.'

I make a little gesture with my hand as if to push away the memories of those days. 'It's not like it was,' I say. 'We have a good king on the throne now and we are prosperous. You can stay there by choice – not because you have nowhere else to go, not because I can't afford to house you. These are different times.'

'I know,' he says mildly. 'And I thank God that we live in such different times.'

'But don't listen to gossip there,' I warn him. 'It was said that they hold a document with an old prophecy about the family, about us. I suppose it's been destroyed; but don't listen to anything about it.'

He smiles and shakes his head at me as if I am an old foolish woman, fretting over shadows. 'I need not listen, but the whole country is talking about the Holy Maid of Kent who prophesies the future and warns the king against leaving his wife.'

'It doesn't matter what she says.' I deny the truth – there are thousands flocking to hear what she says. I am only determined that Reginald shall not be among them. 'Don't listen to gossip.'

'Lady Mother,' he reminds me. 'They are a silent order. There are no gossips there. You are not allowed to say one word.'

I think of the duke, my cousin, beheaded for listening to talk of the end of the Tudors in this very monastery. 'Something must have been said there, something dangerous.'

He shakes his head. 'That must be a lie.'

'It cost your kinsman his life,' I remark.

'A wicked lie then,' he says.

RICHMOND PALACE, WEST OF LONDON, SPRING 1529

We receive few visitors from London this spring but one day I look from my window to the view of the river, swollen with the rains, and see a barge approaching. At the bow and stern are the Darcy colours. Thomas Lord Darcy, the old Lord of the North, is coming to pay us the compliments of the season.

I call the princess and we go out to meet him as he stamps down the gangway of the barge, waves his three guests to follow him, and drops to his knee before her. We both watch with some anxiety the slow creaking down and then the painful rise, but I frown when one of the grooms of the household steps forward to help him. Tom Darcy may be more than sixty years old, but he does not like anyone to remark on it.

'I thought I'd bring you some plover eggs,' he says to the princess. 'From my moors. In the north.'

He speaks as if he owns all the moorland in the north of England, and indeed he owns a good share of it. Thomas Lord Darcy is one of the great northern lords whose life is dedicated to keeping the Scots on their side of the border. I first met him when I lived in Middleham Castle with my uncle King Richard, and Tom Darcy was one of the Council of the North. Now I step forward and kiss him on both ruddy cheeks.

He smiles, pleased at the attention, and gives me a wink. 'I have brought these gentlemen to see your court,' he says, as the French visitors line up and bow, proferring little gifts. Mary's lady in waiting takes them with a curtsey and we lead the way into the palace. The princess goes ahead into her presence chamber and then, after a brief conversation, leaves us. The Frenchmen stroll about and look at the tapestries and the silver plate, the precious objects on the sideboards, and chat to the ladies in waiting. Lord Darcy leans towards me.

'Troubled times,' he says shortly. 'I never thought I would live to see them.'

I nod. I lead him to the window so that he can enjoy the view of the knot gardens and the river beyond.

'They asked me what I knew of the wedding night!' he complains. 'A wedding night a quarter of a century ago! And I was in the north anyway.'

'Indeed,' I say. 'But why are they asking?'

'They're going to sit in judgement,' he says unhappily. 'There's some cardinal, trailing all the way from Rome, to tell our queen that she wasn't truly married, telling the king that he's been a bachelor for the last twenty years and can marry whoever he likes. Amazing what they think of, isn't it?'

'Amazing,' I agree.

'I've got no time for it,' he says abruptly. 'Nor for that fat churchman Wolsey.' He looks at me with his shrewd twinkling glare. 'I'd have thought you'd have had something to say about it. You and yours.'

'No-one has asked me for my opinion,' I say cautiously.

'Well, when they do, if you answer that the queen is his wife and his wife is the queen, you can call on Tom Darcy to support you,' he says. 'And others. The king should be advised by his peers. Not by some fat fool in cherry red.'

'I hope that the king will be well advised.'

The old baron puts out his hand. 'Give me your pretty brooch,' he says.

I unpin the insignia of my husband's house, a deep purple

enamelled pansy, that I wear at my belt. I drop it into Darcy's cal-
loused hand.

'I'll send it with a messenger, if I ever need to warn you,' he
says. 'So you know it's truly from me.'

I am wary. 'I should always be glad to hear from you, my lord.
But I hope that we will never need such a sign.'

He nods towards the closed door to the princess's privy chamber. 'I hope so too. But for all that, we might as well be prepared.
For her,' he says shortly. 'Bonny little thing. England's rose.'

RICHMOND PALACE, WEST OF LONDON, JUNE 1529

Montague comes from Blackfriars to Richmond on our family
barge to bring me the news from London, and I order the servants to bring him directly into my own private room and leave
my ladies and their sewing and their gossip outside the closed
door. Princess Mary is in her rooms and will not come to me
unless I send for her; I have told her ladies to keep her busy today
and to make sure that she speaks to no-one coming from London.
We are all trying to protect her from the nightmare that is being
enacted just downriver. Her own tutor, Dr Richard Fetherston,
has gone to London to represent the queen but agreed with me
that we should keep his mission from her daughter if we can. But,
I know that bad news travels fast, and I am expecting bad news.
Lord Darcy was not the only lord that was questioned, and now
a cardinal has arrived from Rome and set up a court to rule on
the royal marriage.

'What's happened?' I ask the minute the door is closed tightly
shut behind us.

'There was a court, a proper hearing, before Wolsey and

Cardinal Campeggio,' he begins. 'The place was packed. It was like a fair, packed so tightly you could hardly breathe. Everyone wanted to be there, it was like a public beheading when everyone is crowding to see the scaffold. Awful.'

I see he is genuinely distressed. I pour him a glass of wine and press him into a chair at the fireside. 'Sit. Sit, my son. Take a breath.'

'They called the queen into court and she was magnificent. She completely ignored the cardinals sitting in judgement and she walked past them and knelt before the king—'

'She did?'

'Knelt and asked him in what way she had displeased him. Said that she had greeted his friends as her own, done whatever he wanted, and if she had not given him a son it wasn't her fault.'

'My God – she said that in public?'

'Clear as a tolling bell. She said that he had found her an untouched virgin, as she was when she came from Spain. He said nothing. She asked him in what way she had ever failed him as a wife. He said nothing. What could he say? She has been everything to him for twenty years.'

I find I am smiling at the thought of Katherine speaking the truth to a king who has become accustomed to a diet of flattering lies.

'She asked if she could appeal to Rome, and then she rose to her feet and walked out, and left him silenced.'

'She just walked out?'

'They shouted her name to call her back into court, but she walked out and went back to her rooms as if she thought nothing of them. It was the greatest moment. Lady Mother, she has been a great queen all her life but that was her finest moment. And everyone outside the court, all the common people, were cheering and blessing her name and cursing the Lady for a whore who has brought nothing but trouble. And all the people inside the court were just stunned, or longing to laugh, or wanting to cheer too – but not daring while the king sat there, looking like a fool.'

'Hush,' I say at once.

'I know,' he says, snapping his fingers as if irritated at his own indiscretion. 'Sorry. This has shaken me more than I thought. I felt . . .'

'What?' I ask. Montague is not Geoffrey; he is not ready with his feelings, quick to tears, quick to anger. If Montague is distressed, then he has witnessed something very great indeed. If Montague is distressed, then the whole court will be rocked with emotion. The queen has let them see her sorrow, she has shown them her heartbreak, and now they will be as troubled as children who see their mother cry for the first time.

'I feel as if something terrible is happening,' he says wonderingly. 'As if nothing will ever be the same again. For the king to try to end his marriage to a faultless wife is somehow . . . if the king loses her he will lose . . .' He breaks off. 'How will he be without her? How will he behave without her advice? Even when he does not consult her we all know what she thinks. Even when she doesn't speak, there is still the sense of her at court, we know she is there. She is his conscience, she is his exemplar.' He pauses again. 'She's his soul.'

'He hasn't listened to her advice for years.'

'No, but even so, even so, she doesn't have to speak, does she? He knows what she thinks. We know what she thinks. She's like an anchor that he has forgotten, but still it keeps him steady. What is the Lady but just another of his fancies? He's had half a dozen of them but he always goes back to the queen, she always welcomes his return. She's his haven. Nobody believes that this time is any different. And to distress her like this . . .'

There is a little silence as we think what Henry would be without Katherine's loving, patient constancy.

'But you yourself said that she should consider stepping aside,' I accuse him. 'When this all started.'

'I see that the king wants a son and heir. Nobody can blame him for that. But he can't put a wife like this aside for a woman like that. For a princess from Spain or France or Portugal? Yes, then she should consider it. Then he might propose it to her, and she might consider it. But for a woman like that? Driven by nothing but sinful lust? And to try to trick the queen into saying that they were never married? Asking everyone of their opinion?'

'It's wrong.'

'Very wrong.' Montague rests his face in his hands.

'So what happens now?'

'The hearing goes on. I should think it will take days, maybe weeks. They're going to hear from all sorts of theologians, and the king has books and manuscripts coming in from all over Christendom to prove his case. He's commissioned Reginald to find and buy books for him. Sent him to Paris to consult with scholars.'

'Reginald is going to Paris? Why, when will he leave?'

'He's gone already. The king sent him the moment that the queen walked out of the court. She's going to appeal to Rome, she won't accept Wolsey's judgement in an English court. So the king will need foreign advisors, admired writers from all over Christendom. England won't be enough. That's his only hope. Otherwise the Pope will say that they were married in the sight of God, and nothing can put them apart.'

My son and I look at each other, as if the world we know is changing beyond recognition.

'How can he do this?' I ask simply. 'It's against everything he has ever believed in.'

Montague shakes his head. 'He's talked himself into it,' he says shrewdly. 'Like his love poems. He strikes a pose and then he persuades himself it's true. Now he wants to believe that God speaks to him directly, that his conscience is a greater guide than anything else, he's talked himself into love with this woman, and he has talked himself out of marriage, and now he wants everyone to agree.'

'And who will disagree?' I ask.

'Archbishop Fisher might, Thomas More probably not, Reginald can't,' Montague says, ticking off the great scholars on his fingers. 'We should,' he says, surprisingly.

'We can't,' I say. 'We're not experts. We're just family.'

RICHMOND PALACE, WEST OF LONDON, SUMMER 1529

The king, bitterly disappointed by Wolsey and the cardinal he brought from Rome to try to find a compromise, goes on progress without the queen. He takes a riding court, Anne Boleyn among them. They are said to be very merry. He does not send for his daughter and she asks me if I think she will be summoned to join him and her mother this summer.

'I don't think so,' I say gently. 'I don't think that they are travelling together this year.'

'Then may I go and stay with my mother, the queen?'

She looks up from her sewing, where she is doing blackwork embroidery on a shirt for her father, just as her mother taught her to do.

'I will write to ask,' I say. 'But it may be that your father prefers you to stay here.'

'And not see him or my mother?'

It is impossible to lie to her when she looks at me with that straight, honest York gaze.

'I think so, my dear,' is all I say. 'These are difficult times. We have to be patient.'

She folds her lips together as if to stop any word of criticism escaping. She bends a little lower over her work. 'Is my father to be divorced from my mother?' she asks.

That word in her mouth is like a blasphemous oath. She looks up at me as if she expects me to correct her speech, as if the very word is dirty.

'The case has been referred to Rome,' I say. 'Did you know that?'

A little nod tells me that she heard this from somewhere.

'The Holy Father will make a judgement. We just have to wait and see what he thinks. God will guide him. We have to have faith.

The Holy Father knows what is right in this; God will speak to him.'

She gives a little sigh, and shifts in her seat.

'Are you in pain?' I ask, seeing her bend forward a little, as if to ease a cramp in her belly.

At once she straightens up, her shoulders down, her head held like a princess. 'Not at all,' she says.

My son Geoffrey is honoured as the court leaves London. He is knighted for his services to the king in parliament. Geoffrey becomes Sir Geoffrey, as he should be. I think how proud my husband would be, and I cannot stop myself smiling all day at the honour done to his son.

Montague travels with the court as they ride down the sunlit valley of the Thames, calling at the great houses, hunting every day, dancing every night. Anne Boleyn is the mistress of everything she sees. He writes me one scribbled note:

Stop paying Wolsey's bribe, the Lady has turned against him and he's certain to fall. Send another of your little notes to Thomas More, I bet you a noble that he'll be the new Lord Chancellor.

The princess knows that a messenger has come from court, and sees the gladness in my face. 'Good news?' she asks.

'It is good news,' I tell her. 'This day a very honest man has come into your father's service and he, at least, will advise him well.'

'Your son Reginald?' she asks hopefully.

'His friend and fellow-scholar,' I say. 'Thomas More.'

'What has happened to Cardinal Wolsey?' she asks me.

'He has left court,' I say. I don't tell her that the Holy Maid of Kent predicted he would die miserably alone if he encouraged the king to leave his wife; and now the cardinal is all alone, and his health is failing.

GREENWICH PALACE, LONDON, CHRISTMAS 1529

Dressed in her best gown, wrapped in furs, I take Princess Mary by royal barge down the river to Greenwich for Christmas and we go straight to her mother's rooms.

The queen is waiting for us. Her ladies smile as Princess Mary runs through the presence chamber into the private rooms and mother and daughter hold each other tightly, as if they cannot bear to be parted ever again.

Katherine looks over her daughter's bowed head to me, and her blue eyes are filled with tears. 'Why, Margaret, you are raising a beauty for me,' she says. 'Merry Christmas, my dear.'

I am so moved by the sight of the two of them, together after such a long time, that I can barely reply.

'Are you all right?' is all that the little princess asks her mother, pulling back to look at her weary face. 'Mama? Are you all right?'

She smiles, and I know that she is going to lie to her daughter, as we all do these days. She is going to tell a brave lie in the hope that this little girl will grow to be a woman without the heartbreak of knowing that her father is wrong in his thoughts and wrong in his life and wrong in his faith.

'I am very well,' she says emphatically. 'And more importantly, I am sure that I am doing the right thing in the sight of God. And that must make me happy.'

'Does it?' the little princess asks doubtfully.

'Of course,' her mother says.

It is a great feast, as if Henry is trying to show the world the unity of his family, his wealth and power, and the beauty of his court.

He leads the queen to her throne with his usual grace, he talks most charmingly to her as they dine, and nobody seeing them seated side by side smiling would dream that this was an estranged couple.

His children, the bastard and the true heir, are honoured equally in an insane subverting of the rules of precedence. I watch as Princess Mary enters the great hall with a nobody: the ten-year-old boy, Bessie Blount's bastard. But they make a handsome pair. The princess is so dainty and slight and the boy so handsome and tall for his age that they walk at the same pace, their copper heads aligned. Little Henry Fitzroy is referred to everywhere as the Duke of Richmond; this brass-headed smiling child is the greatest duke in the country.

Princess Mary holds his hand as they enter for the Christmas feast, and when he opens his New Year's gift from his father the king – a magnificent set of gilt cups and pots – she smiles and applauds as if she is pleased to see him so highly rewarded. She glances across at me and sees my small nod of approval. If a princess of England is required to treat her father's bastard as an honoured half-brother, the Lord Lieutenant of Ireland, the head of the Council of the North, then my little princess – the true princess of England, Wales, Ireland and France – can rise to this ordeal.

The Lady is not present, so we are spared her pushing in front of her betters; but there is no need for anyone to hope that the king is tired of her yet, for her father is everywhere, flaunting his new title.

Thomas Boleyn, the man who was once very glad to serve me as steward of my lands, is now the Earl of Wiltshire and Ormonde, while his handsome but quite useless son George is Lord Rochford, appointed to the privy chamber with my cousin Henry Courtenay – where I doubt they will agree. The thankfully absent daughter becomes Lady Anne and the previous Boleyn whore, Mary Carey, now serves in two contradictory posts: chief companion and sole confidante to her sister, and as a rather sheepish lady in waiting to the queen.

Montague tells me that at the banquet held before Christmas, to celebrate Thomas Boleyn's remarkable rise, his daughter Anne walked before a princess born: the Dowager Queen of France, Mary. I cannot imagine the king's mistress walking ahead of the king's sister, the daughter of my steward preceding a dowager queen. My only comfort when Montague tells me of this is that I know Anne Boleyn has made herself a formidable enemy. The dowager queen is accustomed to being the first at court for rank, beauty and wit, and no Norfolk-born slut is going to take that off her without a battle.

RICHMOND PALACE, WEST OF LONDON, SUMMER 1530

The first sign of the royal visit is the arrival of the household: the grooms with the cantering horses, ridden four abreast, the man in the king's livery at the centre, holding four sets of reins, the horses going steadily forward. Behind them come the men at arms, first the mounted riders in light riding armour, then – after a long pause – the slower carts carrying the hawks for hunting, with the hounds running alongside, a cart for the little dogs and pets, and then the household goods. The king's luxuries go before him, his linen, his furniture, his carpets, his tapestries, the great riches of the treasury. The Lady's gowns, headdresses and jewels take two carts of their own and her serving women ride alongside, not daring to take their eyes off her wardrobe.

Behind them come the cooks with all the utensils for the kitchens, and the stores for today's feast and tomorrow.

Princess Mary, standing beside me on the tower at Richmond Palace looking down at this winding cavalcade as it heads towards us, says hopefully: 'Is he staying for a long time?'

I tighten my arm around her waist. 'No. He's going on from here. He's just coming for the day.'

'Where's he going?' she asks, forlorn.

'He'll travel this summer,' I guess. 'There's news of the Sweat in London. He'll go from one place to another again.'

'Then will he send for my mother and for me and it will be like the year when it was just us?' She looks up at me, suddenly hopeful.

I shake my head. 'Not this year, I don't think,' I say.

The king is determined to be charming to his daughter, you would almost think he wanted to win her to his side. From the moment his barge draws up to the pier with a shout of trumpets, to the moment he leaves at dusk, he is beaming at her, her hand tucked into the crook of his arm, his head cocked to hear her speech. He looks as if he is sitting for a portrait entitled 'A Loving Father', he looks as if he is an actor performing in a masque, and his role is 'The Righteous Parent'.

He has only a handful of companions with him: his usual friends, Charles Brandon and his wife Mary the Dowager Queen of France, my cousin Henry Courtenay and his wife Gertrude, my son Montague and a few other gentlemen of the privy chamber. The Boleyn men are on the royal barge but there is no mention of either of the Boleyn whores, and the only ladies who dine with us are those in attendance on the king's sister.

As soon as the king arrives, his breakfast is served, and he himself cuts the best meats and pours the sweetest watered wine for Princess Mary. He commands her to say grace for him and she does so quietly, in Greek, and he praises her learning and her composure. He nods his thanks to me. 'You are polishing my jewel,' he says. 'I thank you, Lady Margaret, you are a dear friend and kinswoman. I don't forget that you have been watching over me and mine, like a loving mother, from my childhood.'

I bow. 'It is a pleasure to serve the princess,' I say.

He smiles roguishly. 'Not like me, when I was her age,' he twin-
kles, and I think, how urgently you move the conversation to you.
How eagerly you prompt praise.

'Your Grace was the finest prince in the nursery,' I respond.
'And so naughty! And so beloved!'

He chuckles and pats Mary's hand. 'I loved sport,' he says. 'But
I never neglected my studies. Everyone said that I excelled at
everything I did. But,' he stages a shrug and a little laugh, 'people
always praise princes.'

They take the horses and go out hunting, and I command a
picnic to be ready for them when they are tired. We meet in the
woods to dine, and the musicians, hidden in the trees, play music
that has been composed by the king himself. He asks the princess
to sing for him and she makes a little curtsey to her aunt, the
dowager queen, and sings a song in French, to please her.

The dowager queen, who was once a Princess Mary herself,
rises from the table and kisses her niece, and gives her a gold and
diamond bracelet. 'She's a delight,' she says quietly to me. 'A
princess through and through,' and I know we are both thinking
of the little boy who is not and never can be a prince.

There is dancing after they have dined and I find Montague at
my side, as we watch the princess with her young ladies. 'The
queen stays at Windsor Castle,' he says. 'But we have to go on. We
are to meet up with the Lady and her court tonight.'

'But nothing changes?'

He shakes his head. 'Nothing changes. This is how it is now: the
queen at court and us trailing around with the Lady. There's no
joy in the summer any more. It's as if we are children who have
run away from home. We're tired of the adventure but we have to
endlessly pretend that we are having a wonderful time.'

'Is he not happy? Does she not make him happy?' I ask hopefully. If the king is not satisfied then he will look elsewhere.

'He's still not had her,' Montague says bluntly. 'She's got him
dancing on a thread. She's a prize he has to win. He's still, night
and day, on the hunt, hoping that this day, this night, she will say
yes. My God, but she knows how to entrap a man! She is always

about to fall, but she keeps always a hand-breadth, a moment out of his reach.'

The king seems to be delighted with the hunting, with the day, with the weather, with the music. The king is delighted with everything but especially with the company of his daughter.

'How I wish I could take you with me,' he says fondly. 'But your mother will not allow it.'

'I am sure my Lady Mother would allow it,' she says. 'I am sure that she would, Your Grace. And my Lady Governess could have my things packed and me ready to leave in a moment.' She laughs, a thin, hopeful, little nervous sound. 'I could come at once. You have only to say the word.'

He shakes his head. 'We have had some differences,' he says carefully. 'Your Lady Mother does not understand the difficulty that I am in. I am guided by God, my daughter. I am commanded by Him to ask your mother to take up a holy life, a sacred life, a life filled with respect and comfort that would honour her.

'Most people would say that she is lucky to be able to leave this troubled world and live at her ease in respect and holiness. I, for one, can't just give up. I have to stay and struggle in this world. I have to guard the country and continue my line. But your mother could be freed of her duty, she can be happy, she can live a life that would please her. You could stay with her often. Not I. I cannot put down my burden.'

She folds her lower lip under her little white teeth as if she is afraid of saying the wrong thing. She is frowning with concentration on his words. Henry laughs and chucks her under the chin. 'Don't look so grave, little princess!' he exclaims. 'These are worries for your parents, not for you. Time enough for you to understand the heavy burdens that I bear. But, believe this: your mother cannot travel with me while she writes to the Pope and tells him to command me, while she writes to her nephew the emperor and tells him to reprove me. She complains of me to others – that's not loyal, now, is it? Complains of me when I am trying to do the right thing, God's will! And so she cannot travel with me, though I would like her to be with me. And you cannot travel with me either. It is very cruel of her to separate us to prove her point. It is not a woman's role to enter into discourse. It is very cruel of her to send me out on progress alone. And wrong of her, against the commandment of God, to set up her opinion against her husband.

'It is hard,' the king continues, his voice deepening with pity for himself. 'It is a hard road for me, with no wife at my side. Your mother does not think of this when she sets herself against me.'

'I am sure . . .' Princess Mary begins, but her father raises his hand for her silence.

'Be very sure of this: I am doing the right thing for you, for the kingdom and for your mother,' he interrupts her. 'And I am doing God's will. God speaks directly to kings, you know. So anyone who speaks against me is speaking against the will of God Himself. They all say that – the men of the new learning. They all write it. It is indisputable. I am obeying the will of God and your mother, mistakenly, is following her own ambition. But at least I know I can count on your love and obedience. My little daughter. My princess. My only true love.'

Her eyes fill with tears, her lip trembles; she is torn between her loyalty to her mother and the intensely powerful charm of her father. She cannot argue against his authority, she curtseys to the father she loves. 'Of course,' she says.

RICHMOND PALACE, WEST OF LONDON, AUTUMN 1530

The former cardinal, Wolsey, has died on the road to London, before he could face trial, just as the Holy Maid of Kent predicted. Thank

God that we are spared the sight of a cardinal on trial. Cousin Henry Courtenay had been told he would have to present the charges of corruption and witchcraft; but God is merciful, and our family will not have his blood on our hands. We could not send a cardinal to the scaffold, though Tom Darcy says he could have done it.

The Boleyns, brother and sisters, danced in celebration before the court, in a masque of the damned. They looked as if they had come up from hell with sooty faces and hands like talons. God knows what we are coming to. Wolsey was bad enough but now the king's councillors are a family of nobodies who dress themselves as devils to celebrate the death of an innocent man. Burn this.

GREENWICH PALACE, LONDON, DECEMBER 1530

We spend Christmas at Greenwich as usual, the king his charming regal self, loving with the queen, doting on Mary, and proudly warm to his son the double duke, young Fitzroy, the Duke of Richmond. He is now a boy of eleven years, of soaring importance, and nobody who sees him could mistake him for anyone but his father's son; he is tall like a York, copper-headed like a Tudor, with the Plantagenet love of sport, music and learning.

I cannot imagine what the king means to do with him, unless it is to hold him in reserve as an heir, in case he gets no other. The fortune that is spent on his household and on his goods, even on his New Year gifts, shows that he is to be regarded highly, even as royal as the Princess Mary. Worse, it shows that the king wants everyone to see this – and what this means for my princess and her future leaves me puzzled. Every ambassador at court, every foreign visitor knows the princess is the only legitimate child, the daughter of the queen, a little crown on her head, the king's acknowledged daughter and heiress. But at the same time, walking beside her like an equal, is the king's bastard, dressed in cloth of gold, served like a prince, seated beside his father. What is anyone to make of this but that the king is training up his bastard child for the throne? And what is to become of his daughter if she is not to be Princess of Wales? And, if Henry Fitzroy is the next king, what is she?

The queen is outwardly serene, hiding her anguish at the

299

supplanting of her daughter with a nameless bastard. She takes her place on the throne beside her smiling husband and nods to her many friends. The ladies of the court, from the Dowager Queen of France down to Bessie Blount, show her every respect; most of them show her a special tenderness. Every woman knows that if a husband can set his wife aside and say it is the will of God then not one of them will ever be safe, not even with a wedding ring on her finger.

The noblemen of the court are scrupulous in their respect. They dare not openly oppose her husband, but the way that they bow when she walks by, and lean towards her to listen when she speaks, shows everyone that they know this is a Princess of Spain and a Queen of England and nothing can ever change that. Only the Boleyn family avoid her, the Boleyns and their kinsman Thomas Howard, the new young Duke of Norfolk – he has none of his father's fidelity to the queen, but thinks only of his own family's growing power. Everyone knows that the Howard interests are bound to the success of the young women that they have planted in the king's bed; their opinion of the queen is worthless.

They keep out of the queen's rooms but they are everywhere else at court, as if it were their own house, as if the magnificent Greenwich Palace were poky little Hever Castle. I hear from one of the ladies that the Boleyn woman, Anne, has sworn that she wishes all Spaniards were at the bottom of the sea, and that she will never serve the queen again. I think that if refusing to serve is the worst thing that Anne Boleyn can threaten, then we have nothing to fear.

But the loss of the cardinal and the dominance of the Howard faction at court means that the king has only one good advisor: Thomas More. He is at the king's side through the day but tries to go home to the City to be with his family. 'Tell your son that I am writing a long essay in reply to his,' he informs me one day as he walks to the stable yard, calling for his horse. 'Tell him I am sorry to be late in my reply. I have been writing too many letters for the king to write my own.'

'Do you write everything as he bids, or do you tell him your own opinions?' I ask curiously.

He gives me a small, wary smile. 'I choose my words carefully, Lady Margaret, both when I write as he commands, and when I tell him what I think.'

'And do you and Reginald still agree?' I ask him, thinking of Reginald travelling in France, consulting with churchmen, asking them for the advice that Thomas More avoids offering in England.

More smiles. 'Reginald and I love to differ over detail,' he says. 'But in general, we agree, my lady. And as long as he agrees with me, I am bound to think your son a very brilliant man.'

I am to take a new young woman into my care in the princess's household. Lady Margaret Douglas, the commoner daughter of the king's sister the Dowager Queen of Scotland. She was Cardinal Wolsey's ward and now has to live somewhere. The king chooses to put her in our household, living with our princess, under my care.

I welcome her with pleasure. She is a pretty girl, sixteen this year, desperate to be at court, eager to grow up. I think she will make a charming companion for our princess who is naturally serious and sometimes, in these hard days, troubled. But I hope that her wardship is not a sign to me that the importance of the princess is being diminished. I take my worries to the queen's chapel, kneeling at her altar and looking at the golden crucifix gleaming with rubies, and I pray, wordlessly, that the king has not sent one girl who is half-Tudor and half-commoner into the house of a princess because he may one day argue she is the same: half-Tudor, half-Spanish and no royal heir.

RICHMOND PALACE, WEST OF LONDON, SPRING 1531

Geoffrey rides out to see me, in the twilight, as if he does not want to be observed. I see him from my window that faces over the London road and I go down to meet him. He is handing over his horse in the stable yard and he kneels for my blessing on the cobbles and then draws me into the cold grey garden, as if he dare not speak to me indoors.

'What's the matter? What's happened?' I ask him urgently.

His face is pale in the gloom. 'I have to tell you something terrible.'

'The queen?'

'Safe, thank God. But someone has tried to kill Bishop Fisher, with poison.'

I grip his arm as I stagger in shock. 'Who would do such a thing? He cannot have an enemy in the world.'

'The Lady,' Geoffrey says grimly. 'He defends the queen from her, and he defends his faith from her, and he is the only man who dares to oppose the king. She, or her family, must be behind this.'

'It can't be! How do you know?'

'Because two men died eating from the bishop's bowl of porridge. God Himself saved John Fisher. He was fasting that day and didn't touch it.'

'I can hardly believe it. I *cannot* believe it! Are we Italians now?'

'No-one can believe it. But someone is prepared to kill a bishop to make the way easy for the Boleyn woman.'

'He is unharmed, God bless him?'

'Unhurt for now. But Lady Mother, if she would kill a bishop, would she dare attempt a queen? Or a princess?'

I feel myself grow cold in the cold garden; my hands begin to shake. 'She would not. She would not attempt the life of the queen or the princess?'

'Someone poisoned the bishop's porridge. Someone was prepared to do that.'

'You must warn the queen.'

'I have done so, and I told the Spanish ambassador, and Lord
Darcy had the same idea and came to me.'

'We can't be seen to plot with Spain. More so now than ever.'

'You mean, now that we know it is so dangerous to oppose
Anne Boleyn? Now that we know that the king uses the axe and
she uses poison?'

Numbly, I nod.

RICHMOND PALACE, WEST OF LONDON, SUMMER 1531

Reginald comes home from Paris, in the furred robe of a scholar,
with an entourage of clerks and learned advisors, bringing the
opinions of the French churchmen and universities, after months
of debate, research and discussion. He sends me a brief note to
tell me that he will see the king to make his report, and then come
to visit me and the princess.

Montague brings him, travelling by our barge on an inflowing
tide, with the sound of the drum keeping the rowers to their stroke
echoing over the cool water at the grey time of the evening. I am
waiting for them on the pier at Richmond, Princess Mary and her
ladies with me, her hand in the crook of my elbow, both of us
smiling a welcome.

As soon as the barge is close enough for me to see Montague's
white face and grimly set jaw I know that something is terribly
wrong. 'Go inside,' I say to the princess. I nod to Lady Margaret
Douglas. 'You go too.'

'I wanted to greet Lord Montague, and . . .'

'Not today. Go.'

She does as she is told and the two of them make their way slowly and unwillingly towards the palace, so I can turn my attention to the barge, to Montague's stiff figure, and the crumpled heap of his brother, my son Reginald, in the seat at the rear. On the pier the sentries present arms and snap to attention. The drum rolls, the rowers ship their oars, and hold them upward in salute as Montague hauls Reginald to his feet and helps him down the gangway.

My scholarly son staggers as if he is sick, he can hardly stand. The captain of the barge has to take his other arm and the two of them half lift him towards me as I stand on the pier.

Reginald's legs give way, he collapses to his knees at my feet, his head bowed. 'Forgive me,' he says.

I exchange one aghast look with Montague. 'What's happened?'

The face that Reginald turns up to me is as white as if he were dying of the Sweat. His hands that grip mine are damp and shaking. 'Are you sick?' I demand in sudden fear. I turn on Montague. 'How could you bring him here with a disease? The princess . . .'

Grimly, Montague shakes his head. 'He's not ill,' he says. 'He's been in a fight. He was knocked down.'

I clutch Reginald's shaking hands. 'Who dared to hurt him?'

'The king struck him,' Montague says shortly. 'The king drew a dagger on him.'

I am wordless. I look from Montague to Reginald. 'What did you say?' I whisper. 'What have you done?'

He bows his head, his shoulders convulse, and he gives a sob like a dry choking heave. 'I am sorry, Lady Mother. I offended him.'

'How?'

'I told him that there could be no reason in God's law, in the Bible, or in common justice, for him to put the queen aside,' he said. 'I told him that was the opinion of everyone. And he pounded his fist in my face, and snatched up a dagger from his table. If Thomas Howard had not caught him he would have run me through.'

'But you were only to report what the French theologians believe!'

'That's what they believe,' he says. He sits back on his heels and looks up at me, and now I see a great bruise slowly forming on the side of his pale handsome face. My son's delicate cheek bears the mark of the Tudor fist. Anger curdles in my belly like vomit.

'He had a dagger? He drew on you?'

The only man allowed to bear arms at court is the king. He knows that if he ever draws a sword he will be attacking a defence-less man. And so no king has ever drawn sword or dagger in court. It is against every tenet of chivalry that Henry learned as a boy. It is not in his nature to take up a blade against an unarmed opponent, it is not in his nature to bully with his fists. He is strong, he is big, but he has always managed his temper and controlled his strength. I can't believe he would have been violent, not to a younger, slighter man, not to a scholar, not to one of his own. I can't believe that he would have pulled out a blade on Reginald, of all people. This is not one of his wenching, fighting, drinking cronies; this is Reginald, his scholar.

'You taunted him,' I accuse Reginald.

He keeps his face down, he shakes his head.

'You must have driven him to anger.'

'I did nothing! He went in a moment,' he mutters.

'Was he drunk?' I ask Montague.

Montague is grim as if he took the blow himself. 'No. The Duke of Norfolk practically threw Reginald into my arms. Dragged him out of the privy chamber and thrust him at me. I could hear the king roaring behind him like an animal. I really think the king would have killed him.'

I cannot imagine this, I cannot believe it.

Reginald looks up at me, the bruise darkening on his cheek, his eyes horrified. 'I think he is gone mad,' he says. 'He was like a man insane. I think our king has gone mad.'

We bundle Reginald into the Carthusian monastery at Sheen where he can pray in silence among his brothers and let his bruises fade. As soon as he is well enough to travel we send him back to Padua, without a word to the court. There was some thought that he might be made Archbishop of York; but this will not happen now. He will never be the princess's tutor. I doubt that he will ever come to court or live in England.

'Better that he's out of the country,' Montague says firmly. 'I don't dare speak of him to the king. He's in a state of fury, all the time. He curses Norfolk for driving Wolsey to his death, he curses his own sister for her affection for the queen. He won't even see the Duchess of Norfolk, who has declared her loyalty to the queen, he won't ask Thomas More's opinion for fear of what he would say. He says he can trust nobody, none of us. Better for our family and for Reginald himself that he should be out of sight and forgotten for a little while.'

'He said that the king has run mad,' I say very quietly.

Montague checks that the door behind us is tightly closed. 'In truth, Lady Mother, I think the king has lost his wits. He loves the queen, he has relied on her judgement and he has always done so. She has been at his side without fail since he first came to the throne at seventeen. He cannot imagine being king without her. He's never done it without her. But he is madly in love with the Lady and she torments him night and day with desire and arguments. And he's not a youth, he's not a boy who can fall lightly into love and out again. He's not a good age for greensickness. This isn't poetry and singing songs under her window. She tortures him with her body and her brain. He's beside himself with desire for her, there are times when I think he's going to injure himself. Reginald caught him on the raw.'

'The more pity for us,' I say, thinking of Montague at court, Ursula struggling with the Stafford name, and Geoffrey, always at odds with his neighbours, trying to lead parliament when they are more frightened and troubled than they have ever been. 'It would have been better if we had gone unnoticed for a little while.'

'He had to report,' Montague says firmly. 'And it took great courage to say the truth. But he's better out of the country. Then at least we'll know that he can't upset the king again.'

WINDSOR CASTLE, BERKSHIRE, SUMMER 1531

Princess Mary and I, with our ladies, travel to Windsor to visit her mother while the king is on progress with his riding court. Once again the court is divided, once again the king and his mistress rattle around the great houses of England, hunting all day and dancing all night and assuring each other that they are wonderfully happy. I wonder how long Henry will tolerate this. I wonder when the emptiness of this life will drive him home to his wife.

The queen meets us at the castle gate, the great door behind her, the portcullis hanging above her, and even at a distance, as we ride up the hill to the great grey walls, I can see there is something about the straightness of her bearing and the turn of her head that tells me she has gripped tight onto her courage and that is all that is sustaining her.

We dismount from our horses and I drop into a curtsey, while the queen and her daughter cling to each other wordlessly, as if Katherine of Aragon, the doubly royal queen, does not care for formality any more but wants to hold her daughter in her arms and never let her go.

She and I cannot talk privately until after dinner when Princess Mary has been sent to say her prayers and to bed; then Katherine calls me into her bedroom as if to pray together, and we draw up two stools to the fireside, close the door, and are quite alone.

'He sent the young Duke of Norfolk to reason with me,' she says. I see the humour in her face and for a moment, forgetting the horror of her situation, we both smile, and then we laugh outright.

'And was he very very brilliant?' I ask.

She holds my hand and laughs aloud. 'Lord, how I miss his father!' she says, heartfelt. 'He was a man with no learning and much heart. But this duke, his son, has neither!' She breaks off.

'He kept saying: "Highest theological authorities, highest theological authorities", and when I asked him what he meant, he said: "Levitiaticus, Levitiaticus".'

I gasp with laughter.

'And when I said that I thought it was generally accepted that the passage from Deuteronomy indicated that a man should marry his deceased brother's wife, he said, "What? Deuteronomous? What, Suffolk? Do you mean Deuteronomous? Don't talk to me about scripture, I've never damn well read them. I have a priest to do that. I have a priest to do that for me."'

'The Duke of Suffolk, Charles Brandon, was here too?' I ask, sobering quickly.

'Of course. Charles would do anything for the king,' she says. 'He always has done. He has no judgement at all. He's torn, of course. His wife the dowager queen remains my friend, I know.'

'Half the country is your friend,' I say. 'All the women.'

'But it makes no difference,' she says steadily. 'Whether the country thinks I am right or wrong can make no difference. I have to live my life in the position that God appointed. I have no choice. My mother said I should be Queen of England when I was a little girl of no more than four, Prince Arthur himself chose this destiny for me from his deathbed, God placed me here at my coronation. Only the Holy Father can command me differently, and he has yet to speak. But how d'you think Mary is taking this?'

'Badly,' I say truthfully. 'She bleeds heavily with her courses and they give her much pain. I have consulted with wise women and even spoken to a physician but nothing they suggest seems to make any difference. And when she knows that there is trouble between you and her father she can't eat. She is sick with distress. If I force her to eat anything she vomits it up again. She knows something of what is happening, Our Lady alone knows what she imagines. The king himself spoke of it to her as you failing in your duty. It's terrible to see. She loves her father, she adores him, and she is loyal to him as the King of England. And she cannot live without you, she cannot be happy knowing that you are fighting for your name and your honour. This is destroying her health.' I pause, looking at her downturned face. 'And it goes on and on and on, and I cannot tell her that there will be an end to it.'

'I can do nothing but serve God,' she says stubbornly. 'Whatever it costs, I can do nothing but follow His laws. It blights my life too, and the king's. Everyone says he is like a man possessed. This isn't love, we've seen him in love. This is like a sickness. She does not call to his heart, to his true, loving heart. She calls to his vanity and she feeds it as if it were a monster. She calls to his scholarship and tricks him with words. I pray every day that the Holy Father writes simply and clearly to the king to tell him to put that woman aside. For Henry's sake now, not even for mine. For his own dear sake, for she is destroying him.'

'Has he gone on progress with her?'

'Gone on progress leaving Thomas More to chase heretics through London and burn them for questioning the Church. The London tradesmen are persecuted but she is allowed to read forbidden books.'

For a moment I don't see the weariness in her face, the lines around her eyes, or the paleness of her cheeks. I see the princess who lost the young man she loved, her first love, and the girl who kept her promise to him. 'Ah, Katherine,' I say tenderly. 'How have we come to this? However did this come about?'

'D'you know, he left without saying goodbye?' she says wonderingly. 'He has never done that before. Never in all his life. Not even these last few years. However angry he was, however troubled, he would never go to bed without saying goodnight to me, and he would never leave without saying goodbye. But this time he rode away and when I sent after him to say that I wished him well, he replied . . .' She breaks off, her voice weakened. 'He said that he did not want my good wishes.'

We are silent. I think that it is not like Henry to be rude. His mother taught him the perfect manners of royalty. He prizes himself on his courtesy, on his chivalry. That he should be discourteous – publicly and crudely discourteous to his wife, the queen – is another distinct line of paint in the portrait of this new king that is emerging: a king who will draw a blade on an unarmed younger man, who will allow his court to hound an old friend to his death, who watched his favourite and her brother and sister miming the act of dragging a cardinal of the Church down to hell.

I shake my head at the folly of men, at their cruelty, the pointless, bullying cruelty of a stupid man. 'He's showing off,' I say certainly. 'In some ways he's still the little prince I knew. He's showing off to please her.'

'He was cold,' the queen says. She draws her shawl around her shoulders as if she feels his coldness in her chamber even now. 'My messenger said that when the king turned away, his eyes were bright and cold.'

Only a few weeks later, just as we are about to go out riding, we get a message from the king. Katherine sees the royal seal and tears it open in the stable yard, her face alight with hope. For a moment I think that the king is commanding us to join him on progress, he has recovered from his ill temper and wants to see his wife and daughter.

Slowly, as she reads the letter, her face falls. 'It's not good news,' is all she says.

I see Mary put her hand to her belly as if she is suddenly queasy, and she turns from her horse as if she cannot bear the thought of sitting in a saddle. The queen hands me the letter and walks from the stable yard and into the palace without another word.

I read. It is a terse command from one of the king's secretaries: the queen is to pack up and leave Greenwich Palace at once and go to the More, one of the houses of the late cardinal. But Mary and I are not to go with her. We are to return to Richmond Palace, where the king will visit us when he passes on his progress.

'What can I do?' Mary asks, looking after her mother. 'What should I do?'

She is only fifteen years old; there is nothing that she can do. 'We have to obey the king,' I say. 'As your mother will do. She will obey him.'

'She will never agree to a divorce.' Mary rounds on me, her voice raised, her face anguished.

'She will obey him in everything that her conscience allows,' I correct myself.

RICHMOND PALACE, WEST OF LONDON, SUMMER 1531

We get home and I have a sense of a storm about to break as soon as the door to Mary's bedroom is closed behind us. All the way home, in the royal barge with people cheering her from the river-bank, she was dignified and steady. She took her seat at the rear of the barge on her gold throne, turning her head to right and left. When the wherrymen cheered her, she raised a hand; when the fishwives at the Lambeth quay shouted: 'God bless you, Princess, and your mother, the queen,' she inclined her head a little, to show that she heard them, but no further to indicate disloyalty to her father. She held herself like a marionette on tight wires, but the moment that we are home and the door is shut behind us she collapses as if all the strings are cut at once.

She drops to the floor in a storm of sobbing; there is no comforting her, there is no silencing her. Her eyes run, her nose, her deep sobs turn to retches and then she vomits out her grief. I fetch a bowl and pat her back, and still she does not stop. She heaves again but nothing comes except bile. 'Stop,' I say. 'Stop this, Mary, stop.'

She has never disobeyed me in her life before, but I see that she cannot stop; it is as if the separation of her parents has torn her apart. She chokes and coughs and sobs some more as if she would spit out her lungs, her heart. 'Stop, Mary,' I say. 'Stop crying.'

I don't believe she can even hear me. She is eviscerating herself as if she were a traitor being disembowelled, choking on her tears, on bile, or phlegm, and her wailing goes on.

I pull her up from the floor and I wrap her in shawls, as tightly as if I were swaddling a baby. I want her to feel held, though her mother cannot hold her, though her father has let her fall. I tighten the scarves around her heaving belly, and she turns her head away from me and gasps for breath as I tighten the fabric around her body and wrap her close. I lie her on her back on the bed, holding her thin shoulders, and still her mouth gapes wide on her unstoppable sobs and still her grief racks her. I rock her, as if she were a swaddled baby, I wipe the tears that come from her red swollen eyes, I wipe her nose, I pat the saliva from her drooling mouth. 'Hush,' I say gently. 'Hush. Hush, little Mary, hush.'

It grows dark outside and her sobs become quieter; she breathes and then she gives a little hiccough of grief, and then she breathes again. I lay my hand on her forehead where she is burning hot, and I think between the two of them they have nearly killed their only child. All through this long night, while Mary sobs herself to sleep and then wakes and cries out again as if she cannot believe that her father has abandoned her mother and they have both left her, I forget that Katherine is in the right, that she is doing the will of God, that she swore to be Queen of England and that God called her to this place just as He calls those that He loves. I forget that my darling Mary is a princess and must never deny her name, that God has called her, and it would be a sin to deny her throne as it would be a sin to deny her life. I just think that this child, this fifteen-year-old girl, is paying a terrible price for her parents' battle; and it would be better for her, as it was better for me, to walk away from a royal name and a royal claim altogether.

The court splits and divides, like a country readying for war. Some are invited to the king's progress around the hunting estates of England, riding all day and merry-making all night. Some stay with the queen at the More, where she keeps a good household and a large court. Very many slip away to go to their own houses and lands and pray that they will not be forced to choose whether to serve the king or the queen.

Montague travels with the king, his place is at his side, but his loyalty is always with the queen. Geoffrey goes home to Sussex, to his wife at Lordington, who gives birth to their first child. They call him Arthur, for the brother that Geoffrey loved best. Geoffrey writes at once to me to ask for an allowance for his baby son. He is a young man who cannot hold money, and I laugh at the thought of his lordly extravagance. He is too generous to his friends and keeps too wealthy a household. I know that I should refuse him; but I cannot. Besides, he has given the family another boy, and that is a gift beyond price.

I stay with Princess Mary at Richmond Palace. She is still hoping to be allowed to join her mother, writing carefully loving letters to her father, receiving only occasional scrawled replies.

I think it is a message from him when I see, from the window of her presence chamber, half a dozen riders on the road below, coming towards the palace and turning in through the great gates. I wait at the door of the presence chamber for the letter to be brought up. I will take it to the princess herself when she comes from her private chapel. I find I am afraid now what news she will read.

Yet it is no royal messenger but old Tom Darcy who comes slowly up the stairs, clutching the small of his back until he sees me waiting, when he straightens up and makes his bow.

'Your lordship!' I say, surprised.

'Margaret Pole, Countess!' he replies, and holds out his arms to me so that I can kiss him on the cheek. 'You look well.'

'I am well,' I say.

He glances towards the closed door of the presence chamber and cocks a grizzled eyebrow. 'Not so well,' I say shortly.

'Anyway, it's you I've come to see,' he says.

I lead the way to my own rooms. My ladies are with the princess in the chapel, so we are quite alone in the pretty, sunny room. 'Can I offer you something to drink?' I ask. 'Or to eat?'

He shakes his head. 'I hope to come and go unobserved,' he says. 'If anyone asks you why I was here you can say that I called in as I was going to London, to pay my respects to the princess, but came away without seeing her because she was ...'

'She's unwell,' I say.

'Sick?'

'Melancholy.'

He nods. 'No surprise. I came to see you about the queen her mother, and about her, poor young woman.'

I wait.

'Next parliament, after Christmas, they are going to try to bring the cause of the king's marriage into the judgement of England, away from the Pope. They're going to ask parliament to support that.'

Lord Darcy sees my small nod.

'They mean to annul the marriage and disinherit the princess,' Darcy says quietly. 'I've told Norfolk that I can't stand by and see it happen. He's told me to keep my old mouth shut. I need others to join with me, if I speak out.' He looks at me. 'Will Geoffrey speak with me? Will Montague?'

I find I am twisting the rings on my fingers, and he takes my hands in his firm grip and holds me still. 'I need your support,' he says.

'I am sorry,' I say eventually. 'You're in the right, I know it, my sons know it. But I don't dare have them speak out.'

'The king will usurp the rights of the Church,' Tom warns me. 'He will usurp the rights of the Church just so that he can give himself permission to abandon a faultless wife and disinherit an innocent child.'

'I know!' I burst out. 'I know! But we don't dare defy him. Not yet!'

'When?' he asks shortly.

'When we have to,' I say. 'When we absolutely have to. At the last moment. Not before. In case the king sees sense, in case something changes, in case the Pope makes a clear ruling, in case the emperor comes, in case we can get through this without standing up to be counted against the most powerful man in England, perhaps the most powerful man in the world.'

He has been listening very carefully and now he nods and puts his arm around my shoulders as if I were still a girl and he were a handsome young Lord of the North. 'Ah, Lady Margaret, my dear, you're afraid,' he says gently.

I nod. 'I am. I am sorry. I can't help it. I am afraid for my boys. I can't risk them going to the Tower. Not them. Not them as well.' I look into his old face for understanding. 'My brother . . .' I whisper. 'My cousin . . .'

'He can't charge us all with treason,' Tom says stoutly. 'If we stand together. He can't charge us all.'

We stand in silence for a moment, and then he releases me and reaches into the inside of his jacket and produces a beautifully embroidered badge, such as a man might pin to his collar before going into battle. It is the five wounds of Christ. Two hands with bleeding palms, two feet, stabbed and bleeding, a bleeding heart with a trail of red embroidery, and then, like a halo over it all, a white rose. Gently, he puts it into my hands.

'This is beautiful!' I am dazzled by the quality of the work and struck by the imagery that links the sufferings of Christ with the rose of my house.

'I had them embroidered when I was planning an expedition against the Moors,' he said. 'D'you remember? Years ago. Our crusade. The mission came to nothing but I kept the badges. I had this one made with the rose of your house for your cousin who was riding with me.'

I tuck it into the pocket of my gown. 'I am grateful to you. I shall put it with my rosary and pray on it.'

'And I shall pray that I never have to issue it in wartime,' he says grimly. 'Last time I gave it out to my men we were sworn to die to defend the Church against the infidel. Pray God we never have to defend against heresy here.'

Lord Darcy is not our only visitor to Richmond Palace as the hot weather goes on and the king's court stays away from his capital city. Elizabeth, my kinswoman, the Duchess of Norfolk, Thomas Howard's wife comes to visit us and brings a gift of game and much gossip.

She pays her compliments to the princess and then comes to my privy chamber. Her ladies sit with mine at a distance, and she requests two of them to sing. Shielded from observation and with our quiet voices drowned out by the music, she says to me: 'The Boleyn whore has commanded the marriage of my own daughter.'

'No!' I exclaim.

She nods, keeping her face carefully impassive. 'She commands the king, he commands my husband, and nobody consults me at all. In effect she commands me, me: a Stafford by birth. Wait till you hear her choice.'

Obediently, I wait.

'My daughter Mary is to be married to the king's bastard.'

'Henry Fitzroy?' I ask incredulously.

'Yes. My lord is delighted, of course. He has the highest of hopes. I would not have had my Mary mixed up in this for the world. When you next see the queen tell her that I have never wavered in my love and loyalty to her. This betrothal is none of my doing. I think of it as my shame.'

'Mixed up?' I ask cautiously.

'I tell you what I think is going to happen,' she says in a quick, furious whisper. 'I think the king is going to put the queen aside, whatever anyone says, send her to a nunnery and declare himself a single man.'

I sit very still, as if someone was telling me of a new plague at my doorstep.

'I think he will deny the princess, say that she is illegitimate.'

'No,' I whisper.

'I do. I think that he will marry the Boleyn woman and if she gives him a son he will declare that boy his heir.'

'The marriage wouldn't be valid,' I say quietly, holding on to the one thing that I know.

'Not at all. It will be made in hell against the will of God! But who in England is going to tell the king that? Are you?'

I swallow. No-one is going to tell him. Everyone knows what happened to Reginald when he merely reported the opinion of the French universities.

'He will disinherit the princess,' she says. 'God forgive him. But if the king cannot get a son on the Boleyn woman he has Fitzroy in reserve and he will make him his heir.'

'Bessie Blount's boy? In the place of our princess?' I try to sound scathing but I am finding it all too easy to believe her.

'He is the Duke of Richmond and Sommerset,' she reminds me. 'Commander of the North, Lord Lieutenant of Ireland. The king has given him every great title, so why not Prince of Wales among all the others?'

I know this was the cardinal's old plan. I had hoped it had fallen with him. 'No-one would support such a thing,' I say. 'No-one would allow a legitimate heir to be replaced with a bastard.'

'Who would rise against it?' she demands. 'No-one would like it but who would have the courage to rise against it?'

I close my eyes for a moment and I shake my head. I know that it should be us. If anyone, it should be us.

'I'll tell you who would rise if you would lead them,' she says in a quiet, passionate whisper. 'The common people and everyone who would carry a sword at the Pope's command, everyone who would follow the Spanish when they invade for their princess, everyone who loves the queen and supports the princess, and every Plantagenet that has ever been born. One way or another that's nearly everyone in England.'

I put out a hand. 'Your Grace, you know I cannot have this talk in the princess's household. For her sake as well as mine I cannot hear it.'

She nods. 'But it's true.'

'But why would the Boleyn woman want such a match?' I ask her curiously. 'Your daughter Mary brings a great dowry and her father commands great acres of England – and all his tenants. Why would the Boleyn woman give such power to Henry Fitzroy?'

The duchess nods. 'Better for her than his other choice,' she says. 'She can't bear his marriage to the Princess Mary. She can't bear to see the princess as heir.'

'That would never have happened,' I say flatly.

'Who would stop it?' she challenges me.

My hand creeps to my pocket where I keep my rosary and Tom Darcy's badge of the five wounds of Christ under the white rose of my house. Would Tom Darcy stop it? Would we join him? Would I sew this badge onto my son's collar and send him out to fight for the princess?

'Anyway,' she concludes. 'I came to tell you that I don't forget my love and loyalty to the queen. If you see her tell her that I would do anything, I will do everything I can. I speak with the Spanish ambassador, I speak to my kinsmen.'

'I can be no part of it. I am not gathering her supporters.'

'Well, you should be,' the duchess says bluntly.

RICHMOND PALACE, WEST OF LONDON, SUMMER 1531

Lady Margaret Douglas, the king's niece, daughter of the Scottish queen, his sister, is ordered to leave us, though she and the princess have become the firmest of friends. She is not to be sent to her mother, but going into service at court, to wait upon the Boleyn woman, as if she were a queen.

She is excited at the thought of being at court, hopeful that her dark prettiness will turn heads; brunettes are in fashion, with the Boleyn woman's black hair and olive skin being much praised. But she hates the thought of serving a commoner, clinging to Princess Mary and holding me tightly before she steps into the royal barge that has come for her.

'I don't know why I can't stay with you!' she exclaims.

I raise my hand in farewell. I don't know why, either.

I have a summer wedding to prepare, and I turn from my fears for the princess to write the contracts and agree the terms with the same joy that I pick the flowers to make a garland for the bride, my granddaughter, Katherine, Montague's oldest. She is only ten but I am glad to get Francis Hastings for her. Her sister Winifred is betrothed to his brother Thomas Hastings so our fortunes are safely linked to a rising family; the boys' father, my kinsman, has just been made an earl. We have a pretty betrothal ceremony and a wedding feast for the two little girls and Princess Mary smiles when the two couples come hand-fasted down the aisle, as if she were their older sister and as proud of them as I am.

ENGLAND, CHRISTMAS 1531

This Christmas season has little joy in it, not for the princess, nor for her mother the queen. Not even her father the king seems to be happy; he keeps the feast at Greenwich in the most lavish style, but people say that it was a merry court when the queen was on the throne and now he is hag-ridden by a woman who cannot be satisfied and will give him no pleasure.

The queen is at the More, well served and honoured; but alone. Princess Mary and I are ordered to go to Beaulieu in Essex and we keep the Christmas feast there. I make the twelve days of Christmas as happy as I can for her; but through all the wassailing, and dancing, disguising and feasting, the bringing in of the Yule log and the raising of the Christmas crown, I know that

Mary is missing her mother, and praying for her father, and that there is very little joy anywhere in England these days.

RICHMOND PALACE, WEST OF LONDON, MAY 1532

It is a beautiful early summer, as lovely as if the countryside itself wanted to make everyone remember this time. Every morning there is a pearly mist on the river that hides the quietly lapping water and the duck and geese rise out of it with slowly beating wings.

At sunrise the heat burns the mist away and leaves the grass sparkling with dew, every cobweb a work of lace and diamonds. Now I can smell the river, damp and wet and green, and sometimes, if I sit very still on the pier, looking down through the floating weed and the clumps of sweet-smelling watermint, I see schools of little fish and the movement of trout.

In the water meadows running down from the palace to the river the cows wallow hock-deep in thick, lush grass bright with buttercups, and flick their tails against the flies that buzz around them. Amorously, they walk shoulder to shoulder with the bull, and the little calves wobble on unsteady legs after their dams.

First the swifts arrive, and then the swallows and then the martins, and soon on every wall of the palace there is a frenzy of building and rebuilding the little mud cups of nests. All day long the birds are flying from river to eaves, only stopping to preen on the roofs of the stables, pretty as little nuns in their black and white. When the parents fly past the nests the newly hatched chicks bob up their little heads and cry out, each yellow beak wide open.

We are filled with the joy of the season and we bring in the May, and have dances in the woods, rowing races and swimming contests. The courtiers take a fancy to fishing and every young man brings a rod and a line and we have a bonfire by the river, where the cooks seethe the catch in butter in cauldrons set in the ashes, and serve it sizzling hot. As the sun lies low and the little silver moon rises, we go out in the barges and the musicians play for us and the music drifts across the water as the sky turns to peach, and the river becomes a pathway of rose gold that might lead us anywhere, and the tide feels as if it will draw us far away.

We are coming home at dusk, singing softly with the lute player, without torches so the grey of twilight lies on the water and the bats dipping in and out of the silvery river are undisturbed, when I hear a drum for rowers echoing across the water like distant cannon fire, and I see Montague's barge carrying torches fore and aft coming swiftly towards us.

Our barges land at the pier and I order Princess Mary into the palace, thinking that I will meet Montague alone, but for once, for the very first time, she does not make the face of a sulky child and slowly go where she is bidden. She stops to face me, and says: 'My dear, my dearest Lady Governess, I think I should meet your son. I think he should tell us both what he has come to tell you. It is time. I am sixteen. I am old enough.'

Montague's barge is at the pier; I can hear the rattle of the gangplank behind me and the footsteps of the rowers as they make a guard of honour, their oars held high.

'I am brave enough,' she promises. 'Whatever he has to say.'

'Let me find out what is happening, and I will come at once and tell you,' I temporise. 'You are old enough. It is time. But . . .' I break off, I make a little gesture as if to say, you are so slight, you are so fragile, how are you going to bear bad news?

She raises her head, she puts back her shoulders. She is her mother's daughter in the way that she prepares herself for the very worst. 'I can bear anything,' she says. 'I can bear any trial that God sends to me. I was raised for this; you yourself educated me for this. Tell your son to come and report to me, his future sovereign.'

Montague stands before us, bows to us both and waits, looking from one to the other: the mother whose judgement he trusts, and the young royal in my keeping.

She nods her head to him as if she were a queen already. She turns and seats herself in a little bower that we have made, a seat for lovers to enjoy the river in the shade of a rose bush and honeysuckle. She sits as if it is a throne, and the flowers breathing their scent into the night air are her canopy of state. 'You can tell me, Lord Montague. What grave news do you have, that you come from London with your oars pulling so fast and the drum beating so loud?' And when she sees him glance at me, she says again: 'You can tell me.'

'It is bad news. I came to tell my Lady Mother.' Almost without thinking he pulls off his cap and drops to one knee before her as if she were queen.

'Of course,' she says steadily. 'I knew it as soon as I saw your barge. But you can tell us both. I am no child, and I am no fool. I know my father is moving against the Holy Church and I need to know what has happened. Lord Montague, help me. Be a good advisor to me, and tell me what has happened.'

He looks up at her as if he would spare her this. But he tells her simply and quietly. 'Today the Church surrendered to the king. Only God knows what will happen. But from today the king will rule the Church himself. The Pope is to be disregarded in England. He is no more than a bishop, the Bishop of Rome.' He shakes his head in disbelief as he says it. 'The Pope is overthrown by the king and the king sits below God with the Church below him. Thomas More has returned the seal of Lord Chancellor and resigned his post and gone home.'

She knows that her mother has lost a true friend and her father the last man who would tell him the truth. She is silent as she takes in the news. 'The king has made the Church his own?' she asks. 'All its wealth? And its laws and its courts? This is to take England entirely into his own possession.'

Neither I nor my son can contradict her.

'They are calling it the submission of the clergy,' he says quietly.

'The Church cannot make law, the Church cannot convict heresy, the Church may not pay its wealth to Rome, and it may not take commands from Rome.'

'So that the king can rule on his own marriage,' the princess says. I realise that she has thought deeply on this, and that her mother will have told her the many clever measures that the king and his new advisor Thomas Cromwell have undertaken.

We are silent.

'Jesus Himself appointed his servant Peter to rule the Church,' she observes. 'I know this. Everyone knows this. Is England to disobey Jesus Christ?'

'This is not our battle,' I interrupt. 'This is a matter for churchmen. Not for us.'

Her blue York gaze turns to me as if she hopes that I will tell the truth, but knows that I will not.

'I mean it,' I insist. 'This is a great matter. It is for the king and the Church to decide. It is for the Holy Father to remonstrate, if he thinks best. It is for the king to take advice and make his claim, as he thinks best. It is for the churchmen in parliament to respond to the king. Thomas More must speak out, John Fisher will speak out, your own tutor Richard Fetherston, has spoken out, it is for the men, the bishops and archbishops. Not us.'

'Oh, they have spoken,' Montague says bitterly. 'The churchmen spoke at once. Most of them agreed without an argument, and when it came to a vote they stayed away. That is why Thomas More has gone home to Chelsea.'

The little princess rises from the garden seat and Montague gets to his feet. She does not take his offered arm but turns to me. 'I shall go to my chapel and pray,' she says. 'I shall pray for wisdom to guide me in these difficult days. I wish that I knew what I should do.'

She is silent for a moment looking at us both. 'I shall pray for my tutor, and for Bishop Fisher. And I shall pray for Thomas More,' she says. 'I think that he is a man who does know what he should do.'

RICHMOND PALACE, WEST OF LONDON, SUMMER 1532

That was the end of our carefree summer, and the end of the good weather too, for as the princess prayed in the private chapel, turning over her rosary beads naming her mother, Bishop Fisher, and Thomas More, to St Jude, the saint for the hopeless and the despairing, the clouds rolled up the valley making the river dark and then it started to rain with the thick, heavy drops of a summer storm.

The bad weather lasted for weeks, heavy clouds lay over the city and people grew bad-tempered and exhausted in the heat. When the clouds cleared at night instead of the familiar stars there was a succession of constant burning comets crossing the sky. People watching the troubled stars saw standards and banners and unmistakable signs of war. One of Reginald's former friends, one of the Carthusian monks, told my confessor that he had clearly seen a burning red globe hanging above their church and from this he knew that the king's anger would fall on them for keeping their prophecy safe, and hiding the manuscript.

The fishermen who came to the pier with fresh trout for the household said that they were catching dead bodies in their nets, so many men were throwing themselves into the flood waters of the unusually high tides. 'Heretics,' one said, 'for the Church will burn them if they don't drown themselves. Thomas More will see to that.'

'Not any more,' said the other. 'For More will be burned himself, and the heretics are safe in England now that the king's whore is a Lutheran. It is those who love the old ways and who pray to the Virgin and honour the queen who are drowning themselves in the new tide.'

'That's enough from both of you,' I say, pausing at the kitchen door while the cook picks out her baskets of fish. 'We don't want any talk like that in this household. Take your money and go, and don't come here again or I will report you.'

I can silence the men at the door, but every man, woman and child on the road to or from London who passes our door and calls in for the free food given out at the end of every meal has one story or another, and they all have the same ominous theme.

They are talking of miracles, of prophecies. They believe that the queen is receiving daily messages from her nephew the emperor, promising that he will defend her, and there will be a Spanish fleet sailing up the Thames any dawn. They don't know for sure, but they heard from someone that the Pope is consulting with his advisors, hammering out a compromise because he is afraid that the Christian kings will turn on each other over this matter, while the Turk is at the door of Christendom. They don't know, but everyone seems to be sure that the king is advised only by the Boleyns and by their lawyers and churchmen, and they are telling him wicked lies: that the only way ahead to his desires is to steal the Church, to set aside his coronation oath, to tear up Magna Carta itself and act the tyrant and defy anyone who says that he cannot do such a thing.

No-one knows anything for sure; but they know very well that there are dangerous times ahead, and the smell of danger is in the air, and that every time the thunder rumbles someone, somewhere in England says: 'Listen. Was that guns? Is the war starting again?'

Those who are not afraid of war are afraid of the rising of the dead from their graves. The shallow graves at Bosworth Field, at Towton, at St Albans, at Towcester throw up trophies of silver and gold, badges and keepsakes, tokens and livery buttons. Now they say that the quiet earth itself is disturbed in these old battlefields, as if they are being secretly harrowed in darkness, and the men who died for the Yorks have been released from the damp earth and are standing up, brushing off the clinging soil, mustering in their old troops, and coming back to fight again for their princess and for their Church.

Some fool comes to the stable door and tells the grooms that he has seen my brother, his head back on his shoulders, handsome as a boy, knocking at the door of the Tower of London and asking to come back in. Edward is supposed to have cried out that the Mouldwarp, a wicked, dark animal King of England, has crawled onto his throne; and these are his years. A dragon and a lion and a wolf will have to rise up to defeat him, and the dragon will be the Emperor of Rome, the wolf will be the Scots, and the lion will be our own true princess who, like a girl in a story, will have to kill her wicked father to set her mother and her country free.

'Get that treasonous, foul-mouthed old gossip out of the yard and throw him in the river,' I say shortly. 'And then lock him up in the guardhouse and ask the Duke of Norfolk what he wants done with him. And make sure that everyone knows I never want to hear a word of lions or moles or flaming stars again.'

I speak with such cold fury that everyone obeys me; but that night, as I close the shutters on my bedroom window, I see above our own palace roof a flaming star, like a blue crucifix, above the princess's bedroom, as if St Jude, the saint of the impossible, is shining down on her a sign of hope.

L'ERBER, LONDON, SUMMER 1532

Montague and Geoffrey ask me to meet them at our London house, L'Erber, and I make an excuse to the princess that I need to see a physician, buy some warmer tapestries for the walls of the palace, and get her a winter cloak.

'Will you see anyone in London?' she asks.

'I may see my sons,' I say.

She glances around to be sure that we cannot be overheard. 'Can I give you a letter for my mother?' she whispers.

I hesitate for only a moment. Nobody has told me if the

princess and her mother may exchange letters; but equally no-one has forbidden it.

'I want to write to her and know no-one else reads it,' she says.

'Yes,' I promise. 'I'll try to get it to her.'

She nods and goes to her private chamber. A little while later she comes out with a letter with no name on the front and no seal on the back and gives it to me.

'How will you get it into her hands?' she asks.

'Better that you don't know,' I say, kiss her, and walk through the gardens and down to the pier.

I take our barge downriver to the water stairs above London Bridge and walk though the City, surrounded by my personal guards, to my London home.

It seems like a long time since I was pruning back the vine and hoping for English wine. It was a sunny day when Thomas Boleyn warned me of the danger that my cousin the Duke of Buckingham was running into headlong. I could almost laugh now at the thought of Boleyn's fearful caution, when I think how high he has risen, and how much more danger we are all in as a result of his own ambition – though back then, he was warning me of mine. Who would have thought that a Boleyn could advise the king? Who would have thought that the daughter of my steward should threaten the Queen of England? Who would ever have dreamed that a King of England would overthrow the laws of the land and the Church itself to get such a girl into his bed?

Geoffrey and Montague are waiting for me in my privy chamber, where there is a good fire in the grate and mulled ale in the jug. My house is run as it should be, even though I am here only rarely. I see that everything is just so with a little nod of approval and then I take the great chair and survey my two sons.

Montague looks far older than his forty years. The task of serving this king, as he goes determinedly down the wrong road against the wishes of his people, against the truth of his Church, against the advice of his councillors, is draining my oldest son. It is exhausting him.

Geoffrey is thriving on the challenge. He is where he loves to be, at the centre of things, pursuing something he believes in, arguing the tiniest detail, clamouring for the greatest of principles. He appears to serve the king in parliament, bringing information to the king's clever servant, Thomas Cromwell, chatting to men who have come up from the country, puzzled and anxious with no idea of what is happening at court, and he meets with our friends and kinsmen of the privy council and speaks for the queen whenever he can. Geoffrey loves an argument; I should have sent him to be a lawyer and then perhaps he would have risen as high as Thomas Cromwell, whose plan it is to set the parliament against the priests and so divide them to their ruin.

They both kneel and I put my hand on Montague's head and bless him, and then rest my hand on Geoffrey's head. His hair is still springy under my palm. When he was a baby I used to run my fingers through his hair to see the curls lift up. He always was the prettiest of all my children.

'I have promised the princess to get this into her mother's hands,' I say, showing them the folded paper. 'How can we do this?'

Montague puts out his hand for it. 'I'll give it to Chapuys,' he says, naming the Spanish ambassador. 'He writes to her in secret, and he delivers her letters to the emperor and the Pope.'

'Nobody must know that it has come by us,' I caution him.

'I know,' he says. 'Nobody will.' He tucks the single page inside his doublet.

'So,' I say, gesturing that they can sit. 'We will have been observed, meeting like this. What are we to say we have been discussing, should anyone ask?'

Geoffrey is ready with a lie. 'We can say that we are troubled by Jane, Arthur's widow,' he says. 'She has written me a letter, asking to be released from her vows. She wants to come out of Bisham Priory.'

I raise an eyebrow at Montague. Grimly he nods. 'She wrote to me too. It's not the first time.'

'Why didn't she write to me?'

Geoffrey giggles. 'It's you she blames for putting her inside,' he says. 'She has taken it into her head that you want to secure the fortune of your grandson Henry by keeping her locked up and out of sight forever, her dower lands in your keeping, his inheritance safe from her. She wants to come out and get her fortune back.'

'Well, she can't,' I say flatly. 'She took a vow of poverty for life of her own free will, I won't restore her dower and have her in my house, and Henry's lands and fortune are my safe-keeping until he is a man.'

'Agreed,' Montague says. 'But we can say that is why we met and talked here.'

I nod. 'And so why did you want to see me?' I speak with determination. My boys must not know that I am weary and frightened by the world that we live in now. I did not think that I would ever see the day when a Queen of England did not sit on her throne at her court. I never dreamed that I would see the day when a king's bastard took titles and wealth and paraded himself as an heir to the throne. And nobody, surely nobody in the long history of this country, ever thought that a King of England could set himself up as an English Pope.

'The king is to go to France again, another meeting,' Montague says briefly. 'He hopes to persuade King Francis to support his divorce with the Pope. The hearing is set for Rome this autumn. Henry wants King Francis to represent him. In return, Henry will promise to go on crusade for the Pope against the Turk.'

'Will the King of France support him?'

Geoffrey shakes his head. 'How can he? There is neither logic nor morality to it.'

Montague gives a weary smile. 'That might not discourage him. Or he might promise it, just to get the crusade started. The point is that the king is taking Richmond.'

'Henry Fitzroy? What for?'

'He is to stay at the French court, as a visiting prince, and the French king's son Henri duc d'Orléans is to come home with us.'

I am horrified. 'The French are accepting Fitzroy, Bessie Blount's bastard, in exchange for their prince?'

Montague nods. 'It must be certain that the king plans to name him as his heir, and disinherit the princess.'

I cannot help it. I drop my head into my hands so that my sons cannot see the anguish on my face, then I feel Geoffrey's gentle hand on my shoulder. 'We're not powerless,' he says. 'We can fight this.'

'The king is taking the Lady to France also,' Montague goes on. 'He is going to give her a title and a fortune; she is to be the Marquess of Pembroke.'

'What?' I ask. It is a strange title; this is to make her a lord in her own right. 'And how can he take her to France? She can't be a lady in waiting to the queen, since the queen is not attending. How can she go? What is she to do? What is she to be?'

'What she is – a whore,' Geoffrey sneers.

'A new sort of lady,' Montague says quietly, almost regretfully. 'But the new Queen of France won't meet her, and the King of France's sister won't meet her, so she'll have to stay in Calais when the two kings meet. She'll never meet the King of France at all.'

For a moment I think of the Field of the Cloth of Gold and the queens of England and France going to take Mass together, chattering like girls, kissing each other and promising lifelong friendship. 'It will be such a shadow of what went before,' I say. 'Can the king not see that? Who will attend her?'

Montague allows himself a smile. 'The dowager queen Mary is no friend to the Lady, and says that she's too ill to travel. Even her husband has quarrelled with the king about the Boleyn woman. The Duchess of Norfolk won't go, the duke doesn't even dare to ask her. None of the great ladies will go, they'll all find an excuse. The Lady has only her immediate family: her sister and her sister-in-law. Other than Howards and Boleyns she has no friends.'

Geoffrey and I look blankly at Montague's description of this scratch court. Every great person is always surrounded by a crowd of family, affinity, loyalists, friends, supporters: it is how we parade greatness. A lady without companions signals to the world that she is of no importance. The Boleyn woman is there only at the whim of the king, a very lonely favourite. The king's whore has no queen's court around her. She has no setting. 'Does he not see her for what she is?' I ask helplessly. 'When she has neither friends nor family?'

'He thinks that she prefers him before all company,' Montague says. 'And he likes that. He thinks she is a rare thing, untouchable, a prize that only he can approach, only he might win. He likes it that she is not encircled by noblewomen. It's her strangeness, her Frenchness, her isolation, that he likes.'

'Do you have to go?' I ask Montague.

'Yes,' he says. 'God forgive me, I am commanded to go. And that's why we wanted to see you. Lady Mother, I think the time has come for us to act.'

'Act?' I say blankly.

'We have to defend the queen and the princess against this madness. The time is now. Clearly, if he is parading Henry Fitzroy as his heir he is going to put the princess aside. So I thought that I would take Geoffrey with me, in my household, and when we get to Calais, he can slip away and meet with Reginald. He can give him a report of our friends and kinsmen in England, take a message to the Pope, carry a letter for the queen to her nephew the King of Spain. We can tell Reginald that one strong ruling from the Pope against Henry will put a stop to this whole thing. If the Pope were to decide against Henry, then he would have to take the queen back. The Pope has to speak out. He can delay no longer. The king is pushing on, but he is blind as a mole in a tunnel. He is taking nobody with him.'

'Yet nobody defies him,' I observe.

'That's what we must tell Reginald, that we will defy him.' Montague takes the challenge without flinching. 'It has to be us. If not us, then who will stand against him? It should have been the Duke of Buckingham, the greatest duke in the land, but he is already dead on the scaffold and his son is a broken man. Ursula can do nothing with him – I've already asked her. The Duke of Norfolk should advise the king, but Anne Boleyn is his niece, and his daughter is married to the king's bastard. He's not going to argue against the promotion of the unworthy. Charles Brandon should advise the king, but Henry banished him from court for one word against her.

'As to the Church, it should be defended by the Archbishop of York, or of Canterbury; but Wolsey is dead and Archbishop Warham is dead and the king is going to put the Boleyn's own chaplain in his place. John Fisher is unfailingly brave but the king ignores him and he is old and his health is broken. The Lord Chancellor, Sir Thomas More, handed back his seal of office rather than speak out, our own brother was silenced with a fist, and now the king listens only to men without principle. His greatest advisor, Thomas Cromwell, is neither of the Church nor of the nobility. He's a man from nowhere without education, like an animal. He seeks to serve only the king, like a dog. The king has been seduced and entrapped by bad advisors. We have to win him back from them.'

'It has to be us, there is no-one but us,' Geoffrey exclaims.

'Henry Courtenay?' I suggest, trying to escape the burden of destiny, naming our Plantagenet kinsman, the Marquess of Exeter.

'He's with us,' Montague says shortly. 'Heart and soul.'

'Can't he do it?' I ask cravenly.

'On his own?' Geoffrey mocks me. 'No.'

'He'll do it with us. Together we are the white rose,' Montague says gently. 'We are the Plantagenets, the natural rulers of England. The king is our cousin. We have to bring him back to his own.'

I look at their two eager faces and think that their father kept me in obscurity and short of money so that I would never have to take a decision like this, so that I would never have to take up my duty as a natural leader of the country, so that I would never have to steer the destiny of the kingdom. He hid me from power so that I should not have to make this sort of choice. But I cannot be hidden any longer. I have to defend the princess in my charge, I cannot deny my loyalty to the queen, my friend, and my boys are right – this is the destiny of our family.

Besides – the king was once a little boy and I taught him to walk. I loved his mother and promised I would keep her sons safe. I can't abandon him to the terrible mistakes he is making. I can't let him destroy his inheritance and his honour for the Boleyn bagatelle, I cannot let him put a bastard boy in the place of our true-born princess. I cannot let him enact his own curse by disinheriting a Tudor.

'Very well,' I say at last, and with deep reluctance. 'But you must be very, very careful. Nothing written down, nothing told to anyone except those we can trust, not even a word in confession. This must be absolutely a secret. Not a whisper to your wives, especially I don't want the children to know anything of this.'

'The king doesn't pursue the families of suspects,' Geoffrey reassures me. 'Ursula was unhurt by the sentence against her father-in-law. Her boy is safe.'

I shake my head. I can't bear to remind him that I saw my eleven-year-old brother taken to the Tower and he never came out again. 'Even so. It's secret,' I repeat. 'The children are to know nothing.'

I take out the emblem that Tom Darcy gave me, the embroidered badge of the five wounds of Christ with the white rose of York above it. I spread it flat on the table so that they can see it. 'Swear on this badge, that this remains secret,' I say.

'I so swear.' Montague puts his hand on the badge, and I put my hand on his, and Geoffrey puts his hand on top.

'I swear,' he says.

'I swear,' I say.

We are hand-clasped for a moment and then Montague releases me with a little smile, and examines the badge.

'What is this?' he asks.

'Tom Darcy gave it to me, he had it made when he went on crusade. It's the badge of the defender of the Church against heresy. He had one made for our family.'

'Darcy is with us,' Montague confirms. 'He spoke against the divorce at the last parliament.'

'He was there long before us.'

'And we have brought someone to see you,' Geoffrey says eagerly.

'If you wish,' Montague says more cautiously. 'She's a very holy woman, and she says some extraordinary things.'

'Who?' I ask. 'Who have you brought?'

'Elizabeth Barton,' Geoffrey says quietly. 'The nun that they call the Holy Maid of Kent.'

'Lady Mother, I think you should meet her,' Montague says, forestalling my refusal. 'The king himself has met her, William Warham the archbishop, may he rest in peace, brought her to him. The king listened to her, spoke with her. There is no reason that you should not see her.'

'She preaches that Princess Mary will take the throne,' Geoffrey says. 'And other predictions that she has made have come true, just as she said they would. She has a gift.'

'Our cousin Henry Courtenay has met her, and his wife Gertrude prayed with her,' Montague tells me.

'Where is she now?' I ask.

'She's staying at Syon Abbey,' Geoffrey says. 'She preaches to the Carthusian Brothers, she has visions and understands more than a simple country girl could possible know. But right now, she's in your chapel. She wants to speak with you.'

I glance at Montague. He nods reassuringly. 'She's not under suspicion,' he says. 'She's spoken to everyone at court.'

I rise from my chair and lead the way through the hall and out to my private chapel at the side of the building. The candles are lit on the altar, as always. One candle burns brightly in a glass of red Venice crystal before the memorial stone for my husband. The scent of the church, a hint of incense, a dry smell like leaves, the wisp of smoke from the candles, comforts me. The triptych above the altar gleams with gold leaf and the Christ child smiles down on me as I quietly enter the warm darkness, drop a curtsey, and touch my forehead with holy water in the sign of the cross. A slim figure rises up from her seat at the side of the room, nods her head to the altar as if acknowledging a friend, and then turns and curtseys to me.

'I am glad to meet, your ladyship, for you are doing God's work, guarding the heir to England who will be queen,' she says simply with a soft country accent.

'I am guardian to the Princess Mary,' I say carefully.

She steps towards me into the candlelight. She is dressed in the robes of the Benedictine Order, an undyed wool gown of soft cream tied at the waist with a soft leather belt. A scapular of plain grey wool over the robe falls to the ground at front and back, and her hair is completely covered by a wimple and veil that shade her tanned face and her brown honest eyes. She looks like an ordinary country girl, not like a prophetess.

'I am commanded by the Mother of Heaven to tell you that Princess Mary will come to her throne. No matter what happens, you must assure her that this will come to pass.'

'How do you know this?'

She smiles as if she knows that I have dozens of young women who look just like her working for me on the land, in the dairies or in the laundries of my many houses.

'I was an ordinary girl,' she says. 'Just as I appear to you. An ordinary girl like Martha in the sacred story. But God in His wisdom called on me. I fell into a deep sleep and spoke of things that I couldn't remember when I woke. One time I was speaking in tongues for nine days, without food or drink, like one asleep but awake in heaven.

'Then I could hear my voice and understand what I was saying, and knew it to be true. My master took me to the priest and he called great men to see me. They examined me, my master and my priest, and the Archbishop Warham, and they proved that I was speaking the word of God. God commands me to speak with many great men and women, and nobody has disproved me, and everything that I have said has always come true.'

'Tell her ladyship about your predictions,' Geoffrey urges.

She smiles at him and I see why people are following her in their thousands, why people listen to her. She has a smile of sweetness, but immense confidence. To see that smile is to believe her.

'I told Cardinal Wolsey to his face that if he helped the king to leave his wife, if he supported the king's proposal to marry Mistress Anne Boleyn, then he would be completely destroyed and die ill and alone.'

Geoffrey nods. 'And it happened.'

'Alas for the cardinal, it did come to pass. He should have told the king he must cleave to his wife. I warned Archbishop Warham that if he did not speak out for the queen and her daughter the princess he would die ill and alone, and poor man, poor sinner, he too has gone from us, just as I foresaw. I warned Lord Thomas More that he must take his courage and speak to the king, tell him that he must live with his wife the queen and put his daughter the princess on the throne. I warned Thomas More what would happen if he did not speak out, and that has yet to come.' She looks quite stricken.

'Why, what will happen to Thomas More?' I ask very quietly.

She looks at me and her brown eyes are dark with sorrow as if sentence has been passed. 'God save his soul,' she says. 'I will pray for him too. Poor man, poor sinner. And I spoke to your son Reginald, and told him that if he was brave, braver than anyone else has been, his courage would be rewarded and he would come to be where he was born to be.'

I take her arm and lead her away from my two sons. 'And where is that?' I whisper.

'He will rise through the Church and they will call him Pope. He will be the next Holy Father and he will see Princess Mary on the throne of England and the true religion as the only religion of England once again.'

I can't deny it, this is what I have thought and prayed for. 'Do you know this for a certainty?'

She meets my eyes with such a steady confidence that I have to believe her. 'I've been honoured with visions. God has honoured me with sight of the future. I swear to you that I have seen all this come to pass.'

I cannot help but believe her. 'And how shall the princess come to her own?'

'With your help,' she says quietly. 'You were appointed by the king himself to guard and support her. You must do that. Never leave her. You must prepare her to take the throne, for, believe me, if the king does not return to his wife he will not reign for long.'

'I can't hear such things,' I say flatly.

'I am not telling them to you,' she says. 'I am speaking the words of my vision, and you can listen or not as you wish. God has told me to speak aloud; that is enough for me.'

She pauses. 'I say nothing to you that I have not said to the king himself,' she reminds me. 'They took me to him so that he might know what my visions were. He argued with me, he told me that I was wrong; but he did not order me to be silent. I shall speak and whoever wants to learn may listen. Those who want to stay in the darkness, worming through the earth like the Mouldwarp, can do so. God told me, and I told the king that if he leaves his wife, the queen, and pretends to marry any woman, then he will not live not one day, no, not one hour after his false wedding.'

She nods at my aghast face. 'I said those words to the king himself, and he thanked me for my advice and sent me home. I am allowed to speak such things, for they are the words of God.'

'But the king is not turned from his path,' I point out. 'He may have listened, but he did not come back to us.'

She shrugs. 'He must do as he thinks fit. But I have warned him of the consequences. The day will come, and when that day comes you must be ready, the princess must be ready, and if her throne is not offered to her then she will have to take it.' Her eyelids flutter and for a moment I can see only the whites of her eyes as if she is about to faint. 'She will have to ride her horse at the head of her men, she will have to fortify her house. She will come into London on a white horse and the people will cheer her.' She blinks, and her face loses its entranced dreamy look. 'And your son' – she nods her head to Montague, waiting at the back of the chapel – 'he will be at her side.'

'As her commander?'

She smiles at me. 'As king consort.' Her words drop into the hushed silence of the chapel. 'He is the white rose, he carries royal blood, he is the kinsman of every duke in the kingdom, he is the first among equals, he will marry her and they will be crowned together.'

I am stunned. I turn from her and Montague is at my side at once. 'Take her away,' I say. 'She says too much. She speaks dangerous truths.'

She smiles, quite unperturbed.

'Don't speak of my sons,' I order her. 'Don't speak of us.'

She bows her head; but she does not promise.

'I'll take her back to Syon,' Geoffrey volunteers. 'They think much of her at the abbey. They are studying with her, old documents, legends. And hundreds of people come to the abbey doors to ask her advice. She tells them what is true. They speak of prophecies and curses.'

'Well, we don't,' I say flatly. 'We don't ever speak of such things. Ever.'

RICHMOND PALACE, WEST OF LONDON, SUMMER 1532

It is a hard morning when I come back from London and tell the princess that her father is going to a great council in France in October and taking his court; but not her.

'I am to follow later?' she asks hopefully.

'No,' I say. 'No, you are not. And your mother, the queen, is not attending either.'

'My father is taking only his court?'

'Mostly noblemen,' I temporise.

'Is the Lady going?'

I nod.

'But who will meet her? Not the French queen?'

'No,' I say awkwardly. 'The queen won't, because she's kinswoman to your mother. And the king's sister will not either. So our king will have to meet with the French king alone, and Mistress Boleyn will stay in our fort of Calais and not even enter into France.'

She looks puzzled by this complicated arrangement, as indeed anyone would be. 'And my father's companions?'

'The usual court,' I say uncomfortably. Then I have to tell the truth to her pale, hurt face. 'He's taking Richmond.'

'He is taking Bessie Blount's boy to France but not me?'

Grimly I nod. 'And the Duke of Richmond is to stay in France for a visit.'

'Who will he visit?'

It is the key question. He should visit the French king's mistress. He should be put in a household with noble bastards. He should be paired, like to like, just as we all send our boys to serve as squires to our cousins and friends, so that they can learn their place in a household the match of their own. By all the rules of courtesy Richmond should go to a household that is the match of his own, a noble bastard's house.

'He is going into the king's household,' I say through gritted teeth. 'And the King of France's son will come and stay at our court.'

I would not have thought it possible for her face to go any whiter, and her hand creeps to her belly as if there is a sudden twist in her gut. 'He goes as a prince then,' she says quietly. 'He travels with my father as a prince of England, he stays with the French king as an acknowledged heir; but I am left at home.'

There is nothing to say. She looks at me as if she hopes I will contradict her. 'My own father wants to make me into a nobody, as if I had never been born to him. Or never lived.'

We are silent after this conversation. We are silent when the furrier from London brings Mary her winter cloak and tells us that the king sent to the queen demanding her jewels for Lady Anne to wear in Calais. The queen first refused to give them up, then explained that they were Spanish jewels, then claimed that they were her own jewels given to her by her loving husband, and not part of the royal treasury; and then, finally defeated, she sent them to the king to show her obedience to his will.

'Does he want mine?' Mary asks me bitterly. 'I have a rosary which was a christening gift, I have the gold chain he gave me last Christmas.'

'If he asks, we will send them,' I say levelly, conscious of the listening servants. 'He is the King of England. Everything is his.'

As the furrier leaves, discouraged by the bleak response to the story of the jewels, he tells me that the Lady did not sweep the board, for she sent her chamberlain to get the queen's barge, and he stole it away from its moorings, and had the beautiful carved pomegranates burned off it, and Anne's crest of the falcon imposed in its place. But apparently that was a step too far for the king. He complained that her chamberlain should never have done such a thing, that Katherine's barge was her own possession, that it should not have been taken from her, and the Boleyn woman was forced to apologise.

'So what does he want?' the furrier demands of me, as if I have an answer. 'What does he want, in God's name? How is it well and good to take the old lady's jewels but not her barge?'

'You don't call her the old lady in my house,' I snap at him. 'She's the Queen of England, and she always will be.'

RICHMOND PALACE, WEST OF LONDON, AUTUMN 1532

Neither Montague nor Geoffrey writes me so much as one private note from France. I get a cheerful unsealed letter from Montague talking about the magnificent clothes and the hospitality and the success of the talks. They all swear to one another that they will mount a joint crusade against the Turk, they are the best of friends, they are on their way home.

It is not until Montague comes to Richmond Palace to pay his respects to the princess that he can tell me on their way back from France they stopped for the night at Canterbury, and Elizabeth Barton, the Holy Maid of Kent, walked through crowds of thousands of people and through the guards to the garden where the king was strolling with Anne Boleyn.

'She warned him,' Montague says to me gleefully. We are standing in an oriel window in the princess's rooms. The room is unusually quiet; the princess's ladies are getting ready for dinner, the princess is in her dressing room with her maids choosing her jewels. 'She stood in front of him and then went down on her knees, very respectful, and warned him for his own good.'

'What did she say?'

The little window panes reflect our faces. I turn away in case someone outside in the darkness is looking in.

'She told him that if he put the queen to one side and married the Boleyn woman there would be plagues and the Sweat would destroy us all. She said that he would not live for more than seven months after the wedding and it would be the destruction of the country.'

'My God, what did he say?'

'He was afraid.' Montague's voice is so quiet that I can hardly hear him. 'He was very afraid. I have never seen him like that before. He said: "Seven months? Why would you say seven months?" and he looked at Anne Boleyn as if he would ask her something. She stopped him with one glance, and then the Maid was taken away. But it meant something terrible to the king. He said "Seven months" as they took her away.'

I feel sick. I see the panes of glass before me sway and then recede as if I am about to faint.

'Lady Mother, are you all right?' Montague demands. I feel him get hold of me and seat me in a chair, while someone opens the window and the cold air blows into the room and into my face and I gasp as if I cannot breathe.

'I swear that she's told him she's with child,' I whisper to
Montague. I could weep at the thought of it. 'The Boleyn whore.
She must have lain with him when he made her a marquess and
promised him a boy – seven months from now. That's what the
date means to the king. That's why he was so shocked by the
words "seven months". He's heard them from her. He thinks his
child will be born in seven months and now the Maid has told
him he will die at the birth. That's why he's afraid. He thinks he's
cursed and that he and his heir will die.'

'The Maid speaks of a curse,' Montague says, rubbing my icy
hands in his big palms. 'She says that you know of a curse.'

I turn my head away from his anxious face.

'Do you, Mother?'

'No.'

We don't speak privately again until after dinner, when the
princess complains of weariness and a pain in her belly. I send her
to bed early and take a glass of warm spiced ale to her bedside.
She is praying before her crucifix but she gets up and slides
between the sheets that I hold open for her. 'Go and gossip with
Montague,' she says, smiling. 'I know he is waiting for you.'

'I'll tell you everything that is entertaining in the morning,' I
promise her, and she smiles as if she too can pretend that news of
her father and his mistress triumphant in France could possibly
be amusing.

He is waiting for me in my privy chamber and I order wine and
sweetmeats, before sending everyone away. He gets up and listens
at the door and then he goes down the little stair to the stable
yard. I hear the outer door click and then he comes into the room
with Geoffrey and I lock the door behind them.

Geoffrey comes to me and kneels at my feet, his face bright
with excitement. 'I do hope you're not enjoying this too much,' I
say drily. 'It's not a game.'

'It's the greatest game in the world,' he says. 'For the highest stakes there are. I have just been with the queen. I went to her the moment we landed, to tell her the news.' He draws a letter from his shirt. 'I have this from her to the princess.'

I take it and slip it down the top of my gown. 'Is she well?'

He shakes his head, his excitement draining away. 'Very sorrowful. And I had no joy to bring her. The king has forged an alliance with the French king and we think they'll propose an agreement to the Holy Father: Thomas Cranmer to be made archbishop, and given the power to hear the divorce in England. So the king gets his divorce. In return, he calls off the ruin of the Church, and the monasteries can keep their fortunes and send their fees to Rome. Henry must forgo his claim to be head of the Church, that will be all forgotten.'

'A massive bribe,' Montague says with distaste. 'The Church wins its safety by abandoning the queen.'

'Would the Pope allow Cranmer to put the king's marriage on trial?'

'Unless Reginald can change his mind before the King of France gets there,' Geoffrey says. 'Our brother is working with Spain, he is working with the queen's lawyers. He completely persuaded the scholars at the Sorbonne. He says he thinks he can do it. He has the law of the Church on his side, and the Spanish and God.'

'Henry will insist on a divorce whatever the scholars say, if the Lady is with child,' Montague points out. 'And everyone thinks he's married her already, without waiting for the Pope's licence. Why else would she give herself now, after holding out so long?'

'A haystack wedding,' Geoffrey says scornfully. 'A secret wedding. The queen says that she will never regard such a marriage and none of us is to recognise it either.'

I take this terrible news in silence. Then I ask: 'What else does Reginald say? And how does he look?'

'He's well,' Geoffrey says. 'Nothing wrong with him, don't worry about him, going between Rome and Paris and Padua, dining with the best, everyone agreeing with him. He's at the very heart of all of this, and everyone wants his opinion. He's very influential, very powerful. He's the one that the Holy Father listens to.'

'And what does he advise us?' I ask. 'When you told him that we are ready to rise?'

Geoffrey nods, suddenly sobering. 'He says that Emperor Charles will invade to defend his aunt and we must rise and march with him. The emperor has sworn that if Henry publicly marries the Boleyn woman and sets the princess aside, then he will invade to defend the rights of his aunt and his cousin.'

'Reginald says it is certain to come to war,' Montague says quietly.

'Who is with us?' I ask. I have a sense of everything rushing towards us too quickly, as if, like the prophetess Elizabeth Barton, I can see a future and it is suddenly here and now.

'All our kinsmen, of course,' Montague says. 'Courtenay and the West of England, Arthur Plantagenet in Calais, the Staffords, the Nevilles. Charles Brandon, probably, if we make it clear we are against the advisors and not against the king, all the Church lands and their tenants – that's nearly a third of England alone. Wales of course, because of the princess and you living there, the North and Kent with my uncle Lord Bergavenny. The Percys would rise to defend the Church, and there would be many who would rise up for the princess, more than have ever ridden out before. Lord Tom Darcy, Lord John Hussey, and the old Warwick affinity for you.'

'You have spoken to our kinsmen?'

'I have taken great care,' Montague assures me. 'But I spoke to Arthur Viscount Lisle. He and Courtenay have met with the Maid of Kent and been convinced by her that the king will fall. Everyone else has come to me, to ask what we will do, or spoken to the Spanish ambassador. I am certain that the only lords who would stand with the king are the people he has newly made: the Boleyns and the Howards.'

'How will we know when the emperor is coming?'

Geoffrey beams. 'Reginald will send to me,' he says. 'He knows he has to give us time enough for everyone to arm their tenants. He understands.'

'We wait?' I confirm.

'We wait for now.' Montague looks warningly at Geoffrey. 'And we only speak of it among ourselves. No-one outside the family, only those who we know are already sworn to the queen or the princess.'

RICHMOND PALACE, WEST OF LONDON, WINTER 1532–SUMMER 1533

Like the slow tolling of a funeral bell that rings out sorrowfully again and again as a prisoner is brought from the darkness of the Tower, to walk up to the hill where the headsman waits by the ladder to the scaffold, bad news comes beat by slow beat from the court in London.

In December the king and Anne inspect the works to repair the Tower of London and are reported as saying that the work must be hurried. The City is agog, thinking that the queen is to be taken from the More and imprisoned in the Tower.

She says that she is ready for a trial for treason, and instructs that Princess Mary is never to deny her name or her birth. She knows this means they may both be arrested and taken to the Tower. It is her command. Burn this.

Geoffrey comes to tell me that Anne holds great state at court, wearing the queen's jewels, preceding everyone into dinner. She has come back from Calais holding her head stiffly erect, as if she is bearing the weight of a crown, invisible to everyone but herself. The true ladies of the realm are disregarded, the French dowager queen Mary avoids her own brother's court altogether, and gives out that she is ill. The other ladies of the kingdom – Agnes the Dowager Duchess of Norfolk, Gertrude the Marchioness of Exeter, even I, especially I – are not invited. Anne is guarded by her tight little circle: Norfolk's daughter Mary Howard, her own sister Mary, and her sister-in-law Jane. She spends all her time with the young men of Henry's court and her brother George, a wild circle headed by the one-eyed Sir Francis Bryan whom they call the vicar of hell. It is a feverishly witty, worldly court that the king has allowed to come about that is driven by sexual desire and ambition. There are fearless and bold young men, and women of doubtful virtue, all celebrating their daring in a new world with the new learning. It is a court that is perpetually on tenterhooks for the new fashion, for the new heresy, waiting for the Pope's ruling, and for the king to decide what he will do. A court that has staked everything on the king being able to force the Pope into consent, knowing that this is the greatest sin in the world and the destruction of the kingdom, believing that this is a leap into freedom and into a new way of thinking.

In January, the king's envoy to the Pope returns home wreathed in smiles and with the news that the Holy Father has approved the king's choice for the Archbishop of Canterbury. In place of William Warham, a holy, thoughtful, gentle man, tortured by what the king was doing to his Church, we are to have the Boleyn family chaplain, Thomas Cranmer, whose reading of the Bible so conveniently agrees with the king's and who is nothing less than a heretic Lutheran, like his mistress.

'It's the very agreement that Reginald predicted,' Montague says gloomily. 'The Pope accepts the Boleyn chaplain but he saves the English Church.'

Thomas Cranmer does not look like much of a saviour. With the sacred cope of Archbishop of Canterbury around his shoulders he uses his first ever sermon to tell the court that the king's marriage to the queen is sinful, and that he must make a new and better union.

I cannot keep this from the princess, and anyway, she has to be prepared for bad news from London. It is as if the slow ringing of the bell in my mind has become so loud that I think she must hear it too.

'What does it mean?' she asks me. Her blue eyes have violet shadows under them. She cannot sleep for the pain in her belly, and nothing I can do seems to cure it. When she has her monthly courses she has to go to bed, and she bleeds heavily, as if from a deep wound. Other times she does not bleed at all and I fear for her future. If grief has made her sterile then the king has enacted his own curse.

'What does it mean?'

'I think your father the king must have secretly obtained the permission of the Holy Father to leave your mother, and Thomas Cranmer is announcing this. Perhaps he will make the marquess his wife but not crown her as queen. But it makes no difference to your estate, Your Grace. You were conceived in good faith, you are still his only legitimate child.'

I do not say, your mother requires you to swear this, whatever the cost. I cannot bring myself to repeat the order. I know that I should, but I fail in my duty. I cannot tell a young woman of seventeen years old that to say her name may cost her life; but she must take that risk.

'I know,' she says, in a very small voice. 'I know who I am, and my mother knows that she never did a dishonourable act in her life. Everyone knows that. The only unknown thing is the marquess.'

We learn a little more in spring, when I get a series of notes from Montague in London. They are unsigned, unsealed. They appear at my plate, or pinned to my saddle, or tucked in my jewel box.

The new archbishop has ruled that the marriage of the king to the queen is, and always has been, invalid. Bishop John Fisher argued all day against it and at the end of the day they arrested him. Burn this.

The king is to send the Duke of Norfolk to the queen to tell her that she is now to be known as the Dowager Princess, and that the king is married to Lady Anne, now called Queen Anne. Burn this.

I know what must happen next. I wait for the arrival of the king's herald and when he arrives I take him to the princess's rooms. She is seated at a table with the bright spring sunshine pouring over her bent head, transcribing some music for the lute. She looks up as I come in, and then I see her smile die as she sees the liveried messenger behind me. At once she ages, from a happy young woman to a bitterly suspicious diplomat. She rises to her feet and observes his bow. He bows as low as a herald should bow to a princess. Cautiously, she inspects the name on the front of the sealed letter. She is correctly addressed as Princess Mary. Only then, when she is sure that he is not attempting some trickery of disrespect, does she break the royal seal and impassively read the king's brief scrawl.

From my place at the door I can see it is a few words, signed with a swirling 'H'. She turns and smiles broadly at me, and hands me the letter. 'How very good His Grace is to tell me of his happiness,' she says and her voice is perfectly steady. 'After dinner I shall write to congratulate him.'

'He is married?' I ask, copying her tone of pleased surprise for the benefit of the herald and the ladies in waiting.

'Indeed yes. To Her Grace the Marquess of Pembroke.' She recites the newly invented title without a quaver.

June – I saw her crowned, it's done. Geoffrey was her servitor, I followed the king. I carved at her coronation dinner. The meat choked me. There was not one cheer along the whole procession route. The women cried out for the true queen. Burn this.

Geoffrey comes upriver in a hired boat, wearing a dark cape of worsted and a hat pulled down over his face. He sends my granddaughter Katherine to bring me to him and waits for me by the little pier that the townspeople use.

'I've seen the queen,' he says shortly. 'She gave me this for the princess.'

Silently I take the letter, sealed with wax but the beloved insignia of the pomegranate is missing. 'She's forbidden to write,' he says. 'She's not allowed to visit. She's almost kept as a prisoner. He's going to reduce her household. The Boleyn woman won't tolerate a rival court and a rival queen.'

'Is Anne with child?'

'She carries herself leaning backwards, as if she had twins in there. Yes.'

'Then Charles of Spain must invade before the birth. If it is a son . . .'

'He'll never have a son,' Geoffrey says contemptuously. 'The Tudors aren't like us. There's my sister Ursula with another boy in the cradle, me with another baby on the way. Any Tudor child will be stillborn for sure. The Maid of Kent has sworn it won't happen, there's a curse on the Tudors. Everyone knows it.'

'Do they?' I whisper.

'Yes.'

RICHMOND PALACE, WEST OF LONDON, SUMMER 1533

The Duke of Norfolk himself writes to tell me that the princess's household is to move to Beaulieu, and that we will not be returning to Richmond Palace.

'This is to diminish me,' she says bluntly. 'A princess should live in a palace. I have always lived in a palace or a castle.'

'Beaulieu is a great house,' I remind her. 'In beautiful countryside, it is one of your father's favourite—'

'Hunting lodges,' she finishes for me. 'Yes, exactly.'

'Your mother is to move as well,' I tell her.

She starts up, her face filled with hope. 'Is she coming to Beaulieu?'

'No,' I say hurriedly. 'No, I'm very sorry. No, my dear, she isn't.'

'He's not sending her back to Spain?'

I had not known that she had feared this.

'No, he's not. He's sending her to Buckden.'

'Where's that?'

'Near Cambridge. I am sorry to say it's not an adequate house for her, and he has dismissed her court.'

'Not all of them!' she exclaims. 'Who will serve her?'

'Only a few,' I say. 'And her friends, like Maria de Salinas, Lady Willoughby, are not allowed to visit. Even Ambassador Chapuys is not allowed to see her. And she can only walk in the gardens.'

'She is imprisoned?'

I answer her honestly, but it is a terrible thing to say to a girl who loves her mother and honours her father. 'I am afraid so. I am afraid so.'

She turns her head away. 'We had better pack our things then,' she says quietly. 'For if I don't obey him, perhaps he will imprison me too.'

BEAULIEU, ESSEX, AUGUST 1533

Geoffrey and Montague come openly together to visit me, apparently for a day's hunting in the great park around Beaulieu. As soon as they are announced, the princess comes down to greet them in the walled garden.

It is a beautiful day. The brick walls hold the heat and not a leaf stirs in the windless air. Montague goes down on one knee as the princess comes towards him and smiles up at her. 'I have great news for you,' he says. 'Praise God that I can bring you good news at last. The Pope has ruled in favour of your mother. He has commanded the king to put aside all others and take her back to court.'

She gives a little gasp and the colour comes to her cheeks. 'I am so glad,' she replies. 'God be praised for His mercy, and for speaking to the Pope. God bless the Pope for having the courage to say what he should.' She crosses herself and turns away from my sons, as I put my arms around her thin shoulders and hold her for a moment. Her eyes are filled with tears. 'I'm all right,' she says. 'I am so relieved. I am so glad. At last. At last the Holy Father has spoken, and my father will hear him.'

'If only . . .' I start, and then I trail into silence. It is pointless to wish: if only the Pope had ruled earlier. But at least he has ruled now. The Boleyn woman is with child and has gone through a form of marriage with the king, but this need not prevent the king's return to his wife. We have had pregnant whores at court before; for years the queen lived alongside a favourite mistress and a bastard son.

'My father will return to his obedience to the Holy Father, won't he?' She turns back to Montague, her voice carefully steady.

'I think that he will negotiate,' Montague says shrewdly. 'He will have to come to terms with Rome, and your mother's freedom and position as queen must be restored. The Pope's ruling makes this the business of all Christian kings. Your father is not going to risk France and Spain allying against him.'

She looks as if a great burden has been lifted from her little shoulders. 'This is very good news you bring me, Lord Montague,' she says. 'And you, Sir Geoffrey.' She turns to me. 'You must be glad to see your sons when they bring us such happiness.'

'I am,' I say.

BEAULIEU, ESSEX, SEPTEMBER 1533

It's a girl. All this trouble for a bastard Boleyn girl. They all say it proves that God has turned his face from the king. They're calling her Elizabeth.

After the months of waiting it is an intense relief that the Boleyn woman could not give birth to a boy. A son and heir would have proved to the king that he was right all along, that God had smiled on him whatever the Holy Father said. Now there is nothing to prevent him reconciling with the queen and confirming Princess Mary as his heir. Why should he not do so? He has no legitimate son to put in her place. The Boleyns' great gamble has failed. Their Anne proved to be of no more use than their Mary. The king can return to his wife, she can return to court.

Finally, I think, the wheel of fortune has turned for the princess, and for the queen her mother. The Pope has declared that the Aragon marriage is lawful, that the Boleyn marriage is a charade. The Boleyn child is a bastard and a girl. The shine is taken off the Boleyn woman and the crown will be taken off her too.

I am confident. We are all waiting for Henry to obey the Pope and restore his wife to her throne, but nothing happens. The bastard Elizabeth is to be christened, the whore, her mother, keeps her place at court.

The princess's chamberlain, Lord John Hussey, returns to Beaulieu, riding up the great road from London. 'He's been at the christening,' his wife Anne sourly remarks. 'He carried the canopy because he was commanded to do so. Don't think his heart was in it. Don't think he doesn't love our princess.'

'My cousin's wife Gertrude stood as godmother,' I reply. 'And nobody loves the queen more than her. We all have to take our places and play our parts.'

She glances at me, as if uncertain how much she should say. 'He's met with a northern lord,' she says. 'Better that I don't say who. He says that the North is ready to rise to defend the queen, if the king does not obey the Pope. Shall I tell him that he can come to you?'

I grit my teeth on my fear. In my pocket wrapped around my rosary is Lord Tom Darcy's badge of the five wounds of Christ embroidered with the white rose of my house. 'With great care,' I say. 'Tell him that he can come to me with care.'

The boy who brings in the wood for the fire goes past us carrying his basket and we are immediately silent for a moment.

'Anyway, it's a blessing that the king's sister was not there to see it, poor princess,' Lady Anne remarks. 'She'd never have curt-seyed to a Boleyn baby!'

The dowager queen Mary Brandon died at her home in the summer; some people said it was heartbreak that her brother had married his mistress in secret. Both the queen and the princess have lost a good friend, and the king has lost one of the very few people who would tell him the truth about the England he is making.

'The king loved his sister and would have forgiven her almost anything,' I say. 'The rest of us have to take the greatest care not to offend him.'

We watch John Hussey from the upper window as the troop of horses ride up the long avenue of trees and halts at the front of the house. He dismounts and throws his reins to a groom and then walks slowly and heavily to the front door like a man on a weari-some errand.

'He can't be bringing orders that we have to move again, or to take anything from us,' I say uneasily, watching his heavy stride. 'He won't ask for anything. The queen refused to give them the princess's christening gown for Elizabeth, there's nothing they can want from us.'

'I'm very sure he'd better not ask anything from me,' she says shortly, and turns away from the window to go to the princess's rooms.

I wait on the gallery as I hear Lord John come slowly up the stairs. He almost flinches when he sees me, waiting for him. 'Your ladyship.' He bows.

'Lord John.'

'I have just come from London. From the christening of the Princess Elizabeth.'

I nod, neither confirming nor denying the name, and I think that he cannot have wined and dined very well at the christening feast for he looks sluggish and unhappy.

'The king's secretary, Thomas Cromwell, Cromwell himself, instructs me to get the inventory of the princess's jewels.'

I raise my eyebrows. 'Why would Thomas Cromwell want an inventory of the princess's jewels?'

He stops for a moment. 'He's the Master of the Jewel House, and it is the king's command. He asked me himself. And you can't question that.'

'I can't,' I agree. 'I would not. And so I am sorry to tell you that there is no inventory.'

He takes in the fact that I am going to be difficult. 'There must be.'

'There isn't.'

'But how do you know you have everything safely?'

'Because I myself take out her jewels when she wants them, and then afterwards I put her things away. She's not a goldsmith's shop that has to keep a note of stock. She is a princess. She has jewels as she has gloves. Or lace. I don't have a glove inventory either. I have no register of lace.'

He looks quite baffled. 'I'll tell him,' he says.

'Do.'

But I don't expect that to be the last of it, and it is not.

'Thomas Cromwell says that you are to make an inventory of the princess's jewels,' poor John Hussey says to me a few days later.

His wife, passing us on the stairs, shakes her head with something like disdain and says something under her breath.

'Why?' I ask.

He looks baffled. 'He didn't tell me why. He just said it must be done. And so it must be done.'

'Very well,' I say. 'A thorough inventory? Of everything? Or just the best pieces?'

'I don't know!' he exclaims miserably, but then he gets himself in check. 'A thorough inventory. An inventory of everything.'

'If it is to be done thoroughly, as Master Cromwell wishes, then you had better do it with me, and bring a couple of your clerks.'

'Very well,' he says. 'Tomorrow morning.'

While we go through the princess's wardrobe and open up all the little leather purses with the ropes of pearls and the pretty brooches, Thomas Cromwell is making another inventory. His agents travel up and down the land inquiring into the wealth and practices of the monasteries, discovering what they are worth and where their treasures are kept. Neither here among the princess's boxes nor in the monasteries does anyone explain the purpose of this. Mr Cromwell seems to be a man very interested in the exact value of other people's goods.

I cannot say I am any more helpful than the monasteries who claim holiness and hide their treasures. Indeed, I spin out the inventory for day after day. We bring out all the little boxes, valueless things that she has kept from childhood, a collection of shells from the beach at Dover, some dried berries threaded on silk. Carefully, we list pressed flowers. The diamond brooch from the Emperor Charles turns up as a little ghost from the time when she was the king's heiress and two of the greatest princes of Europe were proposed for her. Out of little boxes at the back of cupboards I bring the hasp of a belt, and one buckle missing its fellow. She has beautiful rosaries, her piety is well known, she has dozens of golden crucifixes. I bring them all, and the little toy crowns made of gold wire and glass, and the pins with silver heads, and the hair combs of ivory and a couple of rusting lucky horseshoes. We annotate her hairpins, a set of ivory toothpicks, and a silver lice comb. Everything I find, I list in exact detail and make Lord John see that his clerk copies it down in his inventory that runs to page after page, each initialled by us both. It takes days before we are done and the princess's treasures, great and small, are spread across all the tables in the treasure room, and every last little pin is recorded.

'Now we have to pack these up and give them to Frances Elmer in the privy chamber,' Lord John says. He sounds exhausted. I'm not surprised. It has been tedious and pointless and long, long drawn out by me.

'Oh no, I can't do that,' I say simply.

'But that is why we made the inventory!'

'It's not why I made the inventory. I made the inventory to obey the instruction of the king from Master Cromwell.'

'Well, now, he tells me to tell you to give the jewels to Mistress Elmer.'

'Why?'

'I don't know why!' It comes out as a bellow like a wounded bull.

I look at him steadily. We both know why. The woman who calls herself queen has decided to take the princess's jewels and give them to her bastard. As if a little coronal of diamonds, small enough to be tied on a baby's head, will transform a child conceived out of wedlock into a princess of England.

'I can't do it without a command from the king,' I say. 'He told me to guard his daughter and keep her estate. I can't hand over her goods just on someone's say-so.'

'It's Thomas Cromwell's say-so!'

'He may seem like a great man to you,' I say condescendingly. 'But I have not sworn to obey him. I could not give up the jewels, against the king's own command, unless I have a command from the king to me, directly. When you give me that, I shall give the jewels to whoever His Grace appoints as worthy of them. But let me ask you, who would that be? Who do you think is worthy of the jewels that were given to our princess?'

Lord John lets rip an oath and flings himself out of the room. The door bangs behind him and we hear his boots stamping down the stairs. We hear the front door bang and his snarl at the sentries as they present arms. Then there is silence.

One of the clerks looks up at me. 'All you can do is delay it,' he says with sudden clarity, speaking for the first time in days of silent work, and impertinently speaking directly to me. 'You have delayed magnificently, your ladyship. But if a man runs mad and wants to dishonour his wife and rob his daughter, it's very hard to stop him.'

BISHAM MANOR, BERKSHIRE, AUTUMN 1533

I travel to my home with a heavy heart, for Arthur's boy Henry has died of a feverish throat, and we are to bury him in the family vault. It seems that he was thirsty, out hunting, and that some fool allowed him to drink water from a village well. Almost as soon as he got home he complained of a swelling and a heat in his throat. The loss of a Plantagenet boy, Arthur's boy, is the result of a moment's carelessness, and I find that I grieve for Arthur all over again and I blame myself that I failed to keep his boy safe.

If his mother Jane had not taken herself into the priory but done her duty by her dead husband and her children then perhaps little Henry would be alive today. As it is, she flings herself down the stone steps to the family vault and clings to the iron grille and cries that she wants to be there with her son, and her husband.

She is beside herself with grief and they have to take her back to the priory and put her to bed to cry herself to sleep. She never speaks one coherent word to me for the whole length of my visit, so I don't have to hear that she wishes she had not joined the nunnery and that she wants to break her vows and come out. Perhaps now she wants to stay inside.

We give a family dinner for those who have come to the funeral and when it is cleared away, Geoffrey and Montague leave their wives in the presence chamber and come to my private room.

'I met with the Spanish ambassador, Eustace Chapuys, last month,' Montague says without preamble. 'Since the Pope has ruled against the king and Henry has ignored him, Chapuys has a suggestion for us.'

Geoffrey brings a chair close to the fireside for me and I sit down and put my feet on the warm fender. Geoffrey rests his hand tenderly on my shoulder, knowing I am feeling the death of Henry like a physical pain.

'Chapuys suggests that Reginald shall come to England in secret, and marry the princess.'

'Reginald?' Geoffrey says blankly. 'Why him?'

'He's unmarried,' Montague says impatiently. 'If it's to be one of our line, it has to be him.'

'Is this the emperor's idea?' I ask. I am quite stunned at the prospect opening before my scholarly son.

Montague nods. 'To make an alliance. You can see his thinking; it's an unbeatable alliance. Tudors and Plantagenets. It's the old solution. It's exactly what the Tudors did when they first came in and married Henry Tudor to Elizabeth of York. Now we do it to exclude the Boleyns.'

'It is!' Geoffrey recovers from his jealousy that Reginald would be king consort to think what we would gain from it. 'The emperor would land to support an uprising?'

'He has promised to do so. The ambassador thinks the time is now. The Boleyn woman has only produced a girl and I hear that she is sickly. The king has no legitimate heir. And the Boleyn woman has spoken out, threatening the life of the queen and the princess. She may have tried to poison Bishop Fisher again, she may make an attempt on the queen. The ambassador thinks they are both in danger. The emperor would come to a country ready and waiting for him, and he'd bring Reginald.'

'They land, they marry. We raise her standard, and our own. All of our affinity turn out for us, all the Plantagenets. Three suns in the sky again, three sons of York on the battlefield. And the emperor lands for the princess, and every honest Englishman fights for the Church,' Geoffrey says excitedly. 'It wouldn't even come to a battle. Howard would turn his coat the moment that he saw the odds against him, and no-one else would fight for the king.'

'Would she agree to marry him?' Montague asks me.

Slowly, I shake my head, knowing that this destroys the plan. 'She won't defy her father. It's too much to ask of her. She's only seventeen. She loves her father, I taught her myself that his word is law. Even though she knows he has betrayed and imprisoned her mother, it makes no difference to a daughter's obedience to her father. He is still king. She would never commit an act of treason against a rightful king, she would never disobey her father.'

'So shall I tell Chapuys no?' Montague asks me. 'Is she trapped by her duty?'

'Don't say no,' Geoffrey says quickly. 'Think what we might be, think if we might return to the throne. Their son would be a Plantagenet, the white rose on the throne of England once again. And we would be the royal family once more.'

'Tell him it's not possible yet,' I temporise. 'I won't even speak to her of it yet.' For a moment only, I think of my son coming home at last, coming home in triumph, a hero of the Church, ready to defend the Church in England, the princess, and the queen. 'I agree, it is a good proposal. It is a great opportunity for the country and, quite unbelievably, a great restoration for us. But the time is not now, not yet. Not until we are released from our obedience to the king. We have to wait for the Pope to enforce his word. Not until Henry is excommunicated – then we are free to act. Then the princess is freed from her duty as a subject and a daughter.'

'That day must come,' Geoffrey declares. 'I'll write to Reginald and tell him to press the Pope. The Pope has to declare that no-one shall obey the king.'

Montague nods. 'He has to be excommunicated. It's our only way ahead.'

BEAULIEU, ESSEX,
AUTUMN 1533

John de Vere, Earl of Oxford, Henry's man through and through, a despised Lancastrian loyalist for generations, rides down the long avenue of trees, through the beautiful great gateway and into the inner courtyard of Beaulieu with two hundred horsemen in light armour trotting behind his standard.

Princess Mary, beside me at the window that overlooks the courtyard, sees the armed men halting and dismounting. 'Does he fear trouble on the road, that he rides with so many?'

'Generally, a de Vere brings trouble rather than meets it,' I say sourly, but I know that the roads are dangerous for the king's officers. The people are sulky and suspicious, they fear the tax collectors, they fear the new officials who come to inspect the churches and the monasteries, they don't cheer when they see the Tudor rose any more, and if they see Anne's badge – she is now showing a falcon pecking at a pomegranate to flaunt her victory over Queen Katherine – they spit on the road before her horses.

'I'll go down to greet him,' I say. 'You wait in your rooms.' I close the door and go slowly down the great stone stairs to the entrance hall where John is tossing his hat on a table and pulling off his leather gloves.

'Lord John.'

'Countess,' he says, pleasantly enough. 'Can I turn my horses out in your fields for the day? We won't stay long.'

'Of course,' I say. 'You'll dine with us?'

'That would be excellent,' he says. The de Veres have always been great trenchermen. The family was in exile with Henry Tudor and came back at Bosworth to devour England. 'I've come to see Lady Mary,' he says flatly.

I find that I am quite chilled to hear him call her that. As if by denying her name, he is announcing the death of the princess. I pause for a moment and give him a long, slow stare. 'I will take you to Her Grace the Princess Mary,' I say steadily.

He puts a hand on my arm. I don't shake it off, I just look at him in silence. He moves his hand awkwardly. 'A word of advice,' he says. 'To a very well-regarded, well-respected, beloved kinswoman of the King of England. One word of advice . . .'

I wait in icy silence.

'The king's will is that she is known as Lady Mary. That is going to happen. It will be the worse for her if she defies him. I am here to tell her that she must obey. She is a bastard. He will guide her and care for her as his bastard daughter, and she will take the name Lady Mary Tudor.'

I feel the blood rush to my face. 'She is no bastard and Queen Katherine was no whore. And any man who says so is a liar.'

He cannot face me with the lie on his lips and my face burning with anger. He turns away from me as if he is ashamed of himself, and he goes up to the presence chamber. I run after him, I have some mad thought of throwing myself in front of the door and barring him from saying the terrible words to our princess.

He enters without announcement. He gives her the smallest bow and I rush in behind him too late to prevent him delivering his shameful message.

She hears him out. She does not respond when he addresses her as Lady Mary. She looks at him steadily, she looks through him with a dark blue gaze that in the end reduces him to repeating himself, to losing his thread, and then to silence.

'I shall write to my father, His Grace,' she says shortly. 'You can carry the letter.'

She rises from her chair and sweeps past him, not waiting to see whether or not he bows. John de Vere, caught between the old habit of respect and the new rules, bobs down, bobs up, and finally stands awkwardly, like a fool.

I follow her to her privy chamber and see her take her seat at the table and draw a piece of paper towards her. She inspects the nib of a quill, dips it in the ink, wipes it carefully and starts to write in her confident, elegant hand.

'Your Grace, think carefully before you write. What will you say?'

She glances up at me, chillingly calm, as if she had prepared herself for this, the worst thing that could happen. 'I will tell him that I will never disobey his commands but that I cannot renounce the rights which God, Nature, and my own parents have given me.' She gives a little shrug. 'Even if I wanted to step aside from my duty, I cannot do so. I was born a Tudor princess. I will die a Tudor princess. Nobody can say differently.'

BEAULIEU, ESSEX, NOVEMBER 1533

Montague comes to Beaulieu, riding through a dark day of mist and freezing rain, with half a dozen men around him, and no standard showing.

I greet him in the stable yard when they clatter in. 'You come disguised?'

'Not exactly disguised, but I don't mind being obscure,' he says. 'I don't think I'm spied on, or followed, and I'd like it to stay that way. But I had to see you, Lady Mother. It's urgent.'

'Come in,' I say. I leave the grooms to take the horses and Montague's men to find their own way into the hall where they can get mulled ale against the cold weather. I lead my son up the small stairs to my privy chamber. Katherine and Winifred, my granddaughters and two other ladies are seated in the window, trying to catch the last of the light on their sewing, and I tell them they can leave it aside and go and practise their dance in the presence chamber. They curtsey and leave, very pleased to be sent to dance, and I turn to my son.

'What is it?'

'Elizabeth Barton, the Maid of Kent, has disappeared from Syon

Abbey. I'm afraid she may have been taken by Cromwell. He's certain to ask her to name those friends of the queen that she has met. He's certain to try to make it look like a plot. Have you seen her at all since the time that I brought her to you?'

'Once,' I say. 'She came with Cousin Henry's wife, Gertrude Courtenay, and we prayed together.'

'Did anyone see you together?'

'No.'

'Are you sure?'

'We were in the chapel at Richmond. The priest was there. But he would never give evidence against me.'

'He would now. Cromwell is using torture to get the confessions that he wants. Did she speak of the king?'

'Torture? He is torturing priests?'

'Yes. Did the Maid speak of the king?'

'She spoke as she always does. That if he tried to set the queen aside his days would be numbered. But she said nothing more than she has said to the king himself.'

'Did she ever say that we would take the throne? Did she ever say that?'

I am not going to tell my son that she foresaw him marrying the princess and becoming king consort. I'm not going to tell him that she predicted that the Plantagenet line would be the royal family of England once again. 'I won't say. Not even to you, my dear.'

'Lady Mother, Thomas More himself warned her against predicting greatness for a family like ours. He reminded her of what happened to the Buckingham chaplain who knew a prophecy and whispered it to Buckingham. He warned her that the false prophet led our cousin on to dream of greatness, and then the king was led on to cut him down. The king cut down both prophet and the hero of his prophecy and now the duke's confessor and the duke are dead.'

'So I don't ever speak of prophecies.' Silently I add: 'Or curses.'

Montague nods, as if he is reassured. 'Half of the court have met with her to have their fortunes told or to pray with her,' he says. 'We've done no more than this. You're sure, aren't you? That we have done no more than this?'

'I don't know what she might have said to Cousin Gertrude. And are you sure of Geoffrey?'

Montague smiles ruefully. 'Well, at any rate, I'm sure that Geoffrey would never betray us,' he says. 'I think he's been to Syon and travelled with her to Canterbury. But so have many others. Fisher and More among them.'

'Thousands have heard her preach,' I point out. 'Thousands have met with her privately. If Thomas Cromwell wants to arrest everyone who has prayed with the Maid of Kent then he will have to arrest most of the kingdom. If he wants to arrest those who think the queen is wrongly put aside he will have to arrest everyone in the kingdom but the Duke of Norfolk, the Boleyns, and the king himself. Surely we would be safe, my son? We'd be lost in the crowd.'

But Thomas Cromwell is a bolder man than I realised. A more ambitious man than I realised. He arrests the Maid of Kent, he arrests seven holy men with her, and once again, he arrests John Fisher, the bishop, and Thomas More, the former Lord Chancellor, as if they were nobodies that he could pick up from the street and fling in the Tower for nothing more than disagreeing with him.

'He can't arrest a bishop for speaking with a nun!' Princess Mary says. 'He simply cannot.'

'They say that he has,' I reply.

BEAULIEU, ESSEX, WINTER 1533

I don't expect us to be invited to court for Christmas, though I hear that they are keeping very great estate and celebrating another pregnancy. They say that the woman who calls herself queen is walking with her head stiffly high, and her hand forever clasped to her belly where they are letting out the laces on her stomacher. They say that she is confident it will be a boy this time. I imagine she is on her knees every night, praying for him.

Under these circumstances I doubt that they will want my assistance. I have attended so many royal lyings-in that disappointment hangs around me like a dark cloak. I doubt that they will want the princess at court either, so I order the household to prepare for the feast at Beaulieu. I don't expect the princess to be very merry – she is not even allowed to send her mother a gift or the good wishes of the season. I suspect that the woman who calls herself queen has warned people not to visit or send gifts; but the princess is a princess to us, and her state demands that we hold a Christmas feast.

Although they are forbidden to pay their respects it's touching to see how the country people send her their love and support. There is a constant stream of apples and cheeses and even smoked hams coming to the door with the good wishes of the local farmers' wives. All my family, even the most distant cousins, send her a little Christmas gift. The churches for miles around pray for her by name and for her mother, and every servant in the house and every visitor refers to her as 'Her Grace the Princess' and serves her on bended knee.

I don't order them to honour her state and defy the king; but in our house at Beaulieu it is as if he never spoke. Many of the people in her service have been with her since she was a little girl. She has always been 'Her Grace' to us; even if we wanted to re-name her, we would not be able to remember it. Lady Anne Hussey boldly calls her by her true title and when anyone remarks on it says that she's forty-three and too old to change her ways.

The princess and I are mounting up to go hunting on a bright winter morning. We are in the central courtyard with her little court on their horses and ready to trot out, passing around the stirrup cup with some hot wine to keep out the cold, the hounds running everywhere, sniffing everything, sometimes bursting into excited yelping. The princess' Master of Horse helps her into the saddle as I stand at the horse's head, patting his neck. Without thinking, I ease my finger under the girth of her horse to check that it is as tight as it can be. The Master of Horse smiles at me and ducks his head in a little bow. 'I wouldn't leave Her Grace's girth loose,' he said. 'Never.'

I have a shamefaced blush. 'I know you wouldn't,' I say. 'But I can't let her mount without checking it.'

Princess Mary laughs. 'She'd have me on a pillion saddle behind you, if she could,' she says naughtily. 'She'd have me ride a donkey.'

'I'm supposed to keep you safe,' I say. 'In the saddle or out of it.'

'She'll be safe enough on Blackie,' he says and then something at the gate catches his eye and he turns and says quietly to me, 'Soldiers!'

I scramble up onto the mounting block so I can see over the tossing heads of the horses that there are soldiers running into the yard, and behind them a man on a great horse with a standard unfurling.

'Thomas Howard, Duke of Norfolk.'

Princess Mary moves, as if she would dismount, but I nod to her to stay in the saddle and I stand tall, like a statue on a pedestal, waiting for the Duke of Norfolk to ride up to me.

'Your Grace,' I say coldly. I loved his father, the old duke, who was a loyal adherent to the queen. I am fond of his wife, my cousin, and he makes her quite miserable. There is nothing I like about him, this man who has stepped into the shoes of a greater father, and inherited all of the ambition and none of the wisdom.

'My Lady Countess,' he says. He looks past me at the princess. 'Lady Mary,' he says very loudly.

There is a stirring as everyone hears him, and everyone wants to contradict him. I see the head of his guard look quickly around, as if to count our numbers and assess his danger. I see him note that we are going hunting and that many of the men have a dagger at their side or a knife in a scabbard. But Howard is safe enough, he has commanded his guard to come fully armed, ready for a fight.

Coolly I count their number, and their weapons, and I look at the hard-faced duke and wonder what he hopes to achieve. The Princess Mary's face is turned slightly away, as if she cannot hear him, as if she does not know that he is there.

'I have brought you news of changes to the household,' he says, loudly enough for her to hear. Still, she does not deign to look at him. 'His Grace the King commands that you are to come to court.'

That catches her; she turns, her face alight, smiling. 'To court?' she asks.

Grimly he goes on. I realise that this is no pleasure to him. This is dirty work that he will have to do, and probably worse than this, if he is going to serve the king and the woman who now calls herself queen.

'You are to go to court to serve the Princess Elizabeth,' he says, his voice clear above the noise of the horses and the hounds, and the swelling discontented murmur from the princess's household.

The joy dies from her face at once. She shakes her head. 'I cannot serve a princess, I am the princess,' she says.

'It's not possible,' I start to say.

Howard turns on me and thrusts into my hands an open sheet of paper with the king's scrawled 'H' at the foot and his seal. 'Read it,' he says rudely.

He dismounts and throws the reins to one of his men and walks without invitation through the open double doors into the great hall beyond.

'I'll see him,' I say quickly to the princess. 'You go riding. I'll see what we have to do.'

She is shaking with rage. I glance at her Master of Horse. 'Take care of her,' I say warningly.

'I am a princess,' she spits. 'I serve no-one but the queen, my mother, and the king, my father. Tell him that.'

'I'll see what we can do,' I promise her, and I jump down from the mounting block, wave my hunter away, and follow Thomas Howard into the darkness of the hall.

'I've not come to dispute the rights and wrongs, I've come to accomplish the king's will,' he says the moment I step into the great room.

I doubt that the duke could dispute the rights and wrongs of anything. He's no great philosopher. He's certainly no Reginald.

I bow my head. 'What is the king's will?'

'There's a new law.'

'Another new law?'

'A new law that determines the heirs of the king.'

'It's not enough that we all know the firstborn son takes the throne?'

'God has told the king that his marriage to Queen Anne is his only valid marriage, and that her children will be his heirs.'

'But Princess Mary can still be a princess,' I point out. 'Just one of two. The senior of two, the oldest of two.'

'No,' the duke says flatly. I can see this puzzles him and immediately he is irritated that I have raised it. 'That's not how it's going to be. I am not here to argue with you, but to do the king's will. I'm to take her to Hatfield Palace. She's to live there, under the supervision of Sir John and Lady Anne Shelton. She's to take a lady's maid, a lady in waiting, a groom for her horses. That's all.'

The Sheltons are kin to the Boleyns. He is taking my girl and putting her in a house run by her enemies.

'But her ladies in waiting? Her chamberlain? Her Master of Horse? Her tutor?'

'She's to take none of them. Her household is to be dismissed.'

'But I'll have to go with her,' I say, startled.

'You won't,' he says flatly.

'The king himself put her in my keeping when she was a baby!'

'That's over. The king says that she's to go and serve Princess

Elizabeth. There's not to be anyone to serve her. You're dismissed. Her household is dismissed.'

I look at his hard face, and think of his armed men in our Christmas courtyard. I think of Princess Mary coming back from her ride, for me to tell her that she has to go and live in the old palace at Hatfield, with none of the entourage or household of a princess, with none of the companions of her childhood. She has to go into service to the Boleyn bastard in a household supervised by Boleyn cousins. 'My God, Thomas Howard, how can you bring yourself to do this?'

'I'm not going to say no to the king,' he says gratingly. 'And neither are you. Any of you.'

She is sick with pain and white-faced. She is too ill to ride and I have to help her into a litter. I put a hot brick under her feet and one wrapped in silk in her lap. She puts out her little hands through the curtains and I cling to her as if I cannot bear to let her go.

'I will send for you as soon as I can,' she says quietly. 'He cannot keep you from me. Everyone knows that we have always been together.'

'I asked them if I could come with you, I said I would come at my own expense, that I will serve you for nothing. I will pay for your household to serve you.' I am gabbling in my anxiety as from the corner of my eye I see Thomas Howard mount up. The litter rocks as the mules move restlessly, and I grab her hands even more tightly.

'I know. But they want to get me alone, like my mother, without a friend in the house.'

'I'll come,' I swear. 'I'll write to you.'

'They won't let me have letters. And I won't read anything that is not addressed to me as princess.'

'I'll write in secret.' I am desperate that she does not see me crying, that I help her to keep her own dignity, as we are dragged apart, in this awful moment.

'Tell my mother I'm well, and that I am not at all frightened,' she says, white as the curtains of the litter and trembling with fear. 'Tell her I never forget that I am her daughter and that she is Queen of England. Tell her that I love her and I will never betray her.'

'Come on!' Thomas Howard shouts from the head of the troop and at once they move off, the litter jerking and rolling as her grip tightens on my hand.

'You may have to obey the king, I can't tell what he will ask of you,' I say quickly, walking alongside, breaking into a run. 'Don't stand against him. Don't anger him.'

'I love you, Margaret!' she calls. 'Give me your blessing!'

My lips form the words but I am choking and cannot speak. 'God bless,' I whisper. 'God bless you, little princess, I love you.'

I step back and I all but fall into a curtsey, my head down so she can't see my face contorted with grief. Behind me, I feel the whole household sink down into the lowest of bows, and the country people lining the avenue, come to see the princess kidnapped from her own house, disobey every shouted order they have heard all day and pull off their caps and drop to their knees to honour the only princess in England as she goes by.

WARBLINGTON CASTLE, HAMPSHIRE, SPRING 1534

I should be glad to be at my own home and pleased to rest. I should be glad to wake with the sun shining through my window panes of clear Venetian glass making the lime-washed room bright and light. I should be glad of the fire in the grate and my clean linen airing before it. I am a wealthy woman, I have a great name and a great title, and now that I am released from my service at court I can stay at home and visit my grandchildren, run my lands, pray in my priory and know that I am safe.

I am not a young woman, my brother dead, my husband dead, my cousin the queen dead. I look in the mirror and see the deep lines in my face and the weariness in my dark eyes. Under my gable hood my hair has gone silver and grey and white like an old dappled mare. I think it is time that I was put out to grass, it is time for me to rest, and I smile at the thought of it and know that I will never prepare myself for death: I am a survivor, I doubt I will ever be ready to quietly turn my face to the wall.

I am glad of my hard-won safety. They charged Thomas More with talking treason to Elizabeth Barton, and he had to find a letter he had written warning her not to speak to prove his innocence so that he could stay at his quiet home. My friend John Fisher could not defend himself against the charge and now sleeps in a stone cell in the Tower in these damp spring days. Elizabeth Barton, and those who were her friends, are in the Tower too, and certain to die.

I should be glad to be safe and free, but I have little joy, for John

Fisher has neither safety nor liberty and somewhere out in the flat, cold lands of Huntingdonshire is the Queen of England, ill served by people who are set about only to guard her. Even worse, at Hatfield Palace Princess Mary is cooking her breakfast over her bedroom fire, afraid to eat at the high table because there are Boleyn cooks in the kitchen poisoning the soup.

She is confined to the house, not even allowed to walk in the grounds, kept from any visitor for fear that they pass her a message or one word of comfort, separated from her mother, exiled from her father. They won't let me go to her, though I have bombarded Thomas Cromwell with begging letters, and asked the Earl of Surrey and the Earl of Essex to intervene with the king. Nobody can do anything. I am to be parted from the princess that I love as a daughter.

I suffer something like an illness, though the physicians can find nothing wrong with me. I take to my bed and find that I cannot easily get up again. I feel as if I have some mysterious illness, a greensickness, a falling sickness. I am so anxious for the princess and for the queen and so powerless to help either of them that my sense of weakness spreads through me till I can barely stand.

Geoffrey comes to visit from his home at nearby Lordington and tells me that he has a message from Reginald, who is in Rome, begging the Pope to excommunicate Henry, as he said he would, so that the people can rise against him, readying the emperor for the moment that he should invade.

Geoffrey tells me that my cousin Henry Courtenay's wife Gertrude has spoken out so strongly in favour of the queen and justice for the princess that the king took Courtenay to one side and warned him that one more word from her would cost him his head. Courtenay told Geoffrey that he assumed at first the king was speaking in jest – for whoever beheads a man for his wife's words? – but it is no laughing matter; now he has ordered his wife to keep silent. Geoffrey is warned by this and does his work in secrecy, going quietly, unseen, along the cold mud tracks to visit the queen and deliver her letter to the princess.

'It didn't cheer her,' he says unhappily to me. 'I fear that it made things worse.'

'How?' I ask. I am lying on a day-bed near the window for the last light of the setting sun. I feel sick at the thought of Geoffrey taking a letter to Mary that made her feel worse. 'How?'

'Because it was a farewell.'

I raise myself up on one elbow. 'A farewell? The queen is leaving?' My head spins at the thought of it. Can it be that her nephew is going to offer her a safe haven abroad? Would she leave Mary alone in England to face her father?

Geoffrey's face is pale with horror. 'No. Worse, far worse. The queen wrote that the princess should not dispute with the king and should obey him in all things except those matters which concerned God and the safety of her soul.'

'Yes,' I say uneasily.

'And she said that for herself, she didn't mind what they did to her, for she was sure that they would meet in heaven.'

I am sitting up now. 'And what do you understand from this?'

'I didn't see the whole letter. This is just what I got from the princess as she read it. She held it to her heart, kissed the signature, and she said that her mother could lead and she would follow, and she would not fail her.'

'Can the queen mean that she will be executed, and is telling the princess to prepare herself too?'

Geoffrey nods. 'She says she won't fail.'

I get to my feet, but the room swims around me, and I cling to the headboard of the bed. I will have to go to Mary. I have to tell her that she must take any oath, make any agreement, she must not risk her life. The one thing that she has, this precious Tudor girl, is her life. I didn't wrap her in swaddling bands as a newborn baby, or carry her in ermine from her christening, or raise her as my own daughter, for her to give up her life. Nothing matters more than life. She must not offer her life against her father's error. She must not die for this.

'There's talk of an oath which everyone is going to have to take. Every one of us is going to have to swear on the Bible that the king's first marriage was invalid, that his second one is good, and that the Princess Elizabeth is the king's only heir and Princess Mary is his bastard.'

'She can't swear to that,' I say flatly. 'Neither can I. Nor can anyone. It's just a lie. She can't put her hand on a Holy Bible and insult her mother.'

'I think she'll have to,' Geoffrey says. 'I think we all will. Because I think they will call it treason to refuse to swear.'

'They can't put a man to death for speaking the truth.' I cannot imagine a country where the hangman would kick out a stool from under a man who was telling a truth that the hangman knows as well as his victim. 'The king is determined, I see that. But he wouldn't do this.'

'I think it will happen,' Geoffrey warns.

'How can she swear that she's not the princess, when everyone knows that she is?' I repeat. 'I can't swear that, nobody can.'

WESTMINSTER PALACE, LONDON, SPRING 1534

I am summoned with the other peers of the realm to the privy council at the Palace of Westminster where the Lord Chancellor, the newly great Thomas Cromwell, stepping into the shoes of Thomas More like a Fool dancing in his master's boots, is to administer the oath of succession to the nobility of England, who stand before him like puzzled children waiting to recite their catechism.

We know the truth of the matter, for the Pope has publicly ruled. He has announced that the marriage of Queen Katherine and King Henry is valid, and that the king must set aside all others and live in peace with his true wife. But he has not excommunicated the king, so though we know that the king is in the wrong, we are not authorised to defy him. We each must do what we think best.

And the Pope is far away, and the king claims that he has no authority in England. The king has ruled that his wife is not his wife, that his mistress is queen and that her bastard is a princess. The king says that by his declaring this, it is so. He is the new pope. He can declare that something is so; and now it is. And we, if we had any courage or even a sure grasp on the material world, would say that the king is mistaken.

Instead, one by one we walk up to a great table and there is the oath written out, and the great seal above it. I take up the pen and dip it in the ink and feel my hand tremble. I am a Judas, a Judas even to take the pen into my hand. The beautifully transcribed words dance before me; I can hardly see them, the paper is a blur, the table seems to sway as I lean over. I think: God save me, I am sixty years old, I am too old for this, I am too frail for this, perhaps I can faint and be carried from the room and spared this.

I glance up, and Montague's steady gaze is on me. He will sign, and Geoffrey will sign after him. We have agreed that we must sign so that no-one can doubt our loyalty; we will sign hoping for better days. Quickly, before I can find the courage to change my mind, I scrawl my name, Margaret, Countess of Salisbury, and so I renew my allegiance to the king, I pledge my loyalty to the children of his marriage with the woman who calls herself queen, and I acknowledge him as head of the Church in England.

These are lies. Every single one of these is a lie. And I am a liar to set my hand to it. I step back from the table and I am no longer wishing I had pretended to faint, I am wishing that I had the courage to step forward and die as the queen told the princess that she must be ready to do.

Later they tell me that the saintly old man, confessor to two Queens of England, and God knows a good friend to me, John Fisher, would not sign the oath when they pulled him out of his prison in the Tower and put it before him. They did not respect his age, nor his long loyalty to the Tudors; they forced the oath on him and when he read and reread it and finally said that he did not think he could deny the authority of the Pope, they took him back to the Tower. Some people say that he will be executed. Most people say that no-one can execute a bishop of the Church. I say nothing at all.

Thomas More refused the oath also, and I think of the warm brown eyes and his joke about filial obedience and his pity for me when Arthur went missing. I wish that I had stood beside him when he told them, like the scholar he is, that he would sign a rewritten version of the oath, that he did not disagree with much of it, but that he could not sign it exactly as it stands.

I think of the sweetness of his spirit that led him on to say that he did not blame those who had drawn up the oath, nor did he have one word of criticism for those who had signed it; but for the sake of his own soul – just his – he could not sign.

The king had faithfully promised his friend Thomas that he would never put him to the test on this. But the king does not keep his word to the man that he loved, that we all love.

BISHAM MANOR, BERKSHIRE, SUMMER 1534

I go back to Bisham, Geoffrey to Lordington. I have a bad taste in my mouth every day on waking and I think it is the odour of cowardice. I am glad to get away from London where my friend John Fisher and Thomas More are held in the Tower, and where

Elizabeth Barton's honest eyes stare from a spike on London Bridge until the ravens and the buzzards peck them away.

They create a new law, one that we never needed before. It is called the Treason Act and it rules that anyone who wishes for the king's death, or wills it, or desires it in either speech or writing or craft, or who promises any bodily harm to the king or his heirs, or who names him as a tyrant, is guilty of treason and will be done to death. When my cousin Henry Courtenay writes to me that this act has been passed and we must take great care in everything we commit to paper, I think that he need not warn me to burn his letter; burning writing is nothing, now we have to learn to forget our thoughts. I must never think that the king is a tyrant, I must forget the words his own mother said when she and his grandmother Queen Elizabeth wished for the end of his line.

Montague travels with the king as he goes on a long progress with his riding court of friends, and Thomas Cromwell sends out his own progress: a handful of his trusted men to discover the value of every religious house in England, of every size and order. Nobody knows exactly why the Lord Chancellor would want to know this; but nobody thinks that it bodes well for the rich, peaceful monasteries.

My poor princess hides in her bedroom at the palace of Hatfield, trying to avoid the bullying of Princess Elizabeth's household. The queen has been moved again. Now she is imprisoned in a castle, Kimbolton in Huntingdonshire, a newly built tower with only one way in and out. Her governors, they might as well call them gaolers, live on one side of the courtyard, the queen and her women and small household on the other side. They tell me she is ill.

The woman who calls herself queen stays at Greenwich Palace for the birth of her child, in the same royal apartments where Katherine and I endured her labours, hoping for a boy.

Apparently, they are certain that this one will be a son and heir. They have had physicians and astrologers and prophecies and they all say that a strong little boy baby is waiting to be born. They are so confident that the queen's apartments at Eltham Palace have been converted into a grand nursery for the expected prince. A cradle of solid silver has been forged for him and the maids in waiting are embroidering his linen with gold thread. He is to be called Henry, after his all-conquering father, he is to be born in the autumn and his christening will prove that the king is blessed by God and the woman who calls herself queen is right to do so.

My chaplain and confessor John Helyar comes to me as they are getting the harvest in. The great stacks are being built in the fields so that we will have hay for the winter; the corn is being brought by the wagonload to the granaries. I am standing at the granary door, my heart lifting with every load that pours down from the cart like golden rain. This will feed my people through the winter, this will make a profit for my estate. This material comfort is so great to me that it feels like the sin of gluttony.

John Helyar does not share my joy; his face is troubled as he begs me for a private word. 'I can't take the oath,' he says. 'They've come to Bisham church, but I can't bring myself to do it.'

'Geoffrey did,' I say. 'And Montague. And me. We were the first to be called in. We did it. Now it is your turn.'

'Do you believe, in your hearts, that the king is the true head of the Church?' he asks me very quietly.

They are singing as the wagons come up the lane, the big oxen pulling in harness now as in spring they pulled the plough.

'I confessed to you the lie that I told,' I say quietly. 'You know the sin that I undertook when I signed the oath. You know that I betrayed God and my queen and my beloved goddaughter the princess. And I failed my friends John Fisher and Thomas More. I repent of it every day of my life. Every day.'

'I know,' he says earnestly. 'And I believe that God knows too, and that He forgives you.'

'But I had to do it. I can't walk towards my death as John Fisher is doing,' I say piteously. 'I can't go willingly to the Tower. I have spent my life trying to keep out of the Tower. I can't do it.'

'Neither can I,' he agrees. 'So, with your permission, I'm going to leave England.'

I am so shocked that I turn and catch his hands. Some bawdy

fool of a labourer whistles and someone else cuffs him. 'We can't talk here,' I say impatiently. 'Come into the garden.'

We walk away from the noise of the granary yard, through the gate to the garden. There is a stone bench set into the wall, late roses still growing fat around it and dropping their scented petals. I sweep them off with my hand and sit down. He stands before me as if he thinks I am going to scold him. 'Oh, sit down!'

He does as he is ordered and then is silent for a moment as if he is praying. 'Truly, I cannot take the oath and I am too afraid of death. I am going to go abroad and I am asking you if there is any way that I can serve you.'

'In what way?'

He chooses his words carefully. 'I can carry messages, for your sons. I can go to your kinsmen in Calais. I can travel to Rome to see the papal court and speak to them of the princess. I can go to the emperor and speak to him of his aunt the queen. I can discover what the English ambassadors are saying about us, and send you reports.'

'You are offering to be my spy,' I say flatly. 'You are presuming that I want or need a spy and a courier. When you, of all people, know that I took the oath to be a loyal subject to the king and Queen Anne, and their heirs.'

He does not say anything. If he had protested that he was only making an offer to keep me in touch with my son I would have known him as a spy from Cromwell, sent to lead us into danger. But he says nothing. He just bows his head and says: 'As you wish, my lady.'

'Will you go anyway, without a commission from me?'

'If you cannot use me in this work then I will try to find someone who can. Lord Thomas Darcy, Lord John Hussey, your kinsmen? I know there are many who have taken the oath against their wills. I will go to the Spanish ambassador and ask him if there is anything I can do. I believe that there are many lords who would want to know what Reginald is thinking and doing, what the Pope plans, what the emperor plans. I will serve the interests of the queen and the princess, whoever is my master.'

I pick a soft-petalled rose, a white rose, and I give it to him. 'There's your answer,' I say. 'That's your badge. Go to Geoffrey's friend, his old steward, Hugh Holland, he will get you safely across the narrow seas. Then go to Reginald, tell him how things are with us, and then serve him and the princess as one. Tell him that the oath is too much for us all, that England is ready to rise, and he must tell us when.'

John Helyar goes the next day, and when people ask after him I say that he left without notice and without warning. I shall have to find another chaplain for the household and a confessor for myself and it is a great nuisance and trouble.

When Prior Richard summons all the household after church on Sunday to administer the king's oath in the priory chapel, I report John Helyar as missing and say that I think he has family in Bristol, so perhaps he has gone there.

I know that we have put another link in the chain that stretches from the queen at Kimbolton Castle to Rome where the Pope must order her rescue.

In September, as the court turns back to London as the weather turns colder, Montague comes to Bisham for a brief visit.

'I thought I would come and tell you myself.' He jumps from his horse and kneels for my blessing. 'I didn't want to write.'

'What's happened?' I am smiling. I can tell from the way he springs to his feet that it is not bad news for us.

'She lost the child,' he says.

Like any woman in the world I feel a pang of sorrow at the news. Anne Boleyn is my worst enemy and the child would have been her triumph but, even so, I have dawdled to the king's rooms too many times with bad news of a dead baby not to remember that sense of terrible loss, of promise unfulfilled, of a future so confidently imagined which will now never happen.

'Oh, God bless him,' I say, and cross myself. 'God bless him, the poor innocent.'

There is to be no Tudor boy this time; the terrible curse that the Plantagenet queen and her witch of a mother put on the Tudor line goes on and on working. I wonder if it will reach its very end as my cousin predicted, and there will be no Tudor boys at all, but only a girl, a barren girl.

'And the king?' I ask after a moment.

'I had thought you would be pleased,' Montague remarks, surprised. 'I had thought you would triumph.'

I make a little gesture with my hand. 'I don't have so hard a heart as to wish for the death of an unborn child,' I say. 'Whatever his begetting. Was it a boy? How did the king take it?'

'He went quite mad,' Montague says steadily. 'He locked himself in his rooms and roared like an injured lion, banging his head against the wooden panelling, we heard him, but we couldn't get in. He raged for a day and a night, weeping and shouting, then he fell asleep like a drunkard with his head in the fireplace.'

I listen to Montague in silence. This is like the rage of a disappointed child, not the grief of a man, a father.

'And then?'

'Then the servers of the body went in to him in the morning, and he comes out, washed and shaved, his hair curled, and says nothing of it,' Montague tells me incredulously.

'He can't bear to have it spoken?'

Montague shakes his head. 'No, he acts as if it never happened. Not the night of tears, not the loss of the baby, not the wife in childbed. It never was. It beggars belief. After the making of the cradle and the painting of the rooms, knocking the queen's apartments at Eltham into a dining room and a privy chamber for a prince, he now says nothing about it, and denies that there was ever a child at all. And we all behave as if it never was. We are merry, we are hoping that she conceives soon. We have everything to hope for and we have never known despair.'

This is more strange than Henry blaming God for forgetting the Tudors. I had thought he would rail against his luck, or even turn on Anne as he turned on the queen. I thought he might claim that she had some terrible fault that she could not give him a son.

But this is the strangest of all. He has had a loss that he cannot bear, and so he is simply denying it. Like a madman facing something that he does not want to see – he denies it is even there.

'And does no-one speak to him? Since you all know that it has happened? Does no-one even express their sympathy for his loss?'

'No,' Montague says heavily. 'There is not a man at court who would dare. Not his old friend Charles Brandon, not even Thomas Cromwell who is with him every day and speaks to him every minute. There is not a man at court who would have the courage to tell the king something that he denies. Because we have allowed him to say what is, and what is not, Lady Mother. We have allowed him to say what the world is like. He's doing it right now.'

'He says that there was no child at all?'

'None at all. And so she has to pretend to be happy and pretend to be well.'

I take a moment to think of a young woman who has lost her child having to behave as if it had never been. 'She acts as if she is happy?'

'Happy is not the half of it. She laughs and dances and flirts with every man at the court. She is in a whirl of excitement, gambling and drinking and dancing and disguising. She has to appear the most desirable, the most beautiful, the wittiest, cleverest, most interesting woman.'

I shake my head at this portrait of a nightmare court, dancing on the very edge of madness. 'She does this?'

'She is frantic. But if she did not, he would see her as flawed,' Montague says quietly. 'Ill. Incapable of bearing a child. She has to deny her loss, because he won't be married to a woman who is not perfect. She has buried a dead baby in secret and she has to look as if she is endlessly beautiful, clever and fertile.'

The process of taking the oath to deny the queen and the princess goes on, from church to courtroom throughout the country. I hear that they arrest Lady Anne Hussey, my kinswoman, who served the princess with me. They charge her with sending letters and little gifts to the princess at Hatfield, and she confesses that she had also called her 'Princess Mary' from habit, not from intent. She has to beg forgiveness and spends long months in the Tower before they let her go.

Then I receive a note from Geoffrey, unsigned and without a seal to identify him.

The queen will not swear the oath, she has refused to deny herself or her daughter and has said that she is ready for any penalty. She thinks they will execute her privately behind the castle walls of Kimbolton and nobody will know. We have to prepare to rescue her and the princess at once.

I think that this is the moment I have longed to avoid. I think that I was born a coward. I think that I am a liar. I think that my husband begged me never to claim my own, never to do my duty, to keep myself and our children safe. But now, I think those days have gone, and though I am sick with fear I write to Geoffrey and to Montague.

Hire men and horses, hire a boat to take them to Flanders. Take every care of yourselves. But get them out of the country.

BISHAM MANOR, BERKSHIRE, CHRISTMAS 1534

I keep the Christmas feast at Bisham as if I were not in a state of frozen anticipation waiting for news from Hatfield and

Kimbolton. It takes time to find a way into a royal palace, to bribe a servant in a royal prison. My sons will need to take the greatest care when they talk with the boatmen along the Thames and find who sails to Flanders, and who is loyal to the true queen. I have to behave as if I am thinking of nothing but the Christmas feast and the baking of the great pudding.

My household pretend to a carelessness that they don't feel. We pretend we are not fearful for our priory, we are not afraid of a visit from Thomas Cromwell's inspectors. We know that every monastery in the country has been inspected and that the money counters are always followed by an inquiry into morals – especially if a priory is rich. They have come to our priory and looked at our treasures and the richness of the lands and gone away again, saying nothing. We try not to fear their return.

The mummers come and play before the fire in the great hall, the wassailers come and sing. We dress up with great hats and capes and prance about pretending to enact stories from long ago. This year nobody enacts a story about the king, or the queen, or the Pope. This year there is no comedy in the Lord of Misrule; nobody knows what is true and what is treason, every-thing is Misrule. The Pope who threatened the king with excommunication is dead and now there is a new Pope in Rome. Nobody knows if God will speak clearly to him, or how he will rule on the king with two wives. He is of the Farnese family: what the world says about him is not fit to be repeated. I pray that he can find holy wisdom. Nobody thinks any more that God speaks to our king, and there are many who say that he is advised by the Mouldwarp in dark and forbidden deeds. Our queen is far away, preparing for her execution, and the woman who calls herself queen can neither bear nor carry a son, prov-ing to everyone that the blessing of God is not on her. Enough here for a hundred masques, but nobody dares even mention these events.

Instead people put on tableaux that tell stories from a time that is safely long ago. The pages plan and perform a masque about a great sea voyage that takes the adventurers past a sea witch, a monster and a fearsome waterspout. The cooks come up from the kitchen and play a throwing game with knives, very fast and dangerous, with no words at all – as if thoughts are more dangerous than blades. When the priest comes in from the priory he reads in Latin from the Bible, incomprehensible to all of the servants, and will not tell us the story of the baby in the manger and the oxen kneeling to him, as if nothing is certain any more, not even the Word that shone in the darkness.

Since truth has become only what the king tells us, and since we have sworn to believe whatever he says – however ridiculous – we are uncertain about everything. His wife is not the queen, his daughter is not a princess, his mistress has a crown on her head, and her bastard is served by his true heir. In a world like this, how can we know anything for sure?

'She's losing her friends,' Geoffrey tells me. 'She has quarrelled with her uncle Thomas Howard. Her sister has been sent away from court in disgrace for marrying some passing soldier, her sister-in-law Jane Boleyn has been exiled by the king himself for starting a quarrel with his new fancy.'

'He's fallen in love again?' I demand eagerly.

'A flirtation; but the Boleyn queen tried to get her sent away and lost her sister-in-law in the attempt.'

'And the girl?'

'I don't even know her name. And now he's courting Madge Shelton,' Geoffrey says. 'Sending her love songs.'

I am suddenly filled with hope. 'This is the best New Year's gift you could have given me,' I say. 'Another Howard girl. This will divide the family. They'll want to push her forward.'

'It leaves the Boleyn woman very alone,' Geoffrey says, sounding almost sympathetic. 'The only people she can count on are her parents and her brother. Everyone else is a rival or a threat.'

BISHAM MANOR, BERKSHIRE, SPRING 1535

I receive an unsigned note from Montague.

We can do nothing, The princess is ill and they fear for her life.

I burn the note at once and I go to the chapel to pray for her. I press the heels of my hands into my hot eyes and I beg God to watch over the princess who is the hope and light of England. She is ill, seriously ill, the princess that I love is said to be so weak that she might die, and nobody knows what is wrong with her.

My cousin Gertrude writes to me that there is a plan to murder the queen by suffocating her in her bed and leave her without a bruise on her body, and that the princess is even now being poisoned by agents of the Boleyns. I can't be sure whether to believe her or not. I know that Queen Anne is insisting that the true queen be accused of treason by an act of attainder and executed behind closed doors. Is she so evil, this woman who was once the daughter of my steward, that she would kill her former mistress in secret?

Not for a moment do I think that Henry has planned any of this. He has sent his own doctor to the princess and said that she can be moved nearer to her mother at Hunsdon, so that the queen's physician can attend her, but he will not let her live with her mother, where the queen could guard her and nurse her back to health. I write again to Thomas Cromwell and I beg to be allowed to go to her and nurse her, just while she is ill. He says that it is not possible. But he assures me that the moment she signs the oath I can join her, she can come to court, she can be a beloved child of her father – like Henry Fitzroy, he adds, as if that would make me feel anything but horror.

I reply to him saying that I will take my own household, my

own physician, at my own cost. That I will set up house for her, that I will advise her to take the oath as I have done. I remind him that I was among the first to do so. I am not like Bishop Fisher, or Lord Thomas More. I am not guided by my conscience. I am one that bends before the storm like a flexible willow. You can call for a heretic, a turncoat, a Judas, and I will answer willingly, consulting my own safety before anything else. I was raised to be faint-hearted, false-hearted; it was the powerful, painful lesson of my childhood. If Thomas Cromwell wants a liar I am here, ready to believe that the king is head of the Church. I will believe that the queen is a dowager princess, that the princess is Lady Mary. I assure him that I am ready to believe anything, anything that the king commands, if he will only let me go to her and taste the food before she eats it.

He replies that he would be glad to oblige me; but it is not possible. He writes that he is sorry to also tell me that Princess Mary's former tutor Richard Fetherston is in the Tower for refusing the oath. 'You had a traitor for a tutor,' he observes like a casual threat. And he remarks, as if an aside, that he is very glad to hear that I will swear to anything; for John Fisher and Thomas More are to go before judges for treason, and that no-one can doubt the outcome.

And, he says at the very end, that the king is going to consult Reginald as to these changes! I almost drop the letter in disbelief. The king has written to Reginald for the benefit of his learned opinion on the marriage with Anne Boleyn, and his thoughts on the ownership of the English Church. They trust that Reginald will confirm the king's view, that the King of England must be head of the Church, since – surely – only a king can rule his kingdom?

At once I fear that it is an entrapment, that they hope to trick Reginald into such words that he will condemn himself. But Lord Cromwell writes smoothly that Reginald has replied to the king and is studying the matter with much interest, and has agreed to reply to the king as soon as he has reached his conclusions. He will read and study and discuss. Lord Cromwell thinks that there can be no doubt what he will recommend, such a loyal and loving churchman has he promised to be.

I call for my horse and for a guard to accompany me. I ride to my London house and I send for Montague.

L'ERBER, LONDON, SPRING–SUMMER 1535

'They put Bishop Fisher and then Thomas More on trial,' Montague tells me wearily. 'It was not hard to see what their verdict would be. The judges were Thomas Howard, the Boleyn uncle, the Boleyn father and Boleyn brother.' He looks tired, as if he is exhausted by these times and by my outrage.

'Why could they not swear it?' I grieve. 'Swear the oath and know that God would forgive them?'

'Fisher could not pretend.' Montague puts his head in his hands. 'The king asks us all to pretend. Sometimes we have to pretend that he is a handsome stranger come to court. Sometimes we have to pretend that his bastard is a duke. Sometimes we have to pretend that there is no dead baby; and now we have to pretend that he is supreme head of the Church. He is calling himself Emperor of England, and no-one may raise their voice to disagree.'

'But he'll never hurt Thomas More,' I argue. 'The king loves Thomas, he allowed him to stay silent when others had to advise about the marriage. He made Reginald speak out, but he allowed Thomas to stay quiet. He allowed him to give up his seal of office and go home. He said that if Thomas was silent then he could live quietly, privately. And Thomas has done this. He lived with his family and told everyone he was glad to be a private scholar. It's not possible that the king should condemn his friend, such a beloved friend, to death.'

'I bet you he will,' Montague says. 'They're just trying to find a day which won't disturb the apprentice boys. They don't dare to execute John Fisher on a saint's day. They fear they are making another saint.'

'For God's sake, why don't they both beg for pardon, submit to the king's will and come out?'

Montague looks at me as if I am a fool. 'You imagine that John Fisher, confessor to Lady Margaret Beaufort, one of the holiest men who ever guided the Church, is going to publicly declare that the Pope is not head of the Church? Swear to a heresy in the sight of God? How could he ever do that?'

I shake my head, blinded by the rush of tears to my eyes. 'So that he might live,' I say despairingly. 'Nothing matters more than that. So that he doesn't have to die! For words!'

Montague shrugs. 'He won't do it. He can't bring himself to it. Nor Thomas More. Don't you think that it will have occurred to him? Thomas? The cleverest man in England? I imagine that he thinks of it every day. I imagine, given Thomas's passion for life and for his children, especially his daughter, that it is his great temptation. I imagine that he puts it aside from him every day of his life, every minute.'

I sink into a chair, and I cover my face with my hands. 'Son, are those good men going to die rather than sign their name on a piece of paper delivered to them by a scoundrel?'

'Yes,' Montague says. 'And if I were more of a man, I would have done the same and I would be in the Tower with them and not let them go as if I were Judas, worse than Judas.'

I raise my face at once. 'Don't wish it,' I say quietly. 'Don't wish yourself in there. Don't ever wish such a thing.'

He pauses. 'Lady Mother, the time is coming when we will have to make a stand, either against the king's advisors or against him himself. John Fisher and Thomas More are making that stand now. We should stand with them.'

'And who will stand with us?' I demand. 'When you tell me that the emperor is setting sail to invade, then we can stand. Alone, I don't dare it.'

I look at his determined pale face and I have to get a grip on myself so that I don't break down. 'Son, you don't know what it's like, you don't know the Tower, you don't know what it's like to look out of the little window. You don't know what it's like to hear them building the scaffold. My father was executed there, my own brother walked across the drawbridge to Tower Hill and laid down his head on the block. I can't risk you, I can't risk Geoffrey. I can't see another Plantagenet walk into that place. We can't stand without the certainty of support, we can't stand without the certainty of victory. We can't go towards death like trusting beasts to slaughter. Promise me that we will not throw ourselves on the scaffold. Promise me that we will only stand against the Tudors if we are certain that we can win.'

The new Holy Father sends the king a message that cannot be mistaken. He makes John Fisher a cardinal of the Church, a sign to everyone that this great man, in failing health in the Tower, must be treated with respect. The Pope is head of the universal Church and the man held as a traitor, praying for strength, is his cardinal, under his explicit protection.

The king swears aloud, before all the court, that if the Pope sends a cardinal's hat then the bishop will be unable to wear it for he will have no head.

It is a brutal, brutish joke. But the gentlemen of the court hear Henry and they do not silence him. Nobody says 'Hush' or 'God forgive you'. The court, my sons shamefully among them, allow the king to say anything, and then in June, beyond belief, they let him do it. They let him execute the saintly man who was his grandmother's greatest friend and chosen confessor. They let him execute the friend who was his wife's spiritual advisor. John Fisher was a good, kind, loving man, he found me a refuge when I was a young woman and desperate for a friend; and I don't stand up and say one word in his defence.

His long vigil in the Tower did not frighten the old man; they say that he never tried to escape the fate that Thomas Cromwell prepared for him. On the morning of his execution he sent for his best clothes as if he were a bridegroom, and went to his death gladly as if to his wedding. I shudder when I hear this and go to my chapel to pray. I couldn't do that. I would never do that. I lack the faith and, besides, I have spent all my life clinging onto life.

In July, Thomas More, after writing and praying and thinking, and finally realising that there is no way to satisfy God and the king, walks out of his cell, looks up at the blue sky and the crying seagulls, and strolls up to Tower Hill quietly, as if taking the air on a summer's day, and lays his head down on the block as he too chooses death rather than deny his Church.

And no-one in England objects. Certainly, we don't say a word. Nothing happens. Nothing. Nothing. Nothing.

I read in a terse note from Reginald that the Holy Father, the King of France and the emperor agree that the King of England must be stopped; not another death can be permitted. It is a horror breaking out in England, and the whole world is shamed by it. The whole of Christendom is stunned that a king should dare to execute a cardinal, should martyr the greatest theologian in his country, his dearest friend. Everyone is horrified and soon they start to ask: if the king can do this, what else will he do? Then they start to ask: what about the queen? What might this tyrant do to his queen?

At the end of August, Reginald writes to us and says that he has achieved the goal he has been working for – the king is to be excommunicated. This could not be more important; it is the declaration of war by the Pope on the king. It is the Pope telling the English, telling all of Christendom, that the king is not blessed by God, is not authorised by the Church, he is outside, he is certain to go to hell. No-one need obey him, no Christian can defend him, no-one should take up arms for him, indeed anyone fighting against him is blessed by the Church as a crusader riding against a heretic.

He is excommunicated but the sentence is suspended. He is to be allowed two months to return to his marriage with the queen. If he persists in his sins the Pope will call on the Christian kings of Spain and France to invade England, and I shall come in with their army and raise the English with you.

Montague has been so sick since the death of Thomas More that his wife writes to me and asks me to come to his bedside. She fears that he might die.

What's the matter with him? I reply heartlessly.

He has turned his face to the wall and will not eat.

He is heartsick, I cannot help him. This is heartbreak, like the Sweat – a disease that came in with the Tudors. Tell him to get up and meet me in London; there is no time for anyone to ill-wish themselves. Burn this.

Montague arises from his sick bed and comes to see me, pale and grave. I call all of us together, as if for a family party to celebrate the birth of two new boys. My daughter Ursula has another boy that she has named Edward, and Geoffrey has a fourth child, Thomas. My cousin Henry Courtenay and his wife Gertrude come with two silver christening cups, and my son-in-law Henry Stafford takes one for his son, with thanks. We look like a family party celebrating the birth of new children.

The court is away from the city, riding with the king and the woman who calls herself queen in a great round of the principal houses going west. Years ago, they would have come to stay with me, and the beautiful royal chamber at Bisham would have housed the handsome young king and my dearest friend, the queen. Now they stay with the men who have built new homes on the wealth that the king has given them, with men who think that the new learning and the new religion are the way to heaven. These are men who do not believe in purgatory, ready to make a hell on earth to prove it, and sleep under stolen slates.

The court on progress is flirtatious. In its desperation to appear triumphantly happy, it is becoming lax. The king has moved on from his infatuation with Madge Shelton and apparently is now favouring one of the Seymour girls, visiting her home at Wulf Hall. I know her, Jane, too shy to take advantage of a lovesick man nearly old enough to be her father, but dutiful enough to receive his poems with a wan smile.

The woman who calls herself queen has to experience the humiliation of watching his eyes go past her, to a younger, prettier woman, just as she once was. Who would know better how dangerous it is when Henry's attention wanders? Who would know better that a lady in waiting can so easily wait in the wrong place, waiting for the king rather than her mistress the queen?

'This means nothing,' I say irritably to Geoffrey, who reports to me that the Seymours say they have a girl that draws the king's gaze as she walks across his wife's rooms. 'If he does not return to the queen he should be excommunicated. Is the Pope going to fulfil his threat?'

Montague, trying to be cheerful, orders the servants to bring the food and invites us to table as a merry family party and then Geoffrey sets the musicians to play loudly in the hall while we step into the private room behind the great table and close the door.

'I have a letter from our Lisle cousins,' Henry Courtenay says. He shows us the seal and then carefully tucks it into the fire, where it blazes and the wax sputters and then it is nothing but ash. 'Arthur Plantagenet says that we have to protect the princess. He will hold Calais for her against the king. If we can get her out of England she will be safe there.'

'Protect her against what?' I ask flatly, as if daring them to say. 'The Lisles are safe in Calais. What do they want us to do?'

'Lady Mother, the next parliament is going to be offered a Bill of Attainder against the queen and the princess,' my son Montague says quietly. 'Then they'll be taken to the Tower. Like More and Fisher. Then they'll be executed.'

There is a shocked silence, but everyone can see the truth in Montague's bleak misery.

'You're sure?' is all I say. I know that he is sure. I don't need his agonised face to tell me that.

He nods.

'Do we have enough support to deny the bill in parliament?' Henry Courtenay asks.

Geoffrey knows. 'There should be enough men for the queen to vote it down. If they dare to speak their minds, there are enough votes. But they have to stand up and speak.'

'How can we make sure that they speak out?' I ask.

'Someone has to take the risk and speak first,' Gertrude says eagerly. 'One of you.'

'You didn't stand up for so very long,' her husband remarks resentfully.

'I know,' she admits. 'I thought I would die in the Tower. I thought that I would die of cold and disease before I was tried and hanged. It's terrible. I was there for weeks. I would be there still if I had not denied everything and begged forgiveness. I said I was a foolish woman.'

'I am afraid that the king is ready to make war on women now, foolish or otherwise,' Montague says grimly. 'Nobody will be allowed that excuse again. But my cousin Gertrude is right. Someone has to speak up. I think it has to be us. I'll approach every friend that I have and tell him that there can be no attainder against the queen or the princess.'

'Tom Darcy will help you,' I say. 'John Hussey too.'

'Yes, but Cromwell will be ahead of us,' Geoffrey warns. 'Nobody manages parliament better than Cromwell. He'll have been before us, and he has deep pockets, and people are terrified of him. He knows some secret about everybody. He has a hold on everyone.'

'Can't Reginald persuade the emperor to come?' Henry Courtenay asks me. 'The princess is begging to be rescued. Can the emperor at least send a ship and take her away?'

'He says that he will,' Geoffrey replies. 'He promised Reginald.'

'But there are guards on both houses. Kimbolton is almost impossible to even get near without being observed,' Montague cautions him. 'Would the princess go without the queen? And from the start of this month all the ports will be guarded. The king knows well enough that the Spanish ambassador is plotting with the princess to try to get her away. She's closely watched, and there's not a port in England that doesn't have a Cromwell spy on duty. I really don't think we can get her out of the country; it will be hard enough to get her out of Hunsdon.'

'Can we take her into hiding in England?' Geoffrey asks. 'Or send her to Scotland?'

'I don't want her sent to Scotland,' I interrupt. 'What if they keep her?'

'We may have to,' Montague says and Courtenay and Stafford nod in agreement. 'One thing is for certain: we can't let her be taken to the Tower, and we have to stop Cromwell's parliament passing a Bill of Attainder and sending her to her death.'

'Reginald is working for the king's excommunication to be publicly declared,' I remind them.

'We need it now,' Montague says.

WARBLINGTON CASTLE, HAMPSHIRE, WINTER 1535

Geoffrey goes visiting all the substantial landlords who live around Warblington or around his own house at Lordington, and speaks to them of the Bill of Attainder against the queen and princess and how it must not come to parliament. In London Montague speaks discreetly to selected friends at court, mentioning that the princess should be allowed to live with her mother, that she should not be so closely guarded. The king's great friend and companion Sir Francis Bryan agrees with him, suggesting that he speak with Nicholas Carew. These are men at the very heart of Henry's court, and they are starting to rebel against the king's malice to his wife and daughter. I begin to think that Cromwell will not dare to propose the arrest of the queen to the parliament. He will know that there is a growing opposition; he will not want an open challenge.

The autumn progress has done its work and she is with child again. No word from Rome, and the king feels safe. He is in and out of her rooms flirting with her ladies; but she does not care. If she has a boy she will be untouchable.

WARBLINGTON CASTLE, HAMPSHIRE, JANUARY 1536

Dearest Lady Mother,

I am sorry to tell you that the Dowager Princess is gravely ill. I have asked Lord Cromwell if you may go to her and he says that he is not authorised to allow any visitors. The Spanish ambassador went just after the Christmas feast, and Maria de Salinas is on her way. I don't think we can do any more?

Your obedient and loving son,

Montague.

L'ERBER, LONDON, JANUARY 1536

I ride up the cold roads to London with my cape over my head and dozens of scarves wound round my face in an effort to keep warm. I fall from the saddle at the doorway of my London house and Geoffrey catches me in his arms and says kindly: 'Here, you're home now, don't even think of going on to Kimbolton.'

'I have to go,' I say. 'I have to say goodbye to her. I have to beg her forgiveness.'

'How have you ever failed her?' he demands, guiding me into the great hall. The fire is lit in the grate; I can feel the flickering heat on my face. My ladies gently lift the heavy cloak from my shoulders and unwind the scarves, take the gloves from my chilled hands and pull off my riding boots. I am aching from cold and weariness. I feel every one of my sixty-two years.

'She left me in charge of the princess and I didn't stay at her side,' I say shortly.

'She knew you did everything that you could.'

'Oh, damn everything to hell!' I suddenly break out in blasphemy. 'I have done nothing for her as I meant to do, and we were young women together and it seems just yesterday, and now she is lying near death and her daughter is in danger and we cannot reach her and I . . . I . . . am just a foolish old woman and I am helpless in this world. Helpless!'

Geoffrey kneels at my feet and his sweet face is torn between laughter and sorrowful pity. 'No woman I know is less helpless in the world,' he says. 'Not one more determined or powerful. And the queen knows that you are thinking of her and praying for her even now.'

'Yes, I can pray,' I say. 'I can pray that at least she is in a state of grace and without pain. I can pray for her.'

I heave myself to my feet, leave the temptation of the fire and the glass of mulled ale and go to my chapel where I kneel on the stone floor, which is how she always prayed, and I put the soul of my dearest friend Katherine of Aragon into the hands of God in the hopes that He will care for her better in heaven than we have cared for her here on earth.

And that is where Montague finds me when he comes to tell me that she is gone.

She went like a woman of great dignity; this has to be a comfort for me and for her. She prepared for her death, she had a long talk with her ambassador and she had the company of dearest Maria, who rode through the winter weather to get to her. She wrote to her nephew and to the king. They tell me that she wrote to Henry that she loved him as she had always done and signed herself as his wife. She prayed with her confessor and he anointed her with holy oil, and administered extreme unction, so that she was, according to her unshakeable faith, ready for her death. In the early afternoon she slipped away from this life that had been such a hard and thankless task for her, and – I am as certain as if I had seen it – joined her husband Arthur in the next.

I think of her as I first met her, a young woman tremulous with anxiety about being Princess of Wales and illuminated with love, her first love, and I think of her going to heaven like that, with her five little angels following her, one of the finest queens that England has ever had.

'Of course, it changes everything for Princess Mary for the worse,' Geoffrey says tempestuously, bursting into my private chamber, throwing off his winter jacket.

'How for the worse?' I feel calm in my grief. I am wearing a gown of dark blue, the royal colour of mourning for my house, though they tell me that the king is in yellow and gold – the mourning colour of Spain, and a bright buttercup shade that suits his mood, freed as he is at last from a faithful wife, and safe from invasion by her nephew.

'She has lost a protector and a witness,' Montague agrees. 'The king would never have moved against her while her mother was alive, he would have had to order that the queen was attainted before his daughter. Now Princess Mary is the only person left in England who refuses to swear to his oath.'

I take the decision that has been waiting for me. 'I know. I know this. We have to get her out of England. Son Montague, the time is now. We have to take the risk. We have to act now. Her life is in danger.'

I stay in London while Montague and Geoffrey hand-pick a guard who will ride to Hunsdon and seize the princess, plan a route skirting London, and hire a ship that will wait for her and take her out of one of the little Thameside villages like Grays. We decide against telling the Spanish ambassador; he loves the princess and he is in deep grief for her mother, but he is a dainty, fearful man, and if Thomas Cromwell were to arrest him I think he would squeeze him like a Spanish orange and the man would tell everything within days, perhaps within hours.

Geoffrey goes to Hunsdon and after waiting patiently, bribing everyone he can, gets the boy who lights the fires in the bed-chambern into his nervioe. He comes home beaming with relief.

'She's safe for the moment,' he says. 'Thank God! Because getting her away would have been near to impossible. But her luck has changed – who would have thought it? She has letters from the Boleyn queen saying that they must be friends, that the princess can turn to her in her grief.'

'What?' I ask incredulously. It is so early in the morning that I am not yet dressed, but am still in my nightgown and furred robe. Geoffrey has come to my bedchamber and we are alone as he stirs up the fire.

'I know.' He is almost laughing. 'I even saw the princess. She is allowed to walk in the garden, by the order of Anne. Apparently the Lady has ordered that the princess is given more freedom and treated more kindly. She can receive visitors and the Spanish ambassador can bring her letters.'

'But why? Why would Anne change like this?'

'Because while Queen Katherine was alive, the king had no choice but to stay with the Lady, he was bound to push through the destruction of the Church. You know what he's like, with everyone saying that it couldn't be done and shouldn't be done he grew more and more obstinate. But now that the queen is dead he is free. His quarrel with the emperor is over, he's safe from invasion, he has no need to quarrel with the Holy Father. He is a widower now, he can legally marry Anne if he wants to, and there is no reason that he should not reconcile with the princess. She is the daughter of his first wife; a son from his second will inherit before her.'

'So that woman is trying to befriend the princess?'

'Says she will intercede with her father, says she will be her friend, says she can come to court and not even be a lady in waiting, but have her own rooms.'

'Precedence over the Boleyn bastards?' I ask, sharp as ever.

'She didn't say that. But why not? If he marries Anne a second time, this time with the blessing of the Church, then both girls will take second place to a legitimate boy.'

I nod slowly. Then as the realisation comes to me, I say quietly, and with such satisfaction: 'Ah. I see it. She will be afraid.'

'Afraid?' Geoffrey turns from the sideboard with a pastry left from last night in his hand. 'Afraid?'

'The king is not married to her. They went through two services but the Holy Father ruled both of them to be invalid. She is just his concubine. Now the queen is dead and he can marry again. But perhaps he won't marry her.'

Geoffrey looks at me with his mouth open, as the pastry sheds crumbs on the floor. I don't even tell him to use a plate. 'Not marry her?'

I count on my fingers the triumphant list. 'She hasn't given him a son, she has only managed to carry a girl, he has fallen out of love with her and started his amours with other women. She has brought him no wisdom of her own and no good friends. She has no powerful foreign relations to protect her, her English family are not reliable. Her uncle has turned against her, her sister is banished from court, her sister-in-law has offended the king, and the moment that she is unsteady then Thomas Cromwell will turn on her, as he will only ever serve a favourite. What if she is favourite no more?'

ON THE GREAT NORTH ROAD, JANUARY 1536

It snows, and the road is very cold out of London, heading north up the great road to Peterborough. The weather is so bad, the snow so blinding and roads so impassable that we are two full days on the journey, rising at dawn and riding all day. In the early dark of the afternoons we stop once at a great house and request hospitality, and once at a good inn. We can no longer count on the monasteries along the way for hospitality and dinner. Some of them are closed altogether, some of the monks are transferred to other houses, some have been turned out of doors. I think that perhaps Thomas Cromwell did not foresee this when he started his great inquiry into religious houses and rifled their fortunes for the king's profit. He claims that he is stamping out ill-doing, but he is destroying a great institution in the country. The abbeys feed the poor, they nurse the sick, they help travellers and they own more land than anyone else but the king, and farm it well. Now nothing is certain on the road any more. No-one is safe on the road any more. Even the pilgrim hostels have put up their shutters as the shrines are being stripped of their wealth and their powers denied.

PETERBOROUGH, CAMBRIDGESHIRE, JANUARY 1536

On the afternoon of the third day I can see the spire of Peterborough Abbey ahead of me, pointing up to an iron grey sky, as my horse dips his head against the cold wind and trudges steadily onward, his big hooves scuffing the snow. I have a dozen men at arms around me and as we enter the gates of the city, the bell tolling for curfew, they close up against the people of the streets who watch resentfully, until they see my banner and start to shout.

For a moment I am afraid that they will shout out against me, seeing me as one of the court, one of the many new lords who have grown rich on the good will of the Tudors, even if I have that good will no more. But a woman leaning out of an overhanging window shrieks down at me: 'God bless the white rose! God bless the white rose!'

Startled, I glance up and see her beam at me. 'God bless Queen Katherine! God bless the princess! God bless the white rose!'

The urchin children and beggars clearing out of the way ahead of the soldiers turn and cheer, though they know nothing of who I am. But out of the little roadside shops, stepping out of workhouses and tumbling out of church and ale-house alike come men pulling off their hats and one or two even kneeling down in the freezing mud as I go by, and they call out blessings on the late queen, on her daughter, and on me and my house.

Someone even sets up the old cry 'À Warwick!' and I know that they have not forgotten, any more than I have, that there was once an England with a York king on the throne who was content to be king and did not pretend to be Pope, who had a mistress who did not pretend to be queen, who had bastards who did not pretend to be heirs.

I understand, as we ride through the little city, why the king commanded that the queen should not be buried, as befits her dignity, in the abbey at Westminster. It is because the City would have risen up to mourn her. Henry was right to be afraid; I think all of London would have rioted against him. The people of England have turned against the Tudors. They loved this young king when he came to the throne to make everything right again, but now he has taken their Church, and taken their monasteries, and taken their best men, put aside his queen and death has taken her. They cheer for her still, they mutter and call her martyred, a saint, and they cheer for me as one of the old royal family who would never have led them so badly astray.

We arrive at the guest house of the abbey, and find it over-crowded with the retinues of other great ladies from London. Maria de Salinas, Countess Willoughby, the queen's faithful friend, is here already and she comes running down the stairs as if she were still a lady in waiting to a Spanish princess and I were mere Lady Pole of Stourton. We hold each other tightly, and I can feel her shake with her sobs. When we pull back to look at each other I know that there are tears in my eyes too.

'She was at peace,' is the first thing she says. 'She was at peace at the end.'

'I knew it.'

'She sent you her love.'

'I tried . . .'

'She knew that you would be thinking of her, and she knew that you would continue to guard her daughter. She wanted to give you . . .' She breaks off, unable to speak, her Spanish accent still strong after years in England and her marriage to an English nobleman. 'I am sorry. She wanted to give you one of her rosaries, but the king has ordered that everything be taken into his keeping.'

'Her bequests?'

'He has taken everything,' she says with a little sigh. 'As is his right, I suppose.'

'It's not his right!' I say at once. 'If she was a widow as he insists, and they were unmarried, then everything she owned at her death was hers to give as she wished!'

There is a little twinkle in Maria's dark eyes as she hears me. I cannot help myself, I always have to defend a woman's estate. I bow my head. 'It's not the things,' I say quietly, knowing well enough that her greatest jewels and treasures had already been taken from her and hung around Anne Boleyn's scrawny neck. 'And it's not that I wanted anything from her, I will remember her without a keepsake. But those things were hers by right.'

'I know,' Maria says and looks up the stairs as Frances Grey, Marchioness of Dorset, daughter of Mary the Dowager Queen of France, comes down the stairs and makes the smallest of bows to me in return to my curtsey. As the daughter of a Tudor princess married to a commoner Frances is cursed with anxiety about her precedence and her position, the more so as her father is now remarried, and to Maria's daughter who is here too.

'You are welcome here,' she says, as if it were her own house. 'The funeral is tomorrow morning. I shall go in first and you behind me and Maria and her daughter Catherine, my step-mother, behind you.'

'Of course,' I say. 'All I want to do is to say goodbye to my friend. Precedence does not matter to me. She was my very dear-est friend.'

'And the Countess of Worcester is here, and the Countess of Surrey,' Frances goes on.

I nod. Frances Howard, Countess of Surrey, is a Tudor sup-porter by birth and by marriage. Elizabeth Somerset, the Countess of Worcester, is one of the Boleyn ladies in waiting in constant attendance upon Anne Boleyn. I imagine that they have been sent to report back to their mistress, who will not be pleased to hear that the people in the street called blessings on the queen as her coffin was drawn to the abbey by six black horses with her household and half the county walking, heads bared to the cold wind, behind.

It is a beautiful day. The wind blows from the east, biting and cold, but the sky is clear with a hard wintry light as we walk to the abbey church and inside the hundreds of candles glow like dull gold. It is a simple funeral, not grand enough for a great queen and the victor of Flodden, not enough to honour an Infanta of Spain who came to England with such high hopes. But there is a quiet beauty in the abbey church where four bishops greet the coffin draped in black velvet with a frieze of cloth of gold. Two heralds walk before the coffin, two behind, carrying banners with her arms: her own crest, the royal arms of Spain, the royal arms of England, and her own insignia, the two royal arms together. Her motto 'Humble and Loyal' is in gold letters beside the stand for the coffin and when the requiem Mass is sung and the last pure notes are slowly dying away on the smoky incense-filled air, they lower the coffin into the vault before the high altar, and I know that my friend has gone.

I put my fist against my mouth to stifle a deep sob that tears from my belly. I never thought that I would see her to the grave. She came into my house when I was the lady of Ludlow and she was a girl, twelve years my junior. I could never have dreamed that I would see her buried so quietly, so peacefully in an abbey far from the city that was proud to be her capital and home.

Nor was it the funeral that she had requested in her will. But I do believe that though she wished to be buried in a church of the Observant Friars and have their devout congregation say memorial Masses for her, she has a place in heaven even without their prayers. The king denied her title, and closed the houses of the friars, but even if they are vagrants on the empty roads tonight, they will still pray for her; and all those of us who loved her will never think of her as anything other than Katherine, Queen of England.

We dine late and are quiet at dinner. Maria and Frances and I talk about her mother, and the old days when Queen Katherine ruled the court and the dowager queen Mary came home from France, so pretty and determined, and disobedient.

'It can't always have been summer, can it?' Maria asks longingly. 'I seem to remember those years as always summer. Can it really have been sunny every day?'

Frances raises her head. 'Someone at the door.'

I can hear too the clatter of a small group of riders, and the door opening, and Frances's steward in the doorway saying apologetically: 'Message from the court.'

'Let him in,' Frances says.

I glance at Maria and wonder if she had permission to be here, or if the king has sent someone to arrest her. I fear for myself. I wonder if information has been laid against me, against my boys, against any one of our family. I wonder if Thomas Cromwell, who pays so many informants, who knows so much, has found out about the ship's master at Grays who is available to hire, who was approached some nights ago and asked if he would sail a lady to France.

'Do you know who this is?' I ask Frances, my voice very low. 'Were you expecting a message?'

'No, I don't know.'

The man walks into the room, brushing the snow from his cape, puts back his hood and bows to us. I recognise the livery of the Marquess of Dorset, Henry Grey, Frances's husband.

'Your Grace, Lady Dorset, Lady Salisbury, Lady Surrey, Lady Worcester, Lady Willoughby.' He bows to each of us. 'I have grave news from Greenwich. I am sorry that it took me so long to get here. We had an accident on the road and had to take a man back to Enfield.' He turns his attention to Frances. 'I am commanded by your lord and husband to bring you to court. Your uncle the king has been gravely wounded. When I left five days ago he was unconscious.'

She stands as if to greet tremendous news. I see her lean on the table as if to steady herself.

'Unconscious?' I repeat.

The man nods. 'The king took a terrible blow and fell from his horse. The horse stumbled and fell on him as he lay. He was running a course in the joust, the blow threw him back, he went down, and his horse on top of him. They were both fully armoured, so the weight . . .' He breaks off and shakes his head. 'When we got the horse off His Grace, he did not speak or move, he was like a dead man. We didn't even know that he was breathing until we carried him into the palace, and sent for physicians. My lord sent me at once to fetch her ladyship.' He thumps his fist into his palm. 'And then we couldn't get through the drifts of snow.'

I look at Frances, who is trembling, a blush rising up into her cheeks. 'A terrible accident,' she observes breathlessly.

The man nods. 'We should leave at first light.' He looks at us. 'The king's condition is a secret.'

'He held a joust after the queen's death, before she was even laid to rest?' Maria remarks coldly.

The messenger bows slightly, as if he does not want to comment on the king and the woman who calls herself queen celebrating the death of her rival. But I don't attend to this, I am looking at Frances. She has been keenly ambitious all her life and hungry for position at court. Now I can almost read what she is thinking as her dark eyes flick, unseeing, from the table to the messenger and back again. If the king dies from this fall then he leaves a baby girl that no-one thinks is legitimate, a baby in the belly of a woman whose chance of ever being accepted as queen dies with him, a bastard boy acknowledged and honoured, and a princess under house arrest. Who would dare to predict which of these claimants will take the throne?

The Boleyn party including Elizabeth Somerset, here at this table, will support the woman who calls herself queen and her baby Elizabeth, but the Howards, with Frances Countess of Surrey, will split apart from their junior branch and press for the male heir, even if he is Bessie Blount's bastard, for he is married into their family. Maria, and all my family, all my affinity, all the old nobility of England, would lay down our lives to put Princess Mary on the throne. Here at this dinner table, at the funeral of the queen, are gathered the parties who will make war against each other if the king is dead tonight. And I, who have seen a country at war, know very well that during the battles, other heirs will emerge. My cousin Henry Courtenay, cousin to the king? My son Montague, cousin to the king? My son Reginald, if he married the princess and brought with him the blessing of the Holy Father and the armies of Spain? Or even Frances herself, who will certainly be thinking of this, as she stands here wide-eyed and glazed with ambition, the daughter of the Dowager Queen of France, the king's niece?

In a moment she recovers. 'At first light,' she agrees.

'I have this for you.' He hands her a letter on which I can see her husband's seal, a standing unicorn. I would give a lot to know what he writes to her privately. She holds the letter in her hand and turns to me. 'Please excuse me,' she says. Carefully we trade measured bobs, and then she hurries from her room to tell her attendants to pack up, and to read her letter.

Maria and I watch her go. 'If His Grace does not recover . . .' Maria says very quietly.

'I think we had better travel with Lady Frances,' I say. 'I think we all need to get back to London. We can travel with her escort.'

'She'll want to hurry.'

'So will I.'

ON THE GREAT NORTH ROAD, JANUARY 1536

We spend one night on the road, riding as fast as we can to London, asking along the way for news but strictly forbidding our servants to say why we are in such haste to get back to court.

'If the people know that the king is gravely injured I fear that they will rise up,' Frances says quietly to me.

'There's no doubt of it,' I reply grimly.

'And your affinity would be . . .'

'Loyal,' I say shortly, without explaining what that might mean.

'There will have to be a regency,' she says. 'A terribly long regency for the Princess Elizabeth. Unless . . .'

I wait to see if she has the courage to finish the sentence.

'Unless,' she says with finality.

'Pray God that His Grace is recovered,' I say simply.

'It is impossible to imagine the country without him,' Frances concurs.

I nod in agreement as I glance around at my companions, and think that clearly it is not impossible; for it is what each and every one of them are thinking.

We halt for the night at an inn which can house the ladies and women servants of our big party but the men will have to go to outlying farms and the guards will have to sleep in barns. So we know we are not fully guarded when we hear the noise of approaching horsemen and then see them cantering down the road at dusk, half a dozen horses ridden hard.

The ladies step back behind the big taproom table but I go out to face whatever is coming. I would rather greet fear than have it come stamping into my hall. Frances, Marchioness of Dorset, usually so anxious to be first, lets me take the precedence for danger, and I stand alone, waiting for the horses to halt before the doorway. In the light spilling out from the door and then in the sudden flicker from a torch held by one of the stable boys running forward I see the royal livery of green and white and my heart skips a beat for fear.

'A message for the Countess of Worcester,' he says.

Elizabeth Somerset hurries forward, and takes the letter sealed with the falcon crest. I let the other women crowd around her as she breaks the Boleyn woman's seal, and leans towards the torches so that she can read in their flickering light; but no-one else can see her message.

I step out into the road and smile at the messenger.

'You've had a long, cold ride,' I observe.

He tosses the reins of his horse to a stable boy. 'We have.'

'And I am afraid there is not a bed to be had in the inn, but I can send your men to a farm nearby where my guard is sleeping. They will see that you get food and somewhere to rest. Are you to return to London with us?'

'I am to take the countess to the court at dawn tomorrow, ahead of you all,' he grumbles. 'And I knew that there would be nowhere to sleep here. And I suppose nothing to eat either.'

'You can send your men to the farm, and I can get you a place at a table here in the hall tonight,' I say. 'I'm the Countess of Salisbury.'

He bows low. 'I know who you are, your ladyship. I'm Thomas Forest.'

'You can be my guest at dinner tonight, Mr Forest.'

'I'd be very grateful for dinner,' he says. He turns and shouts to his men to follow the stable boy with the torch who will show them the way to the farm.

'Yes,' I say, leading the way inside where the trestle tables are being laid out for dinner and the benches drawn up. He can smell meat roasting in the kitchen. 'But what's the hurry? Does the queen need her lady so urgently that she sends you riding cross-country in winter? Or is it just a pregnant woman's whim that you have to serve?'

He leans towards me. 'They don't tell me anything,' he says. 'But I'm a married man. I know the signs. The queen has taken to her bed and they are hurrying in and out with hot water and towels and everyone from the greatest of them to the youngest kitchen maid speaks to every single man as if we are fools or criminals. The midwives are there. But nobody is carrying a cradle in.'

'She is losing her child?' I ask.

'Without a doubt,' he says with brutal honesty. 'Another dead Tudor baby.'

BISHAM MANOR, BERKSHIRE,
SPRING 1536

I leave the ladies to scurry back to court where the king is recovering from his fall and coming to terms with the news of the death of yet another child, and I ride at my leisure to my home. The question now, the only question, is how the king will take the loss of his son – for the baby was a boy. Will he see it as a sign of the disapproval of God and turn against the second wife, as he turned and blamed the first?

I spend some hours on my knees in the priory chapel thinking on this. My household, God bless them, give me the credit to believe that I am praying. Alas, I am not really at prayer. In the quietness and peace of the priory I am turning over and over in my own mind what the boy that I once knew so well will do, now that he is a man and faced with a crushing disappointment.

The boy I knew would recoil in pain from such a blow, but then he would turn to the people he loved and those that loved him and in comforting them, cheer himself.

'But he's not a boy any more,' Geoffrey says quietly to me as he joins my vigil one day and kneels beside me, and I whisper these thoughts to him. 'He's not even a young man. The blow to his head has shaken him deeply. He was going bad, no doubt that he was spoiling like milk souring in the sun; but suddenly, everything is even worse. Montague says it is as if he has realised that he will die just like his wife the queen.'

'Do you think he grieves for her at all?'

'Even though he didn't want to go back to her, he knew she was there, loving him, praying for him, hoping that they would be reconciled. And then suddenly he is near death, and then the baby dies. Montague says that he thinks God has forsaken him. He'll have to find some explanation.'

'He'll blame Anne,' I predict.

Geoffrey is about to reply when Prior Richard comes in quietly and kneels beside me, prays for a moment, crosses himself and says: 'Your Grace, may I interrupt you?'

We turn to him. 'What's the matter?'

'We have a visitation,' he says. He speaks with such disdain that for a moment I think that frogs have come up from the moat and are all over the kitchen garden. 'A visitation?'

'That's what they call it. An inspection. My Lord Cromwell's men have come to see that our priory is well run according to the precepts of its founders and our order.'

I rise to my feet. 'There can be no question of that.'

He leads the way out of the church towards his private room. 'My lady, they do question it.'

He opens the door and two men turn and look at me impertinently, as if I am interrupting them, though they are in my prior's room, in my priory, on my lands. I wait for a moment, without moving or speaking.

'Her Ladyship the Countess of Salisbury,' the prior says. Only then do they bow, and at their grudging courtesy I realise that the priory is in danger.

'And you are?'

'Richard Layton and Thomas Legh,' the older one says smoothly. 'We are working for my Lord Cromwell—'

'I know what you do,' I interrupt him. This is the man who interrogated Thomas More. This is the man who went into Sheen Abbey and interrogated the monks. This is the man who gave witness against the Maid of Kent, Elizabeth Barton. I don't doubt that my name and the names of my sons and my chaplain have been written several times on papers in the little brown satchel that he carries.

He bows, quite without shame. 'I am glad of it,' he says steadily. 'There has been much corruption and wickedness in the Church and Thomas Legh and I are proud to be instruments of purification, of reformation, of God.'

'There's no corruption or wickedness here,' Geoffrey says hotly. 'So you can be on your way.'

Layton makes a funny little nodding gesture with his head. 'You know, Sir Geoffrey, that is what everyone always assures me. And so we will confirm it, and be on our way as fast as we can. We have much to do. We don't want to be here any longer than is necessary.'

He turns to the prior. 'I take it we may use your room for our inquiries? You will send the canons and the nuns in one at a time, the canons first and then the nuns. The oldest first.'

'Why would you speak with the nuns?' Geoffrey asks. None of us wants my daughter-in-law Jane complaining to strangers about her decision to join the priory, or demanding her release.

The quickly suppressed smile that crosses Layton's face tells me that they know of Jane, and they know that we took her dower from her when we encouraged her to enter the nunnery, and they know she wants to be released from her vows and get her fortune back into her own keeping.

'We always speak with everybody,' Richard Layton says quietly. 'That's how we make sure that not a sparrow falls. We are doing God's work, we do it thoroughly.'

'Prior Richard will sit with you, and hear all that is said,' I assert.

'Alas, no. Prior Richard will be our first interview.'

'Look,' I say, in sudden fury. 'You can't come in here to my priory, founded by my family, and ask questions as you like. This is my land, this is my priory. I won't have it.'

'You did sign the oath, didn't you?' Layton asks negligently, turning over the papers on the desk. 'Surely you did? As I recall only Thomas More and John Fisher refused to sign. Thomas More and John Fisher, both dead.'

'Of course My Lady Mother signed.' Geoffrey speaks for me. 'There is no question of our loyalty, there can be no question.'

Richard Layton shrugs. 'Then you accepted the king as the supreme head of the Church. He orders that it be visited. We are here doing his bidding. You are not questioning his right, his divine right, to govern his Church?'

'No, of course not,' I say, driven.

'Then please, your ladyship, let us start,' Layton says with a most agreeable smile, pulls out the prior's chair from behind the prior's table, seats himself, and opens his satchel while Thomas Legh draws a stack of papers towards him and writes a heading on the first page. It says *Visitation of Bisham Priory, April 1536.*

'Oh,' Richard Layton says, as if it has just occurred to him. 'We'll speak to your chaplain too.'

He catches me quite unawares. 'I don't have one,' I say. 'I confess to Prior Richard, as does my household.'

'Did you never have one?' Layton asks. 'I was sure there was a payment, in the priory accounts ...' He turns over pages as if looking for something he vaguely remembers, flicking through them like an actor playing the part of someone looking for a name in old papers.

'I did,' I say firmly. 'But he left. He moved on. He gave me no explanation.' I glance at Geoffrey.

'Most unreliable,' he says firmly.

'Helyar, wasn't it?' Layton asks. 'John Helyar?'

'Was it?'

'Yes.'

They stay in the guest house of the priory for a week. They dine with the canons in the priory dining hall and they are wakened through the night by the priory bell ringing for prayer. I hear with some pleasure that they complain of sleeplessness. The cells are small and stone-walled and there are no fires except in the prior's study room and in the dining hall. I am sure that they are cold and uncomfortable but this is the monastic life that they are investigating; they should be glad that it is poor and rigorous. Thomas Legh is accustomed to grander standards, he travels with fourteen men in his livery and his brother is his constant companion. He says that they should be staying in the manor and I say that they would be welcome but I have an infestation of biting fleas and all the rooms are being smoked and aired.

Clearly, he does not believe me, and I do not try to convince him.

On the third day of their visit Thomas Standish, the clerk of the kitchen, comes bursting into the dairy where I am watching the maids press the cheeses.

'My Lady! The villagers are up at the priory! You'd better come at once!'

I drop the wooden cheese press with a clatter on the well-scrubbed board and strip off my apron.

'I'll come!' says one of the dairymaids eagerly. 'They're going to throw that Crummer man from his horse.'

'No they're not, his name is Cromwell, and you will stay here,' I say firmly.

I stride out of the kitchen, and the clerk takes my arm to guide me over the cobbles of the yard. 'There's just a dozen of them,' he says. 'Nate Ridley and his sons, and a man I don't know, and Old White and his boy. But they're full of it. They say they won't let the visitation happen. They say they know all about it.'

I'm just about to answer when my words are drowned out by a sudden peal of bells. Someone is ringing the bells out of order, out of time, then I hear that they are ringing them backwards.

'It's a sign.' Standish breaks into a run. 'When they ring the bells backwards they signal that the commons have taken command, that the village is up.'

'Stop them!' I order. Thomas Standish runs ahead as I follow him to the priory where the fat bell ropes dangle at the back of the church. There are three Bisham men and one man I don't know, and the clangour of the ill-timed peal is deafening in the small space.

'Stop it!' I shout, but no-one can hear me. I cuff one of my men around the head with a hard backward slap of my hand, and I poke the other with the blunt cheese knife that I still have in my hand. 'Stop it!'

They stop pulling the ropes as soon as they see me and the bells jangle on more and more unevenly until they are stilled. Behind me the two visitors, Legh and Layton, come tumbling into the church, and the men turn on them with a growl of anger.

'You get out,' I say to them briskly. 'Go and sit with the prior. I can't answer for your safety.'

'We are on the king's business,' Legh starts.

'You're on the devil's business!' one of the men exclaims.

'Now then,' I say quietly. 'That's enough.' To the two visitors I say, 'I warn you. Go to the prior. He'll keep you safe.'

They drop their heads and scuttle from the chapel. 'Now,' I say steadily. 'Where are the rest of you?'

'They're in the priory, they're taking the chalice and the vestments,' Standish reports.

'Saving them!' old Farmer White says to me. 'Saving them from those heretical thieves. You should let us do our work. You should let us do God's work.'

'It's not just us,' the stranger tells me. 'We're not alone.'

'And who are you?'

'I'm Goodman, from Somerset,' he says. 'The men of Somerset are defending their monasteries too. We're defending the Church, as the monks and the gentry should do. I came here to tell these good people. They must stand up and defend their own priory. Each one of us must save God's things for better times.'

'No we must not,' I say quickly. 'And I'll tell you why. Because after these two men have run away – and I am sure you can make them scuttle back to London – the king will send an army and they will hang each one of you.'

'He can't hang us all. Not if the whole village rises,' Farmer White objects.

'Yes he can,' I say. 'Do you think that he does not have cannon, and handguns? Do you think he doesn't have horses with lances and soldiers with pikes? Do you think he can't build enough scaffolds for all of you?'

'But what are we to do?' The fight has quite gone out of them. A few villagers straggle in through the church door and look at me as if I will save the priory. 'What are we to do?'

'The king has become the Mouldwarp,' a woman cries out

from the back of the crowd. Her dirty shawl is over her head and her face is turned away. I don't recognise her and I don't want to see her face. I don't want to give evidence against her, as she goes on, shouting treason. 'The king has become a false king, hairy as a goat. He's run mad and eats up all the gold in the land. There will be no May. There will be no May.'

I glance anxiously at the door and see Standish nod reassuringly. The visitors have not heard this; they are cowering in the prior's chamber.

'You are my people,' I say quietly into the unhappy silence. 'And this is my priory. I cannot save the priory but I can save you. Go to your homes. Let the visitation finish. Perhaps they will find no wrongdoing and the canons will stay here and all will be well.'

There is a low groan as if they are all in pain. 'And if they don't?' someone says from the back.

'Then we must beg the king to dismiss his wrong-thinking advisors,' I say. 'And put the country to rights again. As it was, in the old days.'

'Better put it back to the old days before the Tudors,' someone says very quietly.

I put my hand out to order them to be silent before someone shouts 'À Warwick!'.

'Silence!' I say, and it sounds more like a plea than a command. 'There can be no disloyalty to the king.' There is a mutter of agreement to that. 'So we have to allow his servants to do their work.'

Some of the men nod as they follow the logic.

'But will you tell him?' someone asks me. 'Tell the king that we cannot lose our monasteries and our nunneries. Tell him that we want our altars at the roadside and our places of pilgrimage. We need our feast days and the monasteries open and serving the poor. And we want the lords to advise him, not this Crummer, and the princess to be his heir?'

'I'll tell him what I can,' I say.

Unwillingly, uncertainly, like cattle that have broken through a hedge into a strange field and then don't know what to do with their freedom, they allow themselves to be chivvied out of the priory chapel and down the road to the village.

When all is quiet again, the door to the priory opens and the two visitors come out. I feel quite triumphant over their nervous sidle to the door of the church and the way they look around at the traces of unrest, the mud on the floor, the bell ropes hanging, and frown at the echo of the ringing.

'These are a very troubled people,' Legh says to me as if I have stirred them to rebellion. 'Disloyal.'

'No, they're not,' I say flatly. 'They are completely loyal to the king. They misunderstood what you were doing, that is all. They thought that you had come to steal away the church's gold and close down the priory. They thought that the Lord Chancellor was closing down the churches of England for his own benefit.'

Legh smiles at me thinly. 'Of course not,' he says.

Next day, Prior Richard comes to me in my records room at the manor. I am seated at a great round rent table, with each drawer labelled with a letter. Every tenant's deeds are in a drawer labelled with the right letter and the table can spin from A to Z so that I can draw out, in a moment, the document that I need. The prior's arrival distracts me from my pleasure in the well-run business that is my home. 'They are speaking with the nuns today.'

'You don't think there will be a problem?'

'If your daughter-in-law complains . . .'

I close a drawer and push the table a little to the right. 'She can say nothing that is critical of the priory. She might say that she has changed her mind about being a nun, she might say that she wants to come out and draw her dower from my rents, but that is not the sort of corruption they are charged to find.'

'It's the only thing where we might be seen as at fault,' he says tentatively.

'You are not at fault,' I reassure him. 'It was Montague and I who urged her to go in, and Montague and I who have kept here there.'

Still, he looks worried. 'These are troubled times.'

'None worse,' I say, and mean it. 'I've never known worse.'

Thomas Cromwell's men, Richard Layton and Thomas Legh, take their leave of me with perfect civility and mount up to go. I note their good horses and their fine saddlery, I note Legh's men and their smart livery. The king's Church is a profitable service, it appears. Judging poor sinners seems to pay extraordinarily good wages. I wave them off, knowing that they'll be back with a prompt decision, but even so I am surprised that a mere four days later, the prior comes to the manor and tells me that they are returned.

'They want me to leave,' he says. 'They have asked for my resignation.'

'No,' I say flatly. 'They have no right.'

He bows his head. 'Your ladyship, they have a command with the king's seal, signed by Thomas Cromwell. They have the right.'

'Nobody said that the king should be head of the Church to destroy it!' I burst out in sudden anger. 'Nobody swore an oath saying that the monasteries should be closed and good men and women thrown into the world. Nobody wanted the stained glass taken from the windows, nobody wanted the gold taken from the altars, nobody in this country swore an oath calling for the end of the Catholic communion! This is not right!'

'I pray you,' he says, white as his linen, 'I pray you be silent.'

I whirl to the window and I glare out at the sweetness of the green leaves on the trees, at the bobbing white and pink of the apple blossom over the orchard wall. I think of the child that I knew, of the little boy Henry who wanted to serve, who shone with innocence and hope, who was, in his childish way, devout.

I turn back. 'I can't believe this is happening,' I say. 'Send them to me.'

The visitors, Layton and Legh, come into my privy chamber quietly, but without any signs of apprehension. 'Close the door,' I say, and Legh closes it and they stand before me. There are no chairs for them, and I don't move from my seat in the big chair with the canopy of state over my head.

'Prior Richard will not resign,' I say. 'There is nothing wrong with the priory, and he has done nothing wrong. He will stay in his post.'

Richard Layton unrolls a scroll, shows me the seal. 'He is commanded to resign,' he says regretfully.

I let him hold it towards me so that I can read the lengthy sentences. Then I look at him. 'No grounds,' I say. 'And I know you have no evidence. He will appeal.'

He rolls it up again. 'There is no form of appeal,' he says. 'We need no grounds. The decision is final, I am afraid, your ladyship.'

I rise to my feet and I gesture to the door to tell them that they are to go. 'No, *my* decision is final,' I say. 'The prior will not resign unless you can show that he has done something wrong. And you cannot show that. So he is staying.'

They bow, as they have to. 'We will return,' Richard Layton says.

This is a testing time. I know that some monasteries have become lax and their servants a byword for corruption. I know – everyone knows – of the pigeon bones and the duck's blood relics, and the bits of string that are offered to the gullible as the Virgin's girdle. The country is full of fearful fools and the worst of the monasteries and nunneries have battened off them, misled them, exploited them, and lived like lords while preaching poverty. Nobody objects to the king appointing honest men to discover these abuses and stop them. But I shall see now what happens when the king's visitors come to a priory that serves God and the people, where the treasures are used for the glory of God, where the rents taken by the prior are used to feed the poor. My family founded this priory and I will protect it. It is my life: like my children, like my princess, like my house.

Montague writes to me from London, unsealed and unsigned:

He says that he sees that God will not give him a son with her.

I hold the letter in my hand for a moment before I push it deep into the heart of the fire. I know that Anne Boleyn will not call herself queen for long.

In the hour before dinner, when I am sitting with my ladies in my privy chamber and the musician is playing the lute, I hear a great knock on the outer door.

'Go on,' I say to the musician who lets the notes die away as we listen to the sound of feet walking through the hall and coming up the stairs. 'Go on.'

He strikes a chord as the door opens and Cromwell's men Layton and Legh come into the room and bow to me. With them, like a ghost risen from the grave, but a triumphant ghost in new clothes, is my daughter-in-law, the grieving widow of my son Arthur, Jane, last seen clawing at the door of the family crypt and crying for her husband and son.

'Jane? What are you doing here? And what are you wearing?' I ask her.

She gives a little defiant laugh, and tosses her head. 'These gentlemen are escorting me to London,' she says. 'I am betrothed in marriage.'

I feel my breath coming faster as my temper rises. 'You are a novice in a priory,' I say quietly. 'Have you quite lost your mind?' I look at Richard Layton. 'Are you abducting a nun?'

'She has spoken with the prior, and he has released her,' he says smoothly. 'No novice can be held if she changes her mind. Lady Pole is betrothed to marry Sir William Barrantyne and I am commanded to take her to her new husband.'

'I thought William Barrantyne just stole goods and lands from the Church?' I say viciously. 'I am behind the times. I didn't know he captured nuns also.'

'I am no nun, and I should never have been put in there and kept there!' Jane shouts at me.

My ladies jump to their feet, my granddaughter Katherine scuttles towards me as if she would stand between me and Jane, but I gently put her to one side. 'You asked, you begged, you cried to be allowed to withdraw from the world because your heart was broken,' I say steadily. 'Now I see your heart is mended and you beg to come out again. But be very sure to tell your new husband that he takes a poor novice, not an heiress. You will get nothing from me when you marry and your father may leave your inheritance away from a runaway nun. You have no son to bear your name or inherit. You can return to the world if you wish; but it will not return everything to you. You will not find matters as you left them.'

She is horrified. She had not thought of this. I imagine her betrothed will be horrified too, if he even goes ahead with marriage to a woman who is not an heiress. 'You have robbed me of my estate?'

'Not at all, you chose a life of poverty. You took one decision in grief and now are taking another in temper. You cannot seem to take a decision and stay with it.'

'I will get my fortune back!' she rages.

Coolly I look past her to Richard Layton, who has been observing this with growing uneasiness. 'Do you still want her?' I ask indifferently. 'I imagine that your lord Thomas Cromwell did not plan to reward his friend William Barrantyne with a penniless madwoman?'

He is at a loss. I press my advantage. 'And the prior will not have released her,' I say. 'Prior Richard would not do so.'

'Prior Richard has resigned,' Thomas Legh says smoothly,

speaking over his stammering partner. 'Prior William Barlow will take his place and surrender the priory to Lord Cromwell.'

I don't know Barlow, except by reputation as a great supporter of reform, which means, as we now all see, stealing from the Church and expelling good men. His brother serves as a Boleyn spy, and he hears George Boleyn's confession, which must be a pretty tale.

'Prior Richard will not go!' I say hastily. 'Certainly not for a Boleyn chaplain!'

'He has gone. And you will not see him again.'

For a moment I think that they mean that they have taken him to the Tower. 'Arrested?' I ask with sudden fear.

'Wisely, he chose that it should not come to that.' Richard recovers himself. 'Now I will take your daughter-in-law to London.'

'Here,' I say with sudden spite. I reach into my purse and I take a silver sixpence. I toss it straight at him, and Richard catches it without thinking, so that he looks a fool for taking such a little coin from me like a beggar. 'For her expenses on the road. Because she has nothing.'

I write to Reginald and I send it to John Helyar in Flanders for him to take to my son.

They have given our priory to a stranger who will dismiss the priests and close the doors. They have taken Jane away to marry a friend of Cromwell's. The Church cannot survive this treatment. I cannot survive it. Tell the Holy Father that we cannot bear it.

I am still reeling from this attack at the very heart of my home, at the church I love, when I get a note from London:

Lady Mother, please come at once. M.

L'ERBER, LONDON,
APRIL 1536

Montague greets me at the door of my house, the vine showing green leaves all around him as if he is a *planta genista* in an illuminated manuscript, a plant that grows green, whatever the soil or weather.

He helps me from my horse and holds my arm as we go up the shallow steps to the doorway. He feels the stiffness in my stride. 'I am sorry to have made you ride,' he says.

'I'd rather ride to London than hear about it too late in the country,' I say drily. 'Take me to my privy chamber and close the door on the others and tell me what's going on.'

He does as I ask, and in moments I am seated in my chair by the fireside with a glass of mulled wine in my hand and Montague is standing before the fire, leaning against the stone chimney breast, looking into the flames.

'I need your advice,' he says. 'I've been invited to dine with Thomas Cromwell.'

'Take a long spoon,' I reply and earn a wry smile from my son.

'This might be the sign of everything changing.'

I nod.

'I know what it's about,' he says. 'Henry Courtenay is invited with me; he spoke with Thomas Seymour who had been playing cards with Thomas Cromwell, Nicholas Carew and Francis Bryan.'

'Carew and Bryan were Boleyn supporters.'

'Yes. But now, as a cousin to the Seymours, Bryan is advising Jane.'

I nod. 'So Thomas Cromwell is now befriending those of us who support the princess or are kin to Jane Seymour?'

'Tom Seymour promises me that if Jane were to be queen she would recognise the princess, bring her to court, and see her restored as heir.'

I raise my eyebrows. 'How could Jane be queen? How could Cromwell do this?'

Montague lowers his voice though we are behind a closed door in our own house. 'Geoffrey spoke to John Stokesley, the Bishop of London, only yesterday. Cromwell had asked him if the king could legally abandon the Boleyn woman.'

'Legally abandon her?' I repeat. 'What does that even mean? And what did the bishop reply?'

Montague gives a short laugh. 'He's no fool. He'd like to see the Boleyns thrown down, but he said he would only give his opinion to the king, and then only if he knew what it was he wanted to hear.'

'And do any of us know what he wants to hear?'

Montague shakes his head. 'The signs are contradictory. On one hand he's called parliament, and a meeting of his council. And Cromwell is clearly plotting against the Boleyns. But the king got the Spanish ambassador to bow to her as queen, for the first time ever – so, no, we don't know.'

'Then we must wait until we do.'

Thoughtfully I strip off my riding gloves and put them over the arm of my chair. I hold my hands to the warmth of the fire. 'So what does Cromwell want from us? For he owes me a priory at the moment, and I am not feeling kindly towards him.'

'He wants us to promise that Reginald will not write against him, will cease urging the Pope to act against the king.'

I frown. 'Why does he care so much for Reginald's good opinion?'

'Because Reginald speaks for the Pope. And Cromwell is in living terror and the king is in living terror that the Pope will excommunicate them both, and then nobody will obey their commands. Cromwell needs our support for his own safety,' Montague goes on. 'The king says one thing at breakfast and contradicts himself at dinner. Cromwell doesn't want to go the way of Wolsey. If he pulls down Anne, as Wolsey pulled down Katherine, he wants to know that everyone will advise the king that it is a godly thing.'

'If he pulls down Anne and saves our princess then we support him,' I say grudgingly. 'But he must advise the king to return to obedience to Rome. He must restore the Church. We can't live in England without our monasteries.'

'Once Anne is gone then the king will make an alliance with Spain and return the Church to the headship of Rome,' Montague predicts.

'And Cromwell will advise this?' I ask sceptically. 'He has become a faithful papist all at once?'

'He doesn't want the bull of excommunication published,' Montague says quietly. 'He knows that would ruin the king. He wants us to keep it silent, and pave the way for the king to return to Rome.'

For a moment I have a sense of the joy that comes with having, at last, some stake in the game, some power. Ever since Thomas Cromwell started to advise the king to betray our queen, to destroy our princess, we have been shouting against the wind. Now it seems the weather is changing.

'He has to have our friendship against the Boleyns,' Montague says. 'And the Seymours want us to support Jane.'

'Is she the king's new sweetheart?' I ask. 'Do they really think he will marry her?'

'She must be soothing, after Anne,' Montague points out.

'And is it love again?'

He nods. 'He is besotted with her. He thinks she is a quiet country girl, shy, ignorant. He thinks she has no interest in matters that concern men. He looks at her family and thinks she will be fertile.'

The young woman has five brothers. 'But he cannot think that she is the finest woman at court,' I object. 'He has always wanted the very best. He cannot think that Jane outshines all the others.'

'No, he's changed. She is not the best – not by a long way – but she admires him much more than anyone else,' Montague says. 'That's his new benchmark. He likes the way she looks at him.'

'How does she look at him?'

'She's awestruck.'

I take this in. I can see that for the king, shaken by his own mortality after hours of unconsciousness, facing the prospect of his own death without a male heir, the adoration of a pure country girl might be a relief. 'And so?'

'I dine with Cromwell and Henry Courtenay tonight. Shall I tell him that we will join with them against Anne?'

I remember the huge newly accreted power of the Boleyns and the vast wealth of the Howards and I think that, even so, we can face them down. 'Yes,' I say. 'But tell him that our price for this is the restoration of the princess and the abbeys. We will keep the excommunication secret, but the king must return to Rome.'

Montague comes back from his dinner with Cromwell with his feet weaving under him, so drunk that he can hardly stand. I have gone to bed as he raps on my door and asks may he come in, and when I open the door he stands at the threshold and says that he won't intrude.

'Son!' I say, smiling. 'You're drunk as a stable boy.'

'Thomas Cromwell has a head of iron,' he says regretfully.

'I hope you said nothing more than we agreed.'

Montague leans against the door jamb and sighs heavily. A warm gust of ale, wine and I think brandy, for Cromwell has exotic tastes, blows gently into my face. 'Go to bed,' I say. 'You will be sick as a dog in the morning.'

He shakes his head in wonderment. 'He has a head of iron,' he repeats. 'A head of iron and a heart like an anvil. You know what he is doing?'

'No.'

'He is setting her own uncle, her own uncle, Thomas Howard, to gather evidence against her. Thomas Howard is going to find evidence against the marriage. He is going to ask for witnesses against his niece.'

'Men of iron with hearts of stone. And the Princess Mary?'

Owlishly, Montague nods at me. 'I don't forget your love of

her, I never forget, Lady Mother. I raised it at once. I reminded him at once.'

'And what did he say?' I ask, curbing my impatience to dunk my drunken son's head in a bucket of icy water.

'He said that she will get a proper household, and be honoured in her new house. She will be declared legitimate. She will be restored. She will come to court, Queen Jane will be her friend.'

I nearly choke at the new name. 'Queen Jane?'

He nods. ''Mazing, isn't it?'

'You're sure of this?'

'Cromwell is certain.'

I reach up to him, ignoring the odour of wine and brandy and mulled ale. I pat his cheek, as he beams at me. 'Well done. That's good,' I say. 'Perhaps this will end well. And this is not just Cromwell casting bread on the waters? This is the king's will?'

'Cromwell only ever does the king's will,' Montague says confidently. 'You can be sure of that. And now the king wants the princess restored and the Boleyn woman gone.'

'Amen,' I say, and gently push Montague out of the door of my privy chamber where his men are waiting for him. 'Put him to bed,' I say. 'And leave him to sleep in the morning.'

MANOR OF THE ROSE, ST LAWRENCE POUNTNEY, LONDON, APRIL 1536

Hugging this secret, and suddenly filled with hope, I go to visit my cousin Gertrude Courtenay at her house in St Lawrence Pountney, London. Her husband Henry is at court, preparing for the May Day joust, and Montague must stay with the court too. After the joust they are all going on to a great feast to be held in

France, with King Francis as the host. Whatever Cromwell is planning against the Boleyn woman, he is taking his time, and this is no way to further the friendship with Spain or the return to Rome. Since I don't trust Thomas Cromwell any more than I would trust any mercenary soldier from the stews of Putney, I think it very likely that he is playing both sides at once, Boleyn and France against my Princess Mary and Spain, until he can be sure which side will win.

Cousin Gertrude is bursting with gossip. She gets hold of me the moment I am off my horse and walking into the hall. 'Come,' she says. 'Come into the garden, I want to talk to you and we can't be overheard.'

Laughing, I follow her. 'What is it that's so urgent?'

As soon as she turns to speak my laughter dies, she looks so serious. 'Gertrude?'

'The king spoke in private to my husband,' she says. 'I did not dare write it to you. He spoke to him after the concubine lost her child. He said that now he sees that God will not give him a son with her.'

'I know,' I say. 'I heard it too. Even in the country I heard it. Everyone at court must know, and since everyone knows, it can only be that the king and Cromwell must want everyone to know.'

'You won't have heard this: he says that she seduced him with witchcraft, and that this is why they will never have a son together.'

I am stunned. 'Witchcraft?' I drop my voice to repeat the dangerous word. To accuse a woman of witchcraft is tantamount to sentencing her to death, for what woman can prove that a disaster was not of her making? If someone says that they have been overlooked or bewitched, how can one prove that it was not so? If a king says that he has been bewitched who is going to tell him that he is mistaken?

'God save her! What did my cousin Henry say?'

'He said nothing. He was too amazed to speak. Besides, what could he say? We all thought she had driven him mad, we all thought that she was driving everyone mad, he was clearly besotted, he was beside himself, who's to say that it wasn't witchcraft?'

'Because we saw her play him like a fish,' I say irritably. 'There was no mystery, there was no magic. Don't you see Jane Seymour being advised on the same game? Coming forward, going back, half-seduced and then withdrawing? Haven't we seen the king madly in love with half a dozen women? It's not magic, it's what any slut does if she has her wits about her. The difference with Boleyn was that she was quicker-witted than all the others, she had a family who backed her – and the queen, God bless her, was getting old and could have no more children.'

'Yes.' Gertrude steadies herself. 'Yes, you're right. But there again, if the king thinks he was enchanted, and the king thinks she was a witch, and the king thinks that this explains her miscarriages – then that's all that matters.'

'And what matters next is what he will do about it,' I say.

'He'll put her aside,' Gertrude says triumphantly. 'He will blame her for everything, and put her aside. And we and Cromwell and all our affinity will help him to do it.'

'How?' I say. 'For this is the very thing that Montague is working on with Cromwell, and Carew and Seymour.'

She beams at me. 'Not just them,' she points out. 'Dozens of others. And we don't even have to do it. That devil Cromwell will do it for us.'

I stay to dine with Gertrude and I would stay longer but one of Montague's men comes for me in the afternoon and asks me will I return to L'Erber.

'What's happened?' Gertrude comes with me to the stable yard, where my horse is saddled and ready.

'I don't know,' I say.

'But we can be in no danger?' she confirms, thinking of our secret toast at dinner that Anne will fall and the king come to his senses and Princess Mary be named as his one true heir.

'I don't think so,' I say. 'Montague would have warned me. I think he has work for me to do. Perhaps we are on the winning side, at last.'

L'ERBER, LONDON, MAY 1536

Montague strides up and down our private chapel as if he wishes he were running to the coast to the helpful ship's master at Grays and sailing off to his brother Reginald.

'He's gone mad,' he says in a low whisper. 'I really think he has gone mad now. No-one is safe, nobody knows what he is going to do next.'

I am stunned by this sudden reverse. I put my cape to one side and I take my son's hands in my own. 'Be calm. Tell me.'

'Did you hear nothing in the streets?'

'Nothing. A few people cheered for me as I went by, but they were mostly quiet . . .'

'Because it is beyond belief!' He claps his hand over his mouth and looks around. There is no-one in the chapel but us, the candle flames bob up and down, there is no quietly closing door to make them flicker. We are alone.

Montague turns on his heel and drops on his knees before me. I see that he is white and shaking, deeply distressed. 'He has arrested Anne Boleyn for adultery,' he breathes. 'And men of her court with her, for keeping her secrets. We still don't know how many. We still don't know who.'

'"How many"?' I repeat incredulously. 'What do you mean, "how many"?'

He throws out his hands. 'I know! Why would he charge more than one man, even if she had bedded dozens? Why would he let such a thing be known? And what an extraordinary lie for him to tell when he can just put her aside without a word! They've arrested Thomas Wyatt, and Henry Norris, but also the lad who sings in her chamber, and her own brother.' He looks at me. 'You know him! What is he thinking? Why would he do this?'

'Wait,' I say. 'I don't understand.'

I take the priest's chair and I sink down, as my knees go weak underneath me. I think, I am getting too old for this, I am not quick enough to leap to suspicion or conclusions. Henry the king goes too fast for me in a way that Henry the prince never did. For Henry the prince was quick and clever but Henry the king is as fast and as cunning as a madman: wildly decisive.

Slowly, Montague repeats the names to me, adds the names of a couple more men who seem to be missing from court.

'Cromwell is saying that she gave birth to a monster,' my son says. 'As if that proves everything.'

'A monster?' I repeat stupidly.

'Not a stillborn child. Some sort of reptile.'

I look at my son in blank horror. 'My God, how Thomas Cromwell does find sin and sodomy everywhere he looks! In my own priory, in the queen's bedroom! What a mind that man has. What voice does he hear in his prayers?'

'It's the king's mind that matters.' Montague puts his hands on my knees and looks up at me as if I was still his all-powerful mother and could make this better. 'Cromwell only does what the king says that he wants. He's going to try her for adultery.'

'He's going to try her for adultery? His own wife?'

'God help me, I'm going to be on the jury.'

'You're on the jury?'

'We agreed!' he leaps to his feet and bellows. 'All of us who met with Cromwell, who said that we would help him get the marriage annulled, are summoned to judge. We thought we were talking about releasing the king from his false marriage vows. We thought we would inquire into the validity of the marriage and find it wanting. Not this! Not this!'

'He's trying the marriage? He will annul it?' I ask. 'Like he tried to do with the queen?'

'No! No! No! Don't you hear me? He's not trying the marriage, he's putting the woman on trial. He's going to try her for adultery. And her brother, and some other men, God knows who, God knows how many. God knows if they are even our friends or our cousins. Surely only God knows why!'

'Any of us?' I demand urgently. 'Not any of our family or those who are working with us? None of the princess's supporters?'

'No. Not as far as I know. Not arrested yet. That's what's so strange. All those who are missing are those of the Boleyn party who are in and out of her rooms all day.' Montague makes a little face. 'You know the ones. Norris, Brereton . . .'

'Men that Cromwell doesn't like,' I remark. 'But why the lute boy?'

'I don't know!' Montague rubs his face with his hands. 'They took him first. Perhaps because Cromwell can torture him till he confesses? Cromwell can torture him till he names others? Till he gives the names that Cromwell wants?'

'Torture?' I repeat. 'Torture him? The king is using torture? Against a boy? The little musician?'

Montague looks at me as if the country we know and love, our heritage, is tumbling to hell under our feet. 'And I have agreed to be on the jury,' he says.

Not just my son Montague but twenty-five other peers of the realm have to sit in judgement on the woman that they called queen. The panel is chaired by her uncle, grim-faced at the fall of the woman that he pushed onto the throne, who became the queen that he hated. Near him is her former lover, Henry Percy, trembling with ague, muttering that he is too sick to attend, that he should not be forced to attend.

All the lords of my family are there. A good quarter of the jury are of our affinity or party, who support the Princess Mary and have hated the Boleyn woman ever since she usurped the throne. For us, though the accounts of kissing and seduction are shocking enough, the accusation that she poisoned the queen and was planning to poison the princess is a bitter confirmation of our worst fears. The rest of the panel are Henry's men who can be relied on to hate or love as he commands. She made no friends while she was queen, no-one says one word in her defence. There is no possibility of justice for her, as they study the evidence that Thomas Cromwell has so persuasively prepared.

Elizabeth Somerset, the Countess of Worcester, who attended the queen's funeral with me at Peterborough, has turned against her friend Anne and provides a report of flirtations and worse in the queen's bedchamber. Someone speaks of something that someone said on their deathbed. It is a mess of petty gossip and grotesque scandal.

Montague comes home, his face dark and angry. 'The shame of it,' he says shortly. 'The king says that he believes that up to a hundred men have had her. The disgrace.'

I hand him a glass of mulled ale, while I watch him. 'Did you say "guilty"?' I ask him.

'I did,' he says. 'The evidence was inarguable. Lord Cromwell had every detail that one might question. For some reason, which is beyond me, he allowed George Boleyn himself to tell the court out loud that the king was incapable of fathering a child. He announced the king's impotency.'

'Did they prove that she murdered our queen?'

'They accused her of it. Seems that's enough.'

'Will he imprison her? Or send her to a nunnery?'

Montague turns to me and his face is filled with a dark pity. 'No. He's going to kill her.'

BISHAM MANOR, BERKSHIRE, MAY 1536

I leave London. I cannot bear to hear the speculation and the gossip, the constant retelling of the obscene details of the trial, the unending wondering what will happen next. Even the people who have hated the Boleyn woman cannot understand why the king does not call his marriage invalid, name his daughter Elizabeth a bastard, and put the mother away in some distant cold castle where she can die of neglect.

Some of this is done: the marriage is annulled, the child Elizabeth declared a bastard. And yet still the woman is kept in the Tower and the plans for an execution go on.

I am glad to be away from the city but I cannot put the woman in the Tower out of my mind. In the closed and derelict priory I go into the cold chapel and kneel on the stone floor facing east, though the beautiful cross and altar silverware has been taken away. I find myself praying to an empty altar for the woman that I have hated, whose agent stole my holy things.

There is no precedent for the execution of a Queen of England. It is not possible for a queen to be beheaded. No woman has ever walked from the Tower to the little patch of grass before the chapel to her death. I cannot imagine it. I cannot bear to imagine it. And I cannot believe that Henry Tudor, the prince that I knew, could turn against a woman he had loved like this. He is a king whose courtly lovemaking is a byword at his court. He cannot be brutal; it is always love, true love, for Henry. Surely, he cannot sentence his wife, and the mother of his child, to death. I know that he turned against his own good queen, that he sent her away and neglected her. But it is a different thing, a different thing altogether, to ride away from a disappointing woman and ignore her, than to change overnight and command a lover's death.

I pray for Anne, but I find my thoughts turning again and again to the king. I think he must be in a fury of jealous rage, shamed at what men are saying about him, exposed by the spiteful wit of the Boleyns, feeling his age, feeling the good looks of his youth blurred by the fatness of his face. Every day he must look in his mirror and see the young, handsome prince disappearing behind the bloated face of an old, laughable king, the golden child becoming the Mouldwarp. Everyone adored Henry when he was a young king; he cannot understand that his court, the wife that he raised from nothing, could have turned against him and – worse – laughed at him as a fat old cuckold.

But I am mistaken in this. While I think of the sensitive man recoiling with shame, raging at the loss of the woman for whom he destroyed so much, Henry is repairing his pride, courting the Seymour girl. He is not looking in the mirror and mourning his youth. He is going upriver in his barge with lute players twanging away, to dine with her every night. He is sending her little gifts and planning their future as if they are a bride and groom betrothed in May. He is not mourning his youth, he is reclaiming it; and just a few days after the cannon shot from the Tower tells all of London that the king has committed one of the worst crimes a man can do – killed his wife – the king marries again and we have a new queen: Jane.

'The Spanish ambassador told me that Jane will bring the princess to court, and see her honoured,' Geoffrey tells me. We are walking in the fields towards Home Farm, looking at the greening crop. Somewhere among the white hawthorn of the hedgerow there is a blackbird singing defiance to the world, lilting notes, filled with hope.

'Really?'

Geoffrey is beaming. 'Our enemy is dead, and we have survived. The king himself called Henry Fitzroy to him, took him in his arms and said that the Boleyn woman would have killed him and our princess, and that he was lucky to still have them.'

'He'll send for the princess?'

'As soon as Jane is proclaimed queen, and sets up her household. Our princess will live with her new mother, the queen – within days.'

I tuck my hand in the crook of my favourite son's arm and rest my head briefly on his shoulder. 'You know, in a life of such reverses, I find I am almost surprised to still be here. I am very surprised to see it all coming right again.'

He pats my hand. 'Who knows? You might yet see your beloved princess crowned.'

'Shh, shh,' I say, though the fields are empty but for a distant labourer digging out a blocked ditch. It is now treason to even speak of the death of the king. Every day Cromwell makes a new law to protect the king's reputation.

I can hear the sound of hooves on the road and we turn back to the house. I see Montague's standard rippling above the hedgerows and when we walk into the stable yard he is dismounting from his horse. He comes quickly towards the two of us, smiling, drops to his knee for my blessing and then rises. 'I have news from Greenwich,' he says. 'Good news.'

'The princess is to return to court?' Geoffrey guesses. 'Didn't I say so?'

'Even better than that,' Montague says. He turns to me. 'It is you who are invited to return to court,' he says. 'Lady Mother, I am here with the king's own invitation. The exile is over, you are to return.'

I don't know what to say. I look at his smiling face, and I struggle for words. 'A restoration?'

'A complete restoration. It will be as it was before. The princess in her palace, you at her side.'

'God be praised,' Geoffrey exclaims. 'You will command Princess Mary's household again, just as you used to do. You will be where you should be, where we all should be, at court, and places and fees will come your way again, will come to all of us.'

'In debt, Geoffrey?' Montague asks with a slight mocking smile.

'I doubt you could manage on a small estate, constantly going to law with the neighbours,' Geoffrey says irritably. 'All I want is for us to have our own again. Our Lady Mother should be at the head of the court, and we should all be there too. We are Plantagenets; we were born to rule, the least we can do is advise.'

'And I will care for the princess,' I say – the only thing that matters to me.

'Lady Governess to the princess again.' Montague takes my hand and smiles at me. 'Congratulations.'

GREENWICH PALACE, LONDON, JUNE 1536

I return to London with Montague, his standard going before us, the white rose over my head, his guards beautifully mounted and dressed around me, and almost as soon as we are in the city, heading for our barge at the river, I see that people are pointing and running ahead of us, and starting to cheer. By the time we get close to the river there are thousands of people in the streets, shouting my name, shouting blessings, asking for the princess, and finally calling out 'À Warwick! À Warwick!'.

'That's enough.' Montague nods to one of the guards who rides into the crowd, crushing people with his big horse, and takes the flat of his sword and delivers a thudding blow to the young loyalist.

'Montague!' I say, shocked. 'He was just cheering for us.'

'He can't,' Montague says grimly. 'You're back at court, Lady

Mother, and we are restored, but it's not all just as it was. The king is not as he was. I think he will never be the same again.'

'I thought he was so happy with Jane Seymour?' I ask. 'I thought she was the only woman he has ever loved?'

Montague hides a grim smile at my sarcasm. 'He's happy with her,' he says cautiously. 'But he's not so much in love that he can bear even one word of criticism, one word of doubt. And someone shouting for you, or for the princess, or for the Church, is the sort of criticism that he cannot bear to hear.'

My rooms at court are the ones I had before, so long ago, when I was here as lady in waiting to Katherine and she was a queen of only twenty-three years old, pulled out of poverty and despair by a seventeen-year-old king, and we thought that nothing would ever go wrong again.

I go to pay my respects to the new queen in her rooms, and make my curtsey to Jane Seymour, a girl I first met as a shy, rather incompetent maid in waiting to Katherine. From her blanched hauteur, I assume that she remembers being scolded by me for clumsiness, and I make sure I curtsey low, and stay down until she invites me to rise.

I show not the slightest hint of my amusement as I survey her room and her ladies. Every wooden boss that used to bear a falcon or a bold 'A' has been lathed clean and sanded down, and now there is a 'J' or a rising phoenix. Her unctuous motto, 'Bound to Obey and Serve', is being embroidered by her ladies on a banner of Tudor green. They greet me pleasantly. Some of them are old friends. Elizabeth Darrell served Katherine with me, Frances Grey's half-sister Mary Brandon is here and, most surprisingly of all, Jane Boleyn, the widow of George Boleyn, who provided fatal evidence against her own husband and her sister-in-law Anne. She seems to have recovered with remarkable swiftness from her grief and the disaster in her family, and she curtseys to me very politely.

Queen Jane's court amazes me. To appoint Jane Boleyn as your lady in waiting is to knowingly welcome a spy who will stoop to anything. Surely, she must know that since Jane Boleyn sent her own husband and sister-in-law to the gallows she will hardly flinch from entrapping a stranger. But then I understand. These are not ladies of Jane's choosing, these are women placed here by their kinsmen to scoop up patronage and fees and to catch the king's eye; these are vile place-servers inserted here for their reward. This is not an English queen's court in any sense that I would understand it. This is a rat pit.

I am allowed to write to the princess, though I may not visit her yet. I am patient under this ban, certain that the king will bring her to court. Queen Jane speaks kindly of her, and asks my advice about sending her new clothes and a riding cape. Together we choose a new gown and some sleeves of deep red velvet that I know will suit her, and send them by royal messenger north, only thirty miles to Hunsdon, where she is preparing to come to court.

I write to ask of her health, of her happiness. I write telling her that I will see her soon, that we will be happy together again, that I hope the king will let me run her household and it will be as it was before. I say that the court is calm and merry again, and that she will find in Jane a queen and a friend. I don't remark that they have much in common, being only eight years apart in age, except of course that Mary was born and bred a princess and Jane the uninteresting daughter of a country knight, and I wait for a reply.

Dearest Lady Margaret,

I am so sorry, and so sad, that I cannot come to court and be with you again. I have had the misfortune to offend my father the king, and though I would do anything to obey and honour him, I cannot disobey and dishonour my sainted mother or my God. Pray for me.

Mary

I don't understand this at all, so I go at once to the king's rooms to find Montague. He is playing cards with one of the Seymour brothers, who are now great men, and I wait for the game to finish and laugh at Montague's carefully judged losses. Henry Seymour scoops up his winnings, bows to me and strolls away down the gallery.

'What has happened with the princess?' I ask tersely, my hands gripping her letter, hidden deep in my pocket.

'The king won't bring her to court until she takes the oath,' he says shortly. 'He sent Norfolk to her who cursed her to her face and called her a traitor.'

I shake my head in bewilderment. 'Why? Why would the king insist that she take the oath now? Queen Katherine is dead, Anne is dead, Elizabeth declared a bastard, he has a new queen and – please God – she will give him a son and heir. Why would he insist that she take the oath now? What's the point of it?'

Montague turns away from my anxious face and takes a few steps. 'I don't know,' he says simply. 'It makes no sense. I thought that when the Boleyn woman was dead all our troubles would be over. I thought that the king would reconcile with Rome. I don't see why he would persist. Especially, I don't see why he would persist against his daughter. You wouldn't speak to a dog the way that Norfolk spoke to her.'

I put my hand over my mouth to stifle a cry. 'He threatened her?'

'He said that if she were his daughter he would knock her head against the wall till it was as soft as a baked apple.'

'No!' I cannot believe that even Thomas Howard would dare to speak to a princess like this. I cannot believe that any father would allow such a man to threaten his daughter with violence. 'My God, Montague, what are we going to do?'

My son looks like a man being driven gradually, and inexorably, towards danger, a warhorse going reluctantly towards the sound of the cannons. 'I thought that our troubles were over, but they have begun anew,' he says slowly. 'I think we have to get her away. Queen Jane speaks for her, even Cromwell advises that she should come to court, but the king shouted at Jane that the princess should be tried for treason, and that Jane was a fool to be her advocate. I think that the king has turned against her, I think he has decided that she is his enemy. Her very presence, even at a distance, is a reproach to him. He can't see her and forget how he treated her mother. He can't think of her and pretend there was no Anne. He can't pretend that he is not old enough to have fathered her. He can't bear the thought of her defiance. We have to get her away. I don't think she's safe in his kingdom.'

Geoffrey rides once again to the secretive riverside village of Grays and reports back that the boatman is ready to leave at our bidding, and he remains loyal to the princess. Our kinsman in Calais, Arthur Plantagenet, Lord Lisle, writes to me and says that he can receive the consignment of goods that I am preparing to send him, and that a message to his steward in London will warn him when it is due to be delivered. Montague brings half a dozen strong riding horses to court, saying that he is training them for the hunting season. Our cousin Henry Courtenay pays a stable boy at Hunsdon for news, and understands that the princess is now allowed to walk in the garden every morning, for her health.

I am following Queen Jane to chapel before breakfast when I see Montague in the king's train. He comes over to me, kneels for my blessing, and when my hand is on his head he whispers: 'Norfolk has denounced his half-brother to the king and Tom is arrested for treason.'

I keep the shock from my face as Montague rises and gives me his arm. 'Come,' I say quickly.

'No.' He leads me towards the chapel and bows to the queen and steps back. 'Do nothing out of the ordinary,' he reminds me.

While the priest serves Mass, his back to the congregation, the quiet mutter of Latin drifting over us, I find I am gripping my rosary beads and telling them over and over. It surely isn't possible that a Howard has done anything against the king. Tom Howard has risen with his family by doing anything the king asked of them. There are no more loyal, bull-necked henchmen in the country. I can barely hear the Mass, I cannot say a prayer. I glance at the queen's bowed head and I wonder if she knows.

It is not till the court goes to breakfast that I can walk beside Montague and appear to be talking quietly together, a mother and her son. 'What's Tommy Howard done?'

'He's seduced the Scottish queen's daughter, your former ward: Lady Margaret Douglas. They married in secret at Easter.'

'Lady Margaret!' I exclaim. I have rarely seen her since she left my charge to serve Anne Boleyn. For a moment all I can feel is relief that the princess is not threatened by fresh trouble, but then I think of the pretty girl who was in my keeping, but lost at court. 'She would never have done anything which did not befit a princess,' I say fiercely. 'She was our princess's lady in waiting, and she is the daughter of Margaret Tudor. Don't tell me that she has made a secret marriage to a commoner without permission!'

'I do tell you that,' Montague says flatly.

'Married to Tom Howard? In secret? How did the king find out?'

'Everyone is saying that the duke told him. Would Norfolk betray his own half-brother?'

'Yes,' I say instantly. 'Because he can't risk having the king think that there was a plot to marry another royal heir into the Howard family. He's got Henry Fitzroy in his family already; what does it look like if the family traps another Tudor heir?'

'To the king, it looks like they are readying to usurp the throne,' Montague says grimly.

'Better for us that he suspects the Howards than Plantagenets,' I remark. 'But what's going to happen to Lady Margaret? Is the king very angry?'

'He's furious. Worse than I would have expected. And angry with Henry Fitzroy's wife Mary Howard, who helped them to meet.'

'How could they be so foolish?' I shake my head. 'Lady Margaret knows that anyone courting her is putting himself close to the throne. These days, nobody knows how close. If Princess

Elizabeth is declared a bastard and Princess Mary is not restored, then Lady Margaret is third in line for the throne, after her mother and brother.'

'She knows it now,' Montague says. 'The king says that the Duke of Norfolk has put traitorous division into the realm.'

'He used the word "traitor"?'

'He did.'

'But wait,' I say. 'Wait, Montague, let me think.' I take a few steps away from him, and then I come back. 'Think for a moment. Why didn't the Duke of Norfolk snap her up? As you say, if the king denies the princesses then Lady Margaret is in line for the throne. Why didn't Norfolk take advantage of this secret marriage to get the heir to the throne into his family? Why didn't he encourage it and keep it secret?'

Montague is about to answer as I lay out the plot for him. 'Norfolk must be absolutely certain that the king is going to name Henry Fitzroy as his heir – and so make Mary Howard his daughter as Queen of England. Otherwise, he'd have supported the marriage and kept it secret as another useful royal connection.'

'Dangerous words,' Montague says so quietly that I can hardly hear him.

'Norfolk would never have betrayed his brother for anything less than a better chance at the throne – his daughter, married to the king's heir,' I breathe. 'Norfolk would be looking for the greatest opportunity for himself and his family. He knows that is not Lady Margaret. He must be absolutely sure that Henry Fitzroy will be named as heir.'

'And so?' Montague says. 'What does this mean for us?'

I can feel myself grow cold as I realise. 'It means that you are right and we must get the princess out of the country,' I say. 'The king is never going to restore her. And she stands in his way. She is in danger if she stands in his way. Anyone who obstructs him is always in danger.'

I am with the young Queen Jane in her presence chamber, waiting demurely beside her throne as hundreds of people make their bow to her and ask for one favour or another. Jane looks rather blank at this sudden explosion of interest in her health and well-being. Everyone offers a small gift that she takes and then hands to one of her ladies, who puts it on a table behind her. Every now and then she glances at me, to see that I am watching and approving the conduct of her ladies and the decorum of her room. Gently, I nod. Despite the expenses of the princess's household I am still the wealthiest woman at court in my own right, with the greatest title in my own right, and by far the oldest. I am sixty-two years old and Jane is the sixth queen that I have seen on this throne. She is right to glance at me with her shy pale blue gaze and confirm that she is doing everything correctly.

She has started her reign with a terrible error. Lady Margaret Douglas should never have been allowed to meet in secret with Tom Howard. Mary Howard, the young duchess married to Henry Fitzroy, should never have been allowed to encourage them. Queen Jane, stepping up to a throne which was still warm from the frightened sweat of the last incumbent, dazzled by her own rise, did not watch the behaviour of her new court, did not know what was happening. But now Tom is in the Tower charged with treason and Lady Margaret is confined to her rooms and the king is furious with everyone.

'No, she's arrested, she's in the Tower too,' Jane Boleyn tells me cheerfully

I feel the familiar plummet of my heart at the thought of the Tower. 'Lady Margaret? On what charge?'

'Treason.'

That word, from Jane Boleyn, is like a sentence of death.

'How can she be charged with treason when all she did was marry a young man for love?' I ask reasonably. 'Folly, yes. Disobedience, yes. And of course the king is offended. Rightly so. But how is it treason?'

Jane Boleyn lowers her eyes. 'It's treason if the king says it is so,' she states. 'And he says they are guilty. And the punishment is death.'

I am badly shaken. If the king can accuse his beloved niece of treason and put her in the Tower under a sentence of death, he can certainly charge his daughter too. Especially when he calls her his bastard daughter and sends his worst men to threaten her with violence. I am going to the king's rooms to confer with Montague when I hear the tramp of soldiers' feet behind me.

For a moment I think I will faint with fear, and I flinch back against the wall and feel the cold stone, cold as a cell in the Tower, against my back. I wait, my heart pounding as they go by, two dozen yeomen of the guard in the bright Tudor livery, marching in step through the corridors of Greenwich Palace heading to the king's presence chamber.

As soon as they are past me, I am afraid for Montague. I breathe: 'My son,' and I go quickly behind the soldiers as they tramp up the stairs to the king's rooms where the great door to the presence chamber swings open and they go in, two abreast, menacingly strong.

The room is crowded but the king is not there. The throne is empty; he is inside, in his privy chamber, the door closed on his court. He will not witness the arrest. If there are cries and weeping he will not be disturbed. As I look round the busy room, I see with relief that Montague is not here either; he is probably inside with the king.

The soldiers are not here for my son. Instead, the officer walks confidently to Sir Anthony Browne, the king's favourite, his trusted Master of Horse, and asks him, politely enough, to come with them. Anthony gets to his feet from where he has been lounging at the window, smiles like the courtier he is, and asks negligently: 'Why, whatever is the charge?'

'Treason,' comes the quiet reply, and everyone who is near to Anthony seems to melt away.

The officer looks around a court that is suddenly stunned into shocked silence. 'Sir Francis Bryan!' he calls.

'Here,' Sir Francis says. He steps forward and the men he was with slide back, as if they do not know him now, as if they have never known him. He smiles, his black eyepatch looking blindly around the court and seeing no friends. 'How may I be of service to you, officer? Do you need my assistance?'

'You may come with me,' the officer says with a sort of grim humour. 'For you are under arrest also.'

'I?' Francis Bryan says, cousin to this queen, cousin to the former queen, a man secure in royal favour after years of friendship. 'For what? On what possible charge?'

'Treason,' the man says for the second time. 'Treason.'

I watch the two men go out with the guard, and I find the Duke of Norfolk, Thomas Howard, at my elbow. 'What can they possibly have done?' I ask. Bryan in particular has survived a thousand dangers, having been exiled from court at least twice and returned unscathed each time.

'I'm glad that you don't know,' comes the threatening reply. 'They have been conspiring with Lady Mary, the king's bastard daughter. They have been plotting to get her out of Hunsdon and, by ship, away to Flanders. I would have them hanged for it. I would see her hanged for it.'

I go back to the queen's rooms, fear snapping at my heels all the way. The ladies ask me what is happening and I tell them I have seen the arrest of two of the king's firmest friends. I don't tell them what the Duke of Norfolk said. I am too afraid to say the words. Lady Woods tells me that my kinsman Henry Courtenay has been dismissed from the privy council under suspicion of plotting for the princess. I give as good a performance as I can manage of a woman shocked by extraordinary news.

'Don't you write to Lady Mary?' Lady Woods says. 'Don't you stay in touch with her? Your former charge? Though everyone knows that you love her and came back to court to serve her?'

'I write to her only through Lord Cromwell,' I say. 'I have an affection for her, of course. I write with the queen.'

'But you don't encourage her?'

I glance across the room. Jane Boleyn is holding herself very still over her sewing, quite as if she is not thinking about her sewing at all. 'Of course not,' I say. 'I took the oath like everyone else.'

'Not quite everyone,' Jane volunteers, looking up from her work. 'Your son Reginald left England without swearing it.'

'My son Reginald is preparing a report for the king on the marriage of Queen Katherine and the governance of the Church of England,' I say firmly. 'The king himself has commissioned it, and Reginald is going to reply. He is a scholar for the king, as he was raised to be. He is working for him. His loyalty cannot be questioned, and nor can mine.'

'Oh, of course,' Jane says with a little smile, bending her head to her work. 'I didn't mean to suggest anything other.'

I see Montague at dinner but I cannot easily speak with him until the tables are cleared away and the music starts for dancing. The king seems to be happy as he watches Jane dance with her ladies and then, when they beg him, he rises to his feet and invites one of the pretty new girls to dance with him.

I find I am watching him almost as if he were a stranger. He is very unlike the prince that we all loved so much, when his mother was alive and he was a second son, a long, long time ago, forty years ago. He has grown very broad; his legs which were so strong and supple are curved now, the calf muscles bulge under a straining blue garter. His belly is rounded under the jacket, but the jacket is so padded and thickly stitched that he looks grand rather than fat. His shoulders are wide as any great sportsman's under the buckram wadding and the frame of this and the cloth overlaid makes him so big that he can only pass through a double door when it is fully opened. His rich mop of ginger curls is thinning and though he has it carefully combed and curled, still the scalp shines palely through. His beard, starting to be flecked with grey, is growing sparse and curly. Katherine would never let him wear a beard, she complained that it scratched her face. This queen can deny him nothing, and would not dare complain.

And his face – his face, flushed now with his awkward dancing, beaming at the young woman peeping up at him, as if she can think of no greater delight than a man old enough to be her father squeezing her hand and holding her close when the dance allows them to come together – it is his face that makes me hesitate.

He doesn't look like Elizabeth's son any more. The clean beauty of her family profile, our family profile, is smudged by the fat of his cheeks, of his chin. Her defined features are blurred in the collapsing face of her darling Prince Harry. His eyes look smaller in his puffed cheeks, his rosebud mouth is now pursed so often in disapproval that he looks mean. He is still a handsome man, this is still a handsome face, but the expression is not handsome. He looks petty, he looks self-indulgent. Not his mother, not any of our line were ever petty. They were kings and queens on a grand scale; this, their descendant, though he dresses so richly, though he presents himself as such a great power, is – under the padding, under the fat – a little man, with the spite and vindictiveness of a little man. Our trouble, the court's trouble, the country's trouble, is that we have given this small-minded bully the power of the Pope and the army of the king.

'You look very grave, Lady Pole,' Nicholas Carew remarks to me.

At once I move my gaze from the king and smile. 'I was miles away,' I say.

'Indeed, I know of one that I wish was miles away tonight,' he says quietly.

'Oh, do you?'

'I can help you with saving her,' he says earnestly.

'We can't talk of this now, not here,' I say. 'Not after today.'

He nods. 'I'll come to your rooms after breakfast tomorrow, if I may.'

I wait but he doesn't come. I can't be seen to be looking for him, so I go out riding with the ladies of the queen's court and when we meet with the gentleman for a picnic by the river I sit at the ladies' table and barely glance towards the court. I can see at once that he's not there.

At once I look for Montague. The king is at the top table, Queen Jane beside him. He is noisy, laughing, calling for more wine and praising the chef; a huge pastry dish is before him, and he is eating the meat from the inside with the long golden serving spoon, proffering it to Jane, dribbling gravy on her fine gown. I see in a moment that Montague is missing. He is not at the top table, nor with the other gentlemen of the privy chamber. I can feel the sweat prick under my arms and chill. I look at the dozen or so young men and I think that more than Montague and Carew are missing, but I cannot at once see who is absent. It reminds me of the time once before when I looked for Montague, and Thomas More told me that he was exiled from court. Now Thomas More has gone forever, and once again, I don't know if my son is safe.

'You're looking for your son.' Jane Boleyn, seated opposite me, spears a slice of roasted meat on her fork and nibbles the end of it, dainty as a French princess.

'Yes, I expected him to be here.'

'You need not worry. His horse went lame and he went back,' Jane volunteers. 'I don't think he has been taken with the others.'

I look at her slight, teasing smile. 'What others?' I ask. 'What are you saying?'

Her dark eyes are limpid. 'Why, Thomas Cheyney and John Russell have been taken for questioning. Lord Cromwell believes that they have been plotting to encourage Lady Mary to defy her father.'

'That's not possible,' I say coldly. 'They are loyal servants to the king, and what you are describing would be treason.'

She looks directly at me, a mischievous twinkle in her beautiful dark eyes. 'I suppose it would. And anyway, there is worse.'

'What can be worse than this, Lady Rochford?'

'Nicholas Carew has been arrested. Would you have thought him a traitor?'

'I don't know,' I say stupidly.

'And, your friend who served Lady Mary in your household, the wife of the chamberlain, your friend Lady Anne Hussey! She has been arrested for plotting and been taken to the Tower. I fear that they are going to arrest everyone who prided themselves on being Lady Mary's friend. I pray that no-one suspects you.'

'I thank you for your prayers,' I say. 'I hope I never need them.'

Montague comes to my rooms before dinner that evening and I go towards him and lean my forehead against his shoulder. 'Hold me,' I say

He is always shy with me. Geoffrey will take me in a great hug, but Montague is always more reticent. 'Hold me,' I say again. 'I was very afraid today.'

'We're safe so far. No-one has betrayed us and no-one doubts your loyalty to the king. Henry Courtenay is not arrested, just dismissed from the privy council under suspicion. William Fitzwilliam with him. Francis Bryan will be released.'

I take my seat.

'We can't get the princess away now,' Montague says. 'Courtenay's man has been taken, disappeared from the stables. There's no-one with a key to her door, and no-one can get her out of the house. Carew had a maid in his pay but we can't reach her without him. He's under arrest but I don't know where. We'll have to wait.'

'They've arrested Anne Hussey.'

'I heard. I don't know how many of your old household at Richmond are being questioned.'

'God help them. Have you warned Geoffrey?'

'I sent him a message to get in the harvest and keep quiet,' Montague says grimly. 'He mustn't try to see the princess, she's being watched night and day again. They have broken open the plot like a hatching egg. She has a guard on her door and a maid locked into her chamber with her every night. They don't even let her walk in the garden.'

'And the Spanish ambassador?'

Montague's face is grim. 'He tells me that he is trying to get a dispensation from the Pope so that she can swear the oath to say that her parents' marriage was invalid, that she is a bastard, and that the king is head of the Church. Chapuys says that she must swear. She will be arrested if she doesn't.' He sees my horrified expression. 'Arrested and beheaded,' he says. 'That's why Chapuys is telling her that she must swear, buy time, and then we'll get her away.'

She is only twenty years old. Only twenty years old and her mother has not been buried a year. She is separated from her friends and held under arrest like a sinner, like a criminal. She has nothing but her belief in God to support her and she is afraid that it is God's will that she die a martyr for her faith.

A panel of judges, convened to inquire into her treasonous disobedience to the king, struggle briefly with their consciences, and agree to send one more time to Hunsdon where she is now held as a prisoner with no attempt at concealing her disgrace. They prepare a document called 'The Lady Mary's Submission', and tell her that she must sign it or they will charge her with treason. The charge of treason carries a death sentence and she knows that half a dozen men are held in the Tower accused of trying to rescue her, and that their lives depend on what she does next. She believes that her mother was poisoned by her father's wife, she believes that her father will have her beheaded if she does not obey him. No-one can rescue her, no-one can even reach her.

Poor child, poor darling child. She signs the three clauses. First she signs that she accepts her father as King of England and that she will obey all his laws. Then she signs that she recognises him as supreme head on earth of the Church of England, then she signs the last clause:

I do freely and frankly recognise and acknowledge that the marriage between His Majesty and my mother was by God's law and Man's law incestuous and unlawful.

'She signed it?' Geoffrey asks me on a brief visit to London, come to borrow money from me, and horrified at the news.

I nod. 'God only knows what it cost her to swear on His holy name that her mother was an incestuous whore. But she signed it, and she accepts that she is Lady Mary and no princess, and a bastard.'

'We should have taken her away long before this!' Geoffrey exclaims furiously 'We should have gone in before the lawyers got there and snatched her away!'

'We couldn't,' I say. 'You know that we couldn't. We delayed when she was ill, then we delayed because we thought she was safe after the death of Anne, and then the plot was broken wide open. We're lucky not to be in the Tower with the others as it is.'

Lord Cromwell now puts an act before the houses of parliament that rules the king shall nominate his own heir. His heir shall be of his choosing, from Jane, or – as it cheerfully declares – any subsequent wife.

'He's planning to marry again?' Geoffrey demands.

'He's not ruling it out,' Montague says. 'Our princess is denied, and the bastard Elizabeth loses her title. It clearly says that if he has no children with Queen Jane then he can choose his heir. Now he has three children all declared bastards of his own begetting to choose from: the true princess, the bastard princess and the bastard duke.'

'Everyone keeps asking who he means to name,' Geoffrey says.

'In parliament, as they were reading the bill, men kept asking me who the king intended as his heir. Someone even asked me if I thought the king would name our cousin Henry Courtenay as heir and restore our family.'

Montague laughs shortly. 'Does he destroy his children so that he has to turn to cousins?'

'Does no-one think he will get a child from Jane?' I ask. 'Does this act show that he is doubting his own potency?'

Ever since Anne Boleyn went to the scaffold for laughing with her brother that the king could not do the act, we are all well aware that it is illegal to say such a thing. I see Montague glance at the closed door and the barred windows.

'No. He's going to name Fitzroy,' Geoffrey says certainly. 'Fitzroy walked before him at the opening of parliament carrying the king's cap in full sight of everyone. He could not have been more conspicuous. He's been given half of poor Henry Norris's lands and places, and the king is going to set him up at Baynard's Castle with his wife, Mary Howard.'

'That's where Henry Tudor stayed when he first came to London,' I point out. 'Before his coronation as Henry VII, before he moved to Westminster.'

Geoffrey nods. 'It's a signal to everyone. Princess Mary and the bastard Elizabeth and the bastard Fitzroy are all equal bastards, but Princess Mary is only now released from prison and Elizabeth is a weak baby. Fitzroy is the only one with his own castle and his own lands, and now a palace in the heart of London.'

'The king could still get a son from Jane,' Montague points out. 'That's what he'll be hoping for. If this marriage is good in the sight of God why should he not have a son now? She's a young woman of twenty-eight, from good, fertile stock.'

Geoffrey looks at me as if I know why not. 'He'll not get a live son. He never will. There's a curse, isn't there, Lady Mother?'

I say what I always say: 'I don't know.'

'If there ever was such a curse that the king should have no son and heir then it means nothing because he has Fitzroy,' Montague says irritably. 'This talk of curses is a waste of time for there is the duke, on the brink of being named the king's heir and displacing the princess, living proof that there is no curse.'

Geoffrey ignores his brother and turns to me. 'Was there a curse?'

'I don't know.'

KING'S PLACE, HACKNEY, LONDON, JUNE 1536

I am almost singing with hope as we ride out through the city walls into the fields and go north and east to the village of Hackney. It's a summer day, promising good weather and gilded with sunshine, and Geoffrey rides on my right with Montague on my left and for a moment, between my boys, riding away from London and the looming Tower, I have a moment of intense joy.

As soon as Princess Mary denied her mother and denied her faith the king sent for her and gave her his beautiful hunting lodge, only a few miles from Westminster, and promised her a return to court. She is allowed to see her friends, she is allowed to walk and ride as she wishes; she is free. She sends for me at once, and she is allowed to see me.

'You'll be shocked when you see her,' Geoffrey warns me. 'It's been more than two years since you saw her last, and she has been ill and very unhappy.'

'We have both been ill and very unhappy,' I say. 'She will be beautiful to me. My only regret is that I couldn't spare her unhappiness.'

'Mine is that we couldn't get her away,' Geoffrey says grimly.

'Enough of that.' Montague cuts him short. 'Those days are

over, thank God, and we have all survived them, one way or another. Never mention them again.'

'Any news of Carew?' Geoffrey asks Montague, keeping his voice low, though there is no-one near us but half a dozen of our own guards, riding before and behind, too distant to eavesdrop.

Grimly, Montague shakes his head.

'Nothing to link us to him?' Geoffrey presses him.

'Everyone knows that our Lady Mother loves the princess like a daughter,' Montague says irritably. 'Everyone knows that I talked with the plotters. We all dined with Cromwell and plotted the fall of Anne. You don't have to be a Cromwell to make a case against us. We just have to hope that Cromwell doesn't want to make a case against us.'

'Half the privy council opposed the king disinheriting the princess,' Geoffrey complains. 'Most of them spoke against it to me.'

'And if Cromwell wants to bring half the privy council down then you can be sure he'll have evidence.' Montague looks across me to his younger brother. 'And by the sound of it, you'll be the first one he'll come to.'

'Because I am the first to speak up for her!' Geoffrey bursts out. 'I defend her!'

'Hush, boys,' I say. 'Nobody doubts either of you. Montague, don't tease your brother, you're like children again.'

Montague ducks his head in a half-apology and I look ahead, where the old hunting lodge sits on a little rise of ground, the turrets just visible above the trees.

'She is expecting us?' I ask. I find I am nervous.

'Of course,' Montague confirms. 'As soon as she had greeted the king she asked if she could see you. And he agreed. He said that he knew that she loved you and that you had always been a good guardian to her.'

From the edge of the wood we can see the lane leading to the castle, and there are riders coming towards us at a leisurely canter. I think I can see, I shade my eyes against the bright morning sunshine, I can see that there are ladies riding among the men, I can see the flicker of their gowns. I think that they have come out to meet us, and I give a little laugh and press my horse forward into a trot and then into a canter.

'Halloo! Awaaay!' Geoffrey cries out the hunting call and follows me as I ride forward and then I am almost certain, and then I am completely certain, that at the centre of the riders is the princess herself and that she is feeling, just as I am, that she cannot wait for another moment, and she has ridden out to meet me.

'Your Grace!' I call to her, forgetting all about her changed title. 'Mary!'

The horses slow as the two parties come together and I pull up my hunter who snorts excitedly. One of the guards runs to his head and helps me down from the saddle, and my darling princess tumbles from her horse as if she were a child again, jumping down to me, and she dives into my arms and I hold her tightly.

She cries, of course she cries, and I bend my head and put her wet cheek against mine and feel my own grief and sense of loss and fear for her rise up until I am ready to cry too.

'Come,' Montague says gently behind me. 'Come, Lady Mother, come, Lady Mary.' He nods his head as he says this, as if to apologise for the false title. 'Let's all go back to the house and you can talk all day long.'

'You're safe,' Mary says, looking up at me. Now I can see the dark shadows under her eyes and the weariness in her face. She's never going to have the shining look of a lucky child again. The loss of her mother and the sudden cruelty from her father have scarred her, and her pale skin and pinched mouth show a woman who has learned to bear pain with a deep determination too young.

'I am safe, but I have been so afraid for you.'

She shakes her head as if to say that she will never be able to tell me what she has endured. 'You went to my mother's funeral,' she says, handing the reins of her horse to the groom and linking her arm through mine so we walk back to the house in step.

'It was very solemn, very beautifully done, and a number of those of us who loved her were allowed to attend.'

'They wouldn't let me go. They wouldn't even let me pay for her prayers. Besides, they took everything from me.'

'I know.'

'But it's better now,' she says with a brave little smile. 'My father has forgiven my obstinacy and nobody could be kinder than Queen Jane. She has given me a diamond ring and my father gave me a thousand crowns.'

'And you have a proper steward to take care of things for you?' I ask anxiously. 'A chamberlain of your household?'

A shadow crosses her face. 'Sir John Shelton is my chamberlain, Lady Anne, his wife, runs the household.'

I nod. So the gaolers become the servants. I imagine they still report to Lord Cromwell.

'Lord John Hussey is not allowed to serve me, nor his wife,' Mary says.

'His wife is arrested,' I say very quietly. 'In the Tower.'

'And my tutor Richard Fetherston?'

'In the Tower.'

'But you are safe?'

'I am,' I say. 'And so happy to be with you again.'

We talk together all day; we close the door on everyone and speak freely. She asks after my children. I tell her of my little ladies in waiting, my granddaughters Katherine and Winifred. I tell her of my pride and love for Montague's son Henry, who is nine years old. 'We call him Harry,' I tell her. 'You should see him on a horse, he can ride anything. He terrifies me!' I tell her of the loss of Arthur's boy, but his two girls are well. Ursula has given the Staffords a great brood of three boys and a girl, and Geoffrey, my baby, has babies of his own: Arthur who is five years old, Margaret who is four, Elizabeth who is three and our new baby, little Thomas.

She volunteers little stories about her half-sister Elizabeth, smiling at the things that the child says, and praising her quickness and her charm. She asks about the ladies who have come to serve Jane, and laughs when I tell her that they are all Seymour appointments, or Cromwell choices, however unsuitable for the work, and that Jane looks around them sometimes quite dazed that they should all find themselves in the queen's rooms.

'And the Church?' she asks me quietly. 'And the monasteries?'

'Going one by one. We have lost Bisham Priory,' I say. 'Cromwell's men inspected it and found it wanting, and handed it over to a prior who is never there, and whose intention is to declare it corrupt and surrender it to them.'

'It can't be true that so many houses have failed in their faith,' she says. 'Bisham was a good house of prayer, I know it was.'

'None of the inquiries is honest, only a way of persuading the abbess or the prior to resign their living and go. Cromwell's visitors have gone to almost every small monastery. I believe they will go on to inquire at the great houses too. They accuse them of terrible crimes, and then find against them. There have been some places that were trading in relics – you know the sort of thing – and some places where they lived too comfortably for their souls, but this is not a reformation, though that is what they want to call it – it's a destruction.'

'For profit?'

'Yes, only for profit,' I say. 'God knows how much treasure has gone from the altars into the treasury, and the rich farmland, and the buildings have been bought by their neighbours. Cromwell had to create a whole new court to manage the wealth. If you ever inherit, my dear, you will not recognise your kingdom; it has been stripped bare.'

'If I ever inherit, I shall put it right,' she says very quietly. 'I swear it. I will put it right again.'

SITTINGBOURNE, KENT, JULY 1536

The court is on progress to Dover to inspect the new fortifications, then the newly-weds will go hunting. The suspected courtiers have been released from the Tower, and my kinsman Henry Courtenay returns to court but not yet to the privy council.

'Did you prove your innocence?' I ask him very quietly as we mount up and prepare to ride out.

'Nothing was proved or disproved,' he says as he helps me into the saddle and looks up at me, scowling against the bright sunshine. 'I think it was not to test our guilt but to frighten us and throw us into disarray. And,' he says with a wry smile, 'it surely did that.'

This used to be the happiest time of the year for the king, but not this summer. He glances at Jane's plate when she is eating her breakfast, as if he were wishing that she felt queasy, he watches her – his head tipped slightly to the side – as she dances with her ladies, as though he would be better pleased if she were tired. I am not the only person who thinks that he is looking for a fault, wondering why she is not with child, considering that there may be some flaw in her that makes her unworthy to bear a Tudor heir, or even to be crowned as queen. They have been married less than eight weeks, but the king is quick to identify failure in others. He demands perfection – and this is the woman he married because he was certain that she was the perfect contrast to Anne Boleyn.

Sittingbourne is a great town of inns, built on Watling Street, the road from Dover to London, the main pilgrimage route to the Becket shrine at Canterbury. We stay at the Lyon and their banqueting hall is so large and their rooms so many that they can house most of the court on the premises and only the hangers-on and the lower servants have to stay in inns nearby.

For the first time in my life I see that although the pilgrims push back their hoods to uncover their heads for the royal standard, they turn their faces away from the king. They dare do no more, but they do not call out blessings on him, or smile as he rides by. They blame him for closing the smaller monasteries and nunneries, they fear he will go on to destroy the bigger ones. These are devout people, accustomed to praying in an abbey church in their little towns, who now find that the abbey is closed and some hard-faced new Tudor lord is taking the lead from the roof and the glass from the windows. These are people who believe in the saints of little roadside shrines, whose fathers and grandfathers were saved from purgatory by the family chantries that are now destroyed. Who is going to say a Mass for them? These are people who were brought up to revere the local churches, who rented lands from the monasteries, who went to the nunnery hospital when they were sick, who went to the abbey kitchen in hungry times. When the king ordered the visitation and then the closure of the small monasteries and nunneries he tore the heart out of the small communities and handed their treasures over to strangers.

Now these pilgrims are travelling to the shrine of a churchman who was killed by a king, another Henry. They believe that Thomas Becket stood for the Church against the king and the miracles that constantly occur at his celebrated shrine go to prove that the churchman was right and the king was wrong. As the royal guards trot into the village and jump off their big horses and line the village street, the pilgrims whisper of John Fisher, who died for his faith on the royal scaffold, of Thomas More, who could not bring himself to say that the king was the rightful head of the Church, and laid down his life rather than sign his name. As the royal party ride in, nodding to right and left with the usual Tudor charm, there are no beaming faces or excited shouts in reply. Instead they turn their heads away, or they look down, and there is a discontented murmur like a deep embanked stream.

Henry hears it; his head goes up and he looks coldly around at the pilgrims who stand at the doorways of the inns or lean out of the windows to see the man who is destroying their Church. The yeomen of the guard hear it, looking round uneasily, sensing divided loyalties, even in their own ranks.

Many, many people, knowing that I am the princess's governess and head of her household, call out to me: 'God bless her! God bless her!', afraid even to say her true name and her title as they have sworn to deny her, but still wanting to send their love and loyalty.

Henry, usually travelling between his rich palaces, mostly by barge, always heavily guarded, has not heard the rumble of a thousand critical whispers before. It's like a distant thunder, low and yet ominous. He looks around, but he cannot see one person speaking against him. Abruptly, he laughs out loud at nothing, as if he is trying to demonstrate that he is not troubled by this sulky welcome, and he swings himself heavily down from his horse, throws the reins to a groom and stands stock-still, his arms akimbo, a fat block of a man, as if daring anyone to speak against him. He can see no-one to challenge. There is no scowling face in the crowd, no-one is going to stand up to be martyred. If Henry saw an enemy he would cut him down where he stood; he has never lacked courage. But there is no-one opposing him. There is just a dull sourceless whisper of discontent. The people don't like their king any more, they don't trust him with their Church, they don't believe that his will is given to him by God, they miss Queen Katherine, they were horrified by the stories of the guilt and the death of Queen Anne. How can such a woman ever have been the choice of a godly king? He chose her to prove that he was the best, that he could marry the best. Since she is now shown to be the worst, what does that say about him?

They don't know anything about Queen Jane but they have heard that she danced on the night of the execution and married the king eleven days after he beheaded his former wife, her mistress. They think she must be a woman quite without pity. To them, the king is no longer the prince whose coming makes all things right, he is no longer the young man whose follies and sports were a byword for joyous excess. Their love for him has grown doubtful, their love for him has grown fearful; in truth, their love for him has gone.

Henry looks around and tosses his head as if he despises the little town and the lowered heads of the silent pilgrims. He reminds me, for one moment, of the way his father used to look, as if he thought we were all fools, that he had taken the throne and the kingdom by his own quick and cunning wits, and that he despised us all for having allowed it. Henry glances down at Jane who stands at his side, waiting to walk with him through the wide-open doors of the inn. His face does not soften at the sight of her blonde bowed head. He looks at her as if she is another fool who is going to do exactly as he wants, even if it costs her life.

We are following slavishly behind, when there is a disturbance in the crowd outside, horsemen riding down the road and trying to push their way through. I see Montague, following the king, looking back at the noise. It is one of Henry Fitzroy's servants, his horse nearly foundered, looking as if it has been ridden hard, perhaps all the way from St James's Palace, the young duke's London home.

A small nod of Montague's head as he goes into the darkness of the inner hall of the inn prompts me to wait outside and discover the news that has made Fitzroy's servants ride so hard. The man pushes his way through the crowd, while his groom waits behind holding the horse.

At once people gather around him clamouring for news and I stand back to listen. He shakes his head and speaks quietly. I clearly hear him say that nothing could be done, the poor young man, and nothing could be done.

I go into the inn, where the king's presence chamber is filled with the court, talking and wondering what has happened. Jane is seated on the throne, trying to look unconcerned and talking with her ladies. The door to the king's private room is closed, with Montague nearby.

'He went in there with the messenger,' Montague says to me quietly. 'Shut everyone out. What's happened?'

'I think Fitzroy may be dead,' I say.

Montague's eyes widen and he gives a little exclamation but he is such a trained conspirator now that he gives little away. 'An accident?'

'I don't know.'

There is a great bellow from behind the closed door, a terrible roar, like a bull will give when a mastiff has fastened on his throat and he drops to his knees. It is the noise of a man mortally wounded. 'No! No! No!'

Jane whirls around at the cry, jumps to her feet and sways indecisively. The court falls completely silent, and watches her, as she sits back down on her throne and then rises up again. Her brother speaks quickly to her and she obediently goes to the door to the privy chamber, but then she steps back and makes a little gesture with her hand, stopping the guards from opening it. 'I can't,' she says.

She looks across at me, and I go to her side. 'What should I do?' she asks.

There is a single loud sob from inside the room. Jane looks quite terrified. 'Should I go to him? Thomas says I must go to him. What's happening?'

Before I can answer Thomas Seymour is at his sister's side, his hand in the small of her back, literally thrusting her towards the closed door. 'Go in,' he says through his teeth.

She digs in her heels, she rolls her eyes towards me. 'Shouldn't Lord Cromwell go in?' she whispers.

'Not even he can raise the dead!' Thomas snaps. 'You've got to go in.'

'Come with me.' Jane reaches out and grabs my hand as the guard swings the door open. The messenger stumbles out and Thomas Seymour pushes us both in and slams the door behind us.

Henry is on his knees, on the floor, hunched over a richly padded footstool, his face buried in the thick embroidery. He is sobbing convulsively like a child, hoarse-voiced as if his grief is tearing out his heart. 'No!' he says when he catches his breath, and then he gives a great groan.

Cautiously, like someone approaching a wounded beast, Jane

goes towards him. She pauses and bends down, her hand hovering above his heaving shoulders. She looks at me, I nod, and she pats his back so lightly that he will not feel it through the wadding of his jacket.

He rubs his face one way and another against the knots of gold and sequins on the footstool; his clenched fist thumps the stool and then the wooden planks of the floor. 'No! No! No!'

Jane jumps back at this violence, and looks at me. Henry gives a little scream of distress and pushes the footstool away and flings himself face down on the floor, rolling from one side to the other in the strewing herbs and the straw. 'My son! My son! My only son!'

Jane shrinks back from his flailing arms and kicking legs but I go forward and kneel at his head. 'God bless him and keep him, and take him into eternal life,' I say quietly.

'No!' Henry rears up, his hair stuck with herbs and straw, and screams into my face. 'No! Not into eternal life. This is my boy! He is my heir! I need him here.'

He is terrifying in his red-faced frustrated rage but then I see where the footstool cover has scratched his face, torn his eyelid, so blood and tears are running down his face, I see the desperate child that he was when his brother died, when his mother died only a year later. I see Henry the child who had been sheltered from life and now had it breaking into his nursery, into his world. A child who had rarely been refused and now suddenly had everything he loved snatched from him.

'Oh, Harry,' I say and my voice is filled with pity.

He wails and pitches himself into my lap. He grips around my waist as if he would crush me. 'I can't . . .' he says. 'I can't . . .'

'I know,' I say. I think of all the times that I have had to come to this young man and tell him a son has died, and now he is as old as I was then, and once again I have to tell him that he has lost a son.

'My boy!'

I grip him as tightly as he is holding me, I rock him and we move together as if he were a great baby, crying in his mother's lap with the heartbreak of childhood.

'He was my heir,' he wails. 'He was my heir. He was the very spit of me. Everyone said it.'

'He was,' I say gently.

'He was handsome as I was!'

'He was.'

'It was as if I would never die . . .'

'I know.'

A new burst of sobbing follows, and I hold him as he weeps heartbrokenly. I look over his heaving shoulders to Jane. She is simply aghast. She stares at the king, hunched on the floor, crying like a child, as if he is some strange monster from a fairy story, nothing to do with her at all. Her eyes slide to the door; she is wishing herself far away from this.

'There is a curse,' Henry says suddenly, sitting up and scrutinising my face. His eyelids are puffed and red, his face blotchy and scratched, his hair standing up, his cap in the ashes of the fire. 'There must be a curse against me. Why else would I lose everyone I love? Why else am I wretched? How can I be king and the most miserable man in the world?'

Even now, with this bereaved father clinging to my hands, I will not say anything. 'How did Bessie Blount offend God that He strikes at me?' Henry demands of me. 'What did Richmond ever do wrong? Why would God take him away from me if there is not a curse on them?'

'Was he ill?' I ask quietly.

'So fast,' Henry whispers. 'I knew he wasn't well, but it wasn't serious. I sent my physician, I did everything that a father should do . . .' He catches his breath on a little sob. 'I have failed in nothing,' he says more strongly. 'It cannot be anything I have done. It has to be the will of God that he was taken from me. It must be something Bessie has done. There must be some sin.'

He breaks off and takes my hand and puts it to his sore, burning cheek. 'I can't bear it,' he says simply. 'I can't believe it. Say it isn't so.'

The tears are pouring down my own face. Silently I shake my head.

'I won't have it said,' Henry says. 'Say it's not so.'

'I can't deny it,' I say steadily. 'I am sorry. I am sorry, Henry. I am so sorry. But he has gone.'

His mouth gapes and he drools, his eyes raw and filled with tears. He can hardly make a sound. 'I can't bear it,' he whispers. 'What about me?'

I pick myself up from the floor, sit on the footstool and hold out my arms to him as if he were the little boy in the royal nursery once again. He crawls towards me and lays his head in my lap and gives himself up to his tears. I stroke his thinning hair, and I wipe his sore cheeks with the linen sleeve of my gown, and I let him cry and cry while the room goes golden with sunset and grey with dusk and Jane Seymour sits like a little statue at the opposite end of the room, too horrified to move.

As the dusk turns darker and becomes night, the king's sobs gradually turn to whimpers and then shudders until I think he has fallen asleep, but then he stirs again and his shoulders heave. When it is time for dinner he does not move and Jane keeps her strange silent vigil with me, as we witness his heartbreak. Then when the bells in the town toll for Compline, the door opens a crack and Thomas Cromwell slips into the room, and takes in everything in one shrewd glance.

'Oh,' Jane exclaims with relief, rises to her feet and makes a little distracted flapping gesture with her hands as if to show the Lord Secretary that the king has collapsed with grief, and the Lord Secretary had better take charge.

'Would you like to go to dinner, Your Grace?' Cromwell asks her with a bow. 'You can tell the court that the king is dining in his rooms, privately.'

Jane gives a little mew of assent and slips from the room and Cromwell turns to me with the king in my arms, as if I pose a knottier problem.

'Countess,' he says to me, bowing.

I incline my head but I don't speak. It is as if I am holding a sleeping child that I don't want to wake.

'Shall I get the grooms of the bedchamber to put him to bed?' he asks me.

'And his physician with a sleeping draught?' I suggest in a whisper.

The physician comes, and the king raises his head and obediently drinks the measure. He keeps his eyes closed, as if he cannot bear to see the looks, curious, sympathetic or, worst of all, amused, of the grooms of the bedchamber who turn down the bed, pierce it with a sword to prevent assassins, warm it with the hot coals in the pan, and then stand at his head and his feet, waiting for instruction.

'Put His Majesty to bed,' Cromwell says.

I start a little at the new title. Now that the king is the only ruler in England and the Pope is nothing but the vicar of Rome, he has taken to claiming that he is as good as an emperor. He is no longer to be called 'Your Grace' like any duke, though this was good enough for his father, the first Tudor, and good enough for all of my family. Now he has an imperial title: he is 'Majesty'. Now his newly made majesty is so felled by grief that his humble subjects have to lift him into bed, and they are too afraid to touch him.

The grooms hesitate, hardly knowing how to approach him. 'Oh, for God's sake,' Cromwell says irritably.

It takes six of them to lift him from the floor to the bed, and his head lolls and the tears spill from his closed eyes. I order the grooms to pull off his beautifully worked riding boots, and Cromwell tells them to take off the heavy jacket, so we leave him to sleep still half-dressed, like a drunkard. One of the grooms will sleep on a pallet bed on the floor; we see them tossing coins for the unlucky one who has to stay. Nobody wants to be with him through the night as he snores and farts and weeps. There are two yeomen guards on the door.

'He'll sleep,' Cromwell says. 'But when he wakes, what do you think, Lady Margaret? Is his heart broken?'

'It is a terrible loss,' I concede. 'To lose a child is always terrible, but to lose one when he was through the illnesses of child-hood and had everything before him . . .'

'To lose an heir,' Cromwell remarks.

I say nothing. I am not going to share any opinion about the king's heir.

Cromwell nods. 'But from your point of view it is all to the good?'

The question is so heartless that I hesitate and look at him, as if I cannot be sure that I heard him correctly.

'It leaves Lady Mary as the only likely heir,' he points out. 'Or do you say princess?'

'I don't talk of her at all. And I say Lady Mary. I signed the oath, and I know that you passed an act of parliament to say that the king will choose his own heir.'

I order food brought to my private rooms. I can't bear to join the court which is noisy with excited chatter and speculation. Montague comes in with the fruit and sweetmeats, pours a glass of wine and sits opposite me.

'Did he collapse?' he asks coolly.

'Yes,' I say.

'He was like that when he lost the Boleyn baby,' he says. 'He cried and raged and then didn't speak. Then, when he finished with his grief, he denied that it had ever happened. And we had a secret burial.'

'It's a terrible loss for him,' I remark. 'He said he was going to make Fitzroy his heir.'

'And now he has no male heir, just as the curse foretold.'

'I don't know,' I say.

In the morning the king is flushed and sullen, his eyes red and puffy, his face downcast. He completely ignores me. It is as if I am not there at breakfast, and was not there last night. He eats hugely, calling again and again for more meat, more ale, some wine, some fresh baked bread, some pastries, as if he would gobble up the world, and then goes again to his chapel. I sit with the queen and her ladies in our bright rooms which overlook the high street and so we see the messengers in Norfolk livery come and go, but the death of the young duke is not announced to the court and nobody knows if they should wear mourning or not.

For three days we stay at Sittingbourne and still the king says nothing about Fitzroy, though more and more people know that he has died. On the fourth day the court moves on, towards Dover, but still no-one has announced that the duke is dead, and the court has not gone into mourning, and the funeral has not been planned.

It is as if everything is suspended in time, frozen like a winter waterfall with the cascade pouring down one moment and stopped in silence the next. The king says nothing; the court knows everything, but obediently acts as if it is completely ignorant. Fitzroy does not ride to join us from London, he will never ride again and yet we all have to pretend that we are waiting for him to come.

'This is madness,' Montague says to me.

'I don't know what I am supposed to do,' the queen says plaintively to her brother. 'It's not really anything to do with me. I have ordered a mourning gown. But I don't know if I have to put it on.'

'Howard has to speak,' Thomas Seymour rules. 'Fitzroy was his son-in-law. There's no reason for any of us to get the bastard a proper funeral. There's no reason for us to call the king to account.'

Thomas Howard steps up to the throne as Henry sits in the presence chamber before dinner and asks, his voice so quiet that only the men closest to him can hear, if he has permission to leave court to go home and bury his son-in-law.

Carefully, he does not say Fitzroy's name. The king beckons him closer and whispers in his ear, and then turns and waves him away. Thomas Howard leaves court without a word to anyone, and goes to his home in Norfolk. Later, we hear that he buried his son-in-law, and his own hopes, in Thetford Priory, with only two men attending the funeral, a plain wooden coffin and a secret service.

'Why?' Montague asks me. 'Why is it kept so quiet?'

'Because Henry cannot bear to lose another son,' I say. 'And because now he has the court so obedient and we are such fools, if he does not want to think of something then none of us says it. If he loses his son and cannot bear the grief then the boy is buried out of sight. And when he next wants to do something which is completely wrong, we will find that he has grown stronger still. He can deny the truth and nobody will argue with him.'

BISHAM MANOR, BERKSHIRE, JULY 1536

I stay at my home while the court is on progress and walk in my fields, and watch the wheat turn golden. I go out with the reaping gang on the first day of harvesting and watch them stride side by side across the field, their sickles slicing down the waving crop, the hares and the rabbits darting away before them so the boys race after them with yapping terriers.

Behind the men come the women, embracing great armfuls of stooks and tying them with one practised movement, their gowns hitched up so that they can stride, their sleeves rolled up high over their brawny arms. Many of them have a baby strapped to their back, most of them have a couple of children trailing behind with the old people gleaning the fallen heads of wheat so that nothing is wasted.

I feel all the wild joy of a miser watching gold come into the treasury. I would rather have a good crop than all the plate I could steal from an abbey. I sit on my horse and watch the tenants work and I smile when they call out to me and tell me that it is a good year, a good year for us all.

I ride back to the house and notice a strange horse in the stables and a man taking a drink of ale at the kitchen door. He looks up as I ride into the yard and pulls his hat from his head – it's an odd cap, Italian-made I should guess. I dismount and wait for him to come towards me.

'I have a message from your son, Countess,' he says. 'He is well, and sends you good wishes.'

'I am glad to hear from him,' I say, hiding my anxiety. We are all waiting, we have been waiting for months, for Reginald to complete his report on the king's claim to be supreme head of the English Church. Reginald has promised that the work will be finished soon and that it will support the king's views. How he will walk through the maze that lost Thomas More, how he will avoid the trap that snapped shut on John Fisher, I don't know. But there is no-one in Christendom better read than my son Reginald. If there is a precedent for a king like ours in the long history of the Church he will find it, and perhaps he can find a way to restore Princess Mary too.

'I will read this, and write a reply,' I tell him.

He bows. 'I will be ready to take it tomorrow,' he says.

'The steward will find you bed and board for tonight.'

I walk through the door to the inner garden and sit on the seat beneath the roses and break the seal of Reginald's letter to me.

He is in Venice. I rest the letter on my knee, close my eyes and try to imagine my son in a fabulous city of wealth and beauty, where the houses' doors open on the lapping water, and he has to take a boat to go to the great library where he is an honoured scholar.

He writes to me that he is ill and thinking about death. He does not feel sorrow but a sense of peace.

I have completed my report and sent it as a long letter to the king. It is not for publication. It is the opinion that he asked for. It is sharp and loving. The scholar in him will recognise the strength of the logic, the theologian will understand the history. The fool and the sensualist will be shocked that I call him both, but I do believe that the death of his concubine gives him a chance to return to the Church, which he must do to save his soul. I am his prophet, as God sent to David. If he can listen to me he might yet be saved.

I have advised him to give it to his best scholars for them to make a précis for him. It's a long letter and I know that he will not have the patience to read it all! But there are men in England who will read it and ignore the vehement words to hear the truth. They can reply to me and perhaps I will rewrite. This is not a statement for publication for all men to wonder at, this is a document for discussion among men of learning.

I have been ill but I will not rest. There are those who would be glad to see me dead and some days I would be glad to sleep in death. I remember, and I hope that you remember too, that when I was only a little boy you gave me entirely to God and rode away from me, and left me in the hands of God. Don't worry about me now - I am still in His hands, where you left me.

Your loving and obedient son,
Reginald

I hold the letter against my cheek as if I could smell the incense and the candle wax of the study where he wrote it. I kiss the signature in case he kissed it before he sealed it up and sent it away. I think that I have lost him indeed, if he has turned from life and yearns for death. The one thing I would have taught him, if I had kept him at my side, is to never weary of life, but to cling to it. Life: at almost any cost. I have never prepared myself for death, not even going into childbed, and I would never put my head down on the block. I think that I should never have left him with the Carthusian monks, good men though they were, poor though I was and without any other way to feed him. I should have begged on the roadside with my son in my arms before I let him be taken from me. I should never have left him to grow into a man who sees himself in the hands of God and prays to go to heaven.

I lost him when I left him at the priory, I lost him when I sent him to Oxford. I lost him when I sent him to Padua, and now I know the full extent and the finality of my loss. Once, I was married to a good man, I had four handsome boys and now I am an old lady, a widow with only two sons in England, and Reginald, the brightest and the one who needed me the most, is far, far away from me dreaming of his own death.

I hold his letter to my heart and I mourn for the son who is tired of life, and then I start to think. I reread the letter and I wonder what he means by 'vehement words', I wonder what he means by being a prophet to the king. I hope very much that he has not written anything that will stir the king's ever-ready suspicion or wake his restless rage.

WESTMINSTER PALACE, LONDON, OCTOBER 1536

The court returns to London and as soon as the king is in his rooms I am summoned to his privy chamber. Of course, I hope that he is going to appoint me to the princess's household, and I hurry from my rooms, across the courtyard, through a small door and up a stairway, through the great hall, until I come to the king's rooms in the warren that is Westminster Palace.

I go through the crowded presence chamber with a little smile of anticipation on my face. They may have to wait but I have been summoned. Surely, he will appoint me to serve the princess and I can guide her back to her title and her true position.

There are more people than ever waiting to see the king, and most of them have a set of plans or a map in their hands. The monasteries and churches of England are being parcelled out, one after another, and everyone wants their share.

But there are men who look uneasy. I recognise an old friend of my husband's, one of the townsmen of Hull, and I nod to him as I go by.

'Will the king see you?' he asks urgently.

'I am going to him now,' I say.

'Please ask him if I can see him,' the man says. 'We're sick with fear in Hull.'

'I'll tell him if I can,' I say. 'What's the matter?'

'The people can't stand having their churches taken,' he says quickly, one eye on the door of the privy chamber. 'They won't tolerate it. When a monastery is pulled down it robs the whole town. We can't rule the towns, the citizens won't bear it. They're all up in the North, and they are talking of defending the monasteries and throwing out the inspectors who come to close them.'

'You must tell Lord Cromwell, it's his work.'

'He knows. But he doesn't warn the king. He doesn't understand the danger that we are in. I tell you, we can't hold the North against the people if they all join together.'

'Defending the Church?' I say slowly.

He nods. 'Saying it has all been foretold. And speaking for the princess.'

One of the king's grooms opens the privy chamber door and nods to me. I leave the townsman without another word, and go in.

It is cool and dark in the privy chamber, where the shutters are closed against the grey of an autumn afternoon, and the fire is laid in the grate but not yet lit. The king is seated behind a broad black-polished table in a big carved chair, scowling. The table before him is heaped with papers, and a secretary waits at the far end, his pen poised, as if the king had been dictating a letter and had broken off when he heard the sentries knock and swing open the door. Lord Cromwell stands to one side, and politely bows his head to me as I walk in.

I can smell danger, just like a horse can sense weak timbers underfoot on a rotten bridge. I look from Cromwell's downturned gaze to the poised secretary and it is as if we are all posing for a portrait from the court painter, Master Holbein. The title would be 'Judgement'.

I raise my head and I walk towards the table and the dark gaze of the most powerful man in Christendom. I am not afraid. I will not be afraid. I am a Plantagenet. The scent of danger is one that I know as well as I know the rich smell of fresh blood, the sharp smell of rat poison. I smelled it in my nursery; this is the scent of my childhood, of all of my life.

'Your Majesty.' I rise up from my curtsey and I stand before him, my hands clasped before me, my face serene.

He meets my gaze and glares at me, his eyes blank, and I let him hold the silence while I feel salty bile slowly rising in my throat. I swallow it down. Then he speaks first. 'You know what this is,' he says rudely, pushing a bound manuscript towards me.

I step forward and when Lord Cromwell nods, I pick it up. My hands don't tremble.

I see that the title is in Latin. 'Is this my son's letter?' I ask. My voice does not quaver.

Lord Cromwell bows his head.

'Do you know what he has called it?' Henry snaps.

I shake my head.

'*Pro ecclesiasticae unitatis defensione,*' Henry reads aloud. 'Do you know what that means?'

I give him a long look. 'Your Majesty, you know that I do. I used to teach you Latin.'

It is almost as if he loses his balance, as if I have recalled him to the boy that he was. For a moment only he wavers, then he swells into grandeur again. 'For the defence of the unity of the Church,' he says. 'But am I Defender of the Faith or not?'

I find that I can smile at him, my lips don't tremble. 'Of course you are.'

'And Supreme Head of the Church of England?'

'Of course you are.'

'Then is your son not guilty of insult, of treason, when he questions my right to rule my Church and defend it? The very title of his letter is treason, all on its own!'

'I have not seen his letter,' I say.

'He has written to her,' Lord Cromwell says quietly to the king.

'He is my son, of course he writes to me,' I reply to the king, ignoring Cromwell. 'And he told me that he had written you a letter. Not a report, not a book, nothing to be published, nothing with a title. He told me that you had asked for his opinion on certain matters and he had obeyed you, studied, consulted, and written his opinion.'

'It's a treasonous opinion,' the king says flatly. 'He is worse than Thomas More, far worse. Thomas More should never have died for what he said, and he never said anything like this. More should be alive today, the best of my advisors, and your son beheaded in his place.'

I swallow. 'Reginald should not have written anything that even approached treason,' I say quietly. 'I must beg your pardon for him if he has done so. I had no idea what he was writing. I had no idea what he was studying. He has been your scholar for many years, working to your commands.'

'He says what you all think!' Henry rises to his feet and leans towards me. His little eyes are glaring. 'Do you dare to deny it? To my face? To my face?'

'I don't know what he says,' I repeat. 'But none of my family in England speaks or thinks or even dreams a word of treason. We are loyal to you.' I turn to Cromwell. 'We took the oath without delay,' I say. 'You closed Bisham Priory, my own foundation, and I did not complain, not even when you appointed a prior of your choosing and turned out Prior Richard and all the canons and cleared the chapel. You took the Lady Mary's jewels from the list that I made for you, and when you locked her up I obeyed you and never wrote to her. Montague is a loyal servant and friend, Geoffrey serves you in parliament. We are kinsmen, loyal kinsmen, and we have never done anything against you.'

The king suddenly slaps the table with a heavy hand, which sounds like a pistol shot. 'I can't stand this!' he bellows.

I don't jump, I hold myself very still. I turn towards him and face him full on, as the keeper at the Tower faces the wild beasts.

Thomas More once told me: lion or king, never show fear or you are a dead man.

The king leans forward and shouts into my face. 'Everywhere I turn there are people conspiring against me, whispering, writing ...' He sweeps Reginald's manuscript to the floor with another angry gesture. 'Nobody thinks of what I do for the country, nobody thinks of how I suffer, leading the country onward, taking them out of darkness into light, serving God though everyone around me, everyone ...' Suddenly he rounds on Cromwell. 'What are they doing in Lincoln? What are they doing in Yorkshire? What do they say against me? Why don't you keep them silent? Why are they roaming the streets of Hull? And why did you allow Pole to write this?' he yells. 'Why would you be such a fool?'

Cromwell shakes his head as if he is amazed at his own stupidity. And at once, since he is getting the blame for the bad news, he sets about diminishing it. A moment ago he was my prosecutor; now he is my co-defendant, and the offence immediately becomes much less serious. I see him turn, like a dancer in a masque, to skip down the line in the opposite direction.

'The Duke of Norfolk will put down the uprising in the North,' he says soothingly. 'A few peasants shouting for bread, it's nothing. And this from your scholar Reginald Pole – this is nothing. It's only a private letter,' he says. 'It's only the opinion of one man. If Your Majesty would deign to rebut it, how could it stand? Your understanding is naturally greater than his. Who would even read it if you denied it? Who cares what Reginald Pole thinks?'

Henry flings himself to the window and looks out into the soft twilight. The owls that live in the attics of this old building are hooting, and as he watches, a great white barn owl sweeps quietly by on silent snub wings. The bells are tolling all over the great city. I think for one moment what would happen to this king if the bells were to start to peal backwards and the people hear the signal to rise against him?

'You will write to your son,' Henry spits, without looking round. 'And you will tell him to come to England and face me, like a man. You will disown him. You will tell him that he is no child of yours for he speaks against your king. I won't have divided loyalties. Either you serve me, or you are his mother. You can choose.'

'You are my king,' I say simply. 'You were born to be king, you always have been my king. I never deny that. You must judge what is the best for the whole kingdom and for me, as your most humble and loving servant.'

He turns and looks at me, and suddenly it is as if his temper is quite blown away. He is smiling, as if I have said something that makes complete sense to him. 'I *was* born to be king,' he says quietly. 'It is God's will. To say anything else is to fly in the face of God. Tell your son that.'

I nod.

'God put Arthur aside to make me king,' he reminds me, almost shyly. 'Didn't he? You saw Him do it. You were a witness.'

I give no sign of what it costs me to speak of Arthur's death to his younger brother. 'God Himself put you on the throne,' I agree.

'The best choice,' he asserts.

I bow my head in assent.

The king sighs as if he has somehow got to a place where he can be at peace.

I glance at Cromwell; it seems that the audience is over. He nods, his face a little pale. I think that Cromwell must sometimes have to dig deep to find the courage to face this monster he has made.

I curtsey and I am about to turn to go to the door when a little warning gesture of the hand from the silent secretary at the end of the table reminds me that we are not allowed to turn our backs on the king any more. His greatness is such that we have to leave his presence walking backwards.

I am of the old royal family in England. My father was brother to two kings. I think for a moment, for half a moment only, that I will look like a fool showing exaggerated respect for this fat tyrant, whose back is turned to me, who does not even see the homage that I am ordered to give him. Then I think that the only fool is the one who fails to survive in these dangerous times, and

I give Thomas Cromwell a smile which says – if he could but read it – how low shall we stoop, you and I? To keep our heads on our shoulders? And I curtsey again and walk backwards six paces, curtsey, feel blindly behind my back for the handle, and slide out of the door.

Montague comes to my room after Compline, late at night. 'What did he say to you?' he demands. His hair is sticking up as if he has run his hands through it in exasperation. I stroke it down and straighten his cap. He jerks his head away from my touch. 'He tore into me, this letter of Reginald's has all but ruined us. I don't think he'll ever forgive it. He can't bear to hear criticism. He screamed at me.'

'He told me that I had to disown Reginald,' I admit. 'He was angrier than I have ever seen him before.'

'He frightened Cromwell,' Montague says. 'I saw his hands shake. I was kneeling, I swear that my legs would have given way if I had been standing. There was no pleasing him through dinner. The queen spoke to him about a favour for someone and he said that she didn't have enough good will from him to squander it on others. In front of everyone! I thought she was going to cry before all the court. Then after dinner he took me to one side and was beside himself.'

'She's terrified of him,' I remark. 'Not like Queen Katherine, not even like Anne. She can't begin to manage him.'

'What will we do?' Montague demands. 'God knows that we can't manage him. What could possess Reginald to expose us to this?'

'He had to!' I defend him. 'It was either that or write page after page of lies. The king commanded that he give his opinion. He had to say what he thought.'

'He called the king a tyrant and a ravening beast!' Montague raises his voice and then remembers that these words alone are treason, and claps his hand over his mouth.

'We'll have to deny him,' I say unhappily. 'I know we will.'

Montague flings himself into a chair and runs his hands through his hair. 'Doesn't he realise what life is like in England today?'

'He knows very well,' I say. 'Probably nobody knows better. He's warning the king that if he goes on with the destruction of the monasteries the people will rise against him and the emperor will invade. And already the North is up.'

'The commons turned on the bishop's chancellor at Horncastle,' Montague tells me, his voice low. 'They're burning beacons as far as Yorkshire. But Reginald declares against the king too soon. His letter is treason.'

'I don't see what else he could write,' I say. 'The king asked for his opinion. He has given it. He says that the princess should have her title, and the Pope should have the headship of the Church. Would you say any different?'

'Yes! Dear God, I'd never tell the truth to this king.'

'But if you were far away, and ordered to write your honest opinion?'

Montague gets out of his chair and kneels beside mine so that he can whisper into my ear. 'Lady Mother, he is far away; but we are not. I am afraid for you, and for me, and for my son Harry, all my children, and for all our kin. It doesn't matter that Reginald is right – I know he is! It doesn't matter that most of England would agree with him – almost every lord of the land would agree with him. It's not just the commons who are march-ing in Lincolnshire, they're taking the gentry with them and calling on the lords to turn out for them. Every day someone seeks me out or sends me a message or asks me what we are going to do. But telling this truth has put all of us into terrible danger. The king is no longer a thoughtful scholar, he is no longer a devout son of the Church. He has become a man quite out of the control of his teachers, of the priests, perhaps of him-self. There is no point giving the king an honest opinion, he wants nothing but praise of himself. He cannot bear one word of criticism. He is merciless against those who speak against him. It is death to speak the truth in England now. Reginald is far away and enjoying the luxury of speaking out but we are here; it is our lives he is risking.'

I am silent. 'I know,' I say. 'I don't think that he could have done differently, he had to speak out. But I know that he has put us in danger.'

'Geoffrey too,' Montague says. 'Think of your precious Geoffrey. Reginald's letter has endangered us all.'

'What can we do to make ourselves safe?'

'There's no safety for us. We are the royal family, whether we publicly proclaim it as Reginald does, or not. All we can do is draw a line between Reginald and ourselves. All we can say is that he does not speak for us, that we deny what he says, that we urge him to be silent. And we can beg him not to publish, and you can order him not to go to Rome.'

'But what if he publishes this letter, and what if he goes to Rome and persuades the Pope to publish the excommunication and order a crusade against England?'

Montague puts his head in his hands. 'Then I am ready,' he says very quietly. 'When the emperor invades I will raise the tenants and we will march with the commons of England, defend the Church, overthrow the king and put the princess on her throne.'

'We will do it?' I ask, as if I don't know that the answer is yes.

'We have to,' Montague says grimly. Then he looks up at me, and I see my own fear in his face. 'But I am afraid,' he admits honestly.

Both Montague and I write to Reginald. Geoffrey writes too and we send the letters by Thomas Cromwell's messengers, so that he can see how loudly we condemn Reginald for his folly, for the abuse of his position as the king's own scholar, and how clearly we call on him to withdraw everything he has said.

Take another way and serve our master as thy bounden duty is to do, unless thou wilt be the confusion of thy mother.

I leave the letter unsealed, but I kiss my signature and hope that he will know. He will not withdraw one word of what he has written, and I know that he has written nothing but the truth. He will know that I wouldn't have him deny the truth. But he can never come to England while the king lives, and I cannot see him. Perhaps, given my great age, I will never see him again. The only way that my family can be together again will be if Reginald comes with an army from Spain to rouse the commons, restore the Church and put the princess on the throne. 'Come the day!' I whisper, and then I take my letter to Thomas Cromwell for his spies to study for a hidden code of treason.

The great man, Lord Secretary and Vicegerent of the Church, invites me into his privy chamber where three men are bowed over letters and accounts books. The work of the world revolves around Thomas Cromwell, just as it did around his old master, Thomas Wolsey. He takes care of everything.

'The king requests that your son come to court and explain his letter,' he says to me. Out of the corner of my eye I see one of the clerks pause with his pen raised, waiting to copy down my reply.

'I pray that he will come,' I say. 'I will tell him, as his mother, that he should come. He should show every obedience to His Gracious Majesty, as we all do, as he was raised to do.'

'His Majesty is not angry now with his cousin Reginald,' Cromwell says gently. 'He wants to understand the arguments, he wants Reginald to talk with other scholars so that they can agree.'

'What a very good idea.' I look directly into his smiling face. 'I shall tell Reginald to come at once. I will add a note to my letter.'

Cromwell, the great liar, the great heretic, the great pander to his master, bows his head as if he is impressed with my loyalty. I, as bad as he is, bow back.

L'ERBER, LONDON,
OCTOBER 1536

Montague comes to see me at my home early in the morning, while the court is at Mass. He comes into my chapel and kneels beside me on the stone flags while the priest, half-hidden by the rood screen, his back turned towards us, performs the mysteries of the Mass and brings the blessing of God to me and my silently kneeling household.

At the back, untouched and unread, is the Bible that the king has ordered shall be placed in every church. Every one of my household believes that God speaks in Latin to his Church. English is the language of everyday mortals, of the market, of the midden. How can anything that is of God be written down in the language of sheep-farming and money? God is the Word, he is the Pope, the priest, the bread and the wine, the mysterious Latin of the litany, the unreadable Bible. But we do not defy the king on this, we don't defy him on any-thing.

'Queen Jane went down on her knees to the king and begged him to restore the abbeys and not steal them from the people.' Montague bows his head as if in prayer and mutters the news to me over his rosary. 'Lincolnshire is up to defend the abbeys, there's not a village that is not marching.'

'Is it our time?'

Montague bows his head further so that no-one can see him smile. 'Soon,' he says. 'The king is sending Thomas Howard, Duke of Norfolk, to put down the commons. He thinks it will be readily done.'

'Do you?'

'I pray.' Cautiously, Montague does not even say what he prays for. 'And the princess sent you her love. The king has brought her and little Lady Elizabeth to court. For a man who says that the commons will be easily put down it's telling that he should have his daughters brought to him for safety.'

Montague leaves as soon as the service is over, but I don't need him to bring me news. Soon all of London is buzzing. The cook's boy, sent to market to get some nutmeg, comes home with the claim that forty thousand men, armed and horsed, are marching in Boston.

My London steward comes to me to tell me that two lads from Lincolnshire have run away, gone home to join with the commons. 'What did they think they were going to do?' I ask.

'They take an oath,' he says, his voice carefully bland. 'Apparently they swear that the church shall have its fees and funds, that the monasteries shall not be thrown down, but shall be restored, and that the false bishops and false advisors who recommended these wrongs shall be exiled from the king and from the kingdom.'

'Bold demands,' I say, keeping my face quite still.

'Bold demands in the face of danger,' he adds. 'The king has sent his friend Charles Brandon, Duke of Suffolk, to join with the Duke of Norfolk against the rebels.'

'Two dukes against a handful of fools?' I say. 'God save the commons from folly and hurt.'

'The commons may save themselves. They're not unarmed,' he says. 'And there are more than a few of them. The gentry are with them and they have horse and weapons. Perhaps it is the dukes who had better look to their own safety. They say that Yorkshire is ready to rise, and Tom Darcy has sent to the king to ask what his answer must be.'

'Lord Thomas Darcy?' I think of the man who has my pansy badge in his pocket.

'The rebels have a banner,' my steward continues. 'They are marching under the five wounds of Christ. They say it is like a holy war. The Church against the infidel, the commons against the king.'

'And where is Lord Hussey?' I ask, naming one of the lords of the country, the princess's former chamberlain.

'He's with the rebels,' my steward says, nodding at my blank-faced astonishment. 'And his wife is out of the Tower and with him.'

The country is so disturbed with rumours of uprisings, even in the south, that I stay in London in early October. I take my barge downriver one cold day as the mist is lying on the water and the evening sun burning red, and the tide is up and the current strong.

'Best walk round the bridge, my lady,' says the master of my barge, and they set me down on the wet slimy stairs and row the barge out into the middle channel to shoot the stormy waters of the bridge and pick me up on the other side.

One of my granddaughters, Katherine, takes my arm and we have a liveryman before and behind us as we walk the short way around to the water stairs on the other side of the bridge. There are beggars of course, but they clear from the path when they see us coming. I hide my flinch of dismay when I notice a nun's habit, fouled by months of sitting and waiting, and see the strained, desperate face of a woman who had given herself to God and then found herself flung into the gutter. I nod to Katherine's sister Winifred, who, unasked, tosses the woman a coin.

A man comes out of the darkness and stands before us. 'Who's this?' he asks one of my servants.

'I am Margaret Pole, Countess of Salisbury,' I say briskly, 'and you had better let me pass.'

He smiles, as merry as an outlaw in the greenwood, and he bows low. 'Pass, your ladyship, pass with our blessing,' he says. 'For we know who our friends are. And God be with you, for you too are a pilgrim and have a pilgrimage gate to go.'

I stop short. 'What did you say?'

'It's not a rebellion,' he says very quietly. 'You would know that as well as I, perhaps. It is a pilgrimage. We are calling it the Pilgrimage of Grace. And we tell each other that we have to pass through the pilgrimage gate.'

He hesitates and sees my face as I hear the words 'Pilgrimage of Grace'. 'We are marching under the five wounds of Christ,' he says. 'And I know you, and all the good old lords of the white rose, are pilgrims just like us.'

The rebels who say they march on the Pilgrimage of Grace have captured Sir Thomas Percy, or else he has joined with them; nobody seems to know. They are under the leadership of a good man, an honest Yorkshireman, Robert Aske, and in the middle of October we learn that Aske rode into the great northern city of York without an arrow flying in its defence. They threw open the gates to him and to the force that everyone is now calling the pilgrims. They are twenty thousand strong. This is four times the force that took England at Bosworth, this is an army great enough to take all of England.

Their first act was to restore two Benedictine houses in the city, Holy Trinity and the nunnery of St Clement. When they rang the bells at Holy Trinity the people cried for joy as they went in to hear Mass.

My guess is that the king will do anything to avoid an open battle. The rebels in Lincolnshire have been offered a pardon if they will only go home, but why should they do so, now the massive county of Yorkshire is up in arms?

'I'm ordered to muster the tenants and to get ready to march,' Montague says to me. He has come to L'Erber as the servants are clearing away the tables after dinner. The musicians are tuning up and there is a masque to be performed. I beckon Montague to sit beside me, and I lean my head towards him so that he can speak softly against my hood.

'I am commanded to go north and put down the pilgrimage,' he says. 'Geoffrey has to raise a force too.'

'What will you do?' In my pocket I touch the embroidered badge that Lord Darcy gave me, the five wounds of Christ and the white rose of York. 'You can't fire on the pilgrims.'

He shakes his head. 'Never,' he says simply. 'Besides, everyone says that when the king's army sees the pilgrims they'll change sides and join them. It's happening every day. Every letter that the king sends out with orders to his commanders he follows with one asking them if they are staying true to him. He trusts no-one. He's right. It turns out that no-one can be trusted.'

'Who's he got in the field?'

'Thomas Howard, Duke of Norfolk, and the king trusts him no further than he can see him. Talbot, Lord Shrewsbury, is marching in support, but he is for the old religion and the old ways. Charles Brandon refused to go, saying that he wanted to be at home to keep his county down; he's been ordered to Yorkshire against his will. Thomas Lord Darcy says he's pinned down by the rebels in his castle, but since he's been arguing against the pulling down of the monasteries since the first moment of the queen's divorce, nobody knows if he's just waiting for the right moment to join the pilgrims. John Hussey sent a letter to say he's been kidnapped by them, but everyone knows he was the princess's chamberlain and loves her dearly, and his wife is outright on her side. The king is chewing his nails to the quick; he's in a frenzy of rage and self-pity.'

'And what . . .' I break off as a messenger in Montague's livery comes into the hall and walks close to him and waits. Montague beckons him forward, listens intently, and then turns to me.

'Tom Darcy has surrendered his castle to the rebels,' he says. 'The pilgrims have taken Pontefract and everyone under Tom Darcy's command in the castle and in the town has sworn the pilgrim oath. The Archbishop of York is with them.'

He sees my face. 'Old Tom is on his last crusade,' he says wryly. 'He'll be wearing his badge of the five wounds.'

'Tom is wearing his badge?' I ask.

'He had the crusader badges at his castle,' he says. 'He issued it to the pilgrims. They are marching for God against heresy and wearing the five wounds of Christ. No Christian can fire on them under that sacred banner.'

'What should we do?' I ask him.

'You go to the country,' Montague decides. 'If the south rises for the pilgrims they'll need leadership and money and supplies. You can lead them in Berkshire. I'll send to you so you know what's happening in the North. Geoffrey and I will go north with our force, and join the pilgrims when the time is right. I'll send a message to Reginald to come right away.'

'He'll come home?'

'At the head of a Spanish army, please God.'

BISHAM MANOR, BERKSHIRE, OCTOBER 1536

I can get no news in the country but I hear extraordinary stories of thousands of men marching on the destroyed abbeys and rebuilding them while singing the great psalms that were always sung there. People talk of a comet in the sky over Yorkshire, and say that the rising has gone underground in Lincolnshire and King Mouldwarp will have to chase through the earth to find the pilgrims but they are already in the Yorkshire hills and dales and he will never impose his muddy will on them again.

I get a letter from Gertrude who tells me that her husband, my cousin Henry Courtenay, has been commanded by the king to muster an army and put himself under the command of Lord Talbot and march north as soon as possible. The king had said that he would lead his army, but the news from the North is so terrifying that he is sending my kinsmen instead.

It's little and late. The king has not given the commanders money enough to pay the men, and they are so badly shod and there are so few on horses that they can't get north fast enough. Anyway, they all know that when the king's army sees the pilgrim badge they'll desert, taking their weapons with them. And Thomas Howard is complaining that he is supposed to hold down Yorkshire with nothing, while all the money and troops go to George Talbot and the credit will go to Charles Brandon. The king does not know who his friends are, or how to keep them; how should he face his enemies?

Best of all, Norfolk has authority to treat with the rebels and he is

bound to grant them the saving of the abbeys. If we can make the
princess safe too in this moment, then this will be a great victory.

I'll send you news as soon as I have it. The royal army and the
pilgrims are bound to meet in battle and the pilgrims outnumber
them by many thousands. And all the hosts of heaven are on our
side too.

Burn this.

I am in the flesh kitchen at Bisham watching the hunt bring in
the deer. They had two great buck and a hind and they dressed
the meat in the field to stop it spoiling and now hang it in the cool
stone-floored room to drip blood in the gutters.

'They hung our friend Legh just like that,' the Master of the
Hounds remarks quietly to me.

Carefully, I don't turn my head. It looks as if the two of us are
inspecting the flayed carcass.

'Did they?' I ask. 'Thomas Legh who came here, to close the
priory?'

'Yes,' he said with quiet satisfaction. 'On the gates of Lincoln.
And the Bishop of Lincoln's chancellor. He that gave evidence
against the sainted queen. It's like it's all coming to rights, isn't it,
your ladyship?'

I smile, but I take care to say nothing.

'And is your son Reginald coming soon with a holy army?' he
says in the lowest whisper. 'It would make the commons glad to
know it.'

'Soon,' I say, and he bows and leaves.

We have eaten the venison, and made pasties, and made soup
from the bones, and given the bones to the hounds before we get
news from Doncaster where the lords, gentry and commons of
the North drew up in battle order against the king's army, my two
sons on the wrong side, biding their time, ready to cross over.
Montague sends a messenger to me.

The pilgrims brought their demands to Thomas Howard. He was lucky that they agreed to parlay; if they had fought he would have been destroyed. There must have been more than thirty thousand of them, and led by every gentleman and lord in Yorkshire. The king's army is hungry and cold, the countryside around here being very poor and no man wishing us well. I have been given no money to pay my men, and the others are marching for even less than I have promised. The weather is bad too, and they say there is pestilence in the town.

The pilgrims have won this war and now present their demands. They want the faith of our fathers to be restored, that the law should be restored, that the noble advisors to the king should be restored, and that Cromwell, Richard Riche, and the heretic bishops be banished. There is not a man in the king's army, including Thomas Howard, who does not agree. Charles Brandon encourages them also. It's what we've all been thinking since the king first turned against the queen and took Cromwell as his advisor. So Thomas Howard is to ride to the king with the pilgrims' request for general pardon, and an agreement to restore the old ways.

Lady Mother, I am so hopeful.

Burn this.

L'ERBER, LONDON, NOVEMBER 1536

I should be preparing Bisham Manor for Christmas, but I cannot settle to anything when I think of my two sons, the king's army behind them and the pilgrims before them, waiting for the king's agreement to the truce. In the end I take Montague's children, Katherine, Winifred and Harry, and go to London, hoping for news.

I do not promise them the treat of attending a full coronation, but they know that the king has promised to crown his wife, and the ceremony should take place on All Hallows' Day. My own belief is that he will not be able to afford a great coronation while he is sending men and arms north and he will be furious and frightened all at once. He will not be able to stride out in confidence before a crowd, and let everyone admire him and his beautiful new wife. This rebellion has shaken him, and while he is like this, thrown back into his childhood fears that he is not good enough, he simply will not be able to plan a great ceremony.

As soon as I have arrived and prayed in my chapel I go to my presence chamber, to meet with all the tenants and petitioners who want to see me, bid me a merry Christmas, make their requests and pay their seasonal fines and rents. Among them is a man I recognise, a priest and friend of my exiled chaplain, John Helyar.

'You can leave me,' I say to my grandson Harry.

He looks up at me, his face bright and willing. 'I can stay with you, Lady Grandmother, I can be your page. I'm not tired of standing.'

'No,' I say. 'But I could be here all day. You can go down to the stables and you can go out into the streets, you can have a look around.'

He gives a little bow and shoots from the room like a loosed arrow and only then do I nod to Helyar's friend in greeting and indicate to my steward that he can step forward and speak with me.

'Father Richard Langgrische of Havant,' he reminds me.

'Of course,' I smile.

'I have greetings from your son, Geoffrey. I have been with him in the king's army in the North,' he says.

'I am glad to hear of it,' I say clearly. 'I am glad that my son is prospering in the king's service. Is my son well?'

'Both your sons are well,' he says. 'And confident that these troubles will soon be over.'

I nod. 'You can dine in hall tonight, if you wish.'

He bows. 'I thank you.'

Someone else steps forward with some complaint about the cost of ale in one of my tenant ale-houses and the steward steps to my side and takes a note of the problem.

'Get that man to my chamber before dinner,' I say quietly. 'Make sure no-one sees him.'

He does not blink. He merely writes down the claim that the ale has been watered and that the jugs are not full-measure and waves the next petitioner forward.

Langgrische is waiting for me by the little fire in my bedroom, concealed like a secret lover. I can't restrain a smile. It's been a long time since there was a man waiting for me in my bedroom; I have been a widow now for thirty-two years.

'What's the news?' I sit in my chair at the fireside and he stands before me.

Silently he shows me a small piece of cloth, a token like a man might sew to his collar. It is the match of the badge that Tom Darcy gave me, the five wounds of Christ and a white rose above it. Silently I touch it as if it were a relic of faith, and return it to him.

'The pilgrims have dispersed most of their force, waiting for the king to agree to their terms. The king sent a dishonourable command to Tom Darcy, to meet with the pilgrim leader Robert Aske as if to talk in honour, kidnap him, and hand him over to Cromwell's men.'

'What did Tom say?'

'He said that his coat should never have such a spot on it.'

I nod. 'That's Tom. And my sons?'

'Both well, both releasing men from their force to the pilgrim army every day, but both sworn to the king's force and no-one suspecting different. The king has asked for more details of the pilgrim demands and they have explained them.'

'Do Montague and Geoffrey think that the king will grant the demands?'

'He'll have to,' the man said simply. 'The pilgrims could over-whelm the royal army in a moment, they're only waiting for an answer because they don't want to make war on the king.'

'How can they call themselves loyal subjects? In battle array? When they hang his servants?'

'There have been remarkably few deaths,' he says. 'Because hardly anyone disagrees with them.'

'Thomas Legh? Well worth hanging, I agree.'

He laughs. 'They would have hanged him if they had caught him but he got away. He sent out his cook in his place like a coward, and they hanged him instead. The pilgrims don't attack the lords or the king. They blame only his advisors. Cromwell must be banished, the destruction of monasteries reversed, and you and your family restored to the king's council.'

He looks at me almost slyly and smiles. 'I have news of your other son, Reginald, too.'

'Is he in Rome?' I ask eagerly.

He nods. 'He is to be made a cardinal,' he says, awestruck. 'He is to come to England as a cardinal and restore the Church to its glory, as soon as the king agrees to the pilgrims' demands.'

'The Pope will send my son home to restore the Church?'

'To save us all,' Langgrische says devoutly.

L'ERBER, LONDON, DECEMBER 1536

This year we will keep the twelve days of Christmas in the old ways. The priory at Bisham may still be closed, but here in London I open up my chapel and set Advent lights in the window and keep the door open so that anyone can come in and see the altar dressed with cloth of gold, the chalice and the crucifix gleaming in the incense-scented darkness, the shine of the crystal monstrance holding the mystery of the Host, the chapel lined with the smiling, confident painted faces of saints and draped in the banners of the Church and my family. In the darkness of the corner of the chapel the banner of the white rose palely gleams; opposite is the rich pansy of the Pole family in papal imperial purple. And I kneel and bury my face in my hands and think that there is no reason that Reginald should not become Pope.

This Christmas is a great one, for our family and for England. Perhaps this will be the year that my son Reginald comes home to restore the Church to its rightful position, and my sons Montague and Geoffrey restore the king to his true royal place.

I know from a note from my cousin Gertrude, from a messenger from the Spanish ambassador, and from my own people in London that the king has been persuaded there will be no ruling any of England, let alone the North, unless he forges an agreement with the pilgrims. They have told him, simply and respectfully, that the Church has to return to Rome, and the old noble advisors to his chambers. The king may complain that nobody has the right to tell him who to consult, but he knows, as the lords know, as the gentlemen know, as the commons know, that nothing has gone well with his reign since he put lowly clerks in the highest office and pretended to marry the daughter of my steward.

Finally, blustering and angry, he consents – he can do nothing but consent – and Thomas Howard rides back north through flurries of snow in freezing weather, carrying the king's pardon, and has to wait in the cold outside Doncaster while the Lancaster herald offers the king's pardon to the thousands of patient northerners in their massed and silent ranks. Robert Aske, the leader who came from almost nowhere, kneels before his thousands of pilgrims and tells them that they have won a great victory. He asks them to release him from his post as captain. When they agree he tears off the badge of the five wounds and promises that they all will wear no badge but that of the king.

When I hear that, I take the badge that Tom Darcy gave me

from my pocket, and I kiss it and put it at the back of an old chest in my wardrobe rooms. I don't need it as a secret reminder of my loyalty any more. The pilgrimage is over and the pilgrims have won, we can all put our badges away and my sons, all my sons, will be coming home.

London is filled with joy at the news. They ring the church bells for the Christmas service but everyone knows they are pealing out that we have saved the country, and saved the Church, and saved the king from himself. I take my household to watch the court progress from Westminster to Greenwich, and we laugh and walk on the frozen river. It is so cold that the children can slip and slide on the ice and my grandchildren Katherine, Winifred and Harry cling to my arms and beg me to tow them along.

The court, in its golden Christmas glory, walks in the centre of the river, the bishops in their copes with their mitres on their heads and their jewelled crooks sparkling in the light of a thousand torches. The men at arms hold back the crowds so that the horses in their special ice shoes with sharp studs can take to the centre of the river as if it were a great white road curving its way through an ice city, as if they could ride all the way to the Russias. All the roofs of London are crusted with snow; every thatch has a fringe of glistening icicles. The prosperous citizens and their children are brightly dressed in holly colours of red and green, throwing their rosy bonnets in the air and shouting: 'God save the king! God save the queen!'

When the Princess Mary comes out, dressed in white on her white horse, she gets the greatest roar the crowd can raise. 'God save the princess!' My grandson Harry is thrilled to see her, he jumps on the spot and cheers, his eyes bright with loyalty. The people of London don't care that she is to be called Lady Mary, and is a princess no longer. They know that they have restored the Church, they have no doubt but that they will restore the princess too.

She smiles as I taught her to smile, and turns her head left and right so that no-one is neglected. She raises her gloved hand, and I see that she has beautifully embroidered white leather gloves, sewn with pearls; at last she is being kept as a princess should be. Her horse has trappings of deep green, her saddle is green leather. Over her head her standard flaps in the icy wind, and I smile to see that she is flying the Tudor rose, with the red of the centre so small that it looks like a white rose, and she flies her mother's flag too, the pomegranate.

She has the prettiest bonnet on her head, silvery white with a sweeping feather; she has a rich jacket of white embroidered with silver thread and stitched with pearls. Her deep, full skirt is white too, falling either side of the saddle, and she rides well, her reins held firmly in her hand, her head up.

At her side, riding alongside on a little bay pony as if she had a right to be there, is the three-year-old Boleyn girl, her pretty face bright under a scarlet hat, waving her hand to everyone. Mary speaks to her from time to time. It is obvious that she loves her little half-sister Elizabeth. The crowd applauds her for it. Mary has a tender heart, and she is always looking for someone to love.

'Can't I make a bow? Can't I bow to her?' Harry demands.

I shake my head. 'Not today. I will take you to her another time.'

I step back so that she does not see me. I don't want to be a reminder of harder days, and I don't want her to think that I am seeking her attention on this, the day of her triumph. I want her to feel the joy that she should have had from childhood, I want her to be a princess with no regrets. She has had few happy days, none since the coming of the Boleyn whore, but this is one. I don't want it overshadowed by her sorrow that she cannot have me by her side, that still we are parted.

I am content to watch her from the riverbank. I think that at last the king is coming to his senses and we have endured some strange years of mad cruelty, when he did not know what he was doing, when he did not know what he was thinking, and there was no-one with the courage to stop him. But now the people themselves have stopped him. With the courage of the saints, the common people have stood up and warned Henry Tudor that his father conquered the country but cannot take their souls.

Wolsey would not do it, the Boleyn girl could not do it, Cromwell never thought to do it, but the people of England have said to their king that he has come to a line they have drawn. He does not have power over everything in the kingdom. He does not have power over the Church, he does not have power over them.

I don't doubt that the day will come when he sees that he was wrong over Queen Katherine too, and shows justice to her daughter. Of course he will. He gains nothing by naming her as his bastard now. He will name her as his eldest daughter, he will recall me to her service, and he will make a great marriage for her with one of the crowned heads of Europe. I will go with her, and make sure that she is safe and happy in her new palace, wherever she has to go, whoever she has to marry.

'I will be her page,' Harry says, chiming with my thoughts. 'I shall serve her, I will be her page.' I smile down at him and touch his cold cheek.

A great bawl goes up from the waiting crowd as the yeomen of the guard come marching along, keeping time though now and then someone slips. Nobody falls; they sometimes have to use the heel of the pike to stay upright but they look brave and bright in their green-and-white livery, and then finally, at last, there is the king, riding behind them, glorious in imperial purple as if he were the Holy Roman Emperor himself, with Jane beside him, overloaded with furs.

He is a massive figure now. High on the back of a big horse, almost a plough horse, Henry matches the broad shoulders and the huge rump of the horse with his own brawn. His jacket is padded so thick and fat that he is as wide as two men, his hat trimmed all round with fur, like a great basin on his balding head. He wears his cape thrown back, so that we can all see the glory of his jacket and waistcoat, and yet admire the flow of the cape, a rich purple velvet, sweeping almost to the ground.

His hands are on the reins in leather gloves glinting with diamonds and amethysts. He has precious stones in his hat, on the hem of his cape, on his very saddle. He looks like a gloriously triumphant king entering his own, and the citizens and the commons and the gentry of London bellow their approval of this larger-than-life giant astride his giant horse as he rides on a great frozen river.

Jane beside him is tiny. They have dressed her in blue and she looks cold and insubstantial. She has a blue hood that stands high and heavy on her head. She has a rippling blue cloak that catches and jerks her backwards from time to time and makes her clutch at her reins. She is mounted on a beautiful grey horse but she does not ride like a queen; she looks nervous as the horse slides once on the ice, and finds its feet again.

She smiles at the loud cheers but she looks around her, almost as if she thinks they are for someone else. I realise that she has seen two other wives respond to the bellow of 'God save the queen', and she has to remind herself that the loyal shout means her.

We wait till the whole court has ridden by, the lords and their households, and all the bishops, even Cromwell in his modest dark gown lined with hidden rich fur, and then the foreign ambassadors. I see the dainty little Spanish ambassador but I pull up the hood of my fur-lined cape and make sure that he does not see me. I don't want any hidden sign from him; this is not a day for plotting. We have won the victory that we needed: this is a day for celebration. I wait with my household until the last of the soldiers have gone by and all that will follow them are the household wagons and I say: 'That's the end of the show, Harry, Katherine, Winifred. Time to go home.'

'Oh, Lady Grandmother, can't we wait till the huntsmen take the hounds by?' Harry pleads.

'No,' I rule. 'They'll have taken them already, and all the hawks will be on their perches with the curtains drawn against the cold. There's nothing to see and it's getting too late.'

'But why can't we go with the court?' Katherine asks. 'Don't we belong at court?'

I tuck her little hand under my elbow. 'Next year we will,' I promise her. 'I am sure the king will have us back at his side, with all our family, and next year we will have Christmas at court.'

It is Christmas Eve at L'Erber, and I am in the chapel, on my knees, waiting for the moment when I will hear first one, then another, then a hundred bells chime the hour for midnight, and then break into a full peal to celebrate the birth of Our Lord.

I hear the outside door suddenly open, then thud shut and feel the swirl of cold air as the candles bob and then suddenly my son Montague is bowing to the altar and then kneeling before me for my blessing.

'My son! Oh, my son!'

'Lady Mother, blessings of the season.'

'Happy Christmas, Montague. Have you just come from the North?'

'I rode down with Robert Aske himself,' he says.

'He's here? The pilgrims are in London?'

'He's bidden to court. He is the king's guest at the Christmas feast. He is honoured.'

I hear his words but I cannot believe them. 'The king has asked Robert Aske, the leader of the pilgrims, to court for Christmas?'

'As a loyal subject, as an advisor.'

I put out my hand to my son. 'The pilgrim leader and the king?'

'It is peace. It is victory.'

'I can't believe that our troubles are over.'

'Amen,' he says. 'Who would have believed it?'

L'ERBER, LONDON,
JANUARY–FEBRUARY 1537

Montague goes to court himself the next day, taking Harry with him, who trots in his train, very solemn and serious, and when he comes back at the end of the twelve days of Christmas he comes straight to my private rooms to tell me about the meeting between the king and the pilgrim.

'He spoke to the king with unbelievable frankness. You would not think it possible.'

'What did he say?'

Montague glances around, but only my granddaughters are with me, and a couple of ladies, and besides, the time for fearing spies is over.

'He told His Majesty to his face that he was there only to tell him the hearts of the people, and that they cannot tolerate Cromwell as an advisor.'

'Was Cromwell there, listening to this?'

'Yes. That's what made it so brave. Cromwell was furious, swore that all northern men were traitors – and the king looked from one to the other and put his arm around Robert Aske's shoulders.'

'The king favoured Aske over Cromwell?'

'In front of everyone.'

'Cromwell must be beside himself.'

'He's afraid. Think of what happened to his master, Wolsey! If the king turns against him he has no friends. Thomas Howard would see him hanged on his own scaffold tomorrow. He has invented laws that can be bent to catch anyone. If he is caught in his own net none of us would lift a hand to save him.'

'And the king?'

'Gave Aske his own jacket, scarlet satin. Gave him the gold chain from his neck. Asked him what he wanted. My God, but he's a brave man, that Yorkshireman! He bent the knee but he lifted his head and he spoke to the king without fear. He said that Cromwell was a tyrant and the men he had thrown out of the monasteries were good men, thrown into poverty by Cromwell's greed, and the people of England could not live without the abbeys. He said that the Church is the heart of England; it cannot be attacked without hurting us all. The king listened to him, listened to every word, and at the end of it he said that he would make him one of the council.'

I break off to look at Harry's bright face. 'Did you see him? Did you hear this?'

He nods. 'He's very quiet and you don't notice him at first but then you see that he's the most important person there. And he is nice to look at though he's blinded in one eye. He's quiet and smiling. And he's really brave.'

I turn back to Montague. 'I see he's very taking. But – a privy councillor?'

'Why not? He's a Yorkshire gentleman, a kin to the Seymours, better born than Cromwell. But anyway, he refused. Think of it! He bowed and said that it wasn't necessary. What he wants is a free parliament, and that the council should be governed by the old lords, not new upstarts. And the king said that he will hold a free parliament at York to show his good will, and the queen will be crowned there, and the Church convocation will meet there to declare their learning.'

For a moment I am stunned at this change, then, at Montague's quiet certainty, I make the sign of the cross and I bow my head for a moment. 'Everything we have ever asked for.'

'More,' my son confirms. 'More than we dreamed of asking, more than we imagined the king would ever grant.'

'What more?' I ask.

Montague beams at me. 'Reginald is waiting to be called. He's in Flanders, a day's sail away. The moment that the king sends for him, he will come and restore the Church to England.'

'The king will send for him?'

'He will appoint him as the cardinal for the restoration.'

I am so amazed at the thought of Reginald coming home with

honour, to put everything to rights, that I close my eyes for a moment and give thanks to God who has allowed me long enough life to see this. 'How has this come about?' I ask Montague. 'Why is the king doing this, and so easily?'

Montague nods; he has thought about this too. 'I think that he finally understands that he has gone too far. I think Aske told him of the numbers of the pilgrim army and their simple hopes. Aske said that they love the king but blame Cromwell, and the king wants to be loved more than anything. In Aske he sees a good man, a man of principle who is representing good men. He sees a good Englishman, ready to love and follow a good king, driven to rebellion by intolerable changes. When he met Aske he saw another way to be beloved, he saw another way to be kingly. He can throw Cromwell's reputation to them as a sop, he can restore the monasteries. He loves the Church himself, he loves the pilgrim ways. He's never stopped his observance of the liturgy or the rituals. It's as if he suddenly sees a new part in a masque – the king who makes everything well again.'

Montague pauses for a moment, puts a gentle hand on his little son's shoulder. 'Or perhaps, Lady Mother, it's even better than this. Perhaps I am speaking bitterly when I should see a miracle has happened in my lifetime. Perhaps the light has shone on the king, perhaps at last God really has spoken to him, and he has truly changed his mind. Then God be praised, for He has saved England.'

I am normally melancholy in the cold days after the feast of Christmas. The thought of the long winter stretches before me, and I cannot imagine spring. Even when the snow melts on the roof and drips into the gutters I don't think of warmer weather, but gather my furs around me and know that there are many days and weeks of damp and grey mornings before the weather lifts. The thick ice melts and releases the river which is grey and angry, the deep snow clouds roll away from the sky to leave a light which is cold and hard. Normally at this time of year I huddle indoors and complain if anyone leaves a door open anywhere in the house. I can feel the draught, I tell them. I can feel it on my ankles, chilling my feet.

But this year I am contented, like a spoiled cat, soothed by the fire, watching the sleet patter against the window where my grandson Harry draws in the mist on the window panes. This year I imagine Robert Aske riding north, greeted at every inn and house along the way by people wanting to know the news, telling them that the king has come to his senses, that the queen is to be crowned in York, that the king has promised a free parliament and that the abbeys are to be restored to the faithful.

I imagine the monks who hang around the old buildings, begging where they once served, gathering around his horse and asking him to tell them again, to swear that it is true. I think of them opening the doors of the chapel, kneeling before the space where the altar was, promising that they will start again, tolling the bell for the first service. And I think of Robert showing them his golden chain and telling them the king took it from his own neck to put around his shoulders, and told him it was a sign of his favour and offered him a seat on the privy council.

But then we hear of odd reports. Some of the pilgrims who had taken a general pardon seem to have broken the terms of their truce, and are in arms again. Thomas Howard arrests half a dozen ill-doers and sends their names to Thomas Cromwell – and Thomas Cromwell is still in office.

Some of the gentlemen and most of the Northern lords go to talk with Thomas Howard, Duke of Norfolk, and share their concerns about the North becoming unruly in this feast of freedom. Robert Aske assures them, he assures the pilgrims that there is no rebellion against the rule of the king – for see! he carries the king's pardon, he wears the king's scarlet satin jacket. There will always be men who will take advantage of troubled times – they make no difference to the peace and the pardon. The peace will hold, the pardon will hold, the pilgrims have won everything they asked for and the king has given them his word.

And yet Sir Thomas Percy and Sir Ingram Percy, who rode with the pilgrims who marched under the banner of the five wounds, are ordered to come to court, and when they arrive in London, they are arrested immediately and sent to the Tower.

'It means nothing,' Geoffrey says to me as he passes through L'Erber on his way home to Lordington. 'The Percys have always been a law unto themselves, they were using the pilgrims as a shield to defy the king. They are rebels, not pilgrims; they should be in the Tower.'

'But they had been given a pardon?'

'No man would expect the king to honour a pardon to a pair like that.'

I don't argue since Geoffrey is confident, and the news from the North is good. The abbeys are reopening, the pilgrims are dispersing with their pardons, each of them swearing an oath of loyalty to the king, all of them convinced that good times have come at last.. Slowly, quietly, the religious women and men return to the abbeys and they open their doors again. Every village church has the story of a little miracle. People bring a crystal monstrance out of its hiding place under a thatch. Carpenters resurrect the beautiful carvings of saints from where they had been tumbled for safety into the wood piles, farmers dig carefully in the drainage ditches and bring out bright crucifixes. Vestments come out of hidden wardrobes, the monks come back to their cells. They mend the windows, they repair the roofs, I tell my steward to find Prior Richard and invite him back to Bisham.

'Lady Grandmother, do you think my uncle Reginald will come home?' Harry, Montague's boy, asks me. And I answer him smiling: 'Yes. Yes, I think he will.'

But in York in February, nine men are charged with treason by Thomas Howard, Duke of Norfolk, and they are sentenced to be hanged.

'How can they be hanged? Don't they have a pardon?' I ask Geoffrey.

'Lady Mother, the duke is a hard man. He will feel that he has to show the king that though he sympathises with the pilgrims he is hard on the rebels. He'll hang one or two just to show his strength.'

Once again, I don't argue with my son, but I am afraid that the king's pardon is not proving to be a certain guarantee of safety. Certainly, the commons seem to think so, for Carlisle musters its men in desperation and they march against Thomas Howard's army as if they are marching for their lives, staking everything on one last throw of the dice. Hundreds are killed by the well-armed, well-fed, well-mounted lords of the North who were beside them during the pilgrimage, but have abandoned them in the truce.

We get the news in London in the middle of February and the citizens peal the bells in joy that the landless poor men of the North have been defeated by the lords who, only a few months ago, stood by them. They say that Sir Christopher Dacre killed seven hundred men and took the rest prisoner, hanging them on the stunted little trees which is all that grow in the hard north-west, and Thomas Cromwell has promised him an earldom for his service.

Inspired by brutality, Thomas Howard now declares martial law in the North, which means that the magistrates and lords have no power against his rule. Howard can be judge, jury and hang-man to men who have no defence to offer. He declares war on his own countrymen – this is no difficulty for the man who beheaded his own niece and nephew. He holds impromptu hearings in little towns and hands down instant sentences of death. Hundreds of men are forced before him. The chain-makers of Carlisle run out of iron and men have to be hanged wrapped in ropes to signify their shame. Thomas Howard marches out to hang villagers in their own little gardens, so that everyone knows that the pilgrim way led them home to death. His men go into every little village and every hungry hamlet, at the coldest time of year, and demand to know who rode out with the pilgrims and swore an oath? Who rang the church bells backwards? Who prayed for the return of the Church? And who rode out and did not come home again?

Montague writes to me a note from Greenwich, where he is at court.

The king has ordered Norfolk to go to all the monasteries that offered any resistance. He says the monks and canons must be a terrible example for others. I think he means to kill them. Pray for us.

I don't understand the times that I am living in. I read my son's letter, once, twice, three times, and I burn it as soon as I have remembered the terrible words by heart. I go to my chapel and kneel on the cold stone floors and pray, but I find all I am doing is running my beads through my hands and shaking my head, as if I want to deny the terrible things that are happening to the men who called themselves the pilgrims and marched for grace.

The king has heard that some widows and orphans have cut down the bodies of their husbands and fathers, executed as rebels, and buried them secretly, at night, in their churchyards. He has sent to Thomas Howard telling him to find these families and punish them. The bodies are to be dug up out of sanctified ground. He wants the corpses hanged until they rot.

Lady Mother, I think he has run mad.

Thomas Howard, Duke of Norfolk, straining against his own conscience, obeys the king in everything, closing monasteries, and slamming the doors shut on those that had reopened. No-one has any explanation of this, none seems needed. Now the buildings are to be handed to the neighbouring lords for them to use as quarries for stone; the lands are to be sold to nearby farmers. The commons are to look no more to the abbeys for their comfort and help, the monks are to be homeless beggars. Our Lady is not to be invoked in a hundred, a thousand side-chapels and roadside shrines. There are to be no more pilgrimages, there is to be no hope. A song comes out of the North that says there is to be no May, and I look out of the thick glass into the grey courtyard where the snow is slowly melting away, and think that the spring is coming this year without joy, without love, and it is true, the months will change but there will be no merry May.

BISHAM MANOR, BERKSHIRE, SPRING 1537

As soon as the roads are dry enough for travel I leave London and go to Bisham. Harry goes home with his father, his little face puzzled that the season which promised so much does not feel like spring at all. I ride pillion behind my Master of Horse and take some comfort in leaning against the man's broad back as the big horse takes his rolling strides down the muddy road to Berkshire.

So I am out of the city when they bring in Tom Darcy to the Tower, and question him. He has little patience with them, God bless the old man for his fierce temper. He has the king's pardon in his pocket and yet he is under arrest. He looks Thomas Cromwell in the face, and knows him for his judge and jury and yet says to him as they write down his words as evidence against him: 'Cromwell, it is thou that art the very original and chief causer of all this rebellion and mischief.' When the blacksmith's son blinks at this plain speaking, Darcy promises him a certain future death on the scaffold, telling him that if the day comes when there is only one nobleman left alive in England, that single lord will surely behead Thomas Cromwell.

They bring in John Hussey too, the princess's old chamberlain, and I think of him, patiently watching me waste time over the inventory of her jewels, and of his wife's faithful love for her. I pray no-one tells the princess that her former chamberlain is under arrest in the Tower for questioning.

His inquisition, long, detailed, vindictive with petty threats, is of little help to Cromwell, for neither Tom Darcy nor John Hussey will name a single other man or woman. Darcy says nothing about riding with the pilgrims or opening the gates of Pontefract Castle to them. He says that he had the pilgrim badges left in a chest at the castle from his old crusade to the holy land, and he refuses to reveal who received them from his hands. He says: 'Old Tom has not one traitor's tooth in his head,' and he is faithful to the very last.

Henry Courtenay writes to me:

Pray for me, Cousin, for I have been named as Lord High Steward for the trial of those two good lords, John Hussey and Tom Darcy. I have Cromwell's promise that if we find Tom guilty he will have his sentence commuted to banishment – and he can come home later. But there is no hope for John Hussey.

I read the letter standing by the forge, waiting for my horse to be shod, and the moment that I have taken in the meaning I plunge it into the heart of the fire and turn to the messenger in the Exeter livery. 'Are you going straight back to your master?'

He nods.

'Tell him this from me. Make sure you make no mistake. Tell him I recited an old saying; these are not my words but a riddle that the countryfolk say. Tell him the countrymen say not to put a man's head on the block unless you want it struck off. Can you remember that?'

He nods. 'I know it. My grandfather used to say it. He lived in troubled times. "Not to put a man's head on the block unless you want it struck off."'

I give him a penny. 'And don't tell anyone else,' I say. 'And these are not my words.'

I wait for news of the trial. Montague writes to me.

John Hussey is a dead man. Darcy has been found guilty but will be pardoned and spared.

It's a lie from that great liar, Cromwell. And the saying of the people was true – don't put a man's head on the block unless you want it struck off. The lords think they have a promise that will save Tom Darcy and so they find him guilty and wait for the king to commute his sentence of execution into banishment.

But the king fails this great Englishman and he is sent to the block.

BISHAM MANOR, BERKSHIRE, SUMMER 1537

I think of Tom Darcy, and how he hoped he would die on crusade, fighting for his faith, and when they tell me that he was beheaded as a traitor on Tower Hill in June, as the swallows swooped busily from river to Tower building their nests for the summer, I know that he died for his faith, just as he wanted.

A pedlar comes to the back door and says he has a pretty fairing just for me. I go down to the stable yard where he sits on the mounting block with his pack at his feet. He bows when he sees me. 'I have something for you,' he says. 'I said I would give it to you and leave. So now I'm going on.'

'How much?'

He shakes his head and drops a little purse into my hand. 'The man who gave it to me said to wish you luck, and that good times will come,' he says, shoulders his pack and walks from the yard.

I open the purse and tip the little brooch into my hand. It is the pansy brooch that I gave to old Tom Darcy. He never called on me because he thought that he had won a victory and that the king had given his word of pardon. He never called on me because he thought he was guarded by God. I put the brooch in my pocket and walk away.

The culling of the North continues. Eight men and one woman come before the juries charged with treason, lords and gentry, two of them distant kinsmen of mine, all of them known to me, all of them good Christians and loyal subjects. And among them is the Yorkshireman, Robert Aske.

The young man who had the king's satin coat around his shoulders waits for his trial in the Tower of London with no money and no change of clothes and little food. No-one dares to send him anything, and if anyone did, the guards would steal it. He has a full royal pardon for leading the Pilgrimage of Grace and since then, though there have been uprisings and desperate men fighting for their lives, he neither led nor encouraged them. Ever since he returned to the North from the court, he did nothing but try to persuade men to take the pardon and trust the king's word. For this, he is in the Tower. Cleverly, Cromwell suggests that since Aske believed that there would be a parliament in the North, since he swore that the monasteries would be restored, he was assuring people that the pilgrimage had gained its aims, and that this is – must be – treason.

I walk in the hot sunshine in the fields of my home and look at the ripening wheat. It is going to be a good harvest this year. I think of Tom Darcy sending me a message that good times will come, and that Thomas Cromwell has ruled that such a hope is traitorous. I wonder if the seeds of the wheat are planning to ripen and if this is treason? At sunset, a hare bursts out of the crop and runs in a great half-circle before me on the path and then stops, sits on its hinder legs and looks back at me, its eyes dark and intelligent. 'And you?' I say quietly to it. 'Are you biding your time? Are you a traitor, waiting for the good times to return?'

They try everyone that they bring to London and they find everyone guilty. They accuse churchmen: the prior of Guisborough, the abbot of Jervaulx, the abbot of Fountains Abbey. They arrest Margaret Bulmer for loving her husband so much that she begged him to run away when she thought that the pilgrimage had failed. Her own chaplain gives evidence against her and her husband Sir John Bulmer is hanged and quartered at Tyburn as his wife is burned at Smithfield. Sir John is guilty of treason, she is guilty of loving him.

They take Robert Aske from the Tower to the courtroom for his trial and back to prison, though when he was last in London he feasted at the court and was embraced by the king. They take him from the Tower to the North of England, so that he can die in full view of the men who had heard him promise their pardon. They take him to York and parade him around the city that is stunned and silent at the fall of its bravest son. They take him to the very top of Clifford Tower on the walls of York and he reads a confession and they put a rope around his neck where the king put his own chain of gold; they wrap him in chains of iron, and they hang him.

Some of the lords and I spoke to Cromwell for mercy for the Northern men. 'Mercy! Mercy! Mercy!' He has none.

Montague comes to visit me in midsummer. There are fresh rushes down in every room and the windows wide open to the sweet-smelling air so that the house is filled with the singing of birds.

He finds me in the garden, harvesting herbs against the plague, for last summer was terrible, especially for the poor, especially for the North. I have used up all the oils in my physic room and have to make more. Montague kneels before me, and I rest my green-stained hand on his head and notice, for the first time, some silver hairs among the bronze.

'Son Montague, you are going grey,' I say to him severely. 'I can't have a grey-haired son, it will make me feel too old.'

'Well, your darling Geoffrey is going bald,' he says cheerfully, getting up. 'So how will you bear that?'

'How will he bear it?' I smile. Geoffrey has always been dreadfully vain about his good looks.

'He'll wear a cap all the time,' Montague predicts. 'And grow a beard like the king.'

The smile dies from my face. 'How are things at court?' I ask shortly.

'Shall we walk?' He takes my arm and I stroll with him, away from the gardener and the lads, out through the herb garden, through the little wooden gate, and into the meadow that runs down to the river. The mown grass is growing again nearly to our knees; we will take a second crop of hay from this field, rich and green and starred with moon daisies, buttercups and the bright, blowsy heads of poppies.

High above us a lark climbs into the cloudless sky, singing louder and louder with each flutter of its wings. We pause and watch the soaring little dot until it is almost invisible and then the sound abruptly finishes and the bird plunges down to its hidden nest.

'I've been in touch with Reginald,' Montague says. 'The king sent Francis Bryan to capture him, and I had to warn him.'

'Where is he now?'

'He was at Cambrai. He was trapped in the town for some time with Bryan waiting for him to set one foot outside. Bryan said that if he had put one foot into France he would have shot him down.'

'Oh, Montague! Did he get the warning?'

'Yes, but he knows he has to take care. He knows that the king and Cromwell will stop at nothing to silence him. They know that he was in touch with the pilgrims, and that he writes to the princess. They know that he is raising an army against them. Geoffrey wanted to carry the message. Then he told me that he wanted to join Reginald in exile.'

'You told him he couldn't?'

'Of course he can't. But he can't bear this country any longer. The king won't receive him at court, he's in debt again, and he can't bring himself to live under Tudor rule. He was convinced that the pilgrims had won, he thought that the king had seen sense. He doesn't want to stay in England now.'

'And what does he think would become of his children? And what about his wife? And what about his lands?'

Montague smiles. 'Oh, you know what he's like. He flared up and said he would go, and then he thought again and said he would stay and hope for better times. He knows that if another of us were to go into exile it would be even worse for those who stay. He knows he would lose everything if he went.'

'Who took your message to Reginald?'

'Hugh Holland, Geoffrey's old steward. He's set up in shipping wheat in London.'

'I know him.' This is the merchant who trades with Flanders and shipped John Helyar to safety.

'Holland was taking over a load of wheat, and wanted to see Reginald and serve the cause.'

We walk down the little hill, and arrive at the river. A sharp flash of blue like a winged sapphire skims downriver, faster than an arrow, a kingfisher.

'I could never leave,' I say. 'I never even think of leaving. I feel as if I have to bear witness here. I have to be here even when the monasteries are gone, even when the bones of the saints are taken from the shrines and rolled in the gutters.'

'I know,' he says sadly. 'I feel the same. It's my country. Whatever it has to suffer. I have to be here too.'

'He can't go on forever,' I say, knowing that the words are treason, but I am driven to treason. 'He has to die soon. And he has no true heir but our princess.'

'Don't you think that the queen might give him a son?' Montague asks me. 'She's far on. He held a great Te Deum at St Paul's, and then sent her off to Hampton Court for the birth.'

'And our princess?'

'At Hampton Court too, attending the queen. She is kept in her true estate.' He smiles at me. 'The queen is tender to her, and Princess Mary loves her stepmother.'

'And is the king not staying with them?'

'He's afraid of the plague. He's gone off with a riding court.'

'He left the queen to her confinement?'

Montague shrugs. 'Don't you think that if this baby dies too, he would rather be far away? There are enough people saying that he cannot have a healthy son. He won't want to see another baby buried.'

I shake my head at the thought of a young woman left alone to bear her first child and her husband distancing himself from her in case it dies, in case she dies.

'You don't think she will have a healthy boy, do you?' Montague challenges me. 'The pilgrims were all saying that his line is cursed. They said he would never get a living prince because his father had the blood of innocents on his head, because he killed the princes of York, our princes. Is that what you think? That he killed the two York princes and then your brother?'

I shake my head. 'I don't like to think of it,' I say quietly, turning to walk along the little path beside the river. 'I try never to think of it.'

'But do you think the Tudors killed the princes?' he asks, very low. 'Was it My Lady the King's Mother? When she was married to the Constable of the Tower and had her son waiting to invade? Knowing that he could have no claim to the throne while they were alive?'

'Who else?' I reply. 'No-one else gained anything from their deaths. And for sure, we see now that the Tudors have a strong stomach for almost any sin.'

L'ERBER, LONDON, AUTUMN 1537

I am in my great bed in London, with the curtains drawn against the autumn chill, when I hear the bells start to peal, a triumphant clangour that starts up with a single bell and then rings all around the city. I struggle up and wrap a robe around my shoulders as my bedroom door opens and my maid comes in, a candle shaking in her hand in her excitement. 'Your Grace! There is news from Hampton Court! The queen has had a boy! The queen has had a boy!'

'God bless her, and keep her safe,' I say, and I mean it. Nobody could ill-wish Jane Seymour, the mildest of women and a good stepmother to my beloved princess. 'Do they say if the baby is strong?'

The girl smiles and silently shrugs. Of course, under the new laws it is impossible to even ask if the royal baby is well, since this casts a doubt on the king's potency.

'Well, God bless them both,' I say.

'Can we go out?' the girl asks. 'Me and the other girls? There is dancing in the streets and they've built a bonfire.'

'You can go as long as you all stay together,' I tell her. 'And come home at dawn.'

She beams at me. 'Shall you get dressed?' she asks.

I shake my head. It feels as if it is a long, long time since I stayed up all night to watch by the royal bed and took the news of a baby to the king. 'I'll go back to sleep,' I say. 'And we'll say prayers for the health of the queen and the prince in the morning.'

Regular news comes from Hampton Court: the baby is well and thriving, he has been christened Edward, Princess Mary carried him during the ceremony. If he lives, he is the new Tudor heir and she will never be queen; but I know – and who knows better than I, who shared Queen Katherine's five heartbreaks? – that a healthy baby does not mean a future king.

Then we hear, just as I had feared, that the queen's physicians have been called back to Hampton Court. But it is not for the baby; it is the queen who is ill. In those dangerous days after the birth, it seems that the shadow fell on the mother. I go at once to my chapel and pray for Jane Seymour; but she dies that night, only two weeks after the birth of her little son.

They say that the king is devastated, that he has lost the mother of his child and the only woman he truly loved. They say that he will never marry again, that Jane was matchless, perfect, the only true wife he ever had. I think that she has achieved in death the perfection that no woman could show in life. His own perfection is wholly imaginary, now he has an imaginary perfect wife.

'Can he love anyone at all?' Geoffrey asks me. 'This is the king who ordered women tried for treason for the crime of cutting down their husband's corpses and giving them a proper burial. Can he even imagine grief?'

I think of the boy who went white-faced for a year after the death of his mother, but less than a month after the death of his wife he is looking for a new one: a princess of France, or from Spain. Montague, dressed in full mourning, comes to me at L'Erber struggling not to laugh out loud to tell me that the king has asked all the princesses of France to come to Calais so that he can choose the prettiest to be his next bride.

The French are deeply insulted, since it is as if the royal ladies of France were heifers on market day, and no princess is eager to be the fourth queen to a wife-killer; but Henry does not understand that he is no longer highly desirable. He does not realise that he is no longer the handsomest prince in Christendom, famous for his learning and devout life. Now he is ageing – forty-six at the last birthday, fatter every day, and the sworn enemy of the Holy Father, head of the Church. And yet he cannot understand that he is not beloved, not admired, not the centre of all attention.

'Lady Mother, there is one good thing that has come from the death of the queen. You'll find it hard to believe this; but he is restoring the priory,' Montague says.

'What priory?' I ask.

'Ours.'

I don't understand at all. 'He is giving us back Bisham Priory?'

'Yes,' Montague says. 'He called me to his side in the chapel. I went to the royal gallery at Hampton Court where he sits above the chapel in his own little room so he can see the altar. He reads and signs his papers while the priest celebrates the Mass below. He was praying for once, not working, and he crossed himself, kissed his rosary and turned to me with a pleasant smile and said that he wants prayers for Jane's soul and would you oblige him and restore the priory as a chantry for her?'

'But he is closing the great religious houses up and down the country every day! Robert Aske and all the others, hundreds of them, died trying to save the monasteries.'

'Well, now he wants to restore one.'

'But he said that there is no such thing as purgatory and so no need for chantries?'

'Apparently, he wants one for Jane and himself.'

'Cromwell himself appointed the false prior and closed our priory.'

'And that is to be reversed.'

For a moment I am simply stunned, then I see that I am being given the greatest gift for a devout woman: my family's priory back in my keeping. 'This is a great honour to us.' I am quite awed at the thought that we will be allowed to open our beautiful chapel once again, that the monks will sing the plainsong in the echoing gallery, that the sacred Host will stand behind the altar once more in a shining monstrance, and the candles be lit before it, so that the little light shines out of the window into the darkness of a hard world. 'He is really allowing this? Of all the priories and nunneries and monasteries of England that he has closed he is allowing this one light to shine? Our chapel? Where the banners of the white rose hang?'

'He is,' Montague says, smiling. 'I knew it would mean so much to you. I am so glad, Lady Mother.'

'I can make it beautiful again,' I murmur. Already I can imagine the banners hanging once more in the chancel, the quiet shuffle of people coming into the church to hear Mass, the gifts at the door, the hospitality to travellers, and the power and quietness of a place of prayer. 'It is only one place, and only a little place, but I can restore the church at Bisham. It will be the only priory in England, but it will stand, and it will shine a faint holy little light into the dark of Henry's England.'

GREENWICH PALACE, LONDON, CHRISTMAS 1537

Montague and I, accompanied by my grandson Harry as our page boy, visit Greenwich to take our gifts to the king and find a court that is still in mourning for Queen Jane. It is the quietest Christmas that I have ever seen. But the king accepts our gifts with a smile and wishes us the compliments of the season. He asks me if I have seen Prince Edward and gives me permission to visit the little baby in his nursery. He says I may take my grandson and gives a smiling nod to Harry.

The king's fears for his son are painfully evident. There are double guards on the doors and no-one may enter without written permission. No-one at all, not even a duke. I admire the baby who looks well and strong and I press a gold coin into his nurse's hand, saying that I will pray that he stays healthy. I leave him bellowing for a feed, a Tudor in his loud demands.

Having paid my respects I am free to go to the princess's rooms. She has her own little court, her ladies around her, but when she sees me she leaps to her feet and runs to me and I wrap her in my arms and hold her, as I always did.

'And who is this?' She looks down at Harry who is on one knee, his little hand on his heart.

'This is my grandson Harry.'

'I could serve you,' he says breathlessly.

'I should be so pleased to have you in my service.' She gives him her hand and he gets to his feet and bows, his little face dazed with hero-worship.

'Your grandmother will say when you may join my household,' she tells him. 'I expect you are needed at your home.'

'I am no use at home, I am quite idle, they would not miss me at all,' he says, trying to persuade her but succeeding only in making her laugh.

'Then you shall come to me when you are very useful and hard-working,' she says.

She draws me into her privy chamber where we are alone and I can look at her pale face and wipe the tears from her cheeks and smile at her.

'My dearest child.'

'Oh, Lady Margaret!'

At once I can see that she has not been eating properly, there are shadows under her eyes and she is too pale. 'Are you not well?'

She shrugs. 'Nothing out of the ordinary. I was so grieved for the queen. I was so shocked . . . I could not believe that she would die like that . . . for a little while I even doubted my faith. I couldn't see how God could take her . . .'

She breaks off and leans her forehead against my shoulder and I gently pat her back thinking, poor child, to lose such a mother and then to love and lose a stepmother! This girl will spend the rest of her life longing for someone she can trust and love.

'We have to believe that she is with God,' I say gently. 'And we sing Masses for her soul in my own chapel at Bisham.'

She smiles at this. 'Yes, the king told me. I am so glad. But Lady Margaret! The other abbeys!'

I put a finger gently over her lips 'I know. There is much to mourn.'

'Do you hear from your son?' she whispers, her voice so soft that I have to bend to hear her. 'From Reginald?'

'He was raising support for the pilgrims when they made peace and forged their agreement with your father,' I say. 'When he got news of their defeat he was recalled to Rome. He's there now, safe.'

She nods. There is a tap at her door and one of the new maids puts her head into the room. 'We can't talk now,' the princess decides. 'But when you write to him you can tell him that I am well treated, I think I am safe. And now that I have a little brother my father is at peace with me, and with my half-sister, Elizabeth. He has a son, at last. Perhaps he can be happy.'

I take her hand and we go out to where her ladies, some of them friends and some of them spies, all rise and curtsey to us. I smile equably at all of them.

WARBLINGTON CASTLE, HAMPSHIRE, SUMMER 1538

I spend the summer at my house at Warblington. The court on progress passes nearby, but this year there are no Knights Harbinger, riding down the road to make sure that I can house the great party. The king does not want to stay, though the fields are as green and as wide and the forests as richly stocked with game as they were when he said it was his favourite house in England.

I look at the great wing that I built for the comfort of Queen Katherine and her young husband and think that it was money wasted, and love wasted. I think that money or love offered to the Tudors is always wasted, for the Tudor boy who was so well loved by his mother has been spoiled by us all.

I hear from my house at Bisham that Thomas Cromwell has taken the priory away from us, for the second time. The monks who were to pray for Jane Seymour have been told to leave, the chantry that was to stand forever, the only chantry in England, is quiet. The bishop's cope is taken away, our priory is closed again. It was reopened on a Tudor whim; it closes on Cromwell's command. I do not even write to protest.

At least I am confident that the princess is safe at Hampton

Court, visiting her half-brother at Richmond Palace. Without doubt she will have a new stepmother before the year is out and I pray every night that the king chooses a woman who will be kind to our princess. They will be looking for a husband for her too, the Portuguese royal family has been suggested, and Montague and I agree that whatever my age and wherever she is sent, I must go with her to see her settled in her new home.

I am busy this summer in Warblington, preparing for the harvest and bringing the records up to date, but one day my steward comes to tell me that a new patient at our little hospital, a man called Gervase Tyndale, has been asking the surgeon Richard Eyre why there are no books of the new learning in the church or at the hospital. Someone tells him that it is common knowledge that I, and all my family, believe in the old ways, in the priest telling the word of God to the faithful, in the holy Mass, in faith not deeds.

'He asked after that horse groom that you dismissed, my lady. The Lutheran that would have converted half the stable yard? And he asked after your chaplain, John Helyar, and if he ever visits your son Reginald in Rome or wherever he is. And he asks what your son Reginald is doing, staying away from England for so long.'

There is always gossip in a small village. There is always gossip about the big house. But I feel a sense of unease that this is gossip about the castle, about the hospital, about our faith, just as we have come unscathed through the pilgrimage, and just as our princess has found some safety where she belongs

'I think you had better tell this man to mind his manners towards his hosts,' I say to the steward. 'And tell Mr Eyre the surgeon that I don't need my opinions shared with half the country.'

The steward grins. 'No harm done,' he says. 'There's nothing to know. But I'll have a quiet word.'

I think little more of this until I am in my presence chamber, dealing with the business of the estate, Montague at my side, when Geoffrey comes in with Richard Eyre the surgeon, and Hugh Holland, his friend the grain merchant. At the sight of him

I find myself sharply alert, like a deer freezing at the snap of a twig. I wonder why Geoffrey has brought these men to me.

'Lady Mother, I would speak with you,' Geoffrey says, kneeling for my blessing.

I know my smile is strained. 'Is there trouble?' I ask him.

'I don't think so. But the surgeon here says that a patient at the hospital . . .'

'Gervase Tyndale,' the surgeon interrupts with a bow.

'A patient at the hospital wanted to set up a school here for the new learning, and someone told him that there was no call for that here, and that you would not allow it. Now he's gone off full of ill-will, telling everyone that we don't allow the books that the king has licensed, and that Hugh Holland here, my friend, comes and goes between us and Reginald.'

'There's nothing wrong with this,' I say cautiously, glancing at Montague. 'It's gossip that we could do without, but there's no evidence..'

'No, but it can be made to sound wrong,' Geoffrey points out.

'And this is the merchant that went to Reginald with my warning,' Montague says quietly in my ear. 'And he shipped your chaplain overseas for us. So there is a little fire under this smoke.' Aloud he turns to the surgeon. 'And where is this Mr Tyndale now?'

'I sent him away as soon as he was well,' the surgeon says promptly. 'My lady's steward told me that she didn't like gossip.'

'You can be sure that I don't,' I say sharply to him. 'I pay you to heal the poor, not to chatter about me.'

'Nobody knows where he is,' Geoffrey says nervously. 'Or if he has been watching us for a while. Do you think he might have gone to Thomas Cromwell?'

Montague smiles without amusement. 'It's a certainty.'

'How are you so sure?'

'Because anyone with any information always goes to Cromwell.'

'What should we do?' Geoffrey looks from me to his older brother.

'You'd better go to Cromwell yourself. Tell him about this little disagreement, and that this bunch of old women are gossiping about nothing.' I glare at the surgeon. 'Assure him of our loyalty. Remind him that the king himself restored our priory at Bisham and say that we have a Bible in English at the church that anyone may read. Tell him that we teach the new learning in the little school from books that His Majesty licenses. Tell him that the schoolmaster is teaching the children to read so that they may study their prayers in English. And let these good men explain what is said against them, and that we are all loyal servants to the king.'

Geoffrey looks anxious. 'Will you come with me?' he asks Montague very quietly.

'No,' Montague says firmly. 'This is nothing. There is nothing to fear. Better that just one of us goes to tell Cromwell that there is nothing to interest him here, not here at the castle, not at the manor. Tell him that Mr Holland took a message of family news to Reginald, months ago, nothing more. But go today, and tell him everything. He probably knows everything already. But if you go and tell him then you have the appearance of openness.'

'Can't you come?'

Geoffrey asks so pitifully that I turn to Montague and say: 'Son, won't you go with him? You can talk more easily with Thomas Cromwell than Geoffrey can.'

Montague laughs shortly and shakes his head. 'You don't know how Cromwell thinks,' he says. 'If we both go, it looks as if we are worried. You go, Geoffrey, and tell him everything. We've got nothing to hide, and he knows that. But go today, so that you can get our side of the story told before this Tyndale gets there and puts his report in to his master.'

'And take some money,' I say very quietly.

'You know I don't have a penny in the world!' Geoffrey says irritably.

'Montague will give you something from the treasure room,' I say. 'Give Thomas Cromwell a gift and my good wishes.'

'How will I know what to give him?' Geoffrey exclaims. 'He knows I have a pocket full of debt.'

'He will know this comes from me as a pledge of our friend-ship,' I say smoothly. I take my great keys and lead the way to our treasure room.

The door opens with two locks. Geoffrey pauses on the thresh-old and looks around with a sigh of longing. There are shelves of chalices for use in the chapel, there are boxes of coin, copper for the woodcutters and the day labourers, silver for the quarterly wages, and locked chests of gold bolted to the floor. I take a beau-tifully worked cup of silver gilt from its wool cover. 'This is perfect for him.'

'Silver gilt?' Geoffrey asks doubtfully. 'Wouldn't you send something in gold?'

I smile. 'It's flashy, it's new-made, it sparkles more than it shines. It's Cromwell to the life. Take that to him.'

Geoffrey comes back from London, filled with pride at his own cleverness. He tells me how he spoke to Thomas Cromwell – 'not as if I was anxious or anything, but man to man, easily, as one great man to another' – and that Cromwell had understood at once this was the gossip of jealous village people about their bet-ters. He told the Lord Chancellor that of course we wrote to Reginald about family matters, and that Hugh Holland had car-ried messages from us, but that we had never stopped blaming Reginald for his terrible letter to the king, and indeed, had begged him to make sure that it was never published, and that he had promised us that it would be suppressed.

'I told him it was bad theology and badly written!' Geoffrey tells me gleefully. 'I reminded him that you wrote to Reginald and sent a message through Cromwell himself.'

Geoffrey succeeds so well with Thomas Cromwell that Hugh Holland's goods which had been seized on the quayside are returned in full to him, and the three men, Holland, my son and the surgeon, are at liberty to come and go as they please.

Geoffrey and I ride down to Buckinghamshire together to take the good news to Montague, who is at his house at Bockmer. We have half a dozen outriders and my granddaughters Katherine and Winifred come with me to their family home.

We ride towards the familiar fields and trees of Montague's lands and then I see, coming towards us, the rippling royal standard at the head of a guard, riding fast. The captain of my guard shouts: 'Halt!' and 'Stand by!' as we give way to the king's men on the highway, as all good subjects must do.

There are a dozen of them, dressed for riding but wearing breastplates and carrying swords and lances. The rider at the front has the royal standard of the three fleurs-de-lys and the three lions, which he dips in salute to my standard as he sees us waiting for him to pass. They are travelling fast, at a punishing sitting trot, and at the centre of the cavalcade is a prisoner, a man, bare-headed with his jerkin torn at the shoulder, a bruise darkening his cheekbone, his hands tied behind him and his feet lashed under the horse's belly.

'God save me,' Geoffrey breathes. 'It's Hugh Holland, the corn merchant.'

The round, smiling face of the London merchant is blenched and pale, his hands gripping the crupper behind him to hold himself on the swiftly moving horse, as he is badly jolted with the hammering pace.

They ride past us without slowing. The captain throws us a swift suspicious glare, as if he thinks we might have ridden to rescue Hugh Holland. I raise my hand to recognise his authority and this draws Hugh's attention. He sees our standard and my men's livery, and shouts out to Geoffrey: 'Keep on your way, for you'll come after me!'

In the noise of the horses' bits and the jostle of the riders, in the confusion of the dust and the rush of their passing, they are gone before Geoffrey can reply. He turns to me, white-faced, and says: 'But Cromwell was clear. He was satisfied. We explained.'

'This might be something else altogether,' I say, though I don't think that it is. 'Let's get to Montague's house and ask your brother.'

BOCKMER HOUSE, BUCKINGHAMSHIRE, SUMMER 1538

Montague's house is in uproar. The king's men broke tables, settles and benches in the great hall when they arrested Hugh Holland and he fought against them and ran around the hall as they crashed after him like clumsy hounds after a terrified deer.

My daughter-in-law Jane has gone to her private room in tears. Montague is supervising the servants setting up the tables in the hall and trying to make light of it all. But I can tell that he is shaken when Geoffrey bursts in shouting: 'Why have they taken him? What reason did they give?'

'They don't have to give a reason, Geoffrey. You know that.'

'But Cromwell himself assured me!'

'Indeed. And the king pardoned Robert Aske.'

'Hush,' I say instantly. 'There is some mistake here, there is no need for us to fear. This is between Hugh Holland and the law. Nothing to do with us.'

'They searched my private rooms,' Montague says tightly, turning away from the men who are picking up the scattered pewter. 'They tore my house apart. It is to do with us.'

'What did they find?' Geoffrey whispers.

'Nothing,' Montague says tightly. 'I burn my letters as soon as I have read them.' He turns to me. 'You keep nothing, do you, Lady Mother? You burn them as you read?'

I nod. 'I do.'

'Nothing as a keepsake? Not even from Reginald?'

I shake my head. 'Nothing. Ever.'

Geoffrey is pale. 'I have some papers,' he confesses. 'I have kept some papers.'

Montague rounds on him. 'What?' he demands. 'No, don't tell me. I don't want to know. Fool! You're a fool, Geoffrey. Get them destroyed. I don't want to know how.'

He takes me by the arm to lead me from the hall. I hesitate; this is my son, my darling son.

'Send the chaplain, John Collins,' I say quickly to Geoffrey over my shoulder. 'You can trust him. Send him to your steward or, better, to Constance and tell her to burn everything in your room.'

Geoffrey nods, white-faced, and scurries out.

'Why is he such a fool?' Montague demands, dragging me up the stairs to his wife's presence chamber. 'He should never keep anything, he knows that.'

'He's not a fool,' I say, catching my breath and making the men pause before opening the door. 'But he loves the Church as it was. He was raised at Syon Abbey, it was our refuge. You can't blame him for loving his home. He was a little boy and we had nothing, we lived off the Church as if it were our family. And he loves the princess, as I do. He can't help but show it.'

'Not in these times,' Montague says shortly. 'We can't afford to show our love. Not for a moment. The king is a dangerous man, Lady Mother. You never know these days how he will take something. One minute he's suspicious and anxious and the next he's draped around your shoulder and is your best friend. He watches me like he could eat me up, gobble me for his pleasure; and then he sings "Pastime With Good Company" and it's like the old days. You never know where you are with him.

'But he always remembers – he never forgets – that his throne was won on a battlefield by chance and by treason. Chance and treason can turn against him, just as easily. And he has one frail son in a cradle and no-one who would defend him. And he knows that there is a curse, and he knows that it justly falls on his house.'

Montague's wife, Jane, is frightened and crying in her room as I enter with Katherine and Winifred, and she pulls them towards her, blesses them and says that she will never forgive their father for exposing them to danger. Little Harry makes his bow to me and stands staunchly beside his father as if he is afraid of nothing.

'I don't want to hear another word, Jane,' I say flatly to her. 'Not another word.'

That checks her and she curtseys to me. 'I am sorry, Lady Mother. It was a shock. And that terrible man running away from the guard, and they broke some glasses.'

'We must be glad that Lord Cromwell seized him if he is guilty, and if he is innocent he will be quickly freed,' I say stoutly. I drop my hand onto Harry's straight little shoulder. 'We have nothing to fear for we have always been loyal to the king.'

He looks up at me. 'We are loyal cousins,' he volunteers.

'We are, and we always have been.'

Jane follows my cue and for the rest of the day we try to act as if we were making a normal family visit. We dine in the great hall and the household pretends to be merry as we on the high table, looking down on them feasting and drinking, try to smile and chatter.

After dinner we send the children to their rooms, leave the household to their drink and gambling, and go into Montague's private chambers. Geoffrey cannot settle, cannot sit in one place. He prowls about from window to fireplace, from settle to stool.

'I had a copy of a sermon,' he says suddenly. 'But it was preached before the king! There can be no harm in that. And anyway, Collins will have burned it.'

'Peace.' Montague looks up at him.

'I had some letters from Bishop Stokesley, but there was nothing in them,' he says.

'You should have burned them the moment that you got them,' Montague says. 'As I told you. Years ago.'

'There was nothing in them!' Geoffrey exclaims.

'But he, in turn, may have written something to someone else. You don't want to bring trouble to his door, nor for his other friends to bring trouble to yours.'

'Oh, do you burn everything?' Geoffrey suddenly demands, thinking that he will catch out his brother.

'Yes, as I told you, years ago,' Montague replies calmly. He looks at me. 'You do, don't you, Lady Mother?'

'Yes,' I say. 'There is nothing at any of my homes for them to find, should they ever come to look.'

'Why should they ever come to look?' Jane says irritably.

'Because we are who we are,' I answer her. 'And you know that, Jane. You were born a Neville yourself. You know what it means. We are the Plantagenets. We are the white rose, and the king knows that the people love us.'

She turns her bitter face away. 'I thought I was marrying into a great house,' she says. 'I didn't think that I was joining a family in danger.'

'Greatness means danger,' I say simply. 'And I think you knew that then, as now.'

Geoffrey walks to the window, looks out, turns back to the room. 'I think I'll go to London,' he says. 'I'll go and I'll see Thomas Cromwell and find out what he is doing with Hugh Holland, and tell him,' he snatches a breath, he has quite run out of air, 'tell him,' he says more strongly, 'that there is nothing against Holland and nothing against me, and nothing against any of us.'

'I'll come with you,' Montague says, surprisingly.

'Will you?' I ask, as Jane suspends her needle and looks up at her husband as if she would forbid it. Her gaze flicks to me as if she would ask me to send my youngest son without a protector, so that she can keep her husband safe at home.

'Yes,' Montague says. 'Cromwell needs to know that he cannot play cat and mouse with us. He is a great cat in the king's barn, none greater. But still, I think we have credit that we can draw on. And he needs to know he does not frighten us.' He looks at Geoffrey's aghast expression. 'He does not frighten me,' he corrects himself.

'What do you think, Lady Mother?' Jane prompts me to forbid my two sons going together.

'I think it's a very good idea,' I say calmly. 'We have nothing to hide and we have nothing to fear. We have done nothing against the law. We love the Church and honour the princess but that's no crime. Not even Cromwell can compose a law that makes that a crime. You go, Son Montague, you go with my blessing.'

I stay at Bockmer House for a week, waiting for news with Jane and the children. Montague sends us a letter the moment that he arrives in London, but after that there is silence.

'I think I'll go to London myself,' I say to her. 'And I will write to you as soon as I have news.'

'Please do, Lady Mother,' she says stiffly. 'I am always glad to know that you are in good health.'

She comes down with me to the stable yard and stands by my horse as I wearily climb from mounting block to the pillion saddle behind my Master of Horse. In the stable yard my companions mount their horses: my two granddaughters, Jane's girls, Katherine and Winifred. Harry will stay home with his mother, though he is fidgeting from one foot to another, trying to catch my eye, hoping that I will take him with me. I smile down at her pale face. 'Don't be frightened, Jane,' I say. 'We've got through worse than this.'

'Have we?'

I think of the history of my family, of the defeats and battles, the betrayals and executions which stain our history and serve as fingerposts to our ceaseless march on and off the throne of England. 'Oh yes,' I say. 'Much worse.'

L'ERBER, LONDON, SUMMER 1538

Montague comes to me the moment that I arrive in London. We dine in the hall as if this was an ordinary visit, he talks pleasantly of the court and the good health of the baby prince, and then we withdraw to the private room behind the high table and close the door.

'Geoffrey's in the Tower,' he says quietly the moment that I am seated, as if he feared I would fall at the news. He takes my hand and looks into my stunned face. 'Try to be calm, Lady Mother. He's not accused of anything, there is nothing that they can put against him. This is how Cromwell works, remember. He frightens people into rash words.'

I feel as if I am choking, I put my hand to my heart and I can feel the hammering of my pulse under my fingers like a drum. I snatch at a breath and find that I cannot breathe. Montague's worried face looking into mine becomes blurred as my eyesight grows dim, I even think for a moment that I am dying of fear.

Then there is a gust of warm air on my face, and I am breathing again, and Montague says: 'Say nothing, Lady Mother, until you have your breath, for here are Katherine and Winifred that I called to help you when you were taken faint.'

He holds my hand and pinches my fingertip so that I say nothing but smile at my granddaughters and say: 'Oh, I am quite well now. I must have overeaten at dinner for I had such a gripping pain. It serves me right for taking so much of the pudding.'

'Are you sure that you are well?' Katherine says, looking from me to her father. 'You're very pale?'

'I'm quite well now,' I say. 'Would you bring me a little wine and Montague can mull it for me, and I shall be well in a moment.'

They bustle off to fetch it, while Montague closes the window, and the sounds of evening on a London street are cut off. I straighten a shawl around my shoulder and thank them as they come back with the wine and curtscy and go.

We say nothing while Montague plunges the heated rod into the silver jug and it seethes and the scent of the hot wine and spices fills the little room. He hands me a cup and pours his own, and pulls up a stool to sit at my feet, as if he were a boy again, in the boyhood that he never had.

'I am sorry,' I say. 'Behaving like a fool.'

'I was shocked myself. Are you all right now?'

'Yes. You can tell me. You can tell me what is happening.'

'When we got here, we asked to see Cromwell, and he put us off for days. In the end I met him as if by accident, and told him that there were rumours about us, contrary to our good name, and that I would be glad to know that Gervase Tyndale had his tongue slit as a warning to others. He didn't say yes and he didn't say no, but he asked me to bring Geoffrey to his house.'

Montague leans forward and pushes the logs of the fire with the toe of his riding boot. 'You know what the Cromwell house is like,' he says. 'Apprentices everywhere, clerks everywhere, you can't tell who is who, and Cromwell walking through the middle of it all as if he is a lodger.'

'I've never been to his home,' I say disdainfully. 'We're not on dining terms.'

'Well, no,' Montague says with a smile. 'But at any rate, it is a busy, friendly, interesting place, and the people waiting to see him would make your eyes stand out of your head! Everyone of every sort and condition, all of them with business for him or reports for him, or spying for him – who knows?'

'And you and Geoffrey saw him?'

'He talked with us and then he asked us to dine with him, and we stayed and ate a good dinner. Then he had to go and he asked Geoffrey to come back the next day, as there were some few things he wanted to clear up.'

I feel my chest become tight again, and I tap the base of my throat, as if to remind my heart to keep beating. 'And Geoffrey went?'

'I told him to go. I told him to be completely frank. Cromwell had read the message that Holland took to Reginald. He knew it wasn't about the price of wheat in Berkshire last summer. He knew we warned him that Francis Bryan had been sent to capture him. He accused Geoffrey of disloyalty.'

'But not treason?'

'No, not treason. It's not treason to tell a man, your own brother, that someone is coming to kill him.'

'And Geoffrey confessed?'

Montague sighs. 'He denied it to start with, but then it was obvious that Holland had told Cromwell both messages. Geoffrey's message to Reginald, and Reginald's replies to us.'

'But still they are not treason.' I find I am clinging to this fact.

'No. But obviously he must have tortured Holland to get the messages.'

I swallow, thinking of the round-faced man that came to my house, and the bruise on his cheek when he was hurried past us on the road. 'Would Cromwell dare to torture a London merchant?' I ask. 'What about his guild? What about his friends? What about the City merchants? Don't they defend their own?'

'Cromwell must think he's on to something. And apparently he does dare, and that's why, yesterday, he arrested Geoffrey.'

'He won't ... he won't ...' I find I can't name my fear.

'No, he won't torture Geoffrey, he wouldn't dare touch one of us. The king's council would not allow it. But Geoffrey is in a panic. I don't know what he might say.'

'He'd never say anything that would hurt us,' I say. I find I am smiling, even in this danger, at the thought of my son's loving, faithful heart. 'He'd never say anything that would hurt any of us.'

'No, and besides, at the very worst, all we have done is warn a brother that he is in danger. Nobody could blame us for that.'

'What can we do?' I ask. I want to rush to the Tower at once, but my knees are weak, and I can't even rise.

'We're not allowed to visit; only his wife can go into the Tower to see him. So I've sent for Constance. She'll be here tomorrow. And after she's seen him and made sure that he's not said anything, I'll go to Cromwell again. I might even speak with the king when he comes back, if I can catch him in a good mood.'

'Does Henry know of this?'

'It's my hope he knows nothing. It might be that Cromwell has overreached himself and that the king will be furious with him when he finds out. His temper is so unreliable these days that he lashes out at Cromwell as often as he agrees with him. If I can catch him at the right time, if he is feeling loving towards us, and irritated by Cromwell, he might take this as an insult to us, his kinsmen, and knock Cromwell down for it.'

'He is so changeable?'

'Lady Mother, none of us ever knows from dawn to dusk what mood he will be in, nor when or why it will suddenly change.'

I spend the rest of the evening and most of the night on my knees in my chapel, praying to my God for the safety of my son; but I can't be sure that He is listening. I think of the hundreds, thousands of mothers on their knees in England tonight, praying for the safety of their sons, or for the souls of their sons who have died for less than Geoffrey and Montague have done.

I think of the abbey doors banging open in the moonlight of the English summer night, of the sacred chests and holy goods tumbled onto shining cobbles in darkened squares as Cromwell's men pull down the shrines and throw out the relics. They say that Thomas Becket's shrine, which the king himself approached on his knees, has been broken up and the rich offerings and the magnificent jewels have disappeared into Lord Cromwell's new Court of Augmentations, and the saint's sacred bones have been lost.

After a little while I sit back on my heels and feel the ache in my back. I cannot bring myself to trouble God; there is too much for Him to put right tonight. I think of Him, old and weary as I am old and weary, feeling as I do, that there is too much to put right and that England, His own special country, has gone all wrong.

L'ERBER, LONDON, AUTUMN 1538

Constance goes straight to the Tower as soon as she arrives in London, and then comes to L'Erber. I take her into my privy chamber and give her a cup of mulled ale, take her gloves from her cold hands, and unwrap her cape and her shawls from her thin shoulders. She looks from me to Montague as if she thinks the two of us can save her.

'I've never seen him like this before,' she says. 'I don't know what I can do.'

'What is he like?' Montague asks gently.

'Crying,' she says. 'Raging round the room. Banging on the door but no-one comes. Taking hold of the bars of the window and shaking them as if he thinks he might bring down the walls of the Tower. And then he turned and fell on his knees and wept and said he could not bear it.'

I am horrified. 'Have they hurt him?'

She shakes her head. 'They've not touched his body – but his pride . . .'

'Did he say what they put to him?' Montague asks patiently.

She shakes her head. 'Don't you hear me? He's raving. He's in a frenzy.'

'He's not coherent?'

I can hear the hope in Montague's voice.

'He's like a madman,' she says. 'He's praying and crying, and then he suddenly declares that he's done nothing, and then he says that everyone always blames him, and then he says he should have run away but that you stopped him, that you always stop him, and then he says that he cannot stay in England anyway for the debts.' Her eyes slide to me. 'He says that his mother should pay his debts.'

'Could you tell if he has been properly questioned? Has he been charged with any offence?'

She shakes her head. 'We have to send him clothes and food,' she says. 'He's cold. There's no fire in his room, and he has only his riding cape. And he threw that down on the floor and stamped on it.'

'I'll do that at once,' I say.

'But you don't know if he has been properly questioned, nor what he has said?' Montague confirms.

'He says that he has done nothing,' she repeats. 'He says that they come and shout at him every day. But he says nothing for he has done nothing.'

Geoffrey's ordeal goes on another day. I send my steward with a parcel of his warm clothes and with orders to buy food from the bakehouse near the Tower and take in a proper meal for my boy, although he comes back and says that the guards took the clothes but he thought they would keep them, and that he was not allowed to order a meal.

'I'll go with Constance tomorrow, and see if I can command them to take him a dinner at least,' I say to Montague, as I enter the echoing presence chamber at L'Erber. It is empty of anyone, no petitioners, no tenants, no friends. 'And she can take in a winter cape and some linen for him, and some bedding.'

He is standing at the window, his head bowed, in silence.

'Did you see the king?' I ask him. 'Could you speak to him for Geoffrey? Did he know that Geoffrey is under arrest?'

'He knew already,' Montague says dully. 'There was nothing I could say, for he knew already.'

'Cromwell acted with his authority?'

'That we'll never know. Lady Mother. Because the king didn't know about Geoffrey from Cromwell. He knew from Geoffrey himself. Apparently, Geoffrey has written to him.'

'Written to the king?'

'Yes. Cromwell showed me the letter. Geoffrey wrote to the king that if the king will order him some comforts then he will tell all he knows, even though it touches his own mother, or brother.'

For a moment I hear the words but I cannot make out the meaning. Then I understand. 'No!' I am horror-struck. 'It can't be true. It must be a forgery. Cromwell must be tricking you! It's what he would do!'

'No. I saw the note. It was Geoffrey's hand. I am not mistaken. Those were his exact words.'

'He offered to betray me and you for some warm clothes and a good dinner?'

'It seems so.'

'Montague, he must have lost his mind. He would never do such a thing, he would never hurt me. He must be witless. My God, my poor boy, he must be in a delirium.'

'Let's hope so,' Montague says spitefully. 'For if he is mad he cannot testify.'

Constance comes back from the Tower supported by two manservants, unable to walk, unable to speak.

'Is he ill?' I take her by the shoulders and stare into her face as if I can see what is wrong with my son by the blank horror of his wife's expression. 'What's the matter? What's the matter, Constance? Tell me?'

She shakes her head. She moans. 'No, no.'

'Has he lost his wits?'

She hides her face in her hands and sobs.

'Constance, speak to me! Have they racked him?' I name my worst fear.

'No, no.'

'He doesn't have the Sweat, does he?'

She raises her head. 'Lady Mother, he tried to kill himself. He took a knife from the table and he threw himself on it and stabbed himself nearly to his heart.'

Abruptly I let her go and grab a tall chair to support myself. 'Is it fatal? A fatal wound? My boy?'

She nods. 'It's very bad. They wouldn't let me stay with him. I saw thick bandages around his chest, they had him strapped twice. He didn't speak. He couldn't speak. He was lying on his bed, blood seeping through the bandages. They told me what he had done and he didn't speak. He just turned his face to the wall.'

'He has seen a physician? They had bandaged him?'

She nods.

Montague comes into the room behind us, his face ghastly, his smile twisted. 'A knife from his dinner table?'

'Yes,' she says.

'And did he have a good dinner?'

It is a question so odd, so strange to ask in the middle of this tragedy that she turns and stares at him.

She does not know what he means; but I do.

'He had a very good dinner, several dishes, and there was a fire in the grate, and someone had sent him new clothes,' she replies.

'Our clothes?'

'No,' she says, bewildered. 'Someone had sent him some comforts, new things; but they didn't tell me who.'

Montague nods and goes from the room without another word, without looking at me.

Next morning, at a quiet breakfast in my chamber, the two of us close together at the little table before my bedroom fire, Montague tells me that his manservant did not come home last night, and nobody knows where he is.

'What d'you think?' I ask quietly.

'I think that Geoffrey has named him as a servant who takes letters and messages for me, and that he has been arrested,' Montague says quietly.

'Son, I cannot believe that Geoffrey would betray us, or any of our people.'

'Lady Mother, he promised the king that he would betray us both for warm clothes, firewood, and a good dinner. He was served a good dinner yesterday and they have taken his breakfast in to him today. Right now he is being questioned by William Fitzwilliam, the Earl of Southampton. He is leading the inquiry. It would have been better for Geoffrey, and better for us, if he had put the knife in his heart and driven it home.'

'Don't!' I raise my voice to Montague. 'Don't say that! Don't say that foolish thing. Don't say that wicked thing. You speak like a child who knows nothing of death. It is never, *never* better to die. Never think that it is. Son, I know you are afraid. Don't you think I am too? I saw my brother go into that very Tower and he only came out to his death. My own father died in there, charged with treason. Don't you think that the Tower is a constant horror to me, and to think that Geoffrey is in there is like the worst of nightmares? And now I think that they might take me? And now I think that they might take you? My son? My heir?' I fall silent at the sight of his face.

'You know, sometimes I think of it as our family home,' he says very quietly, so quietly that I can hardly hear him. 'Our oldest and truest family seat. And that the Tower graveyard is our family tomb, the Plantagenet vault where we are all, in the end, going.'

Constance visits her husband again but finds him in a haze of fever from his wound. He is well nursed and well served but when she goes to see him there is a woman in the room – the one who usually comes to lay out the dead – and a guard at the door and he can say nothing to her in private.

'But he has nothing to say,' she says quietly to me. 'He didn't look at me, he didn't ask after the children, he didn't even ask after you. He turned his face to the wall and he wept.'

Montague's servant Jerome does not reappear at L'Erber. We have to assume that he is either under arrest or he is held in Cromwell's house, waiting for the day when he will offer evidence.

And then, just after Terce, the doors to the street are flung open and the yeomen of the guard march into the entrance hall, to arrest my son Montague.

We were going to breakfast, and Montague turns as the golden leaves from the vine blow in from the street about the feet of the guards. 'Shall I come at once, or take my breakfast first?' he asks, as if it is a small matter of everyone's convenience.

'Better come now, sir,' the captain says a little awkwardly. He bows to me and to Constance. 'Begging your pardon, your lady-ship, my lady.'

I go to Montague. 'I'll get food and clothing to you,' I promise him. 'And I'll do what I can. I'll go to the king.'

'No. Go back to Bisham,' he says quickly. 'Keep far away from the Tower. Go today, Lady Mother.'

His face is very grave; he looks far older than his forty-six years. I think that they took my brother when he was only a little boy, and killed him when he was a young man; and now here is my son, and it has taken all this long time, all these many years, for them to come for him. I am dizzy with fear, I cannot think what I should do. 'God bless you, my son,' I say.

He kneels before me, as he has done a thousand, thousand times, and I put my hand on his head. 'God bless us all,' he says simply. 'My father lived his life trying to avoid this day. Me too. Perhaps it will end well.'

And he gets up and goes out of the house without a hat or a cape or gloves.

I am in the stable yard, watching them pack the wagons for us to leave, when one of the Courtenay men brings me a message from Gertrude, wife to Henry Courtenay, my cousin.

They have arrested Henry this morning. I will come to you when I can.

I cannot wait for her, so I tell the guards and the household wagons to go ahead, down the frozen roads to Warblington, and that I will follow later on my old horse. I take half a dozen men and my granddaughters Katherine and Winifred and ride through the narrow streets to Gertrude's beautiful London house, the Manor of the Rose. The City is getting ready for Christmas, the chestnut sellers are standing behind glowing braziers stirring the scorching nuts and the evocative scents of the season – mulled wine, cinnamon, woodsmoke, burnt sugar, nutmeg – are hanging in trails of grey smoke on the frosty air.

I leave the horses at the great street door and my granddaughters and I walk into the hall and then into Gertrude's presence chamber. It is oddly quiet and empty. Her steward comes forward to greet me.

'Countess, I am sorry to see you here.'

'Why?' I ask. 'My cousin Lady Courtenay was coming to see me. I have come to say goodbye to her. I am going into the country.' Little Winifred comes close to me and I take her small hand for comfort.

'My lord has been arrested.'

'I knew that. I am certain that he will be released at once. I know that he is innocent of anything.'

The steward bows. 'I know, my lady. There is no more loyal servant to the king than my lord. We all know that. We all said that, when they asked us.'

'So where is my cousin Gertrude?'

He hesitates. 'I am sorry, your ladyship. But she has been arrested too. She has gone to the Tower.'

I suddenly understand that the silence of this room is filled with the echoes of a place that has been abruptly cleared. There are pieces of needlework on the windowseat, and an open book on the reader in the corner of the room.

I look around and I realise that this tyranny is like the other Tudor disease, the Sweat. It comes quickly, it takes those you love without warning, and you cannot defend against it. I have come too late, I should have been earlier. I have not defended her, I did not save Montague, or Geoffrey. I did not speak up for Robert Aske, nor for Tom Darcy, John Hussey, Thomas More, nor for John Fisher.

'I'll take Edward home with me,' I say, thinking of Gertrude's son. He is only twelve, he must be frightened. They should have sent him to me at once, the minute his parents were arrested. 'Fetch him for me. Tell him that his cousin is here to take him home while his mother and father are detained.'

Inexplicably, the steward's eyes fill with tears, and then he tells me why the house is so quiet. 'He's gone,' he says. 'They took him too. The little lord. He's gone to the Tower.'

WARBLINGTON CASTLE, HAMPSHIRE, AUTUMN 1538

My steward comes into my private chamber, tapping on the door and then stepping in, closing the door behind him as if to keep something secret. Outside I can hear the buzz of the people who have come to see me. I am alone, trying to find the courage to go out and face the inquiries about rents, boundaries of land, the crops that should be grown next season, the tithe that should be paid, the hundred little worries of a great estate that has been my pride and joy for all my life but now seems like a pretty cage, where I have worked and lived and been happy while outside the country I love has slipped down to hell.

'What is it?'

His face is scowling with worry. 'The Earl of Southampton and the Bishop of Ely to see you, my lady,' he says.

I rise to my feet, putting my hand to the small of my back where a nagging pain comes and goes with the weather. I think briefly, cravenly, how very tired I am. 'Do they say what they want?'

He shakes his head. I force myself to stand very straight, and I go out into my presence chamber.

I have known William Fitzwilliam since he played with Prince

Henry in the nursery, and now he is a newly made earl. I know how pleased he will be with his honours. He bows to me but there is no warmth in his face. I smile at him and turn to the Bishop of Ely, Thomas Goodrich.

'My lords, you are very welcome to Warblington Castle,' I say easily. 'I hope that you will dine with us? And will you stay tonight?'

William Fitzwilliam has the grace to look slightly uncomfortable. 'We are here to ask you some questions,' he says. 'The king commands that you answer the truth upon your honour.'

I nod, still smiling.

'And we will stay until we have a satisfactory answer,' says the bishop.

'You must stay as long as you wish,' I say insincerely. I nod to my steward. 'See that the lords' people are housed, and their horses stabled,' I say. 'And set extra places at dinner, and the best bedchambers for our two honoured guests.'

He bows and goes out. I look around my crowded presence chamber. There is a murmur, nothing clear, nothing stated, just a sense that the tenants and petitioners in the room do not like the sight of these great gentlemen riding down from London to question me in my own house. Nobody speaks a disloyal word but there is a rustle of whispers like a low growl.

William looks uneasy. 'Shall we go to a more convenient room?' he asks.

I look around and smile at my people. 'I cannot talk with you today,' I say clearly, so that the poorest widow at the back can hear. 'I am sorry for that. I have to answer some questions for these great lords. I will tell them, as I tell you, as you know, that neither I nor my sons have ever thought, done or dreamed anything which was disloyal to the king. And that none of you has ever done anything either. And none of us ever will.'

'Easily said,' the bishop says unpleasantly.

'Because true,' I overrule him, and lead the way into my private room.

Under the oriel window there is a table where I sometimes sit to write, and four chairs. I gesture that they may sit where they please, and take a chair myself, my back to the wintry light, facing the room.

William Fitzwilliam tells me, as if it were a matter of mild interest, that he has been questioning my sons Geoffrey and Montague. I nod at the information, and I ignore the swift pang of murderous rage at the thought of this upstart interrogating my boys, my Plantagenet boys. He says that they have both spoken freely to him; he implies he knows everything about us, and then he presses me to admit that I have heard them speak against the king.

I absolutely deny it, and I say that I have never said a word against His Majesty either. I say that my boys have never said that they wanted to join Reginald, and that I have written no secret letters to my most disappointing son. I know nothing of Geoffrey's steward Hugh Holland except that he left Geoffrey's service and went into business, London, I think, a merchant, I think. He may have carried family letters with family news to Flanders for us. I know that Geoffrey went to Lord Cromwell and explained everything to his satisfaction, that Holland's goods were returned to him. I am glad of that. Lord Cromwell has the keeping of the safety of the king, we all owe him our thanks while he does that great duty. My son was glad to be accountable to him. I have never received secret letters, and so I have never burned secret letters.

Again and again they ask me the same things, and again and again I tell them simply what I have told them already: I have done nothing, my sons have done nothing, and they can prove nothing against us.

Then I rise from the table and tell them that I am accustomed to praying at this time, in my family chapel. We pray here in the new way, and there is a Bible in English for anyone to read. After prayers, we will dine. If they lack anything in their rooms they must ask, and I shall be delighted to ensure their comfort.

A pedlar with Christmas fairings coming from the London goose fair tells the maids at the kitchen door that my cousin Sir

Edward Neville has been arrested and so has Montague's chaplain John Collins, the Chancellor of Chichester Cathedral, George Croftes, a priest, and several of their servants. I tell the maid who whispers this to me to buy whatever fairings she likes and not to listen to gossip. This is nothing to do with us.

We serve a good dinner to our guests, and after the dinner we have carol singing and my ladies and maids dance, then I excuse myself and go outside as the sky is turning grey, to walk around the ricks. It comforts me, when my precious sons are in danger, to see that the straw and the hay are battened down against the winds, and that everything is dry and safe. I step into the barn, the cows shifting quietly among the straw at one end and my valuable handsome tup at the other, and I smell the scent of warm animals safely penned up against cold weather. I wish I could stay here, all night, in the light of the little horn lantern with the quiet breathing of animals, and perhaps on Christmas Eve at midnight I would see them kneel in memory of that other stable, where the animals knelt at the crib and the Light of the World founded the Church which I have honoured all my life and which is not, and has never been, under the command of any king.

Next day, William and the bishop come to my room again and ask me the same questions. I give them the same answers, and they carefully write them down and send them to London. We can do this every day until the end of the world and the harrowing of hell. I am never going to say anything that would throw suspicion on either of my imprisoned sons. It is true that I am weary of my inquisitors and their repeated questions, but I will not fail because of weariness. I will not be putting my head on the block and desiring eternal rest. They can ask me until the dead step out of their graves, they will find me as mute as my headless brother. I am an old woman, sixty-five years old now, but I am not ready for the grave, and I am not so weak as to be bullied by men that I knew as toddlers. I will say nothing.

In the Tower, the prisoners wait too. The newly arrested church-men break down and acknowledge that although they swore the king's oath they never believed in their hearts that Henry was supreme head of the Church. They promise that they did nothing more than break their own hearts over their false swearing; they raised neither money nor men, they did not plot nor speak. Silently, they wished for the restoration of the monasteries and the return of the old ways. Innocently they prayed for better times.

Edward Neville, my cousin, did only a little more than they. Once, only once, he told Geoffrey that he wished the princess could come to the throne and Reginald could come home. Geoffrey tells the inquisitors of this exchange. God forgive him, my beloved, false-hearted, faint-hearted son tells them what his cousin once said, in confidence, years ago, speaking to a man that he trusted as a brother.

My cousin Henry Courtenay cannot be charged for they can find nothing against him. He may have spoken with Neville, or with my son Montague; but neither of them says anything about any conversation, and they confess nothing themselves. They remain true to each other, as kinsmen should. Neither one says anything about the other, nor confesses anything on his own account. Not even when they are told that the other has betrayed him. They smile like the true chivalric lords they are, they know a lie when it is told against the honour of their family. They keep their silence.

Of course, my cousin Henry's wife Gertrude was well known to have visited the Holy Maid of Kent and to pity Queen Katherine; but she has already been pardoned for this. Still, they keep her a prisoner and question her every day as to what the Maid of Kent told her about the death of the king and the failure of his marriage to Anne Boleyn. Her son Edward lives in a little room beside hers and is allowed a tutor and to take exercise in the gardens. I think this is a good sign that they plan to release him soon, for surely they would not keep him at his lessons if they did not think he would some day go to university?

All that they have against Henry Courtenay is one sentence; he is recorded as saying: 'I trust to see a merry world one day.' When I hear this, I go to my chapel and put my head in my hands to think of my cousin Henry hoping for a merry world one day, and that this commonplace optimism should be cited as evidence against him.

As I kneel before the altar, I think, God bless you, Henry Courtenay; and I cannot disagree. God bless you, Henry, and all prisoners who are held for their faith and for their beliefs, wherever they are tonight. God bless you, Henry Courtenay, for I think as you did, and Tom Darcy did. Like you, I still hope for a merry world one day.

Even before my son and his cousin Henry Courtenay come to trial they put Lord Delaware into the Tower for refusing to sit on a jury to try them. There is nothing against him, not even a whisper, nothing that Thomas Cromwell can invent; Delaware simply shows his distaste for these trials. He swore he would not try another old friend after sending Tom Darcy to the scaffold, and now he refuses to sit in judgement on my son. They hold him as a prisoner for a day or two, scouring London for gossip against him, and then they have to release him to his house and command him to stay indoors.

Of course I cannot go to him, I cannot even send a message to thank him while my own inquisitors sit with me between breakfast and dinner and ask me over and over again if I remember eighteen years ago, when Montague said something while walking in the garden with Henry Courtenay, if the clerk of my kitchens Thomas Standish sang songs of hope and rebellion. If anybody mentioned Maytime. If anyone said that May would never come. But my stable boy runs an errand for me to L'Erber, and when Lord Delaware is walking in his garden the next day he finds, flung over the garden wall and lying in his path, a white rosebud made of silk, and he knows that I am grateful to him.

'I am afraid, Countess, that you are to be my guest,' William says to me at dinner.

'No,' I say. 'I have to stay here. There is much work to be done on an estate this large, and my presence here keeps the country calm.'

'We'll have to take that risk,' the bishop says, smiling at his own humour. 'For you are to be imprisoned at Cowdray. You can keep them calm in Sussex. And please, do not be troubled about your estate and your goods for we are seizing them.'

'My home?' I ask. 'You are seizing Warblington Castle?'

'Yes,' William says. 'Please be ready to leave at once.'

I think of Hugh Holland's white face as his horse was dragged from Bockmer to London with him strapped to the saddle. 'I shall need a litter,' I say. 'I cannot ride all that way.'

'You can ride pillion behind my commander,' William says coldly.

'William Fitzwilliam, I am old enough to be your mother, you should not treat me so harshly,' I suddenly burst out, and then I see the quickening of interest in his face.

'Your sons are far worse than me,' he says. 'For they are confessing that they are rebels against the king. That is harsh treatment to a mother for they will be your undoing.'

I draw back, smooth my gown and bite back my temper. 'They are not saying any such thing,' I say quietly. 'And I know nothing against them.'

It takes us two days to ride south to Midhurst, the roads are so bad with mud and flooding, and we lose our way half a dozen times. Only last year we would have been able to stay in comfort at one of the great monasteries on the way, and the monks would have sent a lad with us to put us on the right road, but now we ride past a great abbey church and it is dark, with the stained-glass windows smashed for the lead, and the slates stolen from the roof.

There is nowhere to stay at night but a dirty old inn at Petersfield and the beggars at the kitchen door and in the street bear witness with their hunger and their despair to the closure of the abbey kitchens and the abbey hospital, and the abbey charities.

COWDRAY HOUSE, SUSSEX, WINTER 1538

It is a beautiful frosty evening as we reach the broad fields before Cowdray and ride beneath the leafless trees. The sky is palest pink as the sun sinks behind the thick forested folds of the Rother valley. I miss my own fields as I see the resting pastures of Cowdray. I have to trust that I will see them again, that I will get home, that my sons will come home to me, that this cold sunset will pass into darkness and then a dawn and tomorrow will be a better day for me and mine.

This is Fitzwilliam's new house, and he has all the pride of a man who has entered into a new property. We dismount stiffly before the open door which leads into a dark panelled hall and there is Mabel Clifford, his wife, with her ladies around her, in her best gown, an English hood crushed low on her head, her face dark with bad temper.

I give her the slightest of curtseys and I watch her begrudgingly reply. Clearly, she knows that there is no need for her best manners; but she does not know exactly how she is to behave.

'I have made the tower rooms ready,' she says, speaking past me to her husband as he comes into the hall, throwing off his cape and pulling off his gloves.

'Good,' he says. He turns to me. 'You will dine in your rooms and you will be served by your people. You can walk in the gardens or by the river if you wish, as long as two of my men are with you. You are not allowed to ride.'

'Ride where?' I ask insolently.

He checks. 'Ride anywhere.'

'Obviously, I don't wish to ride anywhere but to my home,' I say. 'If I had wanted to go overseas, as you seem to suggest, I would have done so long ago. I have lived at my home for many years.' I let my gaze go to his wife's flushed, angry face and the new gilding on their woodwork. 'Many years. My family have been there for centuries. And I hope to live there for many years yet. I'm no rebel, and I don't have rebel blood.'

This enrages Mabel, as I knew it would, since her father was in hiding for most of his life as a traitor to my family, the Plantagenets. 'So please show me to my rooms at once, for I'm tired.'

William turns and gives an order and a server of the household leads the way to the side of the building, where the tower rooms are set one above the other around a circular stair. I mount it wearily, slowly, every bone in my body aching. But still, I am not allowed to go alone, and I will not hold the handrail and haul myself upward when someone is watching. William comes with me, and when I am longing to sit before a fire and eat my dinner, he asks me again what I know of Reginald, and whether Geoffrey was planning to run away to him.

Next morning, before breakfast, while I am saying my prayers, he comes to me again, and this time he has papers in his hand. As soon as we left my home at Warblington, they searched my rooms, turning them upside down for anything that might be used against me. They found a letter that I was in the middle of writing to my son Montague; but it says nothing but that he should be loyal to the king and trust in God. They have questioned the clerk of my kitchen, poor Thomas Standish, and made him say that he thought that Geoffrey might slip away. William makes much of this, but I remember the conversation and interrupt him: 'You are mistaken, my lord. This was after Geoffrey had hurt himself while held in the Tower. We were afraid that he might die, that was why Master Standish said that he feared Geoffrey might slip away.'

'I see you chop and change words, my lady,' William says angrily.

'Indeed, I don't,' I say simply. 'And I would rather have no words at all with you.'

I am ready for him to come to me again after breakfast but it is Mabel who comes to my privy chamber where I am listening to Katherine reading the collect for the day, and she says: 'My lord has gone to London and will not question you today, madam.'

'I am glad of it,' I say quietly. 'For it is weary work telling the truth over and over.'

'You won't be glad of it when I tell you where he has gone,' she says in spiteful triumph.

I wait. I take Katherine's hand.

'He has gone to give evidence against your sons at their trials. They will be charged with treason and sentenced to death,' she says.

This is Katherine's father; but I keep her hand in a steady grip and the two of us look straight at Mabel Fitzwilliam. I am not going to weep in front of such a woman, and I am proud of my granddaughter's composure. 'Lady Fitzwilliam, you should be ashamed of yourself,' I say quietly. 'No woman should be so heartless towards another woman's grief. No woman should torment a man's daughter as you are doing. No wonder that you cannot give your lord a child, for since you have no heart you probably have no womb either.'

Her cheeks flame red with temper. 'I may have no sons, but very soon, neither will you,' she shouts, and whirls out of the room.

My son Montague goes before his friends and kinsmen sitting as his jury and is charged with speaking against the king, approving Reginald's doings, and dreaming that the king was dead. It seems that now Cromwell may inquire into a man's sleep. His confessor reported to Cromwell that one morning Montague said to him that he dreamed that his brother had come home and was happy. They have interrogated Montague's sleep and found his dreams guilty. He pleads his innocence but is not allowed to speak in his own defence. Nobody is allowed to speak for him.

Geoffrey, the child that I kept at my side when I sent his brothers away, my favourite child, my spoiled son, my baby, gives evidence against his brother Montague, and against his cousins Henry and Edward, and against us all. God forgive him. He says that his first choice was to kill himself rather than bear witness against his brother but that God so wrought on him that if he had ten brothers, or ten sons, he would bring them all to the peril of death rather than leave his country, his sovereign lord, and his own soul in danger. Geoffrey addresses his friends and kinsmen with tears in his eyes. 'Let us die, we be but few, according to our deserts rather than our whole country be brought to ruin.'

What Montague thinks when Geoffrey argues in favour of his death, and for the death of our cousins and friends, I don't know. I don't think at all. I try very hard not to hear of his trial, and I try not to think what it means. I am on my knees in the little room at Cowdray where I have put my crucifix and my Bible, my clasped hands against my face, praying and praying that God will move the king to pity and that he will let my innocent son go, and send my poor witless son home to his wife. Behind me, Katherine and Winifred pray for their father, their faces dazed and fearful.

I live in silence in my rooms, looking out over the river meadows towards the high green of the South Downs, wishing I was at my home, wishing my sons were with me, wishing I was a young woman again and my life was constrained and my hopes were defined by my dull, safe husband, Sir Richard. I love him now as I failed to love him before. I think now that he set himself his life's task to keep me safe, to keep all of us safe, and that I should have been more grateful. But I am old enough and wise enough to know that all regrets are futile, so I bend my head in my prayers and hope he hears that I acknowledge what he did, when he married a young woman from a family too close to the throne, and that I know what he did when he spent all his time moving us further and further away from its dangerous glamour. I too tried to keep us hidden; but we are the white rose – the bloom shines even in the darkest, thickest hedgerow; it can be seen even in the dark of night like a fallen moon, palely gleaming among thrusting leaves.

COWDRAY HOUSE, SUSSEX, DECEMBER 1538

In my room in the tower at Cowdray, I hear the household start to prepare for Christmas, just as we do at Bisham, just as the king will be doing at Greenwich. They fast for Advent, they cut the boughs from the holly and the ivy, the brambles and the gorse, and weave a green Christmas crown; they drag in a mighty log that will burn in the grate until the end of the Christmas feast, they rehearse their carols and they practise dances. They order special spices and they start the long preparation of the seasonal dishes for the twelve days of feasting. I listen to the household bustling outside my door and I dream that I am at home, until I wake and remember that I am far from home, waiting for William Fitzwilliam to come from London and tell me that my sons are dead and my hopes are ended.

He comes in early December. I hear the clatter of his troop of horse on the track and their shouts for the stable lads, and I crack open the shutter of my bedroom window and look down to see William and his men around him, the bustle of his arrival, and his wife going out to greet him, the horses' breaths smoking in the cold air, the frost crackling on the grass under their feet.

I watch him as he dismounts, his bright cape, his embroidered hat, the way he thumps his fists one against the other as his hands are cold. His absent-minded kiss for his wife, his shouted commands at his men. This is the man who is going to bring me heartbreak. This is the man who is going to tell me that it was all for nothing, that my whole life has been worthless, that my sons are dead.

He comes straight to my room, as if he cannot wait to relish his triumph. His face is solemn, but his eyes are bright.

'Your ladyship, I am sorry to tell you, but your son Lord Montague is dead.'

I face him, dry-eyed. 'I am sorry to hear it,' I say steadily. 'On what charge?'

'Treason,' he says easily. 'Your son and his cousins Henry Courtenay and Edward Neville were brought before their peers and tried and found guilty of treason against the king.'

'Oh, did they plead guilty?' I ask, my voice sharp between my cold lips.

'They were found guilty,' he says, as if this were an answer, as if this could ever be a just answer. 'The king showed them mercy.'

I can feel my heart leap. 'Mercy?'

'He allowed them to be executed on Tower Hill, not at Tyburn.'

'I know that my son and his cousins were innocent of any treason to our most beloved king,' I say. 'Where is Henry's wife, Lady Courtenay, and her son Edward?'

He checks at this. Fool that he is, he had almost forgotten them. 'Still in the Tower of London,' he says sullenly.

'And my son Geoffrey?'

He does not like questions. He blusters. 'Madam, it is not for you to interrogate me. Your son is a dead traitor and you are suspect.'

'Indeed,' I say swiftly. 'It is for you to interrogate me, so skilful as you are. They all pleaded guiltless and you found no evidence against them. I am guiltless and you will find no evidence against me. God help you, William Fitzwilliam, for you are in the wrong. Interrogate me as you wish, though I am old enough to be your mother. You will find that I have done nothing wrong, as my own dear son Montague had done nothing wrong.'

It is a mistake to say his name. I can hear that my voice has grown thin and I am not sure that I can speak again. William swells in his pride at my weakness.

'Be very sure that I will interrogate you again,' he says.

Out of sight, behind my back, I pinch the skin of my palms. 'Be very sure that you will find nothing,' I say bitterly. 'And at the end, this house will fall down around you, and this river will rise against you, and you will regret the day that you came against me in your pomp and stupidity and taunted me with the death of a better man, my son Montague.'

'Do you curse me?' he pants, all white and sweating, shaking with the knowledge that his house is already cursed for the putting down of Cowdray Priory, cursed by fire and water.

I shake my head. 'Of course not. I don't believe in such nonsense. You make your own destiny. But when you bear false witness against a good man like my son, when you put me to the question, when you know that I have done no wrong, you are on the side of the evil in the world and your friend and ally will draw you close.'

Mabel comes to taunt me with the full list of deaths. George Croftes, John Collins and Hugh Holland have been hanged, drawn and quartered at Tyburn, their heads set on London Bridge. My son Montague, my precious son and heir, was beheaded on Tower Hill, his cousins Henry Courtnay and Edward Neville followed him to the scaffold and the axe.

'Dead like traitors,' she says.

'Death instead of evidence,' I reply.

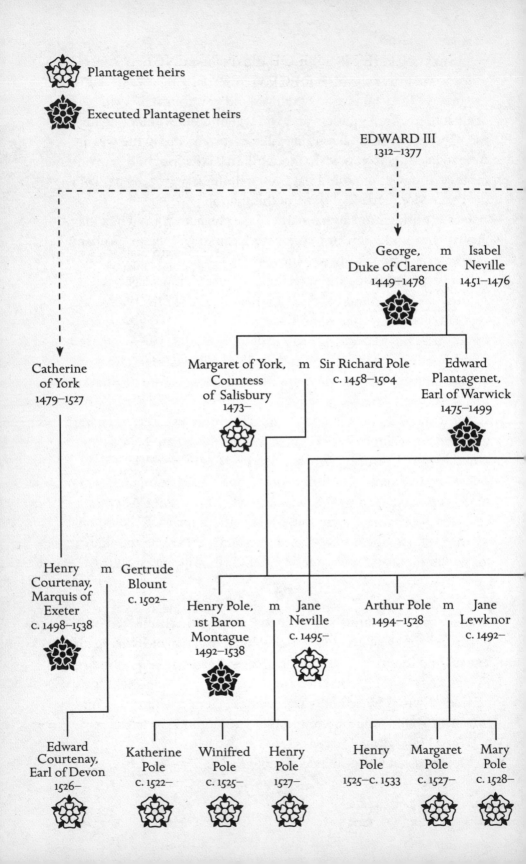

Plantagenet heirs

Executed Plantagenet heirs

EDWARD III
1312–1377

George,   m   Isabel
Duke of Clarence   Neville
1449–1478   1451–1476

Catherine
of York
1479–1527

Margaret of York,   m   Sir Richard Pole   Edward
Countess   c. 1458–1504   Plantagenet,
of Salisbury   Earl of Warwick
1473–   1475–1499

Henry   m   Gertrude
Courtenay,   Blount
Marquis of   c. 1502–
Exeter
c. 1498–1538

Henry Pole,   m   Jane   Arthur Pole   m   Jane
1st Baron   Neville   1494–1528   Lewknor
Montague   c. 1495–   c. 1492–
1492–1538

Edward   Katherine   Winifred   Henry   Henry   Margaret   Mary
Courtenay,   Pole   Pole   Pole   Pole   Pole   Pole
Earl of Devon   c. 1522–   c. 1525–   1527–   1525–c. 1533 c. 1527–   c. 1528–
1526–

THE HOUSE OF PLANTAGENET
ON 9 DECEMBER 1538

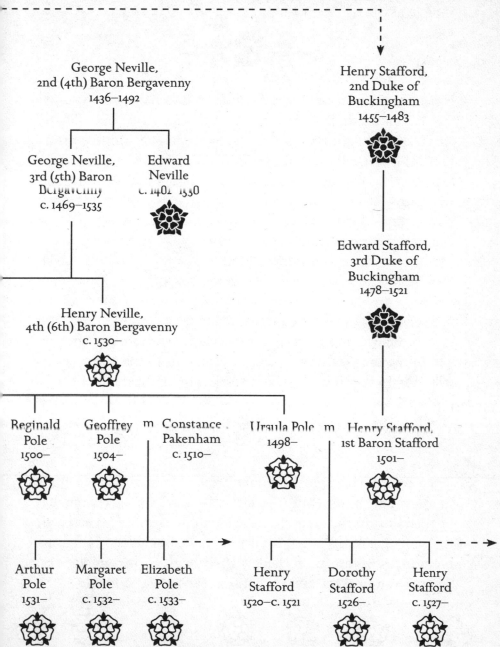

George Neville,
2nd (4th) Baron Bergavenny
1436–1492

Henry Stafford,
2nd Duke of
Buckingham
1455–1483

George Neville,
3rd (5th) Baron
Bergavenny
c. 1469–1535

Edward
Neville
c. 1482–1538

Edward Stafford,
3rd Duke of
Buckingham
1478–1521

Henry Neville,
4th (6th) Baron Bergavenny
c. 1530–

Reginald
Pole
1500–

Geoffrey
Pole
1504–

m Constance
Pakenham
c. 1510–

Ursula Pole
1498–

m Henry Stafford,
1st Baron Stafford
1501–

Arthur
Pole
1531–

Margaret
Pole
c. 1532–

Elizabeth
Pole
c. 1533–

Henry
Stafford
1520–c. 1521

Dorothy
Stafford
1526–

Henry
Stafford
c. 1527–

I spend the day, from dawn till dusk, in the chapel at Cowdray, the de Bohun tomb before me, and the grey quietness of the winter daylight around me. I pray for Montague, for his cousins Edward and Henry, taken out onto Tower Hill where his uncle laid down his innocent head and died. I pray for all our kinsmen who are in danger, today. I pray for their sons, especially Henry Courtenay's son Edward who may have watched from his window and seen his father's last walk across the frosty grass to the outer gate, and beyond that, up to Tower Hill and the block and the black-masked axeman and his death.

I pray for Montague's children, his son Harry, safe with his mother at Bockmer, his daughters Katherine and Winifred who have come with me to this miserable vigil, and more than anyone else I pray for Geoffrey who has brought us to this tragedy and will – for I know my son – be wishing himself dead tonight.

They keep me here, as the winter turns, though my son is in his grave and my boy Geoffrey is left in the Tower. They tell me that he tried to suffocate himself, crushing himself under his bed with the quilt against his face. This is how, it was said, that his cousins the princes in the Tower died, stuffed between two mattresses. But it is not fatal for my son; and perhaps it was not true of the princes either. Geoffrey remains, as he has been for all this winter, a traitor to his king, to his brother, and to himself, a terrible betrayer of his family and me, his mother. They leave him inside the cold walls of the Tower and I know that if they leave him there long enough he will die anyway, of the cold in winter, or of the plague in summer, and it will hardly matter whether his testimony was true or false because this boy, this boy who promised so much, will be dead. As dead as his brother Arthur, who died in the prime of his handsome youth, as dead as his brother Montague, who died keeping the faith, and trying to save his cousins.

They take Sir Nicholas Carew into the Tower and give it out that he has been planning to destroy the king, seize the throne, and marry his son to Princess Mary. William Fitzwilliam tells me this, his eyes all bright, as if I am going to fall to my knees and say that this has been my secret plan all along.

'Nicholas Carew?' I say disbelievingly. 'The king's Master of Horse? That he has loved and trusted every single day these forty years? His best-loved companion in joust and war since they were boys together?'

'Yes,' William says, the glee fading from his face because he was their companion too, and he knows what folly this is. 'The same. Don't you know that Carew loved Queen Katherine and disagreed with the king about his treatment of the princess?'

I shrug, as if it does not matter much. 'Many people loved Queen Katherine,' I say. 'The king loved Queen Katherine. Is your Thomas Cromwell going to put every one of her court to death? For that would be thousands of people. And you among them.'

William flushes. 'You think you're so wise!' he blurts out. 'But you will come to the scaffold at last! Mark my words, Countess. You will come to the scaffold at last!'

I hold my temper and my words for I think there is more here than a young man's frustration at an older woman knowing more than he will ever learn. I look at his face as if I would read the red veins, and the thinning hair, the fat of self-indulgence under the chin, and the petty pout of his face. 'Perhaps I will,' I say quietly.

'But you can tell your master Cromwell that I am guilty of nothing, and that if he kills me, he kills an innocent woman and that my blood and that of my kinsmen will stain his record for all eternity.'

I look at his suddenly pale face. 'And yours too, William Fitzwilliam,' I say. 'People will remember that you held me in your house against my will. I doubt that you will hold your house for long.'

All through the cold weather I mourn for my son Montague, for his honesty, for his steadfast honour, and for his companionship. I blame myself for not having valued him before, for letting him think that my love for Geoffrey was greater than my love for all my boys. I wish I had told Montague how dear he was to me, how I depended on him, how I loved watching him grow and rise to his great position, how his humour warmed me, how his caution warned me, that he was a man his father would have been proud of, that I was proud of him, that I still am.

I write to my daughter-in-law, his widow Jane; she does not reply but she leaves her daughters in my keeping. She has, perhaps, had enough of letters sealed with a white rose. My chamber in the Cowdray tower is small and cramped and my bedroom even smaller, so I insist that my granddaughters walk with me by the cold river in the gardens every day, whatever the weather, and that they ride out twice a week. They are constantly watched in case they send or receive a letter and they become pale and quiet with the caution of habitual prisoners.

Strangely, the loss of Montague recalls the loss of his brother Arthur, and I grieve for him all over again. I am glad in a way that Arthur did not live to see his family's tragedy and the madness of his former friend, the king. Arthur died in the years of sunshine when we thought everything was possible. Now we are in the cold heart of a long winter.

I dream of my brother, who walked to his death where my son walked to his, I dream of my father who died in the Tower too.

Sometimes I just dream of the Tower, its square bullying bulk like a white finger pointing up, accusing the sky, and I think that it is like a tombstone for the young men of my family.

Gertrude Courtenay, now a widow, is still held there, in a freezing cell. The case against her gets worse rather than obscured by time, as Thomas Cromwell keeps finding letters that he says are hers in the rooms of others that he hopes to convict. If Cromwell is to be believed, my cousin Gertrude spent her life writing treason to everyone that Cromwell suspects. But Cromwell cannot be challenged, since he forges the king's whims into reality. When Nicholas Carew comes to trial this spring, they produce with a flourish a sheaf of Gertrude's letters as evidence against him, though no-one looks at them closely but Cromwell.

Nicholas Carew, dearest friend to the king, loving courtier to Queen Katherine, loyal constant friend to the princess, goes to the scaffold on Tower Hill, walking in the footprints of my son, and dies like him, for no cause.

Poor Geoffrey, the saddest of all of my boys, living a life worse than death, receives a pardon and is released. His wife is with child at their home, so he staggers out of the postern gate, hires himself a horse and rides back to her at Lordington. He does not write to me, he sends no message, he does not try to release me, he does not try to clear my name. I imagine that he lives like a dead man, locked inside his failure. I wonder if his wife despises him. I imagine that he hates himself.

This spring I think that I am as low as I have ever been. Sometimes I think of my husband Sir Richard and that he spent his life trying to save me from the destiny of my family and that I have failed him. I did not keep his sons safe, I did not manage to hide my name in his.

'If you were to confess, you would have a pardon and could go free,' Mabel says on one of her regular visits to my little rooms. She comes once a week as if to ensure, like a good hostess, that I have everything I need. In reality, she comes at the bidding of her husband to question me and to torment me with thoughts of escape. 'Just confess, your ladyship. Confess and you can go back to your home. You must long to go to your home. You always say that you miss it so much.'

'I do long to be at home, and I would go, if I could,' I say steadily. 'But I have nothing to confess.'

'But the charge is almost nothing!' she points out. 'You could confess that you once dreamed that the king was not a good king, that's enough, that's all they want to hear. That would be a confession of treason under the new law and they could pardon you for it, like they have done Geoffrey, and you could be freed! Everyone that you loved or plotted with is dead anyway. You save nobody by making your life a misery.'

'But I never dreamed such a thing,' I say steadily. 'I never thought such a thing or said such a thing or wrote such a thing. I never plotted with any man, dead or alive.'

'But you must have been sorry when John Fisher was executed,' she says quickly. 'Such a good man, such a holy man?'

'I was sorry that he opposed the king,' I say. 'But I did not oppose the king.'

'Well then, you were sorry when the king put the Dowager Princess Katherine of Aragon aside?'

'Of course I was. She was my friend. I was sorry that their marriage was invalid. But I said nothing in her defence, and I swore the oath to declare it was invalid.'

'And you wanted to serve the Lady Mary even when the king declared that she was a bastard. I know you did, you can't deny that!'

'I loved the Lady Mary, and I still do,' I reply. 'I would serve her whatever her position in the world may be. But I make no claim for her.'

'But you think of her as a princess,' she presses me. 'In your heart.'

'I think the king must be the one to decide that,' I say.

She pauses, stands up and takes a short turn around the cramped room. 'I won't have you here forever,' she warns me. 'I've told my husband that I can't house you and your ladies forever. And my lord Cromwell will want to make an end to this.'

'I would be happy to leave,' I say quietly. 'I would undertake to stay quietly at my home and see no-one and write to no-one. I have no sons left to me. I would see only my daughter and my grand-children. I could promise that. They could release me on parole.'

She turns and looks at me, her face alive with malice, and she laughs outright at the poverty of my hopes. 'What home?' she asks. 'Traitors don't have homes, they lose everything. Where do you think you will go? Your great castle? Your beautiful manor? Your fine house in London? None of these is yours any more. You won't be going anywhere unless you confess. And I won't have you here. There's only one other place for you.'

I wait in silence for her to name the one place in the world that I most dread.

'The Tower.'

THE ROAD TO THE TOWER,
MAY 1539

They take me, riding pillion behind one of William Fitzwilliam's guard. We leave before dawn as the sky slowly lightens and the birds start to sing. We ride up the narrow lanes of Sussex where the verges are starred with daisies and the hawthorn is foaming white with blossoms in the hedges, past meadows where the grass is growing thick and lush and the flowers are a tumble of colour and the song birds are a ripple of notes as if delighting in life itself. We ride all day, as far as Lambeth where a plain barge is waiting for us with no standard flying at the pole. Clearly Thomas Cromwell does not want the citizens of London to see me follow my sons into the Tower.

It is a strange, almost dreamlike journey on the water. I am alone in an unmarked barge, as if I have shed my family standards and my name, as if I am at last free from my dangerous inheritance. It is dusk and the sun is setting behind us, laying a long finger of golden light along the river, and the waterbirds are flying to the shore and settling down, splashing and quacking, for the night. I can hear a cuckoo somewhere in the water meadows and I remember how Geoffrey used to listen for the first cuckoo of spring when he was a little boy and we lived with the sisters at Syon. Now the abbey is closed, and Geoffrey is destroyed, and only that faithless bird, the cuckoo, is still calling.

I stand at the stern and look back at the swirling grey waters of the wake and watch the setting sun turning the mackerel sky pink and cream. I have sailed down this river many times in my life; I have been in the coronation barge, as an honoured guest, a member of the royal family, I have been in my own barge, under my own standard, I have been the wealthiest woman in England, holding the highest of honours, with four handsome sons standing beside me, each of them fit to inherit my name and my fortune. And now I have almost nothing, and the nameless barge goes quietly down the river unobserved. As the muffled drum sounds and the rowers keep the beat and the barge moves forward with a steady swishing thrust through the water I feel that it has been like a dream, all of it a dream, and that the dream is coming to an end.

As the dark figure of the Tower comes into sight, the great portcullis of the watergate rolls up at our approach; the Constable of the Tower, Sir William Kingston, is waiting on the steps. They run out the gangplank and I walk steadily towards him, my head high. He bows very low as he sees me, and I see his face is pale and strained. He takes my hand to help me to the steps, and as he moves forward I see the boy who was hidden behind him. I see him, and I recognise him, and my heart stops still at the sight of him as if I have been jolted awake and I know that this is not a dream but the worst thing that has ever happened in a long, long life.

It is my grandson Harry. It is my grandson Harry. They have arrested Montague's boy.

He is whooping with joy to see me, that's what makes me weep as his arms come round my waist and he dances around me. He thinks I have come to take him home, and he is laughing with delight. He tries to board the barge, and it takes me a few moments before I can explain to him that I am imprisoned myself, and I see his little face blench with horror as he tries not to cry.

We grip each other's hands and go towards the dark entrance together. They are housing us in the garden tower. I fall back and look at Sir William. 'Not here,' I say. I will not tell him that I cannot bear to be imprisoned where my brother waited and waited for his freedom. 'Not this tower. I cannot manage the stairs. They're too narrow, too steep. I can't go up and down them.'

'You won't be going up and down them,' he says with grim humour. 'You're just going up. We'll help you.'

They half-carry me up the winding circular stair to the first-floor room. Harry has a little room above mine, overlooking the green. I have a larger room, overlooking the green out of one window and the river through a narrow arrow-slit. There is no fire made in either grate, the rooms are cold and cheerless. The walls are bare stone, carved here and there with the names and insignia of previous prisoners. I cannot bear to look for the names of my father or my brother or of my sons.

Harry goes to the window and points out his cousin, Courtenay's boy, in the narrow streets below. He is housed with his mother Gertrude in the Beauchamp Tower; their rooms are more comfortable, Edward is very bored and very lonely but he and his mother get enough to eat and were given warm clothes this winter. With the high spirits of an eleven-year-old boy, Harry is more cheerful already, pleased that I am with him. He asks me to come to visit Gertrude Courtenay and is shocked when I say that I am not allowed to leave my room, that when he comes in to see me, the door will be locked behind him, and he can only go out when a guard comes to release him. He looks at me, his innocent face frowning, as if he is puzzled. 'But we will be able to go home?' he asks. 'We will go home soon?'

I am almost brave enough to assure him that he will go home soon. There may be evidence, real or pretend, against Gertrude, they may concoct something against me, but Harry is only eleven and Edward is thirteen years old and there can be nothing against these boys but the fact that they were born Plantagenets. I think even the king cannot be so far gone in his fear of my family as to keep two boys like this in the Tower as traitors.

But then I pause in my confident reckoning, pause and remember that his father took my brother at just this age, for just this reason, and my brother came out only to walk along the stone path, to Tower Hill, to the scaffold.

THE TOWER, LONDON,
SUMMER 1539

The parliament meets and Cromwell puts before it an Act of Attainder, which declares all of us Plantagenets to be traitors, without trial or evidence. Our good name is a crime, our goods are forfeit to the crown, our children disinherited. Gertrude's name and mine are listed among those of dead men.

They produce the dozens of letters that Gertrude is said to have written, they produce one letter which I wrote to my son Reginald to assure him of my love which was never delivered, and then Thomas Cromwell himself lifts a satchel and like a street magician draws out the badge that Tom Darcy gave me, the white silk badge embroidered with the five wounds of Christ with the white rose above it.

The house is silent as Thomas Cromwell flourishes this. Perhaps he hoped that they would clamour in an uproar, shouting for my head. Cromwell offers it as conclusive evidence of my guilt. He does not accuse me of any crime – even now, having an embroidered badge in an old box in your house is not a crime – and the houses of the commons and the lords barely respond. Perhaps they are sated with attainders, perhaps they are weary of death. Perhaps many of them have a badge just like it, tucked away in an old box in their country houses, from the time when they thought that good times might come, and there were many pilgrims marching for grace. At any rate, it is all that Cromwell has for evidence and I am to be kept in the Tower at His Majesty's wish and my grandson Harry and Gertrude and her little boy must stay too.

THE TOWER, LONDON,
WINTER 1539

It is as though our lives become motionless as the cold weather freezes the water in our jugs and the drips from the slates become long pointed icicles. Harry is allowed to attend Edward's lessons, and stays in the Courtenay rooms for dinner where there is a better table than mine. Gertrude and I exchange messages of good will but we never write one word to each other. My cousin William de la Pole dies alone in the cold cell where he has lived a prisoner, an innocent man, a kinsman. He has been in here for thirty-seven years. I pray for him; but I try not to think about him. I read when the light is good enough, I sew, sitting beside the window overlooking the green. I pray at the little altar in the corner of my room. I don't wonder about my release, about freedom, about the future. I try not to think at all. I study endurance.

Only the outside world moves on. Ursula writes to me that Constance and Geoffrey have a baby, to be called Catherine, and that the king is to marry a new wife. They have found a princess who is prepared to marry a man she has never seen and of whom she can only have heard the worst reports. Anne of Cleves is to make the long journey, from her Protestant homeland to the country that the king and Cromwell are destroying, next spring.

THE TOWER, LONDON,
SPRING 1540

We endure a long year and a bitterly cold winter as prisoners in our cells, seeing the sky only as slats of grey framed by iron bars, smelling the wind from the river in cold draughts under the thick doors, hearing the single call of the winter robin and the ceaseless lament of the seagulls at a distance.

Harry grows taller and taller, out of his hose and out of his shoes, and I have to beg the warder to request new clothes for him. We are only allowed a fire in our rooms when it gets very cold, and I see my fingers thicken and redden with chilblains. It grows dark very early in the little rooms, it stays dark for a long time, dawn comes later and later through this cold winter, and when there is a mist coming off the river or the clouds are very low it never gets light at all.

I try to be cheerful and optimistic for Harry's sake, and read with him in Latin and French; but when he has gone to sleep in his little cell and I am locked in mine, I pull the thin blanket over my head and lie dry-eyed in the fusty darkness and know that I am too beaten by grief to cry.

We wait as spring comes to green the trees in the Tower garden and we can hear the blackbirds singing in the constable's orchard. The two boys are allowed out on the green to play, and someone sets up a butt for them and gives them bows and arrows; someone else gives them a set of bowls and marks out a green for them. Though the days get warmer, it is still very cold in our rooms, and so I ask the warder to allow me to send for some clothes. I am served by my lady in waiting and by the master controller's maid, and I am ashamed that I cannot pay their wages. The warder presents a petition for me and I receive some clothes and some money, and, then, surprisingly, for no reason, Gertrude Courtenay is released.

William Fitzwilliam himself comes in with the warder to tell me the good news.

'Are we to go too?' I ask him calmly. I put my hand on Harry's thin shoulder and feel him shudder like a captive merlin at the thought of freedom.

'I am sorry, your ladyship,' Thomas Philips, the warder, says. 'There are no orders to release you yet.'

I feel Harry's shoulders slump, and Thomas sees the look on my face. 'Maybe soon,' he says. He turns to Harry. 'But you are not to lose your playmate, so you won't be lonely,' he says, trying to sound cheerful.

'Is Edward not going with his mother?' I ask. 'Why would they release Lady Courtenay and keep her little son prisoner?'

As he meets my eyes he realises, as I do, that this is the imprisonment of the Plantagenets, not of traitors. Gertrude can go for she was born a Blount, the daughter of Baron Mountjoy. But her son Edward must stay for his name is Courtenay.

There is no charge, there can be no charge, he is a child and had never even left home. It is the king gathering the Plantagenet sons into his keeping, like the Mouldwarp undermining a house, like a monster in a fairy tale, eating children, one by one.

I think of little Harry and Edward, their bright, eager eyes and Harry's curly auburn hair, and I think of the cold walls of the Tower and the long, long days of captivity, and I find a new level of endurance, of pain. I look at William Fitzwilliam, and I say to him: 'As the king wishes.'

'You don't find this unjust?' he says wonderingly, as if he is my friend and might plead for the boys' release. 'You don't think you should speak out? Appeal?'

I shrug my shoulders. 'He is the king,' I say. 'He is the emperor, the supreme head of the Church. His judgement must be right. Don't you think his judgement is infallible, my lord?'

He blinks at that, blinks like the mole his master, and gulps. 'He's not mistaken,' he says quickly, as if I might spy on him.

'Of course not,' I say.

THE TOWER, LONDON, SUMMER 1540

It is easier in summertime, for though I am not allowed out of my cell, Harry and Edward can come and go as long as they stay within the walls of the Tower. They try to amuse themselves, as boys always will, playing, wrestling, daydreaming, even fishing in the dark depths of the watergate and swimming in the moat. My maid comes and goes from the Tower every day and sometimes brings me the little treats of the season. One day she brings me half a dozen strawberries and the moment I taste them I am back in my fruit garden at Bisham Manor, the warm squashy juice on my tongue, the hot sun on my back, and the world at my feet.

'And I have news,' she says.

I glance at the door where a gaoler may be passing. 'Take care what you say,' I remind her.

'Everyone knows this,' she says. 'The king is to put his new wife aside though she has been in the country only seven months.'

At once I think of my princess, Lady Mary, who will lose another stepmother and friend. 'Put her aside?' I repeat, careful with the words, wondering if she is to be charged with something monstrous and killed.

'They say that the marriage was never a true one,' my maid says, her voice a tiny whisper. 'And she is to be called the king's sister and live at Richmond Palace.'

I know that I look quite blankly at her; but I cannot comprehend a world where a king may call his wife his sister and send her to live on her own in a palace. Is nobody advising Henry at all? Is nobody telling him that the truth is not of his making, cannot be of his own invention? He cannot call a woman wife today, and name her as his sister on the next day. He cannot say that his daughter is not a princess. He cannot say that he is the Pope.

Who is ever going to find the courage to name what is more and more clear: that the king does not see the world as it is, that his vision is unreal, that – though it is treason to say it – the king is quite mad.

The very next day I am gazing out of my arrow-slit window over the river when I see the Howard barge come swiftly downriver, and turn, oars feathering expertly to rush into the inner dock as the watergate creaks open. Some poor new prisoner, taken by Thomas Howard, I think, and watch with interest as a stocky figure is wrestled from the barge, fighting like a drayman, and struggles with half a dozen men onto the quay.

'God help him,' I say as he plunges this way and that like a baited bear with no hope of freedom. They have guards ready to fall on him and he fights them, all the way up the steps and out of sight, under the lee of my window as I press against the stone and push my face against the arrow-slit.

I have a solitary prisoner's curiosity but also I think I recognise this man who flings himself against his gaolers. I knew him the moment that he pitched off the barge, his dark clerkly clothes in the best-cut black, his broad shoulders and black velvet bonnet. I stare down in amazement, my cheek pressed to the cold stone so that I can see Thomas Cromwell, arrested and imprisoned and dragged fighting into the same Tower where he has sent so many others.

I fall back from the arrow-slit, and I stagger to my bed and fall to my knees and put my face in my hands. I find I am crying at last, hot tears running between my fingers. 'Thank God,' I cry softly. 'Thank God who has brought me safe to this day. Harry and Edward are saved, the little boys are safe, for the king's wicked councillor has fallen, and we will be freed.'

Thomas Philips, the warder, will tell me only that Thomas Cromwell, deprived of his chain of office and all his authority, has been arrested and is held in the Tower, crying for pardon, as so many good men have cried before him. He must hear, as I hear, the sound of them building the scaffold on Tower Hill, and on a day as fine and as sunny as the day they took out John Fisher or Thomas More, their enemy, the enemy of the faith of England, walks in their footsteps and goes to his death.

I tell my grandson Harry and his cousin Edward to keep from the windows and not to look out as the defeated enemy of their family walks through the echoing gate, over the draw-bridge, and slowly up the cobbled road to Tower Hill; but we hear the roll of the drums and the jeering roar of the crowd. I kneel before my crucifix and I think of my son Montague pre-dicting that Cromwell, who was deaf to calls for mercy, mercy, mercy, would one day cry out these words, and find none for himself.

I wait for my cell door to be flung open and for us to be released. We were imprisoned on Thomas Cromwell's Act of Attainder; now that he is dead we shall surely be released.

Nobody comes for us yet; but perhaps we are overlooked as the king is married again, and is said to be half-mad with joy in his new bride, another Howard girl, little Kitty Howard, young enough to be his granddaughter, pretty as all the Howard girls are. I think of Geoffrey saying that the Howards to the king are like hare to a Talbot hound, and then I remember to not think of Geoffrey at all.

I wait for the king to return from his honeymoon brimming with a bridegroom's good will, and for someone to remind him of us and for him to sign our release. Then I hear that his happiness has ended abruptly, and that he is ill and has shut himself away in a sort of mad desolation and has imprisoned himself, just as I am confined, inside two small rooms, maddened with pain and tormented with failed hopes, too tired and sick at heart to attend to any business.

All summer I wait to hear that the king has come out of his melancholy, all autumn, then when the weather starts to get cold again, I think that perhaps the king will pardon and free us in the new year, after Christmas, as part of the celebrations of the season; but he does not.

THE TOWER, LONDON, SPRING 1541

The king is to take the bride that he calls his 'rose without a thorn' on a great progress north, to make the journey that he has never dared, to show himself to the people of the North and to accept their apologies for the Pilgrimage of Grace. He will stay with men who have houses newly built with stone from the pulled-down monasteries, he will ride through lands where the bones of traitors still rattle in the chains on the wayside scaffolds. He will go blithely among people whose lives were ended when their Church was destroyed, whose faith has no home, who have no hope. He will dress his hugely fat body in Lincoln green and pretend to be Robin Hood and make the child he has married dance in green like Maid Marian.

I still hope. I still hope, like my dead cousin Henry Courtenay once hoped, for better days and a merry world. Perhaps the king will release Harry and Edward and me before he goes north, as part of his clemency and pardon. If he can forgive York, a Plantagenet city that threw open its gates to the pilgrims, surely he can forgive us, these two innocent boys.

I wake at dawn in these light mornings and I hear the birds

singing outside my window and watch the sunlight slowly walk across the wall. Thomas Philips, the warder, surprises me by knocking on my door and when I have got up and pulled a robe over my nightgown he comes in looking as if he is sick. 'What's the matter?' I ask him, anxious at once. 'Is my grandson ill?'

'He is well, he is well,' he says hastily.

'Edward then?'

'He is well.'

'Then what is the matter, Mr Philips, for you look troubled. What is wrong?'

'I am grieved,' is all that he can say. He turns his head away and shakes his head and clears his throat. Something is distressing him so much that he can barely speak. 'I am grieved to say that you are to be executed.'

'I?' It is quite impossible. The execution of Anne Boleyn was preceded by a trial in which the peers of the realm were convinced that she was an adulterous witch. A noblewoman, one of the royal family, cannot be executed, not without a charge, not without a trial.

'Yes.'

I go to the low window that overlooks the green and look out. 'It cannot be,' I say. 'It cannot be.'

Philips clears this throat again. 'It is commanded.'

'There's no scaffold,' I say simply. I gesture to Tower Hill, beyond the walls. 'There's no scaffold.'

'They're bringing a block,' he says. 'Putting it on the grass.'

I turn and stare at him. 'A block? They're going to put a block on the grass and behead me in hiding?'

He nods.

'There's no charge, there's no trial. There's no scaffold. The man who accused me is dead himself, accused of treason. It cannot be.'

'It is,' he says. 'I beg you to prepare your soul, your ladyship.'

'When?' I ask. I expect him to say the day after tomorrow, or at the end of the week.

He says: 'At seven of the clock. In an hour and a half,' and he goes from the room, his head down.

I cannot comprehend that I have only an hour and a half left of life. The chaplain comes and hears my confession, and I beg him to go at once to the boys and give them my blessing and my love and to tell them to stay away from the windows that face the green and the little block that has been set there. A few people have gathered; I see the chain of the Lord Mayor of London, but it is early in the morning and all unprepared, and so only a few people have been told and only a few have come.

This makes it even worse, I think. The king must have decided it on a whim, perhaps as late as last night, and they must have sent out the order this morning. And nobody has dissuaded him. Of all my numerous fertile family, there was nobody left who could dissuade him.

I try to pray, but my mind skitters around like a foal in a meadow in springtime. I have ordered in my will that my debts should be paid and prayers said for my soul and that I should be buried in my old priory. But I doubt that they will trouble themselves to take my body – I suddenly remember with surprise that my head will be in a basket – all the way to my old chapel. So perhaps I will lie in the Tower chapel with my son, Montague. This comforts me until I remember his son, my grandson Harry, and I wonder who will care for him, and if he will ever be released, or if he will die here, another Plantagenet boy buried in the Tower.

I think all this while my lady in waiting dresses me, puts my new cape over my shoulders, and ties up my hair under my hood so as to leave my neck clear for the axe.

'It's not right,' I say irritably, as if the ties of the dress are wrong, and she drops to her knees and cries, mopping her eyes with the hem of my gown.

'It's wicked!' she cries out.

'Hush,' I say. I feel I cannot be troubled by her sorrow, I cannot understand it. I feel dazed, as if I cannot understand her words nor what is about to happen.

The priest is waiting at the door and the guard. Everything seems to be happening very quickly and I fear I am not prepared. I think of course it may be that just as I get to the grass, a pardon comes from the king. It would be typical of his sense of a grand show to condemn a woman to death after dinner and pardon her before breakfast so that everyone can remark on his power and his mercy.

I dawdle down the stairs, with my lady in waiting's arm under mine, not just because my legs are stiff and unaccustomed to the exercise, but because I want to allow plenty of time for the king's messenger to come in with the scroll and ribbons and the seal. But when we get to the door of the Tower there is no-one there, just the small crowd around the straight stone path, and at the end of the path an impromptu block of wood, and a youth in a black hood with an axe standing beside it.

I have my pennies to pay him cold in my hand as the chaplain precedes me, and we walk the little way towards him. I don't look up at the Beauchamp Tower to see if my grandson has disobeyed me and is looking out of Edward's window. I don't think I would be able to set one foot before another if I saw their little faces looking down on me as I walk to my death.

There is a gust of wind from the river and the standards suddenly flap. I take a deep breath and I think of the others who have walked out of the Tower before me, in the certainty that they were going to heaven. I think of my brother, walking to Tower Hill, feeling the rain on his face and the wet grass under his boots. My little brother, as innocent as my grandson of everything but his name. None of us is imprisoned for what we have done; we are imprisoned for being who we are, and nothing can change that.

We get to the headsman though I have hardly noticed the walk. I wish that I had thought more about my soul and prayed as I walked along. I have no coherent thoughts, I have not completed my prayers, I am not ready for death. I give him the two pennies in his black-leather mittened hand. His eyes glint through the holes in the mask. I notice that his hand is trembling and he thrusts the coins in his pocket and grips tightly to the axe.

I stand before him and I say the words that every condemned person is to say. I stress my loyalty to the king and recommend

579

obedience to him. There is a moment when I feel like laughing out loud at this. How can anyone obey the king when his wishes change by the minute? How can anyone be loyal to a madman? I send my love and my blessings to the little Prince Edward, though I doubt that he will live to be a man, poor boy, poor accursed Tudor boy, and I send my love and blessings to the Princess Mary and I remember to call her Lady Mary and I say that I hope that she blesses me, who has loved her so dearly.

'That's enough,' Philips interrupts. 'I am sorry, your ladyship. You are not allowed to speak for long.'

The headsman steps forward and says: 'Put your head on the block and stretch out your hands when you are ready for it, ma'am.'

Obediently, I put my hands on the block and awkwardly lower myself down to the grass. I can smell the scent of it under my knees. I am aware of the ache in my back and the sound of a seagull crying and someone weeping. And then suddenly, just as I am about to put my forehead against the rough top of the wooden block, and spread my arms wide to signal that he can strike, a rush of joy, a desire for life, suddenly comes over me, and I say: 'No.'

It's too late, the axe is up over his head, he is bringing it down, but I say: 'No,' and I sit up, and pull myself up on the block to get to my feet.

There is a terrible blow on the back of my head, but almost no pain. It fells me to the ground and I say 'No' again and suddenly I am filled with a great ecstasy of rebellion. I do not consent to the will of the madman Henry Tudor and I do not put my head meekly down upon the block, and I never will. I am going to fight for my life and I say 'No!' as I struggle to rise, and 'No' as the blow comes again, and 'No' as I crawl away, blood pouring from the wound in my neck and my head, blinding me but not drowning my joy in fighting for my life even as it is slipping away from me, and witnessing, to the very last moment, to the wrong that Henry Tudor has done to me and mine. 'No!' I cry out. 'No! No! No!'

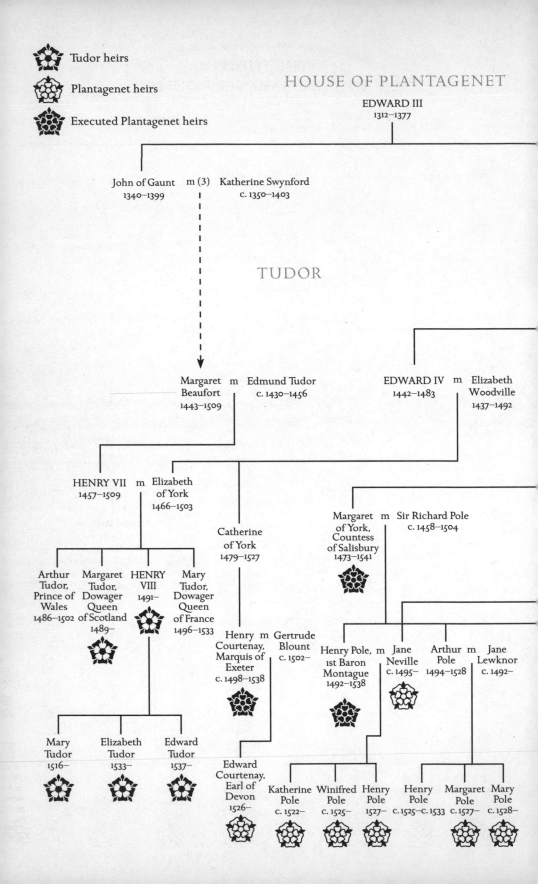

Tudor heirs

Plantagenet heirs

Executed Plantagenet heirs

HOUSE OF PLANTAGENET

EDWARD III
1312–1377

John of Gaunt   m (3)   Katherine Swynford
1340–1399   c. 1350–1403

TUDOR

Margaret   m   Edmund Tudor   EDWARD IV   m   Elizabeth
Beaufort   c. 1430–1456   1442–1483   Woodville
1443–1509   1437–1492

HENRY VII   m   Elizabeth
1457–1509   of York
                          1466–1503   Margaret   m   Sir Richard Pole
                                                          of York,   c. 1458–1504
                                      Catherine   Countess
                                      of York   of Salisbury
                                      1479–1527   1473–1541

Arthur   Margaret   HENRY   Mary
Tudor,   Tudor,   VIII   Tudor,
Prince of   Dowager   1491–   Dowager
Wales   Queen   Queen
1486–1502 of Scotland   of France   Henry   m   Gertrude
                 1489–   1496–1533   Courtenay,   Blount
                                                                  Marquis of   c. 1502–   Henry Pole, m   Jane   Arthur   m   Jane
                                                                  Exeter   1st Baron   Neville   Pole   Lewknor
                                                                  c. 1498–1538   Montague   c. 1495–   1494–1528   c. 1492–
                                                                                                      1492–1538

Mary   Elizabeth   Edward
Tudor   Tudor   Tudor
1516–   1533–   1537–
                                            Edward
                                            Courtenay,
                                            Earl of
                                            Devon   Katherine Winifred Henry   Henry   Margaret Mary
                                            1526–   Pole   Pole   Pole   Pole   Pole   Pole
                                                            c. 1522–   c. 1525– 1527–   c. 1525–c. 1533 c. 1527– c. 1528–

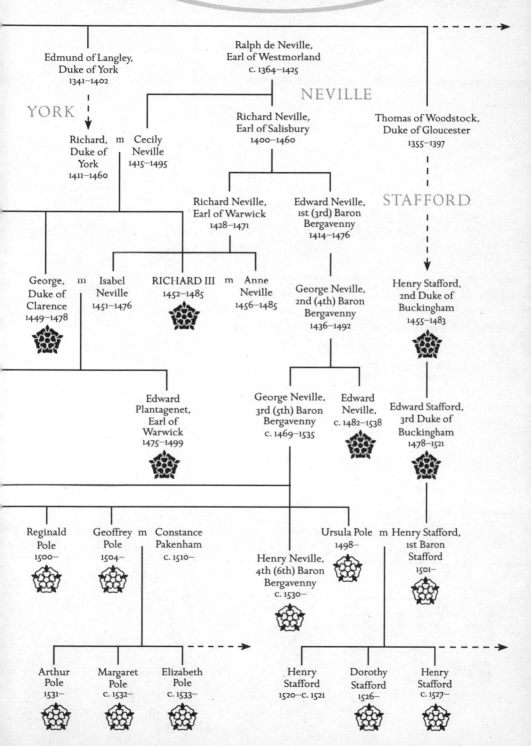

THE TUDOR
AND PLANTAGENET HOUSES
ON 27 MAY 1541

Edmund of Langley,
Duke of York
1341–1402

Ralph de Neville,
Earl of Westmorland
c. 1364–1425

NEVILLE

YORK

Richard Neville,
Earl of Salisbury
1400–1460

Thomas of Woodstock,
Duke of Gloucester
1355–1397

Richard, m Cecily
Duke of Neville
York 1415–1495
1411–1460

Richard Neville,
Earl of Warwick
1428–1471

Edward Neville,
1st (3rd) Baron
Bergavenny
1414–1476

STAFFORD

George, m Isabel
Duke of Neville
Clarence 1451–1476
1449–1478

RICHARD III m Anne
1452–1485 Neville
1456–1485

George Neville,
2nd (4th) Baron
Bergavenny
1436–1492

Henry Stafford,
2nd Duke of
Buckingham
1455–1483

Edward
Plantagenet,
Earl of
Warwick
1475–1499

George Neville,
3rd (5th) Baron
Bergavenny
c. 1469–1535

Edward
Neville,
c. 1482–1538

Edward Stafford,
3rd Duke of
Buckingham
1478–1521

Reginald
Pole
1500–

Geoffrey m Constance
Pole Pakenham
1504– c. 1510–

Ursula Pole m Henry Stafford,
1498– 1st Baron
Stafford
1501–

Henry Neville,
4th (6th) Baron
Bergavenny
c. 1530–

Arthur
Pole
1531–

Margaret
Pole
c. 1532–

Elizabeth
Pole
c. 1533–

Henry
Stafford
1520–c. 1521

Dorothy
Stafford
1526–

Henry
Stafford
c. 1527–

AUTHOR NOTE

This novel is the story of a long life lived at the centre of events which, since it was a woman's life, has been largely ignored by chroniclers at the time and historians since. Margaret Pole's greatest claim to fame was that she was Henry VIII's oldest victim on the scaffold – she was 67 when she was brutally killed on Tower Green – but her life, as I have tried to show here, was lived at the heart of the Tudor court and at the centre of the former royal family.

Indeed, the more I have studied and thought about her life and her wide-ranging family, the Plantagenets, the more I have had to wonder if she was not at the centre of conspiracy: sometimes actively, sometimes quietly, perhaps always conscious of her family's claim to the throne, and always with a claimant in exile, preparing to invade, or under arrest. There was never a time when Henry VII or his son were free from fear of a Plantagenet claimant and although many historians have seen this as Tudor paranoia, I wonder if there was not a constant genuine threat from the old royal family, a sort of resistance movement: sometimes active but always present.

The novel opens with the controversial suggestion that Katherine of Aragon decided to lie about her marriage to Arthur so that she might be married for a second time to his brother Henry. I think that an examination of the agreed facts: the official bedding; the young couple co-habiting at Ludlow; their youth and health; and the absence of any concern about the consummation of their marriage; convincingly indicates that they were wedded and bedded. Certainly, everyone thought so at the time, and Katherine's own mother had requested a dispensation from the Pope that would permit her daughter to re-marry whether or not intercourse had taken place.

Decades later, when she was asked if the marriage to Arthur had been consummated, she had every reason to lie: she was defending her marriage to Henry VIII and the legitimacy of her daughter. It was the stereotyped view of women by later historians (especially the Victorian historians) who suggested that since Katherine was a 'good' woman, she must have been incapable of telling a lie. I tend to take a more liberal view of female mendacity.

As a historian, I can examine one side against the other and share these thoughts with the reader. As a novelist, I have to fix the story with one coherent viewpoint, thus the account of Katherine's first marriage and her decision to marry Prince Harry is fictional and based on my interpretation of the historical facts.

I have drawn from the work of Sir John Dewhurst the dates of Katherine of Aragon's pregnancies. There has been much work on the loss of Henry VIII's babies. Current interesting research from Catrina Banks Whitley and Kyra Kramer suggests that Henry may have had the rare Kell positive blood type which can cause miscarriages, stillbirths and infant deaths, when the mother has the more common Kell negative blood type. Whitley and Kramer also suggest that Henry's later symptoms of paranoia and anger may have been caused by McLeod syndrome – a disease found only in Kell positive individuals. McLeod syndrome usually develops when sufferers are aged around 40 and causes physical degeneration and personality changes resulting in paranoia, depression and irrational behaviour.

Interestingly, Whitley and Kramer trace Kell syndrome back to Jacquetta, Duchess of Bedford, the suspected witch and mother of Elizabeth Woodville. Sometimes, uncannily, fiction creates a metaphor for an historical truth: in a fictional scene in my novel, *The White Queen*, Elizabeth, together with her daughter Elizabeth of York, curse the murderer of her sons, swearing that they shall lose their son and their grandsons, while in real life her genes – unknown and undetectable at the time – entered the Tudor line through her daughter and may have caused the deaths of four Tudor babies to Katherine of Aragon and three to Anne Boleyn.

This novel is about the decline of Henry VIII from the young handsome prince, seen as the saviour of his country, into a sick, obese tyrant. The young king's deterioration has been the subject of many fine histories – I list some of the ones I found most helpful below – but this is the first time in my research that I have fully understood the brutality of the reign and the depth of his corruption. It has made me think about how easily a ruler can slide into tyranny, especially if no-one opposes him. As Henry moved from one advisor to another, as his moods deteriorated and his use of the gallows became an act of terror against his people, one sees in this well-known, well-loved Tudor world the rising of a despot. Henry could hang the faithful men and women of the North because nobody rose up to defend Thomas More, John Fisher or even the Duke of Buckingham. He learned that he could execute two wives, divorce another and threaten his last because no-one effectively defended his first. The picture of the beloved Henry in the primary school histories, of an eccentric glamorous ruler who married six women, is also the ugly portrait of a wife and child abuser and a serial killer who made war against his own people, even against his own family.

Henry's response to the appeal of the Pilgrims for the maintenance of their traditional rulers and religion was to attack the North of England, and the Roman Catholic faithful. The king was consciously dishonest in his persecution of people who believed, firstly, that they could appeal to him for justice and, then, that he had given them a full pardon and would abide by his word. This is one of the worst episodes in our history, yet it is little known, perhaps because it is a history of defeat and tragedy, and the losers rarely tell the story.

Margaret went to the scaffold without a charge, a trial, or even adequate notice, as I describe here. Her execution was clumsy, perhaps because of an incompetent executioner, perhaps because she refused to put her head down on the block. As a tribute to her, and to all woman who refuse to take punishment meted out to them by an unjust world, I have described her in this novel as dying as she may have lived – resisting the Tudor tyranny. She was beatified in 1886 as a martyr for the faith and is honoured by the Church as Blessed Margaret Pole on 28 May each year.

Her grandson Henry disappeared, probably dying in the Tower. Edward Courtenay was released only on the accession of Mary I who freed him and gave him the title Earl of Devon in September, 1553. Geoffrey Pole fled England and obtained absolution from the Pope for betraying his brother, returning only when Mary I came to the throne, as did Reginald who was ordained and became Archbishop of Canterbury, working closely with Mary I to restore the Roman Catholic church to England for the duration of her reign.

There is something in this story – of an old family displaced against their will, of their loyalty to a young woman who suffered extraordinarily unjust treatment, of their adherence to their faith and their attempt to survive – that I have found very moving to research and write. The fiction, as always, is secondary to the history; the real women are always more complex and more conflicted, greater than the heroines of the novel, just as real women now, as then, are often greater than they are reported, sometimes greater than the world wants them to be.

BIBLIOGRAPHY

Ackroyd, Peter, *The Life of Thomas More* (London, Chatto & Windus, 1998)

Alexander, Michael Van Cleave, *The First of the Tudors: A study of Henry VII and His Reign* (London, Croom Helm, 1981, first published 1937)

Amt, Emilie, *Women's Lives in Medieval Europe* (New York, Routledge, 1993)

Bacon, Francis, *The History of the Reign of King Henry VII and selected works* (Cambridge, Cambridge University Press, 1998)

Baer, Ann, *Down the Common: A Year in the Life of a Medieval Woman* (London, Michael O'Mara Books, 1996)

Barnhouse, Rebecca, *The Book of the Knight of the Tower: Manners for Young Medieval Women* (Basingstoke, Palgrave Macmillan, 2006)

Besant, Sir Walter, *London in the Time of The Tudors* (London, Adam & Charles Black, 1904)

Cavendish, George, edited by Lockyer, Roger, *Thomas Wolsey, Late Cardinal: His Life and Death* (London, The Folio Society, 1962, first published 1810)

Childs, Jessie, *Henry VIII's Last Victim: The Life and Times of Henry Howard, Earl of Surrey* (London, Jonathan Cape, 2006)

Chrimes, S. B., *Henry VII* (London, Eyre Methuen, 1972)

Chrimes, S. B., *Lancastrians, Yorkists, and Henry VII* (London, Macmillan, 1964)

Cooper, Charles Henry, *Memoir of Margaret: Countess of Richmond and Derby* (Cambridge, Cambridge Univerity Press, 1874)

Cunningham, Sean, *Henry VII* (London, Routledge, 2007, first published 1967)

Dodds, Madeline Hope, and Dodds, Ruth, *The Pilgrimage of Grace, 1536–1537 and The Exeter Conspiracy, 1538 Volume One* (Cambridge, Cambridge University Press, 1915)

Dodds, Madeline Hope, and Dodds, Ruth, *The Pilgrimage of Grace, 1536–1537 and The Exeter Conspiracy, 1538 Volume Two* (Cambridge, Cambridge University Press, 1915)

Doner, Margaret, *Lies and Lust in The Tudor Court: The Fifth Wife of Henry VIII* (Nebraska, Universe, 2004)

Duggan, Anne J., *Queens and Queenship in Medieval Europe* (Woodbridge, Boydell Press, 1997)

Dutton, Kevin, *The Wisdom of Psychopaths: Lessons in Life from Saints, Spies and Serial Killers* (London, Heinemann, 2012)

Elton, G.R., *England Under the Tudors* (London, Methuen, 1955)

Fellows, Nicholas, *Disorder and Rebellion in Tudor England* (Bath, Hodder & Stoughton Educational, 2001)

Fletcher, A., and MacCulloch, D., *Tudor Rebellions* (Harlow, Pearson Education, 2004, first published 1968)

Fox, Julia, *Jane Boleyn: The Infamous Lady Rochford* (London, Weidenfeld & Nicolson, 2007)

Goodman, Anthony, *The Wars of the Roses: Military Activity and English Society 1452–97* (London, Routledge & Kegan Paul, 1981)

Gregory, P., Jones, M., and Baldwin, D., *Women of the Cousins' War* (London, Simon & Schuster, 2011)

Gristwood, Sarah, *Blood Sisters: The Hidden Lives of the Women Behind the Wars of the Roses* (London, Harper Collins, 2012)

Grummitt, David, *The Calais Garrison, War and Military Service in England, 1436–1558* (Woodbridge, Boydell & Brewer, 2008)

Guy, John, *Tudor England* (Oxford, Oxford University Press, 1988)

Hare, Robert D., *Without Conscience: The Disturbing World of the Psychopath* (New York, Pocket Books, 1995)

Harvey, Nancy L., *Elizabeth of York: Tudor Queen* (London, Arthur Baker, 1973)

Howard, Maurice, *The Tudor Image* (London, Tate Gallery Publishing, 1995)

Hutchinson, Robert, *House of Treason: The Rise and Fall of a Tudor Dynasty* (London, Weidenfeld and Nicolson, 2009)

Hutchinson, Robert, *Young Henry: The Rise of Henry VIII* (London, Weidenfeld and Nicolson, 2011)

Innes, Arthur D., *England Under The Tudors* (London, Methuen, 1905)

Jackman, S.W., *Deviating Voices: Women and Orthodox Religious Tradition* (Cambridge, Lutterworth Press, 2003)

Jones, Michael K., and Underwood, Malcolm G., *The King's Mother: Lady Margaret Beaufort, Countess of Richmond and Derby* (Cambridge, Cambridge University Press, 1992)

Jones, Philippa, *The Other Tudors: Henry VIII's Mistresses and Bastards* (London, New Holland, 2009)

Karras, Ruth Mazo, *Sexuality in Medieval Europe: Doing unto Others* (New York, Routledge, 2005)

Kesselring, K.J., *Mercy and Authority in the Tudor State* (Cambridge, Cambridge University Press, 2003)

Kramer, Kyra C., *Blood Will Tell: A Medical Explanation of the Tyranny of Henry VIII* (Indiana, Ashwood Press, 2012)

Laynesmith, J. L., *The Last Medieval Queens: English Queenship 1445–1503* (Oxford, Oxford University Press, 2004)

Lewis, Katherine J., Menuge, Noel James, Phillips, Kim M., *Young Medieval Women* (Stroud, Sutton Publishing, 1999)

Licence, Amy, *Elizabeth of York: The Forgotten Tudor Queen* (Stroud, Amberley, 2013)

Licence, Amy, *In Bed with the Tudors: The Sex Lives of a Dynasty from Elizabeth of York to Elizabeth I* (Stroud, Amberley, 2012)

Lipscomb, Suzannah, *1536: The Year that Changed Henry VIII* (Oxford, Lion, 2009)

Loades, David, *Henry VIII: Court, Church and Conflict* (London, The National Archive, 2007)

Mayer, Thomas, *Reginald Pole: Prince and Prophet* (Cambridge, Cambridge University Press, 2000)

McKee, John, *Dame Elizabeth Barton OSB, the Holy Maid of Kent* (London, Burns, Oates and Washbourne, 1925)

Mortimer, Ian, *The Time Traveller's Guide to Medieval England* (London, Vintage, 2009)

Mühlbach, Luise, *Henry VIII and His Court [Illustrated]* (New York, D. Appleton & Co., 1867)

Murphy, Beverley A., *Bastard Prince: Henry VIII's Lost Son* (Stroud, Sutton Publishing, 2001)

Neame, Alan, *The Holy Maid of Kent: The Life of Elizabeth Barton, 1506-1534* (London, Hodder and Stoughton, 1971)

Neillands, Robin, *The Wars of the Roses* (London, Cassell, 1992)

Penn, Thomas, *The Winter King* (London, Allen Lane, 2011)

Perry, Maria, *Sisters to the King: The Tumultuous Lives of Henry VIII's Sisters – Margaret of Scotland and Mary of France* (London, André Deutsch, 1998)

Phillips, Kim M., *Medieval Maidens: Young Women and Gender in England, 1270–1540* (Manchester, Manchester University Press, 2003)

Pierce, Hazel, *Margaret Pole: Countess of Salisbury 1473-1541* (Cardiff, University of Wales Press, 2009)

Plowden, Alison, *House of Tudor* (London, Weidenfeld & Nicolson, 1976)

Prestwich, Michael, *Plantagenet England 1225 – 1360* (Oxford, Clarendon Press, 2005)

Reed, Conyers, *The Tudors: Personalities & Practical Politics in 16th Century England* (Oxford, Oxford University Press, 1936)

Ridley, Jasper, *The Tudor Age* (London, Constable, 1988)

Rubin, Miri, *The Hollow Crown: A History of Britain in the Late Middle Ages* (London, Allen Lane, 2005)

Scarisbrick, J J, *Henry VIII* (London, Eyre Methuen, 1968)

Searle, Mark, and Stevenson, Kenneth, *Documents of the Marriage Liturgy* (New York, Pueblo, 1992)

Seward, Desmond, *The Demon's Brood* (London, Constable, 2014)

Seward, Desmond, *The Last White Rose: Dynasty, Rebellion and Treason* (London, Constable, 2010)

Sharpe, Kevin, *Selling the Tudor Monarchy: Authority and Image in 16th Century England* (Yale University Press, 2009)

Sheridan, Thomas, *Puzzling People: The Labyrinth of the Psychopath* (Velluminous Press, 2011)

Simon, Linda, *Of Virtue Rare: Margaret Beaufort: Matriarch of the House of Tudor* (Boston, Houghton Mifflin, 1982)

Simons, Eric N., *Henry VII: The First Tudor King* (New York, Muller, 1968)

Shagan, Ethan H., *Popular Politics in the English Reformation* (Cambridge, Cambridge University Press, 2003)

Skidmore, Chris, *Edward VI: The Lost King of England* (London, Weidenfeld & Nicolson, 2007)

Smith, Lacey Baldwin, *Treason in Tudor England: Politics & Paranoia* (London, Jonathan Cape, 1986)

St Aubyn, Giles, *The Year of Three Kings 1483* (London, Collins, 1983)

Starkey, David, *Henry: Virtuous Prince* (London, Harper Press, 2008)

Starkey, David, *Six Wives: The Queens of Henry VIII* (London, Chatto & Windus, 2003)

Stout, Martha, *The Sociopath Next Door* (New York, Broadway Books, 2005)

Thomas, Paul, *Authority and Disorder in Tudor Times 1485-1603* (Cambridge, Cambridge University Press, 1999)

Vergil, Polydore and Ellis, Henry, *Three Books of Polydore Vergil's English History: Comprising the Reigns of Henry VI, Edward IV and Richard III* (London, Camden Society, 1844)

Ward, Jennifer, *Women in Medieval Europe 1200–1500* (Essex, Pearson Education, 2002)

Warnicke, Retha M., *The Rise and Fall of Anne Boleyn* (Cambridge, Cambridge University Press, 1989)

Watt, Diane, *Secretaries of God* (Cambridge, DS Brewer, 1997)

Weatherford, John W., *Crime and Punishment in the England of Shakespeare and Milton* (North Carolina, McFarland & Co., 2001)

Weightman, Christine, *Margaret of York: The Diabolical Duchess* (London, Amberley, 2009)

Weir, Alison, *Children of England: The Heirs of King Henry VIII* (London, Jonathan Cape, 1996)

Weir, Alison, *Henry VIII: King and Court* (London, Jonathan Jonathan Cape, 2001)

Weir, Alison, *Lancaster and York: The Wars of the Roses* (London, Jonathan Cape, 1995)

Weir, Alison, *The Six Wives of Henry VIII* (London, Bodley Head, 1991)

Whitelock, Anna, *Mary Tudor: England's First Queen* (London, Bloomsbury, 2009)

Williams, Neville and Fraser, Antonia, *The Life and Times of Henry VII* (London, Weidenfeld & Nicolson, 1973)

Williamson, Hugh Ross, *The Cardinal in Exile* (London, Michael Joseph, 1969)

Wilson, Derek, *In the Lion's Court: Power, Ambition and Sudden Death in the Reign of Henry VIII* (London, Hutchinson, 2001)

Wilson, Derek, *The Plantagenets: The Kings that made Britain* (London, Quercus, 2011)

Journals

Cheney, A. Denton, 'The Holy Maid of Kent', *Transactions of the Royal Historical Society*, 18 (1904): 107-129

Dewhurst, John, 'The Alleged Miscarriages of Catherine of Aragon and Anne Boleyn', *Medical History*, 28, 01 (1984): 49-56

Ditchfield, P.H., and Page, William, 'Houses of the Austin Canons, Victorian County History', *A History of the County of Berkshire*, vol 2 (1907): 82-87

Rex, R., 'The Execution of the Holy Maid of Kent', *Historical Research*, vol 64, issue 154 (1991): 216-220

Shagan, Ethan H., 'Print, Orality and Communications in the Maid of Kent Affair', *The Journal of Ecclesiastical History* (2001): 21-33

Whatmore, L.E., 'The sermon against the Holy Maid of Kent and her adherents, delivered at St Paul's Cross November the 23rd 1533 and Canterbury December the 7th', *English Historical Review*, 58 (1943): 463-475

Whitley, Catrina Banks, and Kramer, Kyra, 'A new explanation for the reproductive woes and midlife decline of Henry VIII', *The Historical Journal*, 53 (2010): 827-848

Williams, C.H., 'The Rebellion of Humphrey Stafford in 1486', *The English Historical Review*, vol 43, no 170 (1928): 181-189

GARDENS
FOR THE GAMBIA

Philippa Gregory visited The Gambia, one of the driest and poorest countries of sub-Saharan Africa, in 1993 and paid for a well to be hand-dug in a village primary school at Sika. Now – more than 200 wells later, she continues to raise money and commission wells in village schools, community gardens and in The Gambia's only agricultural college. She works with her representative in The Gambia, headmaster Ismaila Sisay, and their charity now funds pottery and batik classes, bee-keeping and adult literacy programmes.

GARDENS FOR THE GAMBIA is a registered charity in the UK and the US, and a registered NGO in The Gambia. Every donation, however small, goes to The Gambia without any deductions. If you would like to learn more about the work that Philippa calls 'the best thing that I do', visit her website *www.PhilippaGregory.com* and click on GARDENS FOR THE GAMBIA where you can make a donation and join with Philippa in this project.

'Every well we dig provides drinking water for a school of about 600 children, and waters the gardens where they grow vegetables for the school dinners. I don't know of a more direct way to feed hungry children and teach them to farm for their future.'
Philippa Gregory